DREAMLANDER

Join the discussion: #dreamlander

DREAMLANDER

K.M. WEILAND

PenForASword

SCOTTSBLUFF, NEBRASKA

Dedicated to my beloved Savior,
who has made us all with a plan in mind.

And to my brothers.
Derek—who helped me start it.
And Jared—who helped me finish it.

ACKNOWLEDGEMENTS

I WAKE UP every morning and realize how blessed I am, not just to be a writer, spinning worlds out of magic and air, but to be able to count on all the amazing people who have enriched both my writing and my life. *Dreamlander* has been a tremendous journey (or maybe mountain climbing, without any rope, would be the better analogy). I wouldn't be standing here on top of the mountain without the support, suggestions, and occasional smacks on the back of the head offered by the following people:

My sister Amy: my #1 fan, favorite cookie maker, and crunch-time wrist saver.

My brothers: who are just as responsible for this book reaching print as I am. Derek, who came up with the idea that maybe there's more to our dreams than we think. And Jared, whose spot-on story sense and demands for excellence pushed and shoved, poked and prodded me every step of the way.

My editors: Adriela Ashford, Linda Yezak, and CathiLyn Dyck, who encouraged me and educated me.

My beta readers: London Crockett, Lynnda Ell, Daniel Farnum, Holly Heisey, Steve Mathisen, Lorna G. Poston, Braden Russell, Liberty Speidel, April Upton, Laiel Upton (for whom the country of Lael was named in the first place), and Sterling Woomert. Thank you for shooting straight with me, catching my mistakes, and loving the story.

My parents: Ted and Linda, whose support is unfailing.

Dominick Finelle: who created the beautiful cover art.

Robert Altbauer: whose cartography skills much surpass my doodles.

And Wordplayers everywhere: Your comments, questions, and constant encouragement on my blog make me smile and keep me going.

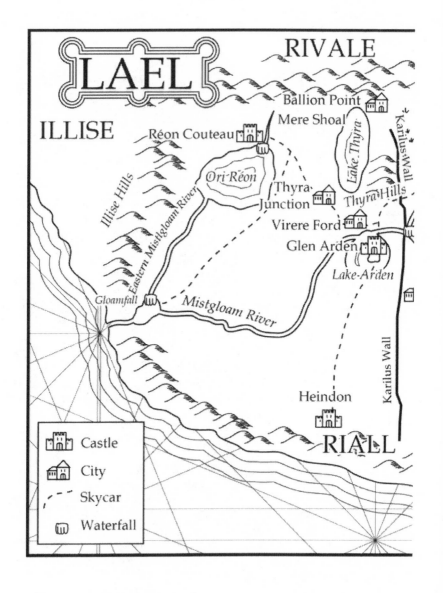

LAEL

RIVALE

ILLISE

Ballion Point

Mere Shoal

Réon Couteau

Karilus Wall

Lake Thyra

Illise Hills

Ori-Réon

Eastern Mistgloam River

Thyra Junction

Thyra Hills

Virere Ford

Glen Arden

Lake Arden

Gloamfall

Mistgloam River

Karilus Wall

Heindon

RIALL

Castle

City

Skycar

Waterfall

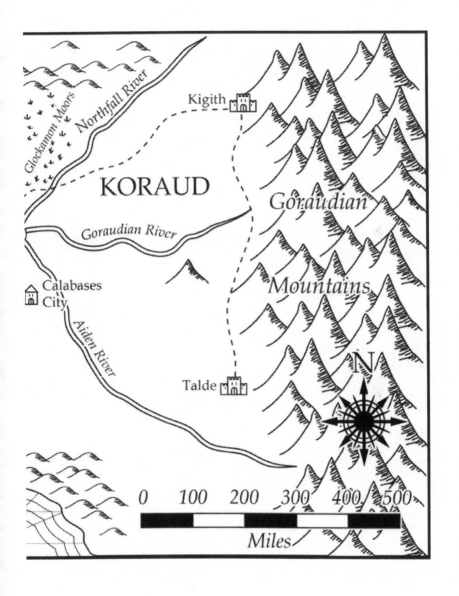

"The real test of a man is not when he plays the role that he wants for himself, but when he plays the role destiny has for him."

—*Vaclav Havel*

1

DREAMS WEREN'T SUPPOSED to be able to kill you. But this one was sure trying its best.

Chris Redston floated in water up to his neck. Cold pounded through his bones, and fog shrouded his vision. He fought to move, but the sludgy water felt like slow-setting concrete. He gritted his teeth and tried to drag his hand free, but it barely shifted. He strained harder.

From out of the mist in front of him rode a woman on a black horse, rifle in hand. She was tall in the saddle, the flow of her white gown accentuating her height. A braided crown of mahogany hair piled atop her head, studded with matching white blossoms.

She drew the horse to a halt. It slid, hind fetlocks buried in the grass, then reared. With her hand on its shoulder, she quieted it. And then she looked up.

She didn't smile, didn't even blink an acknowledgement. She just stared at him, the thunderstorm blue of her eyes never flinching from his face. The sharp angle of her jaw above her neck and the straight slant of her nose exuded a survivor's fierceness. But it couldn't mask something softer and more vulnerable, something almost desperate, in the compression of her mouth.

Her expression bore recognition. She knew him?

Of course not. She was a figment of his imagination. All he had to do was wake up, and she and her gun and her black monster of a horse would disappear.

She pulled back the rifle's bolt lever and thrust it home. A whirring, barely audible over the water, buzzed with a high frequency, and an aquamarine light flickered from a pattern of concentric circles on the rifle stock. She lifted the barrel to point at his forehead.

So maybe she *did* know him. Knew him and didn't like him.

He thrashed against the water and managed to slog toward her maybe an inch.

Panic flickered across her face. "No—"

He struggled harder and tried to speak: "What do you want?" The words came out as a gurgle.

"You're almost here." Her voice held steady—but only barely. Despite the gun in her hand and despite the fact he was paralyzed in the middle of a lake, she looked more afraid of him than he was of her.

"You must listen to me," she said. "We haven't much time."

A wave smashed into his face. He choked and tried to cough the water back up.

"Listen to me!" she said again. "It may be your destiny to cross the worlds, and it may be mine to find you. But I have no faith left in destiny. Stay away from us." Now, her voice wavered. "If you come, you will bring war, you will bring death. And that's not what you're supposed to bring. You're supposed to bring life."

He tried to tell her he wasn't interested in either dreams or destiny. And he certainly wasn't interested in doing her any harm. From the look in her eyes, someone had already done enough of that long ago.

He swallowed more water, and his throat closed up. Mostly, what he was interested in right now was waking up and trying to convince himself he wasn't losing his mind.

Her brows lowered. "Do not come."

She raised the rifle.

He tried to flounder back, to turn and swim away. He tried to shout at her. But all he could do was stare.

She pulled the trigger.

The shot burst from the rifle barrel. It smashed into the center of his forehead. Jagged teeth of pain tore his skin, chewed through the bone, and then—

—he was awake.

Heart hammering, he lurched upright in bed. Sweat drenched the front of his T-shirt and plastered his hair to his temples. Outside the window, in the alley behind the house, a garbage truck's brakes wheezed and an upended dumpster clanked into the hopper.

He squinted against the early morning sunlight and groaned.

Another dream. Another ridiculous dream.

This was the third time he had seen the woman on the black war-horse and the third time she had stared at him down a rifle barrel. But she had never spoken to him before. What did that mean? That he was going crazier faster?

Who dreamt things like this anyway? Who dreamt things that felt as *real* as this?

He tried to swing his feet to the floor, got caught in the sheet, and had to kick free. Finally, bare toes curled in the carpet, he dug his elbows into his knees and scrubbed his hands across his face. The water pipes were humming, which meant his roommate was already back from the gym and in the shower.

Blearily, he looked up at the window. An envelope clung to the screen, held in place by a big X of duct tape. His name was scrawled across the front in black ink.

He frowned and pushed to his feet. Hardly anybody even knew he was back in Chicago. He had just returned a few weeks ago from another investigative journalism assignment in London.

He popped the screen from the windowframe and reached around it to strip the envelope free. It ripped before it came off, and he left the corners of the duct tape to be peeled away later. He leaned out the window to lower the screen to the ground, then pried the single piece of notebook paper from the envelope.

It contained only three lines:

You've been dreaming.
I've been looking for you.
Stay away from the shrink.

Gooseflesh crawled up his arms. He turned the letter over. But there was no explanation. No signature. No return address.

It had to be a coincidence. He had been having weird dreams all his life. He'd never told anyone about them, not even Mike. And he definitely hadn't told anyone the dreams were getting worse. If he was losing his mind, he'd deal with it like he did everything else—on his own.

He tossed the letter back onto the desk and headed to the closet for a clean T-shirt and a pair of cargo pants.

From somewhere in the kitchen, his phone started playing "Folsom Prison Blues"—his dad's ringtone. He closed his eyes. His dad called for only two reasons. Either he needed money for booze or money for bail.

He let the phone ring while he crossed the hall into the kitchen. When it finally stopped, he let it sit for another few minutes, long enough for one of his father's rambling messages, then plucked it from its recharge dock.

The signal for new messages blinked on the screen. He hesitated, finger hovering over the button, then punched it. He raised the phone to his head and braced for his dad's stammering.

"Hi, uh, Chris. Sorry to bother you. I suppose you're working on an article or something . . . Anyway, if you have time, I could really use a ride. I'm down at the jail again." Paul cleared his throat. To his credit, he never took Chris's help for granted. "I'll need you to get me out again. I promise I'll pay you back. Okay? Anyway . . ." His voice faded. "I hope you get this."

Chris breathed out and lowered the phone. His dad didn't need to hope. Chris always showed up to bail him out. He had sworn over and over that was going to end. But he kept right on answering the phone, kept going down to the jail, kept paying bail. This was his father. What was he supposed to do? Walk away?

A door opened down the hall, and Mike Andreola lumbered around the corner into the kitchen. He held his own phone against his ear. "All right, all right, I'll come with you. But for crying out loud, use your head next time, will you? You drive by here and pick me up in half an hour." His face had the pinched look that said he was striving, and mostly failing, to keep hold of his temper.

That meant he could only be talking to his sister.

He snapped the phone shut. "Brooke's got herself into another mess." Phone still in hand, he scratched his bear-sized fingers up his beard and through the curly ash blond hair his sister had been trying to get him to buzz cut ever since grade school.

"What happened?" Chris asked.

Mike crossed the kitchen to the fridge. "She was on the hunt again for that story that's supposed to give her a 'big break' as a reporter."

"What now? She slip past security at the mayor's office?"

From nine to five, Mike's baby sister was a medical transcriptionist. The rest of the time, she was bent on finding the most scandalous, outrageous story possible, one that would turn her into a "real writer."

"Close. She sneaked into the animal shelter and tried to break out two German shepherds, a poodle, a cocker spaniel, and five cats."

"She couldn't just adopt them?"

Pluto, Mike's half-blind Scottish terrier, clicked across the linoleum and growled as he passed Chris.

"Turns out big-hearted animal lovers don't make for front-cover copy." Mike glanced back at him. "What happened to you? Rough night? Those circles under your eyes make you look like the loser in a black-eye contest."

"Bad dreams." He left it at that.

Mike emerged from the fridge with a handful of toaster waffles. "I've got some sleeping pills in the medicine cabinet. Maybe you should give them a try."

Chris waved off the suggestion. He had no trouble sleeping. Sleeping was what brought on the dreams.

Mike stuffed the waffles into the toaster. "You want to come along? Brooke's probably going to need some help to smooth this one over. Besides, she hasn't seen you since you got back from London. You do know half this nutso stuff she pulls is because she's trying to live up to you, right?"

Chris shook his head. The sooner Brooke got over this crush she'd had on him since high school, the better off they'd both be. "Can't. My dad just called."

Mike grunted. He knew what that meant. "You going to bail him out?"

"Somebody's got to." While he was at it, he needed to find out where that letter had come from. Maybe one of the neighbors had seen someone tape it to the window.

Mike drummed his fingers on the countertop, then looked sideways at Chris. "When are you actually going to look into doing something to help your dad? Put him in a rehab center or something?"

Chris's gut clenched up. "If he wanted my help, he'd ask for it."

"Maybe you're never around to *be* asked."

"I'm around. I have to travel for work, but I always come back."

Ever since college, he'd buried himself in his work. His writing was his life, his escape. So long as he was busy chasing journalism assignments around the world, he was happy. Although, up to this point, the busy part was working out better than the happy part.

Mike turned to face him. "I get that you don't like this whole idea of people needing you, but you ever think about staying put for a while, putting down some actual roots?"

Chris stood away from the counter. "Look, if *you* need me, all you have to do is say so."

"This isn't about me, bro." The toaster popped and Mike dropped the waffles onto the countertop. He looked Chris in the eye. "Let up on work for a while. Stay here for a few months in a row. Get your dad clean. Quit the journalism for a while, and write a book, why don't you? I've got a friend in a publishing company. Let me give him a call. You can pitch him an idea or two."

"Maybe." What he wanted to say was "yes." But even the "maybe" came out hard. So his life was careening toward a dead end. So he was using work as an excuse to run away. At least it was safe. At least it was sane. Mostly.

"Maybe someday," he said. The good thing about someday was that it was a long way away. And until it rolled around, leaving was a lot easier than staying—for everyone involved.

He crossed the kitchen. "I've got to go. I'll probably be back late. Good luck with Brooke."

Pluto swung his head blindly and started yapping.

"Wait." Without looking up, Mike held out one of the waffles.

Chris hesitated in the doorway, then turned back and accepted it. "I'll be around for at least a month this time," he promised. "And I'll make time to talk Brooke into being more reasonable about her story chasing."

Mike kept buttering his breakfast, probably embarrassed their conversation had gotten this far. "Don't worry about it. You do what you gotta do."

Chris bit into the waffle and left through the front door. As he started to pocket his phone, it rang again. He glanced at the screen before answering, but the number wasn't familiar. Probably a recorded advertisement, but he hit the button anyway.

A voice creaked in his ear. "Chris Redston. You've been dreaming."

The hair on the back of his neck prickled, and he stopped short.

"I've been looking for you," the voice rasped. "Stay away from the shrink."

His mind raced. A letter was one thing. This phone call to his private number took the game to a new level entirely.

"Who are you?" he demanded. "What do you know about my dreams?"

"I know you don't have much time before you cross over. I know I'm not the only one looking for you, the only one who's spent his life searching for you."

Chris turned on his heel and scanned the neighborhood. "Who's looking for me? Where'd you get my number?"

"If you don't listen to me, Mactalde will find you. And I don't want that. I want victory. Do you understand?" He growled, soft and dark. "But, then, no, of course you don't understand anything."

"No, I don't—"

"I'll see you soon. Just be careful until then."

"Wait a minute—"

The hang-up clanked audibly.

Chris pulled the phone away from his head and stared at it. The chill on his neck crept down his back. This guy *couldn't* be for real. What he was saying about the dreams had to be a coincidence.

He started down the sidewalk. He needed to get out of here, needed to find his dad, needed to figure out how to stop chasing his tail through life. But, first, he searched his call log. He found the number and dialed. The phone rang once, then rang again and again. Either the guy wasn't answering, or he'd called from a pay phone.

Whoever he was, he was good. And whoever he was, Chris would find him.

2

O N THE BANKS of the Mistgloam River, Allara Katadin
sat on the back of her ebony warhorse and watched the
sun sink behind the hills. The Gifted was coming from
across the worlds. She had seen him. She had tried to warn him away.
But that wasn't going to be enough. Today would be her last chance
to find a way to keep her world safe from the destruction he would
have the power to bring with him.

To her right, the Gloamfall splashed into its base pool like chimes
in the wind. High in the Illise foothills, the meadow offered perhaps
only a hundred paces between the waterfall and the trees, but the
gloamwheat here was as tall as her stirrup. In another month or so,
the silvered green heads would be ready to bear a wealth of harvest,
save that no one would dare put a scythe to this meadow.

The gloamwheat that grew here, leagues from the nearest farm,
grew because the Garowai wished it to. As a child, when she had
come here for one of her many lessons, she had asked him what he
wanted with the wheat. Surely, he didn't eat it; his teeth, after all,
were the teeth of a carnivore.

He had looked down at her out of his great green eyes, with their
cat-slit pupils. "I enjoy the smell of it."

"But that's of no use."

"Usefulness, my lovely, reaches far beyond necessity. The gloamwheat is beautiful of sight and smell to me. And that is use enough."

She hadn't said aloud what she was thinking, but he probably knew
that her mind—a child's mind forced to face adult problems—was
already categorizing the immortal likes of the Garowai and his uses

in a far different realm from herself.

Born a princess in a troubled era and chosen by the Garowai himself to be her generation's Searcher, she lived her life by necessities, not luxuries. She had done so when, at nine years of age, she guided her first Gifted across the worlds, and she did so now, as she tried to prevent the coming of an unwelcome second.

Overhead, the sun went black for a moment, and a shadow fell across the meadow. She looked up from the sway of the grass to the arrival of the Garowai. Four times the size of a Koraudian lion, with massive shoulders that rippled beneath smooth black wings twice again as long as his body, he stole the breath from her chest even now, so many years after her father had brought her to the Gloamfall to begin her training.

The sunset glinted off his blue-gray fur as he glided on a wind current before turning and sweeping into the meadow. His green eyes locked on her face, and she dragged air into her lungs. So much depended on the question she had come to ask him. So very, very much.

The wind from his wings brushed through the wheat and swirled her dark hair around her face. Rihawn, her horse, raised his head, then returned to grazing. The big black stallion had been here often enough to know the Garowai presented no threat.

The leathery undersurface of the Garowai's wings cleared her head by barely an arm's span. He swept past her and circled around to land on all fours on the riverbank. The wind from his flight caught at the filmy blue sleeves of her tunic.

She dismounted and dropped her reins, leaving Rihawn ground tied. Touching her thumb and her forefinger to her closed eyes, she slid her hand downward off her face in a gesture of honor and respect.

"Garowai," she said. The ancient Cherazii word translated "teacher" or "master." It wasn't a name, so much as a title, but it was the only name he, or any of the Garowai before him, had ever borne.

There was only ever one Garowai in the world. They rose and fell with the ages, and when one's spirit finally passed into the presence of the God of all, a new Garowai would ascend from its body to share heaven's wisdom, mete its justice, and choose the Searchers who would seek out each generation's Gifted.

On the shore in front of her, the Garowai dropped into a crouch.

He shook his head, ruffling the heavy slate-colored mane that surrounded his face and continued halfway down his back. "Well, now, it's pleasant to return from a long journey to find a sweet face at the end of the flight." He tucked his hindquarters under him and eased his front end down, dropping onto the sand with a faint groan. He was very old—almost seven hundred years if legends were to be believed—and arthritis plagued his bones.

She stepped forward, wanting to help him, to ease his pain.

The corner of his sloped muzzle crinkled with half a smile. "Never mind, dearheart. What brings you all the way from Glen Arden to visit my weary self?"

"Not Glen Arden. Réon Couteau." Glen Arden was the official capital of Lael and the unofficial capital of the civilized world in general. It had been her home since childhood. But, as the Searcher, she spent much of her time in the mountain fortress city of Réon Couteau, high on its cliff above the waterfall that fed Ori Réon, the Lake of Dreams.

After her failure with her first Gifted and his death as a traitor, she had thought never again to use Ori Réon to make contact with the other world. But another Gifted *was* coming, and no matter how much she wanted to stop him, she had no power to do so.

The Garowai blinked, almost sleepily. He was exhausted, no doubt. But he watched her face, waiting without hurrying her. "If you come from Réon Couteau, then you come for business and not for pleasure, I'll warrant."

"Yes." Sweat prickled her hands, and she rubbed them down the soft doe-colored leather of her breeches. "Time is growing short. The Gifted—I can feel him. He's coming. He's almost here. And there's something I need to know."

"Always questions. Does it not strike you as rather unfair you always ask and I always answer?" The crinkle in his muzzle spread to the other side.

Her own smile came hard. What was there to smile about these days? The threat of war from neighboring Koraud on the eastern border? The threat of religious and political unrest from the Nateros protesters within Lael's own borders? The threat of her own failure once again?

She sighed. "Would I were wiser than you, and you were the one who had to come to me for answers."

He breathed a small laugh. "Would that were. But since it is not, what is worrying you?"

"They say Mactalde is returning."

He licked a forked tongue across his fangs, lingering on the chip in the left one. "So they've said ever since he died almost twenty years ago."

"They also know another Gifted is coming." She rubbed her thumb against the crook in her forefinger where she had broken it in a sparring match on her fifteenth birthday—half a lifetime ago. "How can anyone know that?"

"Come now, think. Certainly you've told others. Your father the king, for one."

"He knows better than any how volatile this situation could become." She dropped her hand to her side. "We sent word to the Cherazii, of course. Who knows where the Keepers are these days, but at least one will return to Réon Couteau with the Orimere." The beautiful dreamstone was the tool of the Gifted.

She took a breath and voiced the fear that had been running in her head for over a month now. "What if the Cherazii betrayed us? What if they told Nateros or Mactalde's people in Koraud that another Gifted was coming?"

The Garowai shook his head. "The Cherazii didn't betray, now or before. But if the Keepers are in Koraud and if they are making their way west to bring the stone to the Gifted, is it not plausible their movements were observed?"

She made herself nod. The God of all knew she didn't want the Cherazii as enemies, even after what they had done to the last Gifted. Especially after that. Because, really, weren't they the only ones who *hadn't* failed twenty years ago?

She had failed: as an ignorant nine-year-old she had stood by and watched as her Gifted, Harrison Garnett, turned rogue, allied himself with the Koraudian king Faolan Mactalde, and tried to take the throne of Lael.

Her father had failed: he had botched the war into which Harrison and Mactalde had plunged Lael and Koraud, and, even though he had finally brought Koraud to heel by executing Mactalde, hostilities simmered even now under the war-scarred surface of both kingdoms.

In his own way, even the Garowai had failed: for all his wisdom, his cryptic answers and his passive observances had done nothing to help a bewildered, overwhelmed nine-year-old Searcher stop her Gifted from ripping apart Lael.

Only the Cherazii, as sworn defenders of Ori Réon and Keepers of the Orimere, had succeeded: they had killed the Gifted for his perfidy, banishing him to the other world.

The Garowai was still waiting. He knew these weren't the questions she had ridden all the way from Réon Couteau to ask.

She wet her lips. "How do I stop the Gifted from coming?"

His nostril flaps quivered.

"There shouldn't be another Gifted. Not in my lifetime." Again, she rubbed at her crooked finger. "I fulfilled my duties as Searcher twenty years ago, when Harrison Garnett crossed the worlds."

"Oh, come, I taught you better logic than that. Just because most Searchers are given only one Gifted doesn't mean that it is the way it *must* be."

She held her body very still. What she wanted was to explode into action, to move, to fight, to do something useful. She needed to make this all stop. How could he be so unaffected?

"Nateros will see this second Gifted's coming as witchcraft, or heresy," she said. "It's been centuries since two Gifted crossed in one Searcher's lifetime. People will think it unnatural. And what about Mactalde's prophecy that he would return from the dead?" Her voice came out hoarse, strained.

The Garowai flicked his spiked tail back and forth through the sand. "There is no returning from the dead. Not in this life." He stood and shook himself again, gingerly. He coughed and limped toward the water.

"And the Gifted?" she asked. "I have no power to hold him back. But is there no way to convince him to hold himself away from us?"

"Neither of you can stop what's destined to happen. This Gifted will come, and you will search for him and you will find him, just as you did with the last."

"Just as I did with the last." She choked. "The God of all forbid."

At the water's edge, he twisted his head to look back at her. "You were nine years old, Allara. No one blames you for what happened."

"I blame me."

"Let the Gifted come. Perhaps he will bring peace."

That was something she dared not believe. "One man can't bring peace to Lael. Not now."

"You don't know that. And I didn't say he would bring peace to Lael." His muzzle crinkled again, ever so gently. "Perhaps he will bring peace to *you*. Go along now. Prepare yourself. And when you find this Gifted, bring him to me at Ori Réon. I will know he's come, and I will be waiting."

He padded into the lake. When the water reached his chest, he submerged his head and, with one powerful stroke of his wings, disappeared. The bubbles on the surface faded to froth and then to oblivion. He would resurface in his lair behind the waterfall, and he would not reappear to answer her questions, no matter how much she needed him to.

She stood alone on the riverbank. The evening breeze threaded her hair, and her heart thudded dully. She should have known better than to have expected a way out of this impending disaster. She looked down at her crooked finger and forced an exhale.

If she could write the world as she would, life would go on just as it had since the death of her first Gifted. She would need the rest of her life just to put together the pieces from that one fiasco.

The one thing she didn't need was another Gifted. She didn't need another volatile outsider throwing the world off its axis.

Ever since she had known he was coming, she had tried to contact him through the lake. She had spoken to him. She had even shot at his reflection in the water. She had done her best to scare him away. Perhaps, after all, that would be enough to keep him away from her.

Perhaps.

She turned to mount Rihawn. As she touched her heel to his side, she looked back at the Gloamfall misting up from its silver pool. The Garowai knew more than he was sharing with her. Always he told her only what he thought she needed to hear, and she had grown up trusting his wisdom. But sometimes she wanted to clench her hands in the mane on either side of his head and demand he tell her everything. She wanted to know. Even if the knowing killed her, it had to be better than this blind and deaf struggle.

With a shuddered breath, she turned back and urged Rihawn forward. As he galloped through the gloamwheat into the trees, his hoofbeats seemed to hammer a single message: *You have failed, you have failed, you have failed.*

3

THANKS TO THE Midwest's heat wave, sweat soaked Chris's shirt by the time he reached the El-train.

He was almost to the train's entrance when someone rattled his arm. He looked over his shoulder into the face of a lantern-jawed old man. The man's mouth twitched, almost as if he were trying to hold back a smile.

Goosebumps pinched Chris's skin under his sweat-damp T-shirt. *No way.* Could this be the guy?

The passengers behind squeezed him forward and forced him to turn around and step into the train.

The man's hand closed around his arm. "Do you think the shrink will be able to explain your dreams of the girl on the horse?" His voice was the creak of worn-out bedsprings.

Definitely the guy. Chris whipped around. The man had said Chris would see him soon, but this was way easier than Chris had expected—maybe too easy.

The man released his arm and stepped back. He was lean almost to the point of emaciation. His shoulders jutted against the gray flannel of a knee-length trench coat, and his long white hands and three inches of wrist hung below his sleeves.

Chris shoved back through the loading passengers. "Wait—"

Outside the train, the man walked away, his stride hitching as if he wanted to break into a run but wouldn't let himself. He was here. He knew about the dreams. And he was getting away.

Chris squeezed through the door and broke into a run across the platform.

The man disappeared down the stairs, and Chris followed.

Once past the turnstiles and back on the street, Chris stopped to look both ways. Through the clutter of passing traffic, he caught a glimpse of gray flannel one block down. The streetlight turned red, and traffic came to a halt.

He sprinted, pushing past startled pedestrians. "Hey!"

The old man kept walking, his back straight beneath his coat. In this humidity, the air felt like steam. But this guy, dressed for January, didn't even look damp.

"Stop a minute!" He reached to grab the man's shoulder. One more stride, and he'd have him.

The stranger spun around.

Chris caught a handful of coat. "Who are you? How do you know me?"

"We shouldn't be seen together. It's too dangerous." Lank, greasy hair fell just past his collar.

Chris hung onto the coat. "How do you know about the woman on the black horse? Who are you?"

The man's shoulders drew back, and his chin came up in a vaguely military stance. "My name is Harrison Garnett. But—" His attention seemed to wander. "Don't tell anyone. Until it happens."

"Until what happens?"

Harrison's eyes flicked back. "I told you *not here*. Leave."

"You're the one who came looking for *me*."

Harrison turned half away, then swung back and slammed his fist into Chris's face. "I said leave now!"

Chris tripped backwards. He caught his balance against the brick building behind him and touched the blood oozing from his lip. "You crazy old man—"

On the sidewalk ahead, Harrison ran, already halfway to the next intersection. Chris righted himself and started after him. Harrison crossed the street, the light changed behind him, and the street clogged with traffic.

Chris scrambled to a halt. *Seriously?* This old coot had tracked him down just to whisper threats and smack him in the face?

The guy radiated crazy. But there was something about him . . . something truthful. For whatever it was worth, *Harrison* believed what he was saying—and that was maybe the freakiest part of all.

Chris walked into the commotion of the police station and threaded his way to the queue at the front counter. He'd done this so many times, he could probably fill out the bail forms sleepwalking.

In a few minutes, his father shuffled across the room. Near the door, he stopped and waited. His eyes flitted away from Chris's, and he fingered a bruise on his cheekbone.

Once upon a time, Paul Redston had been a handsome man. Blond, broad-shouldered, brilliant. He had worked as a beat cop by day and moonlighted as a mystery writer during the evenings. Now, his hair had thinned to little more than a ragged skullcap. His shoulders were hunched, his stride a shuffle. The brains Chris had so admired as a kid were spent, drowned in a drunkard's obsession.

Sometimes he couldn't help feeling part of that was his fault. If he had tried harder back when things had started falling apart, if he had done a better job swallowing his own grief, maybe his dad would have held steady.

But then the old anger bit hard. His dad was the one who had walked away, not Chris. His dad was the one who was still walking away.

"Disturbing the peace?" Chris asked.

"Yeah. A brawl, I guess. That's what they told me, anyway."

"You don't remember?"

"Must have been deep into it."

"You usually are."

Exhaustion overwhelmed Chris, as though someone somewhere had spun a dial and quadrupled the gravitational pull. For twenty years, this was the way things had been. When his family's Pontiac had rolled over on a snowy road, killing his mother and his younger sister Jenifer, it had effectively killed his father as well. Paul had disappeared into the bottle and never come up for air.

His dad scratched his whiskered cheek. "I'm sorry about this. Thanks for coming."

"I don't come here to be thanked." Chris brushed past.

Behind him, Paul's steps shambled. "Wait a minute, slow down—"

Chris pushed through the door into the golden day. Noon-hour traffic hummed along the street, and somewhere far away a horn blared, urging everyone to pick up the pace and just *go*, to put a foot down on the accelerator and drive as far and as fast as they could.

At the curb, he stopped. People packed the sidewalks despite the heat, but the crowd opened up around him and flowed on past. If they noticed the old man coming up behind him, they wouldn't much care. What was one more drunk in a city this size?

Paul stopped beside him, wheezing. "I'm sorry. It's the last time, I promise. I promise you."

"Don't promise. We both know you can't keep it."

"No, I mean it." Paul's rumbling voice had once been a powerful bass. Now, it cracked at the end of every word. "I know you give up a lot to come down here and help me out. You've got your own life and everything. You're a smart kid. Smarter than your old man."

"Lisa was the smart one. She stopped bailing you out a long time ago." His older sister had married an investment broker and moved to Los Angeles, probably as much to evade Chris's attempts to take care of her as to escape their father. She had twin daughters and a swimming pool in her backyard. Chris hadn't talked to her in months.

He turned to go.

Behind him, his father's footsteps slapped the sidewalk. "Wait a minute. Chris, wait. You don't mean that."

They passed a sandwich stall, and the smell of old grease clogged in the back of Chris's throat. Maybe he didn't know what he meant anymore. If his dreams were anything to judge by, he was going crazy anyhow, so what did it matter? At least crazy people had an excuse for their messed-up lives.

"I'm sorry I had to call you," Paul persisted. "I *am* sorry. But I couldn't get anybody else to come for me. Maybe you don't believe me, but I've tried to stop. I just—" His voice cracked a little. "I just can't quite bury the past."

Chris turned back. People behind him hesitated, altered their courses, and flowed on by.

"Bury the past." He tamped down on his anger and willed it to stay locked away, deep inside its dark hole. "Why don't we bury it alongside Mom and Jenifer?"

Paul leaned away. His heavy eyebrows knit together, his eyes deep with pain and regret. Or, more likely, just the latest hangover.

"I know you still blame me—" he began.

"I don't want your apologies, and I don't want your thanks." Chris clamped his hands on his hips as he blew out a long breath. "If you really cared about me and my life, you'd just . . . stop calling me."

Paul's head dropped. After a moment, his eyes came back up to look at the traffic. "I would never have hurt you on purpose."

Chris raked his hand through his hair. "Never mind. I shouldn't have said that. Look, I'm tired, you're tired. Why don't you go home, and we can talk about this later."

But they wouldn't talk. They never talked. And maybe that was just as well.

He took a step away. "I'll see you." He started down the sidewalk, made it five paces, then looked back.

His dad stood where he had left him, arms at his sides, shoulders hunched. His button-up shirt and carpenter jeans hung on his body, two sizes too large.

Chris's breath fizzed out between his teeth. He crossed back to his father, dug into his pocket, and came out with a handful of loose papers, a folded-up envelope, and a couple ten-dollar bills.

"Here. Take the bus home." The money would undoubtedly see the inside of a liquor-store cash register sooner than it would the bus till. But did it even really matter anymore? One more bottle wasn't going to change the course of Paul's life.

"Chris, I—" His dad looked into his face, focusing for the first time today. "What happened to your lip?" For a moment, he almost might have been the concerned cop he had been so long ago. "You in a fight, son?"

Chris touched his tongue to the cut. "Just a misunderstanding, of sorts."

"You want to tell me about it?"

He hesitated. Every now and then, his father would give him a glimpse of what might have been between them. They might have had a relationship. They might have talked. Paul might have been the one guiding Chris. Chris might even have told him about the dreams. Paul wouldn't have had an answer for that, but at least Chris could have had the satisfaction of trusting someone else with the burden.

But that was only might-have-been. Reality didn't include such things as second chances. This relationship wasn't father and son.

This was a drunk and the poor sucker who paid his bail.

"No," Chris said. "There's nothing to talk about."

His father looked down at the bills. "I'm not the only one who can ask for help. If you ever want to call me, if I can be there and help, whatever it is, you know I will. I'm still your father."

"Yeah, you're still my father." He managed a smile. "Goodbye, Dad. Go home and sleep it off, okay?"

The corner of his father's mouth tilted up. He turned and shuffled off. With any luck, he was headed to the bus station and not the nearest bar.

Chris watched until his dad disappeared around the corner, then looked at the envelope he had dug out of his pocket along with the money. It was sealed and addressed to him. The scrawl was Harrison's.

He frowned and ripped off the end. How had that old man managed to stuff an envelope into his pocket without his knowing? A sheet of notebook paper, just like the other one, fell into his hand. Its message was a single handwritten sentence and a street address in black ink:

Come ask me. Everything can be explained.

4

CHRIS DROVE SLOWLY, leaning over the steering wheel and checking the numbers on Harrison's note. After leaving his dad, he had gone back home to borrow Mike's Volkswagen Bug. He was crazy to be here. In all likelihood, Harrison was some serial killer with the grand modus operandi of luring chumps out to his abandoned neighborhood and then snuffing them. But right now he wanted answers more than safety.

He nearly missed the shack sporting what had once been an *Eleven* above the door. Most of the letters on the plaque had fallen off, leaving only the *l* and the last two *e*s. He swung over to the curb and winced at the crunch under the wheels. Mike would extract the price of new tires in blood. Deathtrap though it was, the rusty orange Bug was the love of his life.

He cut the engine and sat there. A pallor hung over the street, shrouding it even in the heat of June. The buildings lay colorless and silent, like faces asleep from exhaustion. But if the other buildings on the street were asleep, Harrison's was comatose. Glass jagged the windows against a backdrop of cardboard. The crumbling concrete steps looked like a ragged front tooth. Paint, once blue, had faded to a smutty gray.

He ducked out of the car and pocketed the keys. Probably, he should have told Mike where he was going. He had at least thirty pounds on Harrison, and this time he was more than ready for a fight, but this was the kind of neighborhood where people got mugged by their neighbors and were never heard of again.

Hands loose at his sides, he trudged to the chain-link fence. The gate creaked when he touched it, and the latch refused to budge. He shook it, and the whole fence wobbled.

In a window beside the door, a corner of the cardboard moved. For better or worse, whoever was in there knew he was here. Leaving the latch, he took a step back, braced one hand against the top of the gate, and jumped the thing. The cardboard in the window dropped back into place.

He threaded his way up the walk, kicking newspapers and the occasional soup can out of the way. As he reached the top of the steps, a black pickup roared down the street, and a plastic bag skittered along the gutter. The truck cruised through a stop sign and continued.

At least somebody besides Harrison was alive on this haunted lane.

Chris banged on the screen door, clanking the aluminum frame against the doorjamb.

A long moment passed—long enough that he began to figure Harrison had no intention of opening up. Then the door whooshed inward, and fingers clamped onto his sleeve and hauled him inside.

"You came." Harrison, wearing an undershirt and rumpled brown slacks, shut the door. Without the trench coat, he looked even skinnier than before. The bones of his shoulders and elbows creased his pale, freckled skin. His hair flopped over his forehead and stuck up on top. A thin stink of body odor surrounded him.

Chris stood in a hallway that led all the way to another door in the back of the building. A smudgy darkness hung heavy all over the house, but he could make out waist-high walls partitioning the kitchen on the right side and a living room on the left.

A series of clicks issued from the door as Harrison slammed home a long row of deadbolts.

"Those supposed to keep me in?" Chris asked.

Harrison thrust the last bolt into place and pushed past Chris, headed down the hall. Chris hesitated, shot another glance around, then followed.

The house smelled like the dust from an unused air conditioner. How long had it been since a window had been opened in here? The moth-eaten drapes in the living room shut out any hope of light from the cardboarded windows. A ratty couch and chairs sat stolidly beneath piles of trashed paper plates and cardboard boxes. Mounds of books and notepads flooded the floor, leaving only a narrow path to the lone unencumbered chair.

At the end of the hallway, Harrison knelt in front of the door to unfasten another half-dozen locks.

The silence pressed in on Chris. "Tell me what this is all about."

"Ssh!" With a flourish, Harrison unfastened the last lock, rose to his feet, and threw open the door.

The room inside didn't even seem a part of the same house. Lit with the glare of fluorescent ceiling lamps and carpeted and painted in a grayish blue, it was practically blinding after the murk of the hallway. It was tiny, probably intended for a storage closet, but Harrison had crammed in a bunk, a camp stove, and a desk straining under an old giant of a computer. Sketches, maps, and scrawled notes papered the walls in neat fish-scale rows. Shelves near the ceiling held a collection of wood carvings and strange tools.

Chris stepped inside. "What is all this?"

Harrison slammed the door and turned around. "This is where I live. This is where I survive. I've spent the last twenty years here— searching for you."

Chris shook his head. "I don't get it." He turned, surveying the room, until he was facing Harrison. "Why search for me?"

"You're the Gifted, aren't you? You've crossed, haven't you?"

"What are you talking about?"

"I knew you'd come to me after you crossed. You'd have questions, and I'm the only one who knows the answers." He cackled.

"All right, you want to answer questions, try this one. How'd you know what I was dreaming? I didn't start having those dreams until *you* sent me that letter."

"Don't be an idiot." Harrison crossed his arms. "You've dreamt all your life. Did you never see *me* in your dreams? When you were a child?"

"Thankfully, no—" The word chopped itself off. A slivered memory stabbed his brain: the nightmare battles that had terrified him as a kid. Somewhere in his memory of those battles lurked a young man with Harrison's eyes.

On a shelf, in between two crude wood carvings—one of some kind of winged lion, the other of a castle—glinted a foot-long cylinder of glass, spiraled inside like a strand of DNA. He picked it up and held it to the light. Inside, water ebbed and flowed, like the ocean against the beach. Tiny flames, orange at the tip, blue at the heart, licked up and down inside the glass and danced around the water, never devouring it, never extinguished by it.

He tilted it back and forth. The water and the flames tumbled over the top of each other, only to reappear, intact, at opposite ends of the glass. "What is this?"

"It is a *fawa-radi*, a fire-and-water sculpture. The great artists make them in Glen Arden."

"How does it work?"

"How should I know?" Harrison's thin chest puffed out beneath his undershirt. "I'm a Gifted, not an artist."

Chris looked up. "What's a Gifted?"

"You're a Gifted." Harrison scowled. "Don't tell me you haven't crossed yet?"

He gritted his teeth. He had been an idiot to come here. Harrison was cracked right down the middle, too far gone to even make sense. "Crossed *where*? What are you talking about?"

Harrison grabbed the sculpture. "You shouldn't have come until you crossed. But since you're here, I'll tell you. One of these days you're going to close your eyes and wake up on the other side of your dreams."

"Right. Because I'm a Gifted." He took a careful step toward the door.

Harrison shook the sculpture in Chris's face. "People in this world don't know it, but the human mind has two existences."

Chris stopped in spite of himself. This was so ridiculous it wasn't worth listening to. But he *was* listening. Didn't his dreams feel real? Didn't they *feel* like they could be as real as this life?

He caught himself and sucked in three deep breaths. If he wasn't careful, he was going to end up as daffy as Harrison. "Just tell me what a Gifted is."

"*I* was a Gifted." Pride heated Harrison's words. "One of the chosen who cross the worlds. We're destined to change history! That's our gift! Everyone said I should have been the only Gifted in her lifetime. There's hardly ever two within the same century." His face hardened. "But they were wrong. The Garowai told me. No one else, just me."

"Who's her?" But he had a feeling he already knew. Who else but the woman on the black warhorse?

Harrison propped one hand against his desk chair. "The Searcher." His forefinger tapped the wood and a ligament in his skinny arm jumped. "She was just a child when she called me across." His eyes glazed again. "Now she would be a woman. Twenty-nine." His voice lowered. "What's she look like?"

"Like she likes getting her own way."

Harrison stared at the sculpture in his hand. "She was a strange child. Regal, aloof—a queen. I'll never be able to forget her eyes. I'll go to my grave with those eyes staring at me."

That wasn't a very encouraging thought. Chris gestured around the room. "Why all the secrecy? Nobody's going to believe any of this dream stuff, even if you tell them. Why hide?"

"Stop being naïve. It's not safe out there. Not for a man of my talents. I know too much. I'm too valuable to too many people."

"And these people are . . . ?"

"The government, the CIA, the Mossad—too many people to name."

Chris tried not to laugh. "The government's not going to buy this. Nobody's going to buy it. And even if they believe it, why would they care?"

"It's valuable, sensitive information." Harrison held himself up straight. "They'd kill me for it."

"If it was valuable, they'd keep you alive."

"You don't know what you're talking about." Turning on his heel, Harrison pushed the desk chair aside and knelt in front of a waist-high safe in the corner. "If anyone finds me, I'll blow them up. I've got explosives ready under the floor, out there in the living room."

Chris shot a glance at the closed door. "Explosives." Harrison was just wacky enough to really have a wad of C-4 buried out there. Even worse, he probably *would* set the thing off if provoked. "Okay, I need to go. I only came to ask you if you knew how to make the dreams stop."

"Stop?" Harrison crinked his neck around. "What kind of stupid talk is that? You've never seen a place so magnificent as Lael in all your sloppy city-born life. Most people'd give their life savings to see what you're seeing."

"No. They wouldn't. Schizophrenics don't want their hallucinations. People with dissociative disorder don't want their multiple personalities. And I can tell you right now I don't want these dreams. I'm too busy to go crazy. I've got my own life, my own problems."

Harrison jumped up. "You're a Gifted, you fool! You could rule the worlds! Both of 'em! And I'll show you how." He whirled back to the safe, yanked open the door, and dragged out a double handful of spiral-bound notebooks rubber banded together. "They took my chance from me before I'd even been there a whole year, but I knew you were coming. I've spent the last twenty years making notes, plans, maps!" He shoved the notebooks at Chris. "You can rule Lael, and I'll rule here. Two Gifted, side by side—we'll be unstoppable."

Chris pushed the notebooks back. "I'm sure this will come as a surprise, but I don't want to rule the world. Either of them." He started for the door.

Harrison lunged after him. "You can't go."

"Watch me." He reached the door and unfastened the deadbolt. "What I want is for the dreams to end. If you're not going to tell me how to get it done, I'll find somebody who can." Hand on the doorknob, he paused. "Who's this Mactalde you were talking about earlier?"

Harrison's face paled to gray. "You stay away from him." Spittle welled in the corners of his mouth. "Him and his threats and his grand plans and his high and mighty ways! If you go to him now, he'll ruin everything!"

Chris looked at the maps scrawled in black on the wall. Harrison had spent his life constructing a fantasy, a delirium. "I came here for answers and all you've given me is nonsense. So thanks, but no thanks." He pulled open the door and started down the dark hallway.

Harrison's footsteps slammed the threadbare carpet behind him. "You're a fool! A fool! Mactalde will destroy you if he finds you! Destroy everything!"

Chris reached the front door and started flipping the heavy deadbolts out of their sleeves. They smacked against the doorframe like angry ticks of a clock. Enough was enough. Whatever steps he took to reclaim his sanity were his own business. This deranged old man had no right to lecture him.

"Don't you care about any of that?" Harrison's fingertips stabbed Chris's arm. "Don't you care about the power we can wield?"

Chris hauled the door open and flooded the house with light. He turned back. "No, I don't."

Harrison leaned away. His mouth twisted.

"Listen to me," Chris said, "the dreams are not real. They're a figment of my imagination. For all I know, you're a figment too. I'm going crazy, I'm having a nervous breakdown, I don't know. But I want it to stop. I want it to end. And I'll do whatever I have to do to make it end." His breath came hard. "And it doesn't matter what I do in the dreams because it's *not* real. This is the real world." He pointed at the floor. "This is where we live our lives. What we do in our dreams, no matter how real they *feel*, does not matter."

"Fine. Be that way. Be worse than a fool!" Harrison closed his hands into fists. Before he could swing a punch, he coughed and staggered back against the wall. A round, red hole appeared on the left side of his chest.

Chris jerked back. On the curb, tires squealed. The sound ripped through his mind and blasted him back to full speed. He dropped flat to the floor. Outside, a black pickup sped away from the curb. He batted the door shut.

Across the hall, Harrison clutched his chest as he slid down the wall. "I'm shot, I'm shot—" His pupils shrank into nothing.

Chris scrambled to his feet to catch him. He pulled him away from the wall, and a warm river of blood flooded his hand and arm. The exit wound had ripped through Harrison's shirt, just beneath his shoulder.

"I'm shot, I can't breathe! I'm shot—"

Chris gritted his teeth and tried to channel his thoughts. "Just take it easy." As he lowered Harrison to the rat-eaten carpet, he fumbled his phone out of his pocket. He called 911, pinned the phone against his shoulder, and used both hands to rip open Harrison's thin undershirt.

He'd gotten himself into a whole lot more than he'd bargained for right here.

Ten minutes later, a police car, followed by an ambulance, arrived. After another half an hour, the detective finally got around to talking to Chris. Nobody seemed to know anything about what had happened. At any rate, not anything they wanted to tell him.

It was a whole hour more before they let him walk back up the street to where he'd parked the Bug. He had the key in the lock, turning it, when a footstep sounded behind him.

"Hey," someone said.

He turned to look, and something hard smashed into the back of his head.

5

HE WOKE UP.

Only it wasn't really like waking. It was like closing his eyes on the clout of pain in the back of his head, then blinking them back open to find himself flat on his back, staring up at the soft rustle of very tall trees.

He crooked his head toward his shoulder and narrowed his eyes against the sunlight that streamed through the leaves and lent the green foliage a strangely silver cast. Hanging moss, thin and gray, wafted in the breeze, and the sun shone through it in a way that made it seem to almost glow. It was pretty. Beautiful, really. If this was his latest serving of dreams, it definitely beat getting shot at. He inhaled the same organic spicy smell from the dream of the waterfall.

A face slid into view and blocked out the sun. Shriveled and brown and not too far removed from the underside of a mushroom, the face stretched in surprise, the eyes goggling at him.

"*Ricotée*," scratched a surprised little voice.

"Whoa." He recoiled and scrambled back, crab-like, on his hands and feet, until he smacked into a tree. He blinked hard and willed himself back to the surface of sleep, back to face whatever danger he was in on the street outside Harrison's house. For all he knew, Harrison's assailants might be dismembering him right now.

In front of him, the creature stared, head cocked to the side. "*Ricotée*," it breathed again.

Basically human in form, it stood only a little higher than Chris's knee. Spindly limbs jutted from beneath a long canvas shirt belted at the waist. The legs ended in bare, knobby feet, and the long-fingered hands held the glint of stiletto blades. Framed all about by a mop of mud-colored dreadlocks, the face was the size of Chris's fist, with musty little eyes and a long upper lip.

If this was supposed to be the new-and-improved version of his fair lady on the warhorse, it was a definite misfire.

The creature lifted its lip to reveal two rows of long yellow teeth. It waved its knives in what was either excitement or a threat. "*Ma ta bé?*"

Chris hauled himself to one knee, hands in front of him in a placating gesture. "Just take it easy. I don't know what you want from me. I don't know where I am, I don't know what you are—I just—" His insides eddied. This wasn't real. This couldn't be real. He'd been knocked out. That was what was real. He was dreaming, *dreaming.*

He leaned away from the knife, carefully lifted one hand, and slapped himself in the face. He still didn't wake up. He pinched the skin of his biceps. No go.

His breath came fast. What was it they always told you to do when you were having a nightmare? Tell yourself to wake up? "Wake up, Chris. C'mon, you need to wake up from this one."

He stared around him. Gone were Mike's orange Volkswagen and the gray heat of Harrison's forsaken neighborhood. Instead, he knelt on a rocky hillside, shadowed by trees whose trunks twisted around like whorls of wet caramel taffy. His brain tilt-a-whirled.

"*Ma ta bé?*" The creature flicked one blade toward Chris's chest and shouted over its shoulder. "Raz! *Ci lodden don a tos!* Laeler. *Eck sit cis rotodon!*"

Chris inched a hand out to ease the blade aside. "How about not stabbing me? Because I really don't need to be stabbed right now."

The little figure thrust the blade nearer to Chris's chest. His teeth flashed still more.

A few yards to the left, the underbrush cracked open to reveal his captor's twin. The newcomer thrashed free of the vines and stomped over to stand beside his compatriot.

"*Tuch pua.*" Heavy brows loomed over his eyes, and dark stubble prickled his face. He glared at Chris. "*Ma ta bé?*"

"I come in peace, or whatever it is you want to hear. But I can't understand a word you're saying."

The older one batted his friend's shoulder. "He doesn't speak Cherazii, halfwit."

"Oh." The younger, abashed, lowered his blades a little. "Sorry."

Chris sat back onto his heels and let himself release a long breath. "Okay, then. I really should be going." Somewhere, anywhere.

The blades came back up. "Stay where you are! I have found you, and you are my prisoner!"

"No offense, but I don't quite see how that's going to work." He pushed to his feet. "I'm four times your size and I could squash both of you."

The creature began swaying and parrying the air with his blades. "I have taken your sword while you were sleeping!" This time he was definitely grinning. "It is Riever law. Take a sleeping Laeler's sword, and he is your servant forever!"

"Right." He sidestepped. "I don't want to be rude here, and I really have no desire to squash you, but I don't have a sword, I'm not a Laeler, and I don't know what Riever law is." He took his eyes off his supposed captors long enough to look around.

He was standing on the slope of a wooded hill. Moss sheeted the flat slabs of stone, and a thick fern-like profusion obscured everything else, save for the occasional glimpse of rich black soil. The chittering of little woodland creatures punctuated an almost metallic warbling. In the branches overhead, a flock of sooty-blue birds, about the size of ravens, with carnelian-tipped wingspans twice again as long, hopped and cawed.

He rubbed the smooth, spiraled twist of a tree trunk. "Where am I?"

"Bah." The older one shrugged at his partner. "Pitch, you're an idiot. You would pick the stupidest of the lot."

"Doesn't matter. He's mine, I found him." The one called Pitch bounced around, still brandishing his swords. "Don't be jealous, Raz."

"Where am I?" Chris repeated.

The older one, Raz, replied, "The Thyra hills." He crossed his arms. "If you don't know where you are, how'd you get here?"

Chris managed a laugh that escaped the edge of hysteria. "I'm not here. I'm dreaming. This is all a dream. Just one big fat crazy soon-to-be-woken-up-from dream." He circled the tree. He'd never seen a tree like this in his life. Why would he dream about a tree he'd never seen? "It's a really incredible, convincing dream, but it's just a dream."

"It's not a dream," Pitch said. "If it was a dream, you'd be sleeping.

And you wouldn't dream about us. You'd dream about the other world."

Chris came full circle around the tree. "What other world?"

That, finally, seemed to slow Pitch down a bit. He lowered his blades. "The other world. The one you go to in your dreams. When you sleep here, you dream about the other world. When you're awake here, your body in the other world is dreaming about here."

"You're telling me I have two bodies?" He touched his face. Under a day's growth of whiskers, his features felt the same as always, except . . . He ran his tongue over his lower lip. The copper tang of blood and the sting of saliva in an open cut weren't there.

He slid his hand higher up his face, and his fingers bumped over an unfamiliar knot of bone in the bridge of his nose. "I broke my nose?"

"Stupid *and* delusional," Raz said.

"I broke my nose." He rubbed his fingers against the scar. "I never broke my nose. This is not my nose."

"Could've fooled me."

His hands worked higher. Cheeks, eyes, forehead—everything seemed in order. His hair was longer than when he'd blacked out, just full enough for him to grab a handful on either side. He inspected the rest of his body. Two arms, two legs. Clever of him not to dream about having an amputated limb.

But his clothing was entirely foreign. Instead of T-shirt, jeans, and sneakers, he wore a flowing blouse-like shirt with a wide, unbuttoned collar and voluminous sleeves that were stitched tight at the elbows and the wrists. His pants were made of some kind of dark brown homespun. Heavy leather boots reached to his knees, where they were cuffed down to mid-shin. His belt held a leather pouch and a long thin sword sheath, which, true to Pitch's word, was empty. He made himself keep breathing. At least he *had* clothes. And money. And, apparently, a sword somewhere around here.

"So let me get this straight," he said. "You're telling me everybody moves back and forth between these worlds when they sleep?"

Pitch nodded. "Exactly."

"And you visit my world when *you* dream?" This was where he proved to himself this couldn't possibly be real. The likes of these two had never visited Earth, waking or sleeping.

Raz threw up his hands in disgust and turned back to the hedge.

"No, no." Pitch put both blades in one hand, so he could gesture in the negative with the other. "Rievers don't dream. Neither do Cherazii. Only humans."

"Only humans." So his theory had a loophole. "Why's that?"

"Because Rievers and Cherazii only live *here*. You have to live in both worlds to dream."

Somewhere in the trees in front of Chris, a rhythmic clatter echoed beneath the forest's canopy. "What's that?"

"A horse." Raz glared at Pitch. "Orias said to stay in the thicket until he got back. You want him to find you out larking about?"

Pitch pointed up at Chris. "But he won't fit in the thicket."

"Then leave him. If he's too stupid to take care of himself, you don't want him anyway."

With a flourish, Pitch sheathed his blades. Arms crossed, hands on his hilts, he dropped his head in a bow. "You are my responsibility now, so I will take care of you." He caught two of Chris's fingers in his tiny hand.

"Thanks." Chris looked in the direction of the approaching hoofbeats. "But this sword you say you took from me—maybe it wouldn't be a bad idea for me to have it back."

"It's in the thicket. Come, I'll show you." Pitch ran in a strange, loping pace, doling out three or four strides for every one of Chris's. "I'm Pitch. That's Raz." His remaining blade gestured to the older Riever burrowing into the brush ahead of them. "What's your name?"

"Chris. Chris Redston."

The Riever tilted his head back and forth, blowing air in first one cheek, then the other, as if tasting the words. "Strange name. Your accent is strange too. Where do you come from?"

Before he could answer, a big red horse rounded the corner. On its back rode a giant of a man with skin the color and translucency of an egg white, veined with blue. Sun-bleached brown hair hung past his chin, veiling but not hiding the batwing ears that rose two or three inches above his head. Shoulders and chest swelled against a sleeveless leather tunic that revealed intimidating biceps and corded forearms. Deep scars wormed across the right arm and collarbone.

Eyes of pale, almost luminescent green darted from Chris's face to his hold on Pitch's hand, and, in an instant, the stranger had dropped the dead gazelle-like creature he had dangled from one hand and snatched a battle axe from his belt. "Dougal!"

A black cat, about the size of a wolfhound, bounded up from behind the horse. The muscles in its forequarters bunched and its short white-tufted tail whipped back and forth.

Chris backpedaled, caught his heel on a vine, and fell down flat on his back.

Behind him, Pitch hollered, *"Tulle sit giharde! Eck sit cis rotodon!"*

The hesitation before the newcomer responded could have lasted Chris the rest of his life.

"Dougal! *Eider fon!*"

Chris rolled over and scrambled to regain his feet. Then he dared a look over his shoulder.

The big cat sat on its haunches, blinking rust-colored eyes. Striped ever so faintly in a lighter shade of black, it sported white tassels of fur at the tip of each ear and a beard of white trimmed in black. It licked four-inch fangs.

Its master had returned his axe to his belt. He sat the horse straight-backed, one hand on the reins, the other leaning against the axe head.

Two things were abundantly obvious. First, this hulk could kill Chris, using any number of unsavory methods, in less than a minute. And second, he wasn't going to.

"I apologize." The stranger's voice was deep without being gruff, his inflection weighting the consonants and lengthening the vowels. "In these days, a Cherazim can't afford to mistake an enemy for a friend."

Raz ducked out of the thicket. "Especially humans with strange accents."

The Cherazim's face, with its long planes and sloping jaw, was difficult to read, but something flickered in his eyes, some tiny knitting of the skin above his nose. "I know what my enemies' speech sounds like. And I'll be forsworn if I've ever heard the likes of you."

Pitch ran back to Chris's side and grabbed his hand. "Orias, this is my prisoner Chris Redston. I found him while he was sleeping, and I took his sword. Raz will bear it out."

Raz reached Orias's stirrup and jumped to hook a skinny arm around his boot. "I'll bear out he's near kin to an idiot." He clambered up Orias's leg to stand on the horse's rump, one hand clamped on the baldric across Orias's back. "He doesn't know where he is or how he got here."

Pitch shook his head. "Just because he is not from Lael does not mean he is a worthless find."

The crease between Orias's eyes deepened. "If not from Lael, then where?"

Chris opened his mouth to explain, then closed it and shook his head. "I doubt it's any place you've heard of, even in your wildest dreams."

"He doesn't know anything about the dreams," Pitch said.

"Is that so?" Orias stared on. "Well then, welcome to Lael, Chris Redston. You've chosen a bad time for it, I'm afraid. But that's the way of things."

"There wasn't any choosing in my coming here. I just came. And if I knew how to leave, I would. Like that." He snapped his fingers, part of his mind hoping that would be enough to wake him up.

"My name would be Orias Tarn, and I'll offer you a ride, if you'll take it. But first—" The Cherazim swung his off leg over the horse's neck and slid to the ground. On the ground, his height was even more imposing. "Tell me." He studied Chris. He seemed to be having just as difficult a time believing in Chris's presence here in dreamland as Chris was himself. "Did what you now see as Lael begin for you as a dream—and *grow* into reality?"

Chris nodded. "Not just one dream. All my dreams." That thought caught him up short. *All his dreams.* Why hadn't he realized it before? He'd been so focused on the dreams of the battles and the woman on the black horse that he hadn't given a second thought to the other dreams—the hazy, disjointed *dreamlike* dreams he'd dreamt all the rest of the time.

They'd all been different enough, random enough. But, really, they'd all been the same. Golden threads had always woven through the entire tapestry of his dreamscape and joined them in the common unity of a place. *This* place. This world with its spicy trees and silver leaves and strange beings. Had he dreamt a dream in his life that hadn't taken place here?

What did that mean? That he was lost inside some imaginary world his subconscious had dreamed up? Maybe he was schizophrenic. He was delusional. He was having visions. He was seeing and hearing things that didn't exist. His mind had conjured them up, building them slowly, from his childhood onward, spurred by the catalyst of his mother's and sister's deaths, until suddenly they had taken over his mind.

Sudden sweat slicked his palms, and he forced the air to keep moving in his lungs. Though what did it really matter if he kept breathing? Dream bodies only needed dream air, right?

Pitch's fingers loosened their grip on his hand and slipped away. He stared up with wide eyes. "You're the Gifted?" A grin split his face, and he danced around in a circle. "I have found the Gifted! My servant is the Gifted!" He stopped short and looked at Orias. "Does that mean I can't keep him?"

"A Gifted?" Chris said. That's what Harrison had called him. From the exuberant look on Pitch's face, the bored scowl on Raz's, and the stunned stare Orias was giving him, that might make him anything from a prophet to a plague carrier. "Is that a good thing or a bad thing?"

Orias took a breath. "That depends."

"On what?"

"On the man. But it can't be any coincidence you landed here, right in the lap of a Keeper."

"A Keeper?" Chris shook his head.

"I'm a Keeper. The Tarns have been Keepers of the Orimere for generations." He touched the oval buckle that secured his baldric's chest strap. An upraised wing had been stamped into the burnished silver. "The wing of the Garowai is the Tarn crest. The Searcher sent word two months ago that you were coming."

"The Searcher's the woman on the black horse?"

"Yes. The Searchers are connected to the Gifted. They can feel them. They can sense where they are in the world. You saw her in your dreams before you crossed?"

He rubbed the side of his fist up the center of his forehead, right where the Searcher's bullets always caught him before he woke up. "Yeah, I've seen her."

Orias stepped toward him. "Two months ago, I joined one of the many Cherazii caravans fleeing persecution in Koraud. I came to bring you the Orimere. I never expected to have to bring the Gifted to the Searcher as well."

"We could skip that part as far as I'm concerned."

"You're in a different world now," Orias said. "Takes some getting used to, I suppose. You need to relax, let your subconscious tell you what to do. It's a world you've known all your life. You just don't remember it. When a Gifted crosses over, his conscious mind from the other world usurps the memories from ours. You'll get used to it."

"Get used to it?" He forced a laugh. "This is a dream. I'm going to wake up, and this is all going to be nothing but a long nightmare."

What might have been half a smile raised the corner of Orias's mouth. "Your world is ages behind in understanding the true nature of dreams, but for us here it's common knowledge."

Chris snorted. "It's common knowledge I'm crazy? Of course, if this is some manifestation of my subconscious, it *would* make sense everyone in it would know I was insane before I did."

The smile turned into a grin. "You're not insane."

Raz grunted. "I'll give you good odds."

Pitch shot him a glare.

"This happens to all humans," Orias said. "It's just that most people don't remember it. Each of you lives two separate and distinct lives. And dreams," he tapped his temple, "dreams are the only link. They're your only memories of your life in this other world."

Pitch peered up at Chris, thumbs tucked under his opposite arms. "Only the Gifted can cross the worlds."

"Only the Gifted are able to see and remember what they do in both worlds," Orias said. "For everyone else there are only dreams— just as there were for you before today."

Chris looked around. What he needed right now was some speck of incontrovertible proof that this was a dream. An inconsistency, a flicker in the wall, a crack in the scenery. Even better, he needed to find the magic words that would wake him up.

He faced Orias. "If everyone is living doppelgänger lives, how come you don't live in my world?"

Orias glanced back to where Raz stood on the horse's broad rump. "Perhaps he's not as stupid as you think."

Raz rolled his eyes.

He turned back. "Once, we might have lived in your world. Species, races, countries, they eventually disappear, some never to return. Who is to say the Cherazii were not one of those fatalities of time?" He shrugged. "Only the God of all knows. But it is true the Cherazii dream no longer."

"Okay, fine, so let's say I *am* the Gifted. My lotto number comes up, and I'm the lucky one who gets an express pass to dreamland. What does that mean? What's the point of a Gifted?"

"That's for you to find out. The Gifted are called into our world to change something. Their gift—their destiny—is to launch and sometimes to end epochs."

Pitch's snub-nosed face wrinkled into a smile. "I think your gift is to bring peace to Lael."

"And how am I supposed to do that? I just show up, is that it? I'm here, so now Lael's at peace?" He spread his arms and looked around. "Sounds good to me. So now that the job's done, please point me to the turnoff back to home."

"Stupid *and* arrogant," Raz said. "What do you think you are, human? The blithering Garowai straight from heaven? You don't get nothing for nothing in this world."

"Then what do you want me to do? Find a soapbox and start preaching peace and love?" He glared back. "Just tell me what I'm supposed to do, and I'll do it. I'll follow the ten-step plan, whatever it takes. Just show me what I have to do to wake up."

He would *not* go crazy. He would not end up drunken and slobbering in the gutter like his father. Maybe he'd been pushing himself too hard here lately. Maybe that last trip had tired him out more than he'd realized. Maybe he needed a break. Life was nothing but a fight, and if you had to come out swinging when you were only twelve, it left you with broken knuckles and missing teeth by the time the real battles started.

But this wasn't where it was going to end. He'd fought his way through life this far. He could fight a little farther.

But first he had to play the mind games. He had to stop the dreams.

Pitch reached up and patted his leg. "Don't worry. The Searcher will find you and tell you what you have to do."

Orias's chest lifted with a deep breath. "These are dangerous times into which you've stepped, Chris Redston. Complicated times, and all the more so if you're the Gifted. You find us a weary, war-torn country. I'll explain it to you later. Right now, we'll have to return to my caravan, gather gear, and take our leave."

"And where are we going?"

"The sooner we get you and the Orimere to Réon Couteau, the better."

"What is this Orimere thing anyway?"

Orias reached into his jerkin and pulled out a small green pouch. He tugged loose the drawstrings, then upended the pouch into his palm and closed his fingers over whatever had fallen out. "Only a handful of people in the worlds have ever seen this."

He extended his fist, and his fingers opened to reveal a translucent white stone the size of a turkey egg. Its milky color pulsed with an energy of its own, sometimes veining with green, sometimes deepening to crimson or purple.

"If you are touching it when you sleep, it and anything else your body is in contact with will cross over. The Orimere is the key to the door between the worlds. Only the Gifted are given the power to use it."

Tentatively, Chris held out his hand for the stone. It touched his skin with an electric shock, and he jerked back, nearly dropping it. It purred in his hand, like a kitten curled into a ball. The harder he clenched it, the harder it purred, warming his skin, tingling his nerves.

"Feels like it's going to eat my hand."

"It feels that way only to a Gifted." Orias gave a little nod and touched his fist to his shoulder. "Welcome. I hope your dedication is greater than your predecessor's."

Chris opened his hand. The stone pulsed, a sleepy orange. "What am I supposed to do with it?"

"Keep it. I'm entrusted to deliver it to the Searcher. I'll deliver it and you." Orias circled the horse to reclaim his dead gazelle.

The animal, a little bigger than Dougal, was a steely gray, almost bluish, with a swash of white on both sides of its belly and two sets of antlers, one pointing up and one pointing down. Biceps bulging, Orias lifted it by one hind leg and mounted the horse. As he gathered his reins, Pitch ran to the horse and scrambled up the stirrup to sit in front of the saddle. Raz swung around Orias's body to sit behind Pitch and make room for Chris on the horse's hindquarters.

Orias guided the horse a few steps to the side until it stood next to

Chris. He hesitated, staring into the forest. "Before we go, I'd like you to know something about being a Gifted."

"Like what?" At this point, Orias could tell him they were all on the fifteenth moon of Jupiter, and he wouldn't be surprised.

"What you do as a Gifted will either destroy lives, or it will save them. My people's lives." Orias turned to him. The fierceness in his face softened ever so slightly to reveal a glint of pain. "If you fail, they will die. Hundreds of them, thousands maybe."

That wasn't what Chris had been expecting at all. Whacked-out, convoluted mind games, yes. But not this. This wasn't weird at all. This had the ring of truth. Desperate, pleading, knocked-out-on-its-feet truth.

That was a kind of truth he knew backwards and forwards.

So now he had to choose whether it was better to stay where he was or journey deeper into the rabbit hole. If he stayed here, what then? He'd wander around until he either woke up or one of those big cat things decided to eat him.

Of course, if it was a dream, what did it matter if the cat ate him? Maybe it would just speed things along. Staying here, focusing on waking up, that was the most sensible plan.

But he couldn't make himself look away from the hurt in Orias's face. If he went with Orias, at least he might get some questions answered and actually come up with a notion of what was wrong with him.

"All right." He took hold of Orias's callused palm and swung up behind the saddle.

6

SOMETHING RUMBLED INSIDE Allara's skull. It wasn't a physical sensation, so much as the *sense* of a sensation, like the awareness of someone else's presence. It was a pull, gentle but insistent, telling her to move and in which direction to move. And it was alien, cold—the link of someone else's brain to her own.

Her every nerve burned. The Gifted was in Lael. He had come after all. In spite of all her attempts to stop him, he had come.

She sat very still, wedged in a crenellation atop the ramparts of Réon Couteau. The letter she had been writing to her father dropped into the lap folds of her sea-green gown. To her left, the castle's black granite walls fell away in the roar of a waterfall, leaving only the blue of Ori Réon seven hundred spans below and the silver-green of the forest as far as she could see. Along the shore, the bells signaled midmorning from the blue-roofed monasteries in the Vesper district.

Her lungs quivered. She couldn't mistake this strange rhythmic tremor deep within her brain, this almost magnetic pull, driving her to get up, to move, to *search*. She had been nine years old when last she felt it. The Garowai had told her then it meant a Gifted had arrived in Lael.

Eyes closed, she crimped her fist around the letter to her father. What she needed to do was relax and let the taste of the Gifted wash over her brain. She needed to get a sense of this man who had been summoned here to do . . . something. To save Lael? Or to plunge it even deeper into darkness than had his predecessor?

When Harrison Garnett had crashed into her life twenty years ago, she had spent the first week of her search fighting back nausea. His presence had been a putrescence in her mind, the sense of him like the smell of the vile chemicals used by the embalmers in Glen Arden's slums. Perhaps the taste of him in her mind had been only the foreshadowing of his traitorous personality. Perhaps she should have recognized that. If she had tried harder to overcome her revulsion, she might have done her own job better and prevented the treachery altogether.

This new Gifted's touch upon her mind was sharp and smooth, like the biting smell of fresh-cut heffron wood. It was alien and intrusive, but at least it didn't turn her stomach. His presence in her mind would only strengthen the nearer she was to him physically. What she sensed now were just the first raindrops in a tempest.

She opened her eyes, and for a moment the world swirled. Her inner balance tilted from this new weight inside her head, just as if she'd grown a third arm or a hump on her back. The mid-morning sun warmed the top of her head and prickled cold drops of sweat from the base of her scalp. She stood up slowly and faced the lake far below.

Without the force of a Gifted's dreams pushing through from the other side, she could see no more than the white-edged waves everyone else saw. That was fine with her. She had seen enough, twenty years ago and then again in the last few months, to have no desire to look again.

Toes on the edge of the crenellation, she breathed deep. Fear of the fall rushed over her, and she exalted in the courage that came from being seven hundred spans above the world and only a step away from death. Oh, for wings! Had she them, she would lean forward, over the water, and let gravity pull her into its embrace. She would fall and fall and fall, safe in the certainty that she wouldn't need someone at the bottom to catch her. Had she wings, she would catch herself.

But she hadn't, so she turned to go. Where the Gifted was right now not even she could tell for certain. It was her responsibility to find him, to bring him to her father, and to stand beside him as he learned what it meant to change the worlds.

She scrambled down the battlement ladder onto the parapet and ran the length of it to her dressing chamber's window. Ducking her head, she stepped through the open window onto the cushioned window seat. "Esta!" She tossed the crumpled letter onto her dressing table and ripped at the plaited gold of her gown's sash. "Esta! Where are you?"

Footsteps on the other side of the oaken door heralded the arrival of her lady-in-waiting. The door heaved inward and the tall and imposing Countess Esta Larai puffed into the room, her index finger marking her place in a red leather book. She raised one hand to support her towering blonde wig.

"My lady?" The guilty expression on her rouged cheeks likely meant she had been reading love sonnets.

"Find my riding clothes." Allara pulled her gown over her head and cast it aside. "No, wait, go to Captain Quinnon and tell him to gather the men and saddle the horses."

"We're leaving?" Esta looked at the floor-to-ceiling closets and cupboards, probably calculating the packing she would have to do.

"You'll have to take word to my father in Glen Arden." Allara crossed the room and kicked off her slippers. Packing, indeed. The whole lot of clothes could rot on their manikins, for all she cared. "Tell Quinnon to give you an escort."

Esta, who had stooped to pick up the fallen dress, shot up straight again. "You're not coming with me? What am I to tell your father? He'll think me lax in my duties. He'll have me dismissed from court!"

Esta had been her lady-in-waiting since shortly after Allara's mother, Queen Ranelle, had died in childbirth, along with her infant son. Allara had been thirteen. In many ways, she was already an adult by then. But Esta had still insisted on raising her by hand. Most of her ideas of childrearing and the training of courtly manners failed entirely to take into account the unique responsibilities of a Searcher. Esta was her companion only insofar as Allara was a princess. The moments in which Allara took up the mantle of a Searcher, Esta had to step aside, willingly or no.

"Find Quinnon." Allara yanked riding clothes from an armoire and started for the dressing screen in the far corner. "Tell him it's time. He'll know what I mean. Tell him to gather the men and horses and ready the skycar."

Esta threw up her hands. "Why is it neither you nor your good father listen a wit to me?"

Behind the screen, Allara cast aside her chemise and reached for a russet tunic. She had long since given up trying to explain her responsibilities as a Searcher. "Time is short."

Esta banged the lid on the trunk. "Never mind *I* know it's no job of a princess to be jogging all over the northern counties. Never mind *I* know it isn't right nor proper for you to be off and about without a duenna. Never mind *I'm* the older and wiser—"

"Esta, we're on the brink of war."

"Wars are for men. It's none of the women's concern. Not yours and certainly not mine. I don't know why you haven't the dignity to stop dragging yourself around on horseback—"

"Enough!" Allara stuck her head around the corner of the screen. "For once in your life, *enough!*"

Esta gaped.

Heat flared in her stomach. "Now!"

Esta snatched up her skirts and ran. She left the door open in her haste, and her footsteps thumped down the winding staircase.

Allara breathed out, slowly. She had to get a grip on this new invasion of her mind and quell the swirling in her stomach. Nerves wouldn't help anyone now, not herself, not the Gifted, and certainly not the kingdom. Her fingers trembled as she tied the drawstrings of her yoke collar and left the tassels to hang past the swirls of gold embroidery on the tunic's fitted front.

Far below, the front doors slammed open, and Esta's cries whispered up through the open windows. "Captain Quinnon!"

In the yard, men began to shout. Hooves clattered against the stone pavement. Iron clanged as weapons, armor, and equipages were prepared. A horse whinnied, and Allara recognized her stallion's throaty scream.

All her muscles shuddered. She leaned her forehead against the enameled wood of the dressing screen and listened to the rumble in the back of her skull. "Please," she whispered. "Please, this time, don't let me fail."

She stepped out from behind the screen and collected her sword and her pistol from the glass case beside the door. Then she left the room and marched down three flights of black marble stairs until she reached the ground floor and the great foyer. With a click of their heels, the doormen snapped open the doors and admitted her to the sunlit glare of the courtyard.

Esta, standing beside the door, snagged Allara's sleeve. "Wait, your highness. There's a complication." She jutted her chin to the far end of the courtyard, near the gates, where a lathered horse stood blowing. Beside it, talking fervently to the captain of Allara's bodyguard, stood a bedraggled Cherazim youth.

Allara knit her eyebrows. Ever since the tragedies and misunderstandings surrounding the last Gifted's demise, the Cherazii had avoided Réon Couteau in general and the royal palace in particular. For all their devotion to Ori Réon, they had little use for a Searcher who would allow her Gifted to go rogue. No Cherazim would come here without good reason.

She crossed the courtyard. The men stopped saddling horses and buckling armor to salute her. As she neared, Captain Crea Quinnon stepped aside so she could face the newcomer.

The Cherazim's pale face was flushed blue with the heat of his ride, and sweat glistened against the angular bones of his face. His serrated ears poked up through his white-blond hair to frame a tri-corner hat. He saw her, and the poise and pride of his race pulled back his shoulders. The Cherazii might blame her for the last Gifted's treachery, but they esteemed the time-honored role of Searcher too much not to pay her at least a grudging respect.

"Master Cherazim." She greeted him in the custom of the Cherazii, with her fist against her heart, then looked at Quinnon. "What is it?"

Quinnon raked a hand through his wild gray mane and cocked his mouth to one side, as he always did when weighing information and options. "He says there's Koraudian troops on our side of the border, in the Thyra hills." His good eye gleamed at her from within the scarred and pitted battleground of his face; his bad eye, all but dead in its socket, wandered blindly to the side. "Says they took him prisoner, and by the time he got loose, he was closer to here than Glen Arden."

She clenched her fists. Koraudian troops in Lael right now was tantamount to a declaration of war.

The Cherazim's eyes darted to her face, then away, as if uncertain where to look. "They've been attacking the Cherazii caravans fleeing across the border."

The Koraudian pogrom against the Cherazii had intensified of late with the growing rumors of Mactalde's return. Hundreds of Cherazii, perhaps even thousands, if the worst of the rumors were to be believed, had been killed. Those that could were fleeing Koraud. For all that they disapproved of Allara and her father, they weren't so foolish as to let their pride keep them from the safety Lael offered.

But never before had they asked for help. They would fight and they would die before they submitted themselves to the aid of anyone, especially the monarchy. This young Cherazim wasn't likely to receive accolades from his elders should they learn of his actions.

She licked her lips, then looked him in the eye. "There is no garrison here. But I'll send what men I can." She addressed Quinnon, "Arrange a courier detail to travel back to Glen Arden with the news that Koraudian troops have been seen in the Thyra hills. The rest of my Guard can go to the Cherazii's aid." She left their search for the Gifted unspoken. In days such as these, even a Cherazim could bear tales to the wrong ears. Perhaps especially a Cherazim.

Quinnon swiveled to cast his affirming gaze upon the men, but they were already checking their girths a final time and securing arms. They might technically answer to Quinnon's authority, but they all knew Allara's word was only a whisper away from law.

She and Quinnon stepped back, away from the Cherazim, and Quinnon held her reins as she secured pistol holsters on either side of her saddle pommel.

He stayed by Rihawn's head and steadied the horse as he pawed. "So your Gifted's arrived, then?" He spoke in a gruff undertone.

"Yes." She didn't have to say anything more. He knew what to do.

A professional bodyguard from across the eastern hills in the neighboring country of Rivale, Quinnon had arrived in Lael twenty years ago and taken the job as the captain of her personal guard. He had ridden beside her, fought for her, and protected her every day since. His bad arm and his hunched back belied a dangerous strength and speed, and she had never seen his equal with a rapier.

He had never shown an interest in what she did or felt as a Searcher.

Likely, he didn't even believe in it. But Crea Quinnon would follow her wherever her duties led, be it mountain, ocean, or the darkest reaches of hell. For now, those duties led her to search for a man whom she had never met and whom she would send back to his own world in a twinkling had she the choice.

Quinnon busied himself snugging a buckle on the rifle scabbard attached to her saddle. "Know where he is?"

"Not yet."

At the far end of the courtyard, the glass-encased skycar glided down its steel cables and bobbed to a stop. The skycar trains ran on a basic pulley system, operated by steam engines at stations spaced along the tracks. Depending on variables such as rain and wind, the skycars could maintain the speed of a horse's gallop all the way across half the kingdom, gliding half a league above terrain too rough with hills and lakes to offer straight roads.

Right now, the royal skycar hung from its cable, just above the courtyard paving stones. The engineer and his crew had hitched up the horse cars, which were large enough to hold three mounts side by side. A partition in the front enclosed three green velvet seats, on which the human passengers could ride in comfort.

Allara and her men could take the skycar train all the way to Glen Arden if she so commanded. But should the pull of the Gifted direct her otherwise, she could order the car to a stop and disembark at any station south of Réon Couteau. A shudder touched her skin. She could only hope he would be that near.

To find one particular man, out of all the men in Lael, could take a lifetime. Some Searchers spent years looking for their Gifted. One story, from nearly seven centuries ago, told of a Searcher who scoured the world for her Gifted before finally finding him in the steamy jungles of a land known as Ariad, on the far side of the world. Allara herself had spent eleven months on horseback in her search for Harrison Garnett, tracing him to the rocky Riall coast in the southern reaches of Lael.

Ever since she had known a second Gifted was coming, provisions had been packed in readiness, horses and men standing by to leave at a moment's notice. With another war looming on the horizon, it was a bad time for a princess of Lael to be traveling abroad, but she had no choice. And, anyway, perhaps this Gifted wouldn't be so far away as Harrison had been. His presence wasn't just different from Harrison's; it felt stronger, nearer.

"I think he's in Lael," she murmured. "This side of Glen Arden, even."

"That'd be handy for a change." Quinnon took his own horse from a groom. "The men will stay on the skycar until Thyra Junction. If your laddie's north of Glen Arden, we'll all be headed in the same direction anyway, and I'd like to keep them near you as long as possible."

The company stood at their horses' heads, waiting. Every man among them was a Guardsman, specially chosen to ride as her bodyguard. Over their blouses, they all wore sleeveless tabards: hunter green linen embroidered high on the chest with a rearing stag. The hem hung to mid-thigh, front and back, and, instead of sleeves, an equally long strip of material swung free from either shoulder, also embroidered with the stag.

They stood at attention, eyes on Quinnon, awaiting his order. Their helmets rested on their tall saddle horns, ready to be donned at a moment's notice. Armed with rifles in their saddle scabbards, pistols at one hip, longswords at the other, they appeared every bit as lethal and proud as they had a right to be. Their broad-brimmed leather hats, cocked over one eye with the brim folded up on the right side and cockaded with a sweeping white feather, signaled to the world they were the elite of the elite, the Searcher's personal Guard.

"We move out," Quinnon said. "There may be Koraudian troops awaiting us, so we move with speed and caution. Our lady goes on her own business, and I go with her, so it may be we have to separate before we reach the battle. If that's so, you'll dispatch the enemy with all haste and rejoin your princess as soon as possible."

Tension knotted behind Allara's breastbone. If she failed now—again—all would be lost. Even after she found the Gifted, so very much could go wrong.

Quinnon looked at her, awaiting her signal. "Appears the time's come." His face didn't soften, but the gruff edge left his voice. He had been there for the last Gifted. He knew what she feared. Perhaps he feared it as well.

She took a breath and gave him a smile, as much for her own benefit as the men's. "Yes."

She stepped forward and led Rihawn, prancing, to the first skycar. The groom waiting inside the wide door took the reins from her, and Rihawn leapt aboard without hesitation. At the front of the car, she allowed the conductor the courtesy of offering his hand to help her up the three gilded steps into the snug passenger area. She sat in the farthest seat and swiveled it so she could see through the glass wall.

In the courtyard behind, the men boarded their cars in a clatter of hooves and boots. Her own car rocked on its cable as Quinnon's horse boarded behind her.

Quinnon took the three gilded steps in one stride and slammed the glass door behind him. He stood in front of his seat, arms crossed over his chest, and watched as the engineer and his first mate entered the tiny two-person forecar. At Allara's nod, he raised an arm and circled his forefinger in the air.

The car lurched forward, and she released her held breath.

And so it began. The Gifted's pull on her mind dragged her east. Every second she moved in that direction relieved some of the pressure, even as it filled her head with his presence just a little bit more. Soon she would find him. And she would know the worst of what was to come.

7

CHRIS HUNG ONTO the back of Orias's saddle as the horse crossed a wide dirt road. They plunged back into the trees and emerged, some hundred yards on, into a wide meadow filled with dozens of white canvas tents and maybe a hundred tall, eerily white, long-eared people like Orias.

A squiggle of doubt inched across Chris's spine. "There are humans around here, right?"

"Plenty." Orias's tone was more than a little sardonic. "And not many of them friendly if you're a Cherazim."

"So you're telling me it's humans killing your people?" He looked around. There seemed to be a disproportionate number of warriors compared to the women and children.

"We've had our misunderstandings over the years. But, for the most part, we live in peace with the Laelers. It's the Koraudians in the kingdom to the east who have tried to put their boots to our necks in the last few decades." Orias urged the horse forward. It gathered its weight on its hindquarters, leapt a rivulet, then galloped on through the lush grass to the trampled area where the canvas tents mingled with cooking fires.

Two dozen colorful wagons were parked along the camp's perimeter. They rode past one, and Chris stared at it. Hiked up on spoked wheels, the enclosed wagon was plenty tall enough to allow Orias's six and a half feet to stand up inside. A glass-paned overhang jutted above the driver's bench, and through the overhang's water-spotted windows, Chris could see what appeared to be a child's sleeping pallet made up on the floor.

"You live in those?"

"Not hardly," Raz said. "What do we look like, barbarians? Those are just travel carts."

Pitch hung halfway off the saddle and looked at Chris around Orias's body. "The Cherazii travel a lot. We left Lael because of what happened with the last Gifted, you know. But now you're here, so we're coming home."

"You're coming home because of me?"

"Not because of you," Orias said. "It just worked out that way. The Koraudians have started pushing us harder these last few months." His voice tightened. "But now it will stop."

The Cherazii milled, repairing their wagons, cooking food, and grooming horses. They afforded Orias only a glance, but Chris was rewarded with a second and a third and finally a long stare. One by one, the Cherazii straightened from their work and watched the horse and its four riders pass through their midst.

Most of them dressed similarly to Orias, the men in jerkins and long tunics of variously bright colors. They all wore thick-soled boots, and a few sported leather tri-corn hats over their long hair. All were armed with at least two blades, and one memorable individual sported perhaps a dozen throwing knives in a blood-red baldric across his chest.

The women wore long gowns, the bold colors—vermilion, chartreuse, indigo—in stark contrast to their opalescent skin. Their hair was divided, with one half left to hang free to their waists and the other braided and pulled over their shoulders. Some of them had kilted their skirts in their belts, revealing knee-high boots like the men's, almost all of which offered the glint of a small blade in a sheath at the back of their calves. Children and Rievers roamed about in similar dress.

At the center of the camp, a hulking male, not so tall as Orias, but even broader through the shoulders and chest, stood up from working on a broken wheel. His glance flicked from the dead gazelle and stopped on Chris. His eyes hardened.

A faded red band of cloth wrapped the top of his head, and a heavy silver ring pierced the tip of one tall ear. His face was more angular than Orias's, his nose thick and straight and his mouth demanding.

Orias turned his head to Chris. "It would be best while we're here if you try to blend in. Don't say anything about being the Gifted, and try not to show how strange everything is to you."

The muscles in the small of his back tightened. "They don't like the Gifted?"

"It's not that, exactly. We are sworn to protect the Gifted. But your predecessor was a vile traitor." He hacked in the back of his throat. "So they're not going to trust you without some convincing." He jostled the Rievers. "Mind what I said. Tell no one what he is, and help him blend in."

"Blend in my sweet mother's needle's eye," Raz said.

Orias reined up in front of the stern-faced Cherazim in the red headband and dropped his reins so he could lay his fist to his chest. "Cabahr Laith."

The other Cherazim returned the gesture. "Orias Tarn. You've had good hunting."

"Aye." Orias gave his gazelle a little heft. "As soon as my Rievers butcher it, I'll be taking a haunch for myself as I journey on. The people are welcome to share among the rest."

"You journey on?" Laith's chin lifted. His eyes darted to Chris again and held, as if expecting him to answer. "Why? With rumors that Koraudian detachments have pierced into Lael, our caravans value every sword they can wield, particularly one as proficient as yours. A scout brought word only a few minutes ago," he gestured to a red-haired youth who stood behind him, fiddling with a heavy dagger, "—that Koraudians are near, maybe only a league or two to the east. If they find us, they've no reason for mercy. We're packing as we speak. We leave before nightfall and pray it's not too late."

The muscle under Orias's biceps scar flexed. "It's not you they search for. It's me. It's all the Keepers. If they can find the Orimere, sooner or later, they'll find the Gifted."

Chris's ears tingled. The Orimere hung heavy in the purse on his belt.

Laith shook his head. "They'll settle for slaughtering a random caravan whether they find you among us or not."

Orias shifted in his saddle. "May the God of all allow the raids to end soon." A note of determination underlay his words. "In the meantime, I have no choice. I have come across a man—a farmer from near Ballion—to whom an oath binds me." He inclined his head back toward Chris. "I must see him safely to his home."

"And the human cannot see himself home?"

Chris bit his tongue. These Cherazii seemed like the sort to take offense easily. If he made the wrong move, he'd not only blow his cover as an innocent native, he'd also likely end up challenged to a duel or something. Judging from the size of their swords, not to mention the fact that *his* sword was apparently back in that thicket where Pitch had hidden it, that contest wasn't likely to end well. He had gotten into enough fights over the years to know how to recognize the ones likely to end with him lying flat on his back, busted and woozy.

"This is a private matter," Orias said.

At Laith's feet, a shriveled Riever peered up at them. He hugged a thick fleece, leather side out, around his stick-like body. His arms jutted through arm holes whipstitched with sinew. "And is your oath to him more important than your sacred mission? You're to take the Orimere straight to Réon Couteau. Ballion will carry you leagues out of your way."

"I go where I must." Orias's head tilted back to Laith. "Will you give me my leave?"

Laith pursed his lips. Maybe Chris looked like he didn't belong as much as he felt it. Or maybe it was Orias. Maybe his actions were strange in some way.

Whatever his suspicions, Laith still nodded. "I give you leave. And the human—will he not offer his name while he is among us?"

Orias canted his head back, and Chris took it as permission.

"Chris Redston." On impulse, he mimicked the fist-to-the-chest gesture. "And it is my honor to be welcomed among the Cherazii people." A little bonhomie never hurt.

A smile ghosted across Laith's face. "I never said I welcomed you, Chris Redston. I do not know you, and I do not know your fathers. But one of our own brings you and vouches for you, so be at peace among us." He fisted his chest and turned away.

Orias's shoulders relaxed ever so slightly. "Everybody down." He gave Raz's shoulder a little slap, and the Riever slid down Orias's leg until he was close enough to drop to the ground. "Skin out the zajele. I'll pack up and be back as soon as you've finished."

Pitch peered around Orias's body and motioned with his fingers for Chris to follow. "You come with me."

"No shenanigans," Orias said. "You remember what I told you."

Chris slid off the horse's rump, and Pitch jumped down to claim his hand and lead him forward to where the wizened old Riever had moved into the shade of a tent.

"Jupe, this is Chris Redston," Pitch announced, even though Jupe had been there when Chris introduced himself. "I found him while he was sleeping, and he is my servant now. I wish to proclaim it."

"Wait just a minute," Chris said. "What if I decide I don't want to be your servant?"

Jupe looked at him, askance. "You can't decide. It's Riever law."

"And just what is that?" The question was out of his mouth before he thought about it. Likely, every native with a brain in his head was expected to know the answer.

Jupe's squint deepened, engulfing his eyes entirely. Finally, he gave his head a shake. "We make our own laws."

"I see." Chris tried not to sound like he was humoring a five-year-old. This old Riever was probably seeing right through him anyway. "So you just made up a law that you could claim any human you happen to find?"

"Of course not." Jupe thrust out his chin. "Not any human. Only if he is sleeping, and only if he has a sword to be taken."

Pitch tugged on Chris's hand. "Come on. We have to hurry. We must have the proclaiming before Orias is ready to leave."

"I will gather the others." Jupe hobbled away with a last shake of his head at Chris.

"We'll do it over by the zajele," Pitch said, "so Raz can't get mad at us for not helping."

Chris let Pitch pull him out of the tent's shade. "Listen, I have nothing against you personally. I like you personally. I'm just not so keen on this idea of being proclaimed your servant."

Pitch ran along in front of him, throwing a little skip into his stride every now and then. "It's all right. I will be a good master. I promise."

"I'm not planning to be around here much longer." He gave himself another pinch, just on the off chance it would be enough to wake him up.

"You can't go away unless I say you can. And anyway," Pitch grinned back at him, "Orias said to blend in. This is blending in."

Chris gave up. Riever logic was too blunt a weapon to pierce so much as a piece of paper, but who needed a sharp edge when you could just bludgeon your opponent over the head?

They reached the zajele in the middle of the camp.

"'Bout time," Raz said.

Pitch crossed his arms over his body and, with a flourish, pulled out both his blades. He handed one to Chris, then scrambled on top of the zajele's haunch, stabbed the blade into the flank, and began sawing at the back leg.

Chris hunkered down, one hand on the zajele's neck, and thrust in the knife, just to make it look like he was doing something. Out of the corner of his eye, he watched the movement of the camp: the children playing some kind of game with sticks and hoops, a tall blond male carrying buckets of water from the rivulet, a woman lying on her stomach on top of a wagon and polishing the overhang's glass window. For a dream about blue-blooded aliens, it was remarkably coherent.

Maybe a dozen Rievers filtered in from the edges of the camp and congregated around the zajele. Speaking charitably, they were the ugliest sentient beings he had ever seen. Even the youngest among them had faces pocked and pitted like raisins. Their ears were shaped like a human's, but the round upper halves were too big for the tiny lobes, most of which sported dangling jewelry, made from twisted bits of wire and leather and, in a few instances, teeth. Their eyes were black clear through, like a bird's, with only the faintest darkening at the center to highlight the pupils.

Chris looked down and realized his hands had been moving almost of their own accord. He'd never gutted an animal in his life, but between him and Pitch and Raz, the zajele now lay in neat quarters, skinned and boned.

Raz wiped his knife clean on the grass and glanced sideways at him. "Maybe you're not entirely useless after all."

Chris stared at the bloody knife in his hands. "How'd I do that?"

"Muscle memory. Your mind may not have been here before, but your body has. You've probably skinned out dozens of zajele in your life. But now ain't the time and this ain't the place to be talking on the wonders of it all. Not if you're hoping to pretend you're a farmer from Ballion." He stood up, sheathed his blade, and faced the Riever contingent with crossed arms.

Pitch bounded to Chris's side and took his hand. "It's time." He led Chris forward to where Jupe and the other elderly Rievers fronted their group.

"This is Chris Redston." He held up Chris's hand. "I swear I found him asleep in the hills to the south. I swear I took his sword. I swear he did not wake up until I had done so. I swear I gave him just notification of his claiming. Henceforth he is my servant. Do the Rievers proclaim it?"

Jupe and the other old ones gave a nod of consent, and all the Rievers smacked their fists to their skinny chests. "The Rievers proclaim it!"

Pitch reached a hand into the collar of his tunic and came out with a little leather pouch. He held it up to Chris. "You have to give me something too."

Now they told him. He searched his tunic and then his trousers for pockets. Then he remembered the leather pouch on his belt and pulled out a gold coin.

At his other side, Raz sniffed and shook his head. "Not money. You're his servant. All your money belongs to him anyway."

Of course. Why would he have imagined differently? The Rievers obviously had this subjugation thing down pat. He dug a little deeper into the purse, past the Orimere in its green pouch, and came up with a two-inch triangle of stiff leather. A circle of brass, bearing some kind of letter or symbol, studded the leather, and two thongs hung from either side.

For all he knew, it was money too, but he tilted it toward Pitch. With any luck, the Riever would make some sort of signal before the rest of the clan figured out he had no idea what he was looking at.

Raz raised himself on tiptoe to look, and his brow lifted in frank admiration. "You were in the Guard?"

Chris stopped himself from shrugging his own confusion.

Pitch took the thing in both hands, and a lopsided grin tugged at his mouth. He turned back to his fellow Rievers and held up the triangle. "My servant Chris Redston is a Guardsman!"

The crowd appeared suitably impressed. Probably he was the first Guardsman dumb enough to fall asleep in Riever territory and get his sword stolen.

Pitch's leather pouch still lay in his palm, so he pried open the knot at the top and upended it. A teardrop of glass fell into his hand. When he held it up, the sun showed an interior made of intricate shards of glass twisted around each other. Fire and water danced within, clashing, fighting, but never dying. It was a *fawa-radi* sculpture, like the one Harrison had in his backroom.

"Where'd you get this?" He stared at Pitch, then caught himself. He'd seen Harrison's sculpture just before he'd blacked out. Why *wouldn't* he dream about it?

After leaving Cabahr Laith, Orias packed up his tent and few belongings and bartered a pony away from a shrewd-faced grandmother. If Koraudians were near, then time was blowing away from him like leaves on the wind. He had to get the Gifted away from here before it was too late. But to leave his people like this, under the threat of attack . . .

He snugged his horse's girth, then leaned both hands against the saddle and bowed his head. This Gifted—unlike his predecessor—had done nothing wrong. Chris Redston could hardly be blamed for events that occurred before his own crossing. And did not the very fact that he had landed right in front of a Keeper make it clear what the God of all willed Orias to do?

He was to protect the Gifted and, events being what they were, deliver him safely to the Searcher in Réon Couteau. That was the most sacred responsibility of any Keeper. And yet his heart felt as if it was wringing itself in two.

Koraudians wouldn't venture this far into Lael unless they were tracking someone important. Someone such as a Keeper bearing the Orimere to the Gifted. If Orias left his people now and they were attacked, he would be at fault. But if he stayed to help the caravan fight and the Gifted fell into the hands of Koraudians, would that not be his fault as well?

He straightened up. Duty *must* come first. But his whole body screamed with the need to stay and fight.

He led the horses over to the Rievers' proclaiming caucus and picked up a zajele's canvas-wrapped haunches. *"Kalel ti star nad piuser tulle,"* he told them. Take the rest and disperse it.

He fastened the haunch to the front of his saddle and turned his back on what was left of the meat while a few of the Rievers collected it and carried it away between them. The remaining Rievers hung back to say their farewells to Raz and Pitch.

Orias tossed a glance at the Gifted. Taking the measure of him was still difficult at this point. Today was still only his first day, and he was obviously bewildered and even a little suspicious.

But at least he wasn't hysterical, as the histories suggested some of the Gifted were upon crossing. Beneath the confusion, he seemed to possess a calm confidence and a quick mind. He had not a look of perfidy about him, as the rat-faced Harrison Garnett had possessed from the first. But who knew what weaknesses his heart held? Just because a man was a Gifted was no indication he deserved the honor.

Orias cleared his throat. "We're going to need to move and move fast. If Koraudians find us, they'll as lief slaughter us as they would the caravan." He couldn't keep a muscle from hopping in his cheek.

Chris peered around the caravan, then back to Orias. "They're after me, aren't they?"

"They want you to use the Orimere to bring back their dead leader."

Chris snorted. "Last time I checked I wasn't too handy at the resurrection business."

"He's only dead in our world. In yours, he's still alive." He looked at the *fawa-radi* sculpture in Chris's hand. "Pitch gave you that?" After winning it in a traveling circus last year, Pitch had hardly parted from the bauble. "He must place a high value on his servant."

Chris upended the sculpture. "It's worth a lot then?"

"Not so much in money. You should see the *fawa-radi* in Glen Arden. There's a huge one, twice the size of a Cherazim, in every quarter of the city. Now that is a sight. It's the most beautiful city in the civilized world, let alone Lael." He held out the pony's reins. "Can you ride?"

Chris shook his head.

"Well, I bought you a gentle one. Just keep a leg on both sides and your mind in the middle."

Pitch and Raz trotted over, and Pitch waved the leather triangle. "Look. Orias, he is a Guardsman."

Orias turned for a closer look. If the new Gifted was a Guardsman, that might put things in a more reassuring light. The skill and dedication of the King's Guard almost rivaled the Cherazii's.

He took the triangle and ran his finger over the center medallion. "At least if you get into trouble, you'll know how to handle yourself."

"Why? What do Guardsmen do?" Chris asked.

"They're the king's crack troops." Orias looked him up and down. "You're not in uniform, so you've probably been discharged. All Laeler men are required to train with the army for a two-week period out of every year so they'll be ready to respond if the kingdom comes under attack. But the Guard is the elite." He let the tiniest of grins escape. "I thought you looked like a fighter."

Chris shook his head. "I have a feeling fights around here are a lot different from the ones I'm used to."

"If you get into trouble, blank your mind. Let your body take over. It'll know what to do."

"That's mighty comforting."

Orias handed the Guard badge back to Pitch, who bound it around his upper arm. He had to wrap the thongs twice and hold one end with his teeth while he tied it off.

Orias turned back. "Do the same with the horse. Listen to your body." He mounted slowly, so the Gifted could watch and learn.

Raz scrambled up behind him, but Pitch stood waiting for Chris. He was quite enamored with his new prize. No doubt, he had completely forgotten Chris would be his servant only until the Searcher claimed him.

The pony didn't budge, and the Gifted managed to haul himself aboard without too much difficulty. Pitch clambered up Chris's leg to stand on the horse's hindquarters and rest his hands lightly on Chris's shoulders.

"Kick him," he advised.

Chris did, and the pony lumbered a few steps.

Orias urged his own horse forward before he could change his mind about leaving. But he couldn't stop a long backwards glance. If the Koraudians did attack, his one lone sword could hardly make much of a difference. He told himself that twice over. But he didn't believe it. The strength and power of a single Cherazim had turned the tale in too many battles to count.

He needed to be here with his people.

He needed to be on the road, taking the Gifted far away.

Two impossibly conflicting duties. He had to choose one or the other, so he turned away and rode into the trees.

8

THE ROYAL SKYCAR swung around to begin its approach into Thyra Junction. Allara perched on the edge of her velvet cushion and bounced one knee with the effort of sitting quietly. Every minute was precious now. For all she knew, the Gifted could be in danger—both physically and mentally. If his heart was poisoned before she could get to him, as Harrison's had been, half her battle would be lost.

For seven hours, she had sat, back straight, hands clenched in her lap, as the skycar rushed over the rough hill country between Réon Couteau and Lake Thyra. On horseback, the journey would have taken days, but her heart still screamed at the delay.

Quinnon stood from his seat. "The men will disembark here." He took his sword belt and pistol holster from the hook in the corner and buckled them around his waist. "We riding on?"

"I'm not sure yet."

The Gifted's presence washed over her, flooding her sense of herself. Her thoughts fuzzed around the edges as his emotions eddied with her own. He felt different from when she had first recognized his crossing. Now he felt confused, even defiant. Or maybe those feelings were hers.

When she had met Harrison, as a child, she had nearly panicked, thinking her mind was being swallowed up in this alien essence of another human being. At least now, she had the foreknowledge that a little time and patience would eventually allow her to sort the Gifted's presence from her own thoughts. Once she knew him better and was familiar enough with his presence to recognize its edges and limits, she could separate it from herself and push it out of her way to the back of her mind.

The train swooped into its descent, and Quinnon gripped the brass railing on the ceiling. She swiveled her chair around to face the rear of the compartment and locked it in place so gravity would push her against the seatback instead of spilling her onto the floor.

Outside the window, the white sun hung heavy in the sky, several hours past midday. The scenery had begun to change twenty minutes ago, the hills flattening around the lake. As the car leveled out, she could see the mottled gray of the cobblestone streets running through the city.

Most of the buildings were built of whitewashed wood, their roofs coming to sharp peaks and their walls reinforced with brown planks. Toward the center of town, the buildings grew closer and closer together, and traffic packed the main street. Thyra was a busy district at any time, but especially now given the looming threat of another war.

"Getting out of town on horseback will slow the Guard down," she said.

Quinnon scowled. "They shouldn't *be* getting out. They're not hired to save blues. They're hired to stick around and watch your back."

The train crossed over the many-peaked skycar station. It slowed to a stop momentarily as they waited their turn to be shunted into the docking yard, then moved on as the royal privilege flag on the engineer's car was acknowledged.

"The Cherazii deserve protection," she said.

"As far as I'm concerned, the Cherazii can take care of themselves."

The car glided down into one of the many courtyards behind the station. With a gentle lurch, it bobbed to a stop and dangled above the cobblestones.

Quinnon unlatched the door and jumped down without waiting for the conductor to lower the steps. "I'll tell 'em to take our car off the train soon as the Guard's unloaded. We'll cover more ground without the extra weight."

She followed him to the door. If she sat still any longer, she would explode. Were it not for the infernal weight of her royal dignity, she would run laps around the courtyard. Perhaps the slap of her feet against the stones would numb the jitters in her muscles.

The conductor, in his snug blue doublet and velvet boater hat, rose from securing the steps and offered his hand. "Your highness, you honor us. I trust you had a pleasant journey."

"Very pleasant, Conductor." Her voice sounded tight. She licked her lips and tried again. "Captain Quinnon and I travel on to Virere Ford, so if you'll please make certain our horses are provisioned for another day's ride?"

"Yes, indeed. Would you like to wait in the lobby? I'll have it cleared to ensure your privacy."

She waved him off. "Not necessary. We're in a bit of a hurry, so I'll stay close."

She let him help her down, then walked around to the far end of the car and swung first one leg, then the other over the coupling. Separated from the conductor and his ministrations, she clasped her hands behind her back and leaned against the car. Inside, Rihawn squealed and stomped his impatience, and the whole car swayed on its cable.

The station, with its six sharp peaks adjoined by flat-roofed ticket booths in between, poured out a steady stream of passengers from every ramp. Depending on their destination—north to Réon Couteau, south to Virere Ford and Glen Arden, or west to the Illise coast—they were funneled into various courtyards and loaded into the trains.

Overhead, the skycars threaded their way through a web of cables, their glass walls glistening painfully in the sunlight. They moved with surprising silence, just a low swish and rattle. Except for the shadows sailing across the courtyard and the distant hammer of the mill engines on the far side of the station, she could almost forget where she was.

Thyra was one of the best stations on the line. No train left here without having every window shined, every compartment swept, and every provisions cupboard filled. Men in the station's blue uniform bustled about the royal train, opening the compartment doors and unrolling ramps from the back doors and steps from the front.

The horses unloaded with a clatter, and the Guardsmen exited to check their equipment. A few cast sidelong glances at her, probably wondering what she was up to.

To get back on the skycar and continue south to Virere Ford? Or unload Rihawn and ride out from here? The wrong choice could add days, maybe even weeks, to her search. She closed her eyes and tried to contain the rumbling chaos of the Gifted's presence enough to determine from what direction the pull was coming. The time had come to make her decision.

"There you are, my loveliest."

She started up from resting against the car. "Eroll."

Eroll Leighton, Duke of Thyra, leaned over the coupling behind her. He was an elegant man, slender and fair-haired, with a long face and laughing eyes. A close-trimmed goatee did nothing to hide his grin.

He took her hands in his and kissed them both in turn. "I think you have this nefarious plan to go away from me just so I'll think you're more beautiful when you come back."

"A day of hard traveling never made any of us look the better."

He released one of her hands so he could doff his jaunty cap. A white feather swirled all the way around its brim. Today, his usual frippery took the form of a blue doublet, its ballooning sleeves slashed with gold.

"You see, my princess, that's the difference between us. I am willing to hint at a few—well, not untruths—but *lesser* truths, to ease my lady's mind. You, however, would no doubt let me stagger in after a day of riding and fighting and other such glory-mongering, and tell me to my face I looked like a consumptive Riever."

"I rather think your vanity could stand the blow."

Eroll was her oldest friend—her *only* friend in some ways—the brother she had never had. As a child, she had been betrothed to his older brother, Phlin. After Phlin died in the war, the betrothal should have legally passed to Eroll, but he had understood her heart too well to press the matter. She had no desire to marry and no need. At the moment, her duties as Searcher outweighed her responsibility to produce an heir for her family.

Perhaps someday she would marry Eroll. Better him than anyone else. He was safe, he was familiar, and he understood her more clearly than anyone. More clearly than she understood herself sometimes.

"I'm glad you're here," she said. "I had no idea you'd be in town today."

"On my way to Ballion. Thought I'd get in a little zajele hunting before the season's entirely over. But then I caught a peep of the royal flag fronting a train up there." He pointed to the tracks overhead. "Thought I'd poke around on the off chance you'd decided to leave your behemoth of a black castle after all. And here you are."

He looked around at the Guardsmen. "What is all this anyway? You've been holed up in Réon Couteau for months, and now you're gallivanting through my town without even planning to wave at me on your way out? You do know court's getting beastly dull without you back in Glen Arden."

"Eroll, another Gifted has crossed." Just saying the words lightened the burden.

"What? He's here?" He looked around.

"Not *here* here. I haven't found him yet."

"Dear Garowai in the sky. Not that again." The twinkle disappeared from his eyes, and he actually managed to appear serious, or close to it. He replaced his hat. "You were gone for months last time around. Came home a skinny wreck, if I recall." His voice lowered. "Never seen eyes so big in a face as yours were then."

"I was nine. This is different. He's closer this time, I can tell." She touched his arm reassuringly, though it was really for herself. "It will be better this time. I know it."

"Can hardly be worse, that's for certain." He patted her hand on his arm. "So you're unloading here? Headed where?"

"I don't know." If only she had someone to tell her what to do, someone to guide her. But Eroll was hardly the person to do that. He had followed her lead since they were children. Flirting and dancing and hunting were his areas of expertise, not this. This wasn't anyone's area except hers.

Searchers were never appointed until their predecessors died, so she'd never had the chance to meet and learn from someone who'd experienced the same things she had and made the same decisions. The Garowai knew all about it, of course. But the Garowai kept his own counsel.

She took a breath. "The Guard is riding into the Thyra hills. We've had reports Koraudian troops are attacking Cherazii caravans."

"That's got to be rot, doesn't it? Koraud's not ready to declare war.

Not until—" He caught himself and straightened up.

"Mactalde is *not* coming back." She shot the words at him as if they were bullets.

"'Course not." But his attempt to look convinced only made him appear less so. "Where's your Gifted?"

"I don't know yet." She turned in a slow circle. His presence dragged at her from every which way, but when she faced southward, it concentrated into a decided pull. "South, I think. Still south. I have to decide whether to get off here and ride out with the Guard or stay on the skycar until Virere."

"The farther south he is the better, I say. Be a bad thing if he ran into these Koraudians before you found him—one way or t'other."

An engineer in a black doublet and elbow-high suede gloves stopped behind Eroll and saluted. "Excuse me, my lady, Lord Thyra. Captain Quinnon says I'm to uncouple these cars."

She nodded her consent.

Eroll climbed over the coupling to join her. "Perhaps I'll come along for the ride, eh?"

She shook her head. "Wouldn't want to interfere with your hunt."

"Rot. It'll be jolly fun either way. A hunt's a hunt." He flashed the grin that had famously dazzled the entire female half of the royal court.

Eroll Leighton was one of the most useless men she knew. He'd never done a day's work in his life, never attended Council meetings, probably didn't even know how to remove his own boots. But, for all that, he still managed to be outrageously charming. He made her laugh, something precious few people in this world could do. He would chase sundogs to the ends of the worlds if he thought it would make her happy. And he would never ask a thing in return. As long as he stood beside her, she wasn't alone.

"Thank you," she said.

His grin turned saucy and he gave her a wink. He knew all too well he was a handsome, dashing devil.

Through the glass walls of the car, she could see Quinnon tromping out of the station and across the courtyard. He saw her and Eroll and deviated his path to pass between the newly uncoupled cars and join them.

"Lord Thyra." He gave Eroll a nod, which was about the most

obeisance he gave anyone, noble or not, then addressed Allara. "Time's come. Which way do we go?"

She turned away from them both to face south.

Eroll was right. If the Gifted were farther south than Virere Ford, she could afford to let him wait. But if he were in the Thyra hills, if he were anywhere near that Koraudian troop, she had no time to waste. She had to get to him first, before they killed him or, worse, realized who he was and twisted him to their purposes.

She turned back. "We'll ride out from here. Lord Eroll's coming with us."

Quinnon gnawed the inside of his mouth. "Leaving the train now means a long day's ride yet. And if we find those Koraudians, we're likely in for an ugly fight. You ready for that?"

"No." She moved to the rear of the car to unlatch the horses' ramp. "But since when has that ever mattered?"

9

ORIAS AND THE Gifted hadn't ridden for very long when Orias reined up, head erect. Cherazii could hear far beyond a human's natural range. Even with two leagues separating him from the camp, his ears still caught the sounds he had dreaded every step of the way.

Screams. Iron against iron. The occasional hollow explosion of gunfire.

It had happened after all. The Koraudians had hit the caravan. He trembled. Duty or not, how could he possibly ride on, listening to the slaughter behind him? He must do something, and, if it was to be done, he must do it now.

Behind him, Chris brought his pony to a stop. "What is it?"

Orias hauled his horse around and reached for his battle axe. "The Koraudians just attacked the caravan."

"Where are you going?" Raz demanded from over Orias's shoulder. "Koraudians'll kill us if we go back there. And they'll kill the Gifted too."

Orias's breath came hard. He darted a look at Chris, then stared back in the direction from which the sounds hammered his ears.

These were his people! His blood! How could he just ride away from them? The Gifted was safe here. Orias had done his duty to the Gifted. He'd delivered the Orimere. From here on out, Chris was the Searcher's responsibility. She would find him. She would take care of him.

Battle fire blossomed in his brain, and he tamped it down long enough to look at Chris. "I have to go. They are my people, and I can't remain here and listen. But you need to stay here." He snapped his fingers at his lion. "Dougal!" Then he leaned over his horse's neck and urged it into a gallop before he could change his mind.

Tree branches whipped his face and showered his saddle with leaves. He spurred his horse's sides, and his fingers itched for the basket-hilted broadsword sheathed on his back. His blood thundered in his veins and suffused the oyster white of his skin with its inky blue. Within his mind he found the fiery core of the Cherazii's fighting strength, and he prepared to slip into its calm center where he could access the berserking rage that made them the most feared warriors in the world.

Just in touching the edge of that fire, his vision narrowed to magnify details and his tall ears sucked in sound even beyond their normally exquisite range. The muscles in his shoulders and chest bulged beneath his sleeveless leather jerkin. His reflexes sharpened, and his thoughts refined themselves to razor intensity.

The trail that had taken the better part of an hour to cover flew past in only a few minutes. A skein of smoke wafted through the trees and bit hard in his nostrils.

He burst from the trees into the meadow, knowing what he would find.

A full battalion of troops had cut their way to the center of the camp. Every Cherazim and Riever fought. Every man, woman, and child screamed their battle cries, their blood burning blue under their skin, their minds deep within the berserking fire.

Horses ran loose, wild-eyed and snorting. Fires, started in the tents, spread through the grass. Wagons had been upended, wheels wrenched off, the glass overhangs shattered. Dozens of Cherazii bodies littered the ground. Twice as many Koraudian soldiers lay dead, their bodies hacked open with blows of vicious force.

He galloped through the corpse-strewn meadow and fed his anger. The God of all willing, he would kill as many of these cursed Koraudians as he could bring his blade to meet.

He roared. His sword tore through one Koraudian's chest. His axe severed another's arm. Bodies writhed about him. Horses stumbled and reared as they trod one upon the other. He hacked and shoved, fighting for the space his sword needed to deliver its full potency.

Raz dropped to the ground. His stiletto blades glared as they darted among the horses' legs, slashing tendons. In a black blur, Dougal launched himself at a charging Koraudian and brought him to the ground, teeth clamped in his throat. The horses staggered, and the Koraudians cursed.

Orias swung his sword in abbreviated arcs, catching their blows and flinging them aside.

"Orias!" Raz shouted. "Your back!"

He whipped around to find two Koraudians closing on him, with a dozen more behind them. They shouted their victory and fell upon him, eschewing their ineffective firearms. If they wanted him alive, they would have to fight him on his own ground. With a cry, he drove his horse forward. He buried the axe in one man's chest, and the handle yanked from his grip as the body toppled from its saddle.

Someone seized his right arm, and another Koraudian tried to batter his sword from his hand. Releasing the sword, he threw himself at the soldier who held his arm, and they both plunged to the ground. Hands buried in the man's throat, he dug with his fingers until he could feel the windpipe collapse. Unhorsed and unarmed, he was still the most dangerous foe these cursed Koraudians were likely ever to face.

The ground reverberated with oncoming hoofbeats.

"No!" Raz said.

The horse smashed into Orias. Galaxies flared behind his eyelids, and he rolled away. He shoved to his hands and knees and blinked hard. His lungs refused to expand.

The horse hit him again, legs churning over his body. This time, the pain penetrated his berserking fire and exploded in his left shoulder and along his ribs.

"This is how the mighty Cherazii fight?" A man's voice mocked him. "Where is this legendary skill we've all heard tell about? I didn't think you'd win, but I did have it in my mind you'd put up more of a fight."

The hoofbeats stopped a few strides off and turned for another go. At least twenty Koraudians had formed a loose perimeter around him, boxing him in like a wounded animal to be baited. The battle had waned. His people were either dead or overcome, and now he was to be sport for the victors.

If that was what they wanted, then so be it. He lifted himself to one knee and tried to shake the fuzz from his brain. Someone hit him in the back of the head with a rifle stock. He staggered but didn't fall.

The horse bore down on him again, a shadow looming in the smoke of his vision. His ears caught the sound of the rifle descending for another blow, and he braced. He spun around, hands rising to meet the rifle stock. "Dougal!"

The lion leapt through the ring of horses and clamped his fangs in the forearm of the oncoming rider.

Orias clawed the rifle free of the Koraudian's grasp and fired a blast through his attacker's shoulder.

"Call off the lion!" The voice no longer mocked. "If you want to save your people, call off the lion and surrender!"

Pain thundered through his head. His vision wobbled in and out of focus. He concentrated on the berserking fire and plunged his mind in deeper yet, blocking out the pain and pulling his senses back into clarity. Whatever this man had in mind, it had to be a ploy, a ruse. In these troubled days, any Cherazim would be worse than a fool to trust a Koraudian soldier. His breath gusted, and he turned.

The commander's horse walked forward. He frowned, and his wooly red whiskers clotted around his mouth. He was a greasy man, average in height, with ape arms and an angular face.

A chill melted through the heat of Orias's blood. He knew this man. Every Cherazim knew this man. Glelarn Rotoss, one-time lieutenant of the feared Faolan Mactalde, had famously subscribed to the heresy that Mactalde would one day return from across the worlds to lead his country to final victory against Lael. In the aftermath of the war, Rotoss had seized every opportunity to persecute the Cherazii for the part they had played in Mactalde's and Harrison's executions.

Orias shifted his grip on the empty rifle. This man deserved to die.

Rotoss looked at the baldric buckle that proclaimed Orias a Tarn and a Keeper of the Orimere. "Well." He grinned, and the vein-like scars on his cheeks contorted. "Just the blue I was looking for. Looks like your wretched mother should have taught you to be more considerate of your health."

"Leave his mother out of it, goat-face!" Raz yelled.

A Koraudian grabbed him by one arm and dangled him above the ground like a rooster ready for the axe.

Dizziness threatened at the edge of Orias's berserking fire, and he kept his body still to maintain his mental grip. Rotoss could only be hunting down a Tarn for one reason. If he were going to bring back Mactalde, he needed the Orimere and he needed the Gifted. Could he be aware the Gifted was only a few leagues from here?

"You know—" Rotoss sat back in his saddle, "—you Cherazii hold a vast lot in common with my lord Mactalde."

Orias snarled. "We hated him, and he hated us. That's commonality enough."

"Yes, and he's dead—for the time being—and you're dying." He grinned. "Pity you didn't have the vision to change with the times. If you'd had sense enough to let the last Gifted live even after his so-called 'sin,' you might have ruled us all instead of baring your chests for the sword." His hand fell to his hilt.

Orias's blood rose, and strength flowed through his muscles. He spat on the ground, the Cherazii tradition signifying an oath. "Before I die, I will kill you."

Rotoss didn't move. No one moved. "Oh, now, I'm sure you'd like that. But have you thought about this? How much better—how much more *honorable*—it would be to spare me and save the Cherazii?"

Orias took another step. He would have one chance to reach Rotoss before the rest of the Koraudians swarmed him.

"Give me the Orimere." Rotoss extended his arm. "Put the dreamstone in my hand, and I'll let today's survivors walk, yourself among them."

"You came all this way to save my people?" The rifle hung heavy in his hands, and the buzz of the hydraulic power system in its stock tingled his skin. "Your magnanimity stuns me."

"It should." Rotoss looked up, and his smile fled.

Footsteps whispered behind Orias, the heavy clank of plate armor jostling with each step. He wasn't going to get another chance.

He lunged at Rotoss and twisted the empty rifle in his hands so he held its barrel. The Koraudians behind him cursed and broke into a run. Rotoss's horse tossed its head, whites gleaming in its eyes.

But Rotoss held his ground. He reached to his belt for a pistol and leveled it at Orias's chest. "Stop!"

Orias might be destined to die here, but he would not go down empty-handed. He pivoted his upper body, the rifle a club in his hands. A battle cry swelled his lungs.

Rotoss twitched the pistol up. He fired, and the rifle stock splintered.

Orias hadn't even time to compensate his balance before three Koraudians tackled him from behind. His head hammered into the ground, and his vision flickered.

"Bind him." Rotoss's voice swam in the back of his consciousness.

"You don't just look like a goat, you fight like a pig!" Raz shouted.

The Koraudians lashed his hands behind his back and dragged him to his feet. Not until they slammed his battered shoulder against a tree did the pain blast him out of paralysis. They bound him to the trunk with a thick rope.

Rotoss dismounted and handed his reins to a soldier. He approached Orias's tree as he used his pistol's reloading rod to cram another round down the barrel. "You stupid blues. You never learn." He threaded the reloading rod into the groove on the underside of the pistol barrel and, with a flourish, holstered the gun at his side.

Orias darted a glance to where a Koraudian was stuffing Raz into his saddlebags. Raz bit the man's finger and earned himself another blow to the head.

Orias looked back at Rotoss. "What do you want?"

Rotoss drew his sword and squatted. "I'm here for one thing only." He clanked the tip of the sword against Orias's baldric crest. "And if you're the Tarn this says you are, I've found it." The tip of his blade slipped down from the buckle and bit through Orias's jerkin. With a flick of his wrist, Rotoss sliced the leather open.

Only this morning, that slash would have uncovered the Orimere. But now the inner pocket was empty.

"Where's the Orimere?" Rotoss demanded.

"It's no good to you," Orias said. "Only the Gifted can use it."

Rotoss leaned back on his heels. "That's not your worry. Mactalde is about to return from the dead. And, depending on the choice you make, your people will either die or *survive*."

Orias stared into Rotoss's smile, and his guts twisted. Even after twenty years of silence, even from beyond the grave, Mactalde controlled the fate of the Cherazii.

He shook his head. "I don't have it."

Rotoss stroked his tangled beard. "Well, now, matey, that's an interesting thing for you to say. Because if you haven't got it, that makes me start conjecturing about who has."

Orias met his gaze and held it. "I'm not the only Keeper."

Rotoss grinned. The scars once again warped his face. "You're the only Keeper in Lael. The only Keeper hell-bent for Ori Réon. That means you had the Orimere. And if you don't have it anymore, that means you've given it away." His grin widened. "Ain't that so?"

Orias gave his head the slightest of shakes and immediately regretted it. He and Rotoss both knew the truth. Denial, right now, could only be taken as a sign of weakness.

"All right, then," Rotoss said, "where's the Gifted? If you gave him the Orimere, that means you know where he is. The Searcher couldn't have found him yet. Our informers in Réon Couteau relayed word she left there only this morning." He idly flicked the point of his blade up to the soft flesh beneath Orias's chin. "Let's ponder on this. If she's only just left that great black castle of hers, that means the Gifted's only just crossed. And if the Gifted's only just crossed and you've already given him the Orimere, he must be close by. You going to tell me about it?"

Orias's throat tightened. He shouldn't have come back. He should have taken the Gifted and ridden on to find the Searcher. He had known that in the core of his bones. He knew it now, and yet, even still, he deserved to rot for riding away from his people when he had known trouble was coming. Rot him first—and then the Gifted for coming at all and bringing this upon them. He forced himself to shake his head.

"All right." Rotoss sat back on his heels. "How about I make you a little present then?" He looked back at his men. "Bring a dozen or so of the prisoners. Women, children, and oldings."

A growl built in Orias's throat. He struggled against the rope that bound his hands behind the tree. Blood trickled from his raw wrists, but the ropes held fast.

Rotoss chuckled. "My present to you, loyal Cherazim of the Koraudian Kingdom, is the lives of your people. Provided, of course, you're willing to do a little bartering."

The men who guarded the Cherazii brought them to a halt in front of Orias: four women, six children, and two rickety old men.

They had been defeated, wounded, bereaved. Deep purple bruises formed on several of the women's faces and a child's bare white arms. But they stared at Rotoss, unbroken, watching him like caged lions watch for their chance to devour their whipmaster. They would go to their graves unbowed.

Rotoss gestured to a guard. "We'll start with the children."

"No!" The women started yowling.

A Koraudian dragged over a girl child, her blue-black hair plaited in a Y down her back. Her mother tried to scramble after her, and her strength required two guards to hold her back.

Every muscle in Orias's body stiffened. "Don't do this."

"I'm not doing this. You are." The movement of Rotoss's head tracked the girl as the guards dragged her, kicking and biting, to stand in front of Orias. Then he nodded. "All right."

The guard put a pistol to her head, and, without even waiting to see Orias's response, pulled the trigger.

The clearing erupted in screams and oaths. Orias's blood surged, the berserking fury so strong he could barely see. He fought his bindings. The blood now trickled freely into his hands.

"Shall we try that again?" Rotoss asked. "Before your chattel decrease further?" He gestured to his men. "A little boy this time, I think."

Orias panted. He couldn't do this thing. He was a Tarn, a Keeper of the Orimere. He was sworn to uphold the Gifted. To protect them, even to guide them should the Searcher request his assistance. What Rotoss was asking, it was treason. It was perfidy of the worst kind. He would be betraying the Gifted, the Searcher, the tenets he had lived by all his life, even his people themselves.

The bereaved mother's wails, primal and piercing, clawed his ears. If he let this thing happen, wasn't he betraying them just the same?

Rotoss leaned in nearer. "I'm not just giving you the lives of these people here. I'm promising you the lives of *all* the Cherazii. You can be the savior of your people, and all you have to do is help me bring one man, one lone man, back to his home. What's the harm in that? Who knows, maybe Mactalde won't even want to come back. Maybe he likes this other world so much, he'll call the whole thing off. Really, you've nothing to lose, Master Tarn."

He couldn't do this, he couldn't. And yet—mustn't he? Some force beyond his control dragged the air from his lungs.

A lad so young his ears had yet to grow to a height greater than his head staggered to a stop next to the fallen body of his playmate. The corners of his mouth pinched, but he didn't cry. He stood with the impassivity of a grown Cherazim, his tiny white fists clenched at his sides.

Rotoss nodded to the guard. The pistol pointed at the boy's head.

"Wait!" The word ripped through Orias.

Rotoss laughed. "Ah-ha, you see? I knew you were going to make the right choice."

A groan rent his body. What choice did he *have*? For twenty years, his people had suffered because they had chosen to do the "right" thing, because they had chosen to take the blood of the last Gifted upon their own hands to prevent the forbidden desecration of a living being crossing the worlds by means of the Orimere.

And what had they bought the world with their adherence to duty? A better future? Peace? Prosperity?

Nay, none of that. They had followed the traditions. They had upheld their honor. They had succeeded where others failed. But they had been saddled with a nine-year-old girl for a Searcher. They had been betrayed by a king and a Garowai who failed to give her the guidance she needed. They had followed the path of traditions and honor—and it had blessed no one, least of all themselves.

So what had they to gain by continuing it? What had *he* to gain? Right here, right now, his people died at the feet of their enemies. And he could bear it no more. If he did this thing—if he turned the Gifted over into the hands of Mactalde's chief lackey—he would damn his soul. Perhaps he would even wreak new havocs on the world. But *he would save his people.*

He closed his eyes. "I'll do it."

10

CHRIS DIDN'T HAVE a sword. He didn't know how to ride. He wasn't even sure where he was going. But he wasn't about to stay behind and do nothing while Orias rode away. Besides, maybe getting shot was exactly what needed to happen to wake him up.

He thumped his heels against the pony's ribs, and the horse lumbered into a run that covered only half as much ground as Orias's big mount. Pitch didn't argue. Teeth gritted, Chris attempted to forget about *trying* to ride and just let his muscle memory take over.

He risked a look over his shoulder at Pitch. "What is it these Koraudians have against your people?"

Pitch's face was grim. "They hate us because we helped kill Mactalde in the war."

"And what do they do to you?"

"Kill us."

A cold fist clenched in his stomach. Almost without thinking about it, he rose in his stirrups, his weight centered over the horse's forequarters. He tightened his legs around the pony's girth and smacked the reins against its shoulders. The horse's ears flicked back at him and its body lengthened, its strides reaching farther, its hooves pounding.

After what seemed an eternity, they neared the edge of the trees. Instead of the sounds of battle, he could hear only the tread of heavy feet and the shouting of men. He leaned back and clumsily hauled the pony to a stop. Was the battle over then? Already?

Through the trees ahead, the shadows of mounted horsemen trotted through the smoke. He dismounted.

Pitch clung to his back, then jumped to the ground. "Here." He thrust the hilt of a stiletto toward him. "You better stay here. It's no good if you get yourself killed on your first day."

Chris gripped the light sword. The blade was only a foot long, and the hilt barely accommodated the full breadth of his hand. He tried to relax into the instincts of his body, but the little sword felt unfamiliar, even awkward.

He stood up. His breath came hard, and adrenaline shot through his body. Swords and riding might not be his thing, but he'd thrown himself into enough underdog fights to know how to inflict damage even without a weapon.

"I'm not going to just stand here."

Pitch leapt up and grabbed Chris's free hand. "No! Orias said for you to stay. You'll get killed!"

Hoofbeats drummed toward them, and two horses, side by side, appeared through the trees. Their helmeted riders were humans, dressed in flowing red tabards emblazoned with black eagles. Without pausing to ask questions, the blood-spattered rider nearest to Chris uttered a roar and raised his sword.

Reflex took over. Chris dove headlong. The horse's front feet landed inches from his hand, and the rider's sword slashed overhead. He ratcheted his feet under him and spun to face the horsemen.

Pitch bounced into his peripheral vision, flourishing his remaining stiletto. "Prepare to die, murdering dogs!"

The soldier yanked his horse around to face Chris once again. His friend didn't waste any time following.

"Maybe you should be quiet," Chris said.

"Filthy, brainless, *ugly* murdering dogs!"

The soldier charged, sword rising for the kill. Chris took one step back, lifted the tiny stiletto, and swung to meet the blow. The blades collided, and the stiletto ripped from his hand. The soldier reined his horse closer, and the second knight closed off Chris's escape. He pivoted, trying to keep them both in his line of sight.

Pitch hurled himself at the nearest horse's leg. His blade buried itself in the soft tissue behind the horse's bone and slashed past the tendon. The horse reared and tore the sword from Pitch's grip.

The knight growled. "Should have minded your own business, Laeler."

The other soldier drove his horse forward, shoulder to shoulder with Chris, and hammered his hilt at Chris's temple. Chris hurled himself to the ground. A rock smacked against his head, and fog flooded his brain. He just barely managed to roll over and shove himself to one knee.

More horses broke through the smoke. A rider dismounted and ran to fence off Pitch before he could come to Chris's aid.

The soldier who had taken Chris down dismounted. He pointed his sword at Chris's chest, and his jowls bunched in a grin on either side of his spade-shaped faceplate. "Teach you to fight with Cherazii, eh?"

Half a dozen horsemen gathered around Chris. He wrenched his other foot under him and rose. He wasn't about to make his last stand on his knees. Wishing for a hand grenade or a machine gun or pretty much anything, he launched himself at his attacker and threw him to the ground.

Two of the riders dismounted and ran for him. They raised their swords above his chest, and the sun glinted on the blades as they descended. Blood rushed in his ears. So much for making his last stand on his feet.

"Stop!" That roar could come from no human's chest, and, unless death was clogging his senses, the chest it came from was Orias's.

The two swords halted inches from his heart. He darted a look toward the meadow.

A new squad of Koraudians had ridden into the trees, and Orias and Raz walked beside the lead horse. Blue blood seeped from the corner of Orias's mouth. His face was grim, defeated even, but he wasn't bound.

Chris frowned. He came with these men of his own free will?

The man on the lead horse dismounted. "Aye, stopping would be good." Red-haired, red-bearded, and incongruously grimy beneath the impressive sweep of his hat's feather, he grinned at Chris. "This here is one human I'd hate to see die anytime soon. What'd be your name, bucko?"

A heavy-gutted old fighter hauled Chris to his feet and put a sword to his throat. Chris had a very real urge to sucker punch him. But, under the circumstances, that was probably a fast track to getting himself skewered.

His captor followed his movements with the sword. "Commander Rotoss asked you a question, Laeler. Tell him who you are."

Chris looked to Orias for some kind of indication how to play these people. But Orias stared straight ahead, his face more impassive than before, if that were possible.

The leader glanced at Orias. "Introduce us."

Orias's face never flexed a muscle. "Chris Redston, Glelarn Rotoss."

"Charmed." Rotoss inclined his head and made a bowing gesture with his hand. "I've been waiting twenty years to meet you."

"Seems to be a popular sentiment." Or, more likely, his brain was just using this astonishing dream to process Harrison's similar words from earlier.

Rotoss shrugged one shoulder. "You're the Gifted, matey. Everyone wants to meet you."

Chris hid a frown. Orias hadn't wanted anyone to know he was the Gifted.

Orias stared past him.

What had happened back there? These red-shirted guys had overpowered all those Cherazii? From the looks of Orias, they hadn't just overpowered him, they'd crushed him. But if he was their prisoner, why hadn't they bound his hands? Surely his superior weight and strength would let him take out at least four of these men before they could subdue him again.

Rotoss stepped forward. "You'll think none the worse of me, I warrant, if I ask for a little proof you *are* the Gifted. You have the Orimere?"

That's what this was all about? His palm, hanging inches from the purse on his belt, prickled.

Orias looked at him and lowered his chin in a tight nod.

Chris shrugged. If that was what Orias wanted, that's what he'd get. He untied the leather purse from his belt and tossed it over.

Rotoss upended the contents into his hand. The coins and Pitch's *fawa-radi* sculpture tinkled through his fingers to the ground, but the Orimere's pouch hit his palm with a thump.

"Well." His exhale almost trembled. Long dirty fingernails pried open the drawstrings. He took one look inside, then closed his eyes in an expression somewhere between rapture and relief. "There it be." He opened his eyes, and a smile tugged up the corner of his mouth. "And here you be. I never expected to get this lucky. A Keeper, a Gifted, and an Orimere all in one day. Tell me, how long have you been in our world?"

"Since this morning."

"I see. So the Searcher hasn't found you." Rotoss walked all the way around Chris. "Lucky for you." He cast a thumb back in Orias's direction. "He's told you about the Searcher, I'm sure?"

"I know who she is. She's tried to kill me every time she's seen me."

"She wouldn't kill you. Though I'll say she wasn't able to do much to keep the last Gifted alive." He looked at Orias. "Ain't that right?"

Orias's jaw churned. Then he drew in a breath and conceded with a nod. "The Searcher and her father the king will do everything they can to put the Gifted under their thumbs. To them, you're a political pawn."

"*What?*" Pitch squeaked. His captor clapped a hand over his mouth, and he promptly bit it.

"Pitch." Orias's voice burned. "*Tuch pua.*"

Pitch stared. Slowly, he closed his mouth.

Chris looked at Orias. Something wasn't on the up and up here. He cocked his head toward Rotoss. "And am I so much better off with him rather than the Searcher?"

Rotoss stepped out of Chris's way and gestured for him to move closer to Orias. "I wouldn't hold it against you one jot if you wanted to jaw it over. You don't know me, and we haven't met under the most kindly circumstances. Go ahead. Ask the Tarn."

Chris drew forward a step to meet Orias. "Well?"

Orias let out a long, shuddering breath. "He's here to help you."

"Help me do what? Stop dreaming?"

Rotoss stepped in again. "You telling me you don't want to be a Gifted?"

Chris let himself laugh. "Back where I come from, they'll put you on antipsychotics and lock you up in a mental institution for dreaming something like this."

"Dreaming, is it?" Rotoss paced a few steps, then came back. "All right. In that case, what if I offered you a deal?" The grin returned. "In point of fact, the one and only thing I want from you is the one thing that will give you what you want as well."

"And what is it you want?"

Rotoss winked at Orias. "Tell him, blue."

Orias paused for two long beats, then he looked Chris in the eye. "If you want to make the dreams stop, there's something you have to do in your world. Someone you have to find."

"Mactalde." The name found its way out of his mouth almost of its own accord.

"You've got it," Rotoss crowed. "Faolan Mactalde. Mactalde's life for your freedom."

Chris shook his head. None of this made any sense. "And why's that going to stop the dreams?"

Rotoss dangled the Orimere's green pouch between his fingers. "That's the magic of the dreamstone. Bring back Mactalde, and you will live the dreams no longer. You've my word."

Chris hesitated. Was this his subconscious telling him how to solve its problems? Or was he just devolving further into insanity? Either way, why not give it a shot? Any ticket out of here was one worth buying.

If none of this was real—and it wasn't, he wouldn't let himself believe it was—it didn't matter why Mactalde was the key. But some niggle of doubt made him ask anyway. "Why's this guy so important? What happens when I bring him back?"

Rotoss smiled beatifically. "Lord Faolan Mactalde was a beloved leader. He believed in many beautiful things, including rescuing his people from the tyranny of the Laelers. He was ruthlessly and unjustly cut down in the last war by the Searcher and her father, King Tireus II."

"And after twenty years, you haven't moved on?"

"After twenty years, we find ourselves in need of him again. This is the only way to bring him back. This is the only way to save our people." Rotoss gestured over his shoulder to Orias. "And his."

Ah, so that was it. It was a cinch Orias wasn't siding with this guy because he liked him.

Pitch shook his head vehemently. "You can't use the Orimere to bring people across! That's not allowed. That's what the last Gifted tried to do!"

"Just because it's never been done before doesn't mean it can't be," Orias said. Now that he was finally meeting Chris's eye, the raw, furious intensity of his gaze nearly drove Chris back a step. "Rotoss isn't lying. If you do what he says, you *will* save my people. I told you before you would have to choose whether you save us or destroy us." His whole body trembled. "This is where you choose."

"But—" Pitch sounded desperate. "The Cherazii had to kill the last Gifted when he tried to bring Mactalde back." He looked from Orias to Chris. "This is the worst thing a Gifted can do! Who knows what bad things will happen."

Raz rapped his knuckles against Pitch's shoulder. "*Ci liah spalalal o bé taradu.*"

Pitch opened his mouth, shut it, opened it again, then rolled his lips together and bit down on them. He stared up at Orias.

"Is that true?" Chris asked. Not that it mattered. *It didn't matter.* He clenched his teeth. This was a *dream!* Bad things didn't happen here at all. They were just wisps of color in the back of his mind.

Orias stepped forward. His height, at least six inches above Chris's, loomed. The width and bulk of his shoulders threatened in their massive power even when Chris knew he meant no harm. "Pitch doesn't understand what's happening here."

Chris nodded toward the meadow. "What I want to know is what happened back there?" Dream or not, he needed to figure this thing out. "You said they were your enemies. Pitch said they wanted to kill your people."

"They do, and they will, unless you bring Mactalde back."

"I bring him back, your people are safe, and I don't dream anymore. Is that right?"

Orias hesitated only a second. "That's right."

"Fine." He swallowed the whispered doubt. "I'll do it."

Orias turned away and breathed out. The Rievers exchanged a glance, and Pitch looked at Chris, his eyes wide and wounded.

Behind him, Rotoss clapped his hands together. "That's a bucko! Now, let's get to work on this right away. We haven't the time to waste." He strode over and slapped the Orimere's pouch into Chris's palm. "You know how to use this thing?"

Chris shook his head.

"Fortunately for us, you don't even have to be a fast learner. It's as simple as falling asleep." He guffawed and turned to one of his men. "Bring the wrak."

Chris shook the Orimere out of the pouch. Its electric warmth fell into his hand and tingled all the way up his arm. His heart stuttered. The sensation fell somewhere between painful and exhilarating.

He looked at Orias. "How's this going to work anyway?"

"The stone will cross over with you, along with everything you are touching. It will work the same way when you come back. If you are touching Mactalde when you cross, he will come with you."

"And how am I supposed to find Mactalde? Has anybody here thought about that?"

Rotoss took a large glass vial from one of his men. "If luck be with us, *he'll* find *you*. The last Gifted told him you would be coming. You were his backup plan, so to speak, if Harrison Garnett didn't work out—which, of course, he didn't. You want my gold on it, I'd say Lord Mactalde has known where to find you for a long time past."

Rotoss held up the vial. It was slender in its neck and expanded into a squashed sphere at the bottom. "Now, in the normal course of things, we'd wait until you fell asleep tonight. But with the Searcher coming upon us, we haven't the luxury of time. This here's what we call wrak. It's a knockout drug, used for surgeries and the like. Safe as ever was my own mother's porridge in the bowl. Lie down."

Chris glanced at Orias. If this was a bad idea, this was the last chance the Cherazim would have to tell him so. But Orias stood unmoving except for the twitch of his taut forearms every time he clenched his fists.

With a deep breath, Chris lowered himself to the bedroll someone had spread out.

Rotoss handed the vial back to his man—a medic hopefully—who propped the round base onto a trivet beside Chris's head. Amber liquid sloshed in the vial's globed bottom. The medic slid a metal straw down the vial's neck, then topped it with a flat plate, on which he balanced a chip of wood.

"We light that afire," Rotoss said. "The liquid wrak turns to steam, and you inhale it." He pointed to a nozzled hose connected to the vial's base.

Another man handed the medic an eight-inch cylinder, about as round as Chris's thumb. The medic fitted a wad of dry grass into a notch on the cylinder's base, then rested the grass against the wood chip. He depressed a plunger on the cylinder's other end. Flame spurted against the tinder, and the medic leaned down to blow on it. In a few minutes, he had the woodchip coated in a purple-hearted flame. He covered the chip with a metal dome and handed Chris the spigot at the hose's end.

"Breathe carefully. It'll be hot."

The amber liquid frothed inside the globe and steam fogged the glass. Chris closed his eyes. With any luck this stuff would have the same effect on him as the Searcher's bullet in his face. He was going to wake up, he was going to find out who cracked him over the head, and if at all possible, he was going to get his life back to normal.

He set the silver nozzle between his teeth and inhaled. Steam filled his mouth, not quite hot enough to burn him. It savored of a honeyish sweetness, but when it hit the back of his throat, it burned in his nostrils like the smell of diesel. He coughed and opened his eyes.

"Just keep breathing." The medic put the nozzle back into his mouth.

One more breath was all it took. The trees overhead started to spin. As his head sank back to the ground, he caught one last glimpse of Orias's face. The pale white of his skin blurred and ran like wet paint.

11

CHRIS BLINKED HIS eyes open, expecting to still see Orias's face. But the Cherazim was gone. As a matter of fact, so was the entire forest. It had worked. He was awake again. But he wasn't anywhere he recognized.

Instead of trees, he stared at soaring oak rafters. He blinked, trying to orient himself.

Two things were clear. One of those things was that he could no longer taste the bittersweet wrak steam. The other was that the back of his head felt like someone had clubbed him. Which, come to think of it, someone had.

Gingerly, he turned his head. Sunlight from a wall of picture windows speared his vision, and he squinted. He was lying on a leather couch, his feet propped up on a maroon throw pillow. Across the room, the windows offered a view of a white-capped lake that went on and on. Directly in front of him, a marble fireplace took up at least twelve square feet of wall, crowned by an oil painting of a mountain sunset. Wherever he was, it was swank.

He raised his head and immediately wished he hadn't. Pain thudded at the base of his neck, and black spots smoked up his vision. He lowered his head again and eased a breath past his clenched teeth. Just at this moment, his dream almost seemed preferable. At least whoever had clunked him in the head hadn't also kidnapped him. He wasn't tied up, and this didn't exactly look like a South Side garage.

He swung his legs to the ground and eased himself upright. The whole room swirled, so he let himself hold his head between his hands until the worst of the pounding subsided. That's when he realized his hand was buzzing. In his palm, the Orimere glimmered.

He jumped and dropped it. The fist-sized stone clattered onto the wood floor. In the broad daylight, it was just a milky rock, streaked occasionally with a flicker of lightning. But where had it come from? It couldn't have just materialized.

Scattered all around the floor were the strange clothes he had been wearing in the dream—as well as everything else he had been touching when he'd fallen asleep. His heart pounded. Nausea from the concussion swirled in his head, and he forced himself to breathe slowly.

He looked down at himself. He was wearing the T-shirt and cargo pants he had put on this morning. Maybe he hadn't been asleep after all. Maybe he'd been wandering around Chicago in some kind of daze, wearing those crazy clothes and hallucinating the whole bit with Orias and Rotoss.

Across the room, a door clicked open. He snapped his head back up and shoved the Orimere and all the clothing under the couch. He had zero desire to try to explain any of that stuff right now.

Three men entered. One was a stocky, gray-haired man wearing a rumpled tie and a CPD badge on his belt.

The second was tall, blond, with angular features and an iron gaze. Judging by the buzz haircut and the bulge under his suit coat, he was hired muscle.

The third man was the first to speak, his voice deep and full. "You've awoken." He looked in his mid-forties, his brown hair and close-trimmed beard shot through with gold. Broad shoulders stretched the pin-striped navy of his expensive blazer and led into an equally powerful chest.

He crossed the room, smiling without showing teeth, and held out his hand. "Mr. Redston, I believe? You've had a rough day of it." He had the grip of someone who worked out on a regular basis. The serene slant of his mouth said he was accustomed to viewing life on his own terms, or not at all.

Chris forced himself to sit upright, ready to stand and scram if he needed to. "How'd I get here?"

"Apparently, you were the victim of some random violence in Mr. Garnett's neighborhood."

"You're a detective?"

"No." The man rumbled a laugh. "This is the detective." He gestured back to the rumpled-tie guy. "Detective Dean."

The man shuffled forward. "I'm just here to get your statement. You know who hit you?"

He thought back. His memories of the shooting were clear, right up until he'd been smacked in the head and sent hurtling into his dreams. But he hadn't caught so much as a glimpse of his attacker.

He shook his head. "No, I didn't see him."

Dean scowled. "So you got nothing for me, is that what you're saying?"

"I'll let you know if I remember." He felt his pockets. "Was I robbed? What happened to me?"

Dean scribbled a few notes in his little pad. "No, you weren't robbed. And if you can't tell me, then I have no idea what happened to you, although our best guess is the original shooters were maybe trying to take out their only witness. Even though you didn't see hardly nothing." He paused his scribbling to glare at Chris.

"Where am I?"

The bearded guy smiled. "This is my home. The police allowed me to take care of you. I thought it might be best if you had personal supervision. Also, I thought you might like to talk about your experience after you woke up."

"You're a doctor?"

The detective harrumphed in the back of his throat but didn't look up from his notepad.

"Not to worry, Mr. Redston. You were in good hands. As a matter of fact, I'm quite familiar with your condition." The man pocketed his hands. "I'm a psychologist. Mr. Garnett's personal therapist, as a matter of fact. Hence, my presence at the scene."

Chris cast a sideways glance down at the bottom of the couch, just to make certain the Orimere wasn't showing. "My condition?"

Dean stuffed his notebook and pencil into his coat pocket. "If you think of something that's actually useful to this case, you give me a call. And if you want to go to a hospital, go to a hospital." He waved a hand at the doctor. "I'll show myself out, Dr. Mactalde."

Chris froze. *This* was Mactalde? Mactalde was the shrink? Whatever he'd been expecting, it hadn't been a professional in a power suit.

The doctor chuckled at Chris's expression before turning to the detective. "Thank you, Detective. Flores, show him out." He gestured to someone behind Chris, and a short dark-skinned man with a shoulder-length shag haircut followed the detective to the door. Chris hadn't even realized he was in the room.

Mactalde turned back to Chris. "So now that we know each other, allow me to introduce Geoff Kaufman, who works for me," he indicated the blond bodyguard, "and who will now go find you a glass of water and some ibuprofen, which I'm sure you're in desperate need of."

Kaufman left without comment and closed the door.

Chris's heart started its pounding again, which only ratcheted up the pain in his head even more. He eased out a breath. What were the odds of this guy showing up for the first time right after Chris dreamed he was supposed to go looking for him? He closed his eyes and tried to separate reality from the memory of the dream. But his chat with Rotoss and Orias was still just as vivid as the words he had exchanged with the detective.

Where could he start with Mactalde? What question could he safely ask without immediately looking like the Kook of the Year?

He opened his eyes. "So if you're Harrison's therapist, then he *was* crazy?"

Mactalde laughed. He backed up to the matching couch across from Chris and sank down on the middle cushion. "It's true Mr. Garnett harbored more than his share of delusions. And, as a result, had his share of enemies. I understand you witnessed his unfortunate shooting." His mouth compressed. "Seeing that kind of thing can shake even the best of us, and to be honest, you do look a bit shaken, Mr. Redston. Would you like to tell me about it?"

Stay away from the shrink.

Harrison's scribbled message blinked in his mind. Harrison hadn't mentioned anything about Mactalde being his therapist. He'd seemed to think the man had it out for him.

"What did you treat Harrison for?"

"That's confidential, I'm afraid. However, I can tell you Mr. Garnett happened to mention you the other day. He said you were experiencing some of the same mental problems as he used to."

"And what are those?" Here it came. Schizophrenia, delusional paranoia, psychoses galore. They all seemed like prime candidates if Harrison's problems were anything like his.

Mactalde unbuttoned his coat and spread his arms over the couch's back. His starched shirt pulled tight against his muscled chest. "I think it would be better if you told me. You've been experiencing something strange lately? A delusion of some sort?" He raised his eyebrows, waiting.

When Chris didn't bite, he continued. "You look to me like a man who doesn't sleep well. And I know the look when I see it. Do you have nightmares?"

Chris hesitated. But he had to tell Mactalde sooner or later. Only a few minutes ago, he'd agreed to "bring" Mactalde into his dreams. Now, sitting across from him, looking out onto what had to be Lake Michigan, the whole idea sounded about five miles beyond absurd. More like downright terrifying that any part of his brain had even considered it. Did they still lock people up in padded cells? If they did, he was about to turn into a prime candidate.

"Yeah, I have nightmares. They feel like—" He forced the words out. "Like they're real. And I almost find myself believing them." He couldn't quite squeeze a laugh past his dry throat. "In my dreams, they tell me I'm living two different existences. Is that what Harrison told you?"

"More or less."

A knock sounded on the door, and Mactalde rose to let Kaufman in. The man deposited a glass of water and two pills on the end table beside Chris. Then, at a nod from Mactalde, he left.

Mactalde drifted back across the room. He drew a deep breath, as if considering his words. "Are you aware that before the twentieth century, people believed our minds completely turned off while sleeping? Common logic leads us to believe that, at the very least, our brain waves should decrease during sleep."

Chris downed the painkillers and clinked the glass back onto its coaster. "Makes sense."

Mactalde stopped behind the opposite couch and leaned forward, both hands planted on the back of the seat. "Then perhaps you'll be surprised to learn the exact opposite is true. As we sleep, our brain waves rapidly increase until they're identical to the ones we exhibit when we're wide awake. That's a scientific fact."

Chris's neck prickled. "What's that have to do with my dreams?"

"For all but a select few, dreams will never be anything more than a harmless, random conglomeration of ideas, thoughts, and feelings."

"And for the select few?"

Mactalde's smile deepened. "For them, dreams are everything. Their delusions become so strong, they believe, as you say, they're living two existences. Eventually, their attempts to reconcile these two lives tear them apart."

"Like Harrison." He tried to digest that. "So I'm going crazy?" Maybe he wasn't so different from his dad after all. He looked up at Mactalde. "There are things that have happened, things the people in my dreams said. Like you—they said *you* would find me."

Mactalde shook his head. "Your dreams can only be constructed from the material your waking life supplies it. Did Harrison ever mention my name to you?"

Chris nodded.

"Then no doubt your mind sewed that mention into the tapestry of your dream."

It made sense. Wasn't that what he had been telling himself all this time?

"What about this?" He eased himself onto his knees and tugged his Lael clothes—tunic, trousers, heavy boots, even the money pouch—into the open. Last of all, his hand closed around the Orimere. The shock of it vibrated all the way up his arm.

He pulled it out and turned around, hand outstretched. "You're saying *this* came from my dream?"

Mactalde straightened up from leaning on the back of the couch. "That, if I'm not mistaken, belongs to Mr. Garnett. Did he give it to you?"

Chris drew himself up short. Had Harrison given it to him back at his house? Had he forgotten because of the concussion?

"You've seen this before?" he asked.

"Oh, yes." Mactalde circled the couch to stand in front of him. "He calls it the Orimere. May I?"

After a second's pause, Chris passed it over. Mactalde cradled it in his palm and stroked it with the fingers of his other hand, as if it were a kitten.

"Do you feel that?" Chris asked.

Mactalde looked up. "Feel what?"

"It's kind of a buzz, not quite electric."

A shadow passed over the man's face, annoyance almost. Then he shook his head and handed the stone back. "No. I don't. Possibly it's a carryover from the dream."

"Is there any treatment for this?" Chris asked. He wanted to get out of here. He needed to go back home and sleep—or maybe not, since that was likely to send him straight back to dreamland. But, at any rate, he needed time to let the concussion wear off, so he could give this some logical thought and work out a plan of action.

Mactalde dragged his eyes from the Orimere and tugged his lapels straight. "There are some drugs that may help, but as a psychologist I'm not licensed to provide them. You'd have to go to a psychiatrist for that."

"You worked with Harrison. What'd you tell him?"

Mactalde took a deep breath. He seemed to be bracing himself. "There is one thing you can try. Very often, your brain will tell you what you need to do to fix it." He stepped toward Chris. "Has your brain told you yet what you need to do to stop the dreams?"

"Actually, yes. But it won't work."

"Why not?"

"Because it's impossible." He lifted the Orimere. "It has to do with this. And you."

"How fascinating." Maybe it was just his professional manner, but Mactalde didn't seem surprised in the least. Or maybe he had been through this whole rigmarole before with Harrison.

"I'm supposed to use this to bring you into the world of my dreams."

"Then let's do it," Mactalde said. "Let's pretend. If we can fool your brain into thinking you've accomplished what it wants, that may be all that's required."

Chris frowned. It couldn't be that easy, could it? But, then, did it really matter? What harm could come of giving this a try?

"In my dreams, they say the Orimere only works when I'm asleep."

"Then how about a nap? A little rest would be good for that head of yours right now anyway." Mactalde brought a chair over to the couch. "Go ahead and lie down, make yourself comfortable."

Chris lay back, his head against a maroon pillow. Part of him shouted this was the craziest thing he had done yet. But he hadn't asked for the dreams. He didn't want the dreams. If he could get out from under them, he could change his life. No, he *would* change his life.

Mactalde took off his coat, sat down, and began rolling up his sleeves. "Did they tell you in your dream how this is supposed to work?"

"Whatever's touching me when I fall asleep crosses over."

"Sounds simple enough. "

Minutes passed, and the concussion thumped in the back of Chris's head. His body sagged into the couch pillows. Sleep wasn't far away.

Mactalde touched his wrist. "Thank you."

The vibration from the Orimere crawled up Chris's arm. His head felt like it was stuffed with cotton.

"This is an extraordinary day for me." Mactalde's voice swam in and out of Chris's consciousness. "Should I be so fortunate as to rewrite history, I will certainly remember your name."

A black mist crept across Chris's vision. He was almost there, almost asleep, almost back to sanity. But something twinged in the back of his mind. Rewrite history? What was that supposed to mean?

Mactalde's voice turned golden. "After all, it isn't every day a man gets to rise from the dead. Is it?"

12

CHRIS OPENED HIS eyes. Something was wrong.

The wind soughed in the treetops, harmonizing with the rivulet ulet only a dozen or so yards away. Blue sky blinked overhead. He was back in Lael.

So much for Dr. Mactalde's grand plan.

"Welcome back." The voice was Rotoss's.

Chris turned his head. The soldiers who had watched in silence while he inhaled the wrak had dispersed in a flurry of activity. In his tingling hand, the Orimere winked up at him, now a serene glow of cobalt strobed with violet.

Someone had covered him with the top flap of the bedroll. His chest was bare, and a quick check revealed that so was the rest of him.

"Get dressed." A Koraudian held out a battered gray sneaker.

He sat up. Remnants of the real world littered the ground: his T-shirt, his socks, his cargo pants, the maroon pillow he'd laid his head on, and his heavy metal watch.

The stone *had* worked.

A brown shape, squat and long, caught his attention some three yards away: Mactalde's couch. He hurried into his clothes, stuffed the Orimere into the side pocket of his cargo pants, then left the bedroll and approached the couch. He ran a hand over the leather. The cushions were still warm from his body heat.

A few yards from the couch, half a dozen Koraudians, including Rotoss and the medic, huddled around a prone figure. Mactalde lay on his back, unmoving. His eyes were closed, his breathing shallow.

Rotoss waved Chris over with a jerk of his hand. "How come he's unconscious?"

"He was awake a minute ago." He craned his neck to see around the clustered soldiers. "You're telling me that thing actually worked? It brought him across? He's *here?*"

"It worked, and he's here." Rotoss shoved him away. "And for your health and safety, you better hope he wakes up without scathe."

Chris stumbled back. Mactalde's crisp white shirt and polished Oxfords gleamed incongruously in the dappled sunlight. "But what happened to him in the other world? He just disappeared? He's not there anymore?" It could, of course, be that his crazy dreaming mind had just imagined a facsimile of Mactalde. But the knot in the pit of his stomach said otherwise.

Rotoss pushed him back another step and gestured to one of his men. "Bind him and put him with the blue."

Before Chris could drag himself into comprehension, the soldier twisted his hands behind his back and lashed them together.

"Hey, wait—" He tried to pull away and follow Rotoss as he returned to Mactalde. "If it worked, I shouldn't be here. The dreams should be over! That was the deal."

The soldier hauled him back and toppled him onto his rear end. Chris scrambled to his knees and whirled to face the man, but instead found Orias standing with his back to a tree and his arms secured behind him. The Rievers huddled at his feet, tethered together with a foot of rope between their hands.

Pitch looked at him reproachfully. "You brought him back."

"Of course he did." Raz sat on a gnarled root, arms folded over his knees.

Chris levered his feet under him and stood. "Why am I still here?"

Orias looked at him, slowly, almost as if he were surprised to find him there at all. He appeared completely zoned out. Had they drugged him?

"He's here." Chris faced him. "Mactalde's here. And so am *I.* What went wrong?"

The dazed look snapped, and Orias's eyes went dark—dangerous. "Nothing went wrong."

"You've been lying through your teeth to me. Did this even help your people, or was that a lie too?"

Orias's arms constricted. "I had no choice. I was given the opportunity to stop this slaughter, this pointless persecution the Koraudians have been raining down on us for the last twenty years. I took it." He looked away. "And I'd do it again."

"I thought you were Keeper of the Orimere. You were supposed to protect the Gifted. Lying to me fulfilled what part of that?"

Orias shook his head. "My people are more important to me than any Gifted. If you're anything like the last one, then you wouldn't be worth protecting in the long run."

"And what happened to him?"

"We killed him." Orias's voice was flat.

"So the Cherazii have always been traitors?"

His eyes blazed. "The Cherazii are not traitors. The Cherazii didn't betray you today. *I* am the one who betrayed them and everything they stand for. But I betrayed them to save them. Can you understand that?"

"Maybe Mactalde's dead." Pitch looked up hopefully. "Is he?"

Chris turned half away. "If he is, they're going to kill us."

Pitch slumped on the root beside Raz. "I wish he were dead."

Half hidden in the trees, the Koraudian tabards flashed red as they worked over their lord and master. A collection of shouts filled the woods, and the crisp white shirt rose among them. Mactalde sat up, shaking his head as if to clear cobwebs. Then his men closed in around him again.

Chris stood with his back to Orias and the Rievers. "If the Orimere can't stop the dreams, then what can?"

"Nothing," Orias said. "Dreams are life. So long as you live, so do the dreams. And if you wish to live, then you had better pray you can escape and find someone who cares about keeping you alive. Such as the Searcher."

Chris looked at him. "And become her pawn?"

"We are all pawns." Orias hunched against the scaly bark of the tree. "The only distinction is not everyone bears the ignominy of knowing it."

Pitch peered up at Chris. "Don't you know they lied about the Searcher? She won't hurt you. It's her job to help you."

"Just like it was Orias's?"

"Oh, shut your gob." Raz glared. "If you hadn't wanted out of here so bad, you wouldn't have let yourself believe the lies. But you're here now just like us. You're tied up just like us. And unlike some of us, it's your fault. So whyn't you think on that for a bit."

Chris certainly wasn't in the mood to be taking orders from a shriveled little stick figure with a bad attitude. But what was there left to say anyway? Maybe it *was* his fault just as much as it was Orias's. Like an idiot, he had walked into this thing, and like an idiot, he'd done everything he was told, even when his instincts rebelled. He'd taken a gamble, and he'd lost. Just *what* he'd lost, he wasn't yet quite sure.

He sank down into the crackling leaf bed and waited. It was their move.

The Koraudians left their prisoners for half an hour while they tended Mactalde. They moved with purpose and discipline, but there was a feel about them, a sense of excitement. They joked and laughed as they moved in and out of the meadow, probably looting the camp and securing the surviving Cherazii. They examined the couch, flipped open Chris's cell phone, and rifled through the scant cash in his wallet before casting it aside.

Always, their eyes returned to the clump of trees behind which Mactalde had retired. Occasionally, they glanced at Chris as well. But a crazy dreamer just wasn't as interesting as someone returned from the dead.

A man, tall and broad, stepped into the clearing. He wore a knee-length leather coat, buckled up the front with half a dozen silver closures. A snowy undershirt gleamed through slits in the sleeves. Suede breeches, boots stretched above his knees, and a rapier dangling at his side completed the picture. Only the short trim of his tawny hair and beard spoke of another world.

Chris sat up. Mactalde seemed to have grown six feet. In Chicago, he had been an ordinary man. Now he was a conqueror, a general. He exuded power.

Harrison Garnett's words crackled through his head. *Mactalde will destroy you if he finds you! Destroy Lael!* A fingertip of cold touched the back of his neck. What if the old man had been right?

Behind him, Raz exhaled in a whoosh. "Sweet Garowai in the sky, it is him."

"*Yalarin pitish sé,*" Pitch whispered.

Mactalde made his way through his men, shaking hands and slapping backs. The troops parted before him. They touched thumb and fore-finger to their closed eyes and slid them down their faces in some kind of salute. Mactalde accepted it as if he'd done it all his life. Evidently, he *had*, up until twenty years ago.

When he reached Chris, he clapped his hands in front of him with a smile. His eyes were bright, ecstatic almost, like someone jacked up on crack.

"Well." He raised his voice. "Mr. Redston. How do you like your dream now?"

Chris pushed to his feet and squared his shoulders as much as he could against the tension of his bound hands. "You're telling me this is real? You're real? You're not some conjuring of my subconscious mind?" Even as he said it, he realized how stupid he sounded. If Mactalde *was* a delusion, how was he supposed to tell Chris anything he didn't already know? And if he wasn't . . .

Mactalde just grinned. "Believe what you like. But when you've returned to Chicago, I think you'll find I am no longer there."

What he wouldn't give for a good whack at the guy's smug face. He strained against the rope. "You lied to me."

Mactalde shrugged. "You'll forgive me, won't you?"

"Forgive you." Heat crept up Chris's face. "You tied me up, you lied to me, you manipulated me. What part of that makes you think I'm going to forgive you?"

"Ah, come now. I only told you what you wanted to hear."

Chris snarled. "You knew about this place? You knew about the dreams? How?"

"You forget I lived here."

"*Everyone* is supposed to live here. But not everyone back in our world knows about it. You did." He stepped forward. "From the moment I woke up on your couch, you knew exactly what I was talking about. You knocked me out so I *would* end up on your couch. You probably shot Harrison Garnett too."

"Harrison Garnett served his purpose. He led me to you."

Chris leaned away. "He was in on it?"

Mactalde laughed. "Of course not. I've had him under surveil-lance for the last twenty years because I knew he would try to contact you. Twenty years ago, I made a deal with Harrison Garnett." He exchanged a glance with Rotoss, then looked back at Chris. "I was dying. My body, here in Lael, was not so strong as the one you see me in now." He raised a fist. "But a Gifted—ah, a Gifted can work the magic of giving someone *two* bodies. I promised Harrison Garnett the throne of Lael if he would use the Orimere to bring my other body back from across the worlds after I died here. Unfortunately, he was captured, coerced into revealing his plan—and killed. But we knew you were coming, so all wasn't lost." He spread his arms. "And here we are now."

Chris shook his head. "You're not a Gifted. You shouldn't be able to remember what happened here."

"In Lael for not even a day, and they've already indoctrinated you into the meritocracy of the Gifted." Mactalde paced forward, hands gripping his empty gloves behind his back. "Anyone can break the mental wall between the worlds. The Searcher and her adherents will tell you that's black magic." He shrugged. "So be it."

"What happens to all of us now that you're back?"

Mactalde's smile remained. "Speaking personally, I have a lot of catching up to do." He stepped nearer and lowered his voice almost to a whisper. "You may not understand this, yet, since you haven't been here long, but there's a very good reason I've waited all these twenty years, hoping, keeping faith, forcing myself never to give up that this day would come."

He looked up at the intent faces of his men. The smile that stretched his beard was benevolent, fatherly, as if he were returning to his band of sons after a long captivity. "There's something that must be done in this world, injustices that must be put to rights. The tyranny of Lael must end. It is time Koraud shakes off her shackles and regains her crown. I have not returned to sue for peace. I have returned to crush my enemies beneath my boot."

The troops cheered.

Behind Chris, Raz hacked. "Ah, you're as daft as my Granny Fizz!"

A Koraudian smacked him.

Chris's airways clogged up on him. If this was all true, then what had he unleashed on this world through his stupidity?

Mactalde stepped back. The lift of his mouth hinted at laughter. He raised his voice to address his men, but he looked at Chris. "I've come back to give you victory." He raised a clenched fist. "The corrupted strongholds of Lael will fall! The men who have vilified us, we will trample beneath our horses' feet!"

The Koraudians roared their approval, and Mactalde faced them, arm still raised. "We will bring equality between nations. We will bring an end to tyranny. We will ride to victory!"

"Victory!" Rotoss raised his own fist. "Victory!"

The men took up the cry. "Victory! Victory! Mactalde the Victorious!"

Mactalde laughed and turned back to Chris. "Do join us, won't you? I wouldn't have you think me ungrateful. I'm here now because of you. You've brought me home. You've ended my exile. And ended the voices." For the first time a glitter of pain backlit his ecstasy.

"What voices?" Could it be the shrink needed a shrink?

A frown flicked across Mactalde's face, and he shook his head. "You've helped me, and for that reason I am giving you the opportunity to learn from me and to fight at my right hand."

Chris breathed carefully. "And if I don't?"

"The same thing that happened to Harrison Garnett, I'm afraid."

Chris looked back at Orias and the Rievers.

Orias stared right past him. His face looked like a corpse's. Had he known this was coming? Had he known bringing Mactalde back and saving the Cherazii meant war upon the rest of the country? Or maybe worse, if Pitch was right about bad things happening when a Gifted used the Orimere to bring a living being across the worlds.

Pitch gnawed his lip. His eyes pulled at Chris's, intent and pleading.

Chris breathed out. Raz had been right. He'd been in such a hurry to get out of here he hadn't even listened to Pitch's warning. This was his fault every bit as much as it was Orias's.

He shook his head.

"As you wish." Mactalde shrugged and turned away. "Put them with the rest of the prisoners."

A tubby soldier grabbed Chris's arm. "Come on." He and his fellow soldiers shoved Chris and Orias around and marched them out of the trees and into the meadow.

Armored horsemen surrounded what was left of the Cherazii. All of the survivors—mostly women and children—were bound with their hands behind their backs. The Rievers had been tied together with lengths of rope and draped over Cherazii shoulders.

In the center of the crowd, manacled with iron, the leader Cabahr Laith and a few other warriors stood in the midst of an extra guard. Blue blood seeped from visible wounds, and one male swayed against the shoulder of another, almost unconscious on his feet. All of them glared defiance at their captors.

The Koraudians guarding them never took their eyes away from them. Despite the fact that they outnumbered their prisoners by at least twenty men, they flinched at the crack of every stick.

Near the edge of the trees, Mactalde mounted a white charger. He reined the prancing animal around to face the Cherazii.

"You see I have returned to you. As I prophesied I would."

Their faces paled to gray. Murmurs of disbelief and horror whispered through their ranks. Then, one by one, they looked past Mactalde to Chris and Orias. They knew. They knew now he was the Gifted. They knew what had happened. And they would kill him before Mactalde did if they got so much as half a chance.

He couldn't say he blamed them.

The tubby soldier shepherded Chris and Orias past the group of warriors. Laith lunged forward, and his guards dove to catch his chains and yank him back.

"You." He snarled. "This is how you repay Cherazii hospitality? And so we will repay you! We took the blood of the last Gifted upon our hands for even attempting this sacrilege. You are ten times his worse! No Cherazii will ever serve the Gifted after this day."

The soldiers marched Chris and Orias to the front of the group. Pitch and Raz, their hands still connected by the long cord, were slung over Orias's shoulder like two packs of meat.

Raz snorted. "Serve the Gifted, bah. After today, there won't be no Gifted to serve."

"Shut up, all of you." The fat soldier slapped Raz's head as he turned to go. "Or I'll fricassee you meself."

As soon as he was out of earshot, Raz shouted after him. "Bah! You would choke on my bones, fatgut!"

"Move out!" a guard commanded. As he rode by, he lifted his foot from his stirrup to kick Chris forward.

"Hey!" Pitch said. "Don't you touch my servant!"

Chris staggered to catch his balance. "Planning to fight all these guys for me, are you?"

Pitch twirled around on the end of his tether until he faced Chris. "If I must, I must."

"Even after what I did?"

Pitch blinked hard and tucked his chin. "You'll make it right. I know you will."

A cold weight settled in his guts. He didn't have nearly that much confidence.

13

A LLARA'S HEARTBEAT RACED beneath her skin. He was here. The Gifted was close. And so were the Koraudians. The sense of him in her head pulled her on, southwest more than south now. She didn't have to guide the men because that's where they were headed anyway. The Cherazim youth who had sought help in Réon Couteau led the way through the Thyra hills, his long hair flying behind him as he rode.

For hours, they had pushed the horses hard. Lather flecked the black silk of Rihawn's shoulders and clotted in his mane. But he pounded on, breath gusting from his red nostrils. They passed through the smoking, shattered remnants of the Cherazii caravan, and they left the corpses without a second thought. If survivors were ahead, the dead could wait.

When finally they cleared the forest into the plains, the Cherazim slowed his horse.

"There." He pointed.

She shaded her eyes against the deep gold of the evening sun. The land, suddenly free of the restricting hills, stretched before them, unbroken all the way to the faraway line of trees that marked the Mistgloam River. The last sunrays struck the sway of the gloam-wheat and transformed it into a tapestry of silver. A few sweeta birds—sunshine yellow with curling tail feathers as long as their wingspans—drifted across the sky. They whistled back and forth in two-noted cries, the first deep like a sotti-cello, the second high and questioning.

She found the dark blot about half a league ahead of them and scrabbled in her saddlebags for her spyglass. Eroll handed her his. Through its magnified circlet, she could see the blood red of the Koraudian uniforms, almost two companies strong. In their center walked their Cherazii prisoners, perhaps fifty of them, mostly women and children.

Cold teeth edged the summer warmth of the wind, and bit through her tunic's crepe sleeves. She shivered. "Half a Koraudian battalion this close to Glen Arden. This should never have happened."

Eroll took his spyglass back. "Nateros has heaps of support in the north. And, of course, the border is infested with their followers. Your father's going to have to shut down the border altogether after this."

"And rotate the Guardsmen at the northern posts. Who knows who's loyal anymore."

Quinnon finished conferring with the men and trotted over. "They outnumber us, but not by enough to matter if we can surprise 'em. The Cherazii will fight as soon as they see there's an opportunity to escape, and that'll even the odds considerably. You stay back beside me, you ken?"

The safety of the rear was where she belonged, as both a princess and a Searcher. But that wasn't where she wanted to be. That wasn't where she needed to be. Her palms itched. "He's here. I can feel him."

Eroll looked up from clipping the spyglass to his belt. "The Gifted?"

Quinnon reined around to look, as if he'd be able to recognize one human amidst the dim column ahead. "They've already got him then?"

She gritted her teeth and concentrated. The Gifted's emotions swirled through her head: anger, exhaustion, confusion, maybe even . . . betrayal. Her heart stuttered. "Yes. He's a prisoner."

And if he were a Koraudian prisoner, he was already halfway down the road to bringing Mactalde back.

No. She straightened her shoulders. Perhaps the Koraudians didn't yet know what he was. And even if they did, they would have a long road to travel to convince a hostage to aid them. She allowed herself a nod that was almost confident.

Quinnon reined around. "Good job we got here when we did. I'll tell the lads to keep an eye out for him. Last thing we need is him getting a bullet in the wrong side of him. We'll stick to the gullies as much as we can, stay out of sight until we're on their tails." He rode away to give the order.

She made herself keep breathing. *We're coming. We're coming. Stay alive.* She tried to blast the words across the plain to where the Gifted trudged in the midst of the Cherazii prisoners. He probably couldn't feel them. The channel between Searcher and Gifted only went one way. But right now, it was the only thing she could actually *do* to try to keep him alive and out of danger.

Eroll reached over to tap her forehead. "Stop with the scowling. You'll regret the wrinkles in another ten years. We got here in time, didn't we? The God of all always has a plan. Everything'll come right."

She made herself nod. How long had it been since she believed there was a plan or a purpose to make sense of her life? She fell in beside him at the rear of the troop and urged Rihawn into a trot, down the length of a gully that in the wet months was a tributary of the Mistgloam River. Tall enough to hide all but the hat feathers, it would get them within charging distance of the Koraudians.

At a gruff order from Quinnon, the men replaced their broad-brimmed hats with the helmets affixed to their saddle horns.

She handed hers to Eroll. "Be careful, won't you?"

"That's my knighted name, don't you know?" He tucked his hat into his saddlebags and tugged the too-small helmet over his face. "Sir Careful, that's what all the blokes call me."

"Give me your rapier. You can't fight Koraudians with a blade that light." She pulled her heavier estoc from where it was strapped atop her rifle scabbard.

"Forgot to check my schedule this morning when I got up, so I didn't realize a jolly ol' battle was the order of the evening." He tilted his helmet-heavy head and peered at her from beneath the short brim. "Did you have any more swaps in mind, did you?"

"If I had any plate armor, I'd give it to you." She hadn't been planning on a battle either.

"No matter. Wouldn't fit." He tested the heft of the estoc in his hand and rolled his shoulders. He might not have ever done an honest day's work in his life, but he was still one of the finest swordsmen at court.

She checked the loads on the pistols that hung on either side of her saddle pommel, then pulled her rifle from beneath her leg. With her thumb, she flicked the pea-sized brass lever behind the bolt and turned on the hydraulic system that powered the shots. Aqua light glimmered through the circular vent pattern on the stock and buzzed softly as it pulled moisture from the air. Firearms took too long to reload to be of any use in close combat, but in a fight like this, a few riflemen stationed in the rear could give the Guardsmen just the advantage they needed. Right now, they needed all the aid they could get.

Twenty minutes later, Quinnon called for a halt and signaled with his hand above his head for the men to climb out of the gully.

"Be safe," Allara hissed at Eroll.

He kissed his hand in her direction without looking around. "No worries. Be back with your Gifted before the bounders even know he's gone."

She made herself nod. She should never have let him come along. Never mind that he wasn't dressed for a battle. Of course, he would never dream of staying behind when there were adventures to be had. Life was a game to him. With any luck, today wouldn't be the day he found out differently.

The horses clambered up the wall of the gully, raining pebbles and clods of dirt down on her and Quinnon. Even sweated as he was, Rihawn jerked his head up and down, fighting the bit and half rearing. She held him back. Above, the horses broke into a gallop, and their hoofbeats pounded down through the earth to thump in her chest.

Quinnon trotted the length of the gully to join her. "You could stay down here. Be safer."

"I'm not about to."

"Didn't think you were." He turned his gray to the wall and spurred it forward.

She released Rihawn's head, and the big black followed Quinnon without any urging. His front legs scrabbled up the side of the gully, his hind end lunging to keep up. They broke above the lip, and the setting sun speared her vision. She ducked and blinked hard.

The Guardsmen tore across the field. They stood in their stirrups and leaned over their mounts' necks, swords raised. In front of them, the Koraudian column erupted in chaos. Riders held back their horses and craned to see. In their center, the prisoners churned, already pushing against the perimeter guards.

Quinnon reined up behind the row of sharpshooters that had remained behind the charge. "If they want to stop and gossip, let's give them something to talk about!"

The men dismounted and knelt, their green coats nearly disappearing in the tall grass. Almost as one, their rifles cracked.

The volleys smashed into men and horses alike. Koraudians screamed and fell, and their blood gushed red and invisible against their scarlet tabards. For a long, deadly moment, they swirled in panic. Then someone in the front started shouting and they pulled themselves aright.

Quinnon peered through his spyglass. "*Och.* It's Rotoss heading it then. I can see his pennon."

Allara's chest seized. Rotoss would have led an expedition into Lael for only one reason. He had come hunting the Gifted on purpose. And he had found him. She balanced her rifle across her legs and searched her saddlebags until she found her spyglass. Her fingers shook as she raised it.

The Guard's charge hit the rear lines with a clash of swords and shouts. The Koraudians began to return fire, sporadically, but the Guard was close enough to prevent them from having time to reload.

She glassed the Cherazii. "*Fight,*" she commanded them. A grown Cherazim was worth three men on any day. Even the children could hold their own.

As if they had heard her, they screamed their unintelligible battle cries and hurled themselves at their captors. Their skin burned blue as they sank into the battle fire that banished fear and pain and allowed them to fight with heightened senses. Most of them ran to the rear to hit the beleaguered Koraudians from the back while the Guard entertained them from the front. The Cherazii fell beneath the guards' swords like scythed grass, but even with their hands bound, they fought with a ferocity and a power that stunned their captors.

She swept her glass up the column. The only humans were the Koraudians. Where was the Gifted?

Near the front of the column, a towering Cherazim launched himself at a fat Koraudian's horse. His shoulder caught the man in the ribs, and his momentum hurtled him over the top of the horse and toppled them both to the ground. The Koraudian lurched to his feet and swung his estoc at the Cherazim.

From behind, a human prisoner took the Koraudian down with a shoulder in his back. The sword hurtled into the grass beyond, and the man righted himself in time to smash his knee into the Koraudian's throat.

She couldn't breathe. This man was her Gifted.

The Cherazim used the Koraudian's dagger to hack his bonds loose and buried the blade to its hilt in the man's chest. He snapped something to the Gifted, then turned to where two Rievers, tied together, struggled in the grass. The Gifted rose to his feet, and his fear and excitement pummeled her. He'd quite obviously never been in a fight like this before.

From behind him, a mounted Koraudian bore down. The Gifted turned to face the charge, empty hands clenched uselessly at his sides. The Koraudian's sword arm swung back. In another moment, he would slice the Gifted's head from his body and ride away without a backward glance.

Allara cast aside the spyglass and swung her leg over Rihawn's neck. She dropped to the ground, her rifle already rising to her shoulder. The barrel swung up to find the Koraudian's back. She squeezed the trigger, and her shoulder instinctively softened to absorb the recoil.

The shot slammed the Koraudian's body forward. The sword fell from his hand, and he tipped forward out of the saddle, his back a cavern of exploded flesh.

The riderless horse galloped past, and the Gifted dodged out of the way. His chin lifted and his head turned in her direction. If anything, his stance seemed to widen. Did he think she was going to shoot him, just as she'd done in all of her warnings before he'd crossed?

Quinnon bellowed at the troops. "Regroup! Hit them again!" He caught Rihawn's reins before the horse could bolt.

The Guard thundered into what was left of the enemy, felling the Koraudians like overripe wheat.

Behind the Gifted, the big Cherazim knelt, cutting loose the two Rievers. He shouted something, so loud Allara could almost hear his voice. There was something about him . . . She knelt and snatched her spyglass from where it had fallen.

He rose to his feet and faced her. On his chest, the buckle of his baldric bore an oval crest. And on it—she squinted harder. It could be a Garowai wing, the sign of the Tarns. A Keeper in Lael? What were the odds of Rotoss capturing both a Keeper and the Gifted? The back of her neck iced.

She swerved the spyglass back to the Gifted, his strange clothes, and the tension in his shoulders. Amidst the wary confusion he radiated, something else snaked into her mind. Something that felt like guilt.

"No." It couldn't have come to this. Not already. Not on the first day. She hadn't even had the chance to protect him. To protect Lael. Where was the justice in that? Where was the rotted *plan*?

"Quinnon—" The words were already leaving her mouth, even as she scanned the field. She had to look, had to see if the worst had already happened. But she already knew. "It's Mactalde."

"What?"

The Koraudians fled across the field, headed east to the Karilus Wall. Hanging back, at their rear, a white charger pranced. On his back rode a man who wore the expensive leather coat of a lord. He extended his arm, his pistol pointed across the field, and she knew he aimed at the Gifted.

His pistol fired, and she jerked to see if the Gifted had fallen.

The shot caught the edge of his shoulder and spun him to his knees.

Nearby, a Koraudian fled past, too intent on the pursuing enemy to see the big Cherazim running through the grass behind the Gifted. The Cherazim took two steps forward to meet the horse, grabbed the rider's arm, and stabbed him out of the saddle. He wrenched the horse to a halt and shoved the reins at the Gifted. Then, without awaiting acknowledgement, he ran to meet another fleeing Koraudian, dragged him to the ground, and commandeered his horse.

The Gifted hauled himself into the saddle and spurred his mount, headed toward the gully.

Mactalde's pistol exploded again. The horse's left side fell away. The animal managed to stagger on three legs for a few steps. Then its hind end collapsed, and the rest of its body reared and toppled.

Allara dropped the rifle and the spyglass where she stood. One hand caught hold of her saddle horn, and she vaulted into her saddle without touching the stirrups. She wrenched the reins from Quinnon's grasp.

She may have failed to protect Lael, but she was still sworn to save the devil-taken Gifted, no matter what he had done. Heels to her horse's sides, she charged into the fray.

14

A S THE HORSE tripped and its hind end went down, Chris kicked free of the stirrups and reached out with his bad arm to catch himself. Red pain burst in his vision, but even before his head cleared, he was scrambling to his feet.

Soldiers in green tabards charged past, swords lofted to the fading sun. Horses surrounded him and pounded the ground to pieces beneath his feet. He ran. His arms pumped madly, and the long grass tangled and tore against his legs.

And then the Searcher was upon him. She ground her horse to a jouncing canter. "Get on!"

Without slowing, without even thinking—because if he thought about it once, he would have to think twice—he caught her extended hand and used their opposing momentum to swing himself up behind the saddle. She turned her horse around and urged him back into a run.

Behind them, Mactalde still held back his horse. His newly reloaded shot gushed from the barrel in a cloud of white, and Chris ducked as the bullet tore past. Then Rotoss was grasping his leader's sleeve, urging him on, and they were galloping away.

At the edge of the field, Orias slowed. He looked at Chris, and his hand lifted in what might be either a warning or a farewell. Then he turned his horse's head to the river and left.

Chris stared after him. So that was it then? Orias betrayed him and then left him. To go where? If he continued in the direction he was headed, he would meet up with what was left of the Koraudians sooner or later. Maybe that had been his plan from the start.

The black stallion lurched, and Chris grabbed the back of the saddle to keep his balance. They descended a gully and slowed to a stop.

"Get off." The Searcher swung her leg over her mount's neck and dropped to the ground. "Get off my horse right now."

He braced against the saddle with his good arm and slid off to face her. Gone were the flowing white dress and the flower-studded crown of hair. She wore breeches and knee boots and a brown tunic stitched with gold filigree. A long braid, strands of dark hair coming loose from it, hung over her shoulder. Her breath came fast, and her face whitened until her eyes were dark flames.

"You brought Mactalde across." It was an accusation, not a question.

Déjà vu swarmed him. So this was what it was like to meet someone from your dreams. He leaned a hand against the horse's haunch.

"Listen here, laddies."

Behind her, an old fighter called the green-clad soldiers to him. Coarse gray hair surrounded his craggy face, and one eye leered, white and blind, from within the crevice of its socket. The crest of a golden stag reared against his flowing green tabard.

"Form up and head back out. Seems we ran into more than we bartered for today. We've reason to think that was Faolan Mactalde."

A rumble of surprise and dismay passed through the men.

"If we find him now, we can kill him before he crosses the border into Koraud." The old soldier barked an exhale. "If we find him now, we can end this hash-up before it even begins."

The Searcher turned to him. "Quinnon, you should go with the men."

He gnawed at his lip. But he shook his head. "My responsibility is you. Not Mactalde."

A blond man dressed in a glaringly blue shirt rode up. "I'll go." One of his puffy sleeves was torn from the shoulder down.

"No." The Searcher's word came out too fast.

"Allara. Don't be stubborn." Beneath his mustache, his mouth slanted in half a grin.

She shook her head once, hard to the side. "No. You're not dressed for battle. You shouldn't even be here."

"She's right." Quinnon gestured to a brawny soldier. "Farth, take everyone but Rill with you. Rill can ride to warn the king, and Lord Eroll can come with us." He looked at the tattered nobleman. "When we get back to Thyra, you get your retainers together and take an expedition out from there."

Lord Eroll shrugged. The half smile was still in place, almost as if he'd forgotten it. His gaze flicked to Chris and lingered. Wondering what kind of blind idiot this new Gifted was?

At a signal from Farth, all but one of the Guardsmen urged their horses out of the gully. The one called Rill followed a moment later, and his horse's hoofbeats pounded off in the other direction.

Quinnon shook his head. "They'll never catch 'em. Those Koraudian horses are fresh compared to ours."

Allara rubbed savagely at a crook in her forefinger. "We have to try."

The sun had finished setting minutes ago, and twilight had fallen so quickly Chris hadn't even noticed its arrival. A cold breeze chilled the sweat in his shirt and his hair. He shivered, and, suddenly, from just that tiny movement, exhaustion flooded his body.

His mind hadn't shut off for hours. His bodies apparently rested whenever he fell asleep in one world or another. But what about his mind? From now on, was his mental existence just going to go on and on forever?

He turned back to the Searcher.

In the falling shadows, her features were half hidden, but she looked creased and dirty. She yanked back her shoulders and turned to him. "Did the Koraudians take you with them, or did you go willingly?"

"A little of both."

"And did you know you were bringing back Mactalde? Did you know who he was?" Her hands clenched and unclenched at her sides. "Did you know that was the *one thing* it mattered you not do!"

"Steady on, Alla." Eroll stared at his saddle horn, as if embarrassed.

Chris backed off a step. He needed her to calm down enough to tell him exactly what he'd done in bringing Mactalde back—and what he was supposed to do to fix it. "What do you want from me?"

She turned away and leaned one hand against her saddle. "It's too late. You can't give me what I want. I wanted peace for my country. I wanted a man of honor and courage. What I *wanted* was a Gifted who wouldn't cave to Glelarn Rotoss just to save his own skin!"

"I thought it was all a *dream.*"

"Well, it's not." She was so angry she was shaking. She stood with her shoulders back, impossibly straight, as if shouting she would break before she would bend. Her movements—the twist of her hand as she pushed back her hair, the tilt of her head, the precision of her fingers against her sword hilt—exuded strength and elegance. One glance was enough to tell him what he needed to know about her. She was beautiful, she was smart, and she was dangerous.

Eroll cleared his throat. "Not to take sides or anything, but in all fairness, he couldn't have known all this. He just landed, you know?" His mouth was set in a serious line now, but he offered Chris a wink. "Can't expect him to see the big picture right off, what?" He dipped his head in a bow to Chris. "I'd be Eroll Leighton, Duke of Thyra. This is my lady's personal guardian, Captain Crea Quinnon. And this, of course, is the Princess Allara."

"The Searcher." Chris found himself saying it just because he didn't know what else there was to say.

She gathered herself up and turned around. "And you are?"

He raised an eyebrow. "You don't know? You invade my dreams, my privacy, every night. You follow my scent like a dog after a criminal. But you don't know my name?"

Quinnon raised his head from tightening his girth. "Watch your mouth, bucko. Don't be growing antlers too big for your head." His good eye shone ominously; his milky eye twitched.

Allara stepped forward. "If I invade your dreams, it's because I have no choice. If I follow your scent, it's to save your life."

He bit his tongue and swallowed back his exhaustion and frustration. She *had* saved his life, twice—once when she shot the Koraudian in the back and again when Mactalde killed his horse out from under him. If this was a dream, then maybe—but, no, somehow he couldn't make himself believe that anymore. This was no dream.

So why not admit she was right about the rest of it as well? Nausea gripped the back of his throat. He had done exactly what she accused him of. He'd taken the coward's way out. If Mactalde's return did indeed mean war—or worse—then he was the one to blame. Bile rose, and he swallowed it back.

Perhaps he'd saved a few Cherazii. Perhaps he'd saved a lot of Cherazii. But what he'd done, he'd done more to save himself. He'd turned his back on what he knew, deep down in his heart, was the right choice. He'd walked away.

He faced the Searcher. "I'm sorry."

For a second, her mask cracked and revealed not just anger, but terror. She looked aside, and when she turned back the mask was firmly in place again. "It's too late for apologies."

"Then what can I do to make it right?"

Her laugh sounded as if it were backed by tears. "Kill Mactalde."

"Kill him? Just like that? I've never killed anybody in my life." Surely, there had to be something else. He looked around. "What if I took him back? What if I used the Orimere to take him back to my world?"

"It doesn't work that way. You can be sure you tore the fabric between the worlds by bringing him across once. Who knows what would happen if you tried again."

"It's worth a try though? Better than killing someone."

A bitter smile wrenched her mouth. "You should have considered that before you brought a war to our doorstep. Before this is over, Mactalde won't be the only one to die."

And every single death would be on his head. Sweat sprang up on his forehead. He had made this mistake. What else could he do but put it right? No matter what it took.

A thought struck him. "One of those Rievers back there told me I was a Guardsman. Found a little leather triangle thing in my pouch."

Quinnon cocked a glance at him. "Did he now? That might make things considerably easier."

Chris turned to face him. "What sort of things?"

"Things like keeping you alive. Your troubles are far from over, laddie. I doubt the good people of Lael will take it too kindly should they ever hear about this. Even those who haven't fallen under the sway of Nateros's radical ideas about the Gifted are liable to take a poke at you if they ever figure out what's happened here today."

Allara licked her lips. When she spoke, she was obviously trying to keep her voice level and calm. "I don't know what you've seen of me in your dreams, but, contrary to what you seem to think, I've seen very little of you. Only enough to know you existed. And you were coming. I tried to warn you away." She turned to her horse and shoved her sword into its sheath on top of the rifle scabbard. "That was the best I could do."

"You could have just left me back there. Mactalde would have killed me sooner or later."

"It's not about what I want."

"Then what?"

"It's about duty. You and I both have a duty to this world, and we have no choice but to do it."

"All right." He looked her in the eye. "Tell me what I'm supposed to do, and I will do it. Whatever it takes to make it right. I swear that to you."

Something almost seemed to soften in her face. Or maybe it was a trick of the rising moon. Then she shook her head. She didn't believe him. "What's your name?"

"Chris Redston."

"Well, Chris Redston, I admit I have less faith in you now than even before. But if you'll come with me, I will show you how to fight, how to survive, and perhaps even, if the God of all is with us, how to kill Mactalde and wipe this day from the memory of history."

"That's all I ask." He breathed out.

His left arm throbbed. The adrenaline had worn off, and he was starting to hurt. He craned his neck to peer at the tear in his T-shirt. A cut about three inches long darkened his skin. It was hard to tell its depth without washing away the gelled blood, but, at the very least, it probably needed a handful of stitches.

"You're hurt." She sounded surprisingly concerned, maybe even a shade panicked. Did they need a Gifted, even one like him, around here that badly?

"I'll live."

"Let's see it." Quinnon stalked over, hooked his fingers into the torn sleeve, and ripped it open. "Just a nick."

Eroll dismounted, saddlebags in hand. "Here we are. A little oronborne will get you fixed up right as a rainy day." He dug into the saddlebags and came out with a brass syringe.

Quinnon took the syringe and squirted a thick line of glaucous paste into the wound. The paste hit Chris's raw flesh and burned cold, like the touch of dry ice.

He jerked away. "Ow! What is that stuff?"

"Stops the bleeding." Quinnon grabbed his arm again. "Just shut your gob and try to take it like the Guardsman you say you are."

Glaring, he gritted his teeth and submitted himself to the rest of the dose. "Could have warned me."

Eroll laughed. "It hurts, but it stops the bleeding almost instantly. When it was created forty or so years ago, it revolutionized battle medicine."

Chris tilted his head back toward the rim of the gully and the field beyond. "Maybe we should share it with a few of the Cherazii."

"Doesn't work." Quinnon wrapped a bandage around the wound. "The wondrous properties of oronborne don't combine with Cherazii blood in the same way as ours." He knotted off the bandage and turned back to his mount. "Let's go. The horses are too done in to make good time tonight, but, if we're lucky, we can get back to Thyra Junction in six or seven hours."

Allara mounted and stopped her horse at Chris's side. "A word of advice. Until we're safe within the privacy of the palace at Réon Couteau, keep quiet when we're among others. It's best for your own sake if no one knows what you are just yet."

"Don't tell me I'm not what they expect a Gifted to be?" The words tasted acrid.

Her voice softened until he could hardly hear her. "You're not what *I* expected the Gifted to be."

15

CHRIS WATCHED THE Searcher lay her heels to her mount's sides and canter away to join Quinnon up ahead. She wasn't exactly what he had expected either. She didn't want to shoot him like he'd originally thought, and her idea of duty wasn't going to let her stand by while someone else shot him. But she probably wouldn't mind too much if he got knocked off accidentally while her back was turned.

Eroll rode over. "You've had quite a first day. Most Gifted get speeches and parades." He grinned and offered Chris a hand up. "Don't take her too much to heart. She's strung a bit tight over all this. You're her second Gifted, you know."

Chris swung onto the horse's rump. "So I've gathered."

"This is something of a phenomenon, really. Two Gifted in one Searcher's lifetime. That hasn't happened in five hundred years. There's more than a few of our people who think it's . . . well, to put it lightly, *unnatural.*"

In the darkness ahead, Allara's mounted shadow danced.

"Maybe it is unnatural," Chris said. "Considering how things turned out."

"Not a'tall. Things happen for a reason. And anyway, it doesn't take much imagination to realize how beastly bewildering it would be to wake up one morning and find yourself in a world you hadn't even known was there. Honestly, I can't say I wouldn't have done the same thing you did."

"You don't even know why I did it."

Eroll shrugged. "Don't suppose it matters really. It's done now."

They plodded on in silence for a few minutes, before Eroll spoke again, with a hesitating intake of breath before the words. "You'll forgive her, won't you? The Searchers are sent to guide the Gifted, to support them and protect them, while they're figuring things out. But Alla . . . really, she's the one who needs protecting. She's still shattered from the last Gifted, and she'll crack clean in two if she gets hit hard one more time. Do what she asks you to, eh?"

Chris didn't trust her anymore than she trusted him, but he'd seen her mask slip. He'd seen the raw vulnerability beneath her anger and her confidence. He could relate to that more than he wanted to think about. "I'll try."

For now though, staying awake in the saddle was challenging enough. He blinked hard. His thoughts swirled aimlessly, his physical exhaustion dragging at his mind. He'd been on his feet since early this morning, run ragged by one impossible happening after another. By the time they reached the outskirts of a town, midnight was a few hours past.

Two- and three-story houses loomed, their whitewashed fronts brought into stark relief by dark reinforcing planks. Some were apparently homes, others businesses—a blacksmith's, a post office, a ladies' clothing shop. Large globes of colored glass strung the eaves and lit the cobblestone streets. Only a few horsemen trotted past, headed the opposite direction. Several men in black knee-length coats and wide-brimmed hats walked up and down, iron-tipped canes tucked under their arms.

"Night policemen," Eroll explained.

The shadows at the base of the buildings moved to reveal hunched figures in rags—the destitute and criminal element that combed every town, from the bottom up, at night.

"Where are we?" Chris asked.

"Thyra Junction. It's the biggest town between Glen Arden and Réon Couteau and the only skycar station for a day's ride in any direction. My town, actually. Duke of Thyra and all."

The road led them into a circular piazza. In the center sat a long building with half a dozen ticket windows. White ramps led to the booths, each marked by a sign inked in square-edged symbols.

A shadow overhead blacked out the lights for a moment, and Chris ducked. A web of cables crisscrossed the sky, and chains of glass cable cars glittered.

"That's your ride out of here," Eroll said. "Have to tell you, I'm rather proud of my skycar station. Best in the northern counties. I'd ask you to pardon the bragging, but you can hardly call it that when it's the holy truth, now can you?"

Quinnon circumnavigated the ramps altogether and led them around the corner of the station to where two men in blue uniforms stood guard at a towering iron gate.

"Very sorry, sir," one said, "but ticket counters don't open until morning. You'll have to come around again then."

"I'm Captain Quinnon." He dismounted. "The Princess Allara has urgent business in Réon Couteau, so be good lads and hitch up the royal train. We'll only be needing one car this time around."

The guards peered at Allara. Their halberds snapped straight at their sides and they touched their closed eyes with thumb and forefinger and slid their hands down their faces.

She tipped her chin in response, and they hurried to swing open the double gates.

Inside the cobblestoned courtyard, a man with a close-trimmed gray goatee stumbled out to greet them. He pulled his tabard over his head and replaced his hat as he came.

"Your highness, I'd no idea you'd return tonight. I'll have your train put on the tracks immediately." His gaze wandered back to Eroll's horse and stopped on Chris. A shade of something—confusion, then realization, then shock—passed across his face.

"Thank you, Conductor." Her voice sounded as tight as her shoulders. "We've had a long ride, so if you wouldn't mind hurrying?"

He dragged his attention back to her, twitched his head in a nod, and scampered off.

Chris took the opportunity to unlock his joints and swing his leg over the horse's back. His feet hit the ground and thudded pain all the way up his body to his teeth. The throbbing in his shoulder tightened his throat and flickered black spots across his vision. The bleeding had stopped after Quinnon had jabbed the wound full of that burning stuff, but the pain had only seemed to worsen.

Allara dismounted and handed her reins to Quinnon, who led both horses after the conductor. She walked over to stand at Eroll's stirrup and stared up at him without a glance at Chris. "You're going after Mactalde then?"

"Soon as I get a few winks behind my eyes and gather up the faithful troops."

In the moonlight, her throat glinted white. "I wish you didn't have to. Who knows what trouble you'll run into at the border." She still didn't look at Chris. Sheer force of will was probably the only thing keeping her from glaring accusation at him.

"Not to worry. I'll bring the cheeky rotter's head to you on a platter." Eroll glanced at Chris, then back at Allara. "Don't go too hard on the blighter, what? Whatever went wrong today, you're in the fight together now."

Chris shifted his weight. If Eroll got himself injured or killed out there, that would be his fault as well. And that, more than all the other possible consequences he could see right now, wasn't something he wanted to live with.

He held out his hand. "Good luck. I wish I could come with you."

Eroll gripped it. "Not a bit of it. Gifted have plenty more important things to do with their time."

Allara drew Eroll's gaze back to hers. "Please be safe."

"Forever obedient, my heart's only queen." He doffed his hat, swooping feather and all. "Farewell to you both." With a last grin, he turned the horse about and trotted back down the street.

Side by side in the empty courtyard, Chris and Allara stood in silence. He didn't ask what she was thinking, not that she would have told him. She cared about Eroll Leighton, Duke of Thyra, that much was clear.

"He's a good guy," he said.

She kept staring down the road. "If that means he's more forgiving than I am, then it's true."

The shadow of another train fell over them, and two of the glass-cased cars slid down the cables and stopped a foot or so off the ground, swinging slightly. The front one was about six feet long, backed by a second one three times its size.

Quinnon and a guard led the horses up a ramp at the back end of the long car, and the conductor opened a smaller door at the car's front and flipped out a set of steps. He held the door as Allara crossed the courtyard and climbed them.

Chris followed her inside. Two fist-sized glass candle globes hung from the corners and glittered against the floor-to-ceiling windows that encased the compartment.

Allara stood behind the farthest of the three seats. "It's seven hours yet to Réon Couteau. Best try to sleep. Come morning, you'll have to face the Garowai."

He sat in the middle chair and leaned back. His tired muscles sagged into the soft upholstery. "Who's the Garowai?"

"You'll see for yourself tomorrow."

The car rocked beneath Quinnon's heavy tread as he mounted the stairs. He slammed the door behind him and yanked off his leather gauntlets. "Just as well we got here when the station was closed." He tugged a silken rope attached to the ceiling. "The conductor wouldn't have been the only one who had wonderings about our boy here. Be better if most folks thought Mactalde got here before the Gifted, so's they don't match two and two together and put the finger on him first off."

A bell tinkled distantly, and the car gave one abbreviated lurch, then inched up the cable.

The floor slanted, and Chris nearly toppled out of his chair.

"Swivel it around, so you can lean against the back." Quinnon twisted both his and Allara's empty chairs around and locked them in place with a click.

Allara eased her way across the car and sat down, hands in her lap. She stared out the side windows as they climbed above the town's smoky streets. Her left hand rubbed the crooked finger on her right.

In a few minutes, they reached the peak of their climb and the train leveled out. As they picked up speed—maybe as much as thirty miles per hour—the wind hissed against the windows and the cars swayed on their cables.

Chris slid down in the chair until his head was cushioned against the backrest. His eyelids drifted shut of their own accord. For all he knew the Searcher and her bodyguard would stab him as soon as he was unconscious, but his body was fading out from under him. In another second, he'd be—

—asleep. He blinked his eyes open one more time to glance at Allara in her seat beside him. A ray of sunlight speared his vision, and his heart gave one hard thud. He sat bolt upright.

He was back in Mactalde's living room. The chair Mactalde had sat in was still beside his head, the glass he had drunk from still on the end table behind him. But the couch and everything else he'd been touching when he'd fallen asleep was gone—including his clothes.

"Great." His lip pinched and tore. He raised a fingertip to his mouth, and it came away with a pink thread of blood from where Harrison had punched him two days ago.

Or was it only yesterday?

The muscles that had been wet slag seconds ago were now only stiff from sleeping on the hardwood floor. He pawed at his left shoulder, but the skin was smooth—unmarred by any Koraudian bullet.

So much for any last hope this was all a grand farce. Mactalde's couch was in Lael. *Mactalde* was in Lael. And Chris was in deep trouble. Head hung back, he breathed out hard.

But at least he wasn't crazy. He snorted. Thank heaven for little miracles.

He looked around. No one was in the room, and judging from the slant of the sunlight, the day was already deep into afternoon. He had fallen asleep on Mactalde's couch on Thursday, which meant it was now probably about one or two on Friday afternoon. Why hadn't Mactalde's servants, or at least his bodyguard, tried to get into the room to find their boss? And what were they going to think when Chris came streaking out from behind locked doors with no sign of Mactalde anywhere?

He scrambled to his feet and snagged a maroon throw off the remaining couch to use as a sarong. He cracked the doors open.

The hallway lay in silence. Sunlight the color of old gold pooled on the floor. He pushed the door open another foot and stuck his head around the corner. No one challenged him, so he cinched the blanket a little tighter and stepped into the hall.

Outside, a car with a high-octane engine powered past and its roar magnified the stillness.

Maybe Mactalde had sent the servants and the hired muscle away for the week. Or maybe, in anticipation of his departure, he had dismissed them permanently. Either way, Chris didn't have much choice. He had to get some clothes, and he had to get out of here.

He crossed the hall and ran up the wide staircase, taking the steps two at a time. Under the circumstances, the loan of a polo shirt, a pair of slacks, and some shoes was the least Mactalde owed him.

He found the master bedroom, raided the closet, and started back.

He was halfway down the stairs when a key grated in the front door's lock, and a man's silhouette loomed against the frosted glass. Chris froze for half a second, then grabbed the railing and vaulted into the shadow of the staircase.

The lock thumped open and the door swung inward. He leaned against the curve of the solid mahogany staircase and waited. The man in the doorway stood for a moment, then tugged the key from the door and turned the lock behind him. Footsteps padded against the thick carpet, headed toward the living room.

Chris slid forward and twisted around to see through the rails. Near the office's open door, the broad-shouldered bodyguard, Geoff Kaufman, eased a hand beneath his suit jacket and let it rest against his chest, just where a holstered handgun would ride. At the living room's open door, he stopped, leaned his shoulder into the wall, and eased around the corner.

Of course Mactalde wouldn't just let Chris walk away. If Chris died in Chicago, the Orimere would be useless against the Koraudians. Blood hammered in his muscles. He hissed through his teeth and pulled back.

Kaufman pushed into the living room, and Chris crept to the back of the house. He edged through a swinging door into the empty kitchen. At the far end of the room, a door beckoned, sunlight spilling through the floor-length blinds.

He knew the door would be locked, but he tried the handle anyway. On the wall, a keypad's red light blinked. A house alarm. He grimaced. One way or the other, Kaufman was going to know he'd been here.

He found a bar stool next to the counter, picked it up, and smashed it against the blinds. Somewhere deep in the house, alarms screamed. A door slammed, and footsteps stomped down the hall. He scooped the blinds out of the way and leapt over the ragged edge of glass. He landed on the cement apron outside and started running. He reached the dock at the far end of the lawn and took a turn, headed up the water's edge.

Something chomped into the sand ahead of him, and clods blasted up from the ground. He darted a look over his shoulder.

Midway across Mactalde's yard, the dark-suited bodyguard stood with a noise-suppressed handgun clamped in both hands. The gun rebounded, and another shot ripped past Chris's head.

Adrenaline gushed, and he started veering from side to side. Kaufman wasn't following him, so obviously, he had no intention of pursuing a footrace down the North Shore, gun in hand. Right now, that was about the only reason to hope.

One more shot zipped past, then the shooting stopped. He fought to keep up his speed and make his burning muscles give just a little bit more. Unless Kaufman was inclined to simply give up the chase, he was probably tearing back through Mactalde's house, headed for his vehicle.

Twenty yards ahead, black rails fenced off the end of the neighborhood. Forcing a last burst from his body, he jumped and just managed to catch the top of the fence with both hands and drag himself over. He dropped onto the other side and started running.

Two blocks down, a car horn squawked and brakes squealed. A blur of orange swerved in and out of his vision.

Pulse spiking, he reeled around and blinked at the rusty orange Volkswagen in the middle of the street.

Mike opened the door and stepped out. "Where have you been? I was about ready to call the morgue!"

A ride was exactly what Chris needed right now, but the last place he wanted Mike to be was between him and some psycho assassin. He ran toward the car. "What are you doing here?"

The Bug's other door opened, and Mike's sister bobbed out. Brooke's eyes went wide, and her hand rose to her mouth. "Chris, your lip!"

That made the day just about perfect. If he didn't want Mike in the way when trouble was coming, he didn't want Brooke's dithering attempts at being useful and supportive around, period.

The muscles in Mike's neck bulged, and a flush crept up his face. "Look, bro, it's your life. I don't care what you do with it just about as much as *you* don't care. But you could at least show a little consideration. When you said you'd be back *late*, I had no idea how *late* that really meant."

Brooke rounded the end of the car, already reaching for his arm, as if he were an invalid. "And the police brought the Bug back. They said you got hit on the head, and then this doctor guy took you home. They gave us the address." Her free hand darted to her hairline, smoothing back the little hairs escaped from her ponytail.

She was a pretty enough girl, blonde in a stylish way, her complexion smooth and fair with just a smattering of tomboyish freckles across her nose. But today was really not the kind of day to put him in the mood for her manic affection.

He hustled her back to the car. "We need to get out of here."

She craned her head back so she could look at him. "We tried to call him, but we couldn't get an answer."

"What's up with that?" Mike watched Chris over the roof of the car. "And what's the matter with you? Running through the streets? If you've got a concussion, that's the last thing you should be doing."

"Just get in the car." He reached inside the Bug, pulled the front seat forward, and pushed Brooke into the back. Mike's car wasn't exactly inconspicuous. The sooner they got out of here the better. "We'll talk while we drive." He ducked into the passenger seat.

Mike stood for a few seconds more. "Fine." He slid back inside and slammed the door hard enough to rattle the whole vehicle.

A black truck with tinted windows turned onto the street, and Chris scrunched down. It had to be the same truck that had carried away Harrison's drive-by shooters.

"Get us out of here," he said.

Mike looked at him. "Are you going to tell me what's the matter or what?"

Chris spared a growl. "See that truck? There's a guy with a gun in it."

Brooke clutched at the back of his seat. "A *gun?*"

That was enough to get Mike moving. The truck was almost on top of them by the time he got the engine started and the Bug steered back into the right lane.

Chris kept his head down and stopped breathing. The truck took centuries to creep past, but when he finally dared to look in the rearview mirror, no glare of brake lights lit the truck's bumper. Maybe Kaufman hadn't seen him get into the car. He closed his eyes and breathed out.

Mike drove with both hands clenched on the steering wheel. As soon as he reached the first turn, he stepped on the gas. The Bug bucked once in protest, then leveled out.

He looked at Chris. "All right, let me have it. All of it. There's a guy with a *gun* after you?"

Chris opened his mouth to explain. But the truth would either have Mike laughing or calling the nearest psychiatric ward. Or both. "It's complicated."

"Yeah, I bet it is. But considering I just dragged you out of death's maw, why don't you try uncomplicating it for me."

His mind spun, trying to grapple this thing down to its simplest factor. "It's like the cops told you. I saw someone get shot yesterday down on the South Side. This guy must have tracked me to Dr. Mactalde's. I'm a witness, so he wants to kill me."

Brooke puffed out a breath. "I can't believe it. That's awful."

Mike's eyes were almost as round as hers. "Do the police know? Are they going to give you some kind of protection?"

"No, I don't think they know. Can we head there now?"

Mike slapped his blinker. "And this Dr. Mactalde left you alone?"

"Not exactly. Maybe he just didn't want to answer his phone."

Come to think of it, the first thing the police were going to want to do was talk to Dr. Faolan Mactalde. When they couldn't find him, they were going to start searching for explanations and connections. And *Chris* was the most obvious connection between an attempted murder yesterday and a disappearance today.

He grimaced. "Actually, never mind about the police station. I'll go in later by myself. It'd be better that way. And I should probably get some rest."

"What?" Mike said. "You've got someone gunning you down and you're going to deal with it *later* because you need to *rest*?"

"Maybe he does need to rest," Brooke said. "His lip is bleeding."

Mike ignored her. "What is going on here? Where's this Dr. Mactalde? What are you holding back?"

Chris rubbed at the sweaty grit on his forehead. "I'm not holding back. I just . . . can't tell you right now."

"Why not? Is he in on it too and you're covering for him?"

"*No.*" Chris dropped his hand. "You think I've totally flipped?"

"Of course not," Brooke said.

"Not yet anyway." The steering wheel bobbled in Mike's grip as the Bug argued their straight course. He stared ahead, frowning.

The back of Chris's head thrummed, and his wind-burned throat tickled. He opened the window, and the wind knifed his skin, chilly for the middle of June. It felt like the beginning of autumn, the first whisper of cold that always hugged the tail end of summer.

Other than Lisa, Mike was the only person he had ever been able to count on. But not even Mike was going to buy into the truth.

He took a cooling breath and let it out. "If I told you what was going on, you wouldn't believe me."

Brooke hunched forward between the seats. "Of course we would."

He hesitated. The last thing he needed was her getting her teeth into this. But if he left it hanging, she would probably just keep gnawing at it.

He looked at Mike. "Okay, here it is. Mactalde set me up."

Mike drummed his finger against the steering wheel. "For what?"

"His disappearance." This time he glanced at Brooke, just to see how she was taking it.

Her face had gone serious. "You mean his murder? You're going to investigate it?"

He shook his head. "There's nothing to investigate."

"Yes, there is! A man was shot. You were shot *at* and bashed in the head. Then this Dr. Mactalde disappears." She hung onto the back of his seat. "We could write it into an article together. It could be my big break!"

Mike hacked a disgusted sound. "Your biggest concern here is impressing the editor of *Weekly World News*?"

"Of course not." She leaned back in her seat, her ponytail slinking up and down. "But why can't we kill two birds with one stone? Please, just let me give it a try."

"No way," Mike said. "You're going to be too busy putting in community service hours after that last stunt of yours to do anything that even resembles investigating."

Chris shook his head. "Even if the kind of investigation you're talking about would end up being helpful, I don't want a story like this in any paper."

"Oh, c'mon, don't you want to know the answers?" Her face lit up. "I have contacts that could help us. I used to date this guy who worked for a psychologist."

Mike looked into the rearview mirror. "You talking about that big guy with the crazy eyes?"

She scowled. "He wasn't crazy. Anyway, I'm not dating him anymore." She clasped her hands and pulled her shoulders up in a little shrug. "I've been waiting for a story like this forever!"

Mike batted down his visor. "Oh yeah, great, just great. Chris has some lunatic following him, shooting at him, and beating him up. Most awesome thing I've heard all day."

Chris made a face. "He didn't beat me up. He walked up behind me and hit me on the back of the head."

"Whatever. You're bleeding and he's not." Mike raised his eyebrows at Brooke. "The point is—leave it alone. I mean it. This is none of your business. You'll only dive in and make it worse."

"If Chris wants help, I'm here to give it to him. We'll write the story together."

Chris opened his mouth. He didn't want to burst her bubble—again—but the whole notion of her going all OCD ace reporter was one of the most terrifying ideas in a terrifying day. "Brooke, I don't think so."

Her lips bunched in a pout and she eased all the way back in her seat, arms across her chest. "If you get yourself murdered because you refused to let me take action, it's on your head."

They drove in silence for another mile before Mike looked over at him. "Why do you say Mactalde set you up?"

"Just a hunch." The kind of hunch that came from someone telling you his master plan to your face, then trying to shoot you in the back.

Mike firmed his mouth. "All right. You don't want to tell me everything that's going on, fine. But tell me this. Are you mixed up in something you shouldn't be?"

"Of course he is," Brooke said. "He's being shot at."

"That's not what I mean." Mike looked Chris in the eye. "Are you mixed up on the wrong side?"

Considering he'd spent most of his first day in Lael mixing it up all over the wrong side of things, he couldn't quite manage to meet Mike's gaze.

"Don't worry. I'm sorting it out."

Mike snorted. "I don't believe you."

Chris couldn't blame him. When it came right down to it, he didn't quite believe himself either.

16

EXHAUSTION PULLED AT Chris's body. By the time he got out of the shower, the late summer sun had dropped low into purple clouds. His eyes felt like someone had rubbed a handful of dirt in them, and his eyelids refused to stay open.

He padded back into the kitchen. Except for Pluto growling at shadows in the corner, the house was silent. Through the open window he could hear voices in the driveway, where Mike was checking air pressure on the tires. Maybe whatever Chris had run over back at Harrison's had done damage after all. He winced. He'd dig up the cash for a set of new tires, but for now at least Mike and Brooke were busy where he wouldn't have to avoid their worry and confusion.

A red light gleamed on the oven's panel, and he opened the door to find the white cheese on Brooke's ravioli casserole crisping to golden brown on top. Not bothering to pull it out of the oven, he dug a fork from the dish drainer and helped himself to a few bites of pasta pillows, sweet tomato sauce, and stringy mozzarella.

It tasted great, but when it hit his stomach, the nausea from his overworked concussion swarmed him. He closed the oven door and dropped the fork in the sink. Sleep. He needed sleep—or at least his body did. His mind wasn't likely to have that option for the foreseeable future. He groped through the darkness of the hall to the spare bedroom, flopped facedown on the bed—

—and shivered as a draft hit him. He fumbled for the blankets and instead smacked his hand against the back of the swivel chair bolted into the floor next to him.

The skycar rattled faintly, and the wind hissed past the windows. The whole contraption rocked beneath him, and he caught a faint whiff of some kind of salty meat. He squeezed his eyes shut tighter and tried to slow his breathing and reorient himself.

"Better get him up." Crea Quinnon's throaty voice rumbled behind him. "We'll be pulling into Réon Couteau in another twenty minutes or so."

"What is he dreaming, I wonder?" Allara's voice came from his left, from the same direction as the breeze. "What's it like in the other world? What happens there?"

"Same thing as happens here. Rich and poor, war and peace, this world and that. It's all a balance, isn't it? A balance we can't control. So wake him up and never mind what he's dreaming. What happens on the other side is his own concern."

The door behind Chris opened and shut as Quinnon stepped into the rear compartment with the horses.

Chris turned his head and opened his eyes.

The Searcher stood silhouetted by the sun. "You're awake."

"Depends how you look at it." He started to push himself up, but pain jagged through his body, starting with the wound in his shoulder and slashing down his back, arms, and legs.

Next to an open pane in the glass wall, she leaned against the waist-high gold railing that encircled the compartment. Outside, mist rose from the ground and veiled the soft hills in a reflected orange glow. The country here moved up and down, one hill after another, the horizon blocked by the dark green of tree brakes, with occasionally a glint of water beyond.

"How's your shoulder?" she asked.

It felt like someone had tried to fit a fist inside the wound, but he didn't care to tell her that. "It'll live."

Truth be told, she probably didn't want to hear it either. Dark smudges framed her eyes. Had she slept at all?

He eased to his feet and walked to the front of the compartment. The little engineer car, a third the size of this one, blocked the view in front of them, so he looked out the side wall.

Assuming the sun rose in the east around here, they seemed to be headed more or less north. Below, a herd of zajeles, the gazelle-like creature Orias had brought back to the Cherazii camp, grazed on a hillside. A man who was probably their herdsman lounged on a mossy stone and peered up at the skycar.

The seas of grass had faded while he slept, to be replaced by rolling hills and silver-green forests. Sporadic patches of dark earth, speckled with white and violet flowers, gleamed beneath the bottle green of moss and scrub growth. Through the open windowpane, unseen insects warbled in curtains of metallic sounds. Cold fronted the expected warmth of the wind, just like back in Chicago.

"Feels like a storm's coming," he said, as much to have something to say as anything else. "That usual for this time of year?"

"It's not a storm." She looked up to where the sun, a fat peach swimming in blue cream, burned down at them. In Chicago, a sun like that would melt people all over the pavement. But here, its warmth floated behind the cold edge of the wind. "And it's not usual."

He ran a hand through the sweat-crusted roots of his hair. He was still wearing the cargo pants and T-shirt he'd brought over with Mactalde. Probably he looked as strange as he felt. His stomach growled. The few bites of ravioli casserole he'd eaten back at Mike's definitely hadn't done this body any good.

Allara turned to a floor-to-ceiling cupboard in the corner and pulled out a handkerchief-covered plate. "Here. Break your fast. We'll arrive in Réon Couteau soon."

He cradled the plate against his ribs. The handkerchief hid a hunk of cold sausage the size of his fist and a matching wedge of flaky white cheese. The sausage, made of a dark meat, had a robust smoky flavor, with an almost overpowering aftertaste of spicy mustard. The cheese was as hard as an old brick of parmesan and tasted like the salt had been left out altogether. He ate it anyway.

He leaned his good shoulder against the window. "When we get there, are people going to know what I am?"

"No. You look like an ordinary man, except for your clothes, which we'll soon fix. Why?"

"That conductor last night. He looked surprised to see me."

If possible, her shoulders drew back even more. "We probably shouldn't have brought you straight through town. An ordinary man, riding with me, especially with all the rumors that have been circulating." She shook her head. "He likely guessed the truth."

"Am I supposed to be a national secret or something?"

"The country will know soon enough, but I would like it to be after you're secure behind the city walls."

He didn't really like the sound of that. "Secure behind walls" could mean captivity just as easily as safety. He shouldn't poke her, shouldn't prod her. She was already strung so tight she was probably capable of just about anything. But something in him wanted to push her off balance, if only to crack through that icy façade of hers. If he could get her to react, maybe she would show him what was going on in that head of hers.

He chewed carefully. "A new Gifted wasn't supposed to come this soon, was he?"

She frowned. "How do you know that?"

"Eroll said something about it." He held his breath, debating with himself. If he played his cards now, he might not have anything to put on the table later on. "And so did a man named Harrison Garnett."

She froze. "Harrison Garnett?"

"He introduced himself the other day. Said he'd been searching for me all my life."

Her eyes got big, wild almost. "You know him in the other world? He found you? He couldn't have. He couldn't have known about you. No one knew, not even me."

He wasn't quite certain how he had expected her to react. But this wasn't a little fissure in her defenses. This was a gaping chasm. "He said something about this Garowai of yours. That's how he found out about me."

"The Garowai knew . . . and he didn't tell me . . ." She looked as if someone had slugged her in the stomach and all she wanted to do was curl into a fetal ball and hide from the next blow.

Then the instant ended. The crack closed up, and her voice deepened. "Harrison Garnett was a traitor. He did things no Gifted had a right to do." She lifted her chin. "He deserved to die."

Chris stood away from the window. "Is that what's going to happen to me too?"

Her eyes flickered. "What happens to you is in your hands. I have no reason to trust you. Or any Gifted."

"Or anyone? You might as well say it. You don't trust many people, do you?"

She hesitated the briefest of seconds. "No, I do not. Trust, faith, hope—they get you killed. They get people you love killed. They're not facts, they're fantasies. And I have too much at stake to trust a fantasy."

She meant it. She was playing straight with him even though she might have been wiser to lie. The truths she was flinging at him weren't the kind to make someone want to roll over at her feet. But whatever else she was, she was honest, and he appreciated that.

He appreciated the survivor's soul in her. From the look of it, her life had left her just as battered and broken as his had left him. Maybe more so. On any other day, in any other dream, he would have heard that strangled cry and answered it. He had no desire to hurt this woman. But it was a little too late for that.

Last night, he had said he would do whatever was necessary to fix what had happened. And he'd meant it. But this morning, the enormity of what he had done and what he still had to do if he was going to even attempt to fix it was too big to look in the face. This was exactly the kind of thing he'd steered clear of all his life. Why kid himself? He *couldn't* fix what he'd done. He couldn't save the people who would die in the coming battles. If he tried, he would fail.

He set the plate on the nearest chair. "I don't want to be here anymore than you want me to be. I didn't ask for the dreams. I didn't ask to be lied to and used."

She glared. "Oh, yes, you're absolutely the victim here."

He stood facing her, only a few feet between them. "I'm not saying that."

She was a tall woman. She didn't have to lift her chin very far to look him in the face. "Then what *are* you saying?"

"I'm staying. I'm here. But I'm here now because I *choose* to be here. Don't forget that."

He had hurt her, and he was sorry for it. She was angry with him, and she had a right to be. But he wasn't going to sit around like a dog waiting to be kicked whenever she got steamed. If any of this was going to work—and that was a big *if*—then she needed to come to grips with what he had done. She needed to stop riding him. And she needed to realize the mistake was his to fix—or not—as he saw best.

She tilted her head. "If I told you now you were free to go, would you?"

"If I said yes, would you still let me?"

Her face closed up, and she turned away to lean both hands against the railing. "You say you didn't ask to be a Gifted. Well, I didn't choose to be born a Searcher. The God of all gives us our destinies, and the best we can do is fulfill them. And pray someday He will reward us with freedom."

"Freedom." Sounded good. Sounded impossible too. And judging from her fists clenched around the railing and the muscle hopping in her cheek, it hadn't worked out too well for her up to now. "Is that what you've found?"

The rear compartment's door opened, and Quinnon stepped in. He took in Chris and Allara at a glance and fixed his glare on Chris. "Back off. Haven't you heard of royal distance?" He tilted his head forward. "Réon Couteau yonder."

Chris turned to look just as the forest-covered hills gave way to the wide-open blue of a tremendous lake.

"Ori Réon," Quinnon said. "The Lake of Dreams."

The lake's surface glinted and blurred. Strange half-formed reflections skittered over its surface. Pictures, like streaked watercolors, swayed on the water, then rippled and disappeared, and reappeared once again.

Chris leaned against the glass and craned his neck back to see the sky, but nothing flew overhead that might reflect in the lake. "What's that in the water?"

Allara let out a shuddering breath and unclenched her grip on the railing. "Dreams."

On the nearest shore, a five hundred foot waterfall plunged from a cliff of black stone. Mist cloaked the top, like diaphanous scarves upon ebony shoulders, hiding but not obscuring the city that crowned the summit and spilled down the side of the hill. A wall of the same black stone, almost as tall as the cliff itself, had been built into the hill. It tapered down until it disappeared around the edge of the lake.

The skycar rattled up the shore a few more klicks, then slowed and tilted into an ascent. A few minutes later, it crossed the wall. Long white buildings packed the hillside in haphazard layers, and the morning sun cast its shadow over the blue roofs. The throaty gong of a bell rang out and was answered by another and then another.

"That's the Vesper district," Allara said. "It's where the monks and other religious acolytes live."

"Acolytes?"

She stepped back from the railing and unknotted the gold scarf at the end of her braid. "Réon Couteau is viewed as a sacred place. It's the domain of the Gifted. It's where the worlds meet. Unlike your world, that's common knowledge here." She looked at him. "It's a dangerous time to be a Gifted. More dangerous than ever now that Mactalde's crossed. The people here have their own beliefs about what you're supposed to be."

He gave the blue roofs a long look. "I thought the Gifted were respected."

"They are. The people love the Gifted. You're the stuff of legends. But there's many now who would just as soon see you dead."

"Nateros?" he asked. Quinnon had mentioned something about them last night.

She draped her scarf over her shoulder, combed her hair out with her fingers, and started re-braiding it. "If you're lucky, you'll be able to stay clear of them. They have rather decided ideas about Searchers who bring over more than one Gifted. Even though it's not exactly our choice."

"Do they support Mactalde?"

"No. Or at least not openly." She tightened the scarf with a jerk. "But they're certainly not for us. If Koraud doesn't crush us from the outside, we might just find ourselves in a civil war."

"What is it Nateros wants?"

"Religious and political control. They're fanatical traditionalists, and they want no part of anyone who doesn't play by the rules as they see them." She glanced at him. "And that means you and me. In the aftermath of the last war, they've been a loud voice against my father's regime. You find Lael a disgruntled country, and sometimes disgruntled people believe whoever shouts the loudest."

The skycar moved past the blue roofs of Vesper. Mansions, most of them constructed of the same black stone, stood sentinel within vast courtyards. The houses were all of three or four stories with multiple peaks and chimneys. Crumbled shale covered the yards, criss-crossed by paths of mown grass. The whole neighborhood had a sense of stability and history. Old money.

"This place has been around a while," Chris said.

"Réon Couteau is one of the oldest cities in Lael. It was originally a destination of only the Searchers and the Keepers, but over time, it's become a shrine for pilgrimages from all over the world. A few centuries ago, we started mining the silver out of the Illise hills, and the city's grown even more since then. The farther north you go, the more miners and hunters you'll run into. Here at the southern end, we confine ourselves to religion and wealth."

"Sounds like uncomfortable bed partners."

She shrugged. "It's the way of the world. This is the Manors section. Most of the nobility and wealthy live here. The skycar docks officially in Rockmon, the commercial district. But it has stations all over the city. Our engineer has orders to take us directly to the palace."

As if on cue, the skycar jerked to a stop as another train, this one hauling maybe as many as thirty cars, whooshed past.

"We'll be switching cables." Quinnon dropped into his chair and pulled his gauntlets from his belt. "The royal car claims precedence at all the intersections."

After a wait of only a few seconds, the car lurched forward again and snaked around in a hard right. Twenty minutes later, they began another climb, and Chris got his first glimpse of the palace. It hugged the edge of the cliff, actually straddling the waterfall. From this angle, it seemed to be made up of two separate parts, the large part curving around the edge of the cliff, flat-topped, with two stories of slitted windows glaring blackly from the walls. Branching from there, the construction took on a square, almost boxy look, framed by two turrets, one higher than the other, with a yawning hole of a gate in between.

The skycar crossed between the turrets and descended into the courtyard. Below, a troop of Guardsmen marched in a square ten men deep. As the train glided to a stop just above the ground, their leader called a halt and ordered the men to salute.

Chris dusted a few cheese crumbs from his shirt. Here he was, then. No turning back. From here on in, he wasn't just some guy who'd taken a wrong turn and fouled up massively. From here on in, he would be expected to *be* the Gifted.

The lead Guardsman swept open the door, and Allara faced forward. She shot one glance over her shoulder at Chris, then stepped down from the car onto the wide walkway.

With a deep breath, Chris followed.

"Your highness." The Guardsman stomped one foot and smacked his heels together smartly. "The Garowai flew over the walls just an hour ago." Excitement filled his voice. "We think he's behind the waterfall now."

Her back was ramrod straight again. She nodded without hesitation. "Thank you, Lieutenant." She looked at Quinnon, and Chris caught a glimpse of the steel in her jaw. Whatever she had to say to the Garowai, it wasn't going to be too agreeable.

Quinnon jumped down from the car and moved to the ramp at the end of the horses' compartment. "We'll take these mounts. Save time saddling new ones. These've rested some overnight, and we won't be gone long."

They unloaded the horses, checked their girths, and mounted up. Chris rode behind Allara this time. Almost before they were in their saddles, four of the Guardsmen had run to the far end of the courtyard and hauled open a set of twenty-foot gates.

Chris took a grip on the back of the saddle. "The Garowai doesn't live here?"

Allara reined her big black horse around and urged him after Quinnon's gray. Hooves clopped against the cobblestones.

"He lives at the Gloamfall, far south, but he knew we were coming here."

Once outside the gates, the gravel trail plunged into a steep decline. The waterfall roared not too far away.

"How's he know about me?" Chris asked.

"The Garowai have always been our messengers. They fly nearer heaven than anyone."

"He's what—an angel?"

"In a way."

He braced both hands against the saddle and leaned back as the horse picked its way down the hill. "Seems like having an angel on your side should help tip the odds in your favor."

"The Garowai rarely fight in our battles. Their lives are not connected to ours, and they have been given an indemnity we do not share."

Ten minutes later, the trail leveled out and rounded into view of the waterfall. The horses perked their ears at the scent of water, and Allara's stallion nickered deep within his nostrils, the soft skin quivering.

Quinnon halted his mount and looked at Chris as he spoke to Allara. "Want him to wait with me while you go ahead?"

She reined up at the water's edge and gestured for Chris to dismount. "No, the Garowai knew he was coming."

He braced against the cantle and swung his leg over the stallion's rump. Both feet thumped onto the bank.

"So this guy has a name, I suppose?" he asked.

"No. He is just the Garowai. There is never more than one Garowai in Lael. They rise and fall with the ages. When one dies, another is born from its body." She stared ahead. "The rest he will tell you himself."

He turned to look.

Up close, the surface of the lake was more dizzying than ever. Colors streaked and swirled beneath the waves, dancing incomprehensibly. The waterfall smashed down and raised a cloud of mist that obscured everything.

From within the spray, a blue-gray shadow swam toward them, slowly, almost leisurely. The curtain of mist broke. Through the haze protruded a craggy feline head, framed in a dark mane and a darker beard. Green irises, visible even from across the lake, gleamed. They stared at Chris, unmoving. The milky inner lids blinked, and the Garowai emerged.

17

THE GAROWAI SWAM farther into the lake, and the mist dissipated into white wraiths as the rest of his body followed: black-leather wings folded against his back and a long spiked tail gliding after him. He submerged, and the lake and its strange reflections rolled in to cover his wake.

Chris's breath, trapped in the back of his throat, seeped free. Up to now, the Garowai had sounded like some wise old man or something. But this creature looked like it preferred eating to admonishing.

Allara kicked free of her stirrups and dropped to the shore next to him. "Be polite."

At the edge of the bank, the Garowai surfaced, and water sluiced off the roached mane that continued halfway down his back. He spread his wings and tilted them to let them drain, then shook himself like a dog. His mane fluffed some, but still lay dark and clumped around his face. As he climbed from the shallows to the dry pebbles, his lips peeled back and a double row of needle teeth flashed.

Allara saluted with her thumb and forefinger touching her closed eyes. "Garowai. The Gifted has come. And so has—"

"So I see." The voice grumbled like the first hint of thunder.

Chris took a full step back. It talked? But then again, why not? Before yesterday, he'd never seen Cherazii and Rievers either. He made himself step up again.

The Garowai peered into Chris's face. The wrinkle of fur above his eyes suggested amusement. "So you're the Gifted the God of all sends to us?" His words tapered in a strange accent.

Chris fought the need to do something with his hands, to shove them into his pockets, cross them over his chest, *something* to cover their emptiness.

He cleared his throat. "That seems to be the consensus."

"But, from this tone of yours, I gather you don't grant your approval?"

"I wouldn't go so far as to say anyone consulted me."

"No one consulted you about giving you life either, I think? Or whether or not you wanted to be strong and healthy?" The Garowai laughed deep in his chest. "You take for granted the gifts you like and resent those you do not."

Chris glanced at Allara, but she didn't look back. She'd told him to be polite. She *hadn't* told him he had to agree with everything. "Seems to me if I didn't want it, it wasn't a good gift."

"Well, now, whether or not it's a gift depends entirely on the perspective of the giver, not the receiver." The Garowai's mouth gapped, almost as if he were grinning. He looked at Allara. "How long since he crossed?"

"Yesterday morning. I found him amongst a group of Cherazii taken prisoner by a Koraudian raiding party. And—" her voice tremored, "—Mactalde crossed yestere'en."

The Garowai scraped a foreclaw through the charcoal pebbles into the damp sand beneath. "Did he indeed?"

"You knew." Color drained from her face. Her nostrils flared. "All these years, you *knew* he was coming. But you told Harrison Garnett, and not me. *Why?*"

"I'm not given to know all things. I did not know Mactalde would return."

"I'm not talking about Mactalde. I'm talking about *him*, a second Gifted! He shouldn't be here!"

"And yet he is."

"Yes. And because he is, so is Mactalde."

The Garowai looked at Chris and raised one eyebrow.

Standing before this creature, even the few defenses Chris had tried to offer Allara were stripped away. His gut twisted. He opened his mouth, found his tongue too dry to speak, and tried again. "Someone told me the dreams would stop if I brought him back."

"Who told you this?"

"Orias Tarn."

The Garowai cocked his head at Allara. "A Keeper has betrayed the lake? That does put a different light on things."

She stepped forward. "I don't care about what you didn't know. I only care that you trusted Harrison Garnett and not me! Why? I need to understand that. Just that."

The Garowai stared back at her. Only the twitch of his tail spikes showed movement. "I did not tell you because you did not need to know. Twenty years of preparation wouldn't have changed a thing. You would just have grown twenty years older, fretting over the inevitable. I tell you only what I believe you need to know, only when you need to know it."

The wind scattered loose tendrils of her hair. "Was what I knew enough to stop Harrison from trying to do the forbidden? Did what I know stop *him*—" she pointed at Chris, "—from doing it anyway?"

"Dearheart, I am not the one of us who needs to learn to trust." He lowered his head and snuffled her hair, almost a caress. "Go on into the city. I wish to speak to the Gifted now."

She hesitated. Then she turned and mounted. After she had adjusted her reins, she looked up. The anger still smoldered in her face, but it was tempered now by something else—a desolation almost. "Mactalde would never have returned had you told me."

"Shush yourself." The Garowai sniffed several times, then sneezed. He blinked before turning back to her. "You worry about the Gifted and let him worry about the rest of it. Now get along with you."

She dragged her stallion around and urged him into a trot. At the base of the trail, she stopped to exchange a few words with Quinnon, then laid her heels to the horse's sides. Quinnon remained, leaning forward over his saddle horn, watching Chris and the Garowai.

"Well, now." The Garowai tilted his head down shore as an indication for Chris to follow. "Let us walk."

Chris watched over his shoulder as Allara's stallion lunged up the steep hill. She leaned forward, her hands in his mane. She didn't look back.

"What might your name be?" the Garowai asked.

He turned. "Chris Redston."

The Garowai limped with a heavy stride. He kept his wings folded over his back, and his tail trailed through the sand behind. "I've been watching you a long time, ever since you were a child."

Now that was an unsettling thought—or was it supposed to be comforting?

Chris cleared his throat. "I talked to Harrison Garnett before I crossed, and he said you showed me to him when I was a kid." If the idea of the Garowai watching him was unsettling, the notion of Harrison doing it was downright disturbing. "How does that work?"

"That would be the secret of Ori Réon." The Garowai rocked to a stop and turned to the lake. "What do you see out there?"

Chris looked past the Garowai to the wide expanse of water and the images undulating on its surface. "It's like the lake is reflecting something, or lots of somethings."

"Do you have the Orimere?"

He reached into his pocket for the stone, and electricity shot up his arm. He gritted his teeth. Obviously, this thing was going to take some more getting used to.

The Garowai hobbled two steps back to give him an unobstructed view of the lake. "Look yonder."

Chris nearly dropped the rock. With the Orimere in his hand, the flickering images on the water's surface transformed into absolute clarity. The lake stretched in front of him for miles, and every inch, every ripple, every wave, projected the world he left behind when he slept.

Neon signs and blurred traffic lights sparkled along Michigan Avenue. Sails winked through the darkness beyond North Avenue Beach. Sears Tower melded with the reflection of the black castle high above, separated only by the glint of its backlit windows.

"See that?" The Garowai stretched his muzzle toward the center of the lake, where a man slept facedown on a rumpled bed.

"Me . . ." He eased open his fingers and let the Orimere fall to the sand at his feet. In an instant, the lake returned to blurry shadows. "Can everyone see this?" He bent to pick up the stone.

"The Searcher and the Cherazii can see vague impressions of your world. But only a Gifted can see clearly."

"Harrison saw me in there?"

"Aye. And, with considerably less clarity, so did Allara."

He looked at the crest of the cliff high above, where Allara's silhouette rode the edge. "Why tell Harrison and not her?"

The Garowai sneezed again and turned back down the bank, toward the trail. "The progression life takes isn't always one that makes sense. Sometimes things must happen which at first seem regrettable. I told Harrison he was *not* this generation's only Gifted. That there would be another. He needed to know so he would act in the way that would cause his deceit to be discovered and eliminated."

Chris pocketed the Orimere. "She said he was a traitor."

"He was." The Garowai's forked tongue flicked between his front teeth. "Harrison was ambitious, ruthless, and without honor. Mactalde sought him out as his only means of escaping a dying body. He bribed Harrison with promises of Lael's throne once the war was won."

Chris walked two more steps. "Last time I talked to Harrison, he was pretty interested in staying as far away from Mactalde as possible. And I can't say Mactalde seemed to bear him any love either."

The Garowai's shoulders rippled. "Things didn't go precisely as they planned. Mactalde was captured and executed. So in the end, it didn't matter his body was dying."

Chris digested that. "If Harrison was still alive here, what stopped Mactalde from forcing him to take him across? Why wait for me?"

"By then, rumors were already flying about Mactalde's promise to return from the dead. The Cherazii realized the only way Mactalde could return was if he were aided by a Gifted who lived on both sides of the worlds. This, as you know, is quite forbidden. So they hunted Harrison down and they killed him."

The Garowai's inner eyelids blinked. "And then they left Lael by the thousands in protest against King Tireus, who had refused to slander the name of a Gifted by telling Lael the truth."

That didn't necessarily strike Chris as the worst of decisions for a king to make, especially since most people didn't seem too thrilled with the Gifted these days anyway.

"Was that such a bad thing?"

The Garowai shrugged again. "The truth is always worth the telling, in my mind."

"And subterfuge is always a part of good politics."

"Hmm. We shall see. Perhaps the good or the bad of Tireus's

decision will be dependent on the kind of Gifted you turn out to be. It was for you he preserved among the people the pure legacy of the Gifted." His mouth gapped in another dog-like grin. "What is it you plan to accomplish during your tenure here, young man?"

Chris stopped and faced him. He spread his hands. They were empty, just as he was of knowledge and ideas. "I thought someone was supposed to tell me that. You, for instance."

"Me, for instance." The green eyes twinkled. "Well, for instance, I might tell you the Gifted are summoned to change the worlds. It doesn't always turn out for the best, as you can see from Harrison. But the point is you have the *power* to change history, for better or worse. You're destined to change it."

"Change it how?"

"We never know for certain until it happens. Perhaps you'll bring new technology, new medical discoveries into our world." He leaned nearer. "Or, under the circumstances, perhaps you'll save it."

"Save it?" His skin turned cold.

"We'll see, won't we? At any rate, just know the God of all brings you here for a purpose. Never doubt that." He smiled. "You should also know it's the Searcher's duty to guide the Gifted. Allara and Captain Quinnon will show you what you are to do." He nodded up shore to where Quinnon still waited. "But whatever they may say, they're not responsible for you. What you do and what you don't do is because you and you alone have made the decisions."

Chris watched the lake and its swirl of images. Saving the world was not what he had signed on for here. That was way above his pay grade. And if he had been *chosen* for this, then somebody had just made the mistake of the century.

"Why do you say I'm going to have to save the world?"

The Garowai flicked a glance at the sky. "Tell me, have you ever felt a wind that cold in the middle of summer?"

Chris stared up at the perfect sky and its perfect sun. The cold edge of the wind cut across his unshaven cheek. "It changed after I brought Mactalde across. I noticed it last night."

"These two worlds of ours hang in balance. That's the way of things. A man living two lives and dying two natural deaths in one world is all it takes to tear that balance asunder."

Realization plowed into him so hard it nearly knocked him off his feet. "You mean Mactalde?" He faced the lake. Pitch had told him exactly this, if only he hadn't been too stupid to listen. "I caused the imbalance when I brought him across?"

"You did." The words were calm, without a trace of blame. "And now it's time for you to move on and make it right." The Garowai raised his forepaw in front of Chris, palm up. "Goodbye, Master Gifted. I'm glad to have met you. Perhaps I'll see you again soon."

Chris hesitated, then set his hand against the horny pad. "You're leaving already? You're like a genie—you only answer three questions?"

With a chuckle, the Garowai stepped back. "Answers are overrated. I find it much more effective to ask. And I've already told you what I can: the worlds spin on."

His face scrunched, and his eyes hooded in concentration. Without warning, his skin started to rumple around his joints, as though it were suddenly too large for his body.

Chris stared. The Garowai's body shrunk, the bones telescoping, joints swelling. "What's wrong?"

The Garowai's teeth bulged extra large in his mouth, then shrank to match the new size of his head. His mane and the roach down his back nearly engulfed him, and for an instant his tail was twice as long as his body. His height dropped to half his original size, then half again.

The contortions stopped, and the Garowai, now barely taller than Chris's knee, shook himself and sneezed. He dog-grinned up at Chris. "You'll forgive me. I'm old and my bones hurt. It's easier for me to move about when I'm smaller."

Chris snapped his mouth shut and just nodded.

The black membrane of the Garowai's wings unfolded. Delicate blue veins zigzagged between the phalange bones. "You've less time to work in than many Gifted have, so use it wisely. Tell Allara what I said about the wind." He nodded farewell, then raised his wings to the sky and caught the chill breeze.

Chris backed away from the swirl of air and watched the stroke of the Garowai's wings carry him far away, until he was only a fleck against the horizon. Whatever he had expected of this conversation, a talking monster who preferred to ask rather than answer hadn't been at the top of the list.

So apparently, he'd not only doomed the world to war, but to a new ice age—or worse? He took a careful breath. The first question right now was how was he supposed to fix an imbalance?

The obvious answer seemed to be he needed to remove the cause. That meant Allara was right. He *was* going to have to kill Mactalde. And that meant he was somehow going to have to get into touch with his lost Guardsman skills. If he didn't turn out to be a prodigy of swordplay and battlefield tactics, they might all be in trouble.

He turned back and trudged to where Quinnon stood in front of his horse. At the edge of the lake, he stopped and knelt to raise a handful of water to his mouth.

"He say anything worth listening to?" Quinnon asked.

Chris shook the water from his fingers and stood. "He says there's an imbalance between the worlds. Do you know what that means?"

Quinnon's bushy brows knit. "Aye, I know what it means." He stared after the Garowai. "I don't ken him. He trains her ladyship, practically brings her up, then throws her to her enemies. She was nine years old when first I met her. A nine-year-old girl who was supposed to dedicate her life to the stinking likes of Harrison Garnett." The look he gave Chris made it clear he didn't hold the new Gifted in much better regard.

He mounted, his stiff left arm held close to his body, and sat for a moment adjusting his reins. Then he kneed the horse forward to Chris's side. "Might be best if we got something clear just between the two of us. I don't do what I do for the money. I don't do it for love of country or king, because Lael's neither of mine. And I don't do it because I'm hurrah-happy over any of this Gifted business."

"You do it for her."

"Aye. I do it for her. I've been with her ever since she was that nine-year-old little girl. I know what she is. I know what she does. And I know what she's been through." He leaned his forearm against the saddle horn and bent down. "I'd die for her without a second thought. But I'll tell you this, I'd much rather kill for her."

He'd been waiting all day for Quinnon to stake his territory, and it was just as well the man find out now that he had no intention of pushing him so long as Quinnon didn't push first. He held his ground, feet spread, shoulders back, a position of strength without aggression. "Kill me, you mean?"

Quinnon pursed his lips. "You've caused enough trouble to last you the rest of your life. Cause any more, and you won't be worth the effort as far as I'm concerned. Most people think the Gifted are chosen by the God of all, that they're sacred. But plenty of men will still be more than willing to plant their steel in you." He extended his hand to pull Chris onto the horse. "Not everyone in Lael calls upon God."

Chris swung up behind the saddle. "Good to know where we stand."

Quinnon urged his horse up the path. "Just do your job, and I'll do mine."

Of course, that might end up being easier said than done on both counts.

18

SLEEP HAD ABANDONED Allara halfway through the night. For as long as she could remember, Réon Couteau had been the prison of her soul. Even back in the days when she had been young enough to be a friend to hope, when she had believed being a Searcher was an honor and not a curse, even then she had escaped the shadows of this ancient fortress whenever she could. An oppressive force clung to the very walls here, a sense of history incarnate perhaps. It was a constant presence, an invisible gaze watching over her shoulder, observing her every decision, her every action—and judging her.

She blinked and focused on the half-written papers strewn across her desk. Red dawnlight bled through the curtains on the far side of the room and reflected in the mirror above her head.

Around midnight, she had risen, lit the candle globes, and gotten to work. Time was too short to waste on sleep. But concentration had eluded her as well. She had written and rewritten the letter to her father, only to cast all her attempts aside.

She scanned the last sentence she had written, but she couldn't quite get her mind around it. How was she supposed to drop a fireball like this in his lap? He wasn't likely to understand or care about the whys, and the first thing he would see was that she had once again let a Gifted act outside her control.

Frustrated, she stabbed a period into the paper with the detachable pen nib that slid on and off her fingertip, like a metal fingernail. What was there to say except the truth? She couldn't change it and she couldn't polish it.

Mactalde had returned.

She had only met the man once. He had passed her in a hallway and recognized her. Back then, he had been the Sovereign of Koraud, handsome and young, with his tawny hair and his chiseled chin. But even then, she had seen the crinkled edges of the mortal illness that clawed at his body.

Standing there in the hallway, he had tilted her nine-year-old chin up, as if trying to figure out the cogs in her machine, perhaps searching for weaknesses.

"Bad time to be a Searcher, little one." That's all he had said.

After that, when she saw him again, for the last time, as the executioner's axe descended toward his bowed neck, he had raised his eyes to her, and he had smiled. He didn't look afraid. He had *known* he was coming back. He had believed it with all his heart. And now, twenty years later, here he was.

Someone knocked on the door. The hour was too early to break fast, but whatever new catastrophe had brought the maids to her chambers couldn't be worse than what had already happened.

"Come in."

She slapped the paper down flat on the desk and scribbled just two more lines, "The Gifted has come. So has Mactalde." Before she could change her mind, she folded it up, curled her finger to stamp the paper with the seal on the front side of the pen nib, then pulled the nib from her finger and cast it into its bronze leak pit.

The door opened, and footsteps pattered into the room. Esta, of course. For a tall woman, taller even than Allara herself, she moved with the tiny mincing strides of someone half her size.

"My lady, forgive me, I thought you might be awake."

"I'm awake." She turned around in her chair and draped the long sleeve of her nightgown over its back. "What is it?"

Esta tsked. "Sitting up all night without a robe or a shawl. What are you thinking? Are you hungry?" She was already dressed in a high-waisted gown of dark green with a heavily embroidered brocade underlay showing through the triangular slit up the front of the skirt. Instead of the fashionable blonde wig she usually wore, her dark hair was done up and topped with a crescent headdress.

She didn't wait for Allara to answer before snapping her fingers at the open door and signaling the maids to bring in the breakfast tray and its matching knee table.

Two girls in their early twenties hurried in.

The servants were all schooled by the steward, the housemistress, Esta, Quinnon, and Allara didn't know who else, to keep their eyes respectfully averted in the presence of the royal family. But today they glanced at her not just once, but at least three times before leaving. Their expressions held questions . . . and something else. Anticipation, perhaps.

So every pantry maid knew the Gifted had arrived. Of course it wouldn't have taken long. News flew nowhere faster than downstairs amongst servants. How much longer before the whole city knew? She realized her teeth were clenched and forced them to loosen.

The girls each bobbed an awkward curtsy, finally dropped their eyes, then fled.

"They know," Allara said.

"Of course they know." Esta lifted silver lids to reveal the steam curling from a white fillet of summerton and a peeled sopple floating in its bowl of sweet craniss wine. "To begin with, there's a handsome guest in the western wing. Second, laundry took away a pile of clothes the like of which none of us has ever seen. Third, you come back alone without any of your Guard except Captain Quinnon. Fourth, the Garowai himself flies over our wall. And, fifth, you're up all night in a dither."

"The maids don't know I was up all night." She reached for the china stein of mulled cider and tipped back the hinged lid with her thumb. "And he's not handsome."

"He's a sight better than that weasel-faced one you dragged in last time." Esta lifted a lace handkerchief from a frosted bowl of snow oranges. "This fruit is here all the way from the Goraudian Mountains. I don't suppose we'll be seeing many more shipments any time soon." She held them out. "I've been saving them."

"Thank you." She took the bowl and the offered spoon. Esta knew she had a soft spot for snow oranges. She spooned a smooth wedge into her mouth, broke the bitterness of the skin with her teeth, and bit down on the sweet beads inside. When she swallowed, it stuck in her throat.

She played with the spoon in the bowl. "Esta, I don't know what to do."

Esta sighed. "Seems to me, *you* always know what to do." She threw back first the brocade curtains on the towering bed, then crossed the room to open the matching curtains on the narrow floor-to-ceiling windows. Sunlight streaked the room, searching out the dark corners of the paneled walls and the somber murals on the domed ceiling.

Allara tilted her head to the side and stared up at the pictures.

This room traditionally belonged to the Searcher, whether that person happened to be male or female, royalty or not. The circular ceiling mural was divided into four wedge-shaped pictures, alternating between famous Gifted and their Searchers. One wedge showed Rialla Nialle, an early female Searcher. According to legend, she had spent twenty years searching for her Gifted, Benjamin Webb, before finally finding him in the jungles of Ariad, halfway across the world.

Allara tilted her head farther, to peer into Rialla's eyes. The artist, painting in the Radine style with its sumptuous curves, bland features, and ethereal garments, had envisioned her as an erect, fire-headed woman. Her sky-blue gown blended into the clouds behind her.

Rialla stared right past Allara, searching, still searching. She had found her Gifted. More than that, she had loved him and married him, making their story one of the most romantic and cherished within the canon of Gifted history. But even still, all these centuries after her death, she searched on.

Was that how Allara would be two hundred years from now? Living her life on the ceiling of some forgotten room, still searching for what she had never been able to find in life?

Esta pattered back across the room and rapped the fork against a plate. "The first thing you should do is eat your meal, drink your cider, and take another bath. That mob outside can wait."

Allara sat up. "What mob?"

Esta's rouged lips pinched. "Never mind. I shouldn't have said anything."

Allara set the bowl of snow oranges back onto the tray and shoved her chair back, its feet screeching against the floor's parquetry. "Yes, you should have." She snatched up her dressing gown and threw it on as she left the room.

"My lady! Allara, wait!" Esta scampered behind her.

She strode down the hall, all the way across the building to the windows facing the front courtyard. Even before she could see out, she could hear the sound of people milling and the buzz of their voices.

She unlatched the window. "Who let them in here?"

"No one, my lady." Esta puffed after her.

The liveried footman stationed on this floor hurried to take charge of opening the window.

"You can see they're not in the courtyard," Esta said. "No one would let them in without your or Captain Quinnon's permission. They're all out in the streets."

The courtyard below was empty of anyone save stableboys and Guardsmen. With the window open, the eerie cold of the breeze carried the sound of the crowd into the hall and filled Allara's ears.

"How many are out there?"

"Quite a lot, my lady. I didn't count them, naturally, but if you walk onto the parapet, you can see them packing the streets all the way down into Vesper."

So word had already spread that far. "Nateros?" She made her mouth form the word.

Esta gave a nervous laugh. "I'm sure I don't know, my lady."

Esta didn't have to know. Of course Nateros was there. Headed probably by Crofton Steadman himself. The cool-eyed zealot had become the movement's most popular spokesman in recent years. If Nateros had learned a second Gifted had indeed arrived, they would undoubtedly be whipping themselves into a frenzy against her supposed witchcraft.

She reached past the footman and closed the window herself. Then she turned back down the hall.

Esta followed. "Just give them a glimpse of the Gifted, my lady."

"No."

"That's all they want. They'll see him, everybody will give a cheer, and they'll leave us alone."

"Nobody's seeing this Gifted until he can take care of himself. He's not leaving my sight until I've done every last bit of my duty to him." She hastened through her bedchamber to the dressing room beyond. "After that, if he wants to be seen, the crowds can see all they can stand of him."

She hauled open the doors on an armoire and threw out a thigh-length white blouse and doeskin breeches. "Send someone to get him up. He's slept long enough."

Something crashed. Chris opened his eyes to the darkness of his curtained bed and jerked upright. Footsteps squeaked across the floors in the distinguishable scuff of someone making more noise simply by trying not to. At the foot of the bed, they stopped, and someone cleared his throat, quietly first, then loudly enough to wake any sleeper.

"Excuse me, sir, Master Gifted." The curtains parted, and a ray of sunlight plowed a path up the middle of the bed right into Chris's eyes.

He raised a hand to block the light. "What time is it?"

"Not half past dawn, sir."

The servant, Parry by name, was an ungainly adolescent with a head about half again as big as it should have been. His yellow hair was slicked back, and, above the starched collar of his tight buttoned green doublet, his face had the rawness of a furious scrubbing.

He shifted his weight from one foot to the other. "Sorry to disturb your rest, sir."

"That's all right. I wanted to get up anyway." He rubbed both hands over his face and checked his shoulder.

After his bath last night, Parry had cleaned the wound and packed it with some kind of herbal poultice. Beneath the edge of the bandage, it didn't look inflamed, and he could raise his arm to its full range of motion with only a dull pull of pain. The rest of his body felt considerably better as well, which was nothing short of a miracle after sleeping on this ridiculously soft mattress.

"I'll get your clothes right away, sir," Parry said. "And Cook sent up some breakfast, but you'll have to eat it on the way."

"Way to where?" What memo had he missed this time?

"Her highness wishes to see you in the armory court right away. I'll show you where it is."

"She's one for early starts, isn't she?"

"Yes, sir."

Parry disappeared into an adjoining room and came back out with a pile of clothing folded on one outstretched arm and a pair of boots in the other. "Shall I help you dress, sir?"

"Uh, no thanks. And you don't have to call me sir."

Parry's eyebrow lifted. "And what'd I call you otherwise, sir?"

"Just Chris."

The other eyebrow went up. "Ah." His over-wide mouth hinted at a grin. "All right. I'll just set the clothes here then." He slid them onto a nearby chair and left through the main door.

Chris threw the covers back and wallowed out of the mattress.

The rooms he had been given—bedroom, bathroom, and dressing room—went way past the opulence of even Mactalde's North Shore mansion in Chicago. Lush murals danced across the soaring ceilings, and velvet hangings of alternating blue and black covered the walls. Four chandeliers, each carrying twenty glass globes, hung from the corners. Two big oriel windows, boasting endless views of the lake, spilled sunlight from either end of the room's southern wall.

He went to the straight-backed chair near his bed and started dressing.

Parry had selected a pair of black suede knee breeches and a loose white tunic with green scrollwork embroidered on the cuffs. He felt like a fool, but they were comfortable and easy to move in.

The boots were thick-soled and made of shining black leather that reached all the way to his knee. A seven-inch cuff, laced and knotted in the front, folded back over the top. He stomped his heel down and took a few experimental steps. They were considerably heavier and more cumbersome than his sneakers. Depending on what her highness had in store for the day, he'd probably end up with a nice crop of blisters.

Parry reentered with a covered tray and kicked the door shut behind him. Not that Chris was any expert on hired help, but this kid looked like he had just barely graduated from Servants University. Probably why Allara and Quinnon had assigned him to Chris.

"Here's some zajele cheese on toast and a fresh sopple. Not fancy, I know, but you can eat it quick before her highness gets too impatient."

At any rate, he was a sensible sort.

"What's she want with me?" Chris asked. "The rack or the iron maiden?"

"The what?" Parry pulled the cloth from the tray.

"Never mind." He crossed to the table and picked up a lidded stein. Its contents had a spicy sweet smell, something like cranapple cider.

"I'll tell you something." Parry dropped his voice to a whisper. "Her ladyship's in a bit of a foul mood this morning."

"You mean sometimes she isn't?"

"Well, I'm not actually sure about that. I don't know her, of course. But this morning she puts me in mind of my grandmother whenever she's out to kill a hog for mussing her flower garden."

"I see. Thanks for the warning." He downed the cider in a few swallows and combined the two pieces of melted cheese on toast to make a sandwich. "All right. Lead the way to this hog slaughter."

19

CHRIS FOLLOWED PARRY down a staircase that spiraled into the castle's foundation. After a few minutes, the tight walls fell away to reveal a gymnasium of sorts. Some forty torches illuminated more ceiling murals—these of battles—and a black and white checkerboard pattern, formed of rough slate, on the floor. The far wall dissolved into columns and revealed a thundering white wall of water.

"We're behind the waterfall?"

Parry nodded.

Allara stood in the middle of the room. She wore breeches and a white blouse belted at her waist. Both hands clasped the hilt of a sword propped in front of her.

Parry drew aside and motioned for Chris to pass. From his face, he didn't want to go anywhere near Allara while she had a sword in her hands. She didn't look like she had gotten more than a few hours of sleep last night, and she *did* look like maybe a hog or two had gotten into her flower patch.

Chris crossed the room to join her. "So what's so important it can't wait until after breakfast?"

"Time." She touched the sword's hilt to his chest. "And the lack of it. We've only a matter of weeks, if we're lucky, before all Lael knows you're here. I've written to my father. When he feels the time is right, he'll summon us back to Glen Arden, the capital, for your official investiture. You've a long way to go before you're ready for that."

He slid his hand through the swoop of the hilt's basket and closed his fingers around the leather wrap. "So this is Gifted training?"

She backed away, and her hand fell to her own hilt. The shimmer of firelight intensified against her dark pupils. Likely enough, she'd end up taking a whack at him just for spite.

He instinctively brought his sword up before his face with both hands.

A flicker of movement against the wall caught his attention, and Quinnon stepped away from the weapons rack on the wall, a sword in either hand. "Like the feel of that one, do you?"

He tightened his grip, his palm hot against the leather. It weighed heavy in his hands, but the balance felt right. "What is this? A rapier?"

"It's an estoc," Quinnon said. "A rapier won't get you anywhere in battle. Too light." He set the point of his smaller sword in a crack in the floor and pressed down, bowing the thin blade. "A rapier is the sort of thing folks carry around for personal protection. Light and quick. If you survive long enough, could be we'll get around to training with one later. But we're in a hurry." He jutted his chin. "We'll start you with Allara. She's fast and she's skilled. Could be enough to trigger these Guardsman skills you claim to have."

"Sounds good. I guess."

Quinnon raised both blades to rest against his shoulders. He grinned. "Then watch your back."

Allara struck.

Chris parried reflexively and caught the silver thread of her blade against his.

She held the swords together for a moment and glared at him across the few feet that separated them. Her hair was pinned atop her head, and the loose tendrils clung to the heat of her skin. The look on her face said she wasn't about to cut him any slack.

He gritted his teeth. "So that's how it's going to be."

"That's how it's going to be."

She struck again, and this time he barely caught her blade.

Iron clanged against iron. Echoes reverberated against the stone walls. He staggered back, barely keeping up with her attack. This was no mock battle. One misstep and he'd lose a limb to her hammering blade.

Out of his peripheral vision, he glimpsed Parry at the foot of the stairs, gaping.

Allara had almost backed him into the wall. A few more steps and the fight would be over. He dodged her attack, barely, but the tip of her sword ripped through his left sleeve.

"You're thinking!" Quinnon shouted. "Stop thinking! Your mind's from another world. It doesn't know what in the Garowai's eye it's doing. Listen to your body. Let it do what it wants."

Chris clenched his teeth and tried to sink into the instincts of his muscles.

For an instant, it worked, just as it had in the fight with the Koraudians. Almost of its own accord, his blade spiraled free of Allara's, and he lunged. This time she had to take one step back before catching his sword. But before he could recover his balance, she smacked it aside and nearly ripped it from his grip.

He glared. "Are you *trying* to kill me?"

Her brows lowered over her eyes. This was more than just a bad mood. She wasn't just angry. She was terrified. And it wasn't just a terror born of the events of the last few days. This went deeper. This was something she'd been carrying around for a long time.

He leaned back. "What's got you so afraid?"

Her breathing froze. Then, without even blinking, she hurled another attack into his teeth and beat him back two steps.

"I am fighting a battle I cannot win! Is that not reason to fear?"

He held his sword against hers. "Of course you'll win. You've got me on your side now." He tried on a smile, but the joke didn't take.

"That is such a comfort." She disengaged the blades and pulled back, just out of range. "I've fought all my life to protect my country from another war. And now it's coming." She sidestepped, trying to flank him.

He kept pace with her as they marked a circle on the stone floor. "Who says you have to take the blame?"

She flinched. He half-expected her to hurl the question back in his face. But she didn't. She lowered her sword. "I do. *I* say I do." Her voice thickened. "It was my job to keep this from happening. All of it."

"I thought your job was to find me and show me what to do."

Her nostrils twitched. "Aye. And that's gone well, hasn't it?"

There it was again—that broken look stealing out from behind the edges of her ice-hard façade. Her strength, her confidence, her authority, it was all a mask. She didn't have any more answers than he did. *That's* why she was so angry.

He stepped forward. "I've never been a leader, never wanted to be. I don't follow anyone else and no one follows me. And that's the way I like it." He forced a laugh. "I'll be the first to admit I haven't exactly been a stunning success. Life is hard work, and I'll tell you the truth, it scares the wits out of me."

She gave her head half a shake. "Don't mock me."

"I'm not mocking you. If I could do it over again, I would never bring Mactalde across, even if it really could have gotten me out of here."

He filled his lungs. If he said what he was about to say, the die would be cast irrevocably. He said it anyway. "What I do from here on out, I do because I decide to do it. Not you. Me. Which means whatever happens is my responsibility. So teach me, show me how to survive, tell me what to do, but let's just get it straight that Mactalde is my problem, not yours."

Her cheeks flamed once more. "So you're taking over?" But the anger in her voice was fading.

He lunged, sword lofted. She snapped away, her reflexes a blur. His body reacted, and the sword moved where it was supposed to before he even realized it. They fought all the way back across the floor. The spray from the waterfall beaded his skin with a cool mist.

Then Allara spun away, surprising him with her speed. Before he could lose his position, he clubbed his sword into hers with all the strength he could muster. Her hilt slipped from her hand, and she cried out as it clanged against the floor.

He twitched the tip of his blade up to her throat and grinned. "Yield?"

Her breath fogged his blade. "You'll need more than brute strength to beat Mactalde."

Quinnon walked up behind him, sword in hand. "For a minute there, you almost had it." He had stripped out of his Guardsman tabard into a loose-weave shirt, open at the collar. "But were you and Allara evenly matched in strength and size, she'd have cut your throat before you took two steps."

So much for impressing the veteran. Chris huffed. "I did feel it there at the end. It was like my body just took over. I was reacting without even thinking."

Quinnon brought his sword up and raised his other hand behind his shoulder in an en garde stance. "Let's try again."

Chris caught his breath. "Now?" He gestured to his wounded shoulder. "Maybe I should check to make sure I didn't pull that open again."

Quinnon didn't lower the sword. "Battles have this tendency to not wait until you're rested and well." He lunged.

Chris snapped his sword up and caught the attack.

Quinnon backed off. "So you want to be a leader, do you? I have to tell you, wanting doesn't get the job done." He grinned. "Wanting doesn't make you *my* leader."

Chris stepped to the right, his eyes on Quinnon's. His nerves whispered fire up his arms.

"People believe the Gifted are deliverers," Quinnon said, "sent by the God of all. But I only believe what I see." His sword moved to indicate the tear in Chris's sleeve where Allara's blade had gotten past his defenses. "What I'm seeing is a man who wasn't good enough."

Chris sensed the attack coming before Quinnon barely moved. He caught it, parried, and drove Quinnon back a full step. But if he had been stunned by Allara's speed and ferocity, the addition of Quinnon's strength left him reeling.

They fought in a mindless blur. Some part of his consciousness registered the burn of his muscles, the sweat soaking his hair and his clothes, and the dragging weight of encroaching exhaustion. But still he fought. Quinnon responded with none of Allara's white-hot fury. The corner of his mouth twisted in a hint of amusement and never altered. They fought all the way across the floor, Quinnon sometimes giving ground, but mostly taking.

Chris didn't have time to think. He fell into the rhythms of his body and felt muscle memory take over. His body wasn't his anymore. It responded to the training someone else—some other Chris—had given it. It responded with strength and precision, confidence even. Maybe he was a swordsman after all.

But just the realization was enough to pull his brain out of instinctive response and back into his conscious control. He stumbled, and Quinnon delivered a sideswipe that wrenched open his grip. His sword spun away, and he stopped. His breath rasped in his ragged throat. Technically, he'd just died, of course. But it was still an improvement.

Quinnon poked Chris's chest with his sword. "Don't just stand there! When you drop your sword, go after it." He looked Chris up and down. "Not bad. Not good, but not bad. I wonder where you served your term with the Guard."

Chris used his sleeve to wipe the sweat from his forehead. "Not with you, apparently."

"If you had, you'd have known better than to stand still for that last thrust." Quinnon leaned his blade against his shoulder. "But you know it now, don't you?" When Chris nodded, he nodded back. "We'll take a break. Get yourself a drink." He jutted his chin toward the waterfall. "She's got you a whole lesson plan worked out, and fencing's just the start of it. Firearms, equitation, tactics, political history, and not forgetting everyone's favorite—etiquette." He sounded rather entertained by the whole litany. "You're about to become a busy boyo."

Chris turned to the waterfall. "At least I won't sprain my thumbs from twiddling."

"Fetch your sword first. And don't ever let me catch you with it out of your sight." He stalked off, back toward the weapons wall.

Allara had picked up Chris's sword for him and was holding it out, hilt first. He accepted it and peeled his collar back to check the bandage on his shoulder. No blood, but it didn't feel quite as good as it had an hour ago.

"I see what you meant about brute strength," he said.

The globe flickering overhead shadowed her eyes and masked her thoughts. "I've had a sword in my hand all my life. Not many can best me, disparity in strength notwithstanding."

If he didn't know better, he'd say that was almost, not quite, but maybe a compliment. He walked toward the pillars and the waterfall beyond. The mist engulfed him. It wasn't thick enough to get a drink, but it dampened his tunic and cooled his skin.

She led him to the corner, where a two-inch hole in the rock ceiling let in a steady stream of water. She bent and twisted her head to catch a mouthful. When she straightened, she touched the back of her hand to her mouth and looked up at him. "Quinnon told me what the Garowai said about the wind and the imbalance."

Chris hadn't seen her after leaving the Garowai yesterday. By the time he and Quinnon got back to the palace, she had been barricaded in some private sector of the castle, with obviously no desire to talk to him, and he hadn't asked for an audience.

Now, he stepped up next to her and leaned forward for his own drink. The water was cold and sweet. He swallowed and stood up. "I guess that means things are worse than we thought."

"Time will tell. But it can't be good." Her eyes charted his face. She had every right to explode into another outburst. If he had really rocked two worlds out of balance, that was definitely fuel for a verbal filleting. But, for a change, she didn't seem ready to behead him. She looked like she had actually believed what he said about taking charge.

He chose his words carefully. "If Mactalde being here is what's causing the imbalance, his death should solve the problem, shouldn't it?"

"Is that what the Garowai said?"

"More or less."

She watched the white rush of water. Beyond, silver-sailed ships glinted vaguely against the lake as they maneuvered in or out of the port on the western side of the falls. "Sometimes what the Garowai says is open to interpretation."

"You got any other ideas?"

"Killing Mactalde is as good a place to start as any." She dabbled her fingers in the spray overhead. "It's hard to believe the worlds could really be out of balance. How could that happen? How could that be allowed to happen? And all over a little nothing like one person being where he's not supposed to be." She looked at him. "Bringing living beings over from the other world is forbidden. Everyone knows that. But there's nothing written about it causing the worlds to tear."

"Maybe they aren't tearing. Maybe it's just a cold front or something." From here, the lake's blurred images of the other world were indistinguishable aside from the wash of colors. "Maybe Harrison Garnett knows something about it."

"He's still in contact with you?"

"He got shot by Mactalde's men just before I crossed over. But he was still alive. Maybe tonight, when I wake up, I can find a way to talk to him if I can get out of the house."

She frowned. "You can't leave your house?"

"Mactalde's got some thug after me."

Realization dawned in her face. "He wants to kill you. If you don't live in both worlds, you're not a Gifted anymore. You're just a man."

He shrugged. "That's what I feel like most of the time anyway."

She turned away. "I'll have Parry bring down some decent food. Then we'll get back to it." She stopped and looked over her shoulder. "Master Redston."

He faced her. "Yeah?"

"Stay alive—in both worlds."

20

CHRIS WOKE WITH the bedsheets twisted around his body. A moment ago, he had collapsed into the softness of that big bed in his quarters at Réon Couteau, exhausted from a day of trying to learn a lifetime's worth of knowledge about Lael. Now he was here.

He rolled over and made himself breathe while his brain scrambled to once more snag ahold of his shifting reality. Then he kicked free of the sheets and crossed to the door, pulling his clothes back on in the order he'd tossed them off last night. While his body slept in Lael, he was going to wring some answers from a certain former Gifted.

His cell phone was moldering somewhere in Lael, so he borrowed Mike's from its recharging dock in the kitchen. A call to the hospital was all he needed to get Harrison's room number. He was alive, he was in ICU, and he wasn't taking any phone calls, which meant Chris would have to risk running into Kaufman if he left the house. He put the phone back.

Mike shuffled into the kitchen, wearing the duck-flipper slippers Brooke had given him for his last birthday. "You're up early." He yawned and rubbed a hand over his hair. "Why didn't you get the coffee started?"

"Sorry, just got up myself. I lost my phone, so I borrowed yours."

Mike waved it off and reached into the cupboard for a coffee filter. He glanced back. "How's the dream machine coming along?"

"Wha-at?" Chris stuttered. There was no way Mike could know about the dreams.

"A few days ago you were going on about bad dreams. I thought maybe the excitement of someone trying to murder you knocked them out of your head."

"Oh, right. The dreams." He leaned back against the sink and tried for a casual look. "Um, they're good, actually. Haven't been dreaming much at all." Which was technically true, since they couldn't rightly be called dreams anymore.

Mike shrugged. "Always a silver lining."

"Speaking of silver linings—" although he would be hard-pressed to explain the connection, "—would you mind dropping me by the hospital on your way to work? I'd like to see Harrison Garnett."

"I thought you were staying incommunicado for a while, until the creepy bodyguard backed off."

"Yeah, well, I stayed inside yesterday. He doesn't know I'm here, so that's probably the end of that. And I just feel like I should go check on Harrison." Check on him and pump him for whatever useful information he could cough up about Mactalde and this possible imbalance.

"I thought you didn't know him."

"I don't. But I *met* him, and I just think that's what I should do."

Mike wrenched the lid off the coffee and dumped four heaping spoonfuls into the coffeemaker. "What you *should* do is call the cops, but, of course, you're not going to do that no matter what I say."

"The cops aren't going to protect me. They're probably going to accuse me."

Mike brought the carafe over to the sink and stuck it under the tap. He watched Chris sidelong while he filled it up. "Brooke was going to come by and keep you company this afternoon."

"And you think that's an argument?"

Thirty minutes later, Mike dropped Chris at Mercy General Hospital. "Remember to play on your own side of the street this time, huh?"

Chris checked to make sure he didn't see anyone tall, blond, and armed, then pulled up the hood on his jacket. At least, the wind made it cool enough he could wear a hoodie without standing out. If he kept his face covered and his head down, maybe he could get in and out of here without any problem. With any luck, Kaufman would have called his losses and given up after his one failed attempt anyway.

"You want me to pick you up when I get off work?" Mike asked.

"No, that's all right. I've got enough for a taxi home." It was about *all* he had, since his wallet, along with his credit card and his extra cash, was on its way to decomposition in Lael alongside his cell phone. "I'll see you later."

He climbed out and headed for the entrance. Three days had passed since Harrison Garnett's shooting. According to the nurse he talked to over the phone, the old man was in stable condition, but the doctors wanted him in ICU for at least another week. Chris had been told he could visit so long as he didn't upset the patient.

Yeah, right.

Once inside, he headed for the doors that separated the whispers of the waiting room from the controlled chaos of the ICU. On a bench next to the window, a small dark-skinned man read a magazine. A short beard covered his face, and he wore his sunglasses pushed back on his head.

Chris hesitated. Either he was being incredibly paranoid, or there was something familiar about this man. He'd seen him—recently. An EMT who had answered his 911 call the other day? But why would an EMT be out here?

Before the man could look up, Chris retreated a couple of steps and fell into stride with a middle-aged couple and their two teenagers.

The dad gave him a smile. "How's it going?"

"Just fine." Chris kept up the banalities, head averted from the bench, and managed to pass into the ICU without catching more than a glance from the stranger.

Letting the family walk on, he ducked into Harrison's room, the first on the right.

In the center of the room's white glow, the old man lay on his bed, his mouth slouched open, his skin faded to the gray of an X-ray. The weight of the bedclothes seemed to have compressed him to half his original body mass. Only jutting bones and the wisp of his breath raised the blanket. Compared to the muted commotion outside the door, the methodical beep of the IV throbbed against the room's silence.

Chris eased the door shut and stepped to a window in the right wall. He pried the blinds open far enough to see into the waiting room on the other side of the glass. The magazine reader, his profile to the window, turned a page and scratched his cheek. Chris's skin crawled. Definitely familiar and definitely a recent acquaintance.

He gave his head a shake. He *was* being paranoid. Unless Kaufman was such a master of disguises that he was able to lose twelve inches and change his skin color, there was no way this was him.

Behind Chris, the mummy on the bed woke with an explosion of breath. "Who are you? What are you doing here?"

Speaking of justifiable paranoia. Chris released the blinds. "It's just me."

Harrison, his finger halfway to the call button, slumped back against his pillow. "You? Just *you*? I was shot, and it was your fault."

Chris walked to the foot of the bed. "Yeah, well, I'm being shot *at*, and that's partly your fault."

Harrison sank deeper into the pillow, bottom lip sucked into a pout. "Did you tell the police who did it?"

"Our proof isn't the kind the police are going to buy." He leaned both hands against the foot of the bed. "Especially since they're not going to find a trace of our prime suspect anywhere in this world."

Harrison's eyes bulged. "You took him across? You idiot! You're a bigger fool than even I took you for."

Chris stood up and made himself breathe evenly. "What I'm here for is answers. And if you can manage to stomach it, I'd like them straight for a change."

"This would never have happened if you'd listened to me! I'm going to tell the cops *you* shot me."

"Yeah, why not? Once a traitor, always a traitor, isn't that right?"

Harrison stilled. "What do you mean?"

"I mean people in Lael don't seem to remember you too fondly." Chris walked around the bed. "You want to make yourself out to be a big fat martyr, dying at the hands of the evil Mactalde. But that's not quite the version I'm hearing from anybody."

"Get out." Harrison groped for the call button. "If you don't get out, I'll call the nurse."

Chris leaned forward and snagged the remote. "Just stop. I don't even care about whatever you did or didn't do. I really don't. I've got my hands full trying to fix my own mistakes."

"Yeah, I'll say you made a mistake." Harrison dragged his sheet up to his chin. "You're gonna get us all killed. I'd say that's a mistake."

Chris circled to the side of the bed and kept the remote cord stretched between him and Harrison. "In this world, Mactalde shouldn't even have been able to remember what happened in Lael. But he knew. How did he know?"

"He talked to himself in his dreams."

"He did what?"

Harrison shrugged a bony shoulder. "Everybody remembers their dreams. It's just most people don't remember all the details. It all gets filtered and interpreted by their waking minds in the opposite world. But they do remember. Mactalde took it from there and figured out one side of his brain could send messages to the other."

"Messages?" It made sense, almost. "But I thought only Gifted can break the mental wall."

"Don't be stupid. Gifted don't break the wall. Our minds don't merge. Our minds from this world completely overtake the minds from the other world. If you think about it, Mactalde's got one up on us on this one."

"How'd he do it?"

"All I know is he'd get into a sort of trance, talking to himself over and over again about Lael. Sooner or later, it penetrated his dreams, and his other self started to believe it."

"So he remembers everything." If Mactalde remembered what had been done to him in Lael, he'd have plenty of incentive for protracted revenge. Where was the silver lining there?

The oxygen tube in Harrison's nose hissed. "Yeah, and he went bonkers because of it, hearing voices, seeing things."

That explained Mactalde's comment about wanting the voices to stop.

"There's something else." Chris tossed the remote back onto the bed. He crossed the room and opened the drapes to reveal the gray sky outside. "The weather isn't right."

"So what? I'm a Gifted, not a weatherman. What do you want me to do about it?"

"Something's wrong with it in Lael too."

"The worlds are connected. Haven't they told you nothing?"

"Yeah, I heard about that." Chris turned back. "According to the Garowai, bringing Mactalde back into Lael knocked the worlds out of balance. I don't suppose you'd have any idea what that means?"

"Of course I know what it means!" Harrison flailed around in the bed and groped for the call button. "It means the worlds are going to tumble down around our ears, that's what it means!" He stabbed the button with his thumb. "If you don't get it fixed, everything will tear itself to pieces!"

Harrison was just a crazy old man who spouted crazy ideas. Why would he know what the Garowai had meant when even Allara hadn't? Chris wet his lips. "Do you know what you're saying? You're talking about an apocalypse or something. How do you know this?"

Sweat stood out on Harrison's ashen forehead. "The Garowai told me. The Garowai tells every Gifted." He lurched halfway off his pillow. "He would have told you if you hadn't messed everything up first. *I* would have told you if you hadn't gotten me shot." He flopped back. "I was going to be your mentor. I was going to help you, and together we could have beaten Mactalde, Tireus, the whole lot of them!"

"If you knew this is what would happen, why did you promise to take Mactalde across?"

"He was *dying!* How was he supposed to be able to make me keep my end of the deal? How was I supposed to know he'd be able to find me here? But by the time he did, it was too late for both of us. They'd already killed me in Lael too, and the only reason Mactalde didn't kill me here was because he knew I would be able to find you."

"And you did that just beautifully, didn't you?"

Harrison sulked. "I tried to warn you."

The door behind Chris opened to admit both the noise of the ICU and a trim nurse in lavender scrubs.

She frowned at Harrison's excitement. "What's the problem?"

Chris stepped back. "I'm not sure. I think his heart rate's elevated."

Harrison's wasn't the only one. If what he was saying was true . . . No, it couldn't be true. A cold breeze in the summertime hardly signified the end of one world, let alone two. But if he *was* right, what did that mean? Chris made himself breathe. For one thing, it meant Allara was more accurate than she knew about time being short.

So now what did he do? Tell Allara? He shook his head. The woman didn't need another reason to hate him. He'd already promised to take responsibility, and right now there was absolutely nothing she could do that she wasn't already doing. If things were headed the direction Harrison thought they were, they'd start seeing problems that went far beyond unseasonably cool temperatures.

He stepped back against the wall and lifted the blinds away from the window. In the waiting room, the stranger with the beard sat in the same place on the same bench. A little girl skidded past on pink roller shoes and stopped to study a picture in the magazine. She pointed and asked a question. The man turned his head to her and gave Chris a full look at his face.

Chris stared. He *had* seen this guy before—in Mactalde's living room the day he'd woken up on the couch with a concussion. Probably a concussion this guy had helped give him.

He snatched his hand away from the blinds and let them fall back in place. The other day, he had only caught a glimpse of the guy as he had walked past the couch on his way out of the room. Mactalde had called him Flores.

The nurse looked up from injecting something into Harrison's IV bag. "Are you all right?"

Chris gestured to the window. "Who is that guy? There's a little guy in the waiting room. He's Mexican, Cuban, or something."

She shrugged and turned back. "Oh, him. He's been there for the last couple days. Must have family in here."

He took another peek. The man hadn't moved. He didn't appear armed, and if he knew Chris was in here talking to Harrison, it didn't seem to bother him in the least. But his relation to Mactalde made any chance of a coincidence out of the question. Was he staking out the place?

"He never comes in to visit anyone?"

"Not that I've seen." She finished with the IV and tugged Harrison's blanket higher. "Would you like me to turn up the heat?"

Harrison grunted. "No. Just shut the drapes."

Chris looked at Harrison. "You know anybody named Flores?"

"No."

The nurse smoothed the drapes over the window and headed for the door. Her gaze speared Chris as she passed. "I think you should leave and let your friend rest now. We don't need him getting tired."

"All right. Just give me a minute to say goodbye."

Harrison glowered at him. "Goodbye. Now get out. And don't come back until you've put everything back together the way it's supposed to be."

Chris waited until the door eased shut behind the nurse. Then he crossed the room and leaned over the bed railing. "I think that guy out there works for Mactalde."

Harrison hitched his head and shoulders up from the pillow. "What?"

"I saw him at Mactalde's house. I think he works for him." He dropped his voice. "Mactalde's got Kaufman coming after me, and this guy coming after you. He wants us both dead." Coming here today was beginning to look about as dumb as Mike had warned him.

Harrison's eyes got big again. "And you led him right to me? Why didn't you just shoot me yourself?" His good hand fumbled for the nightstand. He found his water jug and hurled it. "It would have saved time!"

The jug smacked the wall behind Chris, and he bent to pick it up. "Cut it out. You're going to have every nurse in the place swarming in here." He fished the lid out of the puddle and stood up in time for Harrison to thwack him in the chest with a box of tissues.

"I hope they do swarm in here!" Harrison hammered his thumb against the call button. "I hope they throw you out and give you to that guy!"

Chris grabbed Harrison's arm before he could find another missile. He snatched the remote and flicked off the call button above the bed, but not before the door clicked back open.

The nurse stepped inside. "What is going on here?" She elbowed past Chris. "You need to leave now. I told you I didn't want him getting excited."

Chris backed off from the bed. "I'm sorry. But that guy out there— I think he might have been involved in Mr. Garnett's shooting. I think Mr. Garnett's still in danger."

She stared at him over her shoulder. "What?"

He pressed his advantage. "You need to call the cops in here and make sure somebody's watching this room."

She nodded, eyes wide. "I had no idea."

"Mind if I take the back way out?" He started toward the door. The last thing he needed was to be here when the cops showed up.

He hooked a thumb toward the waiting room. "Make sure you keep that punk out of here." Hand on the doorknob, he glanced at Harrison. "Stay healthy."

Harrison glared at the ceiling. "Easy for you to say."

Chris left the room and resisted the urge to jog down the hall to the rear exit. When the door closed behind him, he stood for a moment and scoped out the parking lot, just to make sure Kaufman wasn't waiting for him. But he was alone on the gray asphalt of an employee parking lot.

He shivered. The last time he'd been in this hospital had been the night of the wreck that had killed his mom and sister. He zipped up the hoodie and started walking. The last time he'd been here, he'd thought losing two of the most important people in his life was the worst thing that could happen. But if Harrison was right about the worlds breaking apart, he might learn to be glad his mom and Jenifer had gotten out when they did.

Silver linings were just everywhere today.

21

SOMETHING'S WRONG WITH the wind."

Orias didn't respond, despite the fact it was practically the first thing Pitch had said for a week.

"It's just a storm coming in," Raz said.

"No. Doesn't feel like a storm. Feels . . . wrong."

"Just shut your gob before you get us killed. What's *wrong* is we're close enough to the bloody Koraudians to poke 'em in the eye!"

Orias sat his horse and listened to the faint ripple of voices through the darkness. To his right, river trees rustled their night spells, unaware of the intruders into their peace.

Mactalde had resurrected. And Orias was the one who had brought him back. For days, that knowledge had been hissing in his brain.

After the Searcher had rescued the Cherazii prisoners and taken the Gifted away, Orias had headed north. The Gifted was safe. Whatever protection Orias could have given him would have paled and died in comparison to his treachery.

He could do nothing more to help. Chris would tell the Searcher what Orias had done, and she would have him executed for treason if he ever showed his face. The Cherazii already knew the truth about him, and they wouldn't wait even for a trial to administer their justice. That was as it should be. He deserved to die for what he had done.

But what choice had he? What good had protecting the Gifted and honoring the traditions done the Cherazii up to now? The Koraudians slaughtered them for those very actions.

He had chosen the only path that made sense. He might not have acted with honor. But he had acted with courage. Hadn't he?

He already knew the answer. The self-hatred burning in his guts told him all he needed to know.

After leaving the Gifted, he had turned his horse's face in the same direction as the retreating Koraudians. At the time, he couldn't have quite said why, but some sense of fatalism drew him after Mactalde and Rotoss. What would they do now? Where would they go? What crimes would they make him guilty of now that he'd helped bring Mactalde back?

He had followed them for days. The first night, they had ridden along the edge of the Karilus Wall, the cliff face that separated Lael's high lake country from the fertile farmland beneath—and Koraud beyond. There was only one way up and down the Wall, a narrow switchback path controlled by Glen Arden at the top and Calabases City at the bottom. The Koraudians hadn't bothered with it. They rode right on past and kept on riding for days until they reached the Ballion hills where the Wall tapered into nothing.

Tonight, they had reached the Northfall River and, on its far side, Koraud. Tonight, Mactalde was home.

The wind raised gooseflesh on Orias's skin. For all these days, he had ridden far behind the Koraudians. His keen perceptions, heightened by an occasional plunge into his battle fire, allowed him to follow from so far back they would never be able to see him, much less hear him.

But now he had caught up, because now he had to decide why he had followed them. He pulled his tricorn down over his forehead and hunched into the protection of his coat's tall collar.

Kill Mactalde—that had been his best idea.

But now, staring upriver at the glow of a hundred campfires, the hope died and rotted. Even if he could have done it without undermining the only reason for everything he'd just sacrificed, he'd waited too long. One Cherazim might have had a fighting chance of dropping into the midst of a Koraudian platoon and killing Mactalde before being killed himself. But perhaps another full battalion had been waiting across the river. The Koraudians would escort their sovereign lord home in style.

The wind from across the river filled his ears with their midnight celebrations. And why not? Hadn't their vaunted general come back to them from the dead?

"I still don't understand what we're doing here," Raz grumbled. "I'm hungry."

Pitch shivered. "The wind shouldn't be this cold."

Rievers were worse than useless on a hunt. Their attention span was too short, and they ran out of patience and silence far too soon to be useful. But he couldn't very well leave them behind. Rievers chose the Cherazii who would care for them, and it was an honored responsibility to make certain they were protected. Of late, he hadn't done too well at that either.

His stomach turned over. Only a few weeks ago, he had been one of the Cherazii's proudest sons. A Tarn. A Keeper of the Orimere. He had spent his entire life pledged to and preparing for the day when he would be called to protect the dreamstone and deliver it into the hands of the Searcher. This was the life the God of all had chosen for him, and it was a life he had embraced.

When the last Gifted had turned rogue and the Cherazii left Lael in protest against the king's handling of the situation, Orias had yet clung to hope. The God of all was in control. He had a plan and a purpose, and the worlds could not turn except upon that plan.

But what had happened last week—what Orias himself had chosen to do—could not be a part of any plan. The God of all should have struck him dead before such a thing could come to pass. Even better, He should have delivered the Cherazii Himself, so Orias would have had no need to take matters into his own hands.

But He hadn't.

Instead, He had left Orias to pick up the scattered pieces of his faith, his life, and the world. Were they pieces that had any worth in being put back together?

"Why are we waiting here?" Raz asked. "If we're gonna ride in there and kill all the blokes, let's get it over with. If we die, at least we'll be sainted. *Anybody* who dies on an empty stomach should be sainted."

Pitch's voice whispered behind Orias's ear: "Why did you do it?" He had been asking that question ever since Chris had brought Mactalde across.

This was the first time Orias answered. "I had to." The words scraped in his throat.

The wind blew on, and the joy of the Koraudians pummeled his ears.

Pitch hesitated a long moment. Then he leaned forward, and one little hand patted Orias's shoulder. "I forgive you."

The wrong wasn't Pitch's to forgive, but Orias's heart lurched anyway. If only it were that simple.

Raz poked his other shoulder. "Well, *are* we going to kill them?"

It was tempting: to die a martyr's death by making right his heinous wrong in one glorious swoop. But he couldn't.

So long as Mactalde lived, so did the Cherazii. From now on, there would be no more attacks like the one against the caravan. Rotoss had promised him that, and Orias had no choice but to believe it. The Cherazii no longer had the numbers to defend themselves. If they were ever to become the feared people they once had been, they needed a reprieve long enough to marshal their strength. And he had to believe he had given them that chance.

He lifted his reins to go. "No. Not tonight."

"Wise decision, blue." From the windswept swirl of the long grass, a Koraudian rose with a rifle propped in both hands. Crouched on the horse's opposite side, Dougal hissed and spat.

Orias's dirk was in his hand before the stranger had finished speaking. How long had this man crouched there, listening to Raz's and Pitch's babbling? He had to have been there when they rode up, else Orias would have heard his approach.

"My guess'd be you're the Tarn, eh?" The Koraudian moved a little closer, though still out of reach of Orias's sword. "My guess is you'd be hunting for Lord Mactalde. And my guess is he'd be happy to meet you. Not many of us get the pleasure of seeing a humbled Cherazim." The cloud-streaked moon glinted off his grin. He gestured upstream with his rifle. "Move along. And remember, I'd just as soon bring in a dead blue as a live one." His glance shifted to Raz and Pitch. "And maybe Lord Mactalde'd like a couple of Rievers to toast on a stick for brekkers."

Raz hawked his spit, and Orias nudged the horse forward, out of range. Battle fire churned in the center of his brain. He could leap at the Koraudian, rifle or no rifle, and twist his head from his body. Let him fight, let him die. Let it all be over.

But he didn't move. He had brought himself this far. What

mattered a few more minutes? He kept his horse to a walk. He didn't sheathe his dirk, and he didn't soften the proud set of his shoulders.

The Koraudian trudged through the grass behind him, and the hydraulic system in his rifle purred a constant warning.

"Orias." Pitch gave his shoulder a little shake. "What are you doing?"

Raz muttered, "Does he look like he knows what he's doing?"

Orias had to agree.

They forded the river in a flurry of splashes and clambered onto the far bank, where a hundred golden campfires glinted through the trees. The raucous clanking of the two-handed keysaras, a musical instrument popular in Koraud for bewildering reasons, accompanied the battle songs belted out by a hundred voices. The smell of roast zajele and boiling gasa stew mingled with the smoke and the crisp scent of the hespera trees.

As they neared the campfires, the sentries jolted to attention and snapped their rifles to their shoulders. Orias's captor shouted to them, and they backed off. A few glared in suspicion. Most jeered.

"A new recruit!"

"A little blue come crawling to beg mercy while he still can!"

Pitch trembled with pent-up fury. "You cowards! We don't beg and we don't crawl!"

"Hush," Orias said.

"What, and you're not thinking the same thing?" Raz demanded.

Orias crawled. Orias begged. He had no defense.

They emerged into the riot of light and laughter that was the camp headquarters. He reined to a stop. At each campfire, one by one, the conversations and songs ceased. Men turned to stare at him, most of them slack-jawed, more than a few tight with sudden fear.

In the middle of the opening, at a campfire next to Glelarn Rotoss, one man rose.

Orias had been not quite thirteen years old when he had stood in the palace courtyard in Glen Arden and watched Mactalde bow his head to the axeman's block. He had seen a thin, handsome young man, barely into his twenties then, kneel and brace himself against the block. He had seen the axe fall, and he had believed in his child's heart he would never again see this man. The invaders had been defeated; the war had been won. But somehow, peace had escaped Lael.

And now Orias again faced Faolan Mactalde.

The sovereign of Koraud was older now, thicker through the chest and shoulders. His face glowed with a health he had never enjoyed in this world. But the laughing, lying, bewitching smile hadn't changed. It was the kind of smile you saw from a man before he stabbed you in the back.

"Well, well." His clipped accent carried across the camp. "We weren't expecting such exalted visitors this evening. Join us, Master Tarn."

The Koraudian who had found Orias raised his rifle. "Drop your weapons."

Orias kept his gaze on Mactalde. "No." He had surrendered his weapons, his dignity, and his pride once before—to the worm Glelarn Rotoss. He would not do it again.

The rifle snapped to the Koraudian's shoulder, but Mactalde raised a hand. "It's all right, soldier. Master Tarn may join us tonight as a friend. Come forward please."

The Koraudian didn't lower the rifle. "Put the dirk away."

That Orias did. He withered the Koraudian with a glance, then kneed his horse forward. The men stared at him, silent, their hands on their weapons. Most of them had probably never seen a Cherazim they hadn't been commanded to kill.

Beside Mactalde's neat beard and clean leather doublet, Rotoss, in his feathered hat and rumpled tabard, looked a scraggly crow next to a hunting kelter. Like a crow, his eyes glittered, black and cunning.

Orias quivered. It was all he could do to restrain himself from whipping his dirk free once more and leaping from his horse to plunge the blade into Rotoss's chest. *So die all worms*, he would whisper in the man's face as he slumped to the ground.

But not tonight.

Mactalde turned to his army and gestured to Orias with a gloved hand. "We find ourselves with a strange guest in our midst. An enemy, at first glance. A Cherazim, who like all Cherazii stands opposed to our quest for conquest and freedom."

A rumble passed through the men.

"But when I introduce to you Orias Tarn, Keeper of the Orimere, I tell you I am introducing an ally. So, for tonight, let us put aside our prejudices and welcome someone without whom I would not have been able to return to you." He reached behind him, and an orderly handed him a silver goblet stamped in black with the Koraudian eagle. "I toast him." He raised the glass.

Orias stiffened. So this was how Mactalde twisted the knife?

Mactalde's laughing eyes met Orias's as he addressed his men. "Will you toast him with me?"

They could not refuse him. Wasn't he their beloved leader, Mactalde the Resurrected? What cared they if he asked them to toast a hated Cherazim? Tonight, they would do anything for their lord.

They clambered to their feet in a great clatter of arms and armor and raised their glasses. "To the Cherazim!"

Orias could hardly breathe. He had colluded with his enemies. Now they hailed him for it. Wasn't it a reward he deserved?

Mactalde tossed back a swallow and turned to Orias. "Share our fire, Master Tarn? The night is cold for the season." He glanced at the orderly. "Get him some venison. And a beaker of cranok."

"We don't want any of your rotten food," Pitch said.

"And some for his charming companions as well."

Orias dismounted, the Rievers clinging to his back, and he waited as they jumped to the ground. Pitch filled his little fist with a handful of Orias's long coat. Raz stomped along behind.

At the fire, Orias squatted, a Riever on either side and his lion at his back. The tip of the broadsword strapped across his shoulders bumped the ground. Oh, to be able to free it from its baldric and lay waste to the whole blood-sodden camp! How many Cherazii had died at the hands of these men? How many of Lael's soldiers would die in the weeks to come? Maybe even the Gifted and the Searcher.

The orderly brought the trencher of venison and a beaker dripping red with cranok. Orias transferred the trencher to the ground in front of Raz. He tilted the cranok to his face and downed half the potent liquor in two swallows. It tasted like lemons and iron filings, and its bitter heat burned all the way to his empty stomach.

He lowered the cup and met first Rotoss's smirking gaze, then Mactalde's knowing one. With a flick of his wrist, he tossed the remainder of the cranok into the fire. The flames leapt, showering sparks all around.

Both men recoiled from the heat, and Rotoss swore. Orias didn't move, even as the sparks bit into his face and hands. Likely, neither Mactalde nor Rotoss would know the gesture signified eternal enmity.

Rotoss slapped at his already soiled red tabard. "What's the matter, blue? Our cranok isn't to your liking?"

"Nay. And neither is your company."

"You prefer skinny rodents, no doubt?"

Raz spoke through a mouthful. "Better than fat murderers. A murderer is a bad enough blighter, but a fat one . . . bah!"

Mactalde looked at Orias. "I have always wondered why the Cherazii should ally themselves so disproportionately." The tilt of his chin indicated the Rievers.

"It is a custom of old. And the Cherazii do not go back on their covenants."

"Indeed not. Are you implying I do?"

Ah, here it was. *This* was why he had come then—to make certain the bargain for which he had sacrificed so much would be honored by Mactalde as well as Rotoss.

"I imply only that it would surprise me not."

Mactalde still smiled, but he watched Orias like a lion would watch its prey, judging, calculating, taunting, waiting. "You forget, Master Tarn, *I* have made no covenants with you."

Could it be as simple as that? As blatant as that? The muscles in his arms tightened. He pushed to his feet, and his hand fell to the dirk. Pitch and Raz snatched their stilettos from their belts and stood at the ready.

Behind him, men scrambled away from their fires and drew their weapons. The buzz of firearms filled the clearing.

Rotoss drew his sword. "You filthy fool. I should have killed you back in Lael."

Only Mactalde remained sitting, a hand propped on either booted knee. "You're short-tempered, my friend. And you wonder why the Cherazii have earned so many enemies? Sit down." He pulled at Rotoss's elbow. "All of you."

Orias didn't move.

Mactalde sipped from his goblet. "*I* have made no covenants with you." He paused, his silence pregnant. "But I understand Rotoss has."

Orias's heartbeat thudded against his ribcage with—what? hope?

"I will respect his decision." Mactalde smiled. "So you may be at ease."

Orias stared down at him. His breath came too fast. This was all he could ask for. If he could walk away from here with such a promise, then at least he could believe he had accomplished some good.

"Then you promise peace to the Cherazii?"

"Indeed."

Relief flooded his veins, like the first cool torrent of rain. All was not in vain, then. Thank the God of all, his sacrifice hadn't been in vain.

He lowered his head in a nod. It was the closest he would allow himself to come in gratitude to this man. He snapped his fingers at Dougal and turned back to his horse. He would leave, he would ride. He would be a stranger from his people henceforth. But he would find some measure of peace after tonight.

"Where are you going?" Mactalde's words were as sweet and smooth as overripe dassberries.

Orias turned to see the glimmer in Mactalde's eye. The flicker of hope in his heart sputtered. He didn't answer the question. He just waited.

At Mactalde's side, Rotoss snorted a laugh.

"You see—" Mactalde sat on his velvet campstool like a king on his throne, "—there is one more condition I must place on this pact of ours. You must stay with me." His smile deepened. "And you must fight with me. A Cherazim at my side—that thought pleases me."

The world turned to silence around Orias. And so there was no hope after all. Not for him. Not in this life. Not in any life.

Not after what he'd done.

Pitch tugged at Orias's coat. "Don't. Don't do it."

Mactalde set his goblet on a nearby table and rose. The fire lit his face from the bottom up. "You've come so far on your quest to save your people. I don't think you can abandon them now."

And the gut-wrenching truth was . . . he couldn't.

22

THE WAY CHRIS figured it, the Orimere had to be good for something other than ruining worlds and getting him in trouble. In the small palace library, where he and Allara had been meeting for the less strenuous of their training sessions, he scrutinized what he had brought over from his world.

They called this the small library, since there was one about three times as big down on the ground floor, but the comparison was the only thing that made it small. Like all the rooms on the third story, its ceiling soared. Stairs near the door hugged the wall on the way up to a balcony that ran around the length of the room and effectively split it into two levels.

The only light in the room came from the iron-wrought chandelier high overhead and three stained glass windows near the eaves. Whoever had built this castle obviously hadn't been too enamored of the sun. Shadows lurked in every corner and the library, of all places, was the worst.

He was beginning to think he should have chosen a different room for his presentation. Or maybe just skipped the idea altogether, especially since he had no guarantee Allara wouldn't take it entirely wrong anyway. He stepped back from the round table at the far end of the room and scrutinized the basket of oranges and the bouquet of white orchids.

Last night, he'd dug the Orimere out of its polished wooden box in the back of his dressing room armoire and gone to sleep with it buzzing in his hand. He wanted to get Allara something. He couldn't explain exactly why. After almost two weeks, they were thankfully past talking about accusations and apologies, so these token gifts from his side of the worlds weren't exactly peace offerings. More like the overtures of friendship.

For the last two weeks, after his pre-breakfast fencing bout with Quinnon and before the equitation classes after lunch and the fire-arms practice before dinner, he and Allara had met in the library for a few hours of politics, geography, and social manners. She was a good teacher, calm and patient, and she never brought up Mactalde. Maybe she'd realized, on the morning of their swordfight, that the door was closed and she had no choice but to move forward.

She was still holding herself back. It wasn't that she seemed to actually dislike him. It was more she didn't think she could afford to be friends with him. Based on past experiences, that probably wasn't an unreasonable assumption on her part. But she was practically the only person he knew in this world. It would be nice if they could be friends.

At any rate, he wanted to thank her for her help. Also, the look on her face—whatever it was—would undoubtedly be worth seeing.

He reevaluated the oranges. Maybe he should just save those for another day. He leaned in to pick up the basket. Behind him, the door opened. He set the basket down and turned around, arms crossed, embarrassed despite himself. So much for presentation.

"Morning," he said.

Allara's eyebrows knit. "Good morning."

Today, she wore a white satin gown with a bodice that laced all the way up the front and rose to a two-inch collar around the back of her neck. Her dark hair was piled high and held in place in the front with a simple silver comb.

She had a kind of effortless beauty that wasn't so much a result of her features as it was a simple unaffectedness and an inner dignity. He'd started noticing about the time she'd stopped wanting to kill him.

She leaned back against the door to latch it, then came forward. "What's going on? You haven't gotten tired of our lessons and de-cided to burn all the books, have you?"

"What makes you think I'd do that?"

She raised a shoulder. "I did it with my tutor's books when I was young."

"You did?" Somehow that wasn't surprising. He cleared his throat and hooked a thumb toward the table. "Actually, I thought you might like to see something from my world."

She stopped next to him. Her eyes flitted from the orchids in their glass vase to the basket of shining oranges. The edge of her mouth tugged in something that was *almost* a smile. "Your world?"

"The flowers are orchids." He attempted to slip his hands into his pockets, only to remember these trousers didn't have pockets. "Maybe you already have them around here, but I hadn't seen anything like them."

"No." Her fingertips caressed a petal. "Nothing like them. They're beautiful. And—" she looked from the basket to him, and this time a definite sparkle lit her face, "—snow oranges?"

She liked it then. He breathed out. "Not quite. Esta said something about you liking oranges. But these are different from yours. Bigger and the flavor's stronger. Thought maybe you'd like to try them."

Her expression was unreadable. "You used the Orimere to bring these across?"

Here it came after all. "Yeah. But that's inside the rules, right?"

"Why are you giving me these?"

"Why not?" He grinned. With any luck, he'd melt the ice princess after all. "I wanted to do something for you. For everything. This was all I knew to do."

She studied the table again, then cast him a sidelong glance. "And what do you expect in return?"

Still suspicious then. She was a politician's daughter after all. "A smile would be nice."

That caught her off guard. She looked away, disquieted. When she looked back, she wasn't quite smiling. But her eyes had softened, and the press of her lips said she had to try *not* to smile.

"Thank you." Her voice was low, husky almost. "I've always wanted to see your world. To see it properly, I mean, and not just blurry images in the lake. I suppose this is the closest I'll ever come. So thank you."

He smiled back. "You're welcome."

She held his gaze for a moment, as if she wanted to say something else. Then she broke contact and turned back to her seat at the table.

Head down, she reached for the big book of maps they were using to study Lael and its border countries: Koraud, Illise, and Rivale. She opened the book and riffled through the faded green and red of the maps to find the one they had left off discussing yesterday.

He sat down across from her, caught the glance she cast at the oranges, and pulled one from the basket for her and started peeling it. From the looks of things around here, princesses seemed to get a lot of bowing and scraping and yes-your-ladyshipping, but not much genuine or spontaneous kindness. That ever-present haggard look in the back of her eyes and the way she was always rubbing at that crooked finger of hers said she needed a little genuine spontaneity.

He tossed the peeling back into the basket, split the orange with a faint puff of sweet-smelling mist, and handed her half. "So what are we learning today that's going to help me bump off evil warlords?"

He craned his head to read the map. His recently acquired grasp of their alphabet system was enough to at least recognize the names of the countries they'd been studying. "Koraud." He sat back and tweaked off an orange wedge. "I've been wondering about that. You talk about Koraud being its own kingdom, but you said it pays tribute to Lael. Because of what happened during the war?"

She took the orange and settled back in her chair, her wide sleeves spread over the armrests. Her face was smooth and unruffled again. Back to business, then. But her fingers were slow as they peeled back the first wedge of the orange. "Yes, more or less." She bit the tip off the wedge and savored it.

"Good?" he asked.

"Yes." For just a second, she almost looked happy. It was a good look. "They're even better than snow oranges." She swallowed and returned to the map. "You have to understand the Koraudian people are fiercely independent. They live in the mountains and eke their living out of the mines and timberlands. Not to generalize, but they love it and they're proud of it. And most of them have always disliked Lael on general purposes. Our position on the coast gives us unrivaled access to the speed and efficiency of oversea export and import. Everyone else on the continent has to go through us."

"Which means Lael has all the money."

"Not all, certainly. But eventually it all surfaces here one way or another. So even before intermarriages and treaties united the other kingdoms under us, we were the de facto capital of the continent."

He sat back, chewing. The long-sleeved jerkin he was wearing squeaked against the leather cover on the chair. "Until Harrison arrived."

She shook her head. "What happened can't honestly be blamed solely on either Harrison or Mactalde. I believe Mactalde would have invaded even had Harrison never come. And Harrison would have tried to steal the throne from my father even if he had never met Mactalde. But, as it was, they were the spark to each other's tinder. They fed off each other—in more ways than one in the end."

He gnawed his lip. "So if this does turn into another war, what kind of odds are we looking at?"

She shrugged. "We've known something like this was coming, with or without Mactalde, for the last twelvemonth. But it takes time to communicate and assemble troop movements over such a great distance. If Mactalde strikes soon—and he's wise enough to know he must—he'll catch Lael at perhaps only half our full strength."

Outside the room, footsteps tromped down the hall. A rap on the door was followed by the high-pitched voice of a woman, and the door opened before Allara could respond.

Lady Esta tiptoed in at double-time, skirt held in front of her like a sail. "My lady, forgive me." She ducked a curtsy. "But young Yemas here tells me we have a bit of a situation outside."

Guardsman Canard Yemas stopped in the middle of the room to salute Allara. He was a narrow-faced kid of nineteen or twenty with soulful eyes that didn't look like they missed much. He had seemed particularly interested in Chris's arrival. More than once, Chris had caught the kid watching him with a strange expression.

"There's a Nateros demonstration in the street, my lady," Yemas said.

Her mouth tightened, but she didn't move. "That's hardly news. They've staged a demonstration every day since the Gifted's arrival."

"This is a bit different, I'm afraid."

Esta cast a long glance at the orchids and oranges, cast a longer one at Chris, then glided to a stop next to Allara's chair. "Crofton Steadman is asking for a private audience with you and the Gifted."

Allara sat up straight and pushed the remainder of her orange back onto the table. "*Och.* I suppose it was only a matter of time."

"Who's Steadman?" Chris asked.

"More or less Nateros's spokesman." She rose. "Where's Captain Quinnon?"

Yemas backed out of her way. "He's aware of the situation, my lady."

"And is he coming?"

"Yes, of course. However, time is of the essence right now if we don't want them tearing apart the Vesper district."

She started rubbing at her finger. Indecision twisted her face.

Chris stood up. "What does he want?"

She shook her head. "I don't know. Nothing good I'm sure."

"Can't hurt to talk to him, right? Maybe we could work out some kind of compromise to get him to calm his people down."

"Not likely. He's a fanatic. His kind doesn't calm down."

Yemas ducked his head in an apologetic bow. "Forgive me, my lady, but I think it would be best if you spoke to him. You'll be perfectly safe. And perhaps what he has to say will be worth your while."

She took a breath, glanced at Chris, then let it out. "All right. Have him escorted into the throne room for an audience. And make sure Captain Quinnon's informed."

Esta plucked at Allara's gown, straightening folds. "I'll send for your crown." She scowled critically at Chris. "And I'll have his man-servant fetch him a formal cape and a dress sword."

Allara waved her off. "Never mind. It doesn't matter. That sort of thing won't impress Steadman anyway."

"Don't be ridiculous. You're representing the sovereignty of Lael. You're going to do it properly." Esta whisked off.

Chris had to admit he'd be happy to have the sword. "Any big protocol issues you want to warn me about?"

Allara started toward the door, her face grim. "Mostly just try not to make him want to kill you any faster than he already does."

———

Réon Couteau's throne room rose through all three of the castle's stories. The elaborate vaulted ceiling was almost lost in the shadows high above. Dusty shafts of light speared from the round stained glass windows amid the eaves and crisscrossed the black and white checkerboard floor. At the far end of the room, three ebony thrones sat side by side, the middle one raised eight inches. Thick, waxy candles on waist-high pillars surrounded the thrones and flickered both light and shadow.

"Cheerful place." Chris sat in one of the outer thrones. "Did you design it to strike fear in supplicants' hearts?"

"Why not?" Allara sat in the other outside chair. She let Esta spread her skirt, then motioned her away. The ridges in her cheek stood out in a firm white line. "If they can't be reverent, at least let them be a little afraid."

He sat on the throne's edge and kept one hand on the scrollwork of his rapier hilt. He tugged at the red velvet-lined cape Parry had tied over one shoulder and under the other. He didn't feel reverent or afraid, just slightly preposterous.

"Why three thrones?"

She stared ahead. "Considering you're sitting in one, isn't it obvious? Réon Couteau is the domain of the Gifted and the Searchers as much as, if not more so, than the kings." She clenched her fists in her lap. "Don't say anything unless you have to."

At the end of the room, liveried footmen swept open the arched doors. The dozen Guardsmen who lined the room snapped to attention and stamped their left boot heels to the floor in unison. Their noisy tradition was probably as much to remind guests of their presence as to respectfully acknowledge them.

Escorted by Yemas, and not Quinnon, who apparently hadn't considered the meeting worth his time, the Nateros delegation of three men entered the room.

The slender man who walked at their front wore a knee-length white coat that contrasted sharply with the dark glare of his eyes and the black hair curling past his ears. He clasped his hands in front of him, and his face was soft, marred only by the twist of a scar in his upper lip. He looked less like a fanatic and more like a wistful monk.

He glanced at Allara when he entered, but his eyes stayed on Chris all the way up the room. His expression wasn't threatening, so much as curious. But it never flinched. It was the look of one man taking the size of the other and making certain the other knew it.

Chris looked right back, even though he wasn't entirely sure *what* he was looking at. For now, Allara's fear of Steadman was good enough reason to be more than a little wary.

At the end of the green carpet that stopped ten feet short of the thrones, Steadman stopped and faced Allara. He didn't do the thumb-and-forefinger salute, but he inclined his head.

"Searcher. Thank you for granting me an audience." He spoke with a slight lisp, probably thanks to the scar.

Allara sat painfully straight. Her expression was impenetrable, every bit the iron-faced royal beneath the green jewels that tipped her crown's circlet. "Let us hope doing so will end these demonstrations in the streets."

He smiled, gently. "We can hope." Then he turned to Chris. "I am honored to stand in the presence of one who has seen both sides of our worlds."

Chris wasn't sure what to say to that, so he just nodded. Nateros was supposed to hate the Gifted, not be honored to stand in the same room.

"I welcome you personally," Steadman said, "and as the spokes-man for Nateros, I welcome you, too, on the behalf of an eager people. We're not certain what you may have heard of us." The fin-gers of one hand rose from where they still clasped each other and gestured briefly to Allara. "But we wish to tell you we embrace your advent with great hope and expectation."

"You're right, that's not exactly what I've been hearing." Chris kept his voice light.

"I apologize for any misunderstanding." Steadman offered a smile. "Nateros has nothing against the Gifted. You are dragged from one world to this, with no choice in the matter. Unlike those who do the dragging." He offered another faint gesture to Allara, who shifted forward in her seat, as if about to rise. "Indeed, we recognize the power of the Gifted to change the times and to work great good for society." His voice was soft and low, mellifluous, but powered from deep in his throat. "You've come to us unwitting, and we forgive you for that, even though you are an accursed second. But now that you're here, we entreat you to use your influence to aid in our mis-sion of freeing Lael."

Chris leaned back in the throne and tried to seem at ease. "Why are you so opposed to the Searcher?"

"You, of all people, need ask that?" Emotion rumbled Steadman's voice.

"I, of all people, know the Searcher doesn't have any more control over my being here than I do."

Steadman stepped forward, one foot off the green carpet. "Why is it that those of you who are entrenched in these antiquated creeds of autocracy—" his arm swept open to include Allara, "—are determined to hoard power into the fallen religion of the dreams and your so-called God of all?"

"I'm not hoarding power. I'm just here trying to do a job. You really think an internal schism is such a great idea right now?"

Steadman's smile faded. "You have much to learn from us, just as perhaps you may have much to offer. Allow me to say what I have come here to say: Join us."

Allara stood so fast she was lucky she didn't fall over. "If this is all you've come to say, then you may leave." Her face burned white, and her nostrils flared.

Steadman ignored her and raised both hands to Chris in entreaty. "I tell you now that no one has the power to stop this coming war except the followers of Nateros. We are the voice of the people! Join us, help us. Bring freedom of mind as well as body to this land. If even a Gifted were to speak out against the old ways, everyone would see their worthlessness!"

Allara snapped her fingers at Yemas. When the Guardsman didn't move from his post by the door, she stepped down from the throne dais and into Steadman's line of sight. "How dare you bring your lies here?"

"They're not lies." He held Chris's gaze.

"They're madness!" Allara said. "You fly in the face of the sacred traditions and expect to be rewarded with peace. But you will find peace with neither God nor man!"

Steadman whirled on her and took the two steps necessary to bring them face to face. "You vixen. You witch. You dare talk to me of the sacred when you twist tradition to conjure forth an unholy second Gifted in your lifetime?"

The Guardsmen finally started forward. The room hummed with their drawn pistols. But Chris was the closest. He reached Steadman and clapped a hand on his shoulder. "Back off. Haven't you heard of royal distance?"

Steadman glared at Allara. "Your day has come. The Searchers hold thrall in Lael no longer."

"I have never held thrall! But if you reject the traditions the God of all has given us, you reject Him—and that you cannot be pardoned for."

Steadman laughed and then, without warning, spat at her. Chris let go of him just long enough to punch him in the face.

Steadman staggered into two Guardsmen, who hauled him to his feet, arms twisted behind his back. "The dungeon, my lady?" one asked.

She shook her head. "Let him go. He hasn't done anything."

Steadman blinked and coughed. "I'll see you again, Searcher." He looked at Chris. "And you too. Perhaps you'll be more sensible about your loyalties by then." He turned and walked out without resisting his Guardsmen escort.

Yemas hovered behind, brows knit over his soulful eyes. "I'm sorry, my lady. He meant no harm, I'm sure."

Chris rubbed his knuckles. "He meant a lot of things."

Yemas watched Steadman leave the room. "I'm glad you met with him. He says many things of sense. But I am sorry it ended this way." He turned and hurried after his men.

Chris watched him go. "Better keep an eye on him. If I didn't know better, I'd say you've got a sympathizer on your hands." He turned to her. "You all right?"

She breathed out. The tense expression on her face was more one of anger than fear. "I'm fine." She looked at the hand he was kneading. The corner of her mouth lifted. "You didn't have to hit him."

"He was out of line."

In her hand, something flashed: a tiny pistol. Maybe she hadn't been as endangered as he thought.

"You always carry that?"

"I always carry something." She lifted the wide part of her sleeve, from the elbow down, and revealed a spring-loaded forearm holster. "People have tried to assassinate me before." She was matter of fact about it, but she didn't look at him. She was embarrassed people tried to kill her?

She fitted the pistol back onto its metal track, then started for the doors. "Where's Quinnon?"

Chris untied his ridiculous cape and followed, still flexing his knuckles.

They found Quinnon entering from the courtyard. He hooked a thumb over his shoulder to where the Guardsmen were just taking Steadman out through the front door. "You want to tell me what's going on? What are Crofton Steadman and his whelps doing here?"

Allara frowned. "I thought you knew."

If Quinnon's temperature rose a few more notches, he would start blowing steam out of his nostrils. "I knew he was *outside*. Not that he was in the same blithering room as you. I was on my way up to talk to you about it, but I got held up at the stables. Don't ever do that again."

"It's all right." She glanced back at Chris. "I was taken care of."

23

ALLARA SAT ON the rough slate floor in the gymnasium and retied the laces that ran all the way up her boot to just below her knee.

In front of her, Quinnon scrutinized Chris's shooting stance. "You're catching on to this firearms business faster than you did the swords. You had a little more practice with that, did you?"

"My dad was a cop—a policeman. He taught me." Chris tilted his hand and scrutinized the heavy chewser pistol. "I learned on a Glock. Nothing like this."

The chewser model was an older gun that carried its hydraulic converter in a thick cylinder under the barrel. It was bulky, loud, and likely enough to break the shooter's thumb if he pulled back the hammer the wrong way. But it was compatible with a wide range of ammunition types—everything from snub-nosed slugs to knuckle-sized buzz-saws to half-span stilettos—and it had the stopping power to take down a Koraudian lion. It was the firearm of choice for Quinnon and many other Guardsmen.

Chris had taken a few minutes to adjust to its bulk, then shredded the leather target set up in front of the waterfall.

He grinned back at Allara. "Think you can best that one?"

"I won't even try. Chewsers are too large for me to handle." She knotted off the lace on her boot and let Quinnon help her up. "I prefer something sleeker."

She selected a straitquin pistol from the nearby rack.

Straitquins were light and elegant, with a slim slug-only barrel and the hydraulics tucked away in the slight curve of the grip. The ivory grip of her personal favorite was carved with an elaborate seraphin rooster, the hydraulic vent holes placed strategically so the light shone through the bird's eyes and open beak.

She traded with Chris. He took a second to examine the gun, but by this time he was familiar with the basic workings of Lael's firearms. He flicked the tiny lever that turned on the hydraulic system and waited a second while it powered up. With the waterfall pumping mist into the room, the hydraulics had access to all the moisture they needed. He extended his arms and braced one fist inside the other.

"Top left corner." His practice with the chewser had already torn up the bull's-eye.

He squeezed the trigger, and the hydraulics' faint hum was replaced with the blast and gush of the steam-powered slug. It slammed into the corner of the target and toppled the framework.

He tossed a grin over his shoulder. "How's that?"

She clapped twice. "Too bad conceit isn't the only requirement for survival."

Quinnon handed Chris a slug for reloading. "You'd be immortal."

"Aw, now, you should be happy I'm a fast learner."

He clicked off the hydraulics and used the pistol's reloading rod to fit the slug down its barrel. Then he flipped the pistol around and handed it back to Allara, grip first, with a little bow and another twinkle in his eye.

"Makes you look like a good teacher, right?" He winked.

She busied herself hanging the pistol on the rack.

Sometimes the things he did and said and the way he looked at her left her feeling more like the student than the teacher. She had grown up in the royal court, where people fawned over her, men courted her, and flattery was a language of its own. She had never been at a loss for how to respond.

But from the moment he had ridden into her life, Chris Redston had thrown her off balance. Now that anger was no longer the most obvious response, she didn't know quite *how* to respond to him.

Aside from their audience with Steadman the other day, life had been calm enough lately. Their days had rocked into a rhythm of fencing, studying, shooting, and riding, and she had to admit Chris had proven a model student. He worked hard, never complained, and between what his body was remembering from this world and what his brain brought over from the other, he was living up to his claim to be a Guardsman. He was turning out to be a better shot than she was and just as good a rider. His fencing still wasn't up to speed, but the raw talent was there, if only he would stop over-thinking.

Any day now, her father would summon them to Glen Arden. Mactalde wouldn't wait much longer to strike, and her father would want to formally acknowledge the Gifted before leaving for battle.

If she observed Chris solely from the perspective of a Searcher gauging her Gifted, he could have been worse at this point—much worse. In another few days, he would be as ready as she could hope to make him in such a short period of time. Any Searcher would be pleased.

But the objectivity of a Searcher was starting to prove elusive. He kept her off balance, and she hated it. But she couldn't quite persuade herself to hate *him*. He wasn't the blackguard she had originally convinced herself he was. He had seemed to mean it when he'd said he was taking full responsibility for what had happened. Time would bear out the truth, of course, but he hadn't faltered so far.

And he wasn't like Harrison Garnett, who had always despised her, feared her, even. When Chris looked at her, she had the eerie feeling he was seeing past all her defenses, straight to the core of her, and whatever it was he saw there—the anger, the fear, the weakness—he accepted it without judgment.

Quinnon bent to pick up the ammunition pouches and the rifles they had been working with earlier. "It'll be time for dinner in less'n an hour. We'll quit for the night, so you can get cleaned up and work on some more of that etiquette."

"You ought to join in," Chris said. "You might learn something."

Quinnon didn't even deign to glare at him. "You've still got a ways to go yourself from what I've been seeing. Bring that lot over here." He carried the equipment back to the racks and piled it for the page-boys to put away.

Chris followed him, toward Allara, and she moved away. She was starting to like Chris Redston, and every preservation instinct in her body demanded she fight it.

"I'm going up." She pulled her sleeveless tunic's hood over her sweat-dampened hair and resisted a shiver. The flush of body heat from their fencing match had faded, and the outside cold seeped into her bones.

He half-turned. "If you wait, I'll come with you."

"No." The word was out almost before she had time to consider it. She pasted on the smiling façade of an experienced courtier. "Thank you, but I'm chilled and I want to speak to Esta about dinner."

Puzzlement passed across his face, but he let it go with a shrug.

She turned and forced herself to hold to a stately walk all the way across the gymnasium to the stairs. As soon as she was around the corner, she bounded up the circular staircase two steps at a time.

By the time she'd run all the way up to the third story, she was sweating and huffing. When she banged into her dressing room and cast the hood back from her head, Esta looked up from her needlework in alarm. "What's the matter with you? Are the Koraudians here?"

Allara waved her off. "I just felt like a run."

"That's hardly befitting your position."

"No one saw me." She started unfastening her tunic's buttons. "Will you draw me a bath?"

Esta made a face and took her time sticking the needle back into her cloth. Then she rose slowly, straightened her wig, and started across the room to ring for the maids. "Sometimes I just don't know what to make of you. You're more hoyden than princess."

"Don't fret yourself. No one knows what to make of me." Except perhaps Chris Redston.

She stalked to the nearest closet and scowled at the dozens of gowns. The last thing she wanted to do was dress up and go down there and teach that man one more rule of etiquette. The way things had been going, she was likely to drop her fork every time he looked at her. And if he winked at her again, she'd slap him.

A flash of white caught her eye, and she turned to the vase of flowers he had brought from his world. Orchids, he called them. The white petals spread around hearts of deep pink, like exotic butterflies. They were beautiful.

She walked over and stroked a finger up the underside of a petal. She still didn't know exactly why he'd done it. Part of her wished he hadn't, and part of her loved that he had, and part of her just wanted to chuck the whole lot out the window. Kindnesses were dangerous. They shattered defenses and left the receiver naked and vulnerable.

If only Eroll were here. He would know what to tell her. He understood this sort of blather far better than she did. He'd probably think it was all some great joke and tease her mercilessly, but at least he would make sense of it.

She closed her eyes and tried not to wonder where he was. If he were in danger, if he came back hurt in any way, she *would* revive her anger toward Chris.

In the meantime, she went back to the closet, sorted through a few gowns, rejected most of them, then pulled out one made of green velvet with a sand-colored over-gown laced loosely across the bodice. She almost put it back too, then slammed the closet door and tossed the gown onto the chaise. She would wear what she always wore and she would *not* fall prey to womanly fussings over whether or not her male dinner guest would find it attractive. She didn't need to be attractive to Chris Redston.

In fact, that was the last thing she needed.

By the time Allara rose from the sunken tub—heated from the coals in the recessed chamber just beneath it—she had completely forgotten to speak to Esta about dinner. Fortunately, it turned out as well as it always did without her well-intentioned interference: a chilled sopple soup, herb and cheese tartlets, baked randar root, seraphin hens stuffed with sweet nuts and marinated in a wine and cream sauce, and a goblet of dassberry syrup for dessert.

When they finished, Quinnon excused himself for his nightly conference with the head of the Guard, and Allara led Esta and Chris into the Red Salon, the only room in the palace she could honestly say she liked. The servants had already lit the globes on the elaborate gold pillars and the fire in the great hearth. The light flickered against the red tapestries that framed landscape windows and their glittering glimpse of the city.

Esta sat on the settee in front of the fire, spread her skirts around her, folded her hands, and promptly fell asleep.

Allara gritted her teeth and prodded at the fire with a poker. This was the first evening she and Chris had been left alone. Of course the one moment she actually wanted someone around for moral support, Esta abandoned her. Quinnon sometimes spent hours talking with the Guard, so she couldn't rely on his appearance either. What was a Searcher supposed to talk about with her Gifted if they weren't at work?

Behind her, he yawned. "I'm beat."

"You could go to bed."

"I keep thinking I'm going to go to bed and actually sleep. But then I wake up on the other side and remember that's never going to happen."

He walked up beside her and leaned one hand against the mantle. He had submitted himself to the proper dinner dress—a leather doublet flared at the waist, voluminous green velvet knee breeches, and a dress scabbard with a jeweled rapier—but as soon as they'd left the dining room, he had unbuttoned the doublet and loosened his tunic collar.

"Besides," he said, "I wanted to ask you if something was wrong. You seemed distracted all through dinner. Didn't harp once when I forgot to keep my chair exactly ten inches from the table."

She cast him a glance. "I didn't notice."

"Yeah, and I noticed you didn't notice. That's the point." His mouth straightened. "You angry with me again?"

"No." The word came out quickly. She looked at the fire and shook her head. The next attempt sounded more modulated. "No." She made herself smile and raise her face. "That is to say, not particularly. As you've found, I'm generally a rather angry person."

He turned his back to the fire and crossed his arms. "And why is that?"

"Why are any of us?" She stabbed the poker into a crumbling log and raised a spray of golden sparks. The last thing she wanted to discuss with him was herself. "Aren't you angry?"

He was quiet until she glanced at him, then he wrinkled his nose. "I suppose, to some extent. Though disengaged might have been the better term."

"Might have been?"

He smiled again, but his expression was serious. "I haven't felt very disengaged these last few weeks."

"And what has changed?"

His eyebrow lifted in incredulity. "You're kidding, right?"

"Just because everything changes doesn't mean we change right along."

"Well, I'm not saying I'm any different. Not yet. But when you see a bigger picture, your perspective does change. Know what I mean?"

"No. I don't." She lowered the poker and found herself standing straighter. "My life has always been the same. I've always known what I would be, and I think, deep down, I've always known what it would bring."

"And that's what makes you angry?"

"I'd rather be angry than apathetic."

He chuckled. "Point taken. But I'm sure being the Searcher and all that wasn't easy to grow up with."

What was this he was giving her? Sympathy? Even Eroll didn't give her that. Eroll loved her unconditionally. Eroll would die on the point of a rapier to defend the slightest dint in her honor. But Eroll didn't like peering too hard at the ugly and the uncomfortable. His philosophy was to put the bad in life behind him as quickly as possible and forget all about it.

She resisted the urge to rub at her crooked finger and made herself look at Chris. In Lael, people braced themselves up and moved on. They didn't wait for assistance. They didn't bemoan their lot to others. They just did what needed doing. She didn't want Chris's sympathy.

But the way he presented it, off-hand almost, it was neither a revelation of his own weakness or an accusation of weakness in her. It was just recognition. And maybe understanding.

"What about you?" she asked. "How did you grow up?"

He stood there for a second, just watching her.

So the Gifted didn't want to talk about himself anymore than she wanted to talk about herself?

He scratched his cheek. "I guess you could say I grew up kind of like you did—all at once. My mother and younger sister died when I was twelve, and my dad pretty much fell apart after that."

"I'm sorry." What else could be said to something like that? "My mother died when I was young too."

Again he smiled the not-quite-a-smile. "Happens to a lot of people so I hear."

"And that's why you're disengaged?"

"I don't know. Can you pin your anger down to just one thing?"

Gifted, Gifted, Gifted. It all came back to the Gifted for her. But, no, that wasn't quite true either. Her anger was born of her fear, and hadn't she been afraid all her life?

She shrugged. "I suppose not."

For a moment, they stared into the crackle and spit of the flames. She stole glances at him. His presence in her head was warm and drowsy, contented almost. He no longer overwhelmed her, even standing side by side, and he didn't feel so alien anymore.

She almost liked the sense of his presence. So long as she could feel him in her head, she wasn't alone. No matter where he went in this world, no matter if she understood him or even liked him, so long as he lived here, she would never be alone. The feeling of unwarranted protection that gave her startled her with its power.

She cleared her throat. "So . . . it would seem you're no longer as adamant in your aversion to Lael."

He lowered himself to a crouch and clasped his hands between his legs. His upward glance pulled her down beside him. "It's hard to be in a strange, new, beautiful place—where I might add, you're fighting for survival from practically the first day—and not find a reason to be interested in life every time you wake up."

She knelt, awkward for a moment, and spread her skirt around her. He took the poker from her and laid it on the hearthstone. She fidgeted with her hands in her lap, then flicked her sleeves behind her and leaned back on her arms. "I think I've always been a little envious of the Gifted. There's this whole other world out there, and we're not allowed even to see it."

"You see it every night when you dream."

"That's not seeing it, not really, and you know it. The gypsy section in Glen Arden is full of interpreters who claim they can tell you about the other world if you share with them the bits and pieces you remember from your dreams. And if you put a gold piece in their palms, of course. But we can't see your world anymore than you saw us before you crossed."

"It's not that different there, really. Even has the same people."

"And how many people have you seen here whom you've recognized?"

He lifted a shoulder. "No one. But they're out there, right? Your other self is knocking around somewhere in my world. Maybe we've even met."

She smiled. "I think not. You, I would have remembered."

"You would have woken up, snapped your fingers, and said, 'Ah, there went history's worst Gifted.'" He was teasing, but the look he cocked at her said he was hoping she would refute him.

In all honesty, she had to. "You've some stout competition in Harrison Garnett."

The set of his mouth turned grim. "Harrison wasn't the one who brought Mactalde across."

"That's not irremediable. Not yet. And anyway Harrison had his own ill-fated gifts to offer in competition."

"Speaking of gifts—" He lowered his crouch onto one knee and turned to face her. "What is it your regular, run-of-the-mill Gifted who don't manage to majorly mess up the worlds on their first day— what do they end up doing here?"

"That depends on the era." She watched him. "Some are warriors who come to fight and win great battles."

"Is that what I am?"

"It does rather seem that way. But you'd think the God of all would have chosen someone who knew more about war. A great tactician or something."

He turned back to the fire. "I have to tell you I wasn't a great anything."

She studied his face in the flicker of the light. "You have your good points."

He raised his eyebrows. "I do, do I?"

The back of her neck warmed, but she held his gaze. "You're smart, you're brave. Stubborn."

"That's a good point?"

"As one stubborn person to another, take it for what it's worth when I say yes."

He flashed a grin, then softened the expression. "Well, I doubt any of those are going to fulfill the purpose of the age. But thanks."

He watched the fire for a moment, his face unreadable. She couldn't interpret his thoughts, even through the sense of him in her head.

Finally, he rose. "It's getting late. I should head to bed and make sure no one's trying to kill me in the other world."

She stayed where she was, looking up at him. "Good night."

He walked away and passed Quinnon in the doorway. They stood outside for a few minutes, their conversation a murmur.

She stared into the heat of the fire, listening to them. She'd said nothing but the truth when she'd told him he was smart, brave, and stubborn. But there was one other thing Chris Redston was. He was kind. That wasn't likely to fulfill the purpose of the era, but it was something else that kept her from feeling all alone. And that wasn't nothing.

She climbed the wide staircase, which was lit with a candle globe embedded on either end of each step. Behind her, boots stamped on the flagstones. She glanced back to find Quinnon following her.

He had removed his Guardsman tabard for the night and slung it over the shoulder of his loose tunic. He looked tired, old even. Sometimes she forgot he was almost old enough to have been someone's grandfather, had he ever bothered to leave her side long enough to have a life of his own.

She turned to him, one hand still on the railing. "You should get some rest. You've been working harder than any of us."

He waved her off and held out the embossed silver cylinder of a royal message. "Thought you might like to see this before morning. Courier brought it in just after dark."

Her heart clinched. She grasped the cylinder and fitted her signet ring into the grooves at one end. Like a key, she turned it, and the lid sprang free. She passed the lid to Quinnon, upended the rolled parchment into her hand, then gave him the cylinder as well. They both knew what the message would say.

She read it at a glance. "Koraud has declared war. Troops are already moving. Father wants us in Glen Arden by tomorrow morning. He'll introduce the Gifted at the ceremony tomorrow night, then leave right away to join the army at Aiden River."

Quinnon didn't seem surprised, or happy. "Why does he have to wait for us before joining the army?"

"The presence of a Gifted can be a great advantage during the time of war. And under the circumstances, it's best if Chris is formally recognized by Father as soon as possible." Her hands shook only a little as she rolled the parchment. "I'm glad he's waiting for us." She held out a hand for the cylinder and tried to organize her thoughts. This was what she had been waiting for, wasn't it? This was what she had been preparing for.

Quinnon watched her. Unlike Chris, he had a way of studying her without giving any indication what he was finding. "I'll go out and alert the engineers to put our train on the cables."

"No, I'll do it. You're tired."

He glared. "Like rotted teeth you'll do it. You wake up your maids and get packed. And get that Gifted back out of his bed. If we leave now and travel all night, we still won't make it to Glen Arden until mid-morning, even by sky."

She touched his shoulder. "Let the Gifted sleep until we have to leave. It's more than sleep to him, and he has problems of his own to tend to in the other world."

"You'd do us all a good turn to keep your head on straight about him."

She pulled back. "What's that supposed to mean?"

"It means you're a lass, and he's a lad who's made a muck of everything in real short order."

Her face stiffened. "We all make mistakes. He's not a bad person."

"I'm not saying he is. But, you mark me, you don't know a thing about him."

Part of her wanted to be outraged. But some other part of her was almost relieved. Hadn't she been telling herself this, over and over again, for the last week?

She straightened herself. "What do you expect him to do before you'll consent to our trusting him? Bring Mactalde's head to me on a pike?"

"Yes." His chin jutted. "I'll forgive a man. But not until he's righted his wrongs. So far, all this Gifted of yours has done is learn how to play Guardsman."

"Don't. You're not just cutting him down. You're cutting me."

He rose a step. "Never that, lass. Never that. And that's why I'm telling you, you're not here to be friends with him. You're here to keep him straight on his path, and don't you forget it, for your sake far more'n his." His good eye drilled her, then he turned to tromp back down the stairs.

He was right. Of course he was right. She agreed with his every word. The Gifted, however smart and brave and kind, was still a rogue marksman in a war that could afford no missed shots. He hadn't done anything to win her trust yet. Bringing flowers from another world and punching Crofton Steadman in the face were all well enough, but they weren't testaments of undying loyalty. Hadn't he told her himself that he was intent on doing things his own way?

She slid the rolled parchment back into the cylinder and screwed it shut. Slowly, she started back down to the salon where Esta still dozed.

The Gifted might be a jolly nice bloke, as Eroll would say, but he was still dangerous. Perhaps more so to her than to any other—if only because he was tempting her with hope. She'd learned the hard way that hope was the sharpest weapon of all.

24

LEN ARDEN WASN'T exactly what Chris expected. But, then, he hadn't exactly expected to spend the night sitting up in the sway of a skycar.

He'd slept soundly enough, only to wake to a stiff back and a crick in his neck. Outside, storm clouds weighted the sky, and flecks of rain dotted the glass panels. Even inside, the temperature was chilly. He hunched into the protection of his leather jerkin and watched Allara surreptitiously.

She was back in full-blown ice mode. All her answers to his attempts at conversation amounted to monosyllables, and she wouldn't even meet his gaze. This was about more than just her father's summons. This was about him. Maybe he'd crossed some invisible line of etiquette last night. He'd thought they were making progress, maybe even to the point where she actually liked him instead of just tolerating him for the sake of her duty.

"You okay?" he asked.

"We're here." She gestured out the window to where yet another lake swelled the horizon. This country was one lake after the other. "Lake Arden."

Mansions drifting in the water bobbed into view.

"The city floats?"

"Not quite." Quinnon went over to the corner cabinet to stack the goblets and plates from their early lunch.

Allara stood and brushed off the front of her fawn-colored traveling gown. "The city has no way to increase its boundaries, so new homes and businesses are built on ship hulls and floated around the perimeter."

"Why can't it increase its boundaries?"

The train began its descent, and their car swung around so he could see for himself. The lake's northeastern shore scooped away from the embrace of the hills in something like the shape of an artist's palette. Where the thumbhole would have been on the palette, the island city of Glen Arden rose from the water and stretched far away into the lake, fading from view in the wisping smoke and steam of industry.

He moved to the window as the skycar carried them over the mile or so of water between the city and the shore. "At least you didn't have to dig a moat."

"It's the most defensible city in the kingdom." She lifted her cloak from a hook in the corner. "Thanks to the fishing and access to fresh water, we're entirely self-sufficient. If we ever needed to, we could cut the skycar cables here and detonate Faramore Bridge on the South Shore and we'd be able to hold out against any land siege."

The skycar reached the edge of the city, and its shadow fell across a parade of small ships with stiff, silver-scaled sails. The ships cruised alongside the island, sometimes half a dozen abreast, in an aquatic highway. A wide white-paved road spanned the beach, populated with the expected horse-drawn carriages, as well as a few litters and even a couple rickshaws. On the other side, the city proper began, its streets looping out in widening semi-circles.

Elegant houses of three and four stories lined the streets. Most of them were made of a pale gray stone, all the corners rounded, the walls carved in a rippling effect. Spiraling columns supported narrow balconies at every level, and behind the delicately wrought railings the gleaming windows curved outward. The place had a decidedly more modern feel than the dark solidity of Réon Couteau.

"The Taïs Quarter," he said. He remembered it from their geography lessons. As the city's wealthiest district, it hugged the palace's hill on the east end of the island.

Another twenty minutes brought them in view of the palace itself. It rose in graduating levels up the hill above the city. Green-shingled towers at either end crowned its stone walls, and two smaller towers framed massive iron gates.

Just outside the gates, the cobblestone roads pooled into a large square. In the center, a fountain spurted a circular waterfall, and naked fire glinted from behind the veil of water and mist.

"*Fawa-radi*," he said. Orias had been right. The capital's sculptures *were* impressive.

"How do you know about *fawa-radi*?" Quinnon sounded suspicious.

"Traded my Guardsman's badge for one in a Riever ceremony. Lost it along the way though."

"You got the rotten end of that deal. Guardsmen don't part with their badges."

The skycar crossed over the palace wall and began another short climb to a tower. It glided to a stop with the doors hanging level with the wall platform.

Allara swung her black cloak over her shoulders and slipped her hands through the arm holes. As a liveried footman opened the door, she shot one unreadable glance over her shoulder at Chris, then stepped down from the car onto the wide walkway.

Quinnon already had the horses' ramp in place. He held Rihawn back as he waited for Esta and Parry and a handful of Guardsmen to disembark from the rearward cars.

A pale Esta staggered onto the walkway and let go of the assisting footman's arm long enough to straighten her wig with both hands.

She emitted a little groan. "You can't tell me this is the civilized way to travel. I don't care if proper horse-drawn vehicles do take twice as long over bumpy roads, these newfangled flying wagons are barbaric. Did you fare all right, my lady?"

"I'm fine," Allara said. She didn't look fine, judging from the tiny white lines straining her mouth. "You can go on up to my chambers." She glanced at Parry, as he jumped from the car, flushed with excitement, his cocked hat a little askew. "You too. I'm going straight to speak with my father, so once you've seen to the luggage, you can take a quick rest. I'm sure the staff here has preparations for tonight's ceremony well under way, and the Gifted and I won't need to dress until late this afternoon."

With a deep breath, she turned around. Head up and shoulders back, she led the way down the rampart. Behind, the horses unloaded in a great clatter of hooves against stone and the occasional clank of the car rocking against the wall.

A heavy door let them into an airy gallery, wallpapered in gold filigree. White columns opened into a great hall with yet another black-and-white checkered marble floor. A massive staircase, carpeted in green, rose at the far end of the hall. Its generous landing divided into two narrower flights that hugged the walls to the left and right.

The mingled voices of noblemen, soldiers, and servants thundered beneath the cavernous ceiling.

"This is your home?" Chris asked. "Is it always like this?"

She kept walking. "There's always a horde here. But this is different. There's a Gifted in our halls and a war on our doorstep."

They waded into the sea of people. The men parted before her like dust on the wind. They bowed and murmured civilities, but their eyes inevitably darted behind her to Chris. Recognition sparked in their faces.

By now, of course, everyone knew who he was, and depending on their ideology, they would either hate him or think he had come to save their world and win their war. One viewpoint was almost as uncomfortable as the other.

He kept his breathing regular and returned every curious look with a nod, daring them to glance away first. They almost always did.

Allara led him down the first flight of stairs, then followed a hallway to a sturdy door. A footman admitted them without question into a surprising hush.

The room was large and windowless, the walls paneled in a warm chestnut wood. Tapestries, worked with intricate maps, covered three of the walls. In the center, a table bore a clutter of parchments and pens, along with goblets and platters from a half-eaten meal.

Two men hunched over the end of the table and spoke in strained undertones. They looked up as Allara and Chris entered.

"Alla." The taller of the two crossed the room. He wore a snug black doublet, buttoned all the way up to its high collar, and a sleeveless gray velvet overcoat collared with white fur.

She let him pull her into his arms, but the set of her shoulders remained taut. "Father."

The king cupped her face in his hand. "Quite a muddle we're in."

"Yes, it is." The way she said it seemed more an acceptance of blame than a simple assent. She turned away from him and gestured to Chris. "This is Master Chris Redston, the Gifted. And this is my father, King Tireus II."

Arms behind his back, Tireus studied Chris.

He had the face of a patrician, lean and craggy. Allara had inherited the strength of her eyes from him, if not the color. His dark hair, cropped almost too short to comb over, was silvering at the front and the sides, and his gray goatee tufted at either corner of his chin. He was a big man, easily a few inches taller than Chris, with the arms and shoulders of someone who had acquired his strength by birth.

"Welcome to Glen Arden." He bowed, the movement practiced and formal.

Chris did as Allara had taught him and touched his thumb and forefinger to his closed eyes and slid them down his face. It was a formal gesture of respect and honor that symbolized the most honored and respected person in Lael—the dreamer.

"Thank you," he said.

Tireus straightened up. "Time is short, Master Gifted, so you'll forgive me if I say what needs to be said without prefacing it with polite nothings. We're in a spot. I won't say it's entirely your fault, although I gather your ignorance and perhaps willful stupidity had more than something to do with it."

Chris made himself stand straight. This was the medicine he had asked for, and he would take it. "I'm prepared to accept full responsibility for making things right, whatever that entails."

Tireus waved him off. "Never mind that. It's all well and good and I'm sure you mean it, but I haven't the time right now." He moved back to the table and pawed through the maps. "The point is, war was coming with Koraud whether Faolan Mactalde returned or not. But now that he's here, I'll tell you straight, the odds are considerably less to my liking."

"What's happening?" Allara asked. "I've had no news. Your missive last night was the first I'd heard of anything."

The other man, a heavyset gent with white hair, propped one hand on his jeweled belt. "Official declaration of war came yestermorn. We've had our eyes on the border and our spies across it, and they've been bringing word of intensified troop movements for the last half month."

Allara gestured to him. "This is my uncle, my mother's brother, Denegar Amras, Duke of Heindon."

Denegar nodded an acknowledgement to Chris. "All signs point to an invasion at Aiden River. If they can get through there, they can march straight up the Karilus Wall and be on the shores of Lake Arden before we've time to pull ourselves back together."

"Forgive me," Chris said, "but won't it take time for them to mass and move a sizable army as far as the Aiden?" If what he'd learned about Koraud and the borderland beneath the Karilus Wall was right, only one skycar track ran from Koraud into Lael. No way Tireus would have let enemy troops get through there, and without the skycar, an army on the march would need at least two weeks to reach the Aiden River.

"I see we're an expert already." Denegar's deep voice rumbled.

Chris faced the big man and caught a hint of Allara in the tilt of his mouth. "Not at all. Just trying to figure it out for myself."

Tireus glanced up from his maps. "Helping you figure it out is my daughter's job. We haven't the time for it, I'm afraid, since what you know and what you don't is hardly crucial to our operations at the moment. Koraudian troops have been massing on the border for months, long before Mactalde crossed—as have our own. They've been on the march ever since he joined them. Your own figures bear out whereabouts that places them."

"You're leaving tomorrow?" Allara asked.

"Yes, as soon as we get this ceremony out of the way tonight. We've already had word of raids along the border towns. I expect full-blown hostilities to erupt at any moment, so it's crucial Denegar and I join our men as quickly as possible."

Chris shifted his weight. Up to now, he'd felt he was *doing* something. Learning to fight and ride and understand Lael's politics and geography had given him a purpose. But maybe he'd just been marking time. Tireus certainly seemed to put much less emphasis on the importance of the Gifted than did Allara, or even Crofton Steadman and his people in Nateros.

He looked at Tireus. "What is it I'm supposed to do in all of this? What's my part? How do I help?"

Allara stepped forward, almost as if to stop him, and Denegar harrumphed in surprise.

For a moment, Tireus and Chris stood with locked gazes, each searching the other out.

Chris didn't budge. King or no king, he wasn't about to knuckle under to this man. He still wasn't sure exactly what it meant to be a Gifted, but this was his fight as much as it was anyone's. This was his *fault*, and he needed to do something about it.

Tireus tossed the maps back down on the table. "Master Redston, let us straighten something between us. You're the third Gifted I've seen in my lifetime. No doubt you've heard of your recent predecessor, Master Garnett. Before him, in the lifetime of the Searcher who preceded Allara, there was Aloyshenka Odarennyi. He spent most of his time out in the woods, talking to birds. So between utter uselessness and downright treachery, I haven't seen much to make me believe the Gifted *can* help."

"Father . . ." Allara murmured.

Tireus blew out a deep breath. "You'll pardon me my cynicism and my impatience, but I'm afraid that's just the way you find us here in Glen Arden. As for what you can do to help, you can do this. You're a Gifted, ergo the people automatically adore you."

"Not all the people." He doubted he needed to mention Nateros by name.

Tireus's frown deepened. "No, not all the people. But enough. So, after tonight, you'll have been introduced to the world, and the world will have been introduced to you. From here on, you're a symbol of this country, this kingdom, this monarchy, and the army that defends all three. So you'll do us all a great favor if you use your winning smile to keep the general population happy in the midst of our national crisis."

Chris kept his voice even. "Public relations."

"Something like that."

Denegar straightened from leaning against the table. "A tour among the troops wouldn't go amiss either."

Chris managed a nod. Tireus's attitude was more than just politic, it was sensible. But this was not what he'd had in mind when he'd taken the reins in this new life of his and promised to right all wrongs.

The king had already returned to sorting his maps.

Chris took a breath and tried to keep the frustration from his voice. "I'll do it."

Tireus grunted. After a moment of paper shuffling, he looked sideways at Chris. "Not exciting or glorious, I'm afraid. And, no doubt, not what you had in mind. I'd apologize if I thought you'd think it worth it. But the point is—" he straightened, "—if you truly want to help us, this is how you do it."

"I understand."

And he did. To be honest, he didn't know quite *what* he'd had in mind. After all, he was just one person among many in this war, and an inexperienced, potentially untrustworthy person at that. But that didn't make his new role any easier to swallow.

"And now," Tireus said, "I'm afraid I'll have to bid you take your leave for the time being. My daughter and Captain Quinnon will see to it you're briefed and prepared for this evening's ceremony." He drew himself upright, stamped one foot like the Guardsmen did when coming to attention, and bowed from the waist.

Chris mirrored the bow back at him, then to Denegar.

Denegar returned the gesture formally and gave Allara's shoulder a pat as she passed him. "Nice to have you back, my dear. Oh, and while I remember, I think we've located his family. You might want to have Quinnon or someone check into it. Reuniting a Gifted with his worried family is always rather good publicity."

Chris looked back and forth between Denegar and Allara. "I have a family?"

"Of course you do," Denegar said. "Where was it you thought you came from? A body in each world, don't you know? That means a family in each world as well. Name of Bowen."

"And where are they?" Allara asked.

"Here in Glen Arden. You can send your lady-in-waiting down to get the address from my man if you're of a mind to investigate further."

She nodded and opened the door. Chris followed her out. Shadowed in the recess of the door, they stood in relative privacy for a moment.

"A family." He mulled the words over in his mouth. "I wasn't expecting that. What if I'm married? Maybe I have kids."

"Perhaps. And perhaps they aren't even the right people." She raised an eyebrow. "Would you like to find out?"

25

AFTER COLLECTING QUINNON, Chris and Allara requisitioned a small windboat from the palace's private subterranean harbor.

The passenger compartment was comprised of two plush benches facing each other and enclosed in an ornate box in the center of the craft, just behind the mast. Painted a rich yellow with green and brown vines twining the framework, it glistened from a recent waxing.

Chris sat across from Allara on the red cushions. Quinnon stayed outside with the steersman and latched the door behind them.

On the edge of the dock, a horse pulled the windboat into the open lake, and the steersman scrambled to unfurl the semicircular sail to the breeze. Misting rain filtered through the open windows on either side.

"These people don't live on the island?" Chris asked.

Allara raised the window glass from its recess inside the door. "No, they do. They're in Trawler's Waterfront in Belkin, not too far from the Taïs Quarter."

He tried to remember. "Belkin's the northern quarter of the city."

"It's a working-class neighborhood. The lakefront there is called Belkin Bay. It's not really a bay, just the shoreline, but it belongs to the fishermen all the way up and down."

"Why take a boat? We could have just ridden there, right?"

She settled back against the seat. "It's faster to take a windboat around, rather than fight the traffic overland. Less conspicuous too."

"You're telling me this thing isn't conspicuous?"

"See for yourself."

Outside, through the gray mizzle, dozens of watercraft surrounded them.

"The white ones are taxis," she said. "Water travel is popular here, for obvious reasons."

The traffic was confined to within a mile of the island. Beyond that, the floating mansions Chris had spotted from the skycar bobbed against the waves. The nearest had to be five hundred feet long and rose out of the water three full stories, only to crown itself with two more levels of diminishing sizes, like layers on a wedding cake. The corners of the eaves curved up jovially, and the flash of crimson paint alternated with the glittering windows.

"How many people live in that thing?"

"Just one family." She tilted her head to see. "That one's a bit garish. It belongs to a man who struck it rich in the Illise silver mines. This is Floating Taïs, and the people who live in the houseboats here are just as wealthy and distinguished as those who live on the land."

"Hope they don't get seasick."

A faint smile touched her mouth. "I heard our silver miner was quite green during his first month here."

He rubbed his damp hands against his pants. Allara had asked him if he wanted to meet this supposed family of his, and he'd said yes without thinking. But who knew what he was about to find in Trawler's Waterfront. A mirror of the broken family he'd left behind in the other world? Or a brigade of strangers for whom he would suddenly and irrevocably be responsible?

"You're sure we have time for this today?" he asked.

"We've several hours before we have to prepare for the dinner. Don't you think this is better than sitting around working up our nerves?"

"You seem to be doing a pretty good job of that anyway."

The muscle in her cheek bunched. She turned her head to stare out the window.

He leaned back. "What's bothering you now?"

"Nothing's bothering me." Even slouched, she managed to look stiff and straight.

"C'mon, you've been in a state all day. And don't tell me it's because your father finally called you home. You've been wanting that ever since we arrived at Réon Couteau. So don't pretend nothing's wrong."

That got her to look at him, but it was a glare more than a concession.

He spread his hands. "If you're angry with me because you think I did something wrong, then just tell me. I'll take it under advisement and maybe even try to mend my ways."

The color drained from her face, like it always did when she was upset. "I'm not angry, and it's not you, so there's nothing for you to take under advisement."

"Then what?" He tried to keep his frustration from his face. "Because I thought we were on good terms. Last night everything was fine, wasn't it? Or am I missing something?"

For a second, he thought she was going to slap his questions right back at him. Then, slowly, the anger faded, and her shoulders slackened. Her eyes held his and sent him coded messages he couldn't decipher.

"You are missing something," she said, "but it's not your fault. And I'm sorry for making you think so. The fact is . . . I can't afford to be friends with you."

That was a slap in the face in itself. "What?"

"We'll work together, because that's the way it must be. But I hope you'll understand me when I say I need to maintain my distance so I can keep things in perspective."

"You can hope all you want. I don't understand."

She stared out the window. "Then don't."

His gut churned. And why not? Of all the Searchers he could have ended up with, she had to be the most ridiculous, unreasonable, frustrating, inconsistent person he'd ever met. She clung to her belief in her duty with an adamance that was almost a stranglehold. Physically, she was fearless. She even seemed to enjoy putting herself into danger, and she talked of battle with a wistfulness that was almost a yearning. And yet she seemed riddled with fear and uncertainty. She was positively crumbling with it.

Outside, the mansions of Floating Taïs had given way to serviceable barges topped with plain barn-like houses and fishing schooners with three and even four silver sails open to the wind. A floating marker bore a large white-washed sign announcing the entry to Belkin Bay.

Still without facing him, Allara gathered up the folds of her cloak and slid forward in her seat. "We're almost there."

He stopped her with his hand on her arm. "Wait."

She looked at him, startled.

"You can't run away from people all your life." His expression felt hard. Her withdrawal gouged him more than he wanted to admit. "Everybody's going to hurt you. I've hurt you, and I'll probably do it again. But the person hurting you the most is *you*. This anger and this fear you keep inside, it's eating you alive."

Her dark eyebrows knit. "You have no room to say these things to me. You told me you *used* to be apathetic. But tell me, what's changed? You arrive in a new place, it's exciting, it's different, everybody who doesn't know better thinks you're a hero. But what have you done so far? What have you even tried to do?" She pulled her arm free. "Apathy is a tide pool that drowns its victims. And you're not free of it yet. So don't talk to me about what you think is eating me alive. You have no idea."

The boat rocked to a stop against a wooden dock, and Quinnon jumped down from the deck to open the door. She gathered her cloak and her skirt, took his hand, and climbed out the passenger box and up onto the dock.

Quinnon glanced from the tightness of her white face to Chris disembarking the boat, and he frowned. He gestured to the buildings on the lakefront. "Any of this familiar?"

Chris looked past Allara as she pulled her cowl over her face. Along the beach, bare-chested men mended fishing nets and scraped barnacles from their upturned hulks. Barefoot children in dirty tunics ran up and down, some of them fetching and carrying for their elders, a few rod fishing at the waterline, most of them just romping.

The dock led all the way across the beach to the street. Tall, narrow buildings were constructed like upside-down ziggurats with each story jutting a little from the one below. Dark beams framed each story and crisscrossed the wide squares of whitewashed planking beside the windows.

On the street, foot traffic and hand-drawn carts bustled across the cobblestones. Vendors with baskets of goods atop their heads and women hurrying home from their shopping jostled for room, all of them adding to the commotion.

He shook his head. "Never seen it before."

The smell, though, that was something different. It tingled in the back of his mind. The deep, organic smell of the water, the rot of piled fish heads, and the tang of wet wood. It all combined, along with the spice of smoke, to be both entirely unique and almost familiar.

Quinnon led the way up the dock. He had left his Guard uniform behind in the interest of inconspicuousness and wore, instead, a black jerkin, similar to Chris's, and a patch over his blind eye.

Allara followed, hands folded under her cloak, head down. They reached the end of the dock and turned up the street.

Two houses from the corner, a tall building boasted a large red sign. Judging from the tables out front, all of them set with a white strip of tablecloth and a big bowl of mixed salt and pepper in the center, the place was a restaurant. Waitresses in brown smocks whirled among the tables with round trays held aloft. A long horizontal window in the ground level of the building revealed the bustle of the kitchen workers. What was probably a menu was chalked on a broad beam next to the window.

He caught a whiff of some kind of battered fish—oil and flour and a hint of sweet. Déjà vu whispered again. He'd seen this place in his dreams, long before he'd crossed. He was sure of it. He'd dreamed about that battered fish.

Beside the long window, a door opened. A woman, her dark hair caught back in a purple kerchief, stepped outside. A wisp of hair fell across her eye, and she swiped it aside with one hand. Her gaze flicked across her customers and landed on Quinnon and Allara.

Chris stayed where he was. He couldn't move. Couldn't breathe. This woman standing in a cafe in the middle of a world that shouldn't exist . . . was his mother.

Quinnon and Allara walked up to her.

She stepped out of the doorway, smiling and nodding, and gestured to an empty table. They were all three speaking, but whatever words they used were lost in the rush of his blood.

Memories flashed through his brain like snapshots:

His mother, Sharlee Redston, laughing because she had set off the smoke alarm with yet another failed casserole.

His mother leaving for work at the hospital, arms piled high with flowers and balloons.

His mother lying on snow-wet pavement, choking to death on her own blood.

She had been dead for nineteen years. But here she was, just as strong and straight and beautiful as he remembered her.

She saw him, and a smile burst her face. She darted through the tables and reached for him with one hand. "Talan! What took you so long? We were so afraid you'd gotten caught up in the fight in the Thyra hills." She reached for him without hesitation and pulled him into her arms. "Thank the God of all you're safe."

He didn't fit in her arms as he once had. Now it was her head that rested against his shoulder, and his arms that encircled her back.

He dropped his face into the crook of her neck. She didn't smell of perfume or shampoo or laundry detergent. But the same musky softness clung to her skin as remained in her clothing back home, hidden beneath the sharpness of cedar balls.

"Mom." He whispered the word he had not spoken for almost twenty years.

"Darling." Her arms tightened, then eased him away. "Are you hurt?" Her eyes narrowed. "What is it? What's happened?"

"You're alive." His voice cracked.

What? Her lips formed the word.

He caught himself up short and stepped away from her. How could she know she'd died in the other world?

Quinnon came forward. "I take it we've stumbled onto the right family."

"This is my mother." He left it at that. She probably wasn't Sharlee Redston here. It was strange, not knowing his own mother's name.

She frowned. "What's going on?"

"We should go inside," Allara said.

His mother glanced from face to face and ended on his. "All right."

She led them through the steamy kitchen, where two middle-aged women prepared the food, and up three steps into the back room. Smoked windows dispersed the day's gray light across a rug worked in a flowered pattern. Chairs and a loom surrounded the fireplace. The walls were hung with the bits and pieces of a fisherman's life. A length of heavy netting had been tacked up against the wall; each square framed a different seashell.

On the floor, two blonde girls played with hook-nosed puppets.

Chris started. These were his twin nieces, his sister Lisa's children. He hadn't seen them in years, not since they were three or four. They must be almost ten by now.

His mother shooed them out. "Miriel, Ireth, leave your play and go along for a few minutes. One of you, find Sirra and tell her to take a break from waiting tables."

The twins obeyed without question, but when they saw Chris, their faces lit up with recognition. They grinned and waved.

His mother closed the door behind them. She turned to him, both hands rigid in her smock pockets. "Now tell me. What is it?"

Allara pushed back her cowl. "Mistress Bowen, do you know who I am?"

His mother stared, then seemed to draw into herself. "My lady." She didn't bow or salute. Her eyes darted back to Chris and widened to something between shock and fear.

"Please prepare yourself." Allara's voice softened. "Your son is the Gifted."

His mother's lips came together in the beginnings of another *what?* She stared at him. "Can this be?" She looked again at Allara, then back at Chris. "Can it?"

He just nodded. His chest was too full for his lungs to work. His mother had just come back from the dead. Whatever he had expected in this new family of his, it hadn't been her. She was dead. She was gone from his life, never to return.

But, then, maybe he *should* have expected her. Before he had crossed, he had dreamt of her sometimes, and in the dreams, she had always been alive and well.

The door from the kitchen opened and let in the clatter and babble from outside. A young woman in her mid-twenties entered. She wore the same brown smock as her mother, and her dark hair was pinned atop her head.

He only needed one glimpse into her eyes to know who she was. "Jeni—"

A grin split through her freckles. "Talan!" She caught his neck with both arms, the force of her tackle swinging him around. "We were beginning to think the Guard was getting greedy of your talents and wasn't going to discharge you after all."

He crushed her against him. She had been five years old when she'd died.

She laughed up at him. "Did you run afoul of that Koraudian raid in the Thyra hills? We're hearing all kinds of stories about a human who fought with the Cherazii before the Guardsmen rescued everyone. Was it you?" Her grin widened. "It was, wasn't it?"

He stared at her, his little sister all grown up.

She made a face. "What?"

"You're beautiful." He looked again at his mother. "Both of you."

Jenifer glanced at their mother. "What's wrong?" She looked at Chris, then over at Allara and Quinnon and back again. "What's going on?"

"Sirra—" Their mother took a deep breath. "Go raise the flag to signal your father in from fishing."

Jenifer's—Sirra's—hands slid from his shoulders. Her brows came together. "Something's wrong?" She stepped back.

"Just go. I'll tell you as soon as your father comes."

With a last glance at Chris, she turned and hurried across the room to a narrow staircase.

The last time he'd seen this little sister of his, she had been inseparable from Boppy the pink teddy bear. Now she was a woman— beautiful, graceful, a stranger.

He faced his mother. "What about Lisa? Is she here?"

"Lisa?" Her frown deepened.

"That's . . . my other sister's name." The thousand swirling pieces of his universe slammed themselves into a new order once again. This woman might share his DNA, but she had no idea that in another life he had seen her destroyed. How could she possibly know he hadn't seen her or Jenifer since a few months after his twelfth birthday and that he hadn't looked his father in the face since shortly after?

"Do you mean Tielle?" Her arms came up to hold herself, one work-hardened hand around her waist and the other clutching her elbow.

She had a plain enough face; but as a boy he had always thought her the loveliest of women. She still was. The warmth of her huge eyes and the soft roundness of her cheeks painted pictures of her kindness and her gentle strength.

Her voice was low now, the fear and confusion only half swallowed. "You don't remember?"

He shook his head. Suddenly, he would have given everything to exchange the memories of this world for those he'd been carrying around for the last twenty years.

He swallowed. "I don't remember anything from this world. My name is Chris. Christian Benjamin Redston."

She didn't move, and he knew it was because if she did move, she would start crying. She had lost a son. Just as he had lost a mother, now she was losing every common bond, every shared memory, with her only son.

She shook her head. "Talan Malchor Bowen. My son." Two tears slipped down her face side by side. She looked at Allara. "Will he ever remember?"

Allara stood very straight, but her face was compassionate, even sorrowful. "I'm afraid not. But he knew you in the other world. He knows who you are." She looked at Chris. "And he loves you."

Sirra bounded back down the stairs. "Papa's almost here. He'd already anchored the boat. He must have a full haul already. Tielle's with him."

Footsteps clomped up from the kitchen. The door opened, and a man and a woman entered.

Here was Lisa—Tielle—blonde, lanky, and angular, the set of her jaw as determined as ever.

And here was his father—strong and straight, his eyes clear, and his face lined by wind not whiskey. He wore baggy pants, a billowing yellow shirt stained almost gray under the arms, and a hat with the brim pinned up in the front.

"Hullo, Lauria," he said. "I was already halfway up the beach when I saw the flag. What's the trouble? That piker Silkar run off again without paying for his croutie pie?"

Then he turned to Chris, and his whole face brightened. "You're home."

The words bore a weight of care Chris hadn't heard from that voice since his childhood.

His father shrugged free of his canvas rucksack and reached out to grip Chris's arm and pull him in. "You're safe."

The old reflexes that would have stopped him from embracing his father back home never kicked in. "Dad—I—" His throat cramped around the words. What was there to say anyway?

"Worick," his mother said. "He's the Gifted."

Behind their father, Tielle's hand darted to her mouth. "What?"

Sirra gaped at Allara. "You're the Searcher?"

Allara nodded. "Yes, I am."

His father saluted hastily. "My lady. Are you sure of this?"

"Quite sure. And I'm sorry. I know it's a lot to absorb. Your lives will all change because of this, just as your son's has. But you're also to be congratulated. Having a Gifted in a family is a great honor."

"What does this mean?" His father clamped a hand around Chris's arm. "If Talan's the Gifted, what happens to him now?"

"He belongs to Lael now, as much as he does you." Whatever confusion or fear Allara harbored for herself, she showed no sign of it now. She was all princess. "He'll be staying at the palace. Tonight, as you may have heard, the king is hosting the official ceremony to welcome him to Lael."

Tielle clenched her fists. "And then the king leaves for war. Does Talan go with him? He was only just discharged after serving his full term with the Guard on the Illisian frontier. He was on his way home when you took him."

His mother wrung her hands. "And Mactalde. They say Lord Mactalde's back now."

"So he is," Allara said.

"The people expect the Gifted to vanquish him."

Allara looked at Chris. Her features were unreadable. "And so he shall."

Behind her, Quinnon coughed, less than discreetly.

Allara took a step. "I'm sorry we haven't more time to share with you this afternoon. I know this is all horribly abrupt, and you'll need time to adjust. But I'm afraid we have to return to the palace and prepare for this evening."

"The ceremony," Sirra said. "Can we attend it?"

"I think it would be better if you didn't." Allara watched Chris. "He'll have enough to deal with this evening as it is. And he needs time to accustom himself to his new idea of you as well."

"I understand." His father, still holding onto Chris's arm, nodded.

He turned to look Chris in the face. "I hope you know without my saying that all you ever have to do is tell me what you need from me, no matter what it is." His expression was one of commendation, approval, and respect.

For the space of a heartbeat, that look whitewashed the memories of twenty years.

Worick turned to Allara. "I mean it. And if the lad's too proud to ask his father's help, you ask it for him."

Allara inclined her head. "If he's proud, I suspect it is because you are too. Your son is a good man." Chris could hear the restraint in her voice even if the others couldn't. But she had to mean the words on at least some level, or she never would have said them.

His father turned back to shake his hand. "If this is the path the God of all has chosen, I cannot argue that. May He go with you."

Sorrow ached in his chest. "Dad, I . . ." Was this the way his father *could* have been? Would Paul have been the drunk he was today if Chris had tried harder to forgive him and love him?

Wondering what might have been was hard enough. *Knowing* left him scraped clean inside.

26

CHRIS SURVEYED HIMSELF in the triptych of floor-length mirrors. "I feel like an idiot."

"You don't look like one. Not too much." Parry stepped back and cocked his head. "You look like a real nobleman."

"Well, I'm not. I'm just a normal, ordinary guy who doesn't even own a tie."

He'd take a tie any day over the getup in which Parry had decked him out. The high-collared doublet was made of black velvet with matching leather sleeves. A border of elaborate gold stitching and dark green velvet lined the buttons down the center, all the way to the stiff hem flared around his waist.

The matching pants—black velvet slashed to show a layer of green beneath—ballooned around his thighs. Really, they were more shorts than pants, since they abruptly stopped above the knee where they met his tall boots. And to top it off, Parry had convinced him he was supposed to wear a short cape, its hem embroidered in gold fully six inches deep, slung over one shoulder and tied under the opposite arm.

"Here's the hat." Parry held out a pancake of green velvet with long gold feathers curled all the way around the brim.

"Forget it." He started unknotting the cape. "Forget all this stuff and give me back the leather shirt."

"The jerkin? That's not for occasions of state."

He tossed the cape and the doublet at a chair and took the jerkin from Parry's protesting grip.

"Her ladyship won't approve."

"Her ladyship is going to have to learn I'm not governed by her approval."

"But the king—"

"Or the king's." He shrugged into the jerkin, and laced it up the front. The mirror showed him a slightly piratical reflection.

A knock sounded on the dressing room door, and Parry scrambled to open it. "My lady." He sounded slightly shocked. No doubt visiting men's dressing rooms wasn't the sort of thing a princess was supposed to do, Searcher or not.

"Is he ready?"

"Um . . . not quite."

"May I come in?"

"Let her in," Chris said. She was going to see his chosen wardrobe sooner or later. Might as well let her finish her grumbling now.

Parry bobbed a series of bows and swept the door open.

Chris didn't turn away from fiddling with his collar, and his first glimpse of her was in the mirror. He froze and stared.

She was an attractive woman at any time. But tonight she was resplendent. The brilliant blue of her gown matched her eyes and deepened the contrast between her hair and her skin. An over-gown of black lace covered the back and the wide sleeves and laced up over her stomach. A matching hood framed her face, pinned to the back of her softly upswept hair. Three blue stones hugged her throat.

She looked at his leather jerkin and stopped short. "What are you wearing?"

He turned to face her, mouth half open, trying to come up with a compliment that wasn't utterly clichéd. The best he could do was a sincere, "Wow."

She stopped midway into working up steam for her harangue. A hint of color rose on her cheeks, and she glanced away, obviously flustered.

"What?" He grinned. "You can't tell me you haven't been hearing compliments all the way up the hall."

She positively blushed. "I—" Then she turned away, caught sight of his discarded cape and doublet, and moved to pick them up. "I'm sorry. I know how you feel about our clothing. But you have to understand how important it is you make a good impression tonight." She met his eyes, back in Searcher mode.

She could meet his eyes when she was playing Searcher, but not when she was an ordinary woman? Was that it? Was that what she was afraid of? That if she let herself know him as a person, she'd have to leave behind the protection of her duty as a Searcher?

"Please," she said. "You have to know half the nobles are already set against you. Not everyone here is orthodox. Even if they don't adhere to Nateros, they'd like nothing more than a chance to make sport of you."

He hesitated. Part of him—a big part of him—hated to capitulate, and hated even more to wear that foofaraw. But she was right. He knew she was.

"All right." He reached for the clothes. "I'll do it for you, how's that?"

In the corner by the door, Parry harrumphed. "Is that all it's going to take?"

Her lips parted, as if she wanted to say something, then she straightened up.

Fine. If that's the way she wanted to be, that's the way it would be. He was here to do a job just as much as she was. As long as they could work together calmly and rationally, that was all that mattered. He'd accomplished what he'd needed to accomplish in winning her trust as far as he had. She was absolutely, completely right: any more would be superfluous. They were on level ground now, and he had no reason to court her favor anymore.

He shrugged out of the jerkin and handed it back to her.

Parry hurried over to take it from her and position himself between her and Chris. His body language made it clear *he* was the manservant here. He was supposed to be helping Chris, and her ladyship needed to back down.

She watched for a second, then turned to go. "Quinnon and I will wait in the hall. Everything will be all right."

"Don't sound so convinced." He raised his arm so Parry could knot the cape's drawstring. "Don't forget, if they start throwing tomatoes, I'm the one they're going to be hitting." His stomach squeezed a little. Truth be told, he was every bit as nervous as she was. At least, she knew what was coming. She'd grown up in this court. She knew the rules of etiquette forward and backward, and even if she slipped, she was princess of Lael. Everybody would forgive her.

He, on the other hand, was an upstart nobody who was already disliked by a good-sized chunk of the population and who would probably be stoned by the rest of it if they ever learned what he'd done on his first day in their world. He breathed out.

"Everything will be all right," she said again, on her way out. "Just be yourself. Be honest."

Parry handed him his sword belt—empty now, so it could be filled ceremonially later this evening.

He grimaced at himself in the mirror, then headed for the door. "Wish me luck."

Parry followed. "Could I watch? I mean, it being an important moment in the history of Lael and all that. Isn't every day a Gifted enters the court. I could tell my grandchildren about it years down the road, and—"

"Come along." He finished buckling his scabbard. "One more person watching me fall on my face isn't going to make much difference."

They headed down the hall to where Allara waited with Quinnon near the first flight of stairs. The muted roar of conversation from below woke the butterflies he'd hoped to keep dormant. What was he going to say to these people? It wasn't going to take an atomic physicist among them to realize he was no Alexander the Great.

Allara raised an eyebrow at Parry.

He tried on a grin. "Chris said I could come."

She looked at Chris, then back to Parry. "Chris?"

"He, uh, said I could call him that."

"Hmph." Quinnon nudged Chris toward the stairs. "You just mind what I've been telling you. You don't have to make friends tonight. You just have to avoid making enemies."

In other words, just put on a good show.

Chris fidgeted with the cape's drawstrings. "What exactly are they expecting me to tell them?"

Quinnon shook out his fingers, as if preparing for a swordfight. "Why not tell them you never picked up a sword in your life until this month, you never rode a horse until this month, and you're the one who brought Mactalde back to begin with."

Allara faced forward and focused on the doors at the foot of the stairs. "Tell them you're the Gifted."

In the room beyond, a horn trumpeted a fanfare. She took a deep breath and started down the stairs.

Chris walked one step ahead, just as she'd instructed him earlier. They reached the foot of the stairs, and two footmen swept open the double doors to the banquet hall.

Beneath its six *fawa-radi* chandeliers, the room glittered. Ceiled in white, enameled in gold, and carpeted in crimson, it boasted a long horseshoe-shaped table arrangement that seated two hundred jeweled and velveted nobles.

At the far end of the room, in an arched recess, King Tireus rose, and in a great scuffle of chairs, everyone followed his example.

Chris would have kept walking, but the touch of Allara's fingers on the back of his arm stopped him. He was supposed to wait until Tireus introduced him.

"Princes of Lael." Tireus's regal bellow carried all through the room. "Princesses, dukes and duchesses, earls and countesses, lords and ladies. I introduce to you a traveler from beyond the worlds. Chosen by the God of all, foreseen by the Garowai, found by the Searcher, and now, appointed by us, he is the Gifted. Chris Redston."

Allara had already gone over the ceremonial introduction with him. These were the words spoken over every Gifted, words most of these people had already heard once before in their lives. But tonight, to Chris, they sounded less an introduction and more a benediction.

With equal formality, the people responded. In unison, men and women alike stamped one foot, like Guardsmen coming to attention, and the sound of their single stomp resounded against the high ceiling. They saluted him with their hands to their eyes and spoke the formal antistrophe:

"Hail the Gifted. Welcome the Gifted." Their applause thundered.

Allara's fingers touched his arm again, and he started forward, down the side of the room. He could breathe again, but he struggled to keep his face neutral and confident. Swords and horses were one thing. Facing a horde of upper-crust society was something else.

They sat behind the table, the king in the middle, with Chris and Allara at his sides and Denegar and another noble beside them. Quinnon, in his Guard uniform, stood at attention behind Allara's chair.

The meal was a parade of silver platters that offered at least three selections for every course. Chris ate capon with olives and chestnuts, roasted salmon, eggs with cream and honey, and chocolate-covered dassberries. A footman hovered over his shoulder with a flagon of craniss wine, but he didn't finish even his first goblet. Tonight, he needed a clear head.

The crowd below watched him and whispered about him without any attempt at concealment. They didn't seem to mean it rudely, but their curiosity obviously remained to be sated.

Halfway through the meal, at a signal from Tireus, the entertainment began. The orchestra, in their balcony, struck up a heroic march, and a troupe of actors entered. Half a dozen were dressed as Cherazii, their skin painted white and veined with blue, with large swords strapped to their backs. A few were dressed in the red uniforms of Koraud. A teenage boy with dark hair wore brown trousers and a loose white tunic stained with red. He carried a big Cherazim sword in one hand and a white rock lofted in the other.

It took Chris a second to realize the boy was supposed to be him and the play was a reenactment of his crossing. The actors spoke no lines, relying instead on the swell of the music and their own stylized body language. For the remainder of the meal, they ran and leapt and jumped across the open floor between the king's table and the nobles.

Whoever put the play together had obviously heard only a secondhand account of events—and nothing about Mactalde's involvement. In this version, Chris woke in the woods to the sounds of the Koraudian attack on the Cherazii. Without hesitation, he jumped into the fray, killing fully half the enemy before being overcome. Enter stage left: a woman in a flowing white gown, accompanied by half a dozen Guardsmen. That pretty much spelled the end for the Koraudians. The rescued Cherazii fled, and the Guardsmen and the Searcher alike knelt to the Gifted's bravery and prowess.

That wasn't quite the way he remembered it.

As the applause died down and the troupe took their bows and ran out of the room, Tireus stood. He motioned for silence and the people hushed expectantly.

"As I'm sure you all know, it is my extreme honor to host an unprecedented second Gifted." He sounded so sincere, Chris almost believed him. Allara's trick of hiding behind a professional mask had obviously been learned from a master.

"The Gifted always come to Lael when we need them most. And as we stand on the brink of war, I think it's apparent our needs are many. We face troubled times. Even this very night, I and Lord Denegar, among others, leave to join our troops on the Aiden River. But I rejoice we do not face the trials of these times alone. We have a Gifted."

He extended his arm toward Chris. "We know not yet what his gifts may be, but we trust he was sent to us because he, and he alone, can bring us the succor we need most. And that, more than anything, is why I am pleased you should all bear witness to the ceremony that welcomes Master Chris Redston to our kingdom and knights him as a lord among us." He gestured Chris forward with his fingers. "Rise."

Chris stood, one hand on his scabbard to keep it from bumping the chair, and trailed Tireus around to the front of the table.

Allara knelt behind her father and held up a jeweled rapier in one hand and a flickering candle globe in the other. She breathed steadily, her features composed, and gave him a little nod.

Servants dimmed the lights by raising nets of black cloth, secured to long poles, to cover the glassed-in chandeliers. Here it was then. His big moment. Tireus took the globe from Allara and held it in both hands as he turned back to Chris.

"I give you your old life. Turn upon it. Blow it out."

He did as he and Allara had practiced earlier that afternoon and put his hands over Tireus's. Then he leaned forward and blew out the candle, dousing the room in darkness.

Tireus slipped his hands out from under Chris's and left him holding the globe, while he reached back for a smoldering punk. Chris balanced the globe in one hand and accepted the punk with the other. He took a deep breath and spoke loudly enough for the whole room to hear him.

"I take my new life. I stride out into it. I ignite it."

He touched the punk to the candle's wick, and it sputtered before catching. As soon as he had a proper flame, he set aside the punk and lowered himself to one knee.

Tireus had accepted the rapier from Allara's upraised hands. He lifted the sword in front of his face.

"You are the Gifted. Sir Chris Redston." He lashed the blade down on each of Chris's shoulders, hard enough to slice through the doublet material without touching skin.

The lights came back on, and Chris rose to face the crowd.

"Will you swear your fealty?" Tireus asked the room.

Every chair slid back. The women knelt immediately, their skirts puffing out around them. The men paused to draw their swords, then clanked to their knees beside their wives and daughters.

"Fealty!" they roared. "To the Gifted, to the king, and to Lael!"

Tireus turned the rapier around and offered Chris the jeweled basket hilt. "Tonight, they're yours," he murmured. "Speak to them."

Now came the part he had been dreading. He steeled himself with a breath and eased to his feet.

Allara remained on her knees behind her father. Her face was passive, tight, but she tucked her chin in a nod probably intended to be reassuring.

He turned to the crowd and raised his sword, still following the script. "Rise, and thank you."

They stood, and he lowered the sword. And now he was supposed to make a speech that would tell them how exceedingly honored he was and what a slam-bang Gifted he was going to turn out to be. He was supposed to inspire them with hope and give them confidence.

"Thank you," he said again. "I, um, I'm honored to be the Gifted." He stared out into the sea of eager, cynical, hopeful, laughing faces. Allara had told him to be honest. "I'm not going to lie. I haven't been here very long, and I still have a lot to learn. But I'm working hard—" He half-glanced back at Allara. "We're working hard, so we'll be ready to meet this threat."

The crowd shifted. Those who had been eager and hopeful frowned and whispered to one another. Those who had been cynical and amused only looked the more so. This was not the speech they'd been expecting.

What was he supposed to say? That he had it all under control? That he was here to save the day and their worries were over?

He gave it another shot. "You have a long history of Gifted coming to your aid and helping in the need of the time. And I promise you I will do everything in my power to meet those expectations."

A man called out, "I've heard you're the son of a Belkin Bay fisherman."

He turned to find the speaker, a big man with several gold medallions strung across his chest.

"Why should that interest you?"

Beneath waxed mustachios, the man's lip twisted. "Why shouldn't it interest me? We're about to go to war with Faolan Mactalde, and the son of a ruddy fisherman is all set to lead us into battle."

He could feel the weight of every gaze in the room. In his peripheral vision, Allara stood. If he wasn't careful, he was going to find himself tripping over that wrong impression she was so worried about and landing flat on his face.

His hand tightened around his hilt. "I'm not leading you into battle. That's not my job."

"Indeed not." Tireus walked up beside him. "The Gifted has his own role to play, as do we all. Please sit, everyone. The footmen will be bringing in mugs of mulled craniss. We will drink to the war, and, more importantly, to peace!"

With a murmur, half satisfaction, half displeasure, the crowd sat.

Across the table from the original heckler, a skinny old man with a pointy cap pulled low over his ears blustered, just loud enough for Chris to hear him. "As lords of the realm, we have every right to know whether we're pledging our allegiance to an incompetent."

Chris glanced up and caught sight of Parry in an empty balcony. The kid grinned and shook his clasped hands above his head. If he thought the speech deserved congratulations, he was the only one.

Chris returned to his seat, drank the sweetness of the mulled craniss to its dregs, and tried to keep his frustration from his face. In the history of Gifted ceremony speeches, his had probably just made the record books as the worst. He'd failed to make a good impression, failed to inspire the troops, and failed to discover what, if any, gifts he was supposed to use to save Lael.

Forty minutes later, the guests trooped out, bowing and curtsying. He bowed right back and looked every single person in the eye. He had made a fool of himself, but he wasn't cowed. And he wasn't quitting, even if that's what half these stuffed shirts wanted him to do.

Finally, Tireus led Chris and Allara into the back hall. Denegar followed.

"Well," Tireus said. "Could have been worse." He touched his hand to the back of Allara's head and pulled her forward so he could kiss her forehead. "And now we're off. We'll take the skycar to the Wall and ride down. With any luck, we'll reach the Aiden River camp in three days."

She touched his hand. "Be careful."

He nodded and turned to Chris. "Keep at your training. Gifted have a way of becoming useful. Whether any of us like it or not, we'll probably be calling you up sooner or later."

After tonight, Tireus wasn't likely to be in any great hurry.

Chris nodded anyway. "I'll be ready."

"See that you are." Tireus turned to go.

Denegar stepped up to shake Chris's hand. "Gifted are good for morale."

"You're sure of that?"

"Just because you can't make a speech doesn't mean a thing. Or not much at any rate." He grunted. "Depending on what things are like at the front, I'll send you a message in the next week or two. In the meantime, do like his majesty says and keep training." He patted Allara's shoulder, then followed Tireus out.

Chris breathed out a sigh. Despite the fact nobody wanted him at the front, he couldn't help feeling he should be going with them. "So much for first impressions."

Allara unpinned her hood and let it fall. Her hands were shaking, and her eyes blazed. "They didn't give you a chance out there tonight."

"Don't tell me you're defending me."

She stabbed a finger at the banquet hall door. "What were they expecting? A bloody rehearsed-and-polished show straight out of the bloody Russo Theater? Do they think Gifted cross over the worlds like avenging angels, born ready to slay dragons and strike heroic poses?"

"Don't they sometimes?"

"No, they're like you." She faced him. "They're all like you. You come across like newborn babes, lost and confused, and it's a rotted wonder you find the strength and the commitment to rise up and *become* heroes and legends. But you do." Some of the fire drained from her face. "Eventually."

She turned around and toyed with the jeweled hairpin in her hand. "You're still rising up. You're still becoming. And if that self-righteous lot had any brains at all, they'd see that."

Of all the reactions he'd expected from her, this hadn't been on the list. He *had* expected her to be angry and frustrated and embarrassed. But, mostly, he'd expected those emotions to be directed at him.

"It wasn't a total loss," he said. "Parry liked the speech."

It took a few seconds for that to penetrate whatever moil of thoughts she was immersed in. Finally, she snorted softly. "Parry liked the speech. Well, that's something."

"I guess we'll be adding speechmaking to my training sessions."

"No. The best speeches aren't the kind you learn. They're the kind that well up from deep inside you, charisma born of passion." She started for the stairs, then stopped, one hand on the newel post. "I asked you to be honest, and you were. But honesty can only speak to honesty. If everyone in that room had been as honest as you, they would have heard you."

He watched her climb the stairs. Honesty. Well, if they were both being honest, they'd have to admit that the moment this war came down to him making a speech, they were sunk.

27

THE FIRST SIGN of trouble came, not from Aiden River, but from Chicago.

Kaufman and Flores hadn't made a squeak in the weeks since Chris had spotted Flores outside Harrison's hospital room. He'd kept a low profile ever since, but he was getting cabin fever.

A week after Tireus and Denegar left for the Aiden River, he went to sleep in Lael, woke up in Chicago, and decided he'd had just about enough of this house arrest business. He left a note for Mike and headed out on foot. He had to stop putting this life on hold while he lived the one in Lael. He had to start writing again, *something*.

He spent the afternoon in a coffee shop, trying to dig up anything he could find on Faolan Mactalde. But, by the end of the day, he'd come up with basically zilch. The few articles he'd uncovered, written by the good doctor, were filled with psychobabble and evasive doublespeak—all of which might have sounded impressive if he hadn't personally seen the other side of the mental wall.

He took a taxi home and stared out the window as the streetlights washed over him one after another.

He needed to see his dad. But that thought choked his heart. His *real* dad—his worn-out, sad, alcoholic dad—was once again an open wound. In Lael, Chris could pretend he was whole again as he sat around the hearth with a full family, all of them happy and smiling save for the underlying tension of his new strangeness to them. He could look at his father, and his father could look back. Strong, merry, powerful, and honest. That was the father that might have been. That was the father he could pretend he'd always had, so long as he didn't ever have to see the other one again.

And yet he needed to. He needed to do . . . what? Apologize? He shook his head, and the old black hole of anger pulled at him. Apologize for what? Paul was the one who had ruined both their lives, not him.

So he kept putting it off.

The other thing he needed to do was stop wasting time. In Lael, he and Allara and Quinnon spent every minute racing the clock to prepare for the day when the war would need him—or, even more ominous, when the world would need him.

The weather was growing slowly, almost infinitesimally, more erratic. The heat of summer had almost completely vanished. Every day dawned cloudy, and every day the clouds darkened. People in the streets stared at the skies and muttered, but most of them shrugged it off. Weather was weather. *You should have seen the storms we had on this lake when I was a lad* . . . If any of them guessed the true cause, they didn't seem to be sharing their conclusions. Or, at any rate, their rumors had yet to spread to the palace hill.

But none of that changed the fact that something had to be done about it, and Chris was probably the person who was supposed to do it.

About ten blocks from home, the taxi meter reached the amount of cash he had on him, so he paid the driver, and started hiking down the sidewalk. His breath turned to blue smoke beneath the lights.

A car passed him, headed the same direction, and he glanced up. The glare of its headlights struck a truck parked across the street from his house.

He stopped short.

It was a black truck, same as the one he'd seen on the North Shore the day Kaufman had shot at him. A man sat outlined in the driver's seat. Mactalde's bodyguard.

His heart rate sped up. He backpedaled, praying the man hadn't already seen him. But no flicker of movement from the cab indicated Kaufman was preparing to give chase.

This wasn't good. Mike would still be working at the radio station, until after his late show, so Kaufman couldn't have gotten to him. Assuming he wanted to get to anybody besides Chris. Chris turned the

fenced corner and kept going until he reached the shadow of an over-
grown willow.

There was no way Chris could go home now. And, with his cell
phone in Lael, he couldn't even give Mike a heads up. His heart
pounded, and he turned around and broke into a jog. With no phone,
no credit card, and no cash, he had no way of getting transportation
or a room for the night. Even if he got a call through, Mike couldn't
come get him without the risk of being tailed.

He'd have to get ahold of somebody else. He definitely wasn't
calling his dad. By this late in the evening, he'd be too sozzled to
drive. And that left Brooke.

Brooke's silver Land Rover turned onto the circular drive at Sher-
man Park, and the doors unlocked with a pop.

Chris opened the passenger door and climbed into the seat. "Did
you call Mike?"

She grinned. "Don't I even get a hello?"

"Brooke." He was in no mood for her oblivious cheerfulness. "Did
you call him?" If Mike got hurt because of him, he would never
forgive himself. He'd made more than his share of stupid decisions
in his life, but not calling the cops on Kaufman, just to save his own
hide, was beginning to look like one of the worst.

Her smile faded a little. "Sure. I left a message with the manager at
the station. Told Mike not to go home until you'd talked to him."
She put the car back into gear and circled the drive to merge with
traffic. "So what's going on?"

"Can I borrow your phone?"

She pouted and nodded to where the phone leaned inside the
drink holder. "You are so exasperating sometimes. You never want
to tell me anything. You act like I'm out to get you half the time."
She glanced at him from the corner of her eye. "When have I ever
not tried to help you?"

"I'm sorry I'm exasperating, and I'm sorry I don't tell you anything." Small white lie there. He punched in Mike's cell number. "It's
not personal, and it never has been. I just don't—" The phone started to ring, and he broke off.

She finished for him. "Trust me."

"That's not it." Actually, it was. But telling her that would be like kicking an adoring puppy.

Mike picked up. "Hey, kiddo. What's up with this crazy message from our crazy friend?"

"It's me," Chris said.

"Oh, the crazy friend himself. Look, I'm hungry and beat. So talk fast because I want to go home."

"You can't go home." He took a breath. "You know that guy who was shooting at me? He's got your place staked out."

Brooke nearly drove off the road. "*What?*"

Chris reached instinctively to steady the wheel. She straightened the car back out and gaped at him.

On the other end of the line, Mike echoed her question, "What's going on? Where are you?"

"With Brooke. Everyone's fine. He didn't see either of us."

"And now you're going to call the cops, right? 'Cause if you won't, I will."

"Yes. We're going there now." He glanced at Brooke, and she obediently hit her blinker.

"And then what?" Mike's mood sounded like it was somewhere near the crossroads of disbelief, frustration, and borderline fear.

"And then Brooke's dropping me at a hotel. And I think you better find one for the night as well."

"And what about Pluto?" Mike's voice bit deep on the bass end.

"I'll get the cops to feed him when they drop by to check it out." Chris dug around for the right thing to say. Unfortunately, at this point, he was fresh out of right things. "Mike, I'm sorry."

Mike heaved an exhale. "I don't know what you're mixed up in, but do me a favor and . . . don't do it again." He hung up.

Chris flipped the phone shut and dropped it back into the drink holder. So much for making good use of his time today. Although if he'd been at home this afternoon, Kaufman might well have plugged him already.

Brooke shot him several glances. "You are okay, right?"

"Just peachy." He rubbed the back of his head. If he'd been at Réon Couteau instead of Glen Arden, would he have been able to see this coming in the lake? "I'm sorry I got you involved in this."

"That's all right." She gave a little shrug. "It's scary, of course. But it's also kind of exciting." She glanced at him again. "You don't really want to go to the cops, do you?"

"What else am I supposed to do? There's no way I'm letting you or Mike get hurt just because I don't want to talk to the police."

She shook her hair back from her face and stared at the ribbon of lights that filled the road ahead. "How about I make you a deal? *I'll* talk to the cops. I'll tell them I went by your place earlier and saw this creepy guy breaking into the house."

"I don't know that he broke in."

She waved him off. "Doesn't matter. That'll get somebody out there. The point is you won't have to talk to them."

He chewed on that. As far as it went, it sounded pretty good. "And what do you get out of this?"

"You tell me what's going on?" The lift of her eyebrows was hopeful.

He fiddled with the heater vent. "That's a long story."

"And unless I'm much mistaken, the next chapter seems to be unfolding in Mercy General Hospital. With a leading actor by the name of . . . Harrison Garnett?"

"Where'd you hear that?" He hadn't told her Harrison's name.

"I told you I have contacts." She sounded as smug as she looked. "I asked around about that shooting."

"You really need to stay out of this. You're wading into water about five feet over your head."

"I'm a reporter!"

"No. You're not."

She careened onto the shoulder, car horns blaring behind her.

He braced both hands against the dash. "Hey!"

She braked hard and slammed the gear into neutral. "I am *going* to be a reporter." This time the pout was paired with a determined knit in her forehead. "Chris." She licked her lips. "You could have been shot. We could all be shot, for that matter. So tell me the truth. Was the bullet that got Harrison Garnett meant for you?"

"It's complicated."

She crossed her arms. "If you don't want to tell me what's going on, fine. Maybe I don't want to be your private chauffeur. You can walk to the cops."

"Brooke . . ." Maybe it had been a mistake to call her in the first place. "Look—"

"No, you look. You tell me what the deal is, or you can forget it. If you can't trust me enough to tell me—"

"What about you trusting *me*?" He glared. "That road goes two ways."

She leaned against the door. "Yeah, but I'm driving right now. Tell me or not."

He hesitated. Brooke wasn't Mike. She had the best of intentions but not the sense to keep her nose in her own business.

Unfortunately, however, his choices were slipping away.

"All right, fine," he said. "This guy who's tailing me, he worked for Mactalde. I saw him there at Mactalde's house the day before he disappeared."

She uncrossed her arms and leaned forward. "And you think he's the one who kidnapped or killed Mactalde?"

"No. I think Mactalde hired Kaufman to kill me and this other guy, Flores, to kill Harrison."

"Kaufman?" That seemed to catch her off guard. She sat back and chewed on her lip.

"You know him?"

"Mmm, maybe. I'll have to investigate it."

"No, don't investigate it." He gave her shoulder a little shake. "I mean it. I would hate myself for the rest of my life if something happened to you because of me."

Her smile bloomed. "That's sweet."

"I am not trying to be sweet here. I wish you'd . . ." He looked out his window, then back. "I wish you'd stop reading things into what I say. I don't mean to be unkind, but what I wish is that you could get over this crush, or whatever it is, you've had on me since we were kids."

The smile faded. She turned away.

"I'm sorry." He touched her shoulder again. "I want to trust you. I see you all the time, almost as much as I see Mike. We should be friends, good friends. But I need you to stand back and be sensible. About us, about everything."

She'd always bruised easily. That was the only reason he'd never said any of this before, no matter how exasperated she made him. But right now this was bigger than just her feelings. For once in her life, she needed to hear the truth, and she needed to believe it.

"Please, Brooke."

A car zipped past, so close it rocked the Land Rover.

She reached for the gear. "I'll take you to a hotel." Her voice sounded both wobbly and resolute. "You can use my credit card, so the room won't be under your name. And I'll take care of everything at the police station. I won't even mention you."

"Thank you." He waited while she put the car back into drive and pulled into traffic. "And you won't investigate any further? You'll promise me you'll stay out of it?"

After a long hesitation, she looked over at him. "I have a question, and you need to answer it. How can everything have gone haywire all of a sudden? Mike told me about the letter and the dreams you've been having. I guess that's why you went to the psychologist, right? So then the psychologist disappears, some guy gets shot, and now you're on the run, and you refuse to talk to the police about any of it. It's all nuts."

"I know." And she didn't understand the half of it. He stared at the blur of headlights. Rain misted the windshield.

She flipped on the windshield wipers. "Even the weather isn't normal!"

And that was his fault too. He cleared his throat. "If that's the question you wanted to ask, I don't have an answer."

"No." She straightened from hunching over the wheel. "That's not my question. My question is—do you know what happened to Mactalde?"

He hesitated. She knew him well enough to recognize in a second if he was lying, but if he didn't tell her something, she'd start digging like a dog after a bone on the other side of a wire fence. Right now, he wasn't in a position to be alienating allies. Especially an ally who was paying for his hotel room.

"Yes, I know what happened."

"Then what was it?"

"He's not dead. Let's just leave it at that."

Her jaw dropped. "You *are* involved with his disappearance!"

"C'mon. You think I killed him? Is that it, huh?"

"Did you?"

"*No.*"

She turned into a hotel parking lot and braked in front of the entrance. "Just tell me whether or not he's safe."

"He's safe. He left of his own free will. And as far as I know he has no intention of coming back. Do you think I'd take advantage of your trust?"

"I don't know." She got out of the car. Before slamming the door, she stuck her head inside. "But I *do* trust you, even if you don't trust me."

Fifteen minutes later, she returned with his card key and room number. "Here." She shoved the key into his hands. "You will try to stay safe, won't you?"

"Yeah, I'll try." He unbuckled his seatbelt and opened the door to the spitting rain. "Thanks for your help."

She shrugged. "That's all I ever really wanted to do for you, you know."

"I know. Thank you."

He climbed out and stood in the parking lot while she drove away. Then he turned his coat collar up and trudged into the hotel. His room was on the third floor—a stale-smelling single. He chucked his coat in the chair, kicked off his shoes, and lay back against the headboard. Sleep was already tugging at his eyes. Lael was calling. Any minute now, he'd fall awake and find—

—a ray of light slamming against his eyelids.

Muttering filtered into his hearing, and something poked his arm. "Chris—Chris—"

He dragged his eyes open and found himself in his bed at Glen Arden.

Parry stood in the gap in the bed curtains. Trepidation twisted his pocked face. "Her ladyship told me to wake you. The battle at Aiden River has started. You have to leave."

28

ALLARA'S WORLD STOPPED in place. She stood atop the Karilus Wall and stared toward the Aiden River, almost twenty leagues away. Columns of smoke tinged the horizon.

In the two days of rocking along the skycar tracks between Glen Arden and the Wall, she had kept her doubts to herself. They had known war was coming. They had known her father would be summoning Chris. Now that he'd done so, it meant nothing more or less than that. The sooner the battle was fought, the sooner it could be won.

But at every station, Quinnon had inquired for news of the battle, and at every station, the faces grew more somber. The armies had dug in between the Goraudian and Aiden Rivers. The battle everyone had believed would be over in days had stretched into weeks.

The country here was wild and barren, more stone than soil. The sheer gray lip of the cliff spread beyond sight in either direction. Behind them lay the Tosh Barrens, a rocky, heath-covered expanse, home only to ascetics and rock goats. Before them, the Karilus Wall sheered away, straight down into the sea of mist that camouflaged the fertile farm country watered by the Mistgloam River's three tributaries: the Northfall, the Goraudian, and the Aiden. Only a narrow switchback, blasted into the cliff face, led down.

The wind shifted and carried to her ears the whispered thud of artillery, but it couldn't keep pace with her heart. This was what she had fought all her life to prevent. And now here it was.

Quinnon led Rihawn over. "Stationmaster says the Koraudians hadn't broken through last he knew. He also says the Wall trail should be clear all the way down. Same with the roads and fords between here and our lines, if luck's with us."

"Do you feel lucky?"

He handed her the reins and turned to mount his own horse.

She checked her girth and swung aboard. Behind her, a squad of Guardsmen mounted and formed up. Chris, on a dappled palomino, trotted over. She almost opened her mouth to say something, if only to have him say something back. She wanted reassurances.

But that was supposed to be her job, not his. And after days of conversations that included no more than a dozen syllables, the words didn't find her tongue easily. This distance between them was of her own making, and she knew it. And loathed it.

He seemed to have accepted her reserve. He never questioned it, and part of her lamented it, for no good reason. If he *had* questioned her, she would just have pushed him even farther away.

Is this what her life had doomed her to? This inability to form normal relationships? Or was this what *she* doomed herself to? She made herself look away from him. Everything came at a price, including protection, for both of them.

He watched the horizon, and his face grew stern. "How far to the river?"

"It will take us the rest of the day." The wind buffeted her, and she turned up the collar of her coat. "Two hours down the Wall, then perhaps another four to the river, if we push the horses all the way."

"And when we get there?"

"God only knows." Some hard and resolute angle in his face sparked a fearful thought. "But we're not here to fight. You're still not ready for that, and it's not your responsibility anyway. You're here to inspire the troops." She watched him, willing him to look at her, and when he did, she willed him to nod, which he didn't.

"Right." He reined away to where Quinnon sat his horse at the edge of the Wall.

Quinnon waited for her, his good eye squinched tighter than usual. He hated heights, hated the Wall path. It was the only thing she'd ever known that could make him flinch. It *could* make him flinch, but he didn't.

When she nodded, he straightened around in his saddle and nudged his horse forward. She followed, Chris behind her, and the Guardsmen behind him.

Down, down, the horses picked their careful way. Even Rihawn kept his head low and his footsteps careful. She gave him the bit and concentrated on keeping her weight centered and her body at an angle that matched the declivity.

The thud of a faraway explosion wafted across the leagues separating her from the Aiden River. Sweat burned around her collar. She shivered anyway. This was the sound of Lael at war. Mactalde had come, and now Lael had no choice but to fight. Somehow the thought of it lit her insides with fire. She had never engaged on a real battlefield or ridden at the front of a charge with sword raised. Never clashed against the enemy lines and screamed herself hoarse with wordless battle cries. She'd never been in battle or killed an enemy when her blood was raging.

But she wanted to.

The wind caught at her coat. She lifted her face to the rain. She wanted to fight until she died fighting. Perhaps there would be release in that. Release and honor and purpose, at last. Chris was right about her fear and her anger. They had fueled her for so long she'd almost forgotten how much she fed off their energy.

The hours slipped past, with a stop every thirty minutes at the flat resting spots. The horses descended the path, nose to tail, and their hooves scattered pebbles down the face of the Wall. In front of them, all the way to forever, the tall gloamwheat of the flatlands glinted silver in the mist. Here and there, purple vinebuds studded the fields.

From behind her, a Guardsman called, "Look!"

Barely fifty spans to the south, a score of Cherazii galloped out of the trees bordering the Northfall River.

Her hand dropped to her estoc, strapped atop her rifle scabbard. Few Cherazii would dare harm a Searcher, but they held no great love for her these days. "Quinnon."

"I see 'em. It's not an attack party. They've got women and children with them."

"Why would Cherazii ride this far out of the hills?"

He slipped his heavy chewser pistol from its holster. His thumb rode the hammer. "River's gotten too hot for 'em today, I reckon."

"Or perhaps they've come hunting the Gifted?"

"I don't think so," Chris said from behind. "They couldn't know I'd be here. And they wouldn't bring women and children on a hunting party."

"Once they figure it out, it won't matter if that's their purpose in being here or not. They'll kill you just the same." She kept herself from even glancing back at him. She couldn't risk drawing attention to him. Twenty Cherazii could overpower their squad of Guardsmen without even trying.

Fifteen minutes later, they reached the Wall's base. Half a dozen warriors, Rievers riding behind them, circled the foot of the path. They dressed alike for the most part, in leather tricorns and long layered coats, split up the back. Every one of them gripped either sword or axe, the blades lackluster from use. In the sward beyond, their women and children waited, the unbraided half of the women's hair loose to the wind and the bold red, green, and purple of their gowns glaring against the gray day. They stared at Allara's group, their expressions hard.

At the center of the defensive semicircle, an elder, his gray hair in two bound braids down his chest, laid his war club across his knees. "You can stop there."

Quinnon cocked the chewser, and its faint hum charged the air. "Did we ask you for trouble, blue?"

"Not today." The elder's voice was as cracked and worn as the wrinkles that cut through his white skin like the grain on a heffron tree. "We seek the high country, you seek the low. And no doubt you crave haste as much as we do."

Allara rode up beside Quinnon. "You come from the Aiden?"

The Cherazim glanced at her and tipped his chin in grudging recognition. "Thereabouts. The Koraudians attacked again at dawn."

She hardly dared say the words: "My father?"

Cherazii faces were notoriously difficult to read. But something in the flicker of his eyes might have hinted at sorrow. "He's fighting a losing battle, Searcher. The Koraudians have his back to the Wall."

Chris's horse moved forward, and Allara stiffened. He needed to stay back. She drew her sword a full hand span from its scabbard before she stopped herself.

He faced the old Cherazim and greeted him with his hand to his chest. "How did you escape the battle?"

If the Cherazim recognized Chris, the carved stolidity of his expression never altered. "We crossed into Lael just before the border was closed. We scented the battle last night and camped this side of the Aiden. It was only a matter of running a few outposts."

Chris regarded him. "Do any of the Cherazii fight with Tireus?"

"Why should we fight for an army that protects heretics and traitors? Justice departed Lael long ago." He tilted his head. "You're an outlander."

Chris nodded.

"How far outland?"

Chris had the wisdom to at least think about his answer. He had to know he was in considerable danger right now. "Far enough."

The old Cherazim sucked his teeth. "We've heard rumors another Gifted has come."

Allara raised her chin. "Would you fight with him if he has?" The Cherazii claimed to be the only true followers of the old traditions. But those traditions demanded they rally to the Gifted. And what did they do now? The Gifted rode to war, and the Cherazii rode away.

"We have never ceased to fight." The Cherazim turned in his saddle and gestured the rest of the group forward. When he turned back, his eyes ran up and down Chris's length. "I have so little faith remaining I'm not even sure it is there at all. But should I hear a worthy Gifted leads what is left of the armies of Lael, perhaps I will ply my sword beneath his banner. Perhaps." His lip curled, and he released his hold on his horse's mouth. "We have also heard rumors this new Gifted is not so worthy."

Allara's breath caught. Beneath the lines of his jerkin, Chris's body tightened.

"However," the Cherazim said, "I do not act upon rumors, no matter what they say. I await proof." As the rest of his party trotted up behind him, he saluted Allara with his war club. "Haste to your battle, Searcher. May the God of all prevail."

"May the God of all prevail." She echoed the formal sentiment and reined away before he could change his mind about the rumors.

As the Cherazii urged their weary horses up the wall in a clatter of pebbles, she touched her spurs to Rihawn's sides and left them behind. So the nightmare had started in earnest. Mactalde was hammering at the gates, and all that stood between him and the uttermost reaches of Lael was a trapped and demoralized army and a Gifted who was barely a month across. She led the way to the banks of the Northfall, the rain misting against her face. Her lungs drew in the cold smell of water, and she closed her mouth and held the breath.

Rihawn hurtled through the trees, and she leaned low over his neck. When he leapt into the river, she straightened and tossed her braid over her shoulder. Water splashed from behind, hoofbeats smashing through the water and into the riverbed. Quinnon, pistol still in hand, galloped past without a glance.

As they clambered up the far bank, Chris's horse fell into stride next to Rihawn. "He knew who I was."

"Yes."

"He'll know the rumor is true if we ever meet again. And I won't blame him for exacting justice."

"I will." The words churned up from deep in her chest.

Together, they emerged from the trees, and the horses lengthened into a desperate gallop, their legs lashing the grass.

By the time they reached the Aiden River crossing, stragglers from the Army of Lael were everywhere. They ran with all the strength left in their bodies, their weapons abandoned behind them.

"Hold!" Quinnon blocked their way. But they ran on, most too blind with fear to notice his officer's medallion.

He galloped after one and dragged him back. "Hold yourself there, and tell me what goes on here."

The soldier, a boy of seventeen or eighteen, groveled on his knees. His bloodshot eyes bulged. "Mactalde *has* come back! I wouldn't have believed it, but I saw it for myself."

Quinnon grabbed his collar and yanked him to his feet. "A lamb-faced bodkin like you wouldn't know Mactalde if you met him at a Commemorating Festival! You weren't even born when he died!"

"I swear it's him! It has to be him! And if'n it ain't, it don't matter, 'cause he's about to win the war! He's going to kill us all!'"

Allara snatched at his sleeve. "What about my father? Where's the king?"

He stared at her, blankly. His breath wheezed.

"Where is he?" She shook his arm.

"I don't know." He almost burst into hysterics. "I swear I don't know. But his banner still flies!"

Chris braced one hand against his horse's steaming shoulder. "Then the order for retreat hasn't been given?"

The foot soldier glanced back and forth between Chris and Allara. "I don't know."

Quinnon hauled him off his feet again and reined his gray around. "Get back across the river and fight, or I'll kill you myself."

They galloped to the Aiden. Battle cries and screams of pain echoed above the crash of artillery. Fires raged in the brush on the far side of the river, and the stench of smoke and blood clogged the air. Allara crowded her sword and her reins into one hand and drew her straitquin pistol with the other.

Ahead, through the veil of smoke, the gaunt frame of an elevated cannon bucked as it launched round after round. Black-faced bombardiers, their eyes wild and white, never ceased from the frantic rhythm of their work. They lowered the great bronze cannon, engraved with Lael's rearing stag, from its towering wooden frame. Once it was within reach, they swung the barrel over so the gaping mouth faced rearwards. They fed it with the smooth black fireballs that, in seconds, would burn across the gray sky.

Quinnon turned to find the chief bombardier. "Where's rear command?"

The man gestured toward the Wall behind. His shout disappeared in the crack of the cannon's launch.

Quinnon checked to make sure Allara followed, then spurred his horse forward. Side by side, she and Chris galloped after him through the confused and wounded troops.

Beyond the gusts of smoke, her uncle, Denegar Amras, sat his horse on a rise of ground. He peered into his spyglass and bellowed orders without looking around to see if they were being followed.

Quinnon stopped in front of him. "Where's the king?"

Denegar spared them barely a glance. "How the devil should I know? Down there someplace." Seeing Allara, he lowered the glass. "What do you think you're doing here? Get yourself to safety!"

On the far side of the smoke-laden meadow, Lael's army floundered, half its men scrambling in a futile retreat back to the Wall. Beyond the meadow, the swell of the plains ran red with charging Koraudians.

Her heart stuttered. If Mactalde was just *now* sending his full strength onto the field, the day was indeed lost.

In the middle of it all, the green and gold royal pennon wavered, disappeared for a moment in the smoke, reappeared, and wavered again.

"The battle's already lost," Quinnon said. "If the army doesn't get off that field, Mactalde will finish this war in one stroke."

Lael's ranks fell before the Koraudians like sand castles before the surf. Men who had held fast until now broke ranks and fled. She choked. Before her eyes, the Army of Lael was disintegrating. She darted her gaze back to the center of the field, where the pennon had waved. But the flash of green no longer blinked through the rolling smoke.

Her muscles twitched. "The flag . . ." Her father would be near it, somewhere. If the flag fell, so did the king, so did the army, so did the battle.

Denegar dragged savagely at his reins. "Get them out of here!" he snapped at Quinnon.

She started to rein away, then caught sight of Chris. He held in his horse with one hand and rooted through his saddlebags with the other.

"What are you doing?" she demanded. "We have to get out of here!"

From the saddlebags, he pulled out a simple black pistol, the like of which she'd never seen before.

Her heart jumped. "Where did you get that?"

He reined away. "I brought it across after word of the battle came. I'm still better with a gun than with a sword, and I can't fight close with the pistols you guys have." His eyes charted the battlefield.

"No." She seized his sleeve. "Are you mad? We're leaving. We have to leave now!"

He looked at her. "You leave. I'm going to do this."

Heat washed over her. "This is not what you're here for! If you die out there, do you think that's going to do anyone any good? Is that going to fix what's happened?"

"I'm not going to sit here. I'm done sitting." His face hardened. "If I stay here and watch while this whole thing comes down around our ears, then that's it, for both of us. I'd be finished just as surely as if I get shot out there."

She looked over her shoulder for Quinnon. "You can't go. I won't let you go." Anger rose to vanquish the fear. "The Koraudians will hack you apart before you can even cross the field!"

"You want to lose your war today?"

"The day is already lost! Nothing you do can save it!"

"I can get that pennon back up." He reined the horse away.

"No." She dug her fingernails into his sleeve. "You have to come with us. If you're killed today, we will have nothing left! *Nothing*. Quinnon!" The cry tore her throat.

He didn't look at her. "I told you before. I make my own decisions about how to act." Almost before she realized what he was doing, he pulled his arm free and laid his heels to his horse.

"No—" She closed her legs around Rihawn's girth, ready to follow. Quinnon blew past her. "Stay there!"

The two horses, gold and gray, thundered across the battleground, one in pursuit of the other, the other in pursuit of folly. The retreating army poured into the meadow at her feet. Most of the men ran for the river. Some scattered into the trees to the south. Behind her, Denegar bellowed for them to regroup.

She spun Rihawn around and spurred him back toward the river. If her Gifted insisted on throwing away his life, she at least had to attempt to keep him from dying in vain.

On the riverbank, the artillery thundered on. Bombardiers on one end loaded the cannons with combustible shells, while their partners dashed buckets of water over the blue glow of the hydraulic core. She galloped up to them and flung herself from her saddle. They stared as she caught hold of the crisscrossed support planks of a cannon's fifty-span frame and started climbing. The machine bucked, rebounding so hard it almost jerked out from beneath her.

Below, the chief bombardier shouted. "My lady, get down!"

"Keep firing!" Almost to the top, she hooked her arm over a plank and tucked her hand to the side to keep it clear of the cannon's rebound.

Running soldiers congested the sward below. They would see her, and they would recognize her as the only woman who could possibly have found her way to their battlefield.

"Listen to me!"

They stared as they ran past. Few slowed.

She filled her lungs. "The Gifted has come! The Gifted fights!" They would hear her. They had to hear her.

The bombardiers' blackened faces tilted up.

"The Gifted!" The cannon jolted, and a few men slowed their frantic pace in uncertainty.

A bombardier took up her cry. "The Gifted! The Searcher says the Gifted is here!"

The shout spread. Soldiers began to falter, to slow. They stared up at her.

"Look!" She pointed with her sword, and the men turned to see the two horsemen tearing across the field to face the Koraudian onslaught. "He rides to battle even now!"

Ripples of disbelief swarmed the army.

"The Gifted fights for Lael!" Her throat ripped on the words. "But he cannot fight alone!"

The retreat trickled to a halt. Men turned to watch Chris and Quinnon flying into death's teeth. They stood there, chests heaving, weapons at their sides, silent.

Then, from somewhere in their midst, a voice bellowed: "Rally!"

"Fight for Lael!" she cried. "Fight for the Gifted!"

The cry spread into a roar. What remained of the Army of Lael turned back to face their enemies. Denegar galloped up on the right flank to take charge of his men.

High above them all, she clung to the cannon's shuddering frame.

"Will you come down now, my lady?" the chief entreated.

"No." If Chris Redston was about to die, she had no choice but to watch until the end.

29

CHRIS'S HORSE LEAPT an artillery crater. He couldn't believe he was doing this. What lamebrain had come up with this plan? Oh, yeah, right, *him*.

The field was a churned-up mess of shell craters, burning grass, and bodies. Everywhere bodies. He forced the air in and out of his lungs. So this was war. That was the only thought his brain could seem to summon, and it ran circles inside his head. *So this is war.*

He'd seen a lot since crossing over. He'd seen people die. He'd held a sword in his hand and fought to survive. But not like this. This was destruction on a scale he had only heard about through the anesthetized fog of the evening news.

The smoke shut out sight for all but a few yards in front of him. The twisted bodies with their caverns of ruptured flesh appeared through the haze like breakers in the sea. Then, just as quickly, before he could look again and verify to his brain that what he was seeing was right, they were gone again.

The smoke couldn't block the sounds. Even the crash of his heart and the smashing of hoofbeats couldn't shut out the thunder of the artillery, the shouts of the living, and the screams of the dying. Blood slicked the ground, the smell of it sweet and sticky in the back of his nostrils. Every few steps, the horse slipped and staggered in its headlong run.

He'd signed on for a war. He'd known that's what this all was likely to lead to. But this wasn't what he'd expected.

Was war ever what people expected?

Quinnon had caught up to within half a length, but they'd come too far to turn back now. Ahead, through the smoke, the two armies' colors swarmed and clashed as Lael's green strained to stave off the red of Koraud's charge. Twice, someone had rushed to the standard and attempted to raise it. Twice, they had fallen.

A flaming padar bomb scored a path through the sky, and Chris ducked instinctively. The shell hit somewhere behind, and the impact chattered up through his teeth. Sparks and sod scattered against his back.

When he straightened, Quinnon had drawn up alongside him. "Are you out of your rotted mind?" His face held anger, but not panic like Allara's. An old fighter like Quinnon would know exactly what to expect from a war.

Chris couldn't say he liked Crea Quinnon. And he had little doubt about Quinnon's dislike for him. But, suddenly, he wanted the man's respect. This field, right here, right now, was probably the only place to earn it.

He breathed out hard and dragged in every ounce of composure he had in him. "You going to cover me or not?"

He caught only a glance of Quinnon's expression. It didn't change.

Twenty feet from the standard, a blood-encrusted Koraudian threw himself into Chris's path and planted his pike in the ground behind him. The spearhead caught Chris's horse full in the chest. The animal tumbled over the top of the Koraudian and hurled Chris from the saddle. The Koraudian squirmed from beneath the horse's legs, and Chris rose to one knee and extended the Glock 35 he'd picked up at a pawnshop back in Chicago.

With a roar, the Koraudian charged, his pike lofted in both hands. Chris fired once. The pistol jumped against his palm, and the bullet ripped through the Koraudian's arm. The soldier hit his knees, screaming, and Chris finished him with another shot to the head.

Then he was moving, swiveling, just as his father had taught him so long ago. Half a dozen shrieking Koraudians converged on him. As far as they were concerned, he'd fired his one shot and was done with the pistol.

He didn't even wait for them to look surprised. He hit another target and another and another until the hammer clicked against the empty magazine. He clicked it twice more, just for good measure, then rammed the pistol in his waistband.

Keeping his head down, he scrambled to where the standard was buried in a barricade of the dead who had tried to rescue it. Almost prone behind the pile of bodies, he dragged his chewser from his bandoleer holster, flicked on the hydraulics, and rolled over to fire again.

"You crazy fool." Quinnon stood over him, a sword in one hand and a dagger in the other. "Where in the rotted Four Kingdoms did you get that pistol?"

"You haven't seen anything yet. Remind me to bring you guys a schematic for an M16." He pried another slug from its slot on his bandoleer, and flipped open the chewser's breech to reload. "Now what?"

Quinnon scoffed. "This is your grand plan, bucko."

"Where's the king? Shouldn't he be around here someplace?"

"If he's alive."

Pistol in one hand, Chris used the other to claw bodies away from the flagstaff. The pole was fully ten feet long and top-heavy. He holstered the pistol, gritted his teeth, and levered it into the air. The flag caught the wind, and he twisted the pole to untangle it.

All around him, Laeler soldiers fled. He hoisted the flag in front of him and waved it furiously. "Stop running! Where's the king? Find the king and turn and fight!"

The pommel of Quinnon's sword hammered into one retreating soldier's temple and felled him in his tracks. "Fight or you'll fall where you bloody stand!"

A few of the men wavered; most didn't even notice. Koraudian cavalry galloped across the field and thundered past their footmen.

Quinnon growled. "*Och.* There he is."

Tireus fought beside the floundering body of a gutted horse. Half his adjutants were already dead on the ground, and the other half fought madly beside their king. One leapt from his horse and thrust the reins at Tireus. The king vaulted into the saddle and spun to face his fleeing troops. The distance obliterated his expression, but his shoulders suddenly straightened.

"Rally to your king!" Quinnon shouted.

The troops faltered in their retreat, even as the Koraudians poured into them.

Chris lofted the pennon against his shoulder. He stiff-armed a

Koraudian and shoved aside a confused Laeler. "Rally!"

Together, he and Quinnon ran. Quinnon plied his blades with the carelessness of skill. Chris drew and emptied his pistol into a hulking Koraudian and used it to club another in the face.

Ahead, Tireus spun his horse in a circle, sword lofted above his head. His screams of encouragement melted into a wordless blare.

Men surged up from behind and nearly knocked Chris over. Quinnon grabbed at his elbow and shoved him upright. He looked back. Hundreds upon hundreds of soldiers had re-crossed the field. Few, if any, remained in the rearguard. Far away, in the shadow of the Wall, the artillery had moved up. The cannons hurled their volleys overhead. Fire and destruction spread among the Koraudians.

Chris's heart tangled somewhere in between his thrashing lungs. Somehow, impossibly, the retreat had reversed.

His shoulders straightened. He bellowed wordless roars from deep in his chest. He ran, caught in the sweep of the charge. He could hear their frenzied battle cries:

"The Gifted, The Gifted, *The Gifted!*"

Even through the heat of blood and fire and sweat, a chill dragged gooseflesh up his back. They were fighting for *him.*

Chewser still in one hand, he drew his sword and kept going. The frontrunners of Lael's army reached Tireus at the same moment as the Koraudian charge. The foremost lines crumpled like paper dolls, cast aside by the men who ran behind so they, in turn, might be crumpled.

Above them all, Tireus led his army. He should be in the rear, protected, but he fought like a warrior and never looked back. He hacked at the Koraudians, cut them off his horse, and flung them back into the maelstrom.

Then Chris reached the fight, and the fight reached him. Shoulder to shoulder with Quinnon on one side and a stranger on the other, he braced for the collision. Quinnon broke from the line and angled in front of Chris, his blades keeping back the worst of the fight.

Chris didn't have time to wonder if he resented or appreciated it. He dropped the chewser and gripped his sword with both hands. For a second, his nerves nearly choked him. What was he doing? He had no idea what he was doing. Unlike all the rest in this world, he hadn't grown up with a sword in his hand.

And yet the blade that had been a stranger to him only a month before suddenly became the most familiar thing in the world. His conscious mind shut down. His brain churned through the whirl of images too fast for thought. His body fell into instinctual rhythms, and his muscles remembered what his mind could not.

Pike and axe handles splintered. Iron clashed against iron. Bones cracked and blood slimed the ground. The battle cries faded into the crackle of adrenaline. Time disappeared. Even the memory of time ceased. Only the ebb and flow of battle remained. The pounding of blade against blade, flesh against flesh, feet against sod. The chill of the wind, the heat of his blood.

So this was war.

He fought. He lunged and parried, hacked and slashed. His sword clashed against other swords. He swept them aside. He severed limbs. He opened chasms of blood. Men fell before him, staggering to their knees, some screaming, some silent as death. He ran on, fighting, shoving, roaring.

And then the moment of timelessness stretched and disintegrated.

"Hold fast!"

He blinked. How long since he had last remembered to draw a breath?

Quinnon yanked one of his blades from the belly of a Koraudian and bellowed an echo to Tireus's cry. "Hold fast in the lines!"

Now it was the Koraudians who fled to regroup their battered forces. A fireball rumbled into their midst, a trail of smoke scarring the sky. It struck hard and the padar—an oily substance supposed to burn through anything and be almost impossible to put out—sheeted the ground with flames.

An officer galloped along the lines. "Carabineers to the front! We must hold this ground until the army can retreat to a defensible position!"

The riflemen unslung their weapons and ran to the front.

Another officer shouted to the troops: "Fall back! Fall back to the river in orderly fashion. One battalion at a time!"

Chris looked down at himself. Blood and offal spattered his leather jerkin, his trousers, and his boots. It stuck to his face and stiffened as it dried. He would have wiped it away, but his clothes offered not a single clean spot. Even now, he could smell the stink of death and sweat upon him. Some of it was his; most of it wasn't.

"Let's move." Quinnon pushed his shoulder to turn him around.

He staggered with his first step and nearly went down. Adrenaline shook through him so hard he could barely stand.

"Well, now." Quinnon marched beside him. "Now you're a Guardsman."

Half an hour later, Chris and Quinnon reached the trees at the river and found Tireus, on horseback, dictating messages in a voice that still roared despite its hoarseness.

"Well." Tireus propped a hand on his hip. "What are you doing out here?"

"Sightseeing." The word cracked in the desert of Chris's throat.

"I called you out here to inspire the troops, not to get yourself killed alongside them."

Chris managed a shrug. "Sometimes it's all the same thing, don't you think?"

A smile tugged at Tireus's mouth, then bloomed into a gaping grin. He threw his head back and shouted with laughter. He was still drunk on the adrenaline.

"You may have some distance to go before you're a master tactician," he said, "but no one can critique your panache!"

Chris sheathed his sword and shook circulation back into his fingers. "Figured I didn't have anything to lose."

Quinnon harrumphed.

Tireus laughed again. "It's possible I may decide to like you after all. What do you say to that?"

"Don't go to too much trouble." He tried to keep the sarcasm from the words.

"Not a'tall. I've you to thank for what happened today." Tireus's grin softened a bit. "You'll find I give credit where credit's due. So hail the Gifted!" He gave his clenched fist a shake.

Chris nodded an acknowledgement.

Tireus snapped his fingers at an adjutant. "Find mounts for Captain Quinnon and the Gifted."

In a few minutes, when the soldier returned with a pair of horses,

Chris and Quinnon mounted and followed Tireus to the river. Violet dusk had begun to fall, hastened by the smoke and the heavy cloud cover. Chris took a last look over his shoulder. The blood and the bodies were fading into the shadows, with only the wail of the wounded to mark their places. The two armies, five hundred yards of churned-up ground between them, were digging in for the night. Artillery continued to hammer on both sides, even though all but the occasional volley fell well short.

He turned back to the river. Giant trees—hesperas they were called—stretched overhead. The thick trunks rose six feet from the mossy ground, then split into dozens of smaller trunks, all of which shot up to a towering height, from which a canopy of leaf-vines fell halfway back to the earth. The foliage's rustling muted the rumble of water over rocks, but his body still tightened at the sound. His thirst threatened to burn away even his drying sweat.

His horse clopped nearer, and whispers spread through the troops. The soldiers who crammed the riverbank turned, like dominoes, to look at his approach. All the way to the water, bloodstained, glassy-eyed survivors parted ranks before him. When he dismounted on the bank and knelt to drink, a burly axeman offered him a leather cup. He accepted it with a nod, and the man backed away with a knuckle against his forehead.

Was this how Gifted were treated in normal times? He wasn't sure if he liked it or not. These men were watching him as if he were their leader. And he wasn't. Even if Tireus decided he wanted to play it that way, that wasn't a role he would willingly take. He was a cog in the wheels here, and what he did to help, he would have to do outside the spotlight. Today had just been a fluke.

Tireus and Quinnon led their horses up on either side of him and crouched.

"Ever fought in a battle before?" Tireus asked.

Chris shook his head. He filled the cup and threw his head back to pour the freshness of the river down his throat. He filled it twice more and gulped the water. Then he filled it again and doused his head. For a moment, he knelt there, head hanging, and just breathed.

Beside him, Quinnon splashed water against a cut on his cheekbone. "You're as courageous as you are cocky, I'll give you that. But you're also bloody lucky. Battles are fickle creatures. You could have gotten yourself killed out here for nothing. A Gifted's not a common foot soldier to be used as cannon fodder, no matter how much *panache* he's got."

Tireus looked back at the troops. "How do we win if we don't risk?" He gripped Chris's shoulder. "Whether they saw you out there today or not, they see you now, stained with battle. They know you fought with them. They know you're the reason for the rally. I'd say you've done a ruddy splendid job inspiring them. I've underestimated you, and for that I'll apologize. You've just become a hero to these men, and for that I'll congratulate you."

Chris shook his head. "I'm just trying to put things right."

All around, the men went on staring, like children waiting for a magician to begin his act.

Tireus stood. "You may not have brought victory today, but at least you staved off defeat. And that's all that matters." He slapped Chris's shoulder and led his horse away.

The ranks opened to let him pass, but the men never took their eyes from the spot on the bank of the Aiden where Chris knelt.

30

THE BAD NEWS came during dinner.

While the grim row of cannons stood sentinel before the camp, the leaders of Lael's ragged army gathered in the king's tent to toast their near escape and plot tomorrow's stratagems. They had almost finished a meal of roast sweeta bird, some kind of baked fish, custard, and cheeses.

An orderly hurried to the head table and whispered in the king's ear.

Most of the officers, lofting their goblets and shouting of the day's exploits, didn't even notice his entrance. Chris, who occupied a seat of honor between Tireus and Denegar, wouldn't have paid him any heed either had he not seen Allara, on Tireus's other side, recoil.

". . . just arrived."

Tireus's goatee tightened around his frown. "Only one came back?"

"The others were left for dead. The man said he saw Lord Thyra fall."

Chris stiffened. This was about Eroll? His patrol had left to pursue Mactalde a month ago. Surely he would have given it up and headed home long before then. Surely he would have known weeks ago that Mactalde was already heading off to rendezvous with his army at the Aiden.

Allara didn't say anything, didn't even move. Her eyes grew huge in her stricken face.

Tireus dropped his napkin beside his plate. "I'll see to him directly." He strode out of the room without a backward glance, but his hand brushed Allara's shoulder as he passed.

For the space of a second, she looked at Chris. Emotions he couldn't quite grasp churned in her face. Then she bowed her head, and her hair dropped in a dark curtain past her cheek. She was afraid, more afraid than he'd ever seen her, with the kind of mindless terror that only hit when a loved one was about to be snatched away. It was a terror he knew intimately. His heart beat a dull rhythm.

She loved Eroll. It had been obvious in her face when she'd been with him. It was obvious in her dread now. Something twisted in his stomach. Something that was partly jealousy, but mostly guilt. If Eroll was indeed dead, Chris was the only one to blame. Eroll had gone chasing Mactalde because of Chris's mistakes, and Chris had just stabbed to the heart one of the best things in Allara's life.

He rose to follow Tireus.

"Eh—" Denegar glanced up, chewing. "What's this about?"

He didn't answer. He passed Allara, but she didn't raise her head.

A servant held aside the green curtain at the end of the tent's partition and dropped it behind him, leaving him in the shadows of the hall. Voices to the left led him to a smaller room near the exit, where a soldier in the purple livery of Thyra sat on a settee, head in his hands. A surgeon sponged the shoulder-to-elbow gash on his other arm.

Tireus stood over the soldier and rested a hand on the man's good arm. "I need to know what happened."

Footsteps tromped up behind Chris, and Quinnon stopped beside him in the doorway. He studied the soldier inside, and his mouth worked back and forth.

The man drew a staggered breath. "They attacked us in the middle of the night. We followed them as silent as sleep. I don't know how they knew we were there. It would've taken a Cherazim to have heard us."

The surgeon drew his first stitch, and he flinched.

"Everyone was killed?" Quinnon asked.

"Except me." He laughed, bitterly. "I think they let me go so I could come back and tell you. They hardly tried to stop me when I rode through their ranks."

Tireus leaned in, his voice husky. "Tell me about young Lord Thyra."

The soldier dropped his head and ran his good hand through his hair. "They shot him. In the back."

"Where did it happen?"

"In the Glockamon Moors, just short of the first bend in the Northfall River." He looked up. "How could this happen? How? Mactalde shouldn't even be here!"

All of Chris's energy balled inside his chest. His breath jammed.

Tireus jostled the soldier's shoulder. His voice, still hoarse from the day's shouting, cracked a bit. "Come now. No one blames you."

Chris's muscles jittered. "How do you know Lord Thyra's dead?"

All three men looked at him.

Tireus turned around. Beneath his beard, hard lines etched his mouth. Whatever approval he had held for Chris disappeared. "Garek saw him fall."

Chris took a breath. "Did you see him die?" He had to know.

Garek looked away. "No."

Tireus stepped away from the settee, his eyes firm against Chris's. "Enough. This isn't Garek's fault." His tone left little doubt whom he blamed. "What's done is done." He glanced back at the surgeon. "Find him a private tent for the night. Longer if he needs it."

He pushed through the door and held the flap, impatiently, as Quinnon and Chris followed. Then he dropped the door back in place and turned on Chris. His eyes were bloodshot from the battle smoke.

"You dare cast blame on that man? He did the only thing that could have been done. One could ask how things might be different had you done the same." He glared at Chris long enough to drive the point home, then stepped into the murky evening beyond the awning.

Chris couldn't halt the words that leapt to his tongue: "What if he's alive?"

Tireus stopped short. "Don't. You have no business with what's happened here. Eroll Leighton's death is a knife more than one of us will feel—Allara more than any, if that means a thing to you. But there isn't a rotted jot we can do about it now. He's a casualty of war. May the God of all bless his passing."

Chris shook his head. "I'm going after him." His mind had been made up even before he'd left Allara at the table.

Behind him, Quinnon stirred.

Tireus scoffed, but he did Chris the honor of taking his words seriously enough to turn around and face him. "You *are* daft. I loved Eroll Leighton like a son. I jest not when I say I would give my right arm to bring him back. But I'm not about to sacrifice a Gifted for a dead man."

"You don't need me right now. I helped you win the battle. I've done what you needed me to do here."

"You won the battle." Tireus hacked a laugh. "Yes, you won the great big bloody battle. But the army that won that battle for us is spent. For days now, they've been in one of the worst fights Lael has seen in a hundred years. We've suffered tremendous casualties. Without you, they would have caved in on themselves today, and we would not be standing here tonight." He advanced on Chris. "Without you, they will have no confidence they can win and no reason to stay and fight."

Desperation clawed Chris's gut. He *had* to go. He wasn't a soldier, and he certainly wasn't a leader. That was Tireus's job, and he was good at it. Chris had his own mistakes to deal with. Whatever fate Eroll had met out there was a direct result of Chris's stupid decisions and failed responsibilities. Right now, that was the only thing he could think about. That was the first and most important thing he could do.

He met Tireus's gaze. "If I leave tonight, I can probably be back before the next battle."

Tireus stared at him. "Why are you doing this?"

"Because it's my fault. Because Eroll was the first friend I made in this place." He hesitated. "And because I owe your daughter that much."

"I respect your courage and your compassion." His voice was flat. "But what you owe my daughter—what you owe Lael—is adherence to your duty as a Gifted. There's a larger battle here than the life of a man who's probably already dead."

"I know." The truth was he *did* know. But the other thing he knew was that if he knuckled under to Tireus right now, if he turned his back on Eroll without even trying, he would never be able to gain the respect of anyone in Lael, including himself. "You don't need me right now." Resolve filled his voice. "The army knows the Gifted is here, and if they don't know I've gone, they'll think I'm *still* here. The vast majority of them will never see me anyway. Rumors of my presence will have to be enough until I get back."

"You're presuming you come back." Tireus dragged his teeth across his lower lip. "And what if I decide to put you under arrest?"

"Then do it. Because otherwise I'm going."

For a long moment, Tireus watched him, the clicking of his thoughts almost audible. Finally, he raised a hand in an abrupt gesture, as if to wave Chris away. "Perhaps it's better if you go, after all. Unwilling Gifted and I do not get on. But if I were certain I would need you, I hope you know I *would* keep you, willing or not. At any rate, if you do make it back, it'll be good propaganda."

Chris breathed out and turned to Quinnon. "Will you get together a small detail, maybe six men? And make sure somebody's familiar with where I'm going."

Quinnon regarded him for a long silent moment. Then, slowly, he nodded. "They'll be ready in twenty minutes." He turned and tramped through the flickering shadows of the hall toward the main room's burst of light and noise.

"You know," Tireus said, "there's such a thing as fighting for the greater good." His tone was thoughtful, but an edge cut through it. "Sooner or later, every leader learns sacrifices must be made."

Chris turned back to him. "I'm not the leader you people are looking for. And I'm not going to let him die."

Tireus shrugged. "Men always die. Sometimes even those who are very close to us. That is war. That is life. Temper your bravery with discretion. Otherwise, you will find, in the end, you will have killed more than you will ever be able to save."

———

After stocking his saddlebags and adding the extra layer of a padded gambeson under his leather jerkin, Chris trudged back across the campsite to the main tent.

His body ached. Aside from a few minor flesh wounds and a motley array of bruises, he hadn't been injured during the battle. But he felt as if the Koraudians had dropped a skycar on him. Right now, the whole notion of sleep, even if curled up on the soggy ground, sounded luxurious. But he'd decided to leave tonight and get at least a few dozen miles behind them. Getting past the Koraudian lines unseen would be easiest in the dark. He would leave immediately, and sleep would have to wait until three or four hours down the trail.

He pushed through the flaps at the front of the king's tent.

Sequestered in the various partitions, officers and their adjutants pored over maps and argued strategy. Sleep wasn't going to be an option for most of them either if they hoped to maneuver themselves into the most advantageous position by morning.

He followed the tent's hallways to the royal quarters in the back.

An ancient Guardsman stepped forward from the canvas door he guarded. "Hold there." His voice quavered with age. "This is the princess's section. No one is allowed here without her invitation."

"Well, ask her if she'll invite me." She probably wouldn't want to even speak to him. He wouldn't have wanted to talk to himself under the circumstances. But she needed to know why he was leaving.

The Guardsman glared. "I should say not. Don't give me no cheek, youngster. Her highness is indisposed. You'll have to wait until morning."

"I'm the Gifted." He strove for patience. "She'll want to see me."

The old Guardsman jutted his cleft chin. "When I say her highness is indisposed, I *mean* she is indisposed to anyone." He hefted his pike away from his shoulder. "And certainly to you."

Chris pondered diplomacy, then cast it aside. He didn't have the time. He didn't have the patience. And he was getting sick of everyone telling him what he could and couldn't do around here. He reached for the door flap. "Is that so?"

The Guardsman snagged his sleeve. "What are you doing? I tell you, she wishes to be left alone!"

"Me too." He pushed aside the door and slipped into the dark room.

The Guardsman scrambled after him, still clutching the pike. "What are you doing? Churl!"

He pushed a chair behind him to block the man's way. "Allara?"

She didn't respond. The large room was cold, and moonlight and a flutter of curtains marked a portico at the far end. Now that he was inside, he realized he should have at least let her know he was coming in. "Indisposed" could have any number of meanings.

"This is not the conduct of a gentleman!" the Guardsman wheezed. "I don't care who you are!"

Chris ignored him and made his way through the big room with its lush appointments of tables, chairs, and looking glasses. Another partition led to a bedchamber. He glanced through the door, found the bed empty, and pushed on through to the open air beneath the awning.

Allara leaned against a support pole, her hair and the red brocade of her gown blown back by the wind. She turned to him, slowly, almost as if she hadn't yet comprehended his presence. Or maybe she just didn't care. A rigid calm sculpted her face. He had expected to find her in tears over Eroll's fate, but she seemed stupefied.

He knew the feeling. The pain would come later.

"M'lady!" The Guardsman grabbed Chris's arm. "He barged in here without my permission! I told him you were indisposed to see anyone, but he wouldn't respect your wishes."

She didn't move.

"I'm sorry," Chris said. "I wouldn't have come if I didn't have to."

"What is it?" Her voice was flat.

"I'm leaving."

For a moment, all the hurt he knew she was feeling filled her face. Then, her expression hardened. "You can't."

He had expected her anger. That too would come before the grief. "Afraid I have to."

"No." She straightened away from the pole. Her chest heaved. "Why? Why would you leave? This here, right now, is why you're here. This is the moment when everything we've given—everything we've lost—" Tears glassed her eyes, and she had to stop for a long moment. Then she surged ahead. "This is the moment when it actually matters. And at the first scent of danger you're abandoning us? What about all your talk? Everything you said about making a difference?"

He had hoped she would understand. He had even hoped she might be thankful. Or at least as much as she could be since they both knew Eroll's death was on his hands.

He drew a breath. "I'm taking a few men and going to the Northfall River."

"Northfall?" She drew herself back. "Why?"

Raising false hope wasn't such a great idea right now, but it was better to just tell her. Besides, he didn't have time to lie. "Turns out there's a chance Eroll's not dead."

Her white breath clouded in front of her face. "What?" She shook her head, as if trying to catch herself. "But what about the army? They need you." The words were too flimsy to sound convincing.

She wasn't going to stop him, then. His going might be against her better judgment—maybe even against the conception of duty to which she clung so frantically. But she wouldn't stop him. Eroll meant that much to her.

"The army doesn't need me," he said. "Eroll might."

She clenched her hands at her sides. "I can't believe you're doing this." Her voice thickened. "I can't believe you're doing this for Eroll . . . and for me."

"I have to."

Allara Katadin was beautiful and brave—and desperately broken. So much of him wanted to be able to fix her. But he couldn't. He was too broken himself. Saving Eroll was the best he could offer either of them right now.

"I'm going to bring him back," he said. "Alive or dead, he's coming back to you."

Her eyes thanked him in a way her words never could. For the first time, hope lit her from the inside out.

But still she shook her head. "You shouldn't do this. The most important thing you can do for Lael is listen to Quinnon and my father."

"I'll try to do that." He offered half a smile and turned for the door. "When I get back."

The old Guardsman hacked. "Incorrigible."

"Wait—" The swish of her skirt followed him. "Wait."

He didn't turn back. "I can't wait. I've got men expecting me."

"You're not going to listen to reason?" She didn't especially sound as if she wanted him to.

"Not at the moment." He pushed aside the chair he had moved to block the Guardsman a few minutes ago.

"Then I have to go with you."

He looked back at her through the shadows. Part of him had hoped she would be content to stay here in safety—or as much safety as a battlefield could offer. But, deep down, he hadn't really expected her to.

She stood in the middle of the room, a black silhouette against the arch of moonlight. "Where the Gifted goes, so does the Searcher."

"If I told you to stay, I don't suppose it would do any good?"

She lifted her chin. "The lords of Lael may have sworn fealty to you. But I'm not a lord."

"And if I talked to your father?" It was a last-ditch attempt and he knew it.

"I was proclaimed Searcher before I was born. My father would never question my responsibilities. That's why I have Quinnon, to protect me wherever those duties may lead."

"Then you'd better hope Quinnon doesn't mind going for a ride tonight."

31

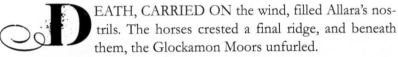

DEATH, CARRIED ON the wind, filled Allara's nostrils. The horses crested a final ridge, and beneath them, the Glockamon Moors unfurled.

On the first night, they had fled through the confusion in the Koraudian lines, then made camp in between the headwaters of the Goraudian and Northfall Rivers. They had followed the river northeast, ever closer to Koraud. Chris had taken the lead, almost without seeming to realize that's what he was doing. He would consult with Quinnon or Canard Yemas or another Guardsman, but it was always Chris who made the decisions.

Here, on the far banks of the Northfall, the rich farmland in the river deltas gave way to the barrens of peat harvesting. Thunderclouds obliterated the sky and shut out the distant Ballion hills. The scrubby, purple-heathed fields lay empty today, as they'd lain empty perhaps for weeks. The peat harvesters had left to huddle in their homes or evacuated to avoid the ravages of the war or maybe even headed south to join the army. Their sharp-edged black rows of earthen rectangles cut order into the tangled land. The peat they'd left behind would have heated a hundred homes. Now it sheltered the bodies of the dead.

Amidst the peat mounds, dark shapes littered the ground. From this distance, they weren't obviously bodies. But they weren't rocks either.

Her heart had leapt when Chris told her of his resolve to rescue Eroll, but deep down, she had known this was a fool's errand. Even if Eroll had somehow survived the attack, what he couldn't have survived was the exposure and blood loss. After all this risk, they would find him dead, if they found him at all. It was time for her to face that.

At her side, Quinnon rumbled. "I don't like this. We've had Koraudians on our trail since dawn. If we get off our horses to start hunting amongst the dead, we're prime targets."

Chris lowered his spyglass. "We came this far. I'm not stopping now."

Quinnon grunted. "Never said we should stop. All I said was I didn't like it."

A rancid taste filled the back of her throat. "I don't like it either." She looked over her shoulder. The Northfall stretched out behind them, its tree-lined banks unruly in the wind. The ghost of a wail floated to her ears, and she stiffened. "Did you hear that?"

Both men looked at her.

"Hear what?" Chris asked.

She tilted her head away from the wind and listened. "Sounded like a . . . horse, perhaps."

Behind her, Canard Yemas said, "Could be anybody. Farmer, or a traveling merchant."

She nodded. She wasn't certain how he'd ended up in this detail. After the laxness Yemas had displayed during their audience with Crofton Steadman back in Réon Couteau, they had investigated his Nateros sympathies without finding anything conclusive. He had been shipped down to the Aiden weeks ago, and that's where she had intended him to stay. But she had never gotten around to telling Quinnon to transfer him from her personal guard.

Chris snapped his glass shut. "I don't see anything threatening down there. Just bodies. But let's get this done as fast as we can." He glanced at her. "You want to stay here?"

If he had known her a little better, he probably wouldn't have bothered to ask, just as Quinnon hadn't bothered. But something inside warmed at his attempt to protect her.

She filled her lungs. "I've seen death before."

"But never Eroll."

"No." She raised one shoulder the tiniest bit.

"All right, then." He gestured to the men. "Let's go."

They trotted down the hillside into the bluster of the wind. She followed Quinnon and deliberately forced her eyes to register, then pass over the blood-blackened corpses of what had been the most elite soldiers in Thyrian livery.

Halfway across the field, she heard it again. The quivering wail. She had left Rihawn at the Aiden camp to rest, but when her new mount twitched his ears forward, she knew she wasn't imagining the sound.

She pulled the horse to a stop and tilted her head to listen. Quinnon moved on to inspect a body, half-hidden in the grass, and left her alone in the middle of the field. Gooseflesh chased across the back of her neck. Her pistol had hardly left her hand since the Aiden. Now, she dropped her thumb onto the hammer, and the hydraulics hissed.

In the expanse of trees to her right, a white face flashed. She turned to get a better look.

Straight and tall in his saddle, his leather greatcoat flapping in the wind, a Cherazim male sat upon a chestnut horse. Her breath caught. Why would a Cherazim risk riding alone in an area that had been recently and heavily raided by Koraudians?

She raised her voice. "Quinnon." But he had moved farther afield, intent on the dead.

She twitched her rein and urged her mount into a trot. As she neared the trees, she could see the medallion buckled to the Cherazim's baldric. It bore the crest of a Garowai's extended wing. Recognition slammed into her like a fist. The Cherazim before her now could only be the traitor who had given Chris the Orimere and fed him with lies.

"You—" Only five paces separated them. "How do you come to be here?"

A tic flexed his cheek. Without a word, he lifted his hand to rein back his horse.

Her pistol twitched up to his chest. "Stop."

He kept going. Behind him, clinging to his baldric, rode two Rievers, stilettos in their free hands. They peered back at her, and one shook his head fervently.

She aimed at the center of the Cherazim's back, between the Rievers' heads. "One more step and you're dead!"

The Cherazim looked over his shoulder, and the dark of his

pupils flashed against his pale skin. "You should leave, Searcher."

One of the Rievers waved his sword to shoo her away. "Please go!"

"Don't be daft, lady," the other one said.

The Cherazim's horse hopped its forequarters over a fallen log.

The deadweight of resolve hurtled through her. But even as she squeezed the trigger and the hammer fell against the firing pin, even as the gun shuddered in her hand and the round that should have killed a traitor jammed and died, she heard two impossible sounds.

In the moors behind: Chris's voice broke above the wind. "I found him! He's alive!"

In the trees to her right: the tread of horses rustled through the undergrowth and the battle cry of twenty Koraudians tore through the wind.

So the trailing Koraudians had found them. So it had been a trap. Perhaps both. Her heart gave one hard thump, and heat flooded her limbs.

She left the Cherazim and spun her horse around. She broke from the trees simultaneously with the enemy's charge. Red tabards filled her vision on either side. Hoofbeats thundered up her spine.

Their triumphant shouts drowned her cry of warning.

Scattered across the meadow, her men turned to look.

On his knees beside Chris, Quinnon bellowed orders, and the men scrambled to horse. Swords loosed, pistols barking, they galloped into the Koraudian charge. Ten paces more, and the lines would collide.

On her left, a Koraudian drew into sight. Two strides carried his horse apace with hers, and, almost as one animal, they leapt a pile of peat bricks. The useless weight of her pistol hung in her hand.

The horses landed, forelegs catching their weight, bodies leaning forward, hind legs plowing into the ground and shoving off. The Koraudian darted a glance from Allara into the face of Canard Yemas.

Yemas stampeded past. His blade disappeared into the Koraudian's chest and glinted red from his back. As Allara galloped one way and Yemas the other, she glimpsed his face, dark with confusion. He wondered, no doubt, why she hadn't used the pistol in her hand. Then their horses carried them apart, and he disappeared somewhere in the melee behind.

She galloped to the center of the field where Quinnon and Chris worked over Eroll's body. He lay, white and unconscious, in front of a hollowed-out peat mound. Had he survived, huddled in there? Her heart twisted.

Before her horse had completely stopped, she threw herself from the saddle. "Six men can't hold twenty for long!" She drew her sword from the scabbard on her saddle and shoved the horse around to stand as a barrier between the men on the ground and the line of Koraudians sweeping across the meadow.

At the Koraudians' center, the traitor Tarn's heavy blade scythed through everything, man and beast, that stood in his way. And so he was truly a traitor. He fought not only with the enemies of Lael and the enemies of his people, but against the Gifted and the Searcher.

"Where the devil did he come from?" Quinnon said.

Chris bent over Eroll's body. With one hand, he shoved a compress against the crusted wound in his back. With the other, he groped for another bandage. "Help me with this!"

The wound had been staunched, badly, with strips of Eroll's blouse, but at some point, either of its own accord or when Chris and Quinnon pulled him from his hole, the blood had started again.

She dropped to her knees. Her hands flew, passing the strip of muslin over Eroll's blood-blackened body, then passing it once more. His head lolled on the ground, eyelids limp. A scraggly beard scuffed his usually immaculate cheek. Somehow that broke her heart more than anything.

"Tie it off!" Chris hauled Eroll halfway to his feet.

She yanked the bandage tight and ducked out from under Chris's arm. Only then did she throw a look over her shoulder. A bare ten paces separated them from the Koraudians. Her men had rallied to present another charge. They would buy her time, and it would cost them their lives.

"Put him on my horse!" Quinnon said. They had brought extra horses to transport Eroll and any other survivors back across the lines, but, in the chaos, they had scattered.

She caught Quinnon's reins from his hand. The horse skittered, wide-eyed, as Chris and Quinnon hefted Eroll to the saddle. She snatched the bridle and held the animal on all fours by sheer force of will. Chris steadied Eroll as Quinnon leapt on behind and took the reins.

"Get out of here!" Quinnon lashed his horse's shoulder.

As one, she and Chris swung into their saddles. Behind them, her surviving men wavered in the face of the attack, then turned and fled. The Koraudians laid their heels to their horses in pursuit. Only the Cherazim and an officer held back. The Cherazim's broad chest heaved, and his sword fell to his side.

Her heart pumped in hot, painful bursts. She could find it in herself to at least respect the Koraudian soldiers. They fought for what they believed. They fought for their country and their people. But this Cherazim could be fighting for nothing worthwhile. The only thing he deserved on this day was death.

She shoved her sword into its sheath and turned her horse.

Chris twisted around in his saddle. "Allara!"

She swept her rifle from her scabbard and raised the stock to her cheek. The God of all willing, the distance wouldn't be too far. Her men stared as the barrel swung around to aim through their fleeing ranks. For just a second she held Yemas in her sights.

"Allara! Move!"

The Koraudians thundered closer. She lifted the rifle to bear on the Cherazim. Her finger closed on the trigger. The gun bucked against her shoulder and spewed its round of death just as the Tarn turned his horse and fled. The shot tore through the empty space where he had been.

Almost before she could look up from her sights, Chris's hand came down on her rein and hauled her horse around. She leaned over the animal's churning forequarters, fingers buried in his mane. They topped the ridge in time to see Quinnon angling upriver.

Chris headed for the nearest bank. "This way!"

"Quinnon will need help if Eroll starts bleeding again!"

"You want to put the Koraudians right on their trail?" The force of his gaze pulled her after him.

They entered the shade of the trees, and the horses leapt into the river. Halfway across, the current caught them and swept them downstream. By the time they finally clambered up the far bank, the Koraudians thudded into the trees.

She spurred into a glen a few paces from the bank. The horse skidded down the slope, crunching old leaves underfoot. She winced.

Chances were one in a thousand the Koraudians would miss the muddy trail of two horses.

"Where are we?" Chris asked.

"I don't know. I've never been here before." She headed for a craggy bluff to the left. If they could get over the escarpment before the Koraudians crossed the river, they might be able to find enough cover to pass unnoticed.

"Here they come," he said.

The wind almost drowned out the splash of the Koraudian horses leaving the water.

She and Chris rounded the bluff, and their horses reached the top in a few bounds. Shrouded in the swaying leaf-vines of a hespera tree, they reined to a stop and waited.

Below, leaves crackled under the horses' feet.

She forced herself to keep breathing. "It was a trap," she muttered. "They knew we were coming. But why? No one in his right mind would have expected us to retrieve dead men. And even then, why should they care about netting half a dozen Guardsmen?"

The cords in Chris's neck were tight. "Mactalde must have recognized Eroll. He must have known someone would come after him, and maybe he's figured out enough about me to know I'm just stupid enough to try it."

"What are you saying?"

"He *knew*. That's why he had Orias here." He shook his head. "I can't believe Orias would do this. Even after everything . . ."

A Koraudian stopped almost directly beneath the hespera's ledge.

She held her breath, her fingers light on the reins. *Stay still, stay still.*

Both horses cocked their ears toward the sound. The rustle of dead leaves stopped, and the Koraudian sat listening. Beside her, Chris's hand whitened against the grip of his otherworld pistol. Then the Koraudian's horse nickered, the sound almost inaudible above the wind. Allara's mount raised its head. She twitched the rein, but it was too late. Her horse rumbled deep in its throat, barely a whinny, but more than loud enough to be heard.

With a shout, the Koraudian kicked his mount forward. Allara and Chris burst from the curtain of leaf-vines. She took the lead, pounding down a nonexistent trail. The forest deepened, the trees thickened. She kept low, both hands braced against her horse's neck. From behind, the Koraudians shouted, and she risked a look over her shoulder to check the distance.

"Watch it!" Chris shouted.

A line of green rushed at the side of her head, and the world imploded into darkness.

32

BEFORE ALLARA EVEN turned to see the tree branch, Chris knew she was going to fall. He hit the ground in a running dismount. His horse shied at her crumpled body, then charged ahead into the trees toward the river. Behind him, the Koraudians crashed through the brush, almost in sight. Barely slowing, he grabbed Allara and rolled both of them over the top of a fallen log.

If the Koraudians had seen him dismount, he was dead. If they spotted his trail over the log, he was even more dead. Tucked in the damp shelter of the log, with Allara pressed between him and the moss-covered bark, he held his breath.

They galloped out of the trees, and their thunder reverberated up through the ground into his shoulder and hipbones. They never slowed.

His breath hissed past his lips, and he leaned away from the tree. Allara rolled, boneless, to the ground beside him. Blood threaded her face from a gash near her hairline. She didn't open her eyes, but a quick check of the pulse in her neck told him she was alive.

They had to get out of here before the Koraudians realized they were chasing riderless horses. Hiding behind a fallen tree would only work once. He got his feet under him and hefted her into his arms.

Behind him, a branch cracked. The carpet of leaves rustled once, then again, and again. Hoofbeats. If it were a lone Koraudian, he'd probably have a better chance trying to fight. He stopped, body poised halfway between running and dropping Allara in favor of his pistol.

A big brown horse trotted into view, reins swinging. Allara's mount. He breathed out and started toward the horse. The animal stopped short and stared, ears pointed so far forward they almost touched at the tips. The wind caught at Allara's long coat, and it scrambled back a step.

"Don't give me that. This was your fault to start with."

The horse took one more step back, then froze and looked over its withers. He took advantage of the moment, dropped Allara's legs, and reached for the reins. The horse jerked its head once but didn't protest as he hefted Allara into the saddle and swung himself on behind her.

From the rear, hoofbeats pounded. The horse bolted. Chris kept his back straight, the reins short in both hands and Allara braced between his arms. The horse seemed to know where it was going, so he let it choose the path, only directing it when a branch threatened a repeat of Allara's concussion. The forest blurred past, the trunks interspersed with the fluffy gray hanging moss.

Minutes later, he reemerged at the spot where they had originally crossed the river. When a quick glance upstream showed no sign of Koraudians, he urged the horse into the water and fought the current to reach the opposite bank.

Only once he was beyond the trees and a good mile upriver did he allow the horse to slow to a walk and breathe. With any luck, his head start would be enough to get him back to Quinnon before the Koraudians could find him. He cast a last glance over his shoulder at the sway of the trees.

In his arms, Allara twitched with the first signs of consciousness. He touched her throat and felt the insistent flutter of her pulse. A spark of relief mingled with his concern. She'd be all right. Probably only five or six minutes had passed since she'd blacked out.

He eased a strand of hair away from the laceration, pinched the edges to stop the bleeding, and held it shut. The bump on her forehead had melted that ice-princess mask she liked so much. She wasn't indomitable any longer; she was vulnerable.

"Where have you been hiding?" The words came out soft, and he found himself admitting what he'd known for weeks now: that with even the slightest nudge, he could fall in love with this woman so irreversibly he would never be able to love again.

It made no sense whatsoever, of course. She was a mess of a

person. She frustrated him out of his mind half the time, with her demands and her commands. She wasn't the kind of woman who would give him—or anybody else, for that matter—an effortless, comfortable relationship. Every day with Allara Katadin was a fight for survival.

But, from the moment he met her, he had known there was more to her than just that. Her defenses might have been stone to others, but to him they were glass. He'd seen the demons she hid in her inner darkness. He'd seen her anger, and he'd known it for fear. And part of him—some protective and probably self-destructive instinct—wanted to shelter her from that fear. He wanted to slay her demons. He wanted to heal her so completely that someday she would wake up and look at him with eyes full of innocence and hope and happiness.

It was impossible nonsense, all of it. That was why he couldn't let himself fall in love with her. That was why he couldn't let himself admit he was already in love with her. He snorted softly.

She whimpered, and her eyelids trembled.

He breathed out and waited for her to focus. "You're okay. Just stay quiet a minute."

"I . . ." She tried to sit up.

"You got knocked out by a tree branch."

She closed her eyes. "Koraudians?"

"We're okay. You slept through all the exciting parts."

"Oh."

With the free fingertips on the hand pinching her cut, he smoothed back the sweat-damp tendrils at her forehead. "You should get hit on the head more often."

She blinked groggily. "What?"

"This is the most cooperative you've been since I met you."

"Oh." She blinked again.

"How's your head?"

"Hurts . . ." Her hand fluttered toward her face and stopped short when she found his fingers on her forehead.

"You've got a nice gash. Probably a nice concussion to go along with it. I haven't got anything to use for a dressing right now, but I don't think it's that deep."

"Why is it so cold?"

"Long story. I'll tell you later, if you don't remember. Can you tell me what day it is?"

"Um . . . the twenty-fourth of . . ." Her eyes drifted shut. "Hearroen?"

He tried to dig back through what he'd learned to figure out if that was right or not, then gave up. "Do you know your name?"

"Allara Katadin."

"Know mine?"

She opened her eyes. Her pupils were beginning to shrink back to normal. "Chris." She said it softly, her tongue lingering on the *s*.

With a little imagination, he could almost believe she said it fondly.

"Yeah." He smiled. Too bad she couldn't stay this way all the time—minus the conk on the head, of course. "Still mad at me?"

She shook her head. "I don't remember."

"Good." Whatever it was that had made her push him away that first day in Glen Arden could disappear from her consciousness and he would never miss it.

Two fine lines feathered the skin above her nose. Her brain hadn't quite rattled back into place.

He held a peace sign in front of her. "How many fingers?"

"Two." But her gaze didn't leave his face. "How did we escape the Koraudians back there?"

"I pulled you over a log before they came around the tree. They followed my horse and gave us enough of a head start to get out of there."

"Oh." Her new favorite word. "Thank you."

"You're welcome."

The fog was beginning to clear. In a moment, the old Allara would be back, hoarfrost and all, and he wouldn't get another chance to see past her walls. But for now, she just lay there, her head against his shoulder, the blood dark against the pallor of her face.

"Why have you shut me out lately?" He asked the question before he could change his mind. If he wanted a straight answer, his only chance might be now. "What are you afraid of?"

The peace that had filled her face began to seep away. Her lips parted, and when she spoke, her voice was a whisper. "You."

"You don't have to be afraid of me."

"Oh, yes, I do actually." A weariness that was almost sadness deepened her eyes. Her shoulders tightened against his arm, and she groped for the saddlebow to pull herself upright. She didn't look at him again. "You can let me down now. I'll ride behind you. There's some oronborne in my saddlebags."

He reined up, and she slid down. While she caught her balance and pressed one hand against the cut on her forehead, he dug out the oronborne. She stood at his stirrup, her hands gripping the saddle, and lifted her face to him, eyes closed. He squirted the paste into the cut and smeared it with his thumb. It burned cold against his skin, and he wiped the excess against his trousers before returning the syringe to the saddlebags.

Then he reached down and pulled her up behind him. She clutched a fist in either side of his jerkin, and at his signal, the horse leaned into a canter. He didn't ask if she was sure she could handle the ride. Already, her walls were rising back into place.

Hours slipped away to the beat of the horse's running feet. Allara held herself still and balled what was left of her strength deep inside her body. She rode with her eyes closed and her pounding forehead against the warm leather of Chris's jerkin. She'd had to encircle his waist with her arms just to keep from falling off, and he'd laid his free hand on top of her wrists.

The pain in her head thrummed with every footfall. Her vision spun in wild circles, and nausea clamped her chest. Her thoughts looped and whirled somewhere in between consciousness and dreams, her mind swimming back and forth between her two bodies. Hopefully she was safe in bed in the other world.

She gripped Chris tighter, and he patted her hand, almost reflexively. The horse slowed. She tilted her head against Chris's back and eased her eyes open.

The wind whipped at the tendrils of hair come loose from her braid, and her long coat flapped noisily. Dusk was falling early, hastened by the storm. A rim of red underlined the wind-driven clouds, as if someone had dragged the edge of a sword through the sky in an attempt to liberate the sun.

When she opened her mouth to speak, the words lodged in her

throat. She swallowed hard, waited for another wave of nausea to pass, then tried again. "Why are we stopping?"

"Thought I heard something." He let go of her hand and drew his otherworld pistol from one of the two bandoleer holsters against his chest.

She straightened and strained against the pain to see into the trees. Leaves rustled. Something was definitely in there. Even as she prayed for it to be a zajele or a scavenging jiswar vixen, the green tabard of a Guardsman materialized from among the trailing hespera vines. His left shoulder hunched from an old wound.

Air rushed from her lungs. "Quinnon."

Chris holstered the pistol and urged the horse forward. "I was beginning to think we weren't going to catch up tonight. How long have you been here?"

Quinnon rubbed a hand up his forehead. "About an hour. We had no choice but to stop and get control of Lord Thyra's bleeding. Wanted to give you a chance to find us too."

Chris reined to a stop beside Quinnon. "Any sign of Koraudians?"

"No. But we need to move out and keep moving, soon as we can. I don't like all these troops we've been seeing these last few days, especially after what happened today." He shook his head. "Could mean things have gone bad back at the Aiden."

Allara leaned down to grip his shoulder. "What about Eroll? Did you stop the bleeding?"

Quinnon shrugged. "Well, he's alive. For the time being. Three of the men made it back with me, and we patched him up best we could. But the wound's bad. I don't know how he kept it clean as long as he did, but it's starting to get inflamed. We could have a full-blown infection on our hands in another twenty-four hours."

Her thoughts flitted around like moths drawn to half a dozen flames. She gritted her teeth and forced herself to focus. "We'll take him straight to the Wall. That will cut nearly two days off what it would have taken us to get back to the Aiden. We can get treatment at the station at the top, then take him back to Glen Arden by skycar."

Quinnon scowled at her. "What in the Garowai's eye happened to you?"

"Ran afoul of a tree." She shook her head. She didn't want to explain.

He turned on Chris. "Lost a horse too, I see." He made a disgusted noise that she knew was mingled frustration and relief. "Come on into camp." He held aside the trailing veil of leaf-vines and frowned up at her. "And get off that horse before you fall off and somebody has to carry you."

They entered the campsite, where Yemas and two other Guardsmen huddled around Eroll's prone body. One, his arm in a sling, rummaged cold rations out of his saddlebags, while Yemas and the other lashed a canvas bedroll between two fresh-cut branches to make a litter. Yemas looked up at her and a strange expression edged his mouth. Anger?

She leaned against Quinnon and slid to the ground. He steadied her until the world stopped spinning and she could think past the throbbing in her head. Then she put one foot in front of the other and sank to her knees beside Eroll.

With both hands crossed over his chest, he looked too much like a sarcophagus. She caught one of his hot hands in hers. His eyes flickered once, then drifted closed.

"Oh, Eroll." If he died, it would cut her heart from her. She'd already grieved his death once. To have him smashed from her life again would be more than she could handle.

Still holding his hand, she scooted back until she could lean against a hespera. Pain, heavy and dark, drummed inside her skull, and the stiffness in her muscles tightened into paralysis. Her every bone felt fractured, every sinew torn.

She looked at Quinnon. "Why would Mactalde move troops away from the Aiden? His quickest way to Glen Arden is up the Karilus Wall."

"If he can split our troops by forcing us to shunt reinforcements to Ballion, he'll have fewer of us to fight all the way around."

Chris tugged loose the horse's girth. "We beat him the last time."

Allara shook her head. "Last time was a drawn battle. Had it not been for you—for the presence of a Gifted—he would have carried the field and won the war in one blow." She slid her free hand inside the warmth of her coat. "And if this ambush could really have been because he knew you'd come for Eroll . . ." She shook her head. "I don't like that he could predict our actions so well." In all honesty, it terrified her.

"What's this?" Quinnon asked.

"All I said was he knew I was a wild card," Chris said. "Maybe he guessed I'd rather charge off after Eroll instead of waiting around for another battle. So he took a chance, let one of Eroll's soldiers escape to bring us the news, and planted an ambush. He didn't have anything to lose."

"He lost us," Quinnon said.

"Barely."

"Well, losing us once is all it's going to take. He's lost us today, and that's the way it's going to stay." Quinnon squatted next to the wounded Guardsman and accepted a muslin-rolled slab of dried whitefish. "Eat and sleep while you can. We'll stay here for six hours, and that's it. I don't care who's bleeding." He glanced at Allara.

She managed a nod.

"We're not going back to the Aiden." He raised his voice to speak to the others. "We're heading for the Wall path, and if we push the pace as much as we can while carrying that litter between two horses, we should be able to make it in a day and a half."

Yemas stood up from the litter. "What about the Koraudians?" He watched Allara. Beneath his carefully blank expression, strong emotion quivered.

What was wrong with him? She knit her brows, then wished she hadn't. A new wave of pain rolled through her head, and she squinched her eyes shut. When she opened them again, Yemas was still watching.

Quinnon unrolled the whitefish into his hand and bit off a large flake. "The faster we move out of here, the less likely we'll get caught in the crossfire. Mactalde will have to break through the king's lines to reach the Wall path, and if he's as smart as he thinks, he won't even try. Ballion's where he's headed. You can bet on it." He laughed grimly. "But the way won't be clear before him. The Cherazii guard the dams in those hills, and they'll open them without thinking twice. Mactalde will come, but only as far as the water lets him. The Cherazii may not be willing to fight with us, but they'll fight against Mactalde, no question."

He chomped on the fish, then glared off at nothing. "Why those poor fools of Koraudians want to follow him, I'll never know. He'll use them up in this war, and at the end of it, they'll find themselves under a king just the same as before."

Yemas was positively trembling. "Following even a fool is better than following a traitor."

Allara's eyebrows came together again, and this time she didn't close her eyes against the pain. Yemas was angry . . . with her. Was this about what happened back in Réon Couteau with Steadman? Was Yemas blaming the war on her father's refusal to negotiate with Nateros? Or had he realized she was planning to transfer him from her personal guard?

Before she could find the right question to ask, he dropped to his knees and yanked tight the thongs securing the bedroll to the litter frame.

Quinnon drank out of his waterskin and didn't seem to heed Yemas's words.

Chris trudged over to her side. He stood over Eroll for a moment, then unfurled his bedroll a few paces off. He lay on his side, his back to her, head cushioned in a pile of leaves.

She had to say something to him. Their conversation after she had woken was foggy, but some niggling in her brain told her she'd said something she shouldn't have. She'd let him see some part of her he was never meant to see. She wasn't exactly sure what it was, but the one thing she did remember was the tender look on his face.

She could withstand many things. She'd taught herself to endure pain, death, betrayal, cruelty, hatred. But the one thing that could undo it all was tenderness, especially from him. He would win her heart, and he would break it. Tears welled up from behind her pain-battered defenses, and she shivered.

Perhaps he'd already undone it, already won it, already broken it. She shivered again.

She made herself speak softly, so only he could hear her: "What I said when I woke up this afternoon, I shouldn't have said it."

He didn't roll over to face her. "And what was that?"

"Everything."

He shifted his weight, and the leaves rustled beneath him. "Are you trying to protect me or yourself? Because, if it's me, don't."

She stared at him through the deepening shadows. Half-formed words caught in her throat. Didn't he yet understand she had to be the strong one? She was the Searcher. The world was falling apart, and *she* was supposed to hold it together.

She drew a shaky breath. "Thank you. For what you did today, for saving Eroll. No matter what happens, I mean that with all my heart."

A long moment passed, so long she thought he wasn't going to answer. Then he burrowed deeper into the bedroll, and the leaves rustled again. "You're welcome."

33

A TELEPHONE YOWLED in Chris's ear, and he scrabbled at his side for a sword that wasn't there. His eyes came open to the white glare of sheets and pillowcases. Lo-mein noodles snaked from the upended Chinese carton beside him. On the nightstand, a digital clock blinked to 3:08, and, beside the clock, the phone shrilled. Only a second ago, he'd fallen asleep on a cold bed of leaves. He groaned. This whole world-shift thing wasn't getting any easier.

He snagged the phone mid-ring and scooted up against the headboard. "Hello?"

"Chris . . ." The voice trailed into a cough.

His heart seized. He had gotten used to hearing that voice without the cough. "Dad?"

"Yeah, it's me."

He sat up straighter and cursed his heart for pounding. "How'd you get this number?"

He'd been dreading this phone call ever since he'd met Worick Bowen. As long as Paul didn't talk to him, Paul didn't have to exist, and he could pretend at least one part of his life was whole. That was the excuse anyway.

His dad cleared his throat. "I—uh, called around. Mike Andreola told me where you are."

If his dad was in jail again, Chris was going to have a hard time getting him out without showing his face. He kicked the comforter aside and swung his legs to the floor. "Where are you? What's going on?"

"I'm home. I'm still home. I been trying to reach you all day. I can't get a signal or nothing from your cell phone. How come you didn't give me your hotel number?"

Because he'd thought he never wanted to see Paul again. For the last few weeks, he'd been trying to come to grips with the idea that these two completely different fathers were really the same man. Even now, he couldn't make himself believe it.

"Um, I didn't know where I would be staying." A trickle of gray light marked the incision where the curtains met in the center of the window. He frowned. The 3:08 on the clock probably meant p.m. instead of a.m. "What time is it?"

"Um, I don't know . . . three o'clock."

"In the afternoon?"

"Yeah."

He had to stretch the phone cord to gather his clothes from where he had dumped them on the loveseat the night before. Mashing the phone between his ear and his shoulder, he tugged on his pants and wrestled his T-shirt right side out. One of his socks had fallen between the end of the loveseat and the wall, and he had to yank open the floor-length drapes to get to it.

Outside, the sky was the color of a soiled eggshell. Frozen rain wormed across the window, and fresh rivulets slid down the glass and swerved to follow the old tracks.

"Chris—" His dad hesitated. "Are you all right?"

He stopped short. The rain tinkled against the window. How long had it been since his dad—his *real* dad, his hopelessly unsalvageable alcoholic father—had asked him that?

"What?" he asked.

Paul coughed, and Chris recognized it as a stalling tactic. He could hear shuffling footsteps and the sucking noise of the fridge door opening.

"Dad, what's going on?"

"Nothing, nothing. I just . . . had a dream last night. Never mind. I shouldn't have called you. I just wanted to make sure you were all right. Sorry."

Chris's heart thudded against his ribs. He sank onto the bed. "What kind of a dream?"

"Oh, nothing much. But in the dream I was—I was worried. About you." A glass clinked on the other end of the line.

Worick was the one who worried about him, not Paul. Paul didn't even think about him. Wasn't that what he'd made himself believe all these years? He closed his eyes. "In the dream, you worried about me."

"Yeah." Paul filled the silence with another self-conscious cough. "Well, you know how dreams are sometimes. Right?"

"Yeah, I know." Boy, did he ever know. "Um, was Lisa there?"

"No, but . . ."

But Mom and Jenifer were. He stared at the window. "Will you do me a favor?"

"Yeah?" His dad's voice perked up just a bit.

How many times had he promised himself he'd stop interfering? It never made any difference. Never.

He took a breath and let it out. "Whatever you've got in your hand right now, will you dump it down the sink?"

His dad's breathing huffed for a long moment. Chris heard a faint clack, as if Paul had pulled the phone away from his ear. Then, one after another, three ice cubes clanged against the stainless steel of the sink, followed by the gurgle of liquid—vodka and orange juice probably—sliding down the drain.

The phone scratched against his dad's ear once more. "There you go."

As soon as he hung up, Paul would be pouring another round. But somehow the moment still felt like a victory, for his own sake as much as his father's. "Thank you," he said.

"Yeah, well. I'll let you go now. I'm glad you're okay. You are okay, right? Mike—he kinda sounded like maybe something wasn't quite right."

"No, everything's fine. Thanks for calling." This was the first time in years his dad had called without an ulterior motive.

He hung up and imagined his father pouring that second screwdriver. How many years since he had let himself feel *anything* about his father? He opened that long-closed door in his soul, just a crack. A crack was more than enough to let him know his family still had the power to break him with his grief. But today the grief wasn't just for his mother and sisters and himself. Today, it was for his father as well.

He pulled his shirt on, and the phone rang again.

"Hi! It's me." The rumble of an engine backed Brooke's voice.

"I'm on my way over. I've got something important to show you."

He stifled a groan. He'd specifically told Mike to keep Brooke away, on the off chance of anyone following her.

"How important is 'important'? I'm kind of trying to keep a low profile."

"Really important." Excitement buzzed in her voice. "Meet me at the front door in ten minutes."

He was waiting in the lobby when Brooke's Land Rover pulled up beneath the apron. After a quick check to make sure she hadn't been followed by the black pickup, he stepped into the bluster of the wind.

Mike climbed out of the passenger side, and Chris stopped short. "Hey."

Mike had his mouth pressed into that I'm-trying-not-to-look-as-annoyed-as-I-feel smile. "Long time, no see."

Chris slid his hands into his pockets. "What's going on? Everything all right?"

"No night ninjas trying to strangle me in my sleep, if that's what you mean."

Chris hadn't seen Mike since he'd gotten a hotel room, and he'd only spoken with him on the phone a few times. The police had investigated the house, and Brooke had apparently even talked them into leaving a patrol car there for a few days. But Mike had been able to move back in, against Chris's recommendation. As far as he knew, there hadn't been any more trouble.

Mike looked him over. "You about had it with being holed up in that hotel? Maybe you ought to come back. The police say it's safe as anything ever is on the South Side." His eyes fidgeted away, then back, and Chris knew it was an apology for his impatience. As if he had anything to apologize for.

He made himself smile. "Thanks. But not yet. So what's this about?"

Mike climbed into the back. "Better ask her."

From inside the vehicle, Brooke beamed at him. "Good afternoon! How come you look like you just woke up?"

He stepped inside and slammed the door. "Been practicing my half-asleep look. Women go for it, don't you know?"

She laughed. "Better wake up anyway." Both hands on the steering wheel, she stepped on the accelerator.

The windshield wipers sloshed across the steamy glass, and Chris reached over to turn the defroster dial. The only thing that gave him the willies more than Brooke on a normal day was Brooke when she was this cheerful. "You've got something up your sleeve, haven't you?"

She cast him a coquettish glance. "I think I've got some answers for you."

"Please tell me you haven't been 'investigating.'"

She was almost purring. "You just wait and see."

"What kind of answers?" When she didn't respond, he glanced over his shoulder.

Mike shrugged. "This is her show. I'm only here because I'm supposed to be moral support."

"Moral support for who?"

"I have a feeling that depends on how you react to whatever she's got in mind."

Whatever she'd done, it must be bad. He stifled a groan. "Brooke?"

She turned into traffic. "All right, here it is. The other day at the hospital, I made a very interesting discovery. Really, all this disaster of yours needed was for someone—" she pointed to herself, "—to look at it logically."

"The hospital? You went to see Harrison?"

Her smile slipped. "Well, no, actually. I tried, but he wasn't accepting visitors." The grin popped back. "But guess who I found waiting for me at my car when I got back outside?"

His chest clenched. "Flores? Brooke, he's a hit man! He's in with Kaufman!"

"What?" Mike demanded.

She wrinkled her nose. "Stop fussing, both of you. Yes, it was Salvidore Flores. But you'll be interested to know he isn't a hit man."

Chris balled his fist against his thigh. "He can *say* he's anything he wants to. How could you be that stupid? He could have killed you!"

"Oh, pooh. He wasn't going to kill me." She tossed him a sidelong glance. "I know him."

"What?"

"A year or two ago I dated a guy he works with." She tapped her blinker and eased into a turning lane. She looked at Mike in the rearview mirror. "A big guy with crazy eyes, as it so happens."

Mike gawked. "You've got to be kidding me. The guy who worked for a *psychologist*?" One hand gripped the back of Chris's seat.

"Ding! You get the prize." She swung the car into a strip mall parking lot. "And his name . . . is Geoff Kaufman."

"Brooke—" Chris's heart revved. "I don't know what you've got in mind. I don't know what they've told you, but this is wrong, this is insane. This is going to get us all killed."

She turned down a long row of cars. "Oh, c'mon already. You should be majorly ashamed for overreacting like this."

A tall blond man in a raincoat stepped out from behind a parked truck.

Chris stopped breathing altogether. "Get us out of here."

She laughed. "Geoff is going to take us out to dinner, and I'm going to properly introduce you. He has some business with you, that's all, and he agrees with me it's time you two sorted out your differences."

Mike grabbed her shoulder. "The man's trying to kill him. You think that's going to get sorted out over dinner?"

She rolled her eyes and turned into a parking slot. "He is *not* trying to kill anyone."

Chris caught hold of her wrist. "Don't park the car! Get us out of here now."

"Brooke," Mike's voice vibrated with intensity, "so help me, if you don't get us out of here—"

Kaufman was only a dozen strides away. His gaze, hard as glass, met Chris's through the window, and his stride lengthened.

Chris unsnapped his seatbelt. "I'm not going to ask you again. Drive away. Now."

"I can't believe you guys." She glared at Mike in the rearview mirror. "And you were supposed to be moral support for me, not him."

Beneath the flutter of Kaufman's raincoat, a concealed handgun bulged. Chris lurched across the console and stomped on Brooke's foot, mashing it down against the accelerator.

"Ow! What are you doing?"

The Land Rover bucked forward into the parking slot and slewed to crash through an opening between two parked cars.

She screamed and grappled with him for the steering wheel. "What are you doing?"

He muscled the steering wheel around, and the car screeched in a tight circle.

"He's getting in his truck!" Mike said.

Chris didn't look back. "Buckle up!"

Brooke kicked him with her free foot and tried to step on the brake. "Stop it right now! You're going to kill us!"

"Let up on the clutch! You'll ruin your engine!"

"My engine! You're driving like a maniac, and you're worried about my engine!"

The street loomed in front of them, and Chris dragged the car around to make the turn. The Land Rover shot off the curb and cut across two lanes of blaring traffic. He let up on Brooke's foot long enough to slam on the brake and haul the car back onto a straight course. Horns blasted from all sides.

"He's following us!" Mike said.

Chris dared a look in the mirror. "Is he waiting for traffic?"

"Yeah, I think— No, here he comes!"

He slapped his blinker and cut through an intersection on a red light. Oncoming cars swerved and skidded.

Brooke shrieked. "Stop it, Chris. I mean it! You have no right to do this!" Her arms snaked between his, and fought for control of the steering wheel. "Mike! Do something!"

"If you don't shut up and let him drive, we'll get demolished out here!"

"You're both insane! If we don't all die, we're going to end up in jail!"

Chris took another hard right onto a side street. "Nobody ends up in jail for running away from a murderer."

"He's not a murderer! I told you, I used to date him." She shoved his arm. "I would never go out with a wacko!"

"Hang on." He swung around another corner, then another, zigzagging through the city. In the rearview mirror, he caught sight of Mike's tight face. "How we doing?"

"I haven't seen him for the last five minutes."

Finally, he turned into a residential district and eased the speedometer needle back.

He looked down to where Brooke's head was wedged between the neck rest and the window. "If I let you have the wheel back, will you promise not to do anything stupid?"

Tears stood out in her eyes. "This is carjacking. *And* kidnapping—because this whole detour was most definitely against my will."

Mike rattled the back of her seat. "And hauling us out here to meet your gun-happy ex-boyfriend wasn't a culpable act on your part?"

"He's not gun-happy! And he was never my boyfriend."

Chris eased the car to a stop on the curb and shifted into neutral. Then he slid back into the passenger seat. He offered Brooke a hand up, but she batted it away.

She used the steering wheel to drag herself upright. Her hands trembled as she slid her hair back from her face. "Geoff has been a professional bodyguard for years. You were right about him working for Faolan Mactalde—who, by the way, happens to be a tremendously respected doctor of psychology and a philanthropist. Do you think someone like that would hire Geoff if he had even the slightest smudge on his record?"

She lowered the visor and touched the beginnings of a bruise on her cheekbone. She looked at Mike in the mirror. "Who's making more sense here, Chris or me?"

Mike glanced once at Chris, then, grudgingly, back at her. "You."

"At least *somebody* here is still rational." She slapped the mirror back and turned to Chris. Her lower lip quivered. "I think you should apologize."

"The man *shot* at me. What am I supposed to do with that? Pretend he was playing laser tag?"

Mike leaned over his knees. "But why is he shooting at you? You say he's after you because Mactalde set you up. But that doesn't make sense. If they set you up, they'd want you alive."

Brooke folded her arms. "Are you trying to cover your tracks? Are you trying to shift the blame onto Geoff?"

"*No.*" He looked at Mike. "You know I wouldn't do that. We've already talked about this."

Mike shook his head. "You can't expect me to back you up if you won't give me a clue about what you're messed up in. As far as I can tell, things are getting way out of control here."

Brooke emitted a little snort that was half sob. "Getting?" She raised her foot to the seat and took off her ballet flat. Her big toe was bleeding from where Chris had stomped on it. "This is way past *getting* out of control."

None of Chris's choices were reassuring. If he told them the facts, they'd think he was lying. If he didn't tell them, they'd know he was holding back.

He stared at the stretch of wet asphalt in front of them. The duplexes that lined the street sat in silence. Except for the mailman walking down the sidewalk, the street was deserted—which was what he was likely to be if he told the truth.

"All right, I'll tell you. You're not going to buy it, but I'll tell you anyway." He twisted in his seat to face them. "Mactalde hired Flores to kill Harrison Garnett. And he hired Kaufman to kill me, because I'm a threat."

"A threat to what?" Mike asked.

"To his plans. To . . . his life."

Brooke's jaw dropped. "You *are* mixed up in his disappearance! You told me he was safe."

"He is." For the moment, anyway. "The only thing I did was help him leave."

"Then where'd he go? And why'd he need your help?"

"Where is he?" Mike kept his voice quiet, but he wasn't asking anymore. He was demanding.

Chris opened his mouth, then closed it. He stared out the windshield and shook his head. How ridiculous was he to think he had a chance of them believing him?

He gestured to the window. "The weather's been really strange lately, right?"

Mike flopped back against his seat. "Chris . . ."

"I'm serious. Everybody's been talking about the weather, right? And not just here. All over the world." He'd watched enough TV over the last week to know the weather was headlining the news. Meteorologists everywhere were scrambling to explain the sudden drop in temperatures.

"So?" Brooke said. "The weather has nothing to do with Dr. Mactalde leaving. Unless he went to the Bahamas."

"The weather isn't why he left. The weather is happening *because* he left."

She stared blankly.

He glanced back at Mike. "Mactalde disappeared—" He ran back over the weeks in his head, trying to separate the time he'd spent in Lael from the time here. "Around the middle of June, right? And that's when the weather started cooling off."

Mike shook his head. "That's coincidence. And if this is supposed to convince me you do, in fact, have things under control, you're doing a pretty rotten job."

He hooked one arm around the neck rest. "You have to promise me you will not just dismiss this out of hand. It's going to sound crazy. It's going to sound beyond crazy."

Brooke rolled her eyes.

"But you have got to at least think about it. Okay?"

Mike shrugged. "Fine. I'll think about it."

Chris looked at Brooke.

She sighed. "Why not?"

"Okay, here it is. What if your dreams are real?"

Mike's expression hesitated a long second, as if he were waiting for Chris to move on to his real explanation. Then his face crinkled. "The dream thing again?"

"Just answer. What if they were real?"

"But—" Brooke shook her head. "They're not."

He turned to her. With her penchant for conspiracy theories and superstitions, she might be able to believe him. "How do you know they're not real?"

"Everybody knows that! Please, please, please tell me you're not trying to say Dr. Mactalde is in dreamland?"

The heating vents hummed between them. He stared at her levelly. "I took him there."

"And that made the weather crummy?" Mike's words were stilted, careful.

He was losing them. Or rather, he'd lost them before he'd even opened his mouth. And why not? A month and a half ago, he would have laughed in their faces had they been the ones telling him his dreams were for real.

He tried again. "It caused some kind of imbalance between that world and this one. The weather's bad there too."

Mike broke eye contact. "Chris, bro . . ."

The ignition ground, and the engine rumbled back to life. Brooke stared out the windshield. She wasn't trembling or fighting back tears anymore. She stared ahead. "I'm glad you didn't talk to Geoff." The words were flat.

He waited a moment, hoping against all reason. "You believe me?"

She shifted into first gear. Then she turned to him, dead serious for maybe the first time in her life. "How can you even ask me to?"

34

TWO DAYS OF riding brought them to the Karilus Wall. For Chris, every minute was a nightmare of senses strained to rupturing. Koraudian troops swarmed everywhere, like red ants to carrion, and Quinnon was right: they were headed for Ballion, almost five hundred miles away, where the Wall's protective fortress tapered into gentle foothills. But Mactalde wasn't *moving* troops. He was *adding* troops. Judging from the direction they were moving, these were fresh troops, straight from Koraud.

They had been able to avoid contact with the troops until the morning of the second day when an advance patrol spotted them and killed the wounded Guardsmen with the first shot. They'd outrun them—keeping Eroll in his litter only because Quinnon had had the foresight to tie him in—but the encounter left Allara shaking and vomiting.

Every night, fireworks lit the western sky with color-coded messages. According to Allara, that meant her father was back in Glen Arden, or maybe even Ballion itself, organizing more troops. If they were lucky, Quinnon was right about the Cherazii opening the dams to keep Mactalde at bay.

When they finally reached the top of the Wall path, it was crawling with Laeler troops, some on their way up, some on guard duty, and some passing through on their own trek to Ballion to try to intercept the Koraudians. They stopped at the aid station long enough to get both Eroll and Allara tended to. Then they'd boarded an express skycar back to Glen Arden.

Chris was asleep on the floor when the car rocked to a stop, late in the second day. He squinted himself awake from the early morning talk show he'd been watching in his hotel. He'd slept for almost the entire forty-eight hours of the trip from the Wall to Glen Arden, and he was about to go nuts sitting around in his hotel, watching TV and eating takeout Chinese. If his body in Lael hadn't needed the rest so desperately, he would have forced himself to stay awake in the skycar. At least here he had Quinnon and Allara to talk to.

He rolled off his stomach and inched himself up to sit against the edge of the corner cabinet. He rubbed at his eyes. He'd been able to take a quick bath at the top of the Wall, while the surgeon had attended Eroll and Allara, but after two days of sleeping in the same clothes, he felt grimy all over again.

Through the glass wall in front of him, the lights of Glen Arden danced in the darkness and reflected against the inky water.

"Why are we stopped?" His voice croaked.

Quinnon stood next to the window. "Not sure yet." He opened a pane and thrust out his head to peer down the length of the train. Cold air blew fat raindrops in around him. He ducked back in and fastened the window. "The tracks are jammed as far up the line as I can see. Probably full of troops and foreign dignitaries and who knows what else." He scratched a hand up the white stubble on his face. "We could be stuck here all night if we try to get straight through to the palace. Might be better to divert to Faramore Station near the bridge and ride up to the palace from there."

From the front of the car, where she was huddled under a mound of blankets, Allara's voice murmured, "That's all the way across the city."

"You decide. Spend another night here, or take a few more hours to cross to Faramore and catch a water taxi up to the palace."

She sat up, and in the dim light of the globes, shadows caverned her cheeks. The laceration on her forehead had faded into a black bump, split down the center with a rough line of red, but two days of hard riding and two more of constant motion in the skycar hadn't done much to speed her concussion on its way to healing.

She sat with the blankets over her knees and her arms over the blankets. "The sooner we get home the better. Tell the engineer."

Quinnon crossed to the corner behind her and tugged the silken cord to ring a bell in the engineer's car. He gave it three hearty tugs, followed by a jingle.

"That's the signal for Faramore Station?" Chris asked.

Quinnon didn't bother to nod. "Go back to sleep, the both of you. I'll wake you when we're close."

Allara nodded and shifted back under her blankets. For her, sleep actually meant closing her eyes and forgetting for a while. But Chris had gotten his fill of talk shows and takeout food.

He eased to his feet and stretched the stiff muscles in his back and legs, then joined Quinnon at the window. "Home again."

Quinnon only grunted.

Of course, it wouldn't take long to get his fill of Quinnon's conversation either. He leaned his shoulder against the window and braced himself for two more hours of one-sided grunting.

Midnight was knocking by the time their train finally reached Faramore Station. The public skycar stations were some of the tallest buildings in the city. The whitewashed Faramore station stretched five stories with half a dozen docks at every level. Even with the right of precedence granted the royal train, it took a full forty minutes to pull into a coveted ground-level slot.

The South Shore of the Hub borough claimed sole access to the only road off the island, via Faramore Bridge. The bridge's proximity to both the upscale Taïs Quarter and the commercial Hub, with its bustling dockyards all along the harbor, made it one of the busiest parts of the city at any time of the day. Tonight, the roar of the people packing the streets drowned out even the clatter of the skycars.

Quinnon sent Yemas and the other Guardsman ahead to secure a taxi, then enlisted two station boys to carry Eroll's litter around the street corner to the taxi stand.

He ducked his head back into the car, where Chris and Allara waited. "All right, let's move. Keep your heads down and don't draw any attention. I don't much like the feel of things out here tonight."

Chris helped Allara to her feet and steadied her. She swayed a moment and gritted her teeth.

"Still having headaches?" he asked.

She gave a tight nod.

"As soon as we get home, you need to go to bed and stay there for a week." Not that she would.

With his hand under her elbow, they moved forward. At the door, Quinnon took her other hand and helped her down. He had turned his Guardsman tabard inside out and belted his sword over the top of it. Beneath his wide-brimmed hat, his scarred face looked less like a princess's bodyguard and more like a dissolute footpad.

Chris's face wasn't well known, so he had little fear of being identified. Allara might be more of a problem, especially since her coat had no cowl for her to hide behind. But tousled and wan, on foot in the midst of a civilian crush, she wasn't immediately recognizable either.

They walked down the covered platform—with the footsteps of the passengers from the level above clunking overhead—and through the double doors. Every building along the main thoroughfare, every shop and every home, flickered beneath glass-encased flames strung overhead. The lights smeared the slate of the night, darkened only by the massing shadows of people.

Chris knew enough about the South Shore to know it was always buzzing, even in the dark of night, but tonight a manic energy leapt through the crowds. The drone of voices was deafening—a shout without anyone in particular seeming to be shouting. Glimpsed expressions showed in one face the glitter of wide, ecstatic eyes, and in another the stolid determination to push on through and be done with this place and this night as soon as possible.

"What's going on here?" he asked.

Quinnon plowed down the street without answering. He opened a passage through the crowd by dint of either his forceful "make ways" or, when that didn't work, even more forceful shoves.

Chris followed on his heels, one hand around Allara's waist, and the other under her elbow. She could probably have walked under her own power if she had to. Over the last few days, she'd shown just how much she could accomplish with sheer willpower when she wanted to. But the very fact that she didn't try to avoid leaning against him showed how exhausted she was. Her eyes were buttoned closed against the lights, and she gnawed her lower lip.

"Hang in there," he said. "You're almost home."

She nodded.

They rounded a corner into a large square. Beneath the three domed towers of what appeared to be a university, the mob came to a head.

A dozen men stood on the steps with their feet spread and their hands on their swords.

At their fore, a slender man in a white coat leaned toward the crowd. "Why should Lael grovel in fear while her leaders prostitute themselves to treachery?"

Allara stopped before Chris did. "Steadman."

He released her elbow and reached for the pistol holstered against his chest. "What's he doing here?"

In front of them, Quinnon cursed and kept ramming through the crowd.

"We are a free people, are we not?" Steadman shouted. "We are an intelligent people, an educated people! Is it right our government should shackle us with the outmoded traditions of religion?"

With every question, the people crowded nearer. Even those who stared askance were dragged forward at the sound of his voice. Murmurs of agreement swept from lip to lip.

Steadman raised a fist. Globes swayed on their wires, and the guttering light illuminated his eyes and the scar on his upper lip. "We are tired of waiting, Lael! Are we not tired of waiting? Mactalde is at our door even now. But it is not he who will destroy us!"

At the edge of the crowd, almost lost in the shadows of a sculpture gallery, the green of a Guardsman uniform glimmered. Quinnon angled toward it, but the Guardsman stared at Steadman, rapt.

Two more steps, and Chris recognized Yemas. They'd suspected him of Nateros sympathies before. Now, Chris had no doubt. Yemas panted, his face flushed. If Steadman demanded the crowd to throw themselves into the lake, Yemas appeared ready to comply.

Allara breathed out. "If they knew we were here, they'd stone us all."

"They don't know we're here." Chris tried to sound reassuring.

On the steps, Steadman clapped his hand against the rapier at his hip. "I ask you. Is it right—is it decent—is it *natural* that men should be dragged across the worlds, unwilling and unprepared? It is witchcraft! Is not this war a judgment upon Lael?"

Quinnon reached Yemas and shook his shoulder. "What are you doing here? I told you and Rantim to find a decent taxi and make certain those station boys got Lord Thyra safe into it."

Yemas dragged his attention away from Steadman. "Rantim's with the taxi. I returned to show you the way."

"You so sure about that?"

Yemas looked back at Steadman, then past Quinnon, past Chris, straight at Allara. Sweat glistened on his lip, and something near to hatred crawled across his face.

When had that happened? Back in Réon Couteau, he had at least remained respectful to Allara.

Allara's steps dragged, and Chris let her pull him to a stop.

"We have borne enough of this villainy!" Steadman shouted. "We have borne enough of this infamy! In our own city, our own capital, the witch and her minions cavort in freedom, piling upon us new abominations!"

Chris's hand sweated against his pistol grip. "He shouldn't get away with this."

"It's all right," Allara said. "Just keep moving."

Steadman railed on: "Lael has suffered under the necromancy of the Searchers for thousands of years, but it is upon our generation that the vilest of these is visited! She has conjured not one, but *two* Gifted! Is this not an atrocity in the sight of all educated men?"

"This is about you?" Chris said. "Why's this about you? This should be about me."

Yemas turned on them. Beneath his hat, sweat matted his sideburns. He shook off Quinnon and stalked close enough to Allara to stab a finger at her. "She's the one who's a traitor!"

Chris thrust him away. "Back off."

Quinnon snagged Yemas's arm from behind. "How dare you?" He pitched his voice low, but anger quivered through its hoarseness. "Your service in the Guard is finished after this."

"Then it's finished!" Yemas panted. "I won't serve her! They're right about her. They've always been right about her!"

She stood away from Chris. "What are you talking about?"

"You're a traitor! I saw it with my own eyes!"

People began to stare.

"Shut up." Quinnon hauled him around.

"No, I won't!" Blood suffused Yemas's face. His body shook, and the muscles in his neck and arms ridged. "I saw what she did at the Glockamon Moors! She wasn't there to save the duke. She was there to meet the Koraudians. She signaled them. She charged from the trees with them. And she shot at her own men!"

Quinnon hit him. Bone cracked against bone. Yemas caught himself with a hand against the pavement.

Chris let go of Allara and plunged after him. He tangled his hand in Yemas's tabard.

Quinnon pushed him back. "Leave him, and get her out of here!"

Already, the crowd was turning toward them. Murmurs spread out, rolling like the ripples of a sound wave, on and on, spreading to every corner of the square. Any attempt to pass unnoticed would be futile now. Even if these people failed to recognize Allara, they were hearing Yemas's words. Before long, everyone in the square, including Steadman, would have heard them, if only because these were the words they wanted to hear. The damage had been done.

Chris drew his pistol and grabbed her arm. "Come on."

She stared at Yemas as she passed him. "You're wrong. That isn't what happened. And if you would have asked me, I would have told you."

He wheezed. "You would have told me lies!"

Her nostrils flared. "You're infected."

Chris yanked her after him. He didn't have the luxury of slowly supporting her anymore. They had to move fast if they wanted to get out of here before Nateros's little demonstration turned into a full-blown riot.

Nearby people shouted at them, but only a few seemed to realize who they were. Chris elbowed through them, all but knocking them over. That inner resilience of Allara's would have to keep her on her feet and moving after him.

A burgher blocked his way and puffed a beery breath into his face. "Where you off to then? Don't want to stay and hear a little honest talk?"

Chris pushed him aside.

Allara must have looked back, because the next thing he heard was a collective gasp.

"That's her," the woman said. "That's the princess!"

Chris gritted his teeth and shoved through one last knot of people to gain the edge of the quay, where the white water taxis bobbed in their stalls. Twenty yards down the boardwalk, the Guardsman Rantim beckoned them. Chris reached back to slide his arm around Allara's waist, then pulled her up beside him. He ran, lifting her just enough to help her keep pace. Behind them, half a dozen footsteps beat against the boards.

Ahead, Rantim scrambled down the short ramp to the boat.

Chris thrust Allara in front of him. "Tell the captain to take off!" He jumped in after her, kicked the ramp free, and turned to see what he was leaving in his wake.

The crowd spilled into the quayside. Most of them had no idea what they were chasing, but they had all been whipped to a fury by Steadman's speeches and probably their evening's share of ale.

"What about Quinnon?" Allara said.

"He's coming."

The white feather atop Quinnon's hat slid through the crowd like the fin of a shark. He'd been closer behind them than Chris had realized. Now he emerged and headed for the next taxi in line. He had Yemas in front of him, arm twisted behind his back, and he hurled him into the boat and leapt the distance from the dock without touching the ramp. He saw Chris and Allara on the taxi ahead and raised a finger to motion them forward.

The water taxi was a trim little craft, not quite as big as the one they had taken from the palace to Belkin Bay. Its half circle of sail caught the breeze and drifted away from the quay.

Someone in the mob threw a clay jug at them, but it only clipped the gunnel. Pursuers crowded the bank. A few tried to hail taxis in order to follow. The rest shoved and shuffled, shouting vulgarities and echoing Steadman's platitudes.

Chris's blood buzzed, and his tired muscles filled with new energy. He turned to find Allara already crouching inside the passenger box, checking Eroll, where he lay on the floor.

"What did Yemas mean?" he asked.

She hung her head back. "I don't know. I think . . . I think he saw me leave the trees with the Koraudians. My pistol had misfired. I suppose—" She exhaled. "I suppose it might have appeared as though I had signaled the Koraudians, then charged from the trees with them. Yemas killed the nearest Koraudian before the man could threaten me and make it clear we weren't allies."

"You've got to be kidding me. He's a soldier. He's got to understand guns jam all the time. It happens."

She raised a shoulder. "You and I both know that sometimes we believe the truth we want rather than the one that is."

35

IF ALLARA PRETENDED she didn't need to breathe, then everything was fine. She sat on the rumpled edge of her bed with her hands folded between her knees and her head bowed.

But the moment of reprieve stretched too far, and her empty lungs were forced to suck in a new breath and a new wave of pain. Her pulse throbbed in her head, her brain swelling against her skull, then receding.

Her rooms in the Glen Arden palace were completely different from the heavy shadows of her Réon Couteau chambers. Here, everything was blindingly white: the marble floors, the snow bear rugs, the bas reliefs on the walls, the bedclothes and pillows, the filmy bed curtains. Gray morning light blared through the wall of windows near the bed and ignited all the white in the room into a burn that stabbed her eyes every time she opened them. At this moment, Réon Couteau actually seemed preferable.

She didn't even remember crumpling into bed last night. She'd slept in a black abyss and only woken when Esta poked her ten minutes ago to make certain she was still alive. Muttering threats against Koraudians and promising a hot bath, Esta had helped her shuck her filthy riding clothes in exchange for a dressing gown, then headed to the kitchen in search of a hearty breakfast Allara didn't even want to think about.

Someone knocked on the door, and she forced her eyelids open. She'd had concussions before. She'd muscled through them then, and she could muscle through this one now.

"Come in."

The ornate ivory of the doors swung inward, and Chris stepped around the corner.

Instinct yanked her backbone straight, and her head thudded in protest. Nausea swirled through her skull; her brain felt as though someone was stirring it into mush. She raised a hand to clasp the collar of her dressing gown. "I thought you were Esta."

He didn't look abashed. "I think I saw her downstairs, getting breakfast or something." He left the door open a crack and stopped between her bed and the door. "I came to see how you're doing before I left."

"Where are you going?"

"To Trawler's Waterfront. Thought today might be my only chance to see my family for a while." He wore a sleeveless gray doublet, ruched and buckled in red, over a loose-sleeved white blouse. His appearance was decent and refined, but not to a degree that would draw attention on the streets.

She dropped her head to rest against the hand propped on her leg and tilted her face to look at him past the veil of her tangled hair. It smelled of smoke and grease and sweat and she didn't want to think about what else.

"I'm sorry you haven't had more time with them," she said.

"Not your fault." He shifted his weight and peered around the room, then broke the silence. "Your father left at daybreak."

She raised her head. "Without seeing me?"

"He didn't want to wake you, and he was in a bit of a hurry."

"Where was he going?"

"Ballion. Mactalde has pushed through the hills there, but Quinnon was right about the Cherazii opening their dams and flooding the canyons. It will be awhile before the Koraudians can find a way through. For now, both armies are dug in. I'm planning to head out there myself tomorrow. I told your father I'd be there for the next battle, and, since I missed that, maybe at least I can get there in time for this one."

"Ballion." She eased a breath past her lips. "I need to come with you." Just the thought of it was exhausting, but by tomorrow things would be better.

He clucked. "You're not in much of a condition to do anything except sleep this thing off. Your head's hurting bad, is it?"

"I can deal with the pain once the nausea stops."

"You should just stay and get your health back together."

"Perhaps."

"If you give up that easily, I'm going to worry there's something really wrong with you."

She peeked up at him, and he gave her a grin that didn't quite ease the lines of concern between his eyes.

"Don't trouble yourself." She made the words gruff. "In the overall scheme of things right now, my headache is a very small issue, hardly worthy of a Gifted's worry."

Just to prove it, she grabbed the edge of the night table and pulled herself to her feet. Dizziness scampered around inside her head like a rodent in a cage. Clamping her eyes shut, she concentrated on fitting the grooves of her top molars with those of her bottom. "I can take care of myself."

"Oh yeah, I can see that." His footsteps crossed the room. "Come here." His hands took hold of her elbows and propelled her backward. The backs of her knees bumped the mattress and buckled. He caught her weight and eased her down.

She scowled enough to wrinkle the cut on her forehead and glared at him. "I don't need to be in bed. I need to be up. I need to take care of things. And I don't need your help."

"Yes, you do." He pushed her back against the pillows once, then once more when she tried to get up.

At the moment, she didn't have the strength to try again.

"I want you to get in this bed and stay in this bed, hear me?" he said.

She opened her mouth and found she had no response. No one told her what to do like this, not even Quinnon. "You have no right to command me."

"Oh, hush." Without so much as a respectful hesitation, he scooped her legs onto the bed and pulled the bedclothes all the way up to her chin. "Here." He dug a white pellet out of his doublet. "This is for you. It's called aspirin." He set it in her palm and closed her fingers over it. "When Esta gets back, tell her to bring you a glass of water so you can swallow it. It'll help the pain." He grinned. "I'll see you later. Be good."

She stared after him as he left and hunted for something to say that would show she had maintained her composure in the midst of this surprising onslaught of forceful tenderness. But the words refused to come.

The door opened just as he reached it and Esta swept in with a breakfast tray. She gaped. "What do you think you're doing in here? This is scandalous!"

"Oh, deeply." He bowed from the waist, held the door for Esta, then strode out.

"Well." Esta tried to sound offended, but two little spots of color shone on her cheeks as she turned back to Allara. "Ah me." She sighed. "I always did favor the rogues."

Instead of commandeering a palace boat, Chris took Parry along as a guide and rode on horseback to Trawler's Waterfront. Yemas's hasty shouts about Allara's supposed treachery had spread like pollen. Nateros demonstrations crowded the streets the whole way. Deeper into the city, some of the demonstrations had turned ugly, with brawls in the streets and rocks hurled through windows.

Many businesses, including the Bowens' restaurant, had been boarded up for the day. Worick had stayed home from fishing to be there for his family if things got out of hand.

His father greeted him with a broad grin and a handshake. "Now I'm glad I had to stay home. No princess today? And I don't blame her."

Chris pushed back his doublet hood and threw his half cape over the back of a chair. They sat around the big table in the restaurant kitchen while his mother bustled around frying croutie in a batter of flour, saffron, salt, and ginger. She served it with heffron nut milk and a pea salad mixed with a salty dark meat.

He watched her cook and tried to find the memories of having watched her a hundred times before. Only the whispered déjà vu of dreams remained—that and the soft, spicy melting of the croutie on his tongue.

Sirra had to leave early to pick up the twins from Tielle's house.

Parry, who had blushed from nose to ears at his first sight of her, knocked his chair over backwards and offered an elbow. "You'll need an escort, my lady, to protect you. The streets are dangerous today, you know."

With a wink at Chris, she threw on her cloak and took his arm.

Worick watched them go. "Seems a nice enough lad."

"Yeah, he is. He's been a good friend. Helped me a lot."

For a few minutes, the only sound in the room was the clink of the utensils against the tin plates, the howl of the wind rattling the windows, and the clatter of passing wagons in the street.

What did you say to people you'd lived with all your life when you knew nothing about them? He caught his mother's eye and saw his own thought reflected back at him. He smiled at her, and she returned it.

"This is very strange," she said.

"You've no idea. I mean, I know it's strange—and difficult—for you, suddenly having a son who doesn't remember anything he used to. But, for me, it's like you're back from the dead."

"I've wondered about that. I stopped dreaming a long, long time ago."

"And my dreams turned to nightmares." Worick spooned in a big bite of sopple and custard pie and thumbed a drop of custard from the corner of his mouth. "I dreamt the nightmares, but you lived them." His head tilted to look at Lauria. "Can't imagine. Don't want to imagine."

Chris's throat closed down, and he lowered his forkful of pie back to his plate. "No. You don't."

"It was very difficult for you," his mother said. She didn't ask.

"Yes. Of course. But I moved on."

Back home, he might have been able to say the words, swallow the lie of them, and change the subject. But, here, he was struck with the need to be honest.

"Actually, I really didn't do that good a job of moving on. My life just sort of ran in circles after the car wreck that killed you and Sirra." He glanced at his mother. "I don't think I realized how true that was until I got here. This whole experience puts everything in a different perspective." He tapped his fork against his plate. "Makes me see how many things I've done wrong."

She made a demurring sound. "I'm sure you haven't done anything wrong."

His father watched him steadily. "What kind of things?"

He forced a laugh and pushed back his plate. Suddenly, this wasn't where he wanted the conversation to go. His family here in Glen Arden was whole; he didn't need to bring over the cracks from Chicago. "Doesn't matter."

"It matters." His father wasn't demanding a response, but the firmness in his words woke faraway childhood memories.

Worick was a man who led his family, a man of patience and kindness, but also a man of bedrock authority. He was a man to respect.

Once, Paul had been that man.

His mother folded her callused hands on the table. "Tell us." Her expression was soft and ever so faintly guarded, as if she knew she would be hurt by the pain he would share.

"Well." He struggled to find the words. "There's not too much to tell, really. The car wreck happened when I was twelve. After that," he glanced at his father, "you sort of went missing in action. I mean, it wasn't you, it was my other father."

Worick's heavy eyebrows, bleached from his long days in the sun, pulled tight. "We're the same person."

How could he put this into words they would understand? "No. You would never have done what he did. I know that. I can tell it by looking at you. You would have stood strong. You would have been there for Lisa and me. You wouldn't have fallen into the bottle and left us fatherless as well as motherless."

His mother released a shuddery breath.

Who wouldn't be upset to hear their children had been mistreated? He deliberately didn't look at her.

His father's fingers steepled, then slid back to clasp each other, over and over. "You don't know I wouldn't have done that."

"Yes, I do." He couldn't keep the bitterness from his voice. "I look at you and see the father I wanted, not the father I had."

"You did have me, Talan. I'm the same person. Only the situation, the surroundings were different."

Chris shook his head.

His father lowered his hands to the edge of the table and leaned back. "If I had done the same in this world, if the Searcher had brought you here and you discovered your mother was dead here too and I was a sot, would you have let your life run by? Same as you did in the other world?"

Chris frowned. "No."

"And you know why not? Because you said yourself you were given a second chance, the opportunity to see your life anew and make your choices over. And that's the key right there." He pointed at Chris. "You make your choices, in this world as well as the other. Just as I do." The creases in his jowls deepened. "I've made my own wrong choices, in both worlds. Mostly in the other, apparently. And I'm sorry for that."

How many times had Chris wanted to hear those words from that mouth?

He shook his head. "It's not yours to be sorry for."

"Yes, it is." Worick drew a tremendous breath. "And when I ask you to forgive me, I'm asking you to forgive all of me."

What Worick was asking was something he had stopped trying to do years ago. He could forgive Worick with all his heart. But Paul was a different matter. He glanced at his mother, and she gave him a little nod.

He turned back. "I don't know if I can." His father wanted him to be honest, so he would be. "But I'll try."

"That's all I ask."

Outside, childish voices shouted, and Chris caught Sirra's laugh. The door opened on a cold gust of wind, and everyone clambered inside. The twins, excited from their walk and some confectionary canes Parry had purchased in a burst of gallant extravagance, ran around the kitchen, shouting, until their grandmother shooed them into the sitting room.

Parry had his chest puffed out and was regaling Sirra with some story about how he had single-handedly protected Chris from the mobs on their ride over. Her grin said she was thoroughly enjoying it, and the glances she threw at Chris said she wasn't believing a word.

Chris didn't want to leave. He wanted to stay here forever. This was where he belonged. He was safe here. He was loved. But the day was already stretching. If he wanted to get back to the palace in good time and prepare for his journey to Ballion tomorrow morning, he needed to get a move on. He eased himself to his feet.

"Time to go then?" his father asked.

"Looks like. I'm off to Ballion tomorrow to join the army."

His father lowered his voice, so the women wouldn't hear. "It's getting serious, isn't it?"

"I think so."

"What would you say if I was to come with you? If it's come to an invasion, then it's time for every able-bodied man to fight for his home. Been awhile since my training with the militia. Don't know as the recruiting centers here in the city would take an oldster like me." He rolled his hulking shoulders. "But I can still throw a punch with the best of them. And, the truth of the matter is, if I'm going to fight, then I'd like to fight at your side."

Chris took his hand and shook it. "I don't want you to get hurt."

"And neither I you." His father gripped his hand and smiled. "When do you leave?"

The last thing he wanted was his father on the front lines, but a familiar face at his side and more time with Worick would improve that long lonely trip to Ballion considerably.

He smiled back. "Skycar leaves the palace midmorning. I'll tell the Guardsmen to expect you."

36

BY THE TIME Chris made it back through the crowds to the palace, the sun had set in a smudge of gray light on the horizon. The palace buzzed with talk, most of it about Nateros's accusations against Allara. When he asked the doormen about her, their eyes turned opaque and they shook their heads and backed away.

On his way up the big staircase, he unslung his cape and handed it back to Parry. Anger burned in his gut. A dithery young nobleman had stopped him in the main hall to ask, all innocence, if he had heard the rumors that the Princess Allara was Mactalde's mistress. Only Parry's clutch at his arm under the guise of pulling his glove free stopped him from slugging the peach fuzz right off the idiot's face.

"I can't believe this," he growled.

Parry chattered, probably trying to distract him. "It really was a lovely day. Lovely, wasn't it? And speaking of lovely, your sister—if it's not forward of me to say so—is a vision. No, that's not right, she's the dream of a vision, is what she is. She'd fit right in here at court, fine as any noble lady."

Chris ignored him. "No one would have the guts to let these rumors spread if the king were here."

"But she's *not* a noble lady, right? Even though she's related to you. I mean, because you're only a lord by accident, so to speak. So, maybe it wouldn't be all that improper for me to call on—"

Chris stopped short and turned around. Parry skidded to a halt and leaned back to keep from bumping into him.

Chris caught the kid's arm so he wouldn't topple. "Where would

Allara usually be this time of the evening?" He doubted she had taken his advice and stayed in bed like a good patient.

Parry screwed up his face. "You know, all this talk we've been hearing . . . you don't think it's true, do you?"

"Of course it's not true! You honestly believe a Searcher would betray you?"

Parry shrugged. "Well . . . *I* don't, you know. But there are lots of folks what'd like to blame her for stuff."

Chris gave him a shake. "Don't say that to my face again. If you want to go anywhere near my sister, then you prove to me you're man enough to stand against slander, no matter whose or how many mouths it's spewing out of. You got me?"

Parry's head bobbed up and down. "Yes, sir. I don't believe it, not a word. I was just asking because I wanted to be sure."

"*I'm* sure. Is that good enough for you?"

Another head bob. "Yes. Absolutely. Now I'm sure too." He cleared his throat. "Um, if she's not in her quarters, perhaps she's with Lord Thyra." He pointed down the hall.

Chris released him and turned away.

Parry exhaled audibly, then called after him, "Your clothes are all dusty. Don't you want to change them before dinner?"

"No." He glanced back as he walked away. "Parry."

"Aye?"

"If anybody says any of that garbage to you again, you break his nose."

"Um, okay. Unless he's bigger'n me."

Chris kept going until he found Eroll's room in the south wing.

A bespectacled surgeon's aide answered his knock. He straightened his shoulders in recognition. "Lord Thyra's awake right now, but he's in and out of consciousness. Since it's you, I'll give you a few minutes. But please don't rouse him too much." He gave his head a shake and his wiry hair flopped against his temples. "Somehow or other, he's heard these ghastly whisperings about her highness. It hasn't done him any good, I assure you."

At the end of the room, near the balcony door, a canopied bed rested in shadows. Beneath the coverlet, Eroll lay on his stomach, one hand on the pillow beside his face. His breath raised the sheet in little puffs. The bedclothes had been drawn up to his chin, but the white swathe of the bandage was visible across his shoulder. Perspiration pearled the flush of his skin and darkened his fair hair.

As Chris approached, his eyes fluttered open. He stared for a moment, then the corner of his mouth lifted. "There you are, old fellow."

Here Chris was, whole and standing, while Eroll lay there a broken wreck. He stopped next to the bed. "I'm glad to see you awake."

The gray hollow of Eroll's cheek quivered in a laugh. "To be perfectly frank, sleep's better. Hurts like the devil to be awake." His words slurred.

Chris shifted. "What's the doctor say?"

"Oh, he says I'll pull through. Of course, they tell you that when you're dying same as not." His eyelids drifted shut, but he smiled again, as if to be reassuring. "I hear tell I wouldn't be here a'tall if not for you."

Chris fingered his doublet's bottom buckle. "If not for me, you wouldn't have been shot in the first place." If he could snap his fingers and make it happen, he would trade places with Eroll in a second. His stomach twisted. "I'm sorry. You were a friend when I didn't deserve one. And this is what I do to you."

"Don't be daft. Koraud has been wanting to mount the head of a Thyrian duke in their throne room for eons. Hardly your fault they don't like the cut of my jib."

This wasn't a forgiveness Chris merited. Risking himself to save Eroll after the fact was small recompense for the pain Eroll had endured and the death he still faced. But how was he supposed to reject the only gift of a man flat out in bed from a shot in the back?

He cleared his throat. "I'll let you get your rest now. You'll pull through in no time and be ready to deliver the death blow to the Koraudian army when the time comes."

"Can't ruddy wait." Eroll took a careful breath and opened his eyes. "What's this I hear about Allara? They're saying she's betrayed Lael, aren't they?"

Chris hesitated, then nodded. "Yes. But she didn't."

"'Course she didn't. But at the moment, we might be the only two people in Glen Arden to believe that. There are those who have been waiting a very long time to destroy her. This is their chance, and they know it."

"I promise I'll keep her safe for you."

Eroll focused on him from the corner of his eye. "Keep her safe for her own sake. She needs someone in her life, you know. A man to take care of her. She never would let me do it properly. Might just be she'll let you." He raised his fingers from the pillow. "She's out on the balcony. I think she's waiting for you."

Chris dug around for a response and found he didn't have one. So she and Eroll weren't an item after all? But an Allara whose heart was free still didn't mean she was an Allara who would ever let him inside her walls.

Footsteps padded in the carpet behind, and the surgeon's aide approached. "I think it would be best if we let Lord Thyra rest now." He gestured to where the surgeon was wheeling in a tray of equipment. "Doctor Vanoy has come."

Chris leaned forward to give Eroll's wrist a squeeze, then crossed to the balcony's glass doors and pushed through. The wind blew against his face, carrying both the hum of the city and the faraway thud of artillery at Ballion.

On the balcony ledge in the corner, Allara sat with her back against the wall and her knees drawn up in front of her.

He walked to the end of the balcony, across from her, and tried on a smile. "There you are. What are you doing out here?"

She held one arm out, and her long scarlet sleeve spread in the breeze like a wing. "Trying to fly away. I came out to be alone."

"I didn't mean to intrude."

"You didn't intrude. I knew you were coming." The dark blue of her bodice and skirt blended with the night. Her face was still pale, but the gaunt look of pain had faded. "I can feel you, you know."

"What?"

She spared a tiny smile. "In my head. I feel your presence. That's how the Searchers are able to find the Gifted."

He tried to absorb that. "What's it like?"

"Different." She tilted her head back and forth as if trying to think of a way to explain it. "It's like sharing your mind with someone. I can sense an essence of who you are. Sometimes I catch hints of what you're feeling, thinking."

Instinctively, he tried to damp his thoughts and pull them away from her. She laughed softly, and he tried harder.

"I'm sorry." She sounded like she meant it. "I shouldn't have told you."

He gave up and released his thoughts. If she'd been reading his mind all this time, it hardly mattered if he couldn't hide it from her now.

"Seems like that puts you at an unfair advantage," he said.

"Perhaps I need an advantage." When she smiled, her exhaustion showed through the cracks.

"You shouldn't be out here with a concussion."

The glow from Eroll's room masked her face: her features half in the light, half in the dark.

"I've had concussions before. I know how much I can handle."

"From the sound of things, you're going to have to handle a lot." He wished the words back as soon as he'd said them. If she didn't know what the city was saying about her, so much the better.

Her smile faded. "You've heard the rumors?"

"Yes, unfortunately." He couldn't help a note of bitterness. "And the people are scarfing it down without a second thought."

"All they needed to vilify me was an excuse." She stared past him at the glitter of the cityscape. "It doesn't take long for rumors to become fact around here."

"So what's all this mean for you?"

"I've had death threats on my head since I was a child. Doesn't matter. The people don't have to love or even respect me. So long as they trust *you*, that's the important thing."

"You must have laws to protect you against slander."

"How do you know it's slander?" Her features were perfectly still. If he didn't know better, he'd say she was asking the question seriously.

"You don't really think I believe you're a traitor?"

"You can't know I didn't do what they're saying I did."

"I know it."

She clasped her hands in her lap. "You're the only person who's said that to me all day."

"What about Quinnon and Esta?"

"The point is no one *said* it."

The fine bones of her face creased hard against her skin. Moonlight flickered through the racing clouds and turned her complexion to the color of a washed-out star. She usually wore her hair in a braid or coiled on top of her head to keep it from the wind. But tonight it hung over her shoulders, halfway down her back, and the dark strands that would have swirled with red and gold in the daylight now looked as if they had been spun from the night.

He spread his hands on the balustrade behind him and leaned back, watching her. This woman had been born to the uppermost echelon of society. She had been bred to a world of sophistication and charm, a world where women were not only allowed but expected to take part in the best things. Had she chosen not to shoulder every last particle of her burden as Searcher, she could have spent her life swirling across marble floors, dancing in silken gowns, and bringing courtier after courtier to his knees in pursuit of her. The lines around her eyes and her mouth could have been laugh lines instead of worry scars.

He cleared his throat. "What happened to Yemas?"

"He'll be dismissed from the Guard certainly. Perhaps put on trial for perjury. But not likely, since we won't want to create a stir. He didn't technically do anything wrong. He believed what he said about me was true."

"Nateros must have puréed his brains. I'd like to kick his teeth in." Maybe she was right about needing an advantage, because he could see every thought in her face. "You look surprised. Why does that surprise you?"

"People don't go around wanting to kick in other people's teeth for me."

"Don't give me that. You're a princess—and a Searcher. You could get anybody to do whatever you want."

She shook her head. Her face had a soft quality, an openness. Aside from when she'd been unconscious, he'd never seen her with her guard down this far. She almost looked happy he'd want to beat up Yemas for her, which somehow made him want to do it all the more.

She was a difficult woman to impress, and, so far, his skill sets in this world hadn't been of a quality that measured up. But, right now, he couldn't help feeling she was pleased with him. Even more than that, she seemed to be reaching out to him for something.

Reassurance maybe? She wouldn't have to reach very far for that. He was already proud of her. She was brave and courageous and honorable. He'd beat up a scumbag like Yemas for her any day.

She must have caught a glimmer of his thoughts, or maybe it was just his smile. She looked away and cleared her throat.

He eyed her, then spoke before he could give himself time to think. "Your life didn't exactly turn out the way you thought it would, did it?"

She darted him a glance. "I suppose if we could control our destinies, all our lives would be much different." She rubbed at her crooked finger.

He ambled toward her. "I would never have chosen . . . this. Any of it. If I'd been given a choice about it, I would have thrown it all away. But I'm realizing this is my world as much as it is yours. It's *my* kingdom, my home."

He stopped beside the railing and looked up at her. "I never thought I'd get another chance with my family. And I certainly never thought I'd meet someone like you. And here I have."

In the darkness, her eyes shimmered.

The clouds overhead rumbled, and the rain began to mist once again.

"You should go to bed," he said. "You're crazy to be out here at all."

She swung her legs over the edge of the railing. "I didn't know what crazy was until I met you."

He grinned. "Is that a compliment? Don't tell me the ice princess is melting."

"What?"

"That mask you like to wear. All ice and stone."

She tensed. "What makes you think it's a mask?"

He took her hands and helped her step down. "Every once in a while, out of the corner of my eye, I catch you without it." He almost left it at that, but something made him go on. "You're happier without it."

She stood in front of him, not quite meeting his look. She was fighting to keep her shields up, to keep him in his old comfortable place at arm's length.

"Happier, perhaps." She looked up. "But not safer."

"Sometimes safety isn't worth the exchange." He watched her, daring her to look away.

"You think you can sacrifice your safety and find happiness?"

"Sometimes you have to take a risk every now and then, just to prove you're still alive." On impulse, he brushed a strand of hair out of her face.

She stared at him, her lips parted. Ever since the day he had met her, she had thrown up layer after icy layer to keep him from understanding her. She had stood unmoving in the face of every kind of physical danger. Her shields had resisted the battering of a thousand people from every side. And now all it took to breach her defenses was a touch?

For a moment, he thought he might kiss her. She needed to be kissed; she needed to be loved. She deserved to have someone hold her in his arms and protect her from a world that had betrayed her at every turn.

"So much is happening right now." He slid the strand back behind her ear. "I suppose it's probably not the best time for me to fall in love with you."

She breathed out, hard. "This isn't—"

He hadn't intended to talk about this right now. He wasn't sure he had intended to talk about it *ever*. But it was out now, and he needed her to respond, one way or the other.

"But—" he began.

The double doors to Eroll's room banged open, and Quinnon stepped outside. His good eye found them in the corner.

"There you are." His mouth tightened. "If you're going to Ballion in the morning, I need a word with you." He headed back indoors, then glanced at Allara. "And you get back to bed."

Chris turned to her.

She had broken eye contact and stepped away from him. With both hands, she pushed her hair back from her face. Erasing his touch? But when she looked up, her face was clear. She gave a little nod. The moment had passed, and they both knew it. But at least she wasn't running.

He stepped back. They would talk about this later, sometime when they weren't distracted by everything else and she wasn't half dead on her feet.

He wet his lips. "I'll try to see you in the morning before I leave." He turned to go.

Her hand snagged his wrist. "Chris."

He looked back.

Just as quickly, she let him go and pulled her hand back to herself. For once, he couldn't quite read her face.

"Thank you," she said. "For not believing what Nateros is saying."

He smiled. "You're welcome." For now, he would have to leave it at that.

He left her and passed through Eroll's rooms.

As soon as Chris closed the door behind him, Quinnon stepped out of the shadows in the globe-lit corridor. "What's this about you being off to Ballion tomorrow morning?"

"My father's going with me. I've told the Guard to admit him to the palace tomorrow."

Quinnon waved off the information. "Her highness and I won't be going with you."

"I figured as much. She needs a few days to heal up before she goes anywhere." He regarded the old fighter. Even hunched with his bad shoulder and his hands hanging empty at his sides, he looked dangerous. "That isn't what you wanted to talk to me about."

Quinnon worked his jaw. "Something's not right. About you, about this whole imbalance." He pointed to a window, streaked with freezing rain. "You say Mactalde's causing it, but that makes no sense."

"The Garowai said it. Not me."

"What you *think* the Garowai said isn't always what he did say." He studied Chris. "If this imbalance keeps on like it is, it could end up making our little war seem like a Commemorating Ball. There's a lot more necks than just yours on the line here. You're sure there's nothing you're not telling us about Mactalde crossing over?"

Quinnon was a brave man, and maybe even a wise one. But the one thing Chris had learned about him was that if you wanted any chance of having your respect returned, you didn't back down. Ever.

"It happened the way I told you." This time, he was the one who closed the distance between them by a full step. "If I knew another way to fix this thing, I'd do it."

Quinnon didn't look convinced, but at least his expression didn't accuse Chris of lying. He gave a nod of dismissal, but as Chris started down the hall, his voice stopped him. "One other thing. You're here to do a job. That's the only reason you're in this palace. You do anything to hurt her, and I swear to you, I will break your back."

Chris looked at him. "I know it."

37

ORIAS STOOD AT the edge of a gully, on a ledge that, a few days ago, had extended over dry earth. The water was recognizable from the dark sky only by its occasional translucence. It filled the night with a cold, mossy smell. The Cherazii had opened the high country dams in time. They had held back Mactalde's invasion. For now, Mactalde was trapped on this side of the river, while the Laeler army dug themselves into the hills opposite.

He closed his eyes against the needling rain and breathed a prayer of thanks to which he had no right. After three days of hard riding from the ill-fated skirmish at the Glockamon Moors, he had arrived in Ballion with the Koraudian escorts assigned to him by Mactalde. "Escort" was Mactalde's term. These men were his captors, and he their prisoner. He stifled the dull ache of that truth. Would that he were dead.

He did this for his people. That was the only reason he did it. But, at times, even that seemed not reason enough.

Two sets of footsteps crunched in the rocks behind him: Mactalde and Rotoss come to gloat over him again.

"Welcome back, Master Tarn." The hoarse exhaustion of a long battle graveled Mactalde's voice. "I hear you've had poor hunting."

He didn't respond. With all his heart, he rejoiced that Chris Redston and the Searcher had escaped Mactalde's ambush. Likely, Mactalde already knew of his joy. Likely, he blamed Orias for their escape.

Mactalde stepped up abreast with him. "I wonder if you perhaps could elucidate the unexpected presence of this tidal wave?"

Were it not for his oath to Mactalde—and the fact that it kept his people safe—he would cast Mactalde into the rage of the water beneath without a second thought.

"What makes you think I would have any elucidation to offer?"

Mactalde laughed, but the silver of it was tarnished. "I'm afraid I haven't the time or the patience to appreciate the scintillating depths of Cherazii conversation right now. Perhaps we could shorten this, for both our sakes, if I answered my own questions."

Orias stared across the water. What was there left to say?

"In short," Mactalde said, "this would seem to be the work of your esteemed brothers-in-arms, would it not? No, don't bother to answer." A note of sarcasm underlined the words. "I know you must be weary too."

Orias rubbed his thumb against the old scar that wormed his biceps. Aye, he was weary. He was wearier than he would ever have thought possible.

The leather of Mactalde's doublet creaked. "Contrary to popular opinion, wouldn't this turn of events seem to indicate the Cherazii are rethinking their antipathy for Tireus and his allies? And don't you think I have reason to take this apparent breach of—truce, shall we say?—rather indignantly?"

Orias stirred. "My people have no idea of my agreement with you."

"Perhaps someone should inform them."

He stopped the restless movement of his thumb against his arm. His people would never understand, or accept, his covenant with Mactalde. "If they discover the truth, they'll cast aside any neutrality."

"Well, then." Mactalde turned to where Rotoss waited a few strides off with a lantern. "It's time we put you to good use."

Planting him in ambush at the Northfall River hadn't been good use enough? His stomach turned. How much more of this would he be forced to endure? How much deeper into this pit of filth and treachery could he burrow before he could bear no more?

He followed the two men—both a hand shorter than him, both of whom he could crush without even trying—back into the glow of the camp. They threaded their way through the fires to Mactalde's big tent.

Outside the door flaps, a beef-faced sergeant sat on a stool. He held a clay jug of cranok in one hand and the leashes of the two

Rievers in the other. Raz sat cross-legged between the sergeant's feet, his grizzled chin propped in one hand. Pitch, his leash stretched to its limit, waited in the path.

He shook his head at the expectant look in the Riever's eyes. This had not been part of the bargain, and Mactalde had no right to treat the Rievers with contempt just to drive another stake into Orias's heart. He choked on his own breath. At the first opportunity, he would see they were set free of this place. But at present, he could do nothing for them.

He ducked inside the tent. An abundance of candle globes quivered overhead, and the colored glass—scarlet and navy and amber—cast murky shadows against the canvas walls.

Rotoss plunked his lantern amid the rolls of maps on the desk and tugged off his gloves with his teeth. He grinned at Orias. "Enjoying fighting for a winning army for a change?"

"You haven't won yet," Raz muttered from the doorway.

The sergeant yanked the Rievers' leashes and pointed out a chair. "Come on, you."

The Rievers scrambled into the fur-covered seat and sat there, Raz sulking and Pitch glaring at Rotoss.

"You're ugly," he announced.

Raz jammed an elbow into Pitch's side.

Rotoss's smile stiffened. "I can see you're an authority on the subject." He clucked his tongue at Orias. "A culture as militant as yours should've hammered a better idea of respect into your lackeys."

Orias fought the urge to smash the heel of his hand into Rotoss's nose. He could snap the cartilage and drive the bone into the man's brain without even trying. "They had no part in this deal. You've no reason to hold them."

Rotoss scoffed. "You're long past any point of bargaining. What's done is done."

"Precisely." Mactalde rounded the corner of the desk and eased himself into his chair. "And I am indeed prepared to let your companions go."

Orias held his ground. "If . . . ?"

"If you fulfill your next mission. I'm afraid I can't send an escort with you this time. It's a rather delicate situation. I doubt Tireus would allow our soldiers behind his lines."

Orias cocked his head. "Behind the lines?"

"I'm sending you home . . . in a sense. I want you to find the Gifted."

His skin tingled. "You want me to kill him."

Pitch jumped from his chair. "No!"

The guard growled and hauled on the leash.

"You have it exactly." Mactalde steepled his fingers. "If Lael hears another Gifted has been murdered by a Cherazim, it will save you and me the discomfort of having to inform the Cherazii of our rather unconventional pact. Couldn't be any more perfect, don't you agree?"

His sword arm trembled. "No, I do not. I won't kill the Gifted. I fulfilled my part of the agreement. I delivered him into Rotoss's hands. I fed him with lies so he'd bring you back. That was treachery enough."

"Treachery is treachery, Master Tarn." Beneath the flickering candlelight, Mactalde's expression was flat and cold. "You've already damned your soul, so you might as well see this to the finish. You agreed to fight under me and to follow my orders. My orders are to find Chris Redston and kill him." His hands dropped to the desk, and he leaned forward. "If you don't, I'll have no reason to keep my end of the deal."

"You've yet to keep it. None of this was a part of the bargain I made with Rotoss."

Rotoss perched one hip on the edge of the desk and leaned back to dig his dirty fingernails through a bowl of white heffron nuts. "The bargain you made with me and the one you made with Lord Mactalde are two different bargains. We've both of us kept our words. Not a single Cherazim has been killed." He grinned. "We'll try to keep it that way."

Orias wanted to kill this man. He wanted it more than he wanted to live. Was any of this worth the living sacrifice of everything he'd ever believed in or cared about? What reason did he have to believe Mactalde would observe his word any longer than was convenient? Once he overran Lael and tired of his pet Cherazim, he could execute Orias at his leisure, then turn his attention to rooting the Cherazii out of the hills.

His heart pumped battle fire, and he dropped his hand to the dirk at his side. The berserking rage climbed through him, all the way to

his eyes. His vision tunneled around Mactalde. Scenarios and stratagems raced through his brain. He could take them out. If he was
lucky, he could take them both out.

"I wouldn't do that." Mactalde's voice held an iron edge. "I've left
orders with all my commanders to eradicate the Cherazii at the first
possible opportunity should anything happen to me."

Hot bile welled in the back of his throat. His hand dropped from
the dirk, and he spat.

Mactalde scowled. "I hope that means yes."

"Yes," Orias said.

"No." Pitch scrambled from his chair fast enough to yank the
leash away from the sergeant. He caught Orias's hand. "Don't do
this. You can't do this. I found him, remember? He belongs to me.
You can't hurt him."

Orias pulled his hand free and addressed the sergeant, "Let them
go and get my gear together. I want my lion too."

"The Rievers won't be going, I'm afraid," Mactalde said.

"What?" Raz said. "Bad enough you tie us up like dogs. Now
you're going to keep us as hostages?"

"No." Orias's arm returned to his side, and Pitch's hot little hands
caught hold of his fingers once more. "If they don't come with me,
then I don't go at all."

"On the contrary." Mactalde rose from his chair. "If you don't
return in two weeks' time with Redston's head in your saddlebags, I
will kill them both." He walked around the end of the desk to face
Orias. "You'd best dispose of these newfound scruples of yours.
You agree, don't you?"

For two long seconds, Orias listened to his heartbeat. He had no
choice, and he knew it. What he did now was what he had doomed
himself to the moment he had first yielded to Rotoss.

"Aye," he said.

Then he pulled his hand free of Pitch's and walked into the cold
night.

38

CHRIS REINED UP. "Sounds like men in a hurry."

From the trees on the other side of the flooded gorge, brush cracked.

He, his father, and a platoon of Guardsmen on their way to the front had arrived on the northern shores of Lake Thyra last night. They had spent the night in Ballion Point, then saddled up to ride the remaining twenty miles to the rear command post, where they were supposed to find Tireus.

His father stopped beside him. "An enemy in a hurry is always a bad sign."

"Unless they're hurrying in the opposite direction." He turned to address the Guardsmen. "Let's stop. I'd like to take a look at the water."

Technically, these men didn't answer to him. They were headed to join up with a depleted company at the front and were only with Chris because the Gifted was supposed to be protected. But their sergeant nodded, and the men fell out for a few moments' rest.

Chris and his father reined off the road and rode through the underbrush to the newborn river the Cherazii had released from their dams the week before. Not-too-distant artillery thudded over the rumble of the water. Except for a haze of smoke against the clouds, the red peaks of the Ballion hills hid all other signs of the battle.

On the far bank, the undergrowth tore open. A short brown figure tripped in the mud and slid down the steep bank.

Chris frowned. "That's a Riever."

Worick reached for the rifle balanced across his knees. "Where there's Rievers, there's Cherazii. This is their country, and they don't like trespassers. From the sounds of it, there are plenty more in those trees."

Chris pulled his spyglass from his coat pocket. The Riever slid down the bank and disappeared for a moment in a circle of foam. He bounced back into view, dreadlocks spinning like tentacles, and paddled for the far shore.

"It's Pitch." He looked up from the spyglass and blinked just to make sure he was seeing straight. "What's he doing way out here by himself?"

"Who's Pitch?"

The crashing in the brush reached a crescendo, and a squad of Koraudians burst from the trees, shouting. A round of gunshots slashed the water.

The water swallowed Pitch, and Chris shed his coat.

His father reached for his arm. "What are you doing?"

"He's a friend. I have to go after him." Without looking back, he spurred into the water.

Pitch resurfaced near the river's center. Another shot splashed next to him, and he bobbed like a cork. Chris's horse lost its footing, flailed for a second, then launched through the water. Chris slid into the river and gripped the saddlebow with one hand.

"Chris!" A wave hit Pitch in the face, and he sputtered. With his every stroke, the water hurled him a little farther downstream. "Chris! I had to find you!"

"Stop talking and swim!"

The Koraudians' slugs chewed into the water only yards in front of his horse's nose. He stretched for Pitch's hand, caught his fingers, and lost them again. Pitch scrunched his face and strained every muscle in his dog paddle.

A dark shape loomed in the corner of Chris's vision. He jerked around to find his father swimming a few feet behind him.

"What do you think you're doing?"

Worick pulled himself forward in powerful strokes. The current barely moved him. "Giving them another target!" Two or three feet more, and he would be close enough to reach Pitch.

Chris plunged his hand under the water and reached across his body for the chewser pistol. Presumably, the gun's hydraulic power system would only be strengthened by the water. He pulled his horse around, perpendicular to the bank, so the animal was treading against the current, and tried to steady his elbow against his saddle.

As Pitch caught hold of Worick's hand and scrambled up his arm to his shoulders, Chris pulled the trigger. Without looking to see if the shot had managed any damage, he turned to follow his father back to shore. The firing behind him slowed, and the water splashed. He looked back. Two of the Koraudians swam after them. Why would a Riever be worth this kind of pursuit?

With a lurch, his horse caught its footing. Chris let go of the reins and turned around. The Koraudians were halfway across the river. He reloaded, and, with his hands braced one inside the other, he squeezed the trigger. The power system in the cylinder glowed, and the pistol hummed and recoiled. A Koraudian reeled back into the river. The other trod water for a moment, then turned back.

Chris loaded a new slug into the pistol's breech, holstered it, and turned to his father. "What were you thinking? You could have been shot out there."

Worick picked up his tunic from where he'd left it on the ground before jumping into the river. His horse had run off. "You're the one who ought to be turned over my knee for pulling such a reckless stunt."

Chris stared.

Worick glanced at him, sidelong. "Runs in the blood, eh?"

"Maybe so." He unbuckled his pistol bandoleer and cast it on the ground. His short-sleeved leather jerkin had sluiced off most of the water, but the quilted gambeson underneath was soaked. He peeled his shirt away from his goose-pimpled skin and looked down to where Pitch sat next to Worick, wringing out his oversized tunic.

"Where's Orias?" he asked.

Pitch stared at the puddle of water that had run off his shirt. "He's in trouble."

"He should have thought of that before he turned traitor."

"He's not a traitor. I mean, not like that . . ."

"How many shades of traitor do you think there are? It's pretty black and white."

"He didn't mean to hurt anybody."

Chris draped his shirt over the horse's withers and grabbed his jerkin. "He knew exactly what was going to happen."

"No, he didn't."

Worick sat down to empty his boots. "What is all this?"

"Long story," Chris said.

"Too long to tell? Or is it a state secret?"

"Both, more or less." He threaded his arms back into his damp jerkin and fastened the front closures. "We need to get back to the Guard and find some dry clothes before we freeze. We can all ride my horse. They can't be far off."

"What about Orias?" Pitch's chattering teeth mangled his words. "Are you going to help him?"

Chris finished re-buckling his bandoleer and stared at the Riever's wet face. Pitch rolled his lips together and bit down on both of them. His wide eyes stared, unblinking.

Chris shook his head. "If he sets foot in one of our camps or cities, he's dead. If he goes back to the Cherazii, they'll probably hack him apart on sight. What's left for him?"

"He didn't *want* to betray anybody."

"Pitch." Chris made himself breathe. "In the other world, we have a saying. If you make your bed, you have to sleep in it. He made his bed, and there's nothing I can do about it, even if I wanted to." He mounted. "Come on, we need to get out of here."

Pitch stared at the ground and rubbed his shirt in both hands.

Chris frowned. "Where's Raz?"

"Back. With the Koraudians."

"Orias left you with Mactalde?"

"He had to." Tears glassed Pitch's eyes. "They might kill Raz now, because I ran away. They might kill Orias when he gets back."

That made things at least a little clearer. If Mactalde and Rotoss were still holding threats over Orias's head, at least maybe he had an excuse for what he was doing. Not that it changed anything.

Chris ran a hand over his wet hair. "Why'd you come to me? What do you expect me to be able to do?"

"Find Orias."

"I can't. I have to stay with the Guard." He glanced at his father. Worick walked over to Pitch and held out a broad, callused hand.

Pitch took it and followed Worick to the horse. "It wouldn't take long. I know where he's going."

"Put your shirt on." Chris waited while Pitch pulled the damp tunic back over his head. His father lifted the Riever into Chris's lap.

Pitch tipped his head back against Chris's chest and looked up at him. "Why don't you want to help me? You belong to me. You should want to help me."

He was right. Why should the Rievers pay for Orias's treachery? If Chris looked Pitch in the face right now, he'd cave. So he stared down the center of his horse's pricked ears.

"I can't leave now. I promised the king I'd be there for the next battle."

"What if I helped you?" Pitch craned his head back farther. The strange angle distorted his face even more than usual. "If I helped you, would you help me?"

"And how do you propose to help?" Worick asked.

"I know where there's a weak spot. Not a big one. Just a little one. But you could use it. Mactalde set up an artillery redoubt on this side of the river before the waters came. It was too far south for the water to wash it away, I guess."

"This side of the river?" Worick peered up at Chris. "That isn't the Koraudians' weakness. It's ours."

Pitch folded his arms over his chest and chattered his teeth. "It *could* be his weakness if you took it. It's closer to Mactalde's lines than any of your artillery. You could probably knock down a lot of his cannons before the Koraudians could move them. Plus, I know Mactalde was going to go there today himself." He stared up at Chris. "That helps you, doesn't it?"

"I don't know." Making tactical decisions wasn't his job. But if Mactalde was there . . . If this could possibly be Chris's chance to finish him, then didn't he have to take it?

Pitch's directions led them straight to the camouflaged cannon. The Guardsmen made short, silent work of the half dozen Koraudian bombardiers stranded on the southern side of the river, then gestured Chris forward to the embankment, where he could glass the far shore.

At his elbow, Pitch whispered, "I was right, wasn't I?"

He spared a nod. "You were right."

Koraudian soldiers milled just inside the tree line. The sound of hammers and chains carried above the artillery fire from farther upriver.

"They're dismantling the artillery on their side," explained the lead Guardsman, a prematurely gray veteran named Mikkel. "That's so we can't destroy them with this cannon here. They'll probably send a team swimming across to spike this one as soon as it's dark."

Chris scanned the bank. "What about officers? See anyone who could be Mactalde?" He stopped his glass on a leather-clad Koraudian. The man's spyglass glinted right back at him. His skin chilled. "That's him. And he's seen us."

The figure on the far shore lifted a hand, and a cannon's maw wheeled around to face them. The glow of a fireball lurched from its barrel. With a sound like a sudden inhalation, it ripped overhead.

Chris smashed his face into the ground, hands over his head.

The shell exploded behind them, and the acrid scent of padar scorched the air.

Beside him, Mikkel spat sand. "*Och.* Of all the worst timing."

Another fireball screamed over them, and the impact shuddered up through Chris's body. Sweat burned away the chill of his wet clothes. If they didn't get out of here now, they were all dead.

On the other hand, for the first time since he'd come to Lael, he had a clear shot at his single greatest objective. If he could stay alive long enough to pull off one shot, he could possibly end this all right now.

A tugging on his pant leg made him look back down the length of his body. Pitch shouted at him, his mouth forming soundless words through the ringing in Chris's ears. Mikkel crawled back through the brush and waved the rest of the Guardsmen toward the road. Worick crouched a few yards off and gestured frantically.

If Chris stayed here any longer, he might well be a dead man. But if he didn't take this chance, who knew if he'd get another. He pulled the Glock from his bandoleer. It was wet from his swim, but it would still fire. The distance across the river had to be at least a hundred yards. It was a long shot for a pistol, but there was no time to go back for a rifle, even if his horse was still alive and in the vicinity.

"Talan!" He felt more than heard his father's roar.

He pushed to one knee to get a clear shot above the bush. Mactalde still had his glass on him. Chris's pistol came up in both hands and he aimed without even thinking. Mactalde turned and signaled the bombardiers behind him with a closed fist. Chris's shot went wide.

A shell, already in the air, smashed into the middle of the river, and water cascaded over Chris. His heart cramped against his lungs, and then the sudden stillness chased electricity through his muscles.

Behind him, a Guardsman breathed out. "What are they doing?"

Mactalde disappeared into the trees, and a moment later, a cough of smoke trailed into the sky and exploded into a golden hailstorm of sparks.

"A truce." Pitch ran up beside Chris. "They want a truce."

Chris made himself breathe, then checked his father. "You all right?" When he got a grim nod, he looked at Mikkel. "Do you have any way to respond?"

Mikkel produced a fist-sized shell from a waist pouch. Using a small mortar tube, he and one of his men launched an answering firework.

And now what was supposed to happen? Chris stood. His pistol weighted his hand, and he rubbed his thumb against the ridged slide.

Across the river, Mactalde reemerged from the trees with a sword belt held above his head. He made a point of laying it aside.

Mikkel touched Chris's arm. "Your pardon, sir, but I hold the highest military rank here, so I'm the one who needs to respond."

Chris stepped back.

"I wish to speak to the Gifted!" Mactalde's voice carried across the river, amplified by a gleaming copper megaphone.

Mikkel hesitated, then motioned Chris forward. Pitch took a convulsive step after him, but Worick pulled him back.

Overhead, lightning tore thunder from the clouds. Rain shredded the artillery smoke.

Chris sheathed his pistol in his bandoleer, but didn't take it off. He slogged through the thick brush onto the rocky bank.

Head bare to the storm, Mactalde saluted Chris with his hand to his eyes. "Master Redston, I greet you. I've been hoping we might meet." The horn turned his voice tinny. "My apologies for the bombardment, but I suppose you understand, under the circumstances."

Chris only nodded. He didn't have a sound-amplifying horn, and he wasn't about to shout niceties across a river at a man he had just tried to kill.

Mactalde stepped forward. "Who would have thought so much could happen in the time since we last saw each other? This old world spins a little faster every day, doesn't it?"

"It may spin off its axis, thanks to you." The words tumbled off his dry tongue, probably not loud enough for Mactalde to hear. He took a breath and shouted, "What do you want?"

"I want us to stand united, Mr. Redston. I want us to end this war. You and me. We're the only ones who can do it."

"You're telling me you're striving for a legacy of peace?"

"As soon as we've achieved our purpose, you and I can stand as united rulers—the only two Gifted to ever live as contemporaries. I've offered you this once before. I hope you've gained a better perspective since last I saw you."

Chris shook his head. "What you want is impossible, and you know it. You're no Gifted."

"Haven't I crossed the worlds just as surely as you have?"

"You couldn't have done it without me, or without Harrison. You're deliberately twisting the truth to gain yourself a following. One day they're going to wake up from their delusions and realize their leader traded his sanity for power!"

"And what about you?" His voice deepened, not quite angry, but maybe a little peeved. "One day, are you going to wake up and realize what a fool the king and the Searcher have made of you? You—a natural-born Gifted." He almost sounded envious. Perhaps he knew, after all, that he could never be what Chris was.

"And yet," he said, "you willingly bow your head to the yoke of those who deny your right of power." His voice twisted. "You're a leader among men, Chris Redston. You're a Gifted. It is you who should lead Lael's army against me. It is you who should sit on the thrones of Glen Arden and Réon Couteau. So tell me, why do you dance as lackey for that shortsighted tyrant Tireus?"

Chris breathed out. He couldn't say he totally disagreed with that. Tireus had his good points, but he had never exactly embraced Chris or his willingness to help.

"Here's something you should know," Mactalde said. "Something Tireus should know. When the day comes when Lael wishes to bring peace back to her lands, it will only be at the hand of a Gifted that I accept her surrender. Never at the hand of Tireus. You remember that. It is you, not Tireus, whom I recognize as the only true authority in Lael."

Mikkel shot Chris a discreet glance, startled.

Chris gritted his teeth. "That's not how it works."

Mactalde's laugh mingled with the burble of the river. "I'm afraid it is. So you just remember that when I start to crack Lael like a nut, it's you who has the power to end it. Not Tireus."

Across the underside of the clouds, lightning flashed a sickly yellow. A clap of thunder blasted from the clouds to the earth and continued rumbling.

Chris held himself steady. "All right, you've told me your say. Now you can hear mine. The only peace that's ever going to happen between you and me is when one of us is dead."

Mactalde spread his free arm. "You forget I've already died. And you're no killer." What might have been a shade of uncertainty raised his voice a notch. He must know Chris's bullet had come within a foot or two a few minutes ago.

"This is war," Chris said. "I'll do what I have to do."

Behind him, hoofbeats pounded.

Mactalde hacked a laugh. "I know you will. So don't forget what I've said today." He swept a bow, then turned on his heel and stalked back into the trees.

Behind Chris, a horse galloped up from the road, and a young man with a courier's black sash leapt to the ground. "With the king's compliments, he's seen the truce signal and wishes a report immediately."

Chris grimaced. The king was going to be significantly less complimentary once he heard what Mactalde had to say.

39

THE BACK OF Allara's neck crinkled. Something was wrong. After a few days of fighting off stark boredom along with the last of her concussion, she and Quinnon had left Glen Arden for Ballion. According to the captain of the ship that had brought them across Lake Thyra, her father's headquarters was some six leagues deep into the Ballion hills. After unloading their horses, Quinnon had chosen a back road that wouldn't be clogged with artillery and troops.

Now, nearly two hours later, she reined up near a fork in the road and listened. The forest sheltered her body from the wind and the rain, but the roar in the treetops filled her ears. And yet *something* out of the ordinary had penetrated her senses.

She slid her estoc from its scabbard. "Quinnon—"

From the trees on her left, the blurred outline of a rider flashed. She jerked around, and the translucent white of a Cherazim face filled her vision. Instinctively, she lashed out at him.

"Wait. I come only to talk." The Cherazim's blade blocked hers, and even without the weight of attack behind it, his strength so far outmatched hers as to topple her balance.

She kicked free of her stirrup, dropped to the ground, and rolled.

"Hold there!" Quinnon galloped past her.

She staggered to her feet and clawed at her pistol.

Without stopping to ask questions, Quinnon swung his sword.

The Cherazim smashed his broadsword into Quinnon's and sent the smaller blade hurtling into the trees. "I've not come to fight you." He pulled back both his sword and free hand.

Allara started to lower the pistol.

A breath of wind blew his tawny hair out of his face. It was the Tarn. Orias.

"You." She twitched the pistol back up to point at his head.

The corner of his mouth curled. "Going to pull the trigger this time, princess?"

Her breath burned her windpipe. "If the cartridge hadn't jammed when I pulled it that day in the Glockamon Moors, you'd already be dead, you reeking traitor."

"I'm a traitor no longer." His expression was as impenetrable as ever. "I've left Mactalde."

One step at a time, with the straitquin's sights hovering over his face, she approached. "I'd be a fool to believe that."

"You'd be a fool not to." He spared another glance away from Quinnon. "I need to speak with Redston. There are things I must tell him. Things that could change the balance of the war."

"Aye, I just bet you do," Quinnon snarled.

Allara stopped beside Quinnon's horse. "You'll never get within pistol shot of him. You've already done more than your share of damage."

"That's a decision he should make for himself." The arm holding the sword flexed. His voice sounded strained.

"He won't get the chance because you'll be dead."

"You shoot me, and you can be assured you'll have just lost the war for Lael."

She braced both hands around the pistol and lowered it to point at his sternum. At this range, the shot would tear his chest into nothing. "Why should I trust you? You've betrayed your country, your people, your God—in the worst possible way."

"You should trust me because you're both still alive." He glanced at Quinnon. "I could kill you both yet, if you'd so much rather."

Her brain raced. He would do it. He would do it in a second, and not even feel shame for it.

She shook her head. "I'm not taking you to the Gifted."

"Then carry him a message. Let him make his own choices."

Quinnon's laugh rasped. "You blues lie as well as you fight. But we've no reason to believe anything you say."

"That's up to the Gifted. And that's all I have to say." Orias wheeled his horse. "Dougal!"

Before Quinnon could pursue, a big black Koraudian lion leapt out of the trees to cut him off. Quinnon drew his chewser to shoot it.

Allara took a quick step forward. "Wait—not yet."

Two horse's lengths down the road, Orias looked back at her. "I'll wait out the day at Mere Shoal. Tell him to come alone."

"Do you think we would risk his life so foolishly?"

"One man, then." He nodded to Quinnon. "Him. But no more. Dougal, *eider fon!*" He reined around and spurred his horse into a gallop.

Allara's pistol fell to her side. Quinnon raised his to sight the Cherazim's back, but he didn't fire.

She emptied her lungs. "We could have had him."

"Could be he's telling the truth."

"Is the truth worth the risk?"

"Maybe." He turned to face her. "I've been doing some wondering about all this. What if we're wrong about Redston being able to fix what he did? Even if he kills Mactalde?"

She knit her forehead. "What are you saying?"

"All I'm saying is . . . what if Redston *can't* fix it? What happens to the imbalance then?"

"I don't know." The heat of her dry throat squeezed her words. "The worlds might tear apart, I suppose."

"Destroyed?"

"I don't know. The God of all help us." She shook her head. She couldn't afford to believe what he was saying. Where there was hope, there was purpose. Where there was purpose, she could yet survive. "Either way, we cannot risk Chris's life needlessly."

Quinnon stared down the trail where Orias had disappeared. He pursed his lips. "It's his life to risk, if he chooses. The Tarn's right about that."

Artillery hammered on, echoed by thunder and hoofbeats as Chris and Tireus returned to the command post. After Chris's arrival a week ago, Tireus had dragged him to the front lines for the sake of public relations, but they weren't on good terms at the moment. Mactalde's refusal to recognize anyone but Chris as the leader of Lael had found its way to Tireus's ears, and Tireus wasn't happy about it.

They reined up in front of Tireus's big tent, and adjutants and grooms swarmed their horses.

Tireus waved Chris off. "You can return to your quarters now." Beneath his beard, his face was grimed and tired.

"Yes, sir." He tamped his own frustration. He had come up here to Ballion to *do* something, but so far Tireus was keeping him chained like a lap dog. He couldn't really say he blamed him, especially in light of Harrison's grab for power the last time around. But it didn't make the situation any more enjoyable.

Behind him, standing on his horse's rump, Pitch fidgeted. "I wish the sun would shine again."

"Yeah." He reined away, toward the smaller tent he was sharing with his father. Worick had stopped off at the hospital tent to help carry stretchers.

"Look." Pitch pointed over Chris's shoulder. "There's the Searcher."

At the far end of the camp, two horses paused to let their riders speak with a sentry, then trotted ahead.

Chris breathed out. This was the last place he wanted Allara to be for any length of time. This was no pretend battle. Men were dying at staggering rates on the front lines. The hospitals were teeming, and the boats back to Thyra Junction were packed with casualties. Mactalde's assault had eased up a bit in the last few days, but this was only a brief respite, and they all knew it.

He turned back to Tireus. "My lord." When he caught Tireus's eye, he nodded toward Allara's approach.

The king urged his horse past his crowd of attendants, and Chris followed to meet Allara and Quinnon in the middle of the camp. Everyone but Quinnon dismounted.

Tireus took hold of Allara's shoulders. "What's wrong?"

Dark circles still ringed her eyes, but the cut on her forehead had almost healed and she stood without wavering.

She glanced at Chris. "We spoke with Orias Tarn."

Chris looked at Pitch. "He's *here*? On our side of the lines?"

Pitch tugged at one of his cuffs and pulled the too-long sleeve over his hand. He stared at Allara, his lip between his teeth.

Tireus frowned. "I thought he was with Mactalde's men."

"He was," Chris said. "We saw him when we went after Eroll."

Allara plucked at a brass button on her coat. "He wants to speak with you."

"Why?" The last time Chris had seen him, Orias had made it very clear he had nothing more to say.

"He claims he's deserted Mactalde and has information that will dramatically affect the battle."

Chris breathed out a laugh. "Yeah, I bet."

Pitch yanked on Chris's fingers. "I told you! He needs to talk to you."

Allara's lips parted. "You're his Riever? He sent you here to bait his trap—"

"No." Pitch rattled his head back and forth. "I told Chris already. Orias needs help. He doesn't want to be with Mactalde."

Tireus huffed. "This is far too obvious a ploy."

Quinnon shifted his weight, and his saddle creaked. "The Tarn says he can tell you about Mactalde's defenses. Says you'll only get one chance to win the battle, and you won't know what it is unless he tells you." His voice remained flat. "He could be lying."

"Please, please." Pitch tilted his head back to Chris. "He's in trouble. If you help him, he'll help you. And I'll help you too. You can take me with you. Orias won't hurt anyone who comes with me."

"He wants you to go alone." Allara stared at Chris. "It's a trap. He wants to kill you. It will be Harrison Garnett all over again."

"That was different," Chris said. "Harrison Garnett was a traitor." But even as he said it, he had to admit it had an ironic ring. After all, in resurrecting Mactalde he had only finished what Harrison started.

Quinnon dismounted and faced Chris. "The only way to find out is to go. Are you willing to live with the results if he's telling the truth and you stay here?"

Quinnon had been challenging him almost from the moment they'd met. But this was something new. This was more than merely bullying or butting heads. Quinnon was out to prove something. And, when it came right down to it, so was Chris.

"I'll go." One way or another, he and Orias had things to settle.

Quinnon gave him a nod. "I'll ride along with you. The blue allowed that much."

"I'll go too. I have to go with you." Pitch let go of Chris's hand and climbed up the stirrup into the saddle.

Tireus's mouth worked. "I'll need to send a squad with you." He didn't have a squad to spare, and his tone made his irritation clear. But at least he wasn't trying to dissuade Chris.

Quinnon shook his head. "The Tarn'll be gone in a whisper if he smells one man more than me on the trail."

Allara rubbed her crooked finger and looked at Chris. "I knew you'd want to go." Tendrils of hair had fallen from her chignon, and the wind plastered them against her face. "But whatever information he may have isn't worth your life."

Chris spread his hands. "So I'll be careful."

The edge of her mouth lifted the tiniest bit. "I don't believe you."

"Don't worry about it."

"I won't."

"Now we're even, because I don't believe that either." He let his smile fade.

His horse stood fast while he mounted, and Pitch ducked as he swung his leg over.

He adjusted his reins and looked down at Tireus. "Maybe I'll have a new plan for you when I come back."

Tireus pursed his lips and didn't say the obvious: That he might not come back.

Orias heard the rambling of nervous words long before Chris and Quinnon rode into the canyon entrance at Mere Shoal. He leaned back against the blue-gray rock that overhung the trail, and his baldric grated between the stone and his shoulder. If his attack went according to plan, he would have no need to draw it. He would fall upon Chris from the rocks above and use his dirk and axe. The death would be quick. Orias would give Chris—and himself—that much.

The hoofbeats neared, perhaps only a dozen paces from his rock. His every muscle tensed. Beneath his skin, nerve ends tingled like white sparks.

The words below resolved into a familiar voice: "Don't you think we should have met him by now? Orias is always on time."

Pitch had escaped Mactalde? His abdomen clenched.

"He always keeps his word," Pitch continued.

"Yeah, I know." Chris's voice gave a wry twist.

"But maybe it would be a good idea for me to go ahead and find him. I mean, maybe I should talk to him first."

"Why? You afraid he's going to change his mind and take a stab at me instead of spilling Mactalde's secrets?"

"No, not exactly . . ."

"Could it be he doesn't want this help you've been begging me for all week?"

"He does want it. He maybe just doesn't know it."

"He doesn't *know* he needs help?" The horses stopped just shy of Orias's rock. "Before you go running off to find Orias, maybe you better tell me what's going on."

Orias eased around the corner and peered into the narrow gorge.

At the far end, Captain Quinnon reined to a stop. The Searcher's bodyguard leaned against his saddlebow, watching. If he caught sight of Orias waiting in the rocks, he didn't so much as flinch in recognition.

Orias gripped his weapons. With Pitch behind Chris's saddle, he couldn't risk attempting the immediate death he'd hoped for. He'd have to knock Chris out of the saddle and take him on the ground. It was not how he would have chosen to end a Gifted's life.

Chris's saddle creaked, and the scrape of a blade leaving its sheath whispered through the misting rain.

"Tell me the truth," he said. "What do you know about this that I don't?"

Orias screamed and launched himself into the air. The horse shied hard, and Chris shot his sword up in front of his face. Orias caught the blade against his dirk. His weight smashed into Chris and tore him from the saddle. They crashed into the ground, and Orias rolled away and scrambled to his feet.

"Orias!" Pitch shouted.

His vision tunneled around Chris. The Gifted had landed in the rocks at the water's edge, and the leather of his coat had ripped down the side. A dark glare of blood showed through the tear.

Chris scrambled to his feet and faced Orias. "So it *was* all a setup. You made Pitch lie to me?"

"I didn't lie!" Pitch said. "He does need help! You do need help. Tell him, Orias."

Orias tucked the dirk and the axe away in his belt and drew his sword from his back. The bank here was formed of flat black stones, pocked with sinkholes and backed by the canyon's mossy walls. Footing would be at a premium.

He charged and hammered his blade against Chris's. The clangor rebounded off the rocks and filled their private arena with the knell of war.

In the months since his crossing, Chris had obviously learned a thing or two. He had tapped into the memories of his body, and he fought with the skill, if not the experience, of a practiced Guardsman. What he lacked in tactics, he supplemented with aggression.

Orias slowed just a bit. The Searcher was right. He had already turned his back on his God, his duty, and his people. He had condemned his soul and had nothing left to lose except the very thing for which he had sold it. And that he could not lose. Even at the price of a Gifted, he could not lose it.

And yet his heart cried out in him. How many times before had he shed blood as he rejoiced in the rush of the battle? Today, he cringed from it. He could not risk letting the Gifted escape, but he had no desire to kill him.

He drew back. "I came here today with every intention of giving you a death so quick you would never know it happened. But fate is much better than I at deciding who should live and who should die." He brought his sword up in front of his face. "So let it be a contest."

Chris held his ground. He was wise enough, at least, not to fling himself into the face of a stronger opponent. "You lied to me from the start. From the moment you figured out who I was, you took advantage of my ignorance at every turn."

"I promised you that if Mactalde returned to Lael, you would leave our land. And now I'm giving you that opportunity." Orias spun and hurled his weight into the blow.

"That's not what I want anymore." Chris gave way, one step then two, and then he held. He strained against Orias's strength. Rain and sweat beaded his face. "I'm staying."

"Why should you change your mind now?" Hard breaths growled through Orias's throat. His own sweat burned his face. "You wanted the dreams to stop. You wanted to go back to your safe, quiet life in the other world. Back to the serenity of ignorance, back where you neither knew nor believed about this world of ours. And now I'm sending you back."

Chris retreated two steps more. He gripped his sword with both hands. His body coiled around its center of energy, waiting to spring. "I can't go back to the way things were, even if I wanted to. And I don't, not anymore." He shot one glance down the gorge to where Quinnon sat his horse.

The bodyguard made no move. Perhaps he too wanted proof this Gifted was worth believing in. For the last few minutes of his life, Chris Redston would be on his own.

Orias lunged. This must end, one way or the other. It must end so completely it would be as if it had never begun.

Chris met him halfway, and the blades clashed.

Orias never looked away from the Gifted's face. He fought effortlessly, intuitively, but he never sank into the mindless furor of the Cherazii. He would fight on equal terms with the Gifted, and he would pray that in the end, perhaps Mactalde might be thwarted after all.

They battled back into the cold rush of water, and Orias slowed his attack until Chris secured his footing. When the Gifted righted himself, his gaze at last left the slash and thrust of the swordplay and found Orias's eyes. He threw his weight forward, attacking, no longer defending. Orias's berserking fire ignited, and the wearied pull on his muscles disappeared. He responded to the attack.

They fought at a stalemate, calf-deep in the water. Chris's blade slipped, and Orias moved without conscious thought. He twisted his blade beneath Chris's and flipped the sword from the Gifted's hands. It splashed into the shallows of the lake.

Never in his life had he wanted less to kill someone. His innards turned cold, and he raised the blade to the hollow of Chris's throat. "I am sorry."

Chris breathed out.

Pitch darted between them. "Don't you dare!" He leapt to grab Chris's belt and hoisted himself up. One foot propped against Chris's leg, he jabbed his stiletto at Orias. "Let him go—he's mine! I found him, he's mine, and you have no right to hurt him!"

"Get down," Orias said. "This has to be."

"If you hurt him, I'll kill you!"

Orias stared into Pitch's round eyes. Pitch—who loved Orias more than anything and had idolized him from the time Orias had first taken him and Raz under his protection—now looked up at him with a gaze backed by a metal sheet.

"Stop," Pitch said. "You have to stop."

"I cannot." Orias tightened his grip on his hilt. "I've gone too far."

Chris's chest rose. His hands hung empty at his sides. "What happened was my fault. I'm to blame, not you."

Orias shook his head. "You said it yourself. I lied to you. You're to blame for that?"

"I made my own choices. I heard what I wanted to hear. In my heart and my gut, I knew Mactalde was dangerous. I knew it from the very moment I saw him. I shouldn't have brought him across, and I knew it when I did it." Chris's shoulders drew back. "I made my choice. I brought Mactalde across, not you. I may have done what you wanted, but in the end I'm the one who's responsible."

The wind rippled the water into ledges against Orias's legs, and the bones in his feet felt hollow with the cold.

On the bank, Quinnon trotted up to wait alongside Chris's mount.

Chris rested a hand on Pitch's back. He studied Orias's face. "I don't know why you've chosen to throw in with Mactalde. But if you're doing it out of some sense of guilt, you're digging a hole you're never going to reach the bottom of."

The thunder of his heart filled his head. "I finish what I start." He ground out the words.

Chris eased Pitch down to stand on his own feet. Orias's blade followed his movement.

"You don't want to kill me," Chris said, "anymore than you wanted to bring Mactalde back. You made a mistake in the beginning. So did I. But we both get to choose where those mistakes end." He stepped back from the point of the sword. "Where does yours end?"

Orias's sword sank. He watched Chris turn to fetch his sword, then wade to the bank. It wasn't too late. He could still attack. He could cut Chris down and return to Mactalde to vouchsafe one more day of safety for his people.

Chris wiped his sword dry on the lining of his coat and sheathed it at his back. He accepted his reins from Quinnon. "Thanks for all the help."

"You don't need my help. You're the Gifted." The bodyguard's voice held a solid note of respect. He glanced at Orias, and then the horses turned and clattered away.

Orias stood in the water and listened until the hoofbeats faded. Then he looked down to where Pitch stood, shivering.

The Riever put away his stiletto. "I didn't *want* to kill you, you know."

"I know." What Pitch didn't understand was that, given a choice, he would have chosen death.

40

OUTSIDE THE CLOSED tent flap, Allara paced. "I knew it was a trap. I should never have told you about it. We should never have let you go!"

She remained outside, for the sake of decency, while the royal surgeon treated the flesh wound in Chris's side. The wind rattled the tent canvas, and the glow of the globes deformed Chris's and the surgeon's shadows into monsters.

"I'm still in one piece." He sounded like he was gritting his teeth.

"Barely!" In front of the flap, she forced herself to stop. Hands on her hips, she hung her head back and sucked in a breath of the cold night. If he had died out there, it would have been her fault. She was the one who was supposed to protect the Gifted. She was the one who was supposed to stay with him at all times.

He grunted in pain. "Yeah, well, all I promised was I'd come back. And I did that."

"Hah." She went back to pacing.

"Orias didn't want to kill me. If he had, I'd be dead. I think Mactalde's blackmailing him."

"If word of this spreads, it could breed ill will against the Cherazii. Right now, you're a hero to our men. They won't take well to the thought of another Cherazii attack upon a Gifted." If it were possible, they might be even more ready to rip out Orias's throat than she was right now.

"There's only about half a dozen of us who know," Chris said. "As long as everyone keeps their mouths shut, we'll be fine."

She scooped her windblown hair out of her face. "The men saw you come back wounded. And the rumor's already gotten about that you'd gone to meet a Cherazim. It won't go well for any Cherazii who show their faces after this." She choked on a laugh. "They're supposed to protect the Gifted. And now you're the second they've tried to kill."

"You're looking at this through the wrong lens. Ah—" He grunted again. "Orias is acting under coercion. Mactalde's holding his other Riever captive under penalty of death."

"He's a Tarn. If even the Tarns have deserted the traditions, what hope does Lael have?"

"What are we going to do about it?"

"We can't afford to antagonize the Cherazii right now. We can't trust them, but we can't antagonize them. Besides, we haven't the troops or the time to mount an offensive against them just to bring one of their number to justice. Chances are they'll deal with him their own way, sooner or later."

And their way wouldn't be gentle.

"For now," she continued, "it's problem enough to figure out what Mactalde has in mind. Something's not right. I can't put my finger on it, but something's amiss. Father says we've been seeing troop movements all through their rear lines, but none of our outposts have reported sightings of anything. I don't like it."

The surgeon's shadow moved away from Chris's. "There you are," he said. "You'll feel better after the oronborne's burn has worn off. It's not a bad laceration. More contusion than anything. Just keep it clean, and try to avoid any more spills from your horse." A moment later, he emerged from the tent and saluted Allara.

She ducked inside and cast a glance over Chris. He finished tugging his blouse over the neat layers of muslin that swathed his ribs, then slid off the table where he had been sitting.

So close. He'd come so close to death this afternoon. What if he had died? What if she had lost him? Her heart turned over inside of her. She reached for a carafe of craniss.

She poured him a goblet. "Here. You need to get some rest."

"Thanks." He sank onto the edge of his cot and tossed back the craniss. His eyelids drooped, and he flopped back on the bed.

If only he could stay awake, they could talk for a few minutes. She hadn't seen him in a week, not since the night they had spoken on Eroll's balcony. There was so much she wanted to say, most of which she didn't know how to put into words.

He folded his hands over his chest. "I'm glad you're here. But I wish you weren't." His eyes drifted shut almost before he'd finished speaking.

"I know."

For that matter, she wished he were anywhere other than here himself. But she could hardly send him away. He wouldn't listen to her even if she tried. Somewhere along the line, their relationship had shifted. Her time as his teacher and guide had ended. He was the leader now. She was the one who followed. She was the one who sheltered beneath his strength and resilience.

"Be strong," she whispered. "Be resilient."

The tent flap opened, and Worick Bowen entered. His gaze flicked from her, to Chris, and back. Fear twisted his thick features. "Is he—"

"No, he's fine. Just exhausted."

"Thank God." He saluted her belatedly and came to stand beside her. "He's a good lad."

"Yes."

"Do you think he can save us?" He spoke quietly, but his eyes searched her face.

"I don't know." She couldn't look at him. "Perhaps. If that's his gift."

"And if it isn't?"

She moved to drape a blanket over him. "I don't know."

Like a well-trained dog, Orias had come seeking his master once again. But this time the dog would not be fawning at Mactalde's feet.

He galloped through the foothills. Clouds pressed upon the earth and trapped him in darkness as deep as eternity. The winds lashed from every direction, and the rain strafed his hands and face. A glare of lightning backwashed the clouds, and the rock chimneys above Mactalde's camp flashed overhead. He slowed his horse.

Pitch thumped his shoulder. "This is crazy, crazy, *crazy*! Why won't you listen to me?"

"This has to be."

"You said that about Chris, and that *didn't* have to be!"

"It's one or the other. Either Chris dies, or Mactalde does."

"You'll never get close enough."

He was going to die one way or the other now. The best he could do for himself and his people was to take their enemies with him. His battle fire churned. "If I can't get to Mactalde, then at least I can empty Rotoss's veins."

"They'll kill you! And they'll kill Raz, and they'll kill me. And then they'll go attack our people. What about them?"

"You wanted me to leave this business from the beginning. And now I am."

At the outcropping that had marked Mactalde's lines four nights ago, he stopped. No one challenged him. His ears couldn't catch the sound of anyone so much as breathing.

"I wanted you to leave," Pitch said. "But not like this. This is suicide."

"Martyrdom."

"Well, martyrs aren't *always* heroic." Pitch's hand clasped and unclasped the baldric. "What's going to happen to Raz and me?"

"They'll never find you in the dark, and you'll be able to make it far into the hills by morning." The God of all willing. He had to end this, but he would not endanger the Rievers again. He stifled a groan.

"But—" Pitch's voice turned uncertain. "But we've always lived with you."

"My family will house you."

"But . . . I don't want to live with anyone but you."

Loyal Pitch. He could have no idea how much better things would have been had he and Raz adopted a different Cherazim.

Orias eased his horse forward. "Mactalde must have moved the lines back."

"That's dumb. The Laelers' artillery couldn't hit him here."

They trotted to the crest of the hill. Lightning tangled through the storm, and the ground beneath flashed into view. Just last night, the strength of Mactalde's army had camped here. Now, only two or three rows of white tents and a line of artillery crowded the riverbank. Beyond that, all that remained was trampled mud and the detritus of a departed army.

Pitch squeaked. "They've gone! Why would they go?"

Had Mactalde decided to try another attack upon the Aiden River? Orias's heart pounded.

"Maybe they're retreating?" Pitch said. "They're going back to Koraud, think?"

Orias spurred the horse into a gallop. Someone, far to his right, shouted a challenge, but he didn't slow.

He rode straight in the saddle, aware of nothing more than the shift of the horse beneath him. Lightning sheeted the sky almost continuously now. Rocks and trees scattered past the edges of his vision, and the ground began to slant downwards.

When the rocks gave way to the dark soil of the foothills, glimpses of a marching army's trail flickered through his consciousness. The wind shifted and scraped the scent of wet earth through his nostrils.

Where would Mactalde move his troops? And how could the Laelers have missed their presence anywhere else in the country?

At last, the lightning glared against a soldier's unslung rifle, and Orias reined to a walk. He was already deep into the foothills. Within the flicker of the storm, a company of Koraudians marched. This was but a tiny fraction of the troops Mactalde had moved out of Ballion. Where had the rest gone?

Without being told, Pitch clambered down the off side of the horse and stood on Orias's foot. He squirmed about until he was bent over with his head hanging beneath the horse's belly and one hand clinging to the stirrup leathers.

Orias reined to the outside of the troop column and trotted past. The clank of the troops marching double time punctured the wind. Up ahead, a guidon flickered.

He *would* break the lead chain of his mistakes. If Mactalde accompanied these troops, then tonight would be his moment. If not, it would have to wait. But it would come. If he succeeded, perhaps his people would forgive his sin and hail him as a hero. If he failed, then he could fall no lower. He eased a hand to the dirk at his side and caressed the worn etching on the hilt.

Pitch clawed his way up Orias's boot to stand straight. "Raz—it's Raz. I can see Raz!" His blade flashed out of its sheath.

The tunnel of Orias's focus collapsed.

The unmistakable grumble of a Riever's voice reached his ears only seconds before he saw the leashed figure loping along behind a soldier. If he freed Raz now, word of his presence would fly down the line, and he would miss his only chance at surprise.

His hand wavered on the reins. "Get down. See if you can sneak into the column and cut him free."

Pitch dropped to the ground and ran to the troop. The lightning stopped, and Orias counted his heartbeats.

After nearly twenty seconds, a long blue tendril lit the sky. Within the column, Pitch sawed furiously at Raz's tether.

Darkness, he prayed. But the lightning had taken respite enough; it filled the sky.

Raz's tether split just beneath his wrists, and the two Rievers ran. A soldier pointed, his mouth a round hole as the thunder swallowed his words.

Time was up. Orias threw himself into their midst. With dirk and axe, he scythed through their ranks, and they fell without even drawing their weapons. Their cries pierced above the thunder, and all around, soldiers turned to react.

The first blow was struck. He had nothing left but to kill Mactalde and his faithless sycophant. Let this ground drink from a warm red flood of Koraudian blood. By the time they cut him down, the land would be too sated to drink of his own.

He whirled the horse away and broke free of the ranks.

"Orias!"

Before the horse could gather itself into a gallop, Pitch threw one arm over Orias's foot and clung to his spur with the other. "Orias, wait!"

Battle furor hammered inside his body. He couldn't wait, couldn't stop.

"Raz knows where they're going!"

Raz stabbed a finger into the darkness ahead. "Mactalde's moved the whole rotting army up the Wall! He's been moving troops out for days, and I heard them say the regiments they left at Aiden River have already gone up. They could be in Glen Arden by morning!"

Had Mactalde gone completely mad? Orias looked to the guidon under which he would find the army's leaders. Maybe Mactalde would be with them, maybe not. Either way—no matter what was happening up the Wall—he wanted blood on his sword tonight.

"Get down."

Pitch clambered up his leg. "No!"

The Koraudian ranks were closing up around the men Orias had killed. The roar of a sergeant's order reached his ears.

Raz ran past a panting Dougal and scrambled up Orias's other leg to stand behind his saddle. "If we don't warn the Laelers, the Koraudians will take their capital by morning!"

Orias spurred the horse. "If I kill Mactalde, this will all be over!"

Raz almost lost his balance. "*What?*"

"You can't!" Pitch shouted. "Mactalde's already up the Wall! You'll get killed for nothing, and Chris and the king will never know what he's planning!"

Raz smacked Orias's shoulder. "Why didn't you tell me you were going to try to kill Mactalde *before* I got on the horse!"

"Please go back," Pitch said. "Go back and tell them before it's too late!"

If he rode into the Laeler camp, they'd shoot him on sight. Orias's heart pounded so hard he could barely breathe. He cast a glance at the troop column to his right.

Rifles rose to point in his direction, their hydraulics a blue glimmer. Ahead, the officers beneath the guidon turned and pointed and shouted.

Frustration and rage—at himself as much as anyone—boiled in his chest and surged from his mouth in a roar. He choked his horse back and spun around. With Pitch and Raz clutching on behind, he charged across the meadow. The staccato of rifle shots punctured the thunder's rumble, but they never came close.

What he wanted more than anything was Mactalde's and Rotoss's blood on his sword. But what he *needed* was to do the right thing. Even if only this once.

41

ACK IN CHICAGO, someone was pounding on Chris's hotel room door—a door which only two people knew he was behind. He crossed the room, freed the deadbolt, and pulled the door inward, right out from under Brooke's upraised fist.

She stepped back and hoisted her purse strap higher on her shoulder. "Oh. You *are* awake." From the half-determined, half-nervous expression on her face, she looked like she didn't know whether to be happy about that or not.

He set one elbow against the doorjamb and blocked her from any chance of entering. "Don't tell me you've got another psychotic boyfriend you want me to meet. Or that you actually decided to believe me?"

She licked her lips and pasted on a smile that didn't hide the tension in her face. "May I come in?"

Well-meaning or not, she'd already sabotaged any trust he still had in her. He hadn't talked with either her or Mike since her stunt with Kaufman last week. "Brooke . . ."

"Please." She squared her shoulders. "I need to come in. What I have to say is better not broadcasted in the middle of a public hallway."

Against his better judgment, he sighed and stepped back against the door.

She entered and crossed the room to stand in front of the window.

He clicked the door shut. "Well?"

"Well . . . I've been giving a lot of thought to what you told me the other day. And . . ." She stared at the bedspread's striped pattern. "I think you need help."

"Brooke—"

Her eyes darted to his. "And I know you well enough to know you'll never get it on your own."

"I don't need you telling me what I need."

"You don't know what you need anymore! You were absolutely insane last week. That whole stunt with my car, then babbling about dreams and weather and people wanting to shoot you!"

"Did you talk to Mike? Huh? What's he say?" He *had* sounded crazy the last time he talked to them. He knew that. But, even still, Mike wouldn't write him off just like that. Brooke was the one who liked to jump to conclusions, not Mike.

She stared at the bedspread some more. "He thinks you need help too."

That set him back on his heels. He licked his lips. "I notice he seems to trust me enough to let me work this out my own way."

"I think you're past the point of being able to work things out by yourself. Listen to me, it doesn't have to be a psych ward or anything like—"

He gaped. "Psych ward? You're here to try to talk me into voluntary commitment?"

She dragged her fingers up and down her purse strap. "I'll drive you down to Lakeshore Hospital. They have professionals who can evaluate you and coach you through this. Chris, I'm doing this because I care about you."

He clenched his fists to keep from grabbing her shoulders and shaking her. "I asked you to trust me."

"Stop it." She dropped both hands to her hips. "What you *asked* me to do is believe something that's impossible! You are completely out of control, Chris. Completely! You're endangering yourself and everyone around you!"

"You don't understand."

"I've been absolutely understanding." Her earlobes burned red around her hoop earrings. "You asked me to stay off the story—a good story, the kind of story that could have made me a real writer. And that's what I did. I've done everything you've asked me. But this whole dream-world fantasy of yours either means you need serious intervention or you're lying to cover up!"

"This isn't the kind of help I need right now."

She moved to his side and clutched his forearm, her hand hot. "Please, don't do this. Don't you realize that after that stunt you pulled last week, you're dangerous enough to warrant an involuntary commitment?"

He shook his head. "They can't hold me. That's against the law."

"They can hold you long enough for evaluation."

"And after that, you figure it's a sure thing, do you?"

"Don't make this difficult. Please."

He stripped her hand from his arm. "You know what? It *is* difficult, and that's just the way it is." He took her by the elbow and shepherded her to the door.

"All I'm trying to do is help. That's all I want to do! I can't stand by and do nothing!"

He pushed her out, and a wave of dizziness clobbered him in the back of the head. He reeled and caught his balance against the door handle.

"*CHERAZII!*" The cry blasted through his ears.

The stamp of her foot drifted in from far away. "Now what?"

Darkness swarmed his vision, and hoofbeats pounded. Something was happening in Lael. Something was waking him up.

"Chris?" Her voice rose a notch. "What are you doing? You're not going to pass out? *Chris?*"

One more step. Take one more step into his room and shove the door shut. Then he could sleep. But not now, not where he would be at Brooke's mercy. He strained against the door handle.

"*THE GIFTED! WHERE'S THE GIFTED?*"

That voice was familiar. It was . . . Orias's voice.

He was waking up in the other world, whether he wanted to or not. His legs collapsed. Only a pinpoint of light remained in his vision, focused on the cherry wainscot in his room.

"Chris, stop it!" He could barely make out what Brooke was saying. "What's wrong with you?"

His knees hit the thin carpet of his room, and then—

—he opened his eyes to the globe-lit darkness of his tent.

The door flaps burst inward, followed by the outline of a soldier.

"Sir, we've captured a Cherazim! We think he may be the one who tried to kill you this afternoon!"

He shook his head hard to clear away the images of Brooke's panicked expression. "All right, I'm coming." He rolled to his feet and winced at the dull ache in his ribs.

Outside, lightning glared across the chaos in the camp. At the center of a growing mob, the white gleam of a Cherazim face loomed above the crowd. If it *was* Orias, what was he doing here? He must know the Laelers would never welcome him. And if he'd come on another mission for Mactalde, then why hadn't he gone through with killing Chris yesterday afternoon?

"Chris!" A high-pitched Riever voice pierced the din.

He broke into a run.

The soldiers had wrenched Orias's arms behind his back and a blue ribbon of blood inched across his cheekbone. Allara had been right. The men had not been kind, and Orias hadn't fought back. Someone had already clapped a hand over the Rievers' mouths.

"He's a spy!" A man smacked his fist against Orias's chest and grinned at Chris. "He's the one, isn't he? He's the one who tried to kill you this afternoon?"

"Let him go," Chris said.

"What?" The soldier's grin faded. "He's a Cherazim. He'd kill us all if'n he had the chance."

"I said let him go."

At the rear of the crowd, a voice hollered, "Make way for the king!"

Tireus pushed through the crowd. He glanced at Chris for confirmation of Orias's identity, and Chris nodded reluctantly.

"What do you seek here?" Tireus asked.

Orias towered above the soldiers. Beneath his coat his muscles bulged. Even in manacles and surrounded by his captors, he held his chin high and stared over their heads.

"I've come to warn you," he said.

The soldiers guffawed.

Chris's neck prickled. He stepped forward. "Warn us of what?"

Orias ignored Tireus and looked straight at Chris. "Mactalde's left Ballion. He's taken the Aiden River troops up the Karilus to Glen Arden. He may be there already."

A ripple spread through the crowd.

With a growl, Tireus snapped a finger at his aides. "Bring him to my tent." He raised his voice. "All the rest of you, back to your posts."

The four men guarding Orias led him forward.

Under the awning of the big tent, Tireus whirled to face him. "What you're saying is impossible. Mactalde could never have moved that many troops without our outposts knowing. The Wall is highly defensible. A thousand men would die before even one could reach the top."

Chris's gut thickened. "If the outposts between here and Glen Arden were held by Nateros spies, they could have been feeding you all's-well messages for weeks, while Mactalde moved troops. We'd never have known."

For the first time, a look of alarm fluttered across Tireus's face. He stepped nearer to Orias. He was a tall man, but even he was dwarfed by the Cherazim's power.

"Why should we believe you?" he asked. "A Cherazim who abandons his people and their principles to fight with their enemy?"

"If I abandoned them, it was for good reason."

"What reason justifies treachery?"

Orias hesitated.

From behind the muffling hand of his captor, Pitch nodded encouragement.

Orias's shoulders came back even more. "Rotoss gave me a choice. If I helped him find the Gifted and use the Orimere to bring Mactalde back, he would spare the Cherazii. I had a chance to save my people. That's all I could see."

"Then why are you here now?" Chris asked.

"Because." In the darkness, Orias's eyes almost disappeared within the canyons of his face. "I cannot change what has been done. But perhaps I can stop it in its tracks." He glanced at Tireus. "If you heed what I say."

Tireus gestured to an aide. "Send a rider to the outpost at Riadon Heights. Find out what's happening there."

The adjutants behind Chris shifted, and Allara walked through their midst. She stopped beside him and handed him his coat, but her eyes never left Orias.

The Cherazim saw her and inclined his head the tiniest bit.

"Why didn't you kill him this afternoon?" she asked.

His arms strained against his bonds. "Perhaps I need him to make things right just as much as the rest of you."

Tireus paced a few steps away, then back. "How far has Mactalde gotten?"

"He was still in Ballion four days ago. My Riever—" Orias nodded to Raz, who hung in a Guardsman's grip, arms crossed over his chest, "—says Mactalde seems to have been orchestrating this for weeks. He's been moving troops from the Aiden, and a few from here in Ballion. He and Rotoss left to join them the day after I crossed your lines."

Tireus stared at the ground. "With a relay of fast horses, he could have arrived at the Wall path in two to three days."

Allara breathed out. "If he's commandeered the skycar line to Glen Arden, he could reach the city by tomorrow morning. We'd never get there in time."

"*If* that's where he's gone," Tireus said. "I cannot send substantial reinforcements on a four day march to defend a city that may not need defending." He looked back at Orias. "This whole thing may yet be a trick, a diversion to distract us from Mactalde's true destination."

Orias's eyes never flickered.

If he had wanted to fulfill Mactalde's bidding, he would have taken Chris's head back with him yesterday. He could have bested Chris easily had he wanted to. But something had held him back.

"It's not a trick," Chris said. He turned to Tireus. "Let me go."

"What for?" Tireus growled, like a wounded animal at bay. "By the time any of us get there, Mactalde will have been king of the city for days."

"I think I can get there sooner than that." He had an idea—an insane idea—but he could hardly just stand by and do nothing. If he could get himself and a small team to Glen Arden ahead of Mactalde's advance troops, he could at least warn the city. Hadn't Allara once told him Glen Arden was the most defensible city in the realm?

Tireus shook his head. "No. There's no point. I refuse to let you needlessly risk your life again."

Allara stepped up beside Chris. "Let him try. We have nothing to lose."

For a long moment, Tireus looked back and forth between them.

Finally, he nodded. "Fine. Do what you need to do. If you manage to get there, launch a distress signal. It will be relayed back to me, and I'll be ready to move as soon as all this is confirmed." He gestured to the men holding Orias. "Take him away and put him someplace secure until we can get this sorted."

Chris gave Orias a nod. Then he took Allara's arm and hustled her back to his tent.

"What do you need?" she asked.

"Wrak."

She stopped so fast she pulled her arm from his. "What?"

"I need to go to sleep. There's something I need from my world. Get the surgeon."

She hesitated, then turned and ran.

Ten minutes later, he lay, naked, on the ground in his tent. The surgeon stood over him and prepared the anesthetic by lighting a fire atop the vial of amber liquid. In his hand, Chris clutched the tingle of the Orimere. Its white glow strobed through the shadows.

The surgeon slipped the hose nozzle into Chris's mouth, and he bit down and inhaled his first breath of the steam. Sweetness filled the back of his throat, followed by a chemical tang. A few more breaths, and the inside of the tent began to swirl. He closed his eyes—

—and opened them to the brown stain edging a ceiling sprinkler.

"I don't know, I don't know." Somewhere behind him, Brooke's voice squeaked. "He's passed out. I don't know what's wrong with him! Maybe he had a heart attack. He's too heavy for me to move and—"

He rolled over on the floor and found the Orimere in his hand. Since he hadn't been wearing or touching anything in Lael, nothing else had come over with him.

With a squeal, Brooke dropped her cell phone and ran to help him up. Tears streaked her flushed cheeks. "I was so scared. You just fainted, just like that, for no good reason. Are you all right? Do you hurt anywhere? I've called the ambulance. I called Mike. I don't know what else to do." She hiccupped.

"It's okay." He patted her hand on his arm and got his feet under him. "Where are your car keys?" She wasn't going to like what he was about to do, but at least there'd be no more talk of psych wards.

She sniffed. "Right here. Why?"

"Let me have them. We need to go." He guided her toward the door with one arm and took the keys from her with the other.

"But why? I don't understand. You should rest. The ambulance is coming—"

"It's all right. I promise I'm fine. Do you have a full tank of gas?" He left his ground floor room and hurried her down the hall, through the lobby into the parking lot.

"Yes, it's full." She craned her head to look up at him. Her tears had ceased, but she still sniffled. "What's going on?"

He spotted the duct-taped taillight on her Land Rover and let go of her. "Just stay right here for a second."

She stopped. "Why?"

"I'm going to borrow your car."

"What?"

He broke into a jog. The surgeon was supposed to give him ten minutes before administering the antidote to the wrak. He had no idea how much time had passed since he'd woken up, but he had to be getting close. His limbs grew heavy, and whispers from Lael clogged his ears.

"Chris?"

He forced himself to run the last few steps to the Rover. His legs buckled. He hit the pavement on his hands and knees, and the lurch of pain anchored his consciousness for a moment longer.

"*WAKE UP, WAKE UP!*"

Back in Lael, someone slapped him.

He transferred the keys to his teeth, gripped the Orimere as hard as he could, and reached his free hand to touch the tread of the Land Rover's rear tire. His eyes drifted closed, and—

—he woke up with Brooke's scream still in his ears.

"Here you are, sir." The surgeon helped him sit up. "How do you feel?"

He rubbed a hand over his face and tried to dispel the leftover fuzz from the wrak. The antidote buzzed under his skin, like a caffeine high. "All right, I guess. Did it work?"

"Judging from the commotion, I'd say yes." With a wry smile, the surgeon handed over Chris's clothes.

Outside the tent, shouts of fear and excitement mingled with a hubbub of running feet. He stomped into his boots, tucked the Orimere away, and ducked through the flaps.

Brooke's Land Rover sat in the middle of the camp. Soldiers swarmed it, gaping and gesturing, all of them talking. Those who saw him emerge stared at him with new eyes. Whispers spread through the group. Making an exotic two-ton vehicle appear out of nowhere seemed to be good for the Gifted business.

Allara met him. Her eyes were big, but she kept her voice calm. "What is this?"

He shrugged into first his jerkin, then his pistol bandoleer. "Think of it as a skycar that runs on the ground. A fast skycar. We'll keep to the wagon thoroughfares as long as we can and go off-road where we can't. If we cut straight down to Glen Arden from here, we might just be able to get there before Mactalde does."

Quinnon walked over with Chris's sword belt in one hand. It was hard to tell in the shadows, but he might actually be a little impressed.

He tossed the sword at Chris. "Thought I told you never to let that out of your sight."

"And I thought you told me I didn't need help." He couldn't hold back a little grin as he belted on the sword. "You and Allara coming with me? We'll have to leave the horses."

"That's all right. We'll pick up new mounts when we get there." Quinnon stalked forward and dispersed the gawking soldiers with a terse order.

"Where's Orias?" Chris asked.

"Over there. Why?" With a frown, Allara pointed to where a Guardsman was driving a metal ring into a tree, while one of his buddies prepared to attach Orias's manacles to it. Orias stood motionless, but even he couldn't seem to look away from the Land Rover.

"I'm thinking we could use his sword when we get to Glen Arden."

"Not if it's aimed at you."

Maybe he was stupid to trust Orias after all he'd done, but if he left him here among these angry, frightened troops, the Cherazim would be lucky to live through the night.

"He just saved us from an ambush," Chris said.

Allara shook her head. "But he tried—"

"But he didn't." He snagged an orderly and sent him to first secure Orias's release, then fetch Worick.

A moment later, they were all crammed into the Land Rover, Chris and Allara in the front, Orias, Quinnon, and Worick hunched in the back, and the Rievers standing up in the cargo area. Chris set both hands on the steering wheel and steadied himself with a breath. The scent of stale French fries and Brooke's cinnamon air freshener seemed dizzyingly out of place here.

He glanced at Allara, then turned the key in the ignition. "Here goes nothing."

42

T HEY MADE BETTER time from Ballion than Chris had hoped. Hours of jouncing over cobbled roads, dirt roads, and no roads had left him with cramps in his back, his arms, and his brain. After the first hour, the buzz from the wrak antidote wore off, and after the second, he began to agree with Tireus's opinion of his plan. It wasn't just crazy, it was probably suicidal.

By the time he gunned the Land Rover over the crest of the last hill and into view of Glen Arden, Brooke's full tank of gas had evaporated into fumes. He shut down the engine and unbent himself to open the door and step up onto the running board.

Blood roses filled Faramore Flats, the meadow that funneled down to the lakeshore. With their upright petals and black centers, the flowers bloomed by the thousands, rippling in the wind like a stained sea. Overhead, a strange crimson dawn stormed across the sky and cast a contorted reflection into the lake around Glen Arden. Faramore Bridge hung eerily empty, and the semicircle of sunken redoubts on the shore lay in silence.

Then he raised his gaze. At the far end of the meadow, Koraudian troops plowed through the blood roses. Little more than five miles of open ground lay between them and the subjugation of their enemy's capital. He forced the air out of his lungs.

"God in heaven," Worick murmured.

Hanging out of the opposite door, Allara peered through her spyglass. "There's Mactalde."

Chris groped for his own spyglass.

A battalion or so to the rear, Mactalde sat his horse by the side of

382 – K.M. WEILAND

the road. He leaned to his left, reading a map held by one of his aides. Every few seconds, he glanced up to scan his troops.

Chris lowered the spyglass. "All right. Here's what we're going to do." His pulse pounded against his bandaged ribs. "I want you all to run down to the nearest redoubt. Alert any troops you can find to get out here and make a stand. Then all of you get into the city." He looked at Allara. "Blow the bridge and cut the skycar cables."

Her eyebrows formed a dark line. "What about you?"

"Mactalde's just sitting out there. If I can get through the trees fast enough, I might get a shot at him."

Behind him, Quinnon rumbled. "You get that close and you're a dead man, one way or t'other."

"How are you going to get down there fast enough?" Allara asked. "That's a league and a half, at least."

"They're coming my way anyway. We'll meet in the middle."

He shucked out of his coat and checked the load on his Glock. He only had ten more rounds. He'd meant to bring over more am- munition today, but with all the commotion in camp and Brooke's unsolicited visit back in Chicago, he hadn't managed it. He snapped the magazine back into place and steeled himself with a breath. Ten shots would have to do. If not, he'd have to fall back on chewser and estoc.

He turned to see his father leaning through the gap between the front seats. Worick's frown furrowed his face, but he didn't say any- thing to stop him. Chris hadn't expected him to. Worick knew the score here. He knew what Chris was going to have to do sooner or later, and as much as his father might want to protect him, he would probably be disappointed in him had he chosen to do anything else.

"When you get into the city," Chris told him, "get Mom and the girls and bring them up to the palace. The waterfront's probably not going to be the safest place for a while."

Worick tucked his chin in a tight nod. His face conveyed all the worry his voice didn't, but it also offered something else: a spark of pride. "Be careful."

Allara ducked back inside the car and leaned across the seats to snatch Chris's sleeve. "What about the Tarn?"

In the backseat, Orias sat motionless, his bound hands resting on his thighs. He might have seemed calm if not for the slow blue flush rising under his milky skin.

Chris looked back at Allara. "Keep him with you. If you get into any trouble, let him go."

She shook her head. "I don't trust him."

He touched her hand. "Then do it because you trust me."

"I . . ." She let him pull her hand free of his sleeve. The blue of her eyes stared up at him, and he realized for the first time what maybe even she didn't know herself—that she *did* trust him. When had that happened?

He shot Orias one last glance. "Keep them safe?"

Quinnon emitted a soft snort, but Orias inclined his head, almost regally.

That was all he had time for. In less than an hour, the red in the meadows wouldn't be just from the roses. He jumped down from the running board and sucked the cold wind into his lungs. Then he hunkered down and slipped into the trees.

He tore through the underbrush, trying to find a balance between pacing himself and pushing himself. He was in good shape, but not for running miles after a sleepless night on top of a recent injury, however minor. When he reached Mactalde—*if* he reached Mactalde—he needed to be steady.

For the first mile or so, he kept within view of the meadow. Periodic glances over his shoulder showed him Allara and the others abandoning the Land Rover and running downhill to the circular redoubts sunk into the ground on either side of Faramore Bridge.

Both redoubts were supposed to hold a full complement of Guardsmen, but who knew how many Tireus had pulled out to defend Ballion. Of those who were left, who knew how many were still loyal? The lookouts had obviously been bought out or incapacitated, since no one in the city had yet raised the alarm. With any luck, Allara would find enough men still able and willing to slam the brakes on Mactalde's advance.

By the time he was near enough to hear the Koraudians' marching tread, the cold had seared his lungs. He angled deeper into the woods, where they couldn't see him, and slowed so they couldn't hear him. With his pistol clamped in his numb fingers, he crouched and listened.

The pop of a signal flare and the crackle of its explosion echoed from the redoubt. So Allara had gotten that far. He closed his eyes and breathed out. The signal would both alert the city and be relayed back to Tireus. Not that he would ever get here in time.

Commotion swept through the troops in the meadow. A faint sound, like the growing rumble of thunder, reached him more as a feeling in the soles of his feet than a sound. Then it grew and the shouts of men joined it. It wasn't the storm, but a charge. The Koraudians were charging.

He rose and angled back toward the edge of the meadow. Red tabards flashed between the trees. The thud of their footsteps and the roar of their battle cries washed over him. He broke into a run.

Half a dozen Koraudian foot soldiers, prowling within the tree line, heard his approach and turned. He raised the Glock and took a wild shot at the first. The man ducked, and the shot went wide. The Koraudian shouted at his companions, and they all started toward him. As far as they knew he'd have to reload before firing again.

He forced himself to stop and place his next shots deliberately, just as Paul had taught him. He dropped all six men in eight shots. That left him just one bullet for Mactalde.

Blood roaring in his ears, he left the carnage he had just created and ran to the tree line. The Koraudian charge flooded the meadow. A thin battalion of Laeler soldiers had emerged from the city. They crashed into the Koraudians and shattered against the sheer weight of overpowering numbers. Blood roses engulfed them, drowning men and horses up to their knees and swallowing the dead.

Chris scanned back through the Koraudian lines. On a knoll, not fifty yards away, Mactalde sat on his horse and glassed the field. Aides milled around him. Rotoss was nowhere to be seen.

Chris was only going to get one shot, and he needed to get as close as he could. He breathed deep, bounced once on the balls of his feet, then ran. He made it all of twenty yards before someone saw him and shouted. Without hesitating, he dropped to one knee and raised the pistol to Mactalde's chest.

Mactalde glanced around. His eye found Chris's, and Chris pulled the trigger. One of the three aides threw himself in front of Mactalde, and the bullet crashed through him.

Almost before the aide fell, Chris cast aside the Glock and drew the chewser from his second bandoleer holster. Mactalde and his aides were already moving, already spurring their horses, but not to get away. Sword in one hand and a flanged mace in the other, Mactalde spun to face Chris and charged. Chris pulled the chewser's trigger, and the heavy caliber slug ripped into the second aide's horse, cartwheeling it over the top of its rider.

The third aide reached him, before he could reload. He hurled the heavy chewser into the man's face, even as he leapt. With one hand, he shoved the aide from the saddle and with the other he caught the saddlebow and pulled himself up and over. He dragged the horse around to trample its rider and to face Mactalde. He drew his sword.

Thunder shredded the sky, and for a millisecond, lightning froze the world in its glare. He passed Mactalde at a gallop and leaned halfway out of the saddle to hammer his blade at him. In one blow, he could decapitate the enemy of Lael once and forever and save the worlds from breaking.

But, of course, it couldn't be that easy. Mactalde caught the sword against his crossguard and pounded the mace down on the flat of Chris's blade. The sword caught fast between Mactalde's weapons and yanked from Chris's grip.

Chris grabbed at his saddlebow to save his balance and drove his horse forward. He galloped past a Koraudian who was fighting with a Laeler footman, snatched the Koraudian's second sword from the sheath on his back, and turned.

Mactalde bowed over his horse's neck. "And so we do battle." His spurs lanced his horse.

Chris watched Mactalde's eyes, watched his weapons. He hadn't really expected to get this far. Now that he had, he had to figure out a way to match swords with a man who seemed fated to conquer, no matter what he tried his hand at.

The two horses swept abreast of each other, and the wind pounded around them. Chris ducked the scythe of Mactalde's blade and shot up his own sword barely in time to catch the mace. For the second time, the blow nearly destroyed his grip.

"Had rather a difficult time of it since you arrived here, haven't you, Master Gifted?" The wind howled at Mactalde's back and catapulted his words into Chris's ears. He bared his teeth. "Everyone lies to you. Everyone wants to kill you." He beat his sword and his mace—one, two—against Chris's upraised blade. "But lately I seem to find you playing the knight-errant every time I turn around."

Chris fought to breathe. He'd never engaged in swordplay on horseback. Quinnon's abbreviated curriculum had skipped that lesson, and his body didn't seem to be remembering anything useful. He caught up his reins and dragged the horse back to place a buffer of space between his inexperience and Mactalde.

"Don't look so shocked," Mactalde said. "You asked for this fight, you know. You came hunting for me, not I you." His horse tossed its head, and Mactalde held its chin almost to its neck. The horse half-reared, hopping on its front legs, refusing to stand.

Chris blinked away his sweat. "You need to listen to me—for your own sake. You being here again isn't natural."

Mactalde trotted forward. "Miracles are seldom natural."

Chris held his ground. "Did you know the worlds are out of balance? Did you know they're breaking apart?"

A dark ripple crossed Mactalde's face. "The worlds cannot break. One cannot be without the other to balance it."

"They're out of balance because of *you*. You can't stay here."

Mactalde's eyes glared, unblinking, from his face. He trembled, not from fear, not from exhaustion, but from sheer passionate conviction. "I died so I might stay here."

Chris held his sword in front of him. In his chest, his lungs burned like a kiln. "You're destroying Lael."

"I will rebuild Lael."

"Look around you!" He pointed to the maelstrom overhead. The wind whipped through the clouds and spun the red dawn back into gray. "Don't you realize more is going on than just this war?" He pulled his horse back one step, then another. He couldn't beat Mactalde in a fair fight. He'd missed his opportunity when he'd missed his shot. The only chance he had left was to make the man see reason. From Mactalde's fevered expression, that choice didn't offer much hope either. His mind raced. "I could take you back to Chicago. What if I just took you back? It might be like none of it ever happened."

Mactalde shook his head. "Why would I go back?"

Thunder rent the sky, and rain spattered Chris's face. "Because you can stop the worlds from breaking."

"Oh, you are a fool." Mactalde flexed his fingers around his sword. "I can't stop the breaking now."

Chris blew the raindrops from his lips. "Then I have to."

This time he didn't wait for Mactalde to attack. He swung hard and fast. Their swords collided again and again. He fought instinctively, reflexively. He had no defenses.

Mactalde's sword crashed once more into his. His mace's silver head flicked across the corner of Chris's vision. He would need only one direct hit to lay Chris open.

Chris flung his free arm to meet the mace, and his forearm smashed against Mactalde's knuckles. The mace hurtled end over end to land among the bloodstained roses. The wound in Chris's side stretched and tore, and pain jagged up his ribcage. Choking it down, he turned just in time to meet Mactalde's boot against his chest.

He hit the ground too hard to remember why he had fallen. When he looked back up, Mactalde's blade plunged toward his heart.

———

The wind shrieked in Orias's ears. He stood on the far wall of the Western Faramore Redoubt and searched for Chris in the meadow's ominous carpeting of red.

Pitch hoisted himself onto a merlon, one hand on Orias's shoulder. "You see him? I don't see him."

The Searcher led two horses up the stone ramp to the wall that encircled the sunken fort. She stopped beside him and scanned the field. Her hands were bone white around the reins. "If we'd come five minutes later, they'd have taken the city." On her orders, the city's troops had charged to meet the Koraudians.

Raz clambered up beside Pitch. "They may take it yet. Then you'll wish you *had* gotten here five minutes later and saved yourselves a cartload of lives."

Quinnon, followed by Worick, clomped up the ramp. "Since when is it that Lael needs the likes of you as a battle advisor?" He pushed Orias's shoulder. "Move."

"Wait!" Pitch bounced. "I see him! There he is!" He scrambled up

Orias's arm onto his shoulder and clung to his ear for balance. "See him?"

Orias squinted. The faraway figure of a man in a leather jerkin, running, edged into focus against the field of windswept red. Chris dropped to one knee and raised a handgun. His first shot felled a soldier who hurled himself in front of another. His second shot, with a second pistol, took out a horse. The remaining Koraudians charged, and Chris dragged the front one from his saddle and commandeered his horse. He turned to face the oncoming Koraudian.

Allara exhaled. "That's Mactalde."

Pitch yanked at Orias's ear. "He's found Mactalde! He's going to kill him!"

Orias's innards thickened. Chris couldn't kill Mactalde. As much as the Gifted had learned since he had arrived, he was inexperienced and untried. Twenty years ago, Mactalde had been a master swordsman. Even the Cherazii respected his skill.

He turned to Allara. "Let me go."

She stared at him. "I can't. How can you expect me to trust you? Even after what you did for us last night."

Quinnon's hand fell onto Orias's manacled wrist. "I said move."

Orias held her gaze. She must realize this was their only chance. *Orias* was Chris's only chance. "If you don't let me go, Mactalde will kill him."

She looked across the battlefield, and her teeth worried her lower lip. "He can take care of himself."

"We both know he can't beat Mactalde in a fair fight."

"You see him having another option, do you?" Quinnon asked.

"Change the odds. Nobody says he has to do this by himself. Besides, he's wounded."

Her chin came up. "And who wounded him?"

"I need Lael to survive as much as you do." He twisted his hands free of Quinnon's grasp.

She darted a look to the meadow. Chris passed Mactalde at a gallop, and Mactalde not only parried his blow but wrenched Chris's sword from his hands. Her pulse quivered in her temple.

Worick pushed forward to stand beside her. "Let him go, my lady. Somebody has to go. Let him go."

"Yes," she said. "I know." She drew the keys from her belt and turned to Orias. "This isn't because I trust you. It's because Chris does." She freed his hands from the manacles.

He looked at the Rievers. "Stay."

They nodded, reluctantly.

Without a backward glance, he swung onto a horse and clattered across the stone platform that bridged the redoubt wall and the earth outside. He turned the horse's face toward the meadow and galloped onto the field.

Fire flooded his limbs and his brain. Blood burned beneath his skin. Men either scattered before him or were trampled underfoot. He cared not who fell, be they Koraudians or Laelers. He would justify any casualty, any risk, if it meant saving the Gifted. That was all he had left now.

He watched Chris fight, watched him parry Mactalde's onslaught with more raw grit than skill. Too occupied with the swordplay, Chris failed to see Mactalde's mace arcing toward his head. Almost too late, his arm snapped up to stay Mactalde's hand, and the mace hurtled free.

Orias read Mactalde's next move in every taut line of his body. He saw the man's weight tilt to the outside, saw his hand drop to the saddlebow. His foot came free of the stirrup, and Chris turned back to catch the full force of the kick against his chest.

As Mactalde rode forward to loom over Chris, thunder cracked open the ashen skies. Rain pelted Orias's face like needles of ice. The wind ripped through the blood roses, and petals scattered like drops of blood. Probably some *were* blood.

He opened his mouth in a roar. The horse gave one more burst of speed, gathered its hindquarters, and leapt a line of fallen bodies. Mactalde flipped his sword in his grip. Its point hovered above Chris's chest. If he had any final words to offer, they were torn away in the howling duet of wind and thunder.

Pebbles of hail spattered against Orias's back. He swung off his horse, his feet running before they ever touched the ground. Mactalde's blade plunged, and, without slowing, Orias bellowed and swung.

His sword hit Mactalde's and ripped it away, seconds before it would have pierced the Gifted's chest. Still running, he spun around and fought to bring his balance and speed under control.

With a snarl, Mactalde urged his charger after Orias. Orias sliced the horse's front legs out from under him in one clean swing. Mactalde hurtled over the horse's head and rolled to his feet in the blood roses beyond.

On every side, hailstones smashed to the ground, and the roses burst into clouds of black seed. Somewhere at the edge of his senses, Orias recognized Chris collecting his sword and shoving to his feet. But he had no intention of holding Mactalde at bay until the Gifted could get to him. This was his fight now.

Mactalde pulled a dirk from his belt, but they both knew the weapon could be no defense against the length and heft of a Cherazii broadsword.

"You." Mactalde breathed a harsh laugh. "Why am I not surprised to see blues no longer honoring their covenants? Come, let us end this."

Orias took one more stride, planted himself, and canted his body for a final blow. His sword swept through the distance between them.

But it never connected.

A hailstone the size of his fist slammed into the blade. He staggered forward, his balance destroyed, and more hail pounded into his back.

Mactalde gasped a laugh and spread his hands. Rain and sweat beaded his beard. "You see? Even Nature protects me."

A stone struck behind Orias's ear. Warm blood oozed against the ice.

"Orias, watch out!" Chris shouted.

Koraudians bore down on him. Rotoss rode at their front, his face streaked with blood beneath his brimmed helmet. Orias's stomach burned.

"Move!" Chris said.

He dove out of the way, and the horses swept past. Hail battered his shoulders. A stone hit the back of his knee, and his toes went numb. He shoved himself up. Blood thumped in his leg, and sparks tingled up and down his calf.

War cries fragmented into screams and confusion as both Laelers and Koraudians swarmed the meadow. The hail thickened and turned deadly. In an instant, the battle became a mass retreat. One of Rotoss's men had picked up Mactalde, and every Koraudian in sight was running for the lake. The city and its two circular redoubts offered the only protection for leagues.

Chris had reclaimed his mount, and he galloped toward Orias with a second horse in tow. Orias met him halfway, sheathed his sword on his back, and vaulted into the saddle. Soldiers—red and green alike—surged on every side.

A Laeler footman leapt up and grabbed Orias's saddlebow. "A ride! For the love of all that's holy, let me ride! We'll be stoned to death out here!"

Orias pried away the man's hand.

All around, men staggered beneath the rain of hail, screaming and bleeding and begging the riders to stop. Orias saw them only at the edge of his vision. He charted the field's swells and divots and natural barriers. Here and there, knots of soldiers still battled, but for the most part, the armies had surrendered all pretext of fighting. All that mattered now was survival.

Ahead, Mactalde slowed and started shouting. The Koraudians in the front columns began to reform. Farther ahead, Guardsmen gathered at the bridge: one thin line trying to defend a city from the retreat of two desperate armies.

A footman ran between Orias and Chris. "Help me! Help us!" He raised his clasped hands to Chris. "You're the Gifted! You're supposed to help us!"

Chris reached for the man and pulled him up behind his own saddle.

Orias snatched his dirk from his belt. "Don't be a fool! They'll pull the bridge out from under your feet if you don't get there in time!"

"We can't leave them all out here to die!"

Orias snarled. He *could* leave them, and with right good will. He dragged his horse over, knee to knee with Chris, and shoved his dirk beneath the footman's chin. "Get off!"

The man's pupils shrank to almost nothing; his eyes gleamed impossibly white.

"Orias!" Chris's fist clamped his wrist "Let him go!"

"You can't afford the extra weight slowing you down! Mactalde's life may be charmed, but yours isn't!"

"I can't save all the men who are going to die out here today. But I can save one!"

Orias slammed his dirk back into his belt. Before either Chris or the man could resist, he hauled the soldier off Chris's horse and dumped him across his saddlebow.

"You've saved him. Now go!"

Everywhere, men fell, screaming, with broken arms and bleeding heads. A stone the size of a Riever's skull smashed into the eye of a Koraudian horse. The horse catapulted to the ground, bowled over three Guardsmen, and rolled over the top of its rider. The soldiers trampled them all.

Chris leaned out of his saddle, grabbed a fallen Guardsman by the hand, and swung the man up behind him.

Orias swore. Did the Gifted have a death wish or was he truly brainless enough to think he could thumb his nose every time Death rode up behind him? Better that half the army should die than the Gifted.

Orias drew his sword and his axe. If the Gifted refused to protect himself, then Orias would have to do it for him.

43

THE CITY'S COBBLESTONES rang beneath fleeing foot-steps and the clatter of hooves as Allara followed Quinnon through the Taïs Quarter to the palace. People mobbed the streets. Hailstones crashed all around them, some big enough to chip the cobbles. A window exploded overhead, and the glass fragments caught in her hair.

The Rievers huddled against her back. "*Ricotée*," the older one grated, "Mactalde won't even need to float out his artillery after this bombardment."

The younger Riever, the one called Pitch, picked the shards from her hair. "What if Orias and Chris can't get across the bridge?"

"They'll get across." She made herself believe it.

Only a few of the panicked citizens fought the current to bolster the defenses at the bridge. Most of them jostled east toward the protection of the capitol buildings and north toward the inner city districts of the Hub.

"Move yourselves!" Quinnon bellowed, but the crowd's uproar swallowed his words.

A hefty man, dressed in hose and a black velvet doublet, shoved a boy against Allara's horse. The animal, already irritated by the press of the crowd, humped its back and kicked. When the boy screamed in fright, people cursed both Allara and the man in the velvet doublet.

Her throat clamped around a cry of frustration. Was this what Lael had come to? A country of arrogant cowards? Once upon a time, every man in Lael would have been proud to fight for his country. Now, they either prostituted themselves as Nateros's spies and saboteurs, or they fled like children running from goblins.

She urged her horse forward. The crowd shrieked and scattered, but they opened a path to the square in front of the palace. In the square's center, the *fawa-radi* fountain sprayed a circular curtain of water from its heart of fire. Both water and flames whipped in the wind. The hail broke against the fountain's center sculpture, and chunks of ice and granite splattered into the basin. She guided the horse to the fountain, and he leapt onto the wide stone ledge. The Rievers grabbed at her coat collar to keep their balance.

She raised her hand to the crowd below. "Outside our walls, our soldiers are falling by the hundreds! We must hold the bridge to give them time to retreat to safety!" The crowd hurried past, and her words turned shrill. "Every man of you should be standing beside them, helping them fight!"

"Enough of your tripe!" someone shouted. "What right've you got to be telling us these things?"

The crowd turned toward her. Fear twisted their faces. Panic darkened into blame and anger. Once, they would have rallied to the Searcher. Now they wouldn't believe her, much less fight for her.

The wind blew her wet hair into her mouth. "The longer we hold the bridge, the more time we buy for the city! My father is bringing troops from the north!"

Pitch stuck one foot into the laces at the back of her coat and hoisted himself above her shoulder. "You have to listen to her! If you can defend the bridge, you can keep the Koraudians out of your city!"

"Do you want the Koraudians to overrun Glen Arden?" she cried.

"That's what *you* want, no doubt!"

"What *we* want is no more Searchers!"

"No more traitors!"

The words became a roar. Someone flung a hailstone at her. It struck her horse's haunch, and his hindquarters skidded into the pool. More stones flew.

"You reekin' traitor!" someone shouted at her. "You led Mactalde right to us! It's her fault! We wouldn't even have this war, if it wasn't for her!"

Stones clacked against the fountain's basin and splashed into the water. She urged the horse forward. He scrambled over the side of the fountain and jumped back to the street. Hailstones rained from all around—from the earth as well as the sky now.

"Kill her! Kill the Searcher! She deserves to die!"

"Stay those stones!" Quinnon galloped around the fountain to stand between her and the crowd. "No man who raises a hand against the Searcher will find shelter in the palace!"

"Bah!" A lanky youth stood up, a hailstone in one hand. "She betrays us to the wolves, then locks us outside to face their fangs! What's happened to honor? The Searchers used to put the people before themselves!"

"The people used to give their Searchers the respect they're due!"

"What respect's she due?"

"That's right!" someone else shouted. "Even she don't believe in the holy things no more!"

The lingering pain from her concussion rose and fell inside her skull like the thrum of the tide. She opened her mouth to say— what?—a denial?—a refutation of the doubts that had been her constant companions since she was old enough to speak? She ducked a hailstone someone threw. It glanced against her cheekbone.

"*Och.*" Quinnon hurled himself into the crowd, after the perpetrator. She laid her rein to the horse's neck and he broke into a run.

"What about the Gifted?" Pitch shouted at the crowd. "You believe in him, don't you?"

Raz grunted. "People only believe in heroes when they win."

The palace gates swept open, and the palace Guard formed a line to beat back the crowds. Guardsmen were already squared up in the center of the yard, their shields over their heads in a protective testudo.

She reached the ranking officer and swung out of her saddle. The Rievers jumped down behind her.

"These are all the men you have?" she asked. "The bridge is going to fall any moment!"

The officer tilted his shield to cover her. "My lady, we can't even get past the courtyard right now."

"We have to buy time! The longer we can hold off the Koraudians, the more men we can save." And the greater chance Chris had of reaching safety. But she didn't say that. He was the only reason to hope right now, and she couldn't afford to rob anyone, including herself, of that hope for even a moment.

Quinnon galloped up. "Get your men out of here, Lieutenant! If these madmen won't clear the path in front of you, clear it yourselves. Anyone who resists—drag him along with you and force him into the fight." He looked back at the gatemen. "Nobody comes in through those gates until the Guard has a clear exit! Nobody, you hear me?"

A groom darted into the hail to snatch Allara's reins, and she and the Rievers ran to the castle. She shoved through the double doors so hard they crashed back against the walls and clipped a heavy floor vase. It tipped and smashed against the marble parquetry.

Right now, she had no way to help Chris, no way to make certain he crossed the bridge before the Guard was forced to detonate it. The only thing she could do was watch, and the only place from which she could catch a glimpse of the bridge was the southern parapets.

She lunged up the stairs, two at a time, pushing past servants and councilmen and high-ranking nobles. She passed her own quarters on the third floor and hardly paused to see the chaos beyond the open doors.

"My lady!" Esta cried. "The hail! The windows, all the windows are breaking!" The pop of broken glass punctuated her screeches.

Allara kept going. She reached the southern wing and entered the shadows of Eroll's room.

"Alla—" Halfway to his feet, he dragged at the bed hangings and pulled himself upright. His chest heaved against the bandages. "What is it? I saw the signals through the window. What's going on?"

She crossed the room to reach him before he could lose his balance. "What do you think you're doing? Get back in bed."

Sweat sprang up at his hairline and glistened against his pasty skin. "Not until somebody tells me what's going on. Sounds like the whole city is being shelled!"

"Not too far off, if you're asking me," Raz muttered.

She grasped Eroll's arms and eased him back to the bed, facedown. "It's hailing. It's just hail. Now lie still."

He flopped against the pillows with a groan, but managed to grab her wrist. "Mactalde. It's Mactalde, isn't it? He's killed the Gifted?"

"*No.*" She snatched her hand free. "Mactalde is *not* going to kill him. Never say that to me again. Never."

These doubts, these wretched, gnawing, pervasive doubts—would they never cease? Her doubts, Eroll's doubts, Quinnon's doubts, even Chris's doubts. When had something so simple as belief become so wrenchingly unachievable? Her chest felt like it was afire.

"Lie down. And don't move." She threw the blankets over him and pushed through the balcony's glass doors.

The northern wind had kept the hail from smashing the windows and doors on this side of the palace, but stones the size of small melons piled against the balustrade. She climbed onto the railing. Twelve leagues away, across the choppy water of Taïs Bay, the bridge was lost in a blur of rain.

"What do you see?" Raz clambered up beside her. "I can't see anything."

Pitch climbed up on her other side and snapped open a diminutive spyglass. "Allow me, my lady."

"There it goes!" Raz cried.

The grate of stones giving way reached her only as a dull rumble. She snatched Pitch's spyglass and watched through the tiny circle as the bridge buckled beneath a mass of screaming men.

Please, please, please, let him be all right. Let Chris make it to safety in time. Just let this one man survive.

If he survived, she would believe. She would stuff her doubts and her fears away where even she could not cling to their comfort. She would put to shame Nateros, with its taunts about her failures. She would choose faith over fear, no matter how much she had to sacrifice. She would believe the God of all was true to His promises.

"Prove to me," she whispered. "Prove to me You're real. Give me a reason to believe."

The bridge twisted and snapped. Suspension lines recoiled. The turrets at either end toppled into the water and men and horses spilled over the railings. They penetrated the dark water. Foam swarmed up in their wakes, and the debris crashed in on top of them.

Pitch grabbed at Allara's coat. "What do you see? Tell me what you see!"

"The bridge is down." She lowered the glass. From here, it was impossible to distinguish faces in the dark knot of humanity wrangling at the gates. The Guard ran through the streets in pursuit of Korau-dians who had slipped into the city.

"The redoubts," Eroll's voice rasped from the doorway behind. "They're taking the redoubts."

She turned to find him hunched against the doorframe, his blan-ket clutched to his bandaged chest. He listed forward and barely caught his balance by shoving one foot in front of him.

"What are you doing?" She leapt down and tilted her shoulder under his arm before he could take another step.

"Look," he said.

She cast a glance at Faramore Flats and the redoubts on either side of what had once been the bridge. Those who had been strand-ed on the shore fled through the hail. Mactalde had been wise enough to secure the redoubts even as the fight at the bridge raged, and now only Koraudians could find sanctuary there.

The Laelers trapped outside the city fell by the hundreds. Those who did not die beneath the hail were ripped to pieces as soon as they were within rifle shot of the redoubts. Carried away by the northbound wind, the screams and the firing reached Glen Arden as a ghost of a sound.

She turned her face against the hollow of Eroll's shoulder.

He could not raise his arms to hold her, but he laid his cheek against her head. "I'm sorry. I shouldn't have said what I did. I'm sure he's alive. He *is* the Gifted after all."

She wrapped her arms around his waist, loosely, to keep from hurting him, and closed her eyes. She painted white the vision of death that stained the backside of her eyelids and cleared her mind. For just a second, she caught hold of a moment of peace in the midst of chaos, and in that moment she felt the tiny, faraway twinge in the back of her mind—the tingle that meant Chris was alive.

Chris galloped through the crush outside the palace gates. Some-where along the way, a soldier had shoved a shield into his hands, and he held it above his head as he rode. The hail thumping against it wrenched at his grip, and his arm cramped for the dozenth time. All around him, the piazza writhed with sodden, screaming human-ity. He had to rein up to keep from trampling an old man.

Anger weighted his stomach. "If these people had come out to protect their city, we could have held off the Koraudians long enough to bring in all our men!"

Orias rode behind him. "Nateros has been poisoning this city from the inside out. They don't know who they want to follow anymore, much less who they want to fight."

"It's the Gifted!" someone shouted.

Bloodied faces turned in his direction. People thronged his horse, crowding him to a standstill. They flailed their hands and scrabbled their fingernails against his legs, his saddle, his horse.

"Help us! The God of all have pity, help us! We'll die out here!"

A hailstone smashed into the tip of his shield and nearly tore it from his grip. "Go back to your homes!" he shouted. "There's no shelter for you here!"

"The palace! Let us into the palace! We deserve to shelter there just as much as the devil-taken Searcher!"

Inside the courtyard, Quinnon stood in the palace entrance. If he were here, then Allara and Worick must have made it safely into the city as well. Chris breathed.

"Clear a path for the Gifted!" a Guardsman roared.

The people jostled closer, packed so tightly that those struck by the hail remained upright, crushed in place by their neighbors. "Help us!"

Orias growled a word in his own language and dismounted. With the handle of his axe and his own bare hand, he shoved through the crowd on foot to reach the head of Chris's horse.

"Move!" His ears showed blue beneath the tangle of his hair.

People either scrambled out of his way or were thrown aside. Chris's horse lurched into a trot and filled the gap behind Orias. The battered line of soldiers holding the crowd back from the palace gates parted just enough to let them pass.

Chris dismounted, crossed the courtyard, and climbed the steps.

Quinnon looked up and down his length, in what could have either been disappointment or relief. "Mactalde?" he asked.

Chris shook his head. "He got away." Again.

Quinnon's lip twitched. "And now you're trapped in the middle of an island. Be interesting to see how you're going to go about killing him from here."

"If I can't touch him, then at least he can't touch us either. We can stay here in safety until Tireus gets here with more troops."

"Aye. Safety." Quinnon cast a glance at the storm.

Orias propped a foot one step up and leaned against his knee. "Mactalde will bring windboats and float his artillery out within range of the city."

"Why should he?" Quinnon said. "We're trapped here. He can ravage the surrounding country at his leisure, then come back and raze Glen Arden. *If* the city doesn't tear itself apart by then."

The day-old flesh wound in Chris's side pulsed. "Glen Arden can hold together until Tireus gets here."

"Aye. Keep telling yourself that, laddie."

Outside the gates, the people hammered against the barrier of shields, and the line of soldiers staggered.

Someone shouted, "You let a blue in to safety, but you keep lawful Glen Ardeners out!"

Quinnon slung his rifle into the crook of his arm. "Enough of your poundings!"

"You're not in command! The Gifted will let us in!"

Chris turned away from the crowd to the palace's open doors.

Inside, Allara and several noblemen stood in discussion halfway up the staircase. She caught sight of him and reached to steady herself against a six-foot statue of a bird with upraised wings. She offered a tiny smile and mouthed, *You're safe.*

A thread of dried blood darkened her cheekbone, and she looked beleaguered. No doubt the officials were in as much turmoil as the rest of the city, and, in addition to her own high rank, she was the last person to have been in contact with the king. Of course, they all wanted her to tell them what was going on.

Guardsmen ran up and down the outside steps. They saluted Quinnon hastily and shoved into his hands missives from their officers. With his permission, some slipped on past and hastened into the castle to deliver their messages to even bigger brass. The cavernous foyer echoed with voices. Everyone had something to say, and no one seemed to know what to do.

Outside, the people beat farther forward, and the line of Guardsmen staggered a bit.

Chris turned to Quinnon. "Why keep all these people out? Can't they shelter in some of the outer buildings until the storm passes?"

"What makes you think any of them deserve sanctuary in these walls? They're rabble-rousers and cowards, every one. I've never been in the habit of paying out protection to that like."

"Some are innocent."

Quinnon's nostrils flared. "Right now, all that's separating that mob from Allara is my line of soldiers. If you want to just open up the path and let half of them tear through her home until they find her, you're going to have a rotted lot to answer for."

Chris scanned the courtyard. "What if we let in the women and the children? And the old men. If the men of fighting age can't defend their own city, then they can stand out there and get battered to death for all I care."

In between scribbling messages on couriers' tablets, Quinnon cast him two quick searching looks. Then he nodded. "All right, I'll let that many of them pass. You can take command here."

Chris raised an eyebrow. "I don't know about that. Tireus has made it pretty clear he's not too happy about me taking command of anything."

"Tireus ain't here." Quinnon stabbed a final blot of ink with his fingertip stylus. "And I've got to go find the garrison commander. So make yourself useful." He pushed past Orias and started down the steps. "We're running out of time, lad. You have to start putting things right, and you can start here."

From anyone else, that might have sounded like a taunt or a reproach. But from Quinnon it almost—almost—sounded like he was giving Chris a chance to make good.

Chris took a breath and faced the Guardsmen in the courtyard. "Pass all women and children and any man not of fighting age."

The hailstorm was slackening, and the men left in the courtyard wouldn't have much longer to withstand the bombardment. Whatever their injuries, they would still be far better off than if they had shouldered their duties and run to fight at the bridge.

A Guardsman with a black courier's shoulder sash brushed past. "Pardon me. I need to find the Princess Allara."

Chris stopped him. "What for?"

The courier glanced up, recognized him with a start, and saluted.

"Pardon me, sir. Captain Arness from the South Shore Precinct sent me. Everyone's wanting to know what's happening."

"And Captain Arness answers directly to the princess, does he?"

The courier squirmed. "No, sir. But we were there when she entered the city at Faramore Bridge, so we know she knows what's going on."

"Never mind the princess. She's busy. We're all busy. Give me your tablet." He scribbled a response to Arness. "You can take that back to your captain, and next time tell him to go through chain of command. He's not the only one in this city who's wondering what's going on. We'll have every guard station in the city briefed before dawn. All right?"

The courier snapped a salute. "Yes, sir."

Chris turned back into the foyer.

Allara descended from her consultation on the stairs and met him halfway. "We have to pull ourselves into some kind of order. No one knows what they're doing." She looked past his shoulder at the first trickle of Glen Ardeners entering the courtyard. Beneath her clothing, her muscles contracted into hard lines. "What are they doing?"

"We're letting some of them in."

"Why?" The word was harsh, clipped.

"I can't leave all of them out in the hail." He took her elbow and guided her toward the stairs. They needed to start talking to the rest of the bigwigs around here and try to get people briefed and things sorted out as quickly as possible.

Her hand strayed to her sleeve, where she kept her little spring-loaded pistol. "We should go somewhere else."

"I agree." Orias's bulk hovered at Chris's shoulder.

She glanced at him, then back to Chris. "Mactalde?"

"No." He couldn't keep the disappointment from his voice. "Not this time."

"Not this time." She didn't have to tell him what she was thinking.

They were running out of time, and they both knew it.

44

ATE THAT EVENING, Chris left the palace through a side entrance. Twilight covered the courtyard in starless darkness. Sometime during the blur of the last ten hours, the hail had finally stopped, and the palace Guard had cleared the townspeople from the courtyard. The whole place was still abuzz. Soldiers tromped across the cobblestones, and a steady stream of wagons and horses clattered through the stable yards.

He crossed the yard to the long wing that extended from the palace's ground floor. Somewhere in the hubbub, a message had arrived, saying Worick had transported his family to the relative safety of the palace. This was the first opportunity Chris had gotten to check on them himself. He knocked at a curtained window. One of his twin nieces peeked out at him, and he walked the rest of the way down to the door.

Shouts from within the city echoed over the castle gates, and the skyline glowed with the heat of fires. Word had come sometime during the afternoon—he had forgotten exactly when—that riots had broken out. What remained of the Guard was stretched from one end of the island to the other, trying to restore order.

His mother opened the door and stood aside to let him enter. "You're exhausted." Her face was soft in the flicker of the lamps.

He pulled her against his chest and leaned his head into her hair. "What a terrible day."

So many things had gone right. The very fact that he had reached the city in time—that they had held off Mactalde—that they had survived the hailstorm—was something to be grateful for. But exhaustion pulled at his body and mind alike. He needed sleep. Even more, he needed Tireus to get here. He needed the storms to end. He needed the city to stop tearing itself apart. He needed more miracles than he could count.

She patted his back, between his shoulder blades, same as she had when he was twelve years old. "This day is over now. We never have to live it again."

He straightened. "I came by to make sure you all made it here safely."

One of his nieces—Miriel, he thought—sat in the inglenook at the back wall, her legs dangling over the edge of the seat. She peeked one eye around the corner and grinned when he noticed her. The door to an adjoining room stood ajar, and Tielle's and the other twin's voices murmured from the other side.

He walked over to squeeze Miriel's shoulder. "Where's Dad?" he asked his mother.

She shut the front door. "He and Tielle's husband went out again to see what could be done to help. I sent Sirra with their supper not long ago."

He turned back to her. "She shouldn't be out there by herself."

She wrung her hands. "Tell me what happened today."

"We lost the battle for Glen Arden." He studied his dirt- and blood-encrusted fingertips. "Probably the most important battle in the whole war."

Miriel craned her head around to peer up at him. "What'd *you* do all day?"

"Too much, not enough." Same as always.

She pulled the delicate golden fuzz of her eyebrows together in a frown.

He fluffed her hair. "Let's just say I didn't do what I was supposed to do."

"Mactalde?" his mother asked.

"Yeah."

"But you didn't get hurt," Miriel said.

He pressed his thumb against a hailstone bruise on the back of his hand. "Can't say the same for a lot of people."

His mother smoothed both hands down the front of her apron.

"You're wrong, you know. Glen Arden isn't the most important strategic location in Lael."

"Then what is? Réon Couteau?"

She nodded.

"I don't know about that." He sank into the inglenook bench across the hearth from Miriel. "What happened here today . . ." He propped his elbows on his knees and scraped his fingers through his hair. "Glen Arden's the center of the kingdom. It controls the Karilus Wall and the rivers."

"But Réon Couteau is the home of the Gifted."

He chewed on that a minute, trying to find some great positive in Mactalde's having blockaded Glen Arden instead of Réon Couteau. There wasn't one.

The door to the adjoining room swung open, and Tielle and Ireth, his other niece, entered.

Tielle glanced over his face, and a hard line in her forehead eased. "At least you're safe. At least we're all safe. The Searcher too?"

He nodded.

She gripped Ireth's shoulders. "The city's a mess. Just listening to it all is a nightmare. Nateros is behind most of it, did you know that?"

"Not much of a surprise there."

Her direct gaze held him, demanding his attention and a truthful response, just as it had all their lives. "Did you know they tried to kill the Searcher this morning?"

No wonder Allara had tensed when he'd let half the mob into the palace grounds. His scalp prickled.

"No. She didn't tell me." But she should have.

He leaned his forehead on his folded hands, eyes closed. Had he ever been this exhausted in his life? If he managed to lie down tonight, at least his body would get some rest. But his mind would wake up back in Chicago and keep going and going and going. How had the other Gifted sustained a lifestyle like this? Or was it maybe different when someone wasn't trying to kill you every other day?

His mother crossed the room and laid her hand on the back of his head. "Be careful. Please promise me that. I believe we can all survive this. You may be the Gifted, but you're still my son, and I still love you. When this ends, we will start over, and we'll learn to know each other again. *I* promise *you* that."

He reached behind his head to take her hand in his. "Let's just hope this thing ends with people throwing roses in front of my horse, instead of something a little less pleasant." He looked at Tielle and forced a wink. "How often does someone like me get the chance to hobnob with kings and princesses, right?"

She shook her head. "I don't care what you do. Just stay alive."

He sighed. "I've got to go have a look at what's going on in the city." He rose and crossed the room. "I'll only stay out until I find Sirra. Dad and Markham are probably with the Guard. I'll pass word along for them to come back as soon as they can, but if things are bad out there, they may be gone all night."

"*If* they're bad," Tielle muttered.

If she had anything more cheerful to say, the click of the door closing behind him blocked out her words.

———————

Chris left the palace and moved through the square to the streets beyond. One hand gripped his chewser and the other rested on his sword hilt. Guardsmen on horseback blocked the roads to the palace, trying to hold back the mob. Someone lobbed a lit torch at the line of soldiers, and one of the horses spooked and reared, nearly throwing its rider.

Bonfires raged up and down the posh streets of the Taïs district, and the flickering light danced mad quadrilles with the shadows of the men who sparked them. Windows popped and shattered, and homes and businesses alike surrendered their goods to the hands of looters. People darted everywhere—some of them running from Guardsman, some of them just running. The wind swirled the shrieks of laughter and the shrieks of pain and fear into one prolonged wail and smeared it against the night's raw canopy.

A drunk, his arms full of dry goods, staggered against Chris's shoulder, fell to one knee, and dropped half his load. Huffing, the man grabbed with both hands to gather his plunder back to his chest. He snatched once at Chris's foot and, when it didn't move, left it in favor of more portable spoils.

Chris gripped the man's shoulder.

Blindly, the drunk ratcheted up his head. "What d'you want?"

Chris regarded him. "Did you fight in the battle today?"

"No."

"Why not?"

The man's tongue lolled as he licked his lips. "I ain't got no reason to get killed."

"Just reason to steal from your neighbors?"

His expression flickered with uncertainty, then he shrugged. "Here." He dumped his armload at Chris's feet. "You take it, aye? I don't need it." He laughed. "I can get more. Maybe from the palace next time." His eyes wandered to something in the street behind Chris and narrowed.

Chris turned and found Sirra backed into a doorway, something heaped in her arms.

He twisted back around, and the drunk's eyes darted to his. "Go home." He released the man's shoulder. "If I see you again, you'll be arrested."

The drunk scrunched up his face. "You ain't no Guardsman."

Chris left him and jogged across the street. The taut lines in Sirra's face slackened, but her hold tightened on the dark shape in her arms.

If his own sister was out here looting, he might as well feed the whole city to the Koraudians. He seized her elbow. "What are you doing out here?"

"Talan—Chris—it's a jiswar cub. I found it. I don't know where it belongs, but I thought somebody might kill it, just for the sport of it." The pile of blond fur in her arms stared through ice blue eyes. About a foot in length, with upright ears springing from a wide base, it huddled against Sirra's chest. Its bushy tail, ringed by one red stripe near the end, spiraled around her arm.

He breathed out. "This is the last place in the worlds you should be tonight."

"It's all right. Father and Markham are just back there." She nodded over her shoulder to where a group of civilians were helping Guardsmen board up broken windows. "I left them the food Mama sent and was starting back to the palace when I found the jiswar."

"Come on then. We're leaving." He turned and nearly ran into the drunk.

"I think I knows you. You really are a Guardsman, eh?" The man stuck a finger in Sirra's face. "Why you let little girlie here run off with what she wants and make trouble for everybody else?" He yanked one of the jiswar's ears.

The cub yelped and flopped to the ground. Before Chris could reach for the man, Sirra smashed the hard, sensible toe of her shoe into his shin. The man screamed, and Chris grabbed his shirtfront and shoved him aside. Up ahead, Sirra scrambled after the jiswar, chasing him between legs.

"Sirra!"

"Just a minute!"

People turned to investigate the commotion, and he started after her. At the edge of the crowd pressing against the Guard's road-block, a white-clad arm reached down and collared the jiswar by its scruff. Sirra stopped short, and Chris took one more stride to catch up with her.

Crofton Steadman looked from the cub, extended in his hand, to Sirra. "A jiswar is an expensive pet to lose. Though I must say you have a beautiful night for chasing after him." He glanced at Chris. "Wouldn't you agree?"

Chris's hand darted to his holstered pistol. Sirra gathered the cub into her arms, and eased back behind him.

Steadman's eyes never wavered from Chris's. The scar on his upper lip twitched. "Perhaps you didn't know. We're having a riot."

One of the Guardsmen had stepped forward in an attempt to calm the mob, but he had only succeeded in whipping them to a higher frenzy. Their screams filled the plaza.

"Down with the Searcher! Down with the king! Up Nateros!"

Chris's hand sweated around his chewser's grip. "Yeah, I see that."

Steadman stepped closer. "It's time for certain changes to be made in our country. It's time for freedom to replace religious mores. Time for worn-out traditions to give way to a future that does not doom us to the ignorance of superstition and sorcery."

Chris looked at him levelly. He wasn't about to dignify the man's rantings by playing along.

Steadman grinned. "Not even you, a natural-born Gifted, can stand against us. You and your pitiful attempts to lead this people *deserve* to be terminated."

Chris refused to let himself falter. Steadman was just prodding for a weakness. Chris had punched Steadman in the face the last time they'd met, and his knuckles itched for a sequel.

"If you're so sure, why not take me out right now? Why leave it for Mactalde to do?"

Sirra tugged at his sleeve.

Steadman's smile remained frozen, but a muscle in his cheek churned. No doubt, he wouldn't mind repaying that punch one bit. But he shook his head. "No. No, I don't think so. When the time comes, I won't have to kill you." He took a step back, then another, and the crowd swallowed him.

Chris took Sirra's arm and led her away, past the drunk.

The man tottered and leaned his head back to squint at Chris down the length of his nose. "Hey, wait, I do know you! You're the Gifted. Aye? The Gifted, right?"

The last thing Chris needed right here was a Nateros mob knowing who he was. Steadman might be willing to let him go for the time being, but his followers wouldn't be so eager.

The man trotted in front of him. "'Cause if'n you're the Gifted, you should've just said so, governor." His laugh blasted the sour taste of cranok into Chris's face. "I'd've given you the stuff to start with, what?"

They reached the corner of the street, and Chris shoved the man aside. The drunk groped for a windowsill, missed, and toppled to the ground. His laughter chased Chris and Sirra down the alley.

As soon as they were around the corner, Chris pulled her into a run. Their footsteps slapped the cobblestones, and their breath clouded in front of them. The streets twirled past in flashes of fire and shadow and a cacophony of laughter and destruction.

Sirra stumbled behind him, and he reached back to take the jiswar. He hung the cub's hot body in the crook of one elbow, his pistol clenched in the opposite hand. Not until they passed through the roadblock did he slow.

In silence, he crossed the square to the palace gates, and he hung his head back and sucked at the cold air. It seared his throat, and he coughed.

Sirra slid her arm deeper into his. "Was that who I think it is?"

"If you think it's Crofton Steadman, then, yeah."

She clenched her fingers in his sleeve. "He could have killed you!"

Yesterday, Steadman probably wouldn't have had enough support to target a Gifted. But a lot had changed today. Lael had lost its first battle. Who knew how much of the people's faith had been lost along with it?

"Maybe," he said. He shifted his hold on the jiswar. The huge copper ears perked, and the blue eyes studied him. It snuffled at his collar. "I can't believe you risked your neck for this thing."

"I could hardly leave him."

He held the cub at arm's length. The jiswar propped a paw on each of his hands and stretched out his nose.

He let himself smile for maybe the only time today. "Reminds me of a puppy I wanted when I was a kid."

They walked over the cracked and dented stones, past the *fawaradi* fountain at the center of the crossroads. The fire had gone out, and the water had run dry. Now the fountain's decapitated figurehead stood an eerie, useless guard beneath the clouded moonlight.

Sirra clasped his arm. "I've been wanting to tell you I'm sorry I wasn't there for you in the other world."

As if it were her fault she hadn't been. "Doesn't matter." He cradled the jiswar in both arms. "You're here now. We're both here now. Nothing's going to change that, not Crofton Steadman and not Faolan Mactalde."

They didn't say anything more after that. In the aftermath of everything that had happened today, his words were only wishes.

45

DARKNESS HAD LONG since fallen by the time the councilmen released Allara and Quinnon from the war room. Most of the corridors were deserted. People had given up for the night, gone to bed, or delved into the darkness and mayhem of the city.

Quinnon leaned a shoulder against the wall and scratched both hands through his wild hair. "What a day." In the flicker of the candle globes, his skin was as gray as his two days' worth of stubble.

Allara stared at the war room's closed door. "It might have been worse. We could have gotten here too late. We have Chris to thank we didn't." She pulled his eyes to hers and waited for his acknowledgement.

He flashed a frown. "You don't have to tell me that. I know it."

"You've been relentless with him ever since he crossed."

He stood away from the wall and faced her. "And you haven't?"

"We both have." In the beginning, she'd been harder on him than anyone. But if he'd won even her faith, then shouldn't he be able to win anyone's? "Lately, it just seems you've been even more set against him."

"I'm not set against him. I could even learn to like the lad." He paused, almost hesitating. Quinnon never hesitated. He always knew what he wanted to say and do.

He looked away for a second, then back. "I'm going to tell you something, and I want you to remember it. Just because Chris Redston's heart's in the right place doesn't mean he's going to save us all."

The truth of his words trembled all through her. "I know."

His good eye drilled her. "I've a feeling in my blood none of us are going to emerge from this unscathed. I don't want you on the hurting end anymore than you have to be."

She almost reached out to hug him, but stopped herself. Quinnon and his prudish warrior soul would probably be scandalized beyond words by such a display.

He turned to go. "Best get yourself off to a bed. The only good thing Mactalde's given us today is the chance for a whole night's sleep. We can't do much of anything until we see his next move." He brushed past. "Tonight's likely to be the only chance you're going to get for sleep for a long while more. I suggest you take it."

She caught his arm as he passed, wanting to thank him somehow—for everything. "Quinnon—"

He just gave her hand a pat and stumped on down the hall.

Wearily, she turned and trudged up the stairs to the third floor. The surgeon's assistant admitted her to Eroll's darkened bedchamber, then retreated to the sitting room to give them privacy.

Eroll lay facedown, his face smashed in the pillow. When the light from her globe touched his eyes, he looked at her, and the side of his mouth lifted in a smile. "Appears I've died after all and ascended to the realm of angelic beauty. Jolly good."

"That would be neither good nor jolly." She set the globe on the night table and straightened the bedclothes. "How do you feel?"

"If I were going to be honest, I'd have to tell you I feel like someone kicked me off the Karilus Wall. However, since I'm being all gallant and brave, I suppose I'll have to make some noise about never having felt better in my whole ruddy life."

"You shouldn't have gotten out of bed this morning."

"I'll admit to seeing the wisdom in that now. But when one feels the sky is falling, curiosity naturally gets the better of one." He quieted. "It was bad out there today, wasn't it?"

She waited until she had folded the sheet down over the top of the blankets. "Yes. It was. We've detonated Faramore Bridge and cut the skycar cables out of the city. We're essentially stranded until Father arrives. But the good news is the city can hold out for an indeterminate amount of time. Mactalde will lose thousands if he attempts to invade across the water."

She slid a hand between his cheek and the pillow, found it hot, and crossed the room to fetch a fresh pillow from the dressing room. When she returned, he allowed her to switch out the old one.

"Seems we owe a lot to your Gifted, doesn't it?" he said.

She hugged the old pillow. "Yes. I think we do."

A stray lock of hair fell across his forehead and made him look unbearably earnest. "I'm going to tell you something you may not know. You're falling for him."

Heat touched her cheeks, and she shook her head. "Hush. You don't know what you're talking about." She moved forward to give his blankets another tug.

He winked. "I will admit he's not so charming and handsome as my dapper self, but I suppose one can't expect the impossible."

"No one could replace you."

He let out a soft laugh. "Oh, my darling girl, God knows I love you. But I'm not what you need. Never have been, never will be." His eyebrow arched. "Never claimed to be."

"Stop. I mean it." But even as she said it, she could feel the warmth of Chris's presence in the back of her head. Reaching for it was almost a reflex now. When had she allowed him to become such a comfort to her? He felt nearer now than he had been for the last few hours. He was coming to her. She straightened away from the bed and steadied her voice. "I haven't time for this nonsense."

"Of course you do. Soon as this ridiculous war is over, it will be the only thing you'll have time for."

She stooped to smooth back the stray hair and then press a kiss on his forehead. "You're an idiot."

She was all the way up in the back hallway on the fourth floor when Chris found her.

He held a sleepy-eyed jiswar cub in the crook of his arm.

"Where'd you find that?" she asked.

"My sister rescued him in the city. I was looking for Parry to take him to the kitchen for some supper. I'd take him myself, but I can't find the kitchen in this place."

"It's in the basement."

"Ah." He grinned. "Well, I was only off by five levels."

She crossed the hall into a small round room that hid the railed entrance to a downward-spiraling stairway. A skylight, set with blue and silver stained glass, glittered under the moon. More than half the panes had been smashed in the storm, and the wind filtered through the cracks. A double set of glass doors, still whole, lined the wall opposite and revealed a wide terrace.

"This is the servants' staircase." She walked around to the far side of the stair hole and turned back to face him. "It goes down to the kitchen."

He propped his free arm against the railing. "I hear you had a run-in with Nateros today." His voice hit a note somewhere between sternness and concern.

She stiffened. "Not with Nateros exactly. Just some people."

His brows came together. "The same people I let into the palace earlier?"

She shrugged. "You didn't know."

"Tielle said they tried to kill you." This time the note of concern strengthened.

"But they didn't."

"Yet."

She rubbed the thin material of her tunic sleeve. "What happens to me doesn't matter. So long as you survive, it doesn't matter." She looked at him. "Searchers have died for their Gifted before."

"You're not going to be one of them." The set of his jaw was adamant.

The jiswar squirmed in his grip, propped its chin against his arm, and let out a long sigh.

She shivered. A week had passed, and so much had changed, since their conversation on Eroll's balcony. She should have had time to think about what he'd told her, but somehow she hadn't. Perhaps she'd deliberately *not* thought about it.

She'd never planned to marry. She'd never even planned to fall in love, and certainly not with him. But from the moment he had raced into her presence, bloody and defiant, he had been nothing she'd expected him to be. Every time she adjusted her expectations to fit his reality, he changed. She had expected a puppet, and a renegade had arrived. She'd resigned herself to the renegade, and a paladin had arisen.

Eroll said she was falling in love with him. Perhaps she was. Perhaps that was what frightened her more than anything.

She dragged in a breath and turned to the glass doors. "I come here to think, when the weather's inclement."

He circled the stairs. The floor creaked beneath him.

She kept talking if only so she wouldn't have to listen to the rush of her pulse. "The servants don't use these stairs very much in the evening. It's almost the highest place inside the palace. On a clear night, you can see the stars through the skylight."

He stopped beside her and joined her in looking outside to where glass and crushed plants littered the octagonal stones of the terrace.

She rubbed at the shiver spots on her arms. "This war isn't going to last forever. One way or the other, it's going to end soon."

His presence surged in the back of her head. "And when it's over, I'd kind of like you to be alive."

A spark of light bloomed in the center of her chest.

He leaned his shoulder against the wall next to her and canted his head to see her face. "Somebody has to be around to keep me out of trouble, right?"

"Every bit of trouble I've pointed out to you, you've promptly jumped into the middle of."

"Here." He lifted the jiswar into her arms. "You have the distinct appearance of a woman in need of something warm and furry."

The jiswar sniffed her face, and her fingers caressed the snip of white on its nose. It licked her chin, and she murmured a laugh and craned her head back, out of its reach.

Chris stood in front of her, smiling at the jiswar, and then he looked up at her. The smile faded. "Allara." His hand moved to her face and his fingertips touched her cheek, feather-light. He leaned nearer and tilted his face to hers. "What if I were to kiss you?" His voice deepened. "Would that be such a terrible idea?"

She lifted her face. Her words caught in her throat, once, twice. "I don't know."

He lowered his face to hers and kissed her softly. For an instant, he pulled back and his eyes found hers, asking permission. And then he kissed her again, deeper this time.

The sense of him in the back of her head churned and spread and dizzied her with its warmth. She almost pulled back. She wasn't strong enough or brave enough for this. An enemy, with a sword in his hand, she could fight. Hatred and anger, she could wield. This was different by far. This left her bare and defenseless.

But Eroll was right. Somewhere along the way, somehow, she'd let him past her defenses. She'd welcomed him inside her walls and given him the key to her gates. She'd put her trust in him, without even meaning to. And despite all her fears, she couldn't find it in herself to regret it.

He deserved her trust. He'd fallen, made mistakes, but he'd risen from them and faced them. He stood before her as a man, when so many had crumbled all around her when she'd needed them most. He'd seen into her depths. He'd understood her. And he wanted her anyway. Perhaps that was the most terrifying part.

She pulled back and tried to look anywhere but at him. She had to remember how to breathe. Her laugh sounded self-conscious even to herself. "You were right. About a war being a bad time to fall in love." She made herself face him. "We haven't the time for it."

"The war will end." He tilted a smile. "Maybe then we can make time." Her sense of him said he was happy in spite of her rebuff, serene even. He wasn't taking her words seriously at all. He was doing it again, seeing right past her shields and reading her down to her core.

She swallowed and forced a nod. It was a good enough fallacy to hide behind. By the time the war ended, they'd find all the work—and the damage—of falling in love already done.

He leaned away a bit. "You're exhausted."

She looked at her hand, frozen on the jiswar's head, and smoothed it down his back once more.

She cleared her throat. "Does he have a name?"

"He's just a stray."

"Perhaps I'll keep him." She peeked up. "If your sister won't mind."

"I'm sure she'd be honored." He rested both shoulders flat against the wall.

A strand of hair slipped past her cheek, and she slid it behind her ear, smoothing it between her fingertips. Then she looked at him. "What if I named him after you. Christian—that's your full name, isn't it?"

He raised both eyebrows. "You expecting to get rid of me so easily you'll need to name your pet Christian to remind you of me?"

She shook her head. "Better to be safe, just in case."

"I don't know about that." He peered at the skylight, where the glass glinted like shattered diamonds. "All that stuff people say about better safe than sorry. I lived that way for a long time, and it was a mistake. If we want to win, if we want to succeed at anything in life, we have to play all our cards. We can't hold anything back, because we never know what we're going to be dealt in the next hand."

She stroked the jiswar, slowly. She didn't need to hear these arguments from him. She'd spent a lifetime trying to refute them in the depths of her own lightless caverns. All her life, she'd hedged her bets. She never went anywhere without a fallback plan.

"If you don't look at the future, you'll never be ready for it," she said.

"The world doesn't turn on a steady axis." His gaze dropped back to her. "And that makes the future a pretty slippery place. Life has to be more than a series of random coincidences. What's happened to me here—to us . . . There has to be a bigger plan."

She turned away from the glass doors. "I believe in the God of all and I believe He does have a plan."

His eyes charted her face. She sensed his own exhaustion, his own searching. He wasn't speaking to her out of a deep well of conviction, but more from a place of tentative and ongoing discovery.

"Maybe you *want* to believe that," he said. "But you don't. Even right now, there's doubt in your face."

She rubbed her thumb against her crooked forefinger. Her struggles, her failures, her broken dreams—they were a private graveyard she shared with no one, not even Eroll.

"My life has been a cliff." Her lips barely moved around the words. "When I found my first Gifted when I was nine, it was as though someone had shoved me over the edge. I've been hanging there ever since. What I know, what I understand about life, is what I can feel—the rocks I'm clutching. Below me is the future, and, because I cannot see how far down it is, I am afraid to let go, even though I know I'm supposed to."

"You're afraid you'll never stop falling."

"Yes. But what if all these years, I've been hanging over a drop the length of my arm?"

He shrugged one shoulder. "Let go and find out."

"I suppose I can't get past the thought that it's better to hang on to what I know, no matter how much it hurts, rather than risk believing I have ten inches to fall—only to discover it's really ten leagues."

She looked away. She hadn't meant to tell him all this, anymore than she'd meant to kiss him. These were things better not spoken of. If she kept them locked away, where only she could know of them, then she was the only one they could harm. And yet hearing herself saying the words, and watching him listen and accept without judging, was like opening the door of a dark room and letting in a pinprick of light.

In her arms, the jiswar gapped his mouth and curled his tongue in a yawn that ended with a whine.

"I should find him something to eat." She looked up. "And you're as exhausted as I am. We should sleep while we can."

He nodded and pushed up from leaning against the wall. One hand reached out to her. "I'll take him down to the kitchen."

"No. You don't know the way. And you probably need the rest more than I do."

But she didn't move just yet. She wanted to hold onto his assurances for just a moment so the sparks might spread their warmth through the winter of her spirit. She wanted to thank him.

But she had no words, so she only nodded and started down the stairs.

He followed to stand at the entrance. "Alla."

Only her father and Eroll used that nickname. She looked up through moonlight shaded blue and green by the stained glass in the skylight.

He propped both hands on the railing and leaned over the stairs. "Do me a favor."

"Aye?"

"Take care of yourself." His face softened. "Don't jump off the cliff until somebody's around to catch you."

"For an instant today, I found myself believing with all my heart that you will be able to save Lael." She filled her lungs with one great breath of resolve. "When the war is over and done with, perhaps then I'll be able to let go of the cliff without fearing the fall."

"I hope so," he said.

She descended out of his sight, and with every step, the warmth of his presence seeped away a bit more, until only the familiar hum remained. As she walked the cold brick tunnels to the kitchens, that lessened too. But something remained. Something tiny and indefinable. Something different. Something better.

46

CHRIS HAD NO sooner closed his eyes in Lael than Brooke's voice pierced the haze in his head.

"I'm telling you he's gone completely off his rocker!"

He opened his eyes and found himself staring at the off-white wall of what looked distinctly like a hospital room. So Brooke had somehow dragged him to Lakeshore Psychiatric after all. He stifled a groan. He'd almost forgotten about the mess he'd left back in Chicago. Watching her Land Rover disappear apparently hadn't been enough to convince her he was telling the truth.

"Chris might be crazy, but he's not *crazy* crazy." That was Mike. "Not crazy enough to be in here."

"Your assurance on that point seems rather wobbly," interjected an unfamiliar woman, her pronunciation crisp and professional. "Last night, you said perhaps his being here was for his own good."

Brooke didn't give Mike a chance to answer. "You didn't see him the other day." Her voice pitched high. "And you didn't see what happened either. I'm telling you he *took* my car. It just . . . disappeared, along with all his—his clothes. And everything else!"

"Give me a break," Mike said. "Now who's not making any sense?"

The professional woman murmured something.

Chris rolled out of bed. He was wearing only a hospital gown and had to scrounge around until he found the duffel someone must have brought from the hotel. As he hurried into his clothes, he could see, through the mesh-reinforced glass window in the door, Mike towering over Brooke and a woman in aqua scrubs.

"You can't keep him here against his will," Mike said.

"Since he has been unconscious for the past twenty-four hours, the orientation of his will remains rather ambiguous."

"Can't you just try to wake him up? I've got a little bit of an emergency on my hands, and—"

"When and how your friend is woken up is in the hands of specialists. Whatever your emergency may be, I'm sure it could hardly be as important as the state of Chris's mental health."

Mike rubbed the top of his head, a sure sign he was about to lose his temper. "If somebody doesn't let him know what's going on, this whole hospital is going to be in a state of emergency when he wakes up."

The woman clicked her pen against her clipboard. "You're saying he's prone to violence?"

"Well, I'd say, yes—" Brooke said.

Mike snapped her a glare. "*No*, that's not what I'm saying."

Chris buttoned his pants and crossed the room to open the door.

The nurse, a narrow-faced woman with spiked hair, turned around. Practiced placidity ironed the surprise out of her face. She laid a hand on his arm to keep him in the doorway.

"Chris. You've had quite a nap." She glanced at his newly donned clothes. "Why don't we go back into your room. You can sit down, and we can have a talk."

Mike shouldered in front of her. "You okay?"

"I'm fine." He looked past Mike to where Brooke stood back. "About your Land Rover. I'm sorry about that."

Her eyes were wide and she hugged herself. "What'd you do with it?" she asked, then immediately paled, as if sorry she'd asked.

"Um." He glanced at the nurse, then back. "It may be a few days, but let's just say I'll try to return it to you as soon as I can." Assuming, of course, the Koraudians hadn't torn it apart. "I'll explain it all to you then."

"Explain it to me, why don't you?" Mike said. "I can't get anything that makes any kind of sense out of her. And here you are sleeping all day and all night, but nobody can find anything wrong with you."

He took a breath. "You want the long story or the short?"

"What do you think?"

"Okay, short answer: I already explained it, and you didn't believe me."

Brooke let out a hopeless groan, but Mike stared him down. Something in the twitch of his eyelids said he *almost* believed Chris's story from the other day. Or maybe it was more that he believed in Chris, and even Chris's impossible story wasn't quite enough to unseat that belief.

The nurse tried to shepherd him back into his room. "Come on, hon. How about we sit down and talk about all this in a more comfortable setting? You can tell us whatever you want whenever you're ready. How's that sound, hmm?"

Mike rattled his car keys. "Actually, we need to go. You've got yourself a little problem to deal with."

Chris's pulse sped up, and he backed out of the nurse's grip. "Kaufman?"

"Tell you on the way." Mike took Chris's other arm and started walking away. He glanced at Brooke. "You coming?"

She stepped back. "I am not getting in the same car with him." Her gaze darted to Chris. "I'm sorry. But we don't even know how sick you are right now."

Frown lines enclosed the nurse's mouth. "Now, now, we don't need any accusations—"

Mike scowled at Brooke. "How are you going to get home?"

She glared back. "You can pick me up after you've dropped him off."

"Fine." He pulled Chris away.

"Wait!" The nurse's shoes squeaked behind them. "He is in no condition to leave. He just woke up. We haven't established anything about his mental condition!"

"Why do you think I signed his release papers?" Mike said.

They wound their way to the exit and pushed through a door into the cooler air of the foyer.

Mike shot a glance at Chris. "The first thing you should know is I had nothing to do with Brooke showing up at your hotel and trying to talk you into that voluntary commitment. Second thing you should know is I'm not so sure she wasn't right." He stopped at the door. "What happened to her car?"

Chris huffed a sigh. "It's in the same place as Mactalde."

Mike's nod was slow and deliberate. He opened the door. "I shouldn't have asked."

They stepped outside, and the cold smacked Chris in the face.

The sky swirled, and hailstones littered the streets in knee-high piles. Windows, windshields, even traffic lights had broken to fragments.

He stopped short. "No way. Here too?"

Mike's frown deepened. "Weird things are happening everywhere. Tsunamis in Australia, earthquakes in Texas, flooding in South America." Next to his Bug, he stopped and unlocked the driver's door. He watched Chris over the roof. "You wouldn't know anything about that, would you?"

"I just escaped the quack house, and I'd prefer not to make a repeat visit. So forget about me, and tell me about this emergency of yours."

"Harrison Garnett's disappeared." Mike dropped into his seat. He reached across to unlock the passenger door and ground the engine to life while Chris climbed in. "Happened last night."

Chris slammed his door and tried to sort out days and weeks in his mind. "He was released?"

"Not exactly. He ripped out his IVs and oxygen and beat it out of there under his own power." Mike gunned the car in reverse and skidded onto the street. "The police called my house, wanting to know if you knew where he'd gone."

"How do they know he wasn't abducted?"

"They've got a security vid of him leaving by himself." Mike swerved to pass a snowplow clearing away hail. "A nurse seems to think a phone call yesterday afternoon made him go."

Chris thumped the back of his head against his seat. "Flores. Or Kaufman. Paranoid as Harrison is, a threat is all it would take to get him to bolt."

"If he left because Flores called him, he's probably walked right into a trap."

"Maybe, maybe not. Harrison doesn't think in straight lines like other people."

The Bug's rear wheel caught a hailstone pile and bucked. Chris braced both hands against the dashboard to keep from banging his forehead against the windshield.

The last thing he wanted to do right now was go chasing after Harrison Garnett. But Harrison wasn't likely in any shape to be out there on his own. If Chris didn't find him first, Flores probably would. He gnawed the inside of his cheek. He didn't owe Harrison anything, but leaving him out there to get shot didn't quite set well either.

He glanced at Mike. "Where would you go if you were crazy?"

"Of the two people in this car, don't you think you're more qualified to be answering that?"

"Thanks a lot." He racked his brain. "Okay, let's try this. Head for his house. The only place I know he'd go is home."

"That's halfway across the city. There's no way he'd be able to make it there in his condition."

"That's where his safe house is. He's been holed up there for years. He hardly knows how to function outside of it."

He drummed his fist against his thigh and fought the urge to lean across the seats and take control of the wheel like he had the other day with Brooke. Who knew how long Harrison had been wandering the backstreets?

Mike turned on his blinker and eased onto the long stretch of North Lake Shore Drive. "The fact that you're thinking like this guy isn't making me any too sure about the wisdom of signing all those papers guaranteeing your sanity."

Twenty minutes later, Mike pulled the Bug around the corner of Harrison's street. Ahead, a man in a flannel coat hung onto a dog-wire fence and dragged himself down the sidewalk.

"That's him. That's Harrison." Chris levered open the door handle and ducked out of the car before Mike even had a chance to stop.

Harrison tried to push himself upright but only managed to sag double over the fence. His breath wheezed white.

Chris held both hands where Harrison could see them. If the old codger had managed to get hold of any kind of a weapon, it was just possible he might try to use it on Chris before he recognized him. Or maybe after he recognized him.

"It's me. Harrison, it's me."

Harrison blinked hard. "You. Don't come near me, you." He gasped for air.

Chris caught his shoulders before he fell over. "You should never have left the hospital."

Harrison trembled, his bones practically rattling against each other within the sack of his skin. "They were after me. They're still after me. And they're after you too. You're putting me in danger by being here!"

Chris hooked an arm under Harrison's knees and carried him to the curb where Mike had parked the Bug. "What I'm doing is trying to save your life."

Harrison grabbed the front of Chris's T-shirt. "My life wouldn't *need* saving if you hadn't nearly got me killed in the first place!" His teeth chattered. "This is all your stupid, arrogant fault!"

Mike rounded the front of the car to flip the passenger seat forward. Chris bent over and eased Harrison into the backseat.

"Should I call an ambulance?" Mike asked.

"No!" Harrison grabbed the edge of the roof and jerked himself to a stop, smacking Chris's head against the ceiling. "No hospitals! Hospitals are dangerous!"

Chris gritted his teeth. "Fine. No hospitals. Now get in the car before you pass out."

"Maybe we should wait *until* he passes out," Mike said.

Chris propped one knee on the floorboards and settled Harrison onto the narrow seat. Harrison flopped against the duct-taped vinyl. His legs hung over the edge, his back wrinkled at a bad angle.

He stared at the ceiling. "I hate this car."

"Oh, shut up." Chris rubbed the bruise on the back of his head and pushed the passenger seat upright. He stood on the curb for a moment and scanned the street, but Kaufman's black truck was nowhere in sight. If Harrison had managed not to be followed, maybe he was cagier than Chris had given him credit for.

He ducked into his seat and kicked the heater up to full blast, ignoring the tortured whine that chased the heat out of the vents.

"Where to?" Mike said. "We can't take him to my place. Your pals have already got it marked."

"My house," Harrison said. "I have to go to my house. I have things I need there. My notes, my papers."

"You want to take him to your hotel?" Mike asked.

Chris shook his head. "It's not safe for us to be together for too long. I've got to change rooms anyway. Too many people know about that last one."

Harrison smacked the back of Mike's seat. "Are you deaf? I said *my* house. That has to come first. Take me someplace safe afterwards, but first I have to go to my house."

Chris took a deep breath and let it out. "My dad's. We'll take him to my dad's."

Harrison rolled halfway to the floor, snaked his hand between Mike's seat and the door, and groped for the door handle. "Let me out of here. I'm not going there. I got my own business to take care of, and if you don't want to help me, I'll walk the rest of the way myself."

"Just give it a rest already." Chris twisted around and heaved Harrison back onto the seat. "What are you trying to do? Rip your stitches completely out?"

Harrison's fist swung wide, just missing Chris's face. "I'll rip them out if I want to!"

"We never said we wouldn't take you to your house!"

Harrison stopped a second punch in midair. His eyes slanted.

"We'll take you by your house and we'll pick up your papers. And tomorrow I'm coming back to see you, and you're going to tell me everything you know about Mactalde and Lael and anything else that could help, you got that?"

Mike watched them out of the corner of his eye, but didn't say anything.

"For now, we're taking you to stay with my dad," Chris said. "And if you don't like that, then tough."

"If he's anything like you, forget it." But Harrison folded his arms across his chest and lay back on the seat.

Mike cleared his throat. "Since when do you trust your dad?"

Chris swiveled around in the seat and leaned back with a sigh. "I don't know what other choice we have right now. And things have . . . happened, since I saw him last time."

Mike stepped on the gas. "No kidding."

───────────

Chris stood on his dad's doorstep and held his breath for a short eternity while the door swung inward.

Paul, his hair fluffed into disarray, stared at him. "Chris . . ." He screeched open the screen door. His mouth worked, opening and closing, but he couldn't seem to summon the voice to inflate his words.

Chris knew the feeling. The last time he'd seen his dad, he'd been Worick: strong and whole—not this trembling, crumbling wreck. If Chris hadn't known better, he might not have even recognized Paul as being the same person. Except for his eyes. Even swollen and bloodshot, his eyes were the same.

Chris swallowed. "I need a favor."

Paul stepped outside. "I got a call from some hospital downtown, said you was being kept there. I was going to come see you today. I was going to sign the papers to get you out." He looked to where Mike and Harrison waited in the Bug. "Guess I was too late."

A day late, a dollar short, and one shot too many. Story of his dad's life. For the first time in a long time, his heart squeezed at the thought. "Doesn't matter, I'm out now. But you can help me with something else." The Bug's doors slammed behind him. "There's a guy here—his name's Harrison Garnett. He's in trouble, and I need someplace safe for him to stay."

Paul's eyes held steady. "I'll do it."

Mike carried Harrison across the sidewalk.

The old man scowled up at the house and clutched the packet of notebooks they'd retrieved from his safe. "Another hailstorm is all it'll take to bring that roof down on my head."

Chris followed his dad inside. He stopped in the entrance and tried not to breathe. He had never lived in this house, but somehow it still held the scents of his childhood: microwave popcorn, his mother's perfume, vodka.

Mike hauled Harrison inside and followed Paul into the living room. From the entrance, Chris watched as his dad shoved newspapers and red licorice wrappers off the couch and opened the sofa sleeper.

"I'll get some blankets and pillows. This'll be ready in just a minute." Paul disappeared around the corner.

Mike deposited Harrison on the bed, and Harrison folded his arms over his notebooks. "This is a rat hole. This sofa is spider-infested."

"Gimme a break," Mike said. "After living in that garbage dump of a house, you're going to carp about spiders you can't even see?"

Harrison looked at Chris. "How come you think I'm safe with him? He can't protect me. I'd have been better off in the hospital."

"This isn't about protection. It's about hiding. And right now you're as hidden as you're going to get. So try not to pop a blood vessel. I'll be back to see you sometime tomorrow."

"Hmp." Harrison yanked his coat collar up around his chin. "Be just fine with me if I saw you sometime never."

Paul stopped in the doorway with an armful of faded bedding. His expression wavered on the edge of disappointment. "You're not staying?"

Chris shifted his weight. "Um, no, I can't. I'll see you later." He turned to go, Mike right behind him, but then something made him turn back. "But I'll see you tomorrow. All right?"

"You in trouble?" His dad dumped the blankets on the foot of the bed and stood with his arms at his sides.

Chris forced a smile. "Slightly more than usual. Let's just say that."

His dad licked first his lower lip, then his upper. "I've been having more of those dreams, bad dreams, lately. You're always in trouble, in the dreams. More than slightly."

Mike rolled his eyes. "It's genetic. This whole dream craziness. It's genetic, isn't it?"

Harrison snorted.

Chris hesitated: one breath in, one breath out. Right now, two worlds were falling to pieces around him. He didn't have time to try to rebuild what was broken between him and his dad—much less his dad himself. But then again, in some ways, he had no time to wait either.

He shouldered past Mike and stopped in front of his dad. "Listen, I'm going to make you a deal. I'm going to make the nightmares stop. Okay? But you've got to promise me you're going to knock off drinking. What about that?"

Paul curled his thumbs into his palms. He didn't say anything; he only nodded. But for right now, that was enough.

47

RUMBLING FILLED CHRIS'S bones. Caught for an instant between worlds, his mind thought he was dreaming. But then he remembered: he didn't dream anymore.

His body was flung from the bed, and he ripped fully awake. He rolled across the rug, anchored one hand against the bed, and dragged himself to his feet. The bed's canopy fell onto his head. The window shutters cracked and splintered. Stones rained from the ceiling, and paintings and sculptures crashed to the floor.

His brain scrambled to find some kind of sense in all this. Mactalde had brought his artillery into range overnight? He was shelling the castle itself?

He cast aside the bed curtain and lunged for the table where he had left his sword. The floor bucked beneath him and hurled him down.

Someone banged on the door.

"Chris!" Parry shouted. "Let me in! The door's jammed! Bloody let me in! It's an earthquake!"

A great big impossible earthquake. Now why hadn't he thought of that?

He shoved to his feet, sword in hand, and half-rolled, half-scooted across the room. He squeezed his back to a divan and crunched his knees against his chest. "Get away from the door!" he shouted. "Get down beside one of those chairs out there and put your arms over your face!"

The ceiling collapsed. Wood planking and tables and chairs and candle globes flooded down from the room above. A rafter smashed onto the divan and cracked in two, slanting down to form a triangle of space around him. On the far side of the floor, a hole ripped open. The four-poster bed creaked and plummeted.

Was this what it looked like when the worlds were breaking?

Abruptly, as if someone had flipped a switch, the rumbling stopped. Dust and pebbles rained in the corner. In a room above, someone choked and coughed. A woman started wailing. He sucked in a breath—half-air, half-dust—and jumpstarted his heart.

He dragged his sword from beneath the rubble and inched back into the open. Where the outside wall had been, now only ragged stones remained. A pewter expanse of lake glinted through the haze.

"Chris?" Parry called from the other side of the door.

"Yeah, I'm fine." He coughed on the dust and turned away. "What's it like out there?"

Between him and the door, a highboy listed toward the chasm in the floor. The Orimere was in the bottom, right-hand drawer. His breath caught.

"Um," Parry's voice squeaked and cracked. "The ceiling fell down in a couple places!" He rattled the door. "And one side of the hallway completely collapsed!"

"Which side?" Chris lowered himself to his stomach and slid across the floor toward the highboy. "The stairs?"

"No, I can see the stairs." The door rattled harder. Then, with a sudden pop, the whole thing gave way and flew open hard enough to smack Parry into the wall.

The highboy slid closer to the hole. Chris snagged the nearest leg and yanked out the bottom drawer. The floor beneath him creaked and sagged.

Parry squawked. "What are you doing?"

Chris flung the drawer behind him, praying the floorboards would hold, and rolled away. Beneath the highboy, the floor crumbled. He grabbed the drawer and Parry grabbed his leg, just as half the room gave a tortured shriek and plunged into nothing.

He snatched the Orimere's leather purse from the drawer and hauled Parry to his feet. "C'mon."

Rubble strewed the hall. The entire eastern half of the third floor had caved in. Nobility and servants clogged the passage, some of them dazed, some of them crying. Most of them staggered toward the stairs. At the end of the hallway, two men carried Eroll Leighton, dragging half his bedding behind them.

Chris shoved through the crowd, running sideways when they refused to make a path. "Put him down on the blanket. We'll make a hammock of it."

The floor wheezed as they set him down. Eroll's eyes were clenched shut, his hands balled against his chest. Chris and Parry took the blanket's left corners, and together the four of them heaved him into the air.

The crowd lurched down the double flight of stairs, the well supporting the wounded. Something behind them fell with a crash.

Eroll didn't open his eyes. "Appears we've all lived to fight another day, eh?"

"Where's Allara?" Chris demanded. Her rooms were on the northern side of the palace, same as his, but hers were farther east, where everything had been hit harder.

"She's not here." Eroll's breaths came hard. "She left earlier."

Thank God for that, at least. The earthquake had probably rocked the whole city, but just about anywhere would be a better place than here.

Behind them, running footsteps hammered into the already weakened structure. The stones grumbled, and fresh screams swelled. People packed the wide staircase, and a desperate few flung themselves over the railings into the foyer thirty feet below.

They rounded the corner to the second flight of stairs, and the foundation began to shake. It numbed the soles of his feet and vibrated through his body. Screams disappeared in the crash of broken glass and wrecked masonry. The tiles overhead cracked, and white dust fell like flour from a sieve.

Chris crooked one arm over his head to ward off the rain of stones. "Move!" The aftershock's roar swallowed his voice.

They hit the smooth marble of the foyer running, and all around them the palace, once so safe atop its hill, gasped one long breath and fell to pieces.

They burst from the doors into the courtyard. He ran, head down, free arm pumping. Bricks pelted the courtyard. The fragments bounced and ricocheted into what was left of the yard's walls. Gray dust engulfed everything.

He looked back. The palace was gone, the hill ripped in two. Only the western tower remained. It swayed, high above the wreckage, as the stones at its base crumbled. A gust of wind tipped it into the lake.

Not until the tower hit the water did he realize he could hear once again. He threw his head back to breathe. All around him, people were crying, coughing.

Allara and Quinnon galloped through the haze at the gates. She wore a flame-colored gown, probably in the mistaken assumption this day would hold no fighting. She drove Rihawn through the crowd.

Even before she reached him, her lips were moving. ". . . we have no defenses!"

"What?"

She skidded in front of him. "The walls are down. Half the artillery's destroyed. Mactalde can attack us at will!"

Quinnon rode in behind her. "Guardsmen, form up! Two companies to Faramore Station!" He reined his horse around to face Chris. "The redoubts on the shore didn't get hit anywhere near as hard as we did. If Mactalde takes advantage of this, and he will, he could be here inside four hours." He gestured past what was left of the palace to where the lake was now visible. "He'll sail up from the south. If we can get people out, via the taxi boats and whatever we've got left in the palace harbor, we can sail them to shore through Floating Taïs to the north."

Chris was shaking his head before Quinnon finished the words. "Most of these people would be sitting ducks out in the open."

"We'll take horses and ride to Virere Ford." Allara spun Rihawn in a tight circle to keep him from rearing. "From there, we can take the skycar up to Réon Couteau."

The hubbub of astonishment, fear, and grief filled every corner of the courtyard. Those who weren't busy tending wounds or trying to find loved ones clambered through the stones to stand around Quinnon and Allara—or so Chris thought.

When he glanced into their faces, he found the eyes of every person anchored on him. His mouth went dry. Why shouldn't they look to him? He was the Gifted, wasn't he? He was supposed to make everything right.

"Chris!" Pitch ran through the crowd. "You're alive!"

Orias followed, leading a big red charger with Raz standing upright in its saddle. Dougal trotted behind, his stub tail fuzzed out to twice its normal size. The crowd skittered back to give the group a wide berth.

Orias's skin glowed faintly blue with waning adrenaline. He ignored Quinnon and Allara and walked up to Chris. "The Koraudian boats are already in the water, coming our way."

"How can you tell?"

"I can hear them."

A murmur spread through the crowd. They wanted the Gifted to take the lead, because that's what the Gifted of yore did in all the victorious legends where everything always turned out happily ever after.

Chris swallowed and swiveled to look at as many of them as he could. "Captain Quinnon's advice is sound. We're leaving on the boats."

If they wanted him to be their bastion of confidence, they were headed for disappointment. But if they wanted him to be brave, the least he could do was pretend.

Tight nods and tighter faces responded to him.

He looked at Quinnon. "Let's get to it. It won't take Mactalde long to figure this out and send troops after us." He looked around for someone to whom he could hand off his corner of Eroll's blanket.

"Give him to me." Worick pushed through the crowd and hefted the corner away from him.

A wave of relief punched him in the stomach. "Mom? Sirra, Tielle?"

"They're fine. Everyone got out." The gray dust charted maps to nowhere in the wrinkles of Worick's forehead. "I brought my fishing schooner around to this end of the island yesterday. We can cram maybe a hundred aboard."

A Guardsman ran over with a horse. Chris looked at Allara. "There's no way we're going to get everyone out."

"I know." She looked at the rubble of the palace. "But we'll take all we can."

They only managed to get a hundred or so out. Allara's heart broke as they sailed away from what was left of Glen Arden. Refugees clogged the shores, but with Mactalde already in pursuit, what choice had she and Chris but to flee?

As soon as they reached Virere Ford, they launched the fireworks, starting the chain of signals that, God willing, would soon reach her father and his army on their way south from Ballion. Depending on how much distance the army had covered yesterday, it was possible they might be able to cross the short end of Lake Thyra and alter course to join up with the evacuees before the day was out.

Late in the afternoon the refugee train swooped into the Thyra Junction station. She rose from her seat. "Why are we stopping?" The engineers had been ordered to run straight through to Réon Couteau. "We haven't the time to stop. Mactalde's probably right behind us."

Chris stepped outside just as the stationmaster ran up.

"I'm so sorry." He wrung his hands and bobbed little bows. "My lord Gifted." He peered into the car at her. "My lady."

"Why have we stopped?" Chris demanded.

"I thought it best you know." He bobbed another bow. "None of our trains have returned from Réon Couteau for nearly a day."

"What do you mean?" Quinnon shouldered past Allara to stand in the doorway.

She focused on keeping air in her lungs. A skycar stoppage from Réon Couteau could mean any number of things. Chris looked at her, and she saw cold hard reality reflected back at her.

"You think it's Mactalde?" she asked.

"I don't know." His face was grim. "He could have sent a strike force to Réon Couteau from his position in Ballion and maybe taken control of the skycar stations."

Quinnon scratched his stubble. "Nateros has a large following in Réon Couteau. Could be Mactalde had help."

Her mind raced. They couldn't just stay here. Mactalde's men had to be right behind them. Depending on the size of the force, the Guard might be able to fend them off. But the rest of these people—high-ranking statesmen and councilmen—weren't fighters.

She looked at Chris. "What if we just kept going? There might be another reason for the trains not returning."

"No. We can't risk that. If we go and the Koraudians have control of the city, we're finished. If we stay here, at least we have a chance." He turned back to the stationmaster. "Pull the rest of the train down to level ground so we can unload it."

"Yes, my lord."

Without warning, the entire train lurched in a crash of screeching metal and exploding glass. Allara hit the floor on her hands and knees. She started up, only to be hurled forward again.

"Get out!" Chris seized her arm and hauled her out. "Get the horses out!" he shouted at Quinnon. "They're ramming us!"

She staggered onto the pavement, clutching onto him for balance.

High above, the long stretch of their train crumpled and twisted on the wildly swinging cables. From behind, another train backed up a few spans, then surged forward to ram the rearmost car. The Koraudians had been even closer behind than she'd feared.

Everyone in the train would be stranded. The lead car was the only one on level ground.

"We'll have to get the people to climb down through the cars to this one. If we pull forward, the Koraudians will be able to disembark!" Even as she said it, the doors in the Koraudians' train burst open and grappling lines snaked to the ground.

She whirled to the stationmaster. "If we move our train forward, can you switch the tracks before they can follow us down? Can you keep them up there long enough for us to bring all the cars down and start unloading?"

He wobbled back a step and jerked a nod. "I'll try, my lady."

Quinnon unloaded their horses in a clatter of hooves just as the train reeled forward. She caught up Rihawn's reins and, holding her skirts aside, clambered into the saddle. As fast as the cars leveled out, the people poured from them.

Orias and a squad of Guardsmen boiled out of the first few cars, weapons in hand.

Chris swung aboard his horse and raised his sword to them. "The Koraudians are lowering troops into the city. We have to engage them and buy the rest of these people the time to unload." He passed her with only a glance. "Get these people out of here! Get to safety!"

Orias, his face a snarl of bared teeth, galloped after him with the Rievers clinging on behind.

She watched them go, and her heart choked on its blood. She wanted to go with them. What was her own safety, so long as the Gifted was lost under the ravages of Mactalde's shock troops? She could be just as reckless as he when she had nothing to lose. And if she lost him, she would lose Lael, she would lose faith, she would lose everything.

Quinnon, mounted on his gray, reached over and slapped Rihawn's hindquarters. "Move! If we can get these people clear of the city, we'll take them up to the Cairns. We can hold out there until your father's reinforcements get here."

She nodded and spun Rihawn around.

Allara lost track of the precious time it took them to get out of the city. Across the meadows that surrounded Thyra Junction's outskirts, the moist black earth grew steep beneath its coverlet of green. The sky hung low and dark, the clouds racing.

Wind ripped at her hair and her gown, and freezing rain pelted her skin. At the base of the hill, she halted Rihawn amidst the struggling mass of Glen Arden evacuees. Her life was never less her own than in the midst of a crisis. That was the only reason she rode away from the fight and away from Chris. That was why she rode ahead of her people now, her skirts and her coat spread to the wind, and prayed that, in spite of everything, the sight of her might give them hope.

But when she looked back, it was not hope she saw. It was Koraudians.

The world shattered like glass. Chris had not been able to stop them all. Or, worse, they had stopped Chris on their way out.

"Quinnon!"

Behind her, Guardsmen scrambled down the hill to offer a slender perimeter of protection. Rihawn reared, and she leaned over his shoulders, her estoc in her hand. She was screaming something. A battle cry, a prayer. Something. Nothing. It didn't matter. It shook her throat, but she couldn't hear it, couldn't even slow her thoughts long enough to know what shape her lips formed.

The Koraudians swarmed like vultures to carrion. They crashed into the line of Guardsmen. Screams burbled up from mouths full of blood, and green and gold stags fell to the earth. Few red eagles joined them. Gunshots resounded from up the hill, where half a dozen carabineers leaned against the mossy stones. They fired, reloaded, fired.

"Move!" Quinnon bellowed. Behind her, he held in his horse and reached across his body to fire his pistol. "Keep moving! And don't look back!"

But she had to look back. She was leaving too much behind.

The Koraudians were breaking through the line of Guardsmen. Soon, they would chew through the ragged defenses of the noblemen, and they would swallow the evacuee column whole. Her eyes lifted to the city and the sinuous movement of troops in the streets, hundreds of them, maybe even thousands. How had Mactalde been able to send so many? Her blood burned the underside of her skin.

A Koraudian horse charged her, crossing the sward in great pounding strides. Its rider tilted his sword at her chest. Over his shoulder, the first of the troops left the city. They entered the long sweep of the meadow, and she could see the color of their tabards.

Not the red of Koraud, but the hunter green of Lael.

Her heart leapt. Her father had gotten their signaled messages in time after all.

With a shriek, she raised her sword, and Rihawn charged. Her sword crashed into the Koraudian's, and she twisted her wrist and freed her blade. Before he could regain the balance of his heavier weapon, she reversed her sword in her hand, dropped her reins, and plunged the blade into the man's back, all the way to its filigreed guard. The barb near her hilt caught on a rib, and the sword tore from her grip as the horses separated.

Her heart battered her ribcage. She righted her balance and turned back to face the city.

All the way from Virere Ford to Thyra Junction, she had done the figures in her head, over and over again. If her father had moved the army from Ballion early yesterday, he might have made it halfway down Lake Thyra. If he had gotten their messages early today, he might have been able to take the troops across the short end of the lake. If he wasn't stopped, if the winds were in their favor, if the troops moved as they never moved before, they might make it to Thyra in time. If, if, if, if, if.

She hadn't dared to believe any of those ifs.

Now, two companies of Guardsmen charged up the bank with her father's banner unfurled at their fore. They would angle to strike the Koraudians' left flank and force them back from the hill.

She turned Rihawn around. The man she had killed slumped over his horse's neck, blood seeping around her hilt like melted wax. She twisted the sword free and met Quinnon as he was extricating himself from a knot of the enemy.

He tossed aside an empty pistol and drew his last holdout from his pommel. "Get these people to the Cairns!"

Rihawn plunged up the hill, past the mounds of dead and dying and past the defensive thread of Guardsmen. The people didn't need her encouragement to flee. They clawed their way up the hill, climbing faster whenever they looked back.

Three-quarters of the way up, the Cairns stretched for half a league across the face of the hill. The stone piles marked their only hope of reprieve. If Chris and her father could hold back the Koraudians just long enough for them to reach the Cairns, then perhaps they would survive this day.

48

CHRIS SAW THE green flutter of Tireus's personal standard down the street, near the skycar station. He looked around. Chaos churned everywhere. Minutes screamed past, maybe even hours. Hard to tell the difference anymore.

Mactalde had packed the trains with men. They had landed in the streets and tangled with the Laeler soldiers. All through the cobblestone squares and corners, they fought, pistols barking, swords clashing. Even a few hand cannons spewed their fireballs and scattered splinters from wrecked houses.

He hunkered against a demolished shop front and tried to breathe through the smoke. Somewhere along the line, his horse had been shot out from under him, and who knew where Orias and the Rievers had gotten themselves off to.

Bullets zinged overhead. Cobblestone shards stung his face. He switched his chewser back and forth between his hands, so he could swipe his sweaty palms against his pants. He needed to get to Tireus, needed to find out what the plan was. If there *was* a plan . . .

Men ran past, faces black with soot and dirt, uniforms torn and bloodied. They saw him, and they flocked to him. Some stood steadfast and stony-eyed. Some shook with the adrenaline. They were all looking to him. They all wanted him to lead them.

A young footman stared up at him. "Tell us what to do, sir! We'll follow you anywhere." His cheek had been split from the corner of his lip halfway to his ear, and his words burbled through the blood in his mouth.

Chris's insides skidded. How many who followed him had died in the last hour? They would have been better off in Glen Arden. They would have been better off had they never seen his face. Didn't they know they wouldn't be here now if not for him? He had led them, sure enough. And look where it had gotten all of them.

He pointed his sword down the street to where the Laelers had established a temporary headquarters. "We'll join up with the king!" A fireball hit the eaves above them. "Move!"

He ran, and the men followed him up the street to the station. Overhead, the skycar train wobbled on its cable. Two Koraudian soldiers, high above, hacked at one end of the cables.

He gritted his teeth and pelted down the street. There was no version of the story in which any of this could end well. Allara had said his duty was to the God of all. He was the One who had ordained the Gifted. He was the One who chose the few. But why choose *him*? What had he brought to Lael but war and ruin? People were dying all around *because of him*.

Sure, he could be a leader. Any fool could lead. But no matter what choices he made, people would suffer. How had he deluded himself into thinking life could be any different here than it had been back in Chicago?

He reached the station courtyard and found Tireus, on horseback, directing troops.

Chris reached him and saluted. "It's too dangerous for you here."

"That's why we're leaving right now!" Tireus had to shout to be heard above the roar of the hand cannons. "We have to join my daughter and the others in the Cairns!"

Chris nodded relief and turned. Far away down the skycar cables, another train pulled into the center of the city. His gut seized, and he fumbled for his spyglass. The train stopped at an anchor pole, and when the doors opened, more Koraudian soldiers began to climb down. Instead of a red tabard, one of them wore a leather doublet.

His pulse quickened. It couldn't be Mactalde. Why should he follow his troops to Thyra Junction when the glory of Glen Arden was his for the taking?

But what if it *was* Mactalde?

His every breath flooded energy through his body. If that was Mactalde, then here was another chance to end this. *That*'s what he was here for. He was here to kill Mactalde and right the balance. If he could do that, that was all that mattered.

"Form up here in the square!" Tireus shouted. "Pass the word, carabineers to the front! I want covering fire laid down immediately. Bring up a horse for the Gifted."

Someone thrust reins into Chris's hand. Without taking his eyes from the fresh wave of disembarking Koraudians, he swung aboard. "Mactalde's here."

"What?" Tireus reined his horse around in a clatter of hooves. He stabbed Chris with a commanding look. "You stay here with me. Even if it's him, you'd never reach him."

He gathered his reins and laid his heels to his horse's sides. "I may never get another chance."

"Redston!" Tireus's mount stumbled. "Stay that horse!"

Chris galloped through the ranks, and every man turned to follow him.

He wasn't going to dance to Mactalde's tune any longer. He wasn't going to wait for Mactalde to come to him. There was no master plan here, guaranteeing victory. There was only him against the world, just as it had always been. The thunder of his mount's galloping hooves burst inside his body like fireworks.

From out of nowhere, Orias's big red horse smashed into him and knocked Chris's mount to its knees.

"What do you think you're doing?" Orias caught up the horse's reins and dragged him away from the charge. "Stop! This is a trap!" Somewhere during the fight, he had cast aside his long coat; he wore a sleeveless jerkin, and steam rose from his skin. Blue blood edged the corner of his mouth. "They're cutting down the skycars!"

Overhead, cables creaked and groaned. One snapped with a report like a gunshot and whipped through the air. The train plummeted several feet before catching on the remaining cables. The Koraudians hanging onto the support pole hacked more furiously.

From behind, Tireus roared: "Fall back! They're trying to divide the troops!"

Row upon row of red uniforms marched through the surrounding streets. They were converging on the station. They would surround Tireus, and he would never escape. Mactalde would chew him into nothing, then spew him back out. Chris's guts turned to ice.

"*Fall back!*" Tireus's cry wafted through the streets.

Another cable snapped. The skycar yawed dangerously. Troops in the streets scattered.

Chris snatched his rein from Orias and spurred into a side street. "Fall back! Retreat!" They had to circle around and get back to the station. "To the king!"

With a tremendous crack, the last cable snapped. The train's rear end plunged fifty feet into the street. Cobblestones exploded. Glass cars burst into shards. Like the tail of a destroying beast, the writhing train smashed into buildings on both sides. Men fell beneath the crush. Those who escaped were blocked from the station—and the king.

Chris rode around another corner, back into view of the station. The contorted train filled the street, obstructing any chance of passage on horseback.

Koraudian soldiers flooded the station. Tireus's adjutants flocked around him, and the king drew his pistol and fought at their sides. But they were trapped, all of them. As the Laeler army crumbled, a Koraudian pointed at Tireus in recognition. In seconds, the king's was the only green tabard in a sea of red.

Chris flung himself from his horse, snatched up a fallen pistol, and clambered through the wreckage.

A Koraudian toppled Tireus from his saddle, but the Koraudians around him, cavalry and footmen alike, kept him from hitting the ground. Eager hands reached up to grab a piece of him—arms, legs, hair, clothing. They swallowed him up, and then he reappeared, more or less upright, his hands wrenched behind his back.

Chris hauled himself up the side of a car, ignoring the bite of broken glass. He pulled the chewser's trigger, and his shot ripped through a Koraudian's back. The gun, useless after its single shot, rebounded in his hand, and he threw it aside.

Orias leapt onto the car and seized his arm. "You can't fight an entire Koraudian battalion!"

He tried to yank free, but Orias's grip tightened.

From the ground, Raz shouted, "The king's lost! You can't get him back this way!"

He wobbled on the slanted side of the skycar and gasped for air.

Walk away, walk away—that's what they were telling him to do. But wasn't that what he'd already just done? He'd walked away from Tireus, from the men who had pledged allegiance to him, and from the responsibilities he had accepted as the Gifted.

Just like his father had walked away after the car wreck, he had walked away.

Shots ripped past, and more glass exploded. He gave in to Orias's hand on his arm. They leapt back to the street and ran to where the Rievers held the two horses.

Pitch scrambled up behind Chris and gripped his shoulders. "We can't save the king now. If we don't leave, they'll capture you too!"

Chris hauled his horse around to gallop away. Every muscle fiber in his body ripped with the movement.

By the time Chris and Orias reached the protective front of the Cairns, a murky dusk backlit the clouds. Chris galloped through the only opening in the wall of stones, then he dismounted and tossed his reins to an orderly.

"Where are you going?" Pitch asked.

"Allara has to be told what happened back there." And because he was to blame, she would hear it from his mouth.

At the base of the hill, a thread of smoke streaked upwards and tossed gold sparks across the sky—the signal for a truce. A long moment later, a squad of Koraudians galloped across the meadow to within earshot of the Cairns. A man in a leather doublet dismounted and motioned for someone behind him to follow. Even without his spyglass, Chris knew it was Mactalde. Behind him, two soldiers stepped from their horses and yanked a third man out of his saddle.

Tireus.

Chris stopped short.

The orange of Allara's dress flashed. She threw herself against the wall, her face tilted to the man on her right, her neck muscles rigid as she snapped inaudible words.

"Ladies and gentlemen of Lael. I've a proposition for you." Mactalde's voice echoed up the face of the hill. "A twist of fate has left your esteemed monarch in my possession. However, I'm quite prepared to return him to your safekeeping."

The silence of a hundred people holding their breath covered the hillside.

The man with whom Allara had been speaking hauled his bulk up onto the cairn. It was Amras Denegar, her uncle. "What are your terms?"

Mactalde draped his hands over the hilt of his sheathed sword. "All I want is the Gifted."

49

THE SILENCE THAT met Tireus's imprisonment splintered into a buzz of voices. Chris's life for Tireus's, it was fair. It was right. Tireus was the leader Lael needed. Both Tireus and Chris had proven that. Sweat rose on Chris's spine, and he started forward, running, headed for Denegar.

"Are you mad?" Denegar shouted at Mactalde. "You already have our king. Do you think we'd also put into your hands the Gifted?"

Mactalde's body straightened into taut lines. "I've never been inclined to haggle, Lord Heindon. But I'll give you this. If you deliver me the Gifted, everyone on this hill goes free—the king, the Searcher, everyone, down to the lowest jack among you."

The voices rose to a clamor, and Chris shoved through the crowd. "Move! Make way! Get out of the way!"

A few heard him. A few moved. Most were too busy staring down the hill.

Denegar shot a glance down to where Allara's face stood out against the shadows. She shook her head—a tiny, frenzied shake, a demand for more time and more options.

"Well?" Mactalde's voice cut across the distance.

"We cannot surrender the Gifted," Denegar said.

"As I said, I do not haggle. This is your only opportunity to regain your king in one piece. Trade me the Gifted. He's worth nothing to you!"

Denegar planted both hands on his wide girth. "If he's worth something to you, I guarantee he's worth at least that much to us."

Mactalde held perfectly still for a long moment. Then he inclined his head, the movement stiff. "As you wish then."

Chris slammed through a barrier of bodies. "No, wait!"

One of the soldiers flanking Tireus kicked his knees from under him. Mactalde drew his sword. He touched the blade to his forehead in a salute to those on the hill. Then he turned to face the king of Lael.

Tireus knelt with his shoulders back and his head erect. "Stand fast!" His words pierced the cold evening. "We are not conqu—"

Mactalde's blade carved through air and flesh and blood and bone.

"No!" Chris shouted.

Allara shrieked.

Tireus's head fell to the mossy earth, and his body tilted to follow it.

Chris broke free of the mob and leapt onto the cairn. This couldn't be happening. Mactalde was truly out of his mind. What did Tireus's death buy him that wouldn't have been worth more as a bartering chip? He could never hope to gain the support of the rest of the surrounding countries like this.

Mactalde bent to retrieve Tireus's head and mounted. With his gory treasure held aloft, he rode away without a second glance at the body of the enemy he had waited a lifetime to kill. From the Cairns, gunfire chattered, smacking Koraudians from their saddles.

Chris stepped forward. Everything in him wanted to follow Mactalde. He wanted vengeance. He wanted atonement.

Quinnon grabbed his coat sleeve and pulled him back to the ground. "You go out there now and the crossfire will shred you."

Chris yanked his sleeve free. Could Quinnon possibly think he cared about the crossfire?

A muscle in the old warrior's cheek bulged, and he shifted his head so his bad eye was only a glare of white.

Behind him, Allara's hands had fallen from the stone wall to hang at her sides. She took one step back, then another, then just stood there. She was drawing in her air so fast she was choking.

Chris pushed past Quinnon and went to her.

"Allara." His hand touched her shoulder.

She flinched away. "Don't. Not now, not now." She stared at the top of the cairn. Tears, like liquid glass, fell in straight lines down her face. But she wasn't crying. She stood there, staring, panting.

Denegar approached, his face a mosaic of a thousand fractured pieces. He reached out to her, but she backed away. He turned to Chris. "We can't defend these cairns for even a day. We haven't the forces."

Chris made himself nod.

"As soon as it's dark, we should pull out. The deeper we can get into these hills tonight, the better." Denegar took a breath. "With Mactalde holding the skycar lines, we haven't a chance of getting through to Réon Couteau before him."

"It doesn't matter now." Tireus was gone. *Gone.* The word sounded like a pebble cast into the yawning eternity of a never-ending well.

Councilmen, nobility, and high-ranking Guardsmen swarmed Allara. Her skin shivered with every touch. She bowed her head, and strands of hair fallen from her chignon curtained her face. Her breaths still came in gasps, but she was regulating them. She was shoving away her grief and forcing her body back to the responsibilities at hand. She was summoning up that icy core and freezing her pain.

He pressed toward her, and the people opened a path for him. Her eyes were darker than he'd ever seen them, her pupils huge.

"I'm fine." Her voice sounded like sandpaper.

"Allara—Allara, I'm sorry." The words cut his throat so deeply he could almost taste the blood.

Late in the night, the destitute, vagrant horde collapsed, and Chris went looking for Orias. When he finally came upon him at the edge of the camp, the snow was beginning to fall like wet lace. The Rievers slept on either side of a tiny fire. Orias stared into the flames, one hand on his dirk, the other stroking Dougal's head where it rested on his leg.

Chris kicked snow at the fire. "What makes you think I want a bodyguard?" Even as he spat the words, he knew they were profoundly unfair. What had happened out there today wasn't Orias's fault. Orias would never have faltered in the midst of a battle. And if *he* had decided to go after Mactalde, however stupidly, he would not likely have failed to reach his enemy.

Still, the words poured out, and in their place the grief and the anger filled up his chest. "You think you can go from trying to stab me in the back one day to swaddling me in protective padding the next?"

Orias looked up. No doubt he had heard Chris's approach long before he had appeared. "You're no good to any of us dead."

"And what good have I done alive?"

Orias's hand stopped moving across the lion's head. "Lael sold their king's life for you today. I would think you'd want to live long enough to make it worth their while."

The wind swirled his exhales into cobwebs. "Lael didn't sell him. I did." He smacked himself in the chest. "Me!"

"If I hadn't stopped you, you would have landed in Koraudian hands. You wouldn't have accomplished anything."

"I could have tried."

Orias eased the lion aside. The firelight glittered in his eyes. "Some people say to try when there is no hope of success is faith. Others say it is madness."

"You're talking to me about faith? You're the one who abandoned everything your people believed in."

Orias looked away. "I abandoned faith because I thought I had no other choice. I have faith in you now because now there *is* no other choice."

"That's not faith. That's desperation."

"Makes little difference now." Orias rose and dusted the snow off his knees. "Sometimes a Gifted is worth more than a king. Tireus knew that."

Chris shook his head. "I don't accept that." He *couldn't* accept it. He turned away, hands on his hips and paced in front of the fire. He had to tell someone the truth. He had to just *say it*. Maybe that was why he had really come seeking Orias, not to accuse, but to confess.

He looked back. "The one thing I always swore I wouldn't do was walk away." He clenched his hands so hard his arms ached. "But that's what I did today. I walked away back there. I did the one thing I swore I wouldn't."

Orias's face might have been carved from white marble. The snow swirled between them, silent. He breathed in. "Sometimes," his voice was the lowest of rumbles, "we do the one thing we swear we won't. Sometimes we have to spend the rest of our lives trying to make it right." He held Chris's gaze a moment longer, then he turned away. He snapped his fingers at Dougal and disappeared into the trees.

Chris didn't follow him.

Chris wandered back through the knots of people crowding their fires. They had come away from Glen Arden with hardly anything more than the clothes on their backs. Most of them didn't even have a blanket to separate them from the snow.

Next to his own campfire, he found Eroll, watching something halfway across the camp. The duke glanced at him when he crouched beside the fire.

"You all right?" Chris asked.

The firelight cast a deceitful color onto Eroll's wan face. He wore a heavy coat and a fur hat. Unlike so many, he had a blanket as well.

He tried to smile, but the effect was somehow more painful than if he hadn't bothered. "My country has been shorn of her king. Can't say as I feel like a jig, even if I could."

Chris bowed his head and ran a hand over the back of his hair. "He died for me. I know that."

The shadow-flames flickered in the hollows of Eroll's face. "Now what are you going to do?"

There it was again: the challenge to take charge. Every muscle in his body was pleading for rest. The worlds were cracking apart above his very head. And he was suddenly the de facto leader of a ragged group of people on the verge of annihilation. He wasn't the best man for the job. There was no question of that. But who else was there? He was the Gifted. He was here. And he had to do *something*.

He looked up. "In the other world, my mother and my sister died when I was twelve. I couldn't protect them, I couldn't save them. And I couldn't save my dad from the bottle." The snow stung his face wherever it melted. "And maybe I can't save Lael. But I'm going to try. Somehow."

With a groan, Eroll rolled over onto his side, so he was facing Chris. "I'm not a great man myself, as you've probably figured out." His sad little smile almost reached his eyes. "But I'm not such a bad judge of men. And I'll tell you this. You've got off to a bally bad start around here."

Chris could only nod.

"But unlike most of us, you can *become* a great man. What you need to remember is you're only a piece in the puzzle. Nothing more.

The best and only thing you can do for us is to slow down and apply a little patience and wisdom to figuring out that all you have to do is hold up your *place* in that puzzle. You're so caught up in reacting, in trying to fix every tiny leak you run afoul of, that you're being swallowed in the flood."

Chris stood. "I can fight the leaks. I can't fight the flood."

"Stop reacting and start believing. Start surrendering."

"Start surrendering to what? Destiny?" His hands twitched at his sides. "I don't believe in destiny."

"Maybe you should start believing." Eroll looked back into the distance. "If for no other reason than so you'll have some kind of strength to give Allara."

Chris looked up through the spackling of snow. Twenty feet away, Esta stood next to Allara's bedroll.

He stepped toward her, then stopped and looked down at Eroll. "You've been a better friend to me than I deserve."

Eroll gave a little nod and lowered his head to the ground. "Go on with you."

Esta saw Chris approach and lurched toward him. Her face was red from the cold and splotched with tears. "I don't know what to do, what to say—"

At her feet, the mound of blankets trembled.

"Nobody ever does." He sank to his knees.

"She won't stop crying—"

"Would you?"

Esta backed away, into the falling snow, and left him with Allara. He laid his hand on the blanket. "Alla."

Throughout the night, he had caught glimpses of her riding in the darkness. The wind had swirled her coat and her dress, but inside the folds of her garments, her body had been unmovable. Her face could have been carved in stone, in ice. She had clung to her pain, hiding it deep down where it could not touch her or interfere with what had to be done. But she couldn't hold it forever.

Now she breathed in moans, deep and furious. Her body writhed with the sobs. She didn't respond to him, didn't even catch her breath. He pushed the blanket back from her face and pulled her up into his arms. She crushed her face against his chest, and her fingers clenched in the front of his coat.

He rocked her. "I'm sorry." His throat caved in around the words. "I'm sorry I didn't take his place."

Her grip tightened. Her arms slid around him and her fists clamped in the leather at his back.

"I couldn't get there in time." He laid his cheek against her head, and his own tears wet her hair.

Ghosts of snow swirled around them, dancing a silent waltz, bowing and sweeping to the hiss of the wind. Cold fingers scraped a rhythm against bare skin, beating, pounding, demanding they join their dirge dance.

He sat with her until his legs cramped beneath him, and her sobs finally slackened into shudders.

She rested her cheek against his chest. "What happens to us now?"

"We'll deal with tomorrow when it comes." He glanced across the camp. The snow fell through the trees and padded the world in silence.

Her breath trembled. "Tomorrow."

"It will be better than today." He stroked her snow-damp hair. "Has to be."

"There's a lullaby," she said. "The Cherazii sing a lullaby about tomorrow."

For a moment, he thought it was merely a comment, something that had flitted in and out of the weary night. But then the words lifted from her mouth. The notes were the simple, tragic flood of a folk song. Her voice was the color of a broken rose, husky and bruised.

"Don't cry tonight. There are tears enough, and tomorrow brings its own pain. So we laugh tonight, we sing tonight, for tomorrow we weep again."

The notes scattered on the wind, and the snow ghosts danced a little faster. She slid down into her bedroll, and he held her hand in his until she fell asleep.

50

COLD AND WET, Chris closed his eyes beside the camp fire—

—and opened them to find Chicago in the grip of a massive power outage. Word on the street was that lightning had fried at least two power plants and that most of the Midwest was floundering in electrical blindness. At ten in the morning, the streets were surprisingly full of people crowding in the cold. Some of them mobbed the city buildings, demanding answers no one could give. Others just followed along to keep from being alone.

He caught a taxi to the South Side and stopped several neighborhoods from his dad's. He got out to walk the rest of the way, just in case he was being tailed.

Less than a mile later, a car squealed around the corner. It shot past him and swerved to a stop, branding black rubber onto the asphalt.

His pulse spiked and he froze, dropping into a defensive crouch. If Kaufman had followed him after all, he was dead.

But the driver was a woman. Brooke. By comparison, he was actually glad to see her. He released his held breath and straightened.

She burst out of the driver's door, caught herself on the seatbelt, and ducked back inside to unbuckle it. She rounded the back of the car and threw her arms out to him. Tears shone against her mottled face.

His pulse sped up again. The last time he'd seen her, she had been spitting mad and too upset to even talk to him. "What's wrong?" He caught her elbows. "Mike? My dad? What is it?"

"I spent the night in the El!" she wailed.

He pushed her back. "What?"

"The power went out!" She started crying. "I was taking the El through the subway, since I didn't have a car. I was going to a movie with a friend, and then she was going to lend me her car." The tilt of her head indicated the station wagon behind her. "And the power went out! It was pitch black in the tunnels. Nobody could see to get home."

"Brooke . . ." She had always been neurotic, but since when was a power outage enough to conquer her overwhelming optimism? Had his little disappearing act with her Land Rover pushed her over the edge? He patted her arm awkwardly. "It's just a power outage. It happens."

"No." She swiped at her tears. "No, this was different. They couldn't get the backup generators running or anything. I heard on the radio the entire country's shut down!"

"Just the Midwest."

"The Midwest, the entire country, what difference does it make? This sort of thing is not supposed to happen!" A fresh batch of tears glossed her eyes. She trembled.

"Brooke, listen to me." He tried to infuse every ounce of confidence, along with a few ounces of sheer make-believe, into keeping his own voice calm. "It's going to be all right." He steered her around to the station wagon's passenger side. "I'm going to take you over to my dad's. He's got a gas stove. We'll get you some coffee, get you calmed down. Everything'll be fine."

She folded into the seat, then snatched at his sleeve. "What you said . . . about the weather—"

"What—you decided to believe me? After you chucked me into a mental ward?"

She dropped her face into her hands. "I don't know. I don't know what to believe!"

"All right, all right. We'll talk about it later. Just get in the car." He pushed her legs inside.

Mike answered the door. "Hey . . . What do you look so down about?" He glanced over Chris's shoulder to where Brooke was sniffling. "Oh, so you've made up? Would have been nice had you done that *before* you dragged me down to the loony bin yesterday."

"Ha ha." She whimpered a laugh. "You're so uproarious in the middle of a crisis."

He took in her tear-streaked face, and his eyebrows came together. "What's going on? What crisis?"

"It's all right. She got stuck in the subway last night." Chris led her inside by her coat sleeve. The house was cool and stuffy, and all the curtains had been drawn tight across the windows to keep out the cold. "Any trouble here?"

Mike shook his head. "Not except for the power."

Harrison, up to his chin in blankets, glared at them from the sleeper couch in the living room. "If we freeze to death I'd call that trouble enough."

Mike slammed the door. "Give it a rest already. It's August. Nobody's going to freeze to death."

"Yeah, that's right, it's August. And look at that, it's snowing *in August*!"

At the foot of the bed, Brooke stopped and stared at Harrison and the clutter of notebooks scattered on either side of his pillow. With the back of her hand, she rubbed her red nose. "You're the guy who got shot?" A spark of her old curiosity lifted her voice.

Harrison scowled. "Who are you?"

"She's a friend." Chris eased her toward the kitchenette. "Sort of."

His dad stepped into the doorway, drying a tumbler with a ragged blue towel.

Chris shot a glance from the glass to his dad's face. Paul's eyes were bloodshot, but clear. If his dad had actually made it through one whole night without a drink, that was more than Chris had ever given him credit for.

He pushed Brooke forward. "Dad, you remember Mike's sister Brooke?"

She gave him a listless wave. "Hi."

"She needs some coffee. In fact, we could all probably do with some if you've got enough."

"Sure, sure, I've got it." Paul let Brooke sidle between him and the island cabinet. He looked at Chris. "Black, right?"

"Yeah." He nodded, surprised his dad remembered. "Black would be great." He turned back to Mike. "Would you mind giving them a hand? I need to talk to Harrison real quick."

Mike lumbered across the living room. "I'll spend the rest of my life making coffee if it means you talking to him instead of me talking to him."

Chris stopped him as he tromped past. "What are you doing here anyway?"

"I came back after dropping Brooke off with her friend last night. I figured if one of those hoods came around here, your dad might need some help." He shrugged and followed Brooke into the kitchen.

Harrison drummed his fingers against the green notebook at his side. "So why the long face?"

Chris walked back around the bed and dropped into a chair next to the bedroom door. His elbows landed on his knees, and he rubbed his thumbs up the ridge of his nose. "I need your help." Harrison was the last person in the world he wanted to be taking advice from. But under the circumstances, he had no one else he could turn to who would understand the magnitude of what was going on. "Tireus is dead."

Harrison scrunched his face and gave his head a shake, not comprehending. "Dead."

"Mactalde killed him yesterday." Chris leaned his chin on his clamped fists. "And it gets worse. You heard about those earthquakes down in Texas? Well, one hit Glen Arden too."

Harrison's jaw dropped. "Earthquakes don't happen in the high country! What have you done to the worlds?"

"Glen Arden's destroyed. The Searcher and most of the high-ranking officials have evacuated." He closed his eyes. "I've got dozens of people sleeping out in the snow. The army's scattered, and Mactalde's huffing down our collars. I don't know what to do with them. I thought maybe we could find shelter with the Cherazii." That had been his one idea before falling asleep.

"Ha. Don't be brainless. The Cherazii will chase you out of their country with sword and hatchet and laugh at your bloodstained footprints as you go." Harrison scooted down until the blanket overlapped his chin. "The Cherazii aren't going to be interested in helping Gifted."

"Thanks to you." He couldn't keep the bitterness from his voice.

"You'll be thanking me sure enough if you'll just stop trying to think for yourself long enough to listen. Look at this." Harrison pushed the green notebook across the bed. "This is for you. This is all my secrets. Been working on them ever since I died in Lael. Tried to give 'em to you that first day you was at my house, but you were too stuffed full of your own ideas to listen, weren't you?"

Chris reached for the notebook and riffled through pages of notes and diagrams. "What kind of secrets?"

"Secrets that'll keep you from needing the Cherazii." Harrison reached for more of the notebooks piled beside his head. "There's lots of things you don't know about Lael, sonny. Things like the secrets in that big black fortress by the lake."

Chris halted the pages on a sketch of a castle above a waterfall. "Réon Couteau?" A chill touched the back of his neck. Maybe there was something in here he could use after all.

"That's right." Harrison gave the handful of notebooks a little heave toward Chris and settled deeper into the pillows. "And there's other things too. Things like maybe none of this unbalanced stuff is what you think it is. Maybe it's not what anybody thinks—except me."

Chris looked up. "What do you mean?"

"I mean it's a good thing you got me around to direct this crummy show, or you'd all be out in the cold, now wouldn't you?" He guffawed.

Chris set the notebook aside and leaned closer. "All right, I'm listening."

Before Harrison could respond, the front door smashed open.

Salvidore Flores had found them.

A noise-suppressed pistol coughed twice, and wood and plaster spattered in the kitchen. Flores kicked the door shut behind him, swiveled to face the couch, and ripped two shots into an explosion of chicken feathers.

Harrison half-rolled, half-fell off the couch. "You led him right to me!"

Chris hurled himself around the corner into the bedroom. Shots splintered the doorframe.

Brooke shrieked. "Sal! Stop, stop! *It's me!*" Her scream shot up the decibel scale into unintelligibility.

Chris lunged at his dad's nightstand, tore out the top drawer, and caught up the Glock 35 Paul had owned since his days on the force. He ran into the adjoining bathroom, chambering the gun as he went, and crashed through the hall door into the kitchenette. The Glock's sights found Flores in the kitchen doorway, and Chris pulled the trigger.

The hammer clicked against empty steel. He pulled the trigger again and again. Empty.

"Drop that." The long barrel of Flores's pistol pointed at Chris's chest. Above the gun, his eyes were cold and steady.

Chris's hands tightened around the useless gun.

Flores took one step, grabbed the Glock, and prodded his pistol into the flesh beneath Chris's chin. "Everyone, get over against the counter, back of the kitchen. You want to keep him alive, you do as I say."

Paul pulled a fallen chair out of the way and started backing up. A whimpering Brooke clung to him. Mike caught Chris's eyes, his eyebrows a hard line across his face. Chris gave a tiny nod, and Mike promptly backed right over the top of a chair and fell flat on his back.

Brooke yelped, and Flores twitched the pistol in Mike's direction. That was all Chris needed. He twisted back into the hallway and grabbed the first weapon that came to hand: an old cast-iron floor lamp.

"Hey!" his dad shouted, and the gun started coughing again.

Chris made it back to the kitchen just as Flores turned in search of him. Before the little man could bring the gun up to Chris's chest, Chris swung the lamp. The heavy glass shade smashed into Flores's face, and he staggered. Chris came through the doorway and battered the lamp into the man's stomach. Flores's upper body snapped forward. Air rushed from his mouth, and blood spritzed from his smashed face. He toppled to the floor, and Mike landed a knee in the middle of his back.

"Call the cops." Chris dropped the lamp onto the linoleum and kicked the pistol away from Flores's limp hand. He found Brooke clamping her cell phone to her head with one hand and trying to tear open his dad's bloody sleeve with the other.

Chris's heart stuttered. He crossed the kitchen, pushed Brooke's flailing hand out of the way, and ripped the sleeve all the way down.

His dad breathed through his teeth. "It's nothing. Nothing, don't worry."

Chris found the hole, grabbed the last clean towel out of the drawer, and applied pressure. "Went through your triceps." He shot a glance at Brooke. "Tell them to send an ambulance."

She was crying again. "I know, I know!"

Mike looked up from Flores and scanned Paul's wound. "You're one lucky dude. You stepped right in front of that shot."

Chris looked at his dad. The eyes staring back were steady—the kind of steady he hadn't seen from Paul in forever. The kind of steady he saw from Worick every single day.

"He'd have shot me in the back," Chris said.

His dad shrugged. "Guess I have some reflexes left after all."

"Got rope or something to tie him up with?" Mike asked.

Chris led his dad to a chair. "If he wakes up, I'll break his skull." He looked into the living room. "Harrison? Everything all right?"

Brooke's trembling hands had to try twice to close her phone. "They're coming. She said they're coming. I don't understand. Why is this happening? I know Sal! Why would he try to kill me?"

Chris stepped out from between her and his dad. "Here. Hold this for me."

As soon as she had a grip on the bloody towel, he sidestepped Flores's body into the living room. "Harrison? Flores is out of commission. Everybody's okay."

A moan floated across the living room.

Chris darted around the edge of the bed and ripped through the pile of blankets and cushions to find Harrison's chest flooding blood over everything. The shag carpet absorbed the sticky wetness like a sponge.

He thrust the heel of his hand into the wound. "Call the ambulance back! He's bleeding to death!"

Feathers from the exploded pillows spiraled above the bed. They mired wherever they touched the expanding sheen of red that coated Harrison's chest and Chris's arms.

Harrison arched his back. His mouth gaped, his breath rasping. "Mactalde . . . not . . . Mactalde . . ."

Then his eyes drifted shut, and the rattle of his breathing was all Chris could hear.

The hospital glowed in the falling darkness. Thanks to its backup generators, it was the only building on the street that had electricity. Even the traffic lights weren't working.

Chris entered through the main doors and headed up the halls. Mike walked behind, silent except for the jingle of his key ring on his finger. On the second floor, Chris let himself into his dad's room.

The fingers protruding from Paul's elastic sling trembled with the need of a drink. His face was twisted, gaunt, as though the bones had all receded from his skin. But his eyes met Chris's with a quick flash.

"Harrison?" Chris asked.

Brooke huddled in a chair at the foot of the bed. "They're supposed to come tell us as soon as he's out of surgery." The red tear streaks had faded and left her face pale and strained.

Paul raised the bed to a sitting position. "How'd it go with the police?"

Chris leaned his shoulder against the window. Cold from the glass seeped through his coat sleeve. "They're not going to do a thing. They'll keep Flores, but I don't have sufficient evidence against Kaufman, so there's no way they're going to divert men for protection right now."

"The police station was insane," Mike said. "Between the weather and the power outage, the whole city is going nuts."

Chris turned to his dad. "You'll have to stay in the hospital awhile. You and Harrison will be safe here."

Brooke slumped deeper into the chair. "I don't understand. None of this makes sense."

Chris pushed away from the window and balled his hands inside his coat pockets. "Kaufman's after me, not you guys. I'm going off the radar. I'm getting another hotel. This is the last time I endanger any of you."

A petite blonde nurse knocked on the half-opened door and entered the room. Exhaustion pulled at her face. "You're all friends of Harrison Garnett?"

"More or less," Mike said.

Chris stepped forward. "He's out of surgery?"

"Yes."

"And?" He held his breath. He needed Harrison alive. He needed questions answered. He needed help.

The nurse clasped her hands. She shook her head.

Brooke choked.

"I'm sorry." The nurse looked at Chris. "He lost too much blood. The damage was irreparable."

He stared past her. One more dead. Without a word, he squeezed by her into the hall.

"Hey, bro," Mike called. "Where are you going?"

He didn't slow. "To sleep."

His first stop was to fetch Harrison's bloodstained notebooks from the backseat of Mike's Bug. From there, he hiked down the sidewalks to the nearest hotel. He locked himself into the room, sat on the bed, and started flipping through the notebooks, reading by the light of a flashlight between his teeth.

He didn't have time to read them all. It would be morning soon in Lael, and he had to get back. They would need an early start. But there had to be answers in here. Harrison had kept things from him. He'd been hinting at secrets ever since they met.

Chris stopped on the drawing of Réon Couteau. What had Harrison meant when he said Chris didn't know everything about the black fortress above the lake? His eyes snagged on two words:

Subterranean Caverns.

51

BEHIND CHRIS, A gray sun lit the sky. Just as soon as he'd returned to Lael, he'd gotten the people onto their horses and started them running. Their only chance right now was to reach the southern shores of Ori Réon by nightfall. If they could find a ship, they could cross the lake and reach Réon Couteau in another ten to twelve hours. Even if Mactalde had taken the city, they would at least be able to find shelter nearby. Once these people were taken care of, they could come up with some sort of a plan for reclaiming Réon Couteau.

It was a tiny hope and he knew it, but for three hours he'd kept them running. And for three hours, the red glare of Koraudian uniforms dogged them through the snow. Now, deep in the hills, the Koraudians faced off across a canyon from what was left of Chris's forces.

A metal-magnified shout echoed across the distance. "One more time I will say this! One last time, and then my mercy will evaporate as though it had never been!"

Chris dismounted his lathered horse. "What game is this now?"

On the far hillside, well out of rifle range, but within plain view, row upon row of Koraudian soldiers stood waiting. The speaker was invisible within their ranks, but the voice was plainly Mactalde's.

"We saw the quality of your mercy yesterday!" Chris's dry throat cracked around his voice. Mactalde wouldn't be able to make out his words, even if he could hear them.

All around, the people milled uneasily.

Allara led Rihawn up behind him and traded him his reins for a waterskin. Deep lines cut through her face. "Why is he stopping us like this? It makes no sense."

At her side, Quinnon ground his teeth. "He's proving he can finish us off at his leisure."

"I have had enough of this war," Mactalde shouted. "I have had enough of Lael. I wish to go home to Koraud and live in peace. What I want is justice. What I want is the Gifted!"

All across the face of the hill, no one spoke. The Glen Arden evacuees shifted their weight and exchanged glances.

"Give this one life into my hand, and I will spare everything else. I swear it."

"Never!" Worick's voice boomed across the chasm and ricocheted against the far hill. "You're asking the impossible!"

Murmurs passed back and forth. The people had seen Mactalde's ruthlessness yesterday. They knew what he was capable of, and they had every right to fear for their own lives.

"Come, come," Mactalde said. "If every last man of you truly wishes to sacrifice himself for those who brought such destruction on you in the first place, I have no objections. I admire bravery. But I also admire wisdom. I will give you until sunset to make up your minds. Perhaps your leader will decide to be generous and prove how much he cares for you. Perhaps."

"This war is not over!" Chris shouted.

Mactalde must have heard that at least, because his laughter wafted across the chasm. "If you refer to any misguided hope of retreating to Réon Couteau, it would no doubt be kind of me to inform you that, already, my men have secured it."

Among all the red tabards, a white coat flickered.

Chris's gut clenched. Had Crofton Steadman thrown in with Mactalde? Nateros's attempts to undermine Lael's monarchy had already aided Mactalde more than once. Why *not* throw in with him? The enemy of an enemy was a friend and all that.

Steadman's voice floated across the canyon. "Why is it that ever since the Searcher's witchcraft summoned this latest Gifted to our world, destruction and death have hailed down upon us?"

The color drained from Allara's face. "Kill Mactalde and it will stop!"

Steadman continued. "Do you hear the lies they spin to convince you to continue in bondage to their superstitions and sorceries? They want you to sacrifice your lives in pursuit of their devotion to a twisted paradigm! The witch and her minion—they have brought these tragedies upon us! Why should you suffer for their sins? Shall we not cast them out for the judgment they have brought upon their own heads?"

Chris could almost see the curl of Steadman's scarred lip. No doubt he gloried in the sufferings of the Searcher and the Gifted.

The people listened in rapt silence. A change flitted over their features. They were listening. More than that, they were *hearing* what Steadman was telling them, and in their desperation and fear, maybe they were even believing it. They cast sidelong glances at Chris and Allara and whispered among themselves.

Mactalde raised his voice again. "Master Redston, didn't I tell you I would recognize you as the true leader of Lael? I've even cleared the path for you! Tireus can no longer impede your destiny. So take it! Seize it with both hands! Act like the leader these people need and give yourself into my hand."

The people shot furtive, wide-eyed glances at Chris, and their murmurs increased.

These people had no defenses and no hopes. They would all die tonight. Some of them to the cold, most of them to the sword. And wouldn't it be his fault, once again? What choice did he have besides surrender? He dropped the waterskin at his feet and reached back to take his reins.

Allara clamped her hand on his arm. "Think. You can't do this. The worlds are breaking. If you surrender yourself to him to save these people, you condemn the lives of everyone! Mactalde is the one who has to die."

He stared across the canyon. "What if it's not true? What if there's nothing I can do to stop the breaking? What if the only thing I can do for anyone here is what I do right now?"

If he turned and walked away from Mactalde, he was sentencing these people to death, and he knew it. He would have to live with that for the rest of his life. How much easier would it be to gallop straight into the Koraudian lines in exchange for at least the possibility that Mactalde would keep his word?

Sacrificing himself for the immediate good was what he wanted. Staving off the hollow agony of guilt was what he needed. But, in a sense all its own, wasn't that walking away too?

"Chris . . ." Her eyes pled with him. "Don't do it."

He couldn't outgun Mactalde, couldn't even try anymore. But maybe, just maybe, he could outwit him. He had one chance here, and he wasn't about to walk away until he had given it his best shot.

He moved her hand from his sleeve. "No, I won't surrender. Not yet anyway." He turned to mount. "Send somebody to find Orias Tarn."

Allara shook her head. "I don't understand. Where are you going?"

"To the Cherazii."

Orias rode with Chris, up the hills, into the deep forests. This plan would never succeed. The Cherazii were a people of honor and justice, not mercy. And even had they been otherwise, they had been betrayed once too often to remember it. Had not Orias himself betrayed them?

But he rode with Chris anyway. If the Gifted failed, the Laelers would undoubtedly sacrifice him to Mactalde's demands. In their fear, too many of the fine gentleman and high nobles of Lael were falling under the spell of Nateros. The Gifted would die, and the hope of victory would die with him.

And Orias would never find redemption.

So he led Chris back through the rough hill country, five hours south to the nearest of the Cherazii's transient settlements, a camp used by those emigrating from Koraud.

They were within half a league when the rustling he'd been hearing for the past hour materialized into a pair of Cherazii sentinels: Cabahr Laith and a red-haired youth.

Cherazii protocol demanded a civil exchange of greetings between Cherazii and strangers found wandering near a settlement. But before Orias could speak, the youth launched himself at Chris's horse. His leap lifted him almost to eye level with Chris, and his vambrace-clad forearm hammered into Chris's chest and felled him from his horse.

The last spark of Orias's hope blinked into darkness. He galloped to Chris's side. "*Forid!*" Enough.

Laith's lip curled. "Orias Tarn."

The red-haired warrior thrust his knee between Chris's shoulders. He rifled Chris's clothing and cast aside whatever weapons he found.

Pitch clambered halfway over Orias's shoulder. "*Podd! Eck sit ti Retteloj.*" Stop! He's the Gifted.

Laith looked at Chris. "So you're alive yet." The angles and planes of his face betrayed nothing.

But Orias recognized the anger in his eyes. The last time he and Chris had seen Laith had been that long ago day when the Koraudians had massacred Laith's caravan—and Orias had corrupted the Gifted into resurrecting Mactalde. Of all the Cherazii they might have met today, Laith was the one most likely to kill them on sight.

Laith nudged his horse forward. "What business brings our noble Gifted so far into the hills? Did you not know this is Cherazii country?"

Already, the back part of Orias's brain, where his battle fire never completely died down, was charting tactics and identifying the best places to defend and attack.

The youth wrenched Chris to his feet.

Chris spat snow and mud. "I've come in search of an alliance with your people."

Laith barked a laugh. "The only reason I don't kill you right now is because there are more than just a few of us who deserve to watch you fall."

Chris pulled his shoulders back against the hands that restrained him. "Do you think I'd be here if I didn't want to make things right? We only have one chance left—all of us. Take me to your elders, that's all I ask. If they decide to execute me, I'll submit. But first I need them—and you—to listen to me."

For a long windblown moment, Laith watched the Gifted.

Chris stood in the face of almost certain death and obviously knew it, but he never flinched. Any Cherazim would admire that.

"Perhaps we will listen," Laith said. "Perhaps not. But I will take you to Elder Averr." Again, he looked at Orias, but that glance offered no touch of admiration. "Both of you."

They rode the rest of the way to the camp, and as they entered beneath the stone arch, Orias's stomach lurched. How many years since he had ridden the streets of a true Cherazii settlement? The enclaves in Koraud had mimicked the ways of the homeland, but until right now he hadn't realized how much the Cherazii had abandoned in their self-imposed exile.

Dozens of stone longhouses, organized in concentric circles, rode the hilltop, but the heffron trees hid all but the nearest. Most of the walls and roofs had been packed with sod, and beneath the snow, what remained of the summer grass embraced the houses and joined them with the hill itself.

Ornaments hung from every eave: azure birdhouses, scarlet wind chimes, yellow and purple pennons, and candle globes in every imaginable hue. Between the houses, the circular garden plots would normally have bloomed with flowers and vegetables, but now they lay crushed and barren beneath the snowfall. Dogs and Rievers and the occasional donkey ran through the streets.

The people rose from their work and watched, without expression, as Laith led his prisoners through the streets to the circular plaza at the camp's center.

He stopped in front of the elder's longhouse. "Elder Averr, I bring you traitors for judgment by the people!"

The elder's grandson ran through the house's indigo door and brought back his grandfather. Seragon Averr entered the snow glare and watched with only the slightest crook of an eyebrow as Chris and Orias, along with Pitch and Raz, were pulled from their horses and shoved to their knees in the mud-swirled snow.

"It's all right," Pitch whispered. "It's going to be all right."

Raz peered around. "Like rotted eggs it is."

Averr surveyed them without so much as a fine gray wrinkle moving in his face. He wore his hair in two white braids over his shoulders and covered his head with a tricorn cockaded in the same red as his cape. His shoulders and chest were still broad enough to impressively fill the blue wool of his knee-length tunic, and four short-handled stilettos rode in sheaths on both sides of his boots.

He crossed his arms and slid his hands into his opposing sleeves. "So I find myself once again face to face with the Gifted."

Chris tilted his head, confused.

Averr stepped forward. "You remember. The day of the great battle at the Aiden River. We met at the base of the Karilus Wall. I told you I awaited proof of the new Gifted's worthiness."

Recognition flickered in Chris's eyes. "And did you find proof?"

Averr cocked his head. "Yes." He glanced at Laith. "I have heard the eyewitnesses. I have no doubt that you, with the traitorous aid of one of our own, did the forbidden. Do you deny it?"

"No, I do not." Chris met his gaze. "And I am willing to submit myself to whatever punishment you deem fit."

Averr's eyebrow lifted. "This is why you ride to find us?"

"Not exactly. I've come to ask for your help."

More than a few Cherazii broke their impassivity to murmur amongst themselves.

Laith prodded Chris's shoulder with the haft of his poleax. "Why would we help you?"

Chris sat back on his heels, head up, and addressed them all. "I'm here because I'm out of options. We all are. The worlds are breaking."

Laith shook his head. "The Cherazii want no alliance with a traitor and a thief." He opened his fist and revealed the creamy pulse of the Orimere. "He carries it as if it were a common bartering rock."

Averr claimed the stone and looked at Chris. "How did you come by this?"

Orias stiffened. Laith already knew, of course. They all knew. But before they could legally punish Orias, they required definitive proof he had played an active role in Mactalde's return. They needed Chris to hand him over to them.

Raz scowled. "The Orimere has always belonged to the Gifted. Why shouldn't he have it?"

Pitch murmured a shushing breath. "Don't."

The violet scar that threaded Laith's cheek lay perfectly straight. "It is the Cherazii's right to provide the Orimere to the Gifted. But we have not provided it to *you*, I think. The Orimere is never passed on without a great ceremony. We have had no such ceremony since your crossing." He tilted Chris's head back with the tip of his poleax. "The Orimere was stolen."

Chris held his ground. "Not by me."

"Who then?"

Pitch reached over to grip Orias's fingers.

Chris shook his head.

"You protect a traitor," Averr said. "You think that gives us reason to trust you?"

The cold air burned Orias's lungs. Chris was trying to protect him, the God of all knew why. But in protecting him, he would doom himself as well. Couldn't he see that?

If Orias knelt here in silence, if he kept his words buried under his tongue, he would be worse than a traitor and a heretic. What kind of coward accepted protection from the hand of a man whom he had already betrayed once? If his own life must be the price for the Gifted's freedom, then so be it.

He lifted his hand to his collar. "If you seek the traitor—" he unbuttoned his coat and pulled down his jerkin to bare his shoulder, "—then here he is."

When he had agreed to Mactalde's terms, they had marked him forever as a minion in their service. Tattooed in red against the milk white of his skin, the unfurled wings and cawing mouth of the Koraudian Blood Eagle bruited his false allegiances.

Silence roared through the piazza. Chris closed his eyes. But he must know the truth was their only chance. Wasn't *that* why Orias had come with him, in spite of everything? To convince his people to aid the Gifted in a final battle?

"Orias Tarn." Averr's chin dipped in recognition. "I heard the rumors, but I chose not to believe. You have fought with the enemy?"

"Aye, I have fought with the enemy."

Behind him, someone swore. The haft of a pike punched him in the kidney and ripped the air from his lungs. Someone else hit him upside the head.

Raz leapt to his feet. "He did what he had to!"

Laith left his poleax against Chris's throat as he addressed Orias. "And now you ride with the Gifted. What are we supposed to gather from that? That you are a traitor twice over? Or that there is so little difference between the Gifted and the Koraudians that in betraying your people you serve them both alike?"

Orias pushed himself upright and burned the pain away from his mind. "I have done what I have done. I am the one who deserves to be punished. The Gifted fights for Lael, and in fighting for Lael, he fights for the Cherazii. If we do not help, we doom our own lives. Even more, we doom the traditions we have spent our existence protecting."

"Twenty years ago," Averr said, "we were betrayed by a Gifted, and we thought no blacker treachery could darken the pages of our history. Perhaps we were wrong."

"That's not true." With both hands, Pitch held onto Orias's fingers. "Orias has not betrayed you. He has come back. You see?"

Averr shrugged.

What Orias had done, he had done. And what he would suffer for it, he would suffer. That was the Cherazii way.

Averr turned and paced a few steps in front of Chris. "What is it you think you could do against Koraud, even with us at your back? Mactalde has all the odds on his side. We have nothing left with which to fight him."

With his head leaned back on the end of Laith's poleax, Chris could only follow Averr with his eyes. "What if we did?"

Laith hacked. "Once Mactalde's taken Réon Couteau, you'll never shake him loose from behind those walls."

Averr's pacing carried him past Chris, and he turned to walk behind the prisoners. "Not even an army could conquer Réon Couteau. And a siege of attrition would take years. There's not a single way in that won't bring certain death."

"Certain death for an army maybe. But not for me." Chris raised his voice. "We can bring the fortress down around Mactalde's ears."

Pitch stared. "How?"

"I'm going to blow it up." His voice deepened. "There's a secret built into Réon Couteau. It's either a weakness or a strength, depending on who's exploiting it. And, when we're ready, it's going to be a weakness."

Laith pulled the poleax away and exchanged a glance with Averr as the elder circled around Orias and back into view. "What are you talking about?"

"I'm talking about what's behind the waterfall. What's beneath the castle. Caverns that go all the way back into the cliff and undermine the entire fortress."

Something that might almost have been hope tickled at the back of Orias's mind. The Cherazii histories contained rumors, legends almost, passed down from those who had built the fortress. They told of caverns carved by the water, caverns honeycombing the cliff beneath the castle.

"You know how to access the caverns?" he asked.

Chris watched Averr. "I have a map."

"You have a map." Averr stopped in front of Chris and motioned Laith back a step. "You have a map, Master Gifted, and you have courage. Perhaps you even have honor, in spite of everything. I can't say that with any certainty, but what I can say is I believe you when you tell me the worlds are breaking." Above, silent lightning veined the swirl of clouds. "You are not innocent, but you are repentant. And I believe you are the only one who can mend what you have broken. And for that reason alone I release you to your fate—whatever it may be."

Chris eased to his feet. "But you won't come with me? You won't fight?"

"I think you had best take your life as gift enough and run from here."

He hesitated. "What about Orias?"

Averr turned to Orias. He did not hide his disgust. "Tell me, Orias Tarn, will you willingly bow your neck to the blade of justice?"

Pitch jumped up. "No! You don't understand!"

Orias had awaited this from the moment Chris had asked him to come as his guide. The words almost brought a sense of relief. He would atone for his great mistake, and, after that, it would be over at last.

"I come," he said.

Averr motioned to the Cherazim behind Orias. "Bind him."

Hands seized him and twisted his arms behind his back. He didn't fight. So long as Chris was free and so long as a chance remained he might kill Mactalde, that was all he had left to care about.

Chris accepted his chewser and sword. His thumb clicked on the hydraulics, and the blue-lit buzz filled the piazza. He didn't raise the gun, just let it hang at his side.

"Let him go." His words were without threat. He had to know he had no chance of fighting and winning here. He ignited his firearm only to get their attention.

Laith laughed. "Don't renew my opinion of your folly. You ask to flout Cherazim law and still expect us to pardon you?"

"I expect you to look beyond yourselves. Orias made a mistake. So did I."

"Aye, you did at that. And now you stand in our midst and demand exemption for a traitor?"

"I'm not leaving without him."

"Go," Orias said. "This is now between me and my people."

Chris faced Averr. "I need him."

The elder stared back. "You need a traitor?"

Pitch scrambled to stand at Chris's side. "The Gifted belongs to me. I found him. And I belong to Orias. We must be together, we must help each other."

"The worlds are breaking," Chris said. "King Tireus is dead. Lael is staggering with its losses, and Mactalde is calling for my head even as we speak."

"Then give it to him," Laith said. "What do we care?"

"You should care because . . . you're a piece in a larger puzzle."

The Cherazii regarded him in silence.

"Let him go." Chris flicked off the hydraulics and holstered his pistol. "And if you change your minds and decide you want to raise your steel in the greatest battle of your lives, then you'll follow me to Réon Couteau."

A minute passed, a long, interminable minute, and then Averr turned to the men who held Orias. "Let him go." He looked at Orias, and something in his mouth quirked. "For the sake of your misguided friend, I give you back into the hand of the God of all. I pray whatever death He metes to you will be worthy of your sins."

Orias's hands fell free. They were releasing him? Because the Gifted had asked them? Never had he expected that. A single breath burst from his mouth.

Someone forced his reins into his fingers. He mounted, his joints like wooden hinges, and he rode through the ranks to join Chris. In silence, they left the camp through the archway.

"They will not fight so long as I am with you," he said. "You're a fool not to leave me here."

Chris faced the trail before them. "I can't leave a man to die a traitor when I am guilty of the same crimes."

52

ALLARA WATCHED THE sky. All day, wind-whipped clouds of green and purple had hidden the sun. Now, the passage into night was marked only by the gray film fading into shadows—and by the Koraudians gathering at the base of the canyon. Mactalde's time limit was up. And with it, Lael's only hope of respite.

In the back of the makeshift camp, a woman wailed and voices tangled into unintelligibility. A shiver racked Allara's body. Only a remnant of men remained loyal to the Gifted. Most were too fearful to see beyond the Koraudians across the canyon. If Chris returned in the next ten minutes, they would cast him to Mactalde without a second thought.

Her hand trembled, and she closed it into a fist.

"The time has come." The wind carried Mactalde's voice to the center of the camp. "What is your choice?"

Quinnon trotted to her side and dismounted. "As if even a gambler could like the choices he's given us."

"The Gifted in my hand and life in yours?" Mactalde shouted into his loudhailer. "Or death for yourselves and the Gifted alike?"

Denegar had ridden to the edge of the ravine to give the formal answer. The people crowded around him, and their shouts rose above his. "Life! We want life! Have mercy!"

Denegar's soldiers forced the people back, but they could not stop the shouts.

Denegar planted his hand on his thigh and spoke through a makeshift loudhailer someone had manufactured from a thin strip of hammered plate armor. "We will have nothing to do with you, sir-rah! And we spit upon your mercy. Are we not the sovereign people of Lael? Who are you to make demands upon us, and who are we to listen to them?"

"I am the conqueror, and you are the conquered. I should think that rather obvious. Where is the Gifted? Let him speak for himself. Let me hear from his own mouth he sentences these people to death."

"He's not here!" Dozens of voices carried the words. "He's gone!"

Allara clenched her hands together. It had looked badly when Chris and Orias had galloped out of the camp. Only those most loyal to him had not been shaken by the sight of his retreat.

"Your vaunted Gifted has run away? How poetic."

"It is not our fault!" someone screamed. "We would have given him to you!"

"Nay!" Denegar reined his horse away from his post and turned to face the people. "We would not have! We would have fought to the deaths beside him!"

Worick Bowen climbed onto a broken cart. "We have no hope of victory apart from the Gifted! And can any of you wish to live with-out victory?"

"We wish to *live*!" a woman shouted.

"Unfortunately," Mactalde said, "I am a man of my word. And since you have not presented me the Gifted, you leave me no choice."

Someone clambered onto a pile of boulders. "We'll give you the Searcher!"

Allara recoiled.

"Well, then," Mactalde said. "Perhaps you're not as ungenerous as I thought. I'll take her."

Quinnon snarled and snatched his sword. "The rotted devil you will."

"No!" Denegar shouted. "She is not part of the bargain!"

"You're right," Mactalde said. "Which is why I will give you an additional forty-eight hours to fulfill my original terms. Consider the Searcher the price of an extension."

Allara stopped breathing. All around her, the hillside caved in. Some of these people had been waiting for her head for twenty years. Now they descended with the howls of hungry wolfhounds. The few loyal men and women, most of the remaining Guardsmen among them, threw themselves against the flood, but they were sand in a tidal wave.

She ran, trusting Quinnon to cover her back. Nearby, Rihawn danced at the end of his tether, his eyes edged with white. Someone—Esta perhaps—screamed. Hands closed around her arms. She ducked forward and jerked away. Her coat tore.

Behind her, Quinnon bellowed. A gunshot blasted through her hearing. Fingers clawed at her, tearing at her hair, wrenching her limbs. She ripped free and reached Rihawn's side. He tried to dodge, but she managed to grab her saddlebow. Up and over, she lifted herself just far enough to close her fingers on her sword hilt.

Hands clamped around her arms, her waist, her legs and hauled her backwards. She dragged the estoc free of the saddle scabbard and levered her arm back as hard as she could. The hilt smashed into bone, and one set of hands fell away. But others replaced them. Someone grabbed her wrist, and someone else tore away the sword. She writhed in their arms and saw Quinnon fall to a man with a stave.

"No!" she screamed.

They had her on her feet now. They forced her arms behind her back and tied them. She twisted her body down and away, and her shoulders nearly exploded from their sockets. A brawny man hit her across the face. Blood welled behind her teeth, and the world tilted.

Despite the best efforts of her uncle and Worick Bowen, she was dragged down the edge of the ravine. At the bottom, a Koraudian delegation, headed by Glelarn Rotoss, met her.

Rotoss gripped her hair and forced back her head. "Well, well, the lioness at bay." He nodded to one of his soldiers. "Truss her behind your horse."

While he held her, the Koraudians bound her hands in front of her and leashed her behind a horse. He thrust her head farther back, until the vertebrae in her neck ground against each other.

His gaze rose to her Laeler captors. "The Gifted had best arrive at the gates of Réon Couteau within two days, or you're all dead men. You and your wee ones. Don't forget." He propelled Allara forward, and she staggered out of his grasp. "Tell them, your highness. Tell them they're doomed unless they listen. Doomed just like you."

She swiped her bloody chin against her shoulder. "Better doomed than a faithless traitor!"

"Lucky for them, they're not so daft as you." He turned his horse and spurred back up the hill to the Koraudian lines. "Move!"

The horse to which she was tethered yanked her forward, almost off her feet, and she wrapped both hands around the line and used the animal's momentum to lengthen her running strides. Rotoss wasn't likely to wait should she fall.

The Koraudian troops were already withdrawing when Rotoss's party reached the opposite hill. She caught only a glimpse of Mactalde's pennon flickering ahead before her captor fell in at the rear. A single company remained behind to keep watch on the Laelers. It would be more than enough.

They'd taken Allara.

Chris's heart thudded painfully. Well after the sunset deadline, his sweated horse arrived back on the canyon lip where he had left Allara and the others.

Almost everyone had fled. He'd expected that, or maybe even worse—when he'd allowed himself to consider it at all. But he hadn't expected *this*. This changed everything.

How could he even attempt to blow up the palace if she were inside it? He paced through the snow, back and forth, back and forth.

Worick watched him pace. His shoulders sagged, but his eyes were still alert. "Mactalde's using her as bait. You have to know that. If you surrender yourself to free her, he'll kill both of you."

Chris stopped with his back to his father and stared into the trees where what was left of the army had gathered. Less than a hundred Guardsmen and a battered remnant of Glen Ardeners remained to fight.

He hung his hands on his hips. "What other choice do we have? This is a free pass to meet Mactalde face to face."

Orias watched him from the shadow of the trees. "Bound and at swordpoint? That's daft, and you know it. A Riever'd have a better chance in a den of Koraudian lions."

Chris scrubbed a hand up his forehead. Without the Cherazii's support, he would never survive facing Mactalde's troops in the open field. His only chance was to lower the odds.

He turned to face the people. "Nobody says I have to play by his rules."

Quinnon, his forehead seeping red through a bandage, stalked along the camp's perimeter. He hadn't said a word since Chris had arrived.

"What if I call Mactalde out for a duel?" Chris said.

From where he crouched beside a nearby fire, Denegar shook his head. "Why should he agree to that? He has all the advantage right now and no reason to risk himself."

"What if he didn't have the advantage?"

Orias stepped into the firelight. "You mean blowing up the palace."

He ran both hands through his hair. "I don't know. I don't know about that anymore. Maybe not that. Not now that Allara's in there." He clenched his fists in his hair. What was he saying? That he would sacrifice the whole mission, the *only* mission, on the off chance she was in that castle? What if she wasn't? What if Mactalde had taken her to Thyra Junction? What if they abandoned the whole plan for no good reason?

And what if she *was* there, and he went through with it? His body tightened. He couldn't do that. They were *both* supposed to be around after this thing was over. Wasn't that what he had promised her? Except, if he didn't go through with this, it was possible *no* one would be around afterwards.

Tireus's voice rumbled through his head: *Sooner or later, every leader learns sacrifices must be made.* He threw back his head and stifled a soul-deep groan.

His father cleared his throat. "What do you mean blow up Réon Couteau? How? We've no explosives, no padar, nothing. Barely a sword apiece among us."

"You're jolly well cracked," Denegar said. "You'd never get close enough to plant anything. The carabineers and the bombardiers would pick you off from the ramparts."

He took a breath and turned to face them. "The cliff beneath the palace is riddled with caverns, and I know where the entrances are. We can set the charges there."

The survivors murmured. For the first time in days, a faint spark of hope and excitement lit faces.

"And what about Allara?" Quinnon's voice grated across the clearing.

Chris's stomach rolled over on itself once more. He tightened his abdomen and forced it to stop. He *had* to do this. He had no choice. Allara would be the first to agree. He would do it, and he would pray she was anywhere but in that castle.

He met Quinnon's gaze and held it. "This is what she would want."

In the flicker of the firelight, Quinnon seemed almost to tremble. He had made it clear, over and over, that his loyalty was to Allara's safety and not to her cause. But surely he must know that if the cause died, so would she. Surely he must know how much it cost Chris to follow through with this plan when there was even the possibility of her being harmed because of it.

Finally, Quinnon's scraggle-bearded chin dipped. He was nodding. He was agreeing. They had no other choice right now, and they both knew it.

Chris started across the camp to where his horse was tethered. He stopped at the animal's hindquarters and opened his saddlebag. "Mactalde gave us forty-eight hours to comply with his demands. If we leave tonight and move cross-country, we might be able to reach the southern shore of Ori Réon by morning. If we can get a ship from there, we can cross the lake to Réon Couteau in ten to twelve hours. We could be there by tomorrow night."

His father followed him to stand at the horse's haunch. "Even if we can get in under the palace, we've nothing to use to bring it down."

Chris pulled his hand from his saddlebag, and into the darkness floated the white glow of the Orimere. "We will by tomorrow night."

Allara's guards hauled her into the bowels of Réon Couteau. In the damp darkness of the dungeon, they untied her bleeding wrists and shoved her against the stones. She spun back around, wanting to reach them before they closed the door. She wanted to fight them, to kill just one of them before they killed her.

The barred door clanged shut, and a new globe lent its strength to light the cavern. Mactalde, followed by a soldier bearing the globe, entered the narrow corridor.

He smiled. "The princess Allara." In front of the door, he tugged off his gauntlet. "We've long been opponents in this game, have we not? But I believe this is the first time since my return we've had the pleasure of meeting."

She glowered. "The only thing that would give me pleasure is a span of steel through your heart."

"Certainly you must have put your talents for hatred to a better use during the years I've been gone?" He bounced his glove against his bare palm. "And what about my friend Mr. Redston? He's done you some rather bad turns, hasn't he? I should think you'd want to reserve at least a particle of ill will for his particular benefit."

She lifted her chin. Her teeth ached where one of her own people had hit her.

"Perhaps you'll be pleased to know," Mactalde said, "that in bringing you here, I'm giving you a prime opportunity of revenging yourself upon your unruly Gifted. This time tomorrow, you may spit in his eye, if you so choose." He stepped closer to the door, until the bars framed his face. His voice dropped to a whisper. "I'd even give you the honor of stabbing your span of steel into his heart, except, you see, it's become rather important to me to do it myself."

She held her breath. "It is not an honor I crave."

"No. Goes against your maidenly dignity, no doubt. But still, you'll have the satisfaction of knowing you've brought him here—one way or the other. Your countrymen may well turn him over to me, as they've done you." He clanked his signet ring against a bar. "But I have this rather interesting feeling he'll come riding in of his own free will."

"Because I'm the bait in your trap." She clenched her fist to keep from sinking her fingernails into his windpipe.

"Of course." His nostrils flared. "Just as your father was bait."

A pent breath tore free. "The Gifted didn't step into the trap then."

"Doesn't matter." He smiled. "This way, I get all three: the king, the Searcher, and the Gifted."

"You're going to die anyway. The worlds are breaking." Let him consider that.

His smile fled. "If that's so, then the only pleasure left in my rather short life is feeling Chris Redston's neck snap between my hands. Call it my last obsession."

"You're mad."

His hand flashed through the bars and clamped the back of her neck. He smashed her up against the door, her face inches from his.

"Dying does that to a man." His irises were a band of green around the black hole of his pupils. "You think this is what I want? This is not the life I wanted to return to. I wanted revenge, I wanted freedom, I wanted to return to the man I was and forever escape these voices in my head. But, of all these things, I find I am given only the first. And I *will* exact it to the uttermost measure!"

His fingers jagged pain through her skull. She gritted both hands against the bars and tried to push away. "You haven't won yet."

"True. Quite true." His hand slid from her neck down through the tangles of her hair, smoothing them over her shoulder. He smiled. "Until tomorrow, my princess. You will sleep well, I trust?" He tugged his glove back over his hand, then turned and strode down the corridor.

The soldiers followed, taking with them the globes and dousing the dungeon in utter darkness.

She stood rooted in front of the door, gripping the rusted bars. She didn't think, she didn't feel, she just stood, until finally she could no longer do even that. Her hands slipped from the bars and she sank down against the door. The cold of the stones infiltrated her clothes and her skin and touched her bones. She leaned her head against the iron.

Only one plea remained to her. Only one plea mattered anymore: *Don't let Chris come.*

53

THE FIRST THING Chris did when he surfaced in Chicago's pre-dawn darkness was call Mike. "I need you to drive me to Harrison's house."

"What happened to going off the radar?" Mike's voice rasped with sleep.

"It died a quick death. How soon can you get here?" Chris gave him the address.

Mike sighed. "Give me about twenty minutes. And there better not be anybody shooting at me."

Chris hung up and groped through the hotel room to find his clothes and Harrison's bundle of notebooks.

By some miracle, his ragtag group had managed to reach the shores of Ori Réon and commandeer a ship his father referred to as a "sow." But sow or not, Worick had been able to helm it. After a harrowing day crossing the wind-thrashed lake, they arrived on the northern shore under the cover of darkness. Chris had fallen asleep with the Orimere in his hand and a final prayer on his lips that this might all somehow work.

Snow plastered his hotel room's windows, and he had to drag up the sash to watch for the approach of Mike's orange Bug. Thirty minutes later, he glanced outside to see the car idling on the curb.

The power outage had killed the elevators, so he hiked to the nearest stairwell, ran down the first flight of stairs, and turned the corner—right into the noise-suppressed barrel of Geoff Kaufman's handgun.

His breath exploded from his mouth. He ducked and spun back around the corner. Behind him, the gun spat, and a poster of Sears Tower rained glass across the landing.

How had this thug found him? Mike couldn't have been so stupid as to let Kaufman tail him. Or maybe he could. He scrambled up the stairs.

"Why prolong this?" Kaufman's voice was flat. "For what I'm getting paid, I have no reason not to spend the rest of my life hunting you. Why not get it over with?"

Chris reached the top of the stairs and pelted down the hall. Another shot ricocheted against the wall, and he threw himself into the elevator alcove. His thumb worked the button, but no reassuring orange light pinged behind the arrows.

Kaufman's strides measured the hall.

Chris hurled himself around the edge of the elevator. The shot clanked against the doors. He sprinted down the hallway to the stairwell at the opposite end and blasted through the doors. The corner of the first landing provided him cover until Kaufman reached the end of the hallway, and he kept his lead all the way down the stairs and into the shadows of the lobby.

The clerk at the desk gaped as Chris ran past.

Outside, where the Bug waited on the curb, Mike turned from leaning against the car and looked over the roof at Chris. "There you are. I was about to come get you."

"Get in!"

"What's the hurry? We don't even have traffic to contend with this morning."

Chris wrenched open the passenger door. "Just get in!"

Mike looked past Chris, and his mouth flopped open. He ducked into the car and was flooring the gas before his door was even closed. The tires sprayed snow, finally caught traction, and spun off across the empty street. Behind Chris, the rear side window exploded.

Mike swerved into the wrong lane. "You said nobody'd be shooting at me!"

In a minute, the black streak of Kaufman's pickup careened around a corner through the snow.

"He's following," Chris said.

"Wonderful. Perfect. Good thing that makes my life complete, 'cause it doesn't look like I have long to live it!" Mike started to turn left.

Chris snatched his arm. "What are you doing?"

"I'm finding the police, that's what I'm doing!"

"We haven't got time for the police! Go to Harrison's."

"Are you out of your mind? You're still afraid the cops are going to nail you for that whole Mactalde thing? You're willing to risk our lives on that possibility?"

The black truck barreled through the snow behind them.

"No. You're right." Chris grabbed for his seatbelt. Mactalde had hired Kaufman to kill him. If Mactalde wanted him dead, he wouldn't draw attention to Chris by framing him for his disappearance.

He slammed the side of his fist against the glove box, and it fell open in his lap. "Where's your phone?"

"It's on the fritz." Mike swerved onto the highway ramp, and the junk in the glove box tumbled to the floor. "Everything's on the fritz right now because of the storms."

Chris clawed through the mess to find the phone and power it up. "We've got a signal."

"Yeah, and now we've also got traffic to deal with."

"Get in front of that semi and stay there." He dialed the police station and got an earful of static.

Kaufman's truck roared up on the shoulder of the road and loomed in Chris's side mirror.

"The semi's too slow!" Mike yelled.

"Just floor it! Weave in and out of traffic!"

Mike stomped on the gas, and the Bug shuddered into the other lane. "I can hardly *see* the traffic through the snow! How am I supposed to weave in and out?"

The static in Chris's ear dissolved into a choppy female voice. "Hel—lo, this—9—1."

"We've got a man in a black pickup trying to run us down. He's shooting at us." He gave Harrison's address. Static erupted again, and he threw the phone back into the glove box. "Get off at the next exit."

The Bug caught a patch of ice, slid sideways onto the ramp, and lost traction for precious seconds until Mike could pull it back into the turn. The truck juddered behind them as Kaufman fought to brake in time to follow.

Mike smacked the steering wheel. "He overshot it! He missed the exit!"

The truck churned into reverse, snow spewing from its wheels.

"He's pulling back around!" Chris said. "Get off the ramp. We'll try to lose him in the side streets."

Mike kept the gas pedal to the floor as they raced through the streets. His eyes flicked back and forth between the speedometer and the rearview mirror. "We're losing ground! We're not going to make it!"

"Only a couple more blocks." Sirens moaned in the distance. "Cops are coming."

"By the time they get to us, we're going to be too dead to waste tax money saving!"

Kaufman smashed into their rear bumper. Metal crumpled, and cracks spidered the rear window. The Bug's engine wheezed.

Kaufman rammed them again. The Bug spun out on the ice and careened across the street. Barely in time to brace himself, Chris dragged his legs up against the dashboard. The car crashed into a stop sign, and the dirty orange hood and the perforated green pole pretzeled together.

Mike raised his head from the cushion of his arms. "My car!"

"Get out!" Chris shoved through the door.

The truck had caught the same ice patch and crashed into the house across the street.

"If he's not dead, I'm gonna kill him." Mike dragged himself out of the car.

The truck's passenger door sprang open, and a shot smacked into the pavement at Mike's feet.

Chris sprinted down the sidewalk. He dared one look over his shoulder. Mike gasped along behind him. Farther back, Kaufman ran like a trained sprinter, gun in hand, his tie flaring over his shoulder.

Together, Chris and Mike clambered over Harrison's fallen fence and across the yard. Chris pounded a kick just below the doorknob, and the door snapped like brittle cardboard.

"Great." Mike flung out his arms. "Good thinking. Smash the door. Why not let everybody in—including the bad guy!"

"Shut it behind you, and start propping stuff in front of it. Maybe it'll slow him down." Dust from the desecrated door clogged the dark hallway.

"A slow death, just what I wanted." The door banged shut.

Chris ran down the hallway into the living room. Harrison had bragged about the explosives hidden under the floor. Back then, Chris had dismissed it as the ravings of a demented kook. Now, he was banking more than just his life on its truth.

He shoved chairs out of the way, toppling piles of trash. A threadbare rug covered the floor, and he ripped it up and cast it aside. Halfway beneath the one chair Harrison had kept clear for his own use was a trapdoor.

A shot tore through the front of the house, and something heavy hit the floor.

"He's shooting at *me* now!" Mike crawled around the corner, and Kaufman started kicking the door.

Chris dragged open the trapdoor.

"What is this?" Mike peered over the edge. "Panic room?"

Chris snatched a flashlight from his coat pocket and shone it on a long lumpy pile swathed in blue plastic. Outside, sirens howled. He dropped into the shallow hole, up to his chest. Squatting, he tore open a corner of the plastic far enough to make sure it was the explosives he was after, then tied it shut again. The front door splintered, and Mike's improvised barricade crashed.

"Mike." He pulled out the Orimere and the notebook with Harrison's map of Réon Couteau. "I need you to do me one more favor."

Mike shook his head. "I have to tell you, I'm about out of favors, bro."

"I need you to knock me out."

"What?" Mike rocked back on his heels.

Tires screeched outside, and men started yelling.

"Before the cops get here, I need you to knock me out." He held out the heavy flashlight.

"What are you trying to do now? Frame me?"

"Just do it. Please." If Mike had been the one asking him, he probably wouldn't have done it, and he couldn't blame Mike if he didn't either. "Trust me just one more time."

Mike raised both hands and shook his head. "I'm not doing this. This is crazy."

"It's the last time. I promise. You have no idea how much is riding on this."

Footsteps ran up the sidewalk. Kaufman's pistol started coughing, and the staccato report of the officers' weapons replied.

Chris held the flashlight out farther. "We're running out of time. Just give me one good crack behind the ear."

"That could kill you!"

"Mike!" He lunged halfway out of the hole and snagged his friend's sleeve. "I've told you the truth, every bit of it. I don't care if you believe me about the dreams or not, it's true. And if I don't get back there right now, people are going to die!"

"I don't believe you." Mike reached for the flashlight. "I don't. But you do deserve a smack in the head."

The front door rattled. "Anybody in there?" a man called. "Everyone okay?"

Chris clenched the heat of the Orimere in one hand and reached back with the other to touch the mound of explosives. "Tell them I fell and hit my head."

Mike wrapped both hands around the flashlight. "When you wake up with a headache, just remember you asked for this."

"Do it."

The flashlight crashed into the side of his head. His vision flashed into darkness—

—and he jerked upright to find a wild-eyed Parry scrambling toward him.

Harrison's green notebook and the clothes he'd been wearing in Chicago lay scattered around his bedroll.

He propped himself up on one elbow. "Did it happen?"

"Don't know." Parry pointed behind him. "I'm too busy wondering if *that* was supposed to happen."

The tromp of hoofbeats thudded all around the camp.

54

CHRIS SNAGGED HIS clothes and his weapons and levered himself to his feet. Through the moonlit trees, horses trotted into the camp from all directions.

"Women and children to the center!" Denegar bellowed.

Chris threw on his clothes. Had Mactalde been expecting them? Could he have found them already? He gritted his teeth. Why hadn't he prepared for this? He shouldn't have left his people alone for even the few hours he'd spent in Chicago.

"*Eseded!*" The word rolled through the camp like thunder.

In the back somewhere, Pitch squealed. "They've come!"

"*Podd!*" Orias shoved through the crowd. "*Timon kardge bé ta ti yitlog!*"

Chris stopped short. The troops surrounding them weren't wearing the red of Koraud. They weren't wearing any kind of uniform at all. Through the shadows gleamed hundreds of faces, white as marble. His heart pumped hard. The Cherazii had come after all.

He pushed past Parry to follow Orias. From the lakeshore, line upon line of Cherazii horsemen spilled into the camp. At their head rode Cabahr Laith. He drew his white charger to a stop and watched Chris's approach.

"You've come to fight," Chris said. He had never dreamed they would change their minds.

Laith looked at him levelly. "We heard what you said to us, Gifted. And with a little *convincing*, we have decided that if the worlds break, it will not be because the Cherazii had not the foresight to raise their blades. Do not think I trust you—or your choice in companions." He didn't even glance at Orias. "But we will fight with you for the sake of something greater."

Chris saluted them with his fist on his heart. "Thank you." He swiveled around. "Did the Orimere work?"

His father gestured to where the blue mound of explosives had landed a few yards off from his bedroll. "If that was supposed to appear out of nowhere, then, aye, it worked."

Pitch danced up beside Chris. "Huzzah! I knew it would turn out all right! Now what?"

"Now we move." Chris shrugged into his bandoleer and turned to face the people gathering behind him. Their eyes glittered in the snow-reflected moonlight as they watched him and the Cherazii.

He took a breath. His speechmaking hadn't had much of a chance to improve since the Gifted ceremony in Glen Arden, but what he had to say now he meant with all his heart. "Even if I could get more explosives, we're not going to have the chance to try this again. So listen to me and do exactly as I tell you."

Quinnon, standing in the rear, crossed his arms.

Chris continued, "I need as many volunteers as I can get from among the women. They're going to come with me and the Rievers and set the explosives under the waterfall. Captain Quinnon and a squad of Cherazii—" he looked at Laith, "—will breach the Vesper gate beneath the palace. We need to disable any Koraudian sentries. I'll join you before dawn, and as soon as the explosion goes off, we'll ride up the hill to the palace."

He surveyed the ranks of his tiny army. The choice he made now would be irrevocable. "The explosion will get their attention and hopefully weaken their defenses. Only a small portion of Mactalde's troops are in the city, but before we risk the casualties of such a battle, I'm going to challenge Mactalde to fight me one on one. Him against me to decide the war."

Laith frowned. "Have you the experience to defeat Faolan Mactalde in battle?"

The camp held its breath.

The answer, of course, was probably not. But before one more person died in this war, he had to attempt to make things right. If he failed, Denegar, Quinnon, and Laith could still lead the troops to victory. And if he won . . .

"This battle is the reason I'm here."

His sister Tielle pushed through the crowd to stand beside their father. In the darkness, her blonde hair almost glowed. "You needed volunteers. Here's one."

He could only thank her with a nod. Behind her, a dozen women gathered, Lauria and Sirra among them.

Parry trotted over with a horse, and Chris swung aboard. While Pitch and Raz scrambled up behind him, he looked out at the up-turned faces. In his chest, something dark and horrified gripped his heart and his lungs. But he felt something else too, something buoyant, something that was almost peace.

He raised his voice. "When I came here, I didn't believe in any-thing bigger than chance. I didn't believe in destiny. I didn't believe my life had a purpose."

Motionless, they watched him. They were waiting for words of affirmation, a promise that somehow all this insanity would at last bring hope.

"In the months I've been here, something has changed. Today, the very world will change." He raised his sword. "May the God of all help us."

The Cherazii's voices boomed an echo. "*Yalarin pitish sé!*"

They loaded the explosives in saddlebags and on makeshift litters. Chris led the volunteers along the shoreline cliffs, to the place where Harrison's notes showed the caverns' entrance.

Wordlessly, the women worked inside the dank stone, passing the explosives down the hallways, packing them in the recesses beneath the black fortress. The Rievers ran back and forth, squeezing into impossibly small alcoves, carrying torches, and checking fuses. Hours trickled past, marked by the cold sweat down Chris's back and the inaudible footsteps of his men marching up the shore to lay in wait outside the gates.

When finally he'd judged three hours to have passed, he drew his mother aside and showed her how to set off the charge. "At dawn. Get everyone out safely, and set it off at dawn."

The corners of her eyes glistened. "Be safe. Please be safe." She laid her hand against his face. "The God of all shine His grace upon you."

He squeezed her fingers once, then threaded his way back through the tunnels into the cold rush of night. The sky was paling to a bruised purple dawn. In the distance, three falling stars, the color of dead men's bones, streaked to the earth.

He galloped through the remnants of night. The hoofbeats crunched through snow and clattered against stone. They rebounded through the shadows and dragged his thoughts into their remorseless rhythm. The time had come. One way or the other, there could be no escape from this day. What he did now would change the course of the worlds.

As the first streaks of morning stained the wind-tossed sky, he found the men crouched in the shadows of the Vesper district's walls. To the east, beyond the castle on its cliff, more stars fell. Perhaps the sky itself was falling.

In silence, he trotted through his troops, and, in silence, they parted ranks to let him pass. He reined up at their front and glanced at Quinnon and Denegar on one side and Orias on the other.

"When?" Orias asked.

Beneath their feet, the ground rumbled. He took a breath. God willing, it wouldn't be Allara's death knell, anymore than it would be their own.

He loosed his sword from its sheath. "Now."

The blast ripped through Allara's dreams and hurled her against the wall. Another blast and then another—a long chain of them all through the length of the fortress—shook her body. The ceiling collapsed, one huge center piece crashing into pebbles. She huddled against the wall, her head in her lap and her hands over her neck.

When at last the shaking stopped, she peered into the gaping hole overhead. Light dribbled through the breach and flickered over the rubble. She pushed to her feet, and stones clattered from her clothing to the floor. Voices shouted overhead; footsteps hammered.

She held her breath, and her mind touched the warmth of Chris's presence. He was near. He had done this. He had come despite her prayers.

She clambered on top of the rubble in the room's center and caught hold of the hole's edge. The stones crumbled beneath her grip, and she pawed them out of the way until she found a solid handhold. Praying no one above would hear, she kicked off from the pile of rocks, dragged an elbow over the ledge, and rolled herself up and over. The room, a part of the servants' quarters, lay empty and hazy with dust.

Réon Couteau held no surprises for her. She knew every room, every passage. She knew the back corridors Mactalde and his men would not yet have had time to find. Through the ruined hallways, she ran. Higher and higher, she climbed, to the places she knew best, her private haunts high above the rest of the palace.

Finally, she reached the huge outer terrace that swept from the gates above the city entrance to the waterfall on the southern exposure.

"Two days ago, you offered us a bargain!" Chris's shout wafted to her. She stopped short and flattened herself against the wall.

"My bargain included no provision for your blowing up my palace."

She eased her face around the corner. Mactalde leaned against the balustrade, his hands spread. In profile, he was smiling, but everything about his posture radiated anger.

"You said you'd leave Lael in peace if I came to you." Chris had to be standing outside the palace gates, shouting up. "I've come."

No, no, no. Her breath rasped.

"To propose a bargain of my own," he continued.

"What could you possibly want that I would give you?" Mactalde's voice mocked.

"I want a fair fight. You against me. Alone. Winner take all."

Chatter chased through the crowded terrace. A handful of Mactalde's generals stood at his sides, babbling and shaking their heads.

Allara splayed her hands against the stone on either side and clenched her teeth for a moment of interminable silence.

Then, almost abruptly, Mactalde thrust his generals away. "I would hardly call that a fair fight. But fairness doesn't appeal to me nearly so much as inevitability. You have a bargain. Let him into the courtyard!"

She pushed away from the wall. She had to get out of here. How could Chris think he could do this? He had few chances of surviving a duel with Mactalde, and she wasn't about to let him trade his life for hers. Unless the explosion had blocked the way, she might be able to escape through the armory court.

She started to turn away.

In the crowd of Mactalde's disciples, Crofton Steadman's face in its frame of black hair appeared. His eyes locked with hers.

Her muscles turned to rock.

He pointed at her. Mactalde and Rotoss looked around, and before she could flee to the safety of the back corridors, two soldiers caught her and dragged her past Steadman.

"And so I gain a second audience with you, my lady." Steadman grinned. "Only now you are no longer queen here."

The soldiers forced her to a stop in front of Mactalde.

He paused in pulling on his gauntlets only long enough to look her over. What was the lowly Searcher to him now that he had the Gifted within his grasp?

Rotoss hovered at his shoulder. "With respect, this is balmy. Why risk our victory fighting that whelp?"

"You call this a risk? This is no risk." Mactalde smiled at Allara. "Wouldn't you agree, princess?" He turned back to Rotoss. "Alert the men to stand ready. If anything should go amiss, they're to eliminate Redston immediately."

Perspiration beaded Allara's hairline. "You can't do this."

"Of course I can." He gave her nose a tap as he walked past. "Stay here on the walls, my lady. It seems you'll be able to witness your loyal Gifted's demise after all."

She lunged against her captors' arms and filled her lungs with the shout that was her only weapon. "Chris! He's lying! Don't come in here, it's a ploy!"

Rotoss's hand shot out and clamped over her mouth. "You rotted little witchling." He looked at Mactalde. "She can't stay up here."

"Oh, well, give her to Steadman, then." Mactalde glanced back from the doorway. "He'd enjoy that, I'm sure."

"Fine." Rotoss hit her once across the side of her head, hard, then thrust her wrist into Steadman's hand. "Get her out of the way."

Her brain spun, and she squeezed her eyes shut. Orders and the tread of marching feet filled her head. In the courtyard, the gates ground open to admit Chris. Steadman's hand tightened around her coat sleeve, grinding the bones of her wrist.

It wasn't going to end like this. She wasn't going to let it.

She opened her eyes.

Steadman pulled her closer, until his forehead touched hers. His heavy breath heated her skin. "You thought you could blind the people with your witchcraft forever. But you were wrong. The old ways are falling even as we speak."

"No." She pulled back. The length of their arms stretched between them. "There are no old ways. There is only one way, and that way is not yours."

She turned and yanked away. Her wrist slid from her sleeve, and Steadman's grip tore her coat from her body. She crossed the wide terrace to the curve in the balustrade where the spray from the waterfall misted through the rails. A single running step lifted her onto the wrecked banister. Her only escape was a mad, blind dive into the lake, with no one at the bottom to catch her.

"You fool!" Steadman snagged her fingertips. "The fall alone will kill you!"

She launched herself over the edge and dragged Steadman with her.

55

ON THE COBBLESTONES of the palace courtyard, Chris waited.

Mactalde appeared through an arched doorway one level up and started down the stairs that hugged the wall. His footsteps crunched in the snow, and the sound reverberated against the high stone walls. The gray swirling shadows of the morning lit the sprawl of the courtyard.

Mactalde's men had admitted Chris through the gates, but the explosion had crumbled the walls in several places, just as he had hoped. Had they not let him in, he could have climbed over the rubble into the courtyard.

His sword hung loose in his hand, and sweat scalded inside his glove.

Mactalde reached the last step and approached to within a few yards. They were alone in the courtyard. Chris's own men waited in the streets beyond, and Mactalde's troopers were nowhere to be seen.

Mactalde flashed a smile, but the skin around his mouth stayed tight. "Rather an exciting few months it's been." He unbuckled his knee-length doublet and cast it to the wind, leaving himself free to move within the loose weave of his blouse. "As a professional psychologist, I admit this isn't the way I usually like to see my client relationships end." His sword hissed free of its sheath, and he rolled his shoulders before stepping forward. "But at least we solved that troubling little dream question of yours, eh?"

Chris brought his sword up in front of him and fell into his stance. "It's not solved. Not yet."

Mactalde raised his sword in front of his face and touched his forehead to the steel in salute. "Then here's to solving it." He attacked, his blade swiping low, trying to chop Chris's legs out from under him.

Chris leapt back and swung blindly, just nicking Mactalde's blade with his own. He parried Mactalde's salvo and staggered back, one step after the other. He sank into the instinctual rhythms and patterns of his body, but even with all he had learned since crossing over, his brain couldn't keep up. He couldn't afford for it to keep up.

For a split second, the attack slowed, and Mactalde's right side lay open. Chris lunged to the left and swung low. Mactalde's sword snapped down, one-handed, to catch the blow, and he slammed his elbow into Chris's temple. Darkness fluttered across Chris's vision, and he lurched back, automatically dragging the length of his sword in front of his face.

Mactalde laughed. "The heroic Gifted isn't quite good enough, is he?"

The sickening part was . . . he wasn't.

Allara plummeted through the waterfall's spray, Steadman grappling her body. Shouts and gunshots droned from the palace above, and the slugs ripped past. She stopped breathing. In seconds, the sheet of water looming beneath would snap her spine with the impact of the long fall. Water and blood rushed in her ears. She barely heard the faint rattle, like a piece of parchment in the wind.

A shadow the size of a hawk flitted across the water, and the Garowai, in miniature, careened past. He slapped his wings together in front of him and blasted from the cloud of dust in his proper size. With a roar, he dove past. He snagged her arm with his foreclaw, and all her joints seemed to burst.

Steadman lost his hold on her and skidded down her body, one hand clawing her gown, his eyes huge. The Garowai's wings pumped hard and the wind swirled her body like a kite tail. Steadman's grip slipped, and he fell, screaming, into the lake.

More shots howled past. One scored the Garowai's wing and another skittered off his hard ribs. He angled for the top of the city wall, and its iced bricks flew past, so near she could reach out and touch them.

"Warn the Gifted's men," the Garowai said, and then he let her go.

She thudded against a flying buttress and started climbing the rest of the way to the parapet on top. The stones were large and the cracks between just wide enough for a finger hold. Her hands cramped in the snow. The ice tore through her skin and her fingernails, and pink blood trailed her progress.

Below, horses stopped. The rattle of equipment and the buzz of rifle hydraulics could only mean men had been sent after her. Their gunfire had stopped, no doubt because they feared alerting Chris's men to their presence. They would have to climb up after her and kill her by hand.

She screamed out a precious breath: *"Quinnon!"*

The shout echoed back and mocked her as it faded. If she could get Quinnon's attention and tell him of Mactalde's treachery, then at least she would not fall in vain. Her pursuers gained slowly, hampered by their armor and their weapons.

"Quinnon!"

Below her, men cursed. "Shoot her before someone hears!"

Rifle bolts clattered into place. Above her, the edge of the wall leered just out of reach. The gunshots hammered into the stones beneath her.

"Reload!"

A few more handholds and she would be safe.

"Fire!"

Stones split on either side of her, and in her left forearm, skin and muscle pinched. Something that felt like a warm fingertip traced a caress down her arm. The sky, huge and white, expanded over the edge of the parapet.

Almost there, almost there.

She didn't look at her arm. She didn't listen when the muscles insisted they couldn't lift and clamp and brace her weight. One more rung to climb and she would be there.

A hand seized her ankle. Her hold on the rock snapped, and she skidded down the face of the wall. Rolling half onto her side, she caught a buttress, and drove her free heel into the Koraudian's mouth. Sputtering and spitting blood, he slid away. She kicked him again, and his hand scraped free. Oaths howled from below, and the firing once again smacked into the wall. She clawed her way to the top and hoisted herself over the edge.

Below, interspersed among the blue-roofed monasteries of the Vesper district, waited a ragtag army such as she had not seen in twenty years. Her breath caught. They had come. After all these years, the Cherazii had once again joined forces with Lael. She pushed to her feet and ran the length of the parapet to the stairs.

They saw her coming and Quinnon hurried to meet her. He slung his coat around her shoulders and thrust her blood-soaked sleeve back from the half-span bodkin bullet that pierced her forearm between the wrist and elbow.

She gritted her teeth. "Just leave it in for now." She faced the soldiers. "Mactalde has betrayed the bargain."

Alone in the shadows of a monastery's blue eaves, Orias Tarn straightened. He would understand. Better than anyone here, he understood what that meant.

"Even if Chris succeeds, the Koraudians will kill him."

Someone shouted an order. The men mobilized into a hundred tiny fragments.

Quinnon tore away the rest of her sleeve and used it as a tourniquet, but her eyes followed Orias. Before she had finished speaking, he had mounted up and called to his lion. The rest of the men marshaled into ranks, but Orias already galloped up the street, bent low over his horse's mane, his hair blowing out behind him.

The thunder of marching footsteps filled Chris's consciousness, but he dared not look up. One misstep, one blink, and Mactalde would disembowel him.

Mactalde chuckled. "Go on, take a look." He swiveled away a step.

On the walls all around, Koraudian troops tromped into view. Chris's breath heaved from his mouth in long clouds. They were here to either watch him be killed or to kill him themselves if their master failed.

Futility welled in his gut. "You couldn't even keep your word."

"The Gifted are dangerous individuals. They never play fair. So why should I be fair with them?" Mactalde spun in for another attack. "Of course, life hasn't exactly shown justice to you either, has it?" His blade slammed into Chris's, inches from his face. "Tell me, how does it feel to have a path set before you that's not of your choosing? How do you like being *controlled*?"

Mactalde pulled his blade free. He rotated his wrist, and the reflected snow flashed against the glint of steel. "The only difference in our lives these days is I have maintained the right to act, whereas you . . . you can only react." His blade crashed down and nearly ripped Chris's sword from his hands. "Tell me the truth, would you not trade places with me in a heartbeat?"

Chris held, his strength aching against Mactalde's. "No."

"Why not?" Mactalde shoved him back a full step. "You can't truly believe I'm destroying the world."

"How many people have died because of you?"

"Hundreds. How many have died because of you?" The corner of his mouth tilted. "Too many to count, I think?"

"No. Not too many." Chris tightened his hold on the sword. His gloves squeaked against the leather-wrapped hilt. "Just one less than enough."

"Then may it be your death that fills the tally." Mactalde charged, but before he could reach Chris, his attention wavered. He glanced at the crumbled corner of the courtyard wall. The sound of a hundred melded screams filled the air.

This time, Chris didn't turn to follow Mactalde's gaze. He had been given the advantage, if only for a split second. He lunged and thrust.

Mactalde saw his attack, parried in time to save his life, but too late to keep the blade from glancing off his thigh. His wild swing chopped the point of Chris's blade into the snow, then hacked upward and hissed past Chris's head.

Chris pulled back, sword in front of his face. From the corner of his eye, he saw the motley charge of Laelers and Cherazii scrambling over the broken walls to meet the Koraudian defenders.

He filled his lungs with a new breath. "Consider the playing field leveled."

Mactalde stared down at the wash of red on his leg. Then he dropped his hand to his belt and drew his mace. "Not yet, I think. Not yet."

Allara galloped atop the wide city wall, headed toward the palace. On her right, the shoreline vanished, and the mist and thunder of the wind-whipped waterfall burst into view.

Her left arm throbbed against her chest, and her bones ached with the brittleness of cold. Chris's presence roared inside her as it had not done even when he had held her after her father's death. His thoughts rushed with fear, with anger, with a flurry of reflex and instinct.

Quinnon galloped up beside her and yanked her horse to a stop. "This is madness. What good are you to anyone if you kill yourself before the battle's half over?"

She dismounted. "Give me your spyglass!"

In the faraway eastern sky, falling stars rained through the clouds. The sound of their crash disappeared in the collision of troops. Soldiers swept through the snow in the courtyard. They stopped. Staggered. Then red and green tabards and the glare of blue-streaked Cherazii faces blended into the chaos.

She raised Quinnon's spyglass to her face, and clarity unfurled across the field. She saw all their faces. She saw the Commander of the Guard collapse, a pike haft filling a hole in his stomach. She saw her uncle, Amras Denegar, fighting on horseback, cutting through the ranks with sword and mace. She saw Glelarn Rotoss's pistol shot blast through a Cherazim's face. She saw the Cherazii leader, Cabahr Laith, fighting on foot, his black hair swinging around his face as he spun in wide arcs, cutting down everything, man and horse, that neared him. She saw Orias scrambling through the dead, clearing a path before him, but running, always running, through the fight, toward the far end of the courtyard.

She raised the glass, and she saw why he ran.

In the middle of it all, Chris and Mactalde battled on. Mactalde fought with mace and sword against Chris's single blade and a lifetime's lack of experience.

The time had come. This was her time as surely as it was Chris's. She would ride to him. She would fight by his side. She would die on Mactalde's sword if she had to.

The Garowai alighted on the wall's edge, and Quinnon's hand came down hard on her shoulder.

Her heart leapt. "You've come to fight with us."

"I cannot," the Garowai said. "I am allowed only to watch. I have done all I can do in saving you."

"You know Mactalde's the better fighter." She pulled her sword from its sheath on her saddle. "You're here, you can help Chris!"

"No, my dear, I told you: *I will watch*." He sneezed. "I am here because epochs tend to require my presence."

"If Chris does not win today, there will never be another epoch!"

He shuffled around to face the palace. "You can't know that, love." He hooked his claws over the edge of the wall. "You must trust that which is beyond your own senses."

Her stomach cramped. "You may choose to stay here and *watch*. But I cannot." She dragged herself into her saddle. "I was born for this day. I will not live to see it slip away into darkness!"

Quinnon gathered his reins. "You won't live a'tall if you don't start showing some sense." But he had to know she was right. She couldn't stay here. She couldn't watch while the drama she had feared all her life spun itself to an end in a battle she couldn't touch.

"Allara." The Garowai swiveled his head almost backwards over his shoulder. "You need to know this is not your battle." His inner eyelid filmed the bottomless green of his eye. "Your battle is not of flesh and bone and blade. Your battle is coming."

Blood pounded in the broken veins of her left arm. She opened her mouth to ask him what he meant. He stared at her, unblinking.

"Don't you understand?" she said. "I cannot watch him die."

56

BERSERKING FIRE CHURNED through Orias's body as he ran across the courtyard. The red blood of fallen Koraudians glittered against his blade. It streaked his arms and spattered his face. Around him, the battle tilted and spread like a map of strategies. He saw the weaknesses, the strengths, and the shatterpoints of both armies. He felt the blood of his Cherazii brethren as it stained the snow, heard the death howls of the Koraudians, saw the ebb and flow of power as the troops deadlocked.

He knew where he was needed. He saw precisely where the added strength of a single warrior could push Lael into an advantage. But he did not turn to help them. Someone shouted to him, but he ran on. A Koraudian lunged into his path, and he slashed him across the chest and did not look back. What lay behind did not matter.

Ahead, Mactalde and the Gifted were locked in combat. Each of them was flagging, each of them bleeding. Chris had held his own for a long time. But now the ground slipped away beneath his feet. Mactalde rained blows upon him, driving him back into the battle.

Orias roared. His vision tunneled, and the battlefield disappeared. He would save the Gifted. If nothing else could be said of his life, then at least let it be said he had saved the Gifted. His strides lengthened, and his sword and his shoulder thrust a pathway through the thrashing bodies. He hurtled the fallen carcass of a horse and landed with both hands solid around his sword and every muscle dragged taut.

He didn't see what hit him. Something smashed into his left side and spun him around. His ribs cracked like dry tinder, and blood flooded the inside of his coat. Only whispers of pain filtered through the heat of his brain, but for a long, agonizing moment, his lungs refused to draw his next breath. He clamped his free arm over the chasm in his side, and he brought his sword up to face his attacker.

Glelarn Rotoss raised his sword like a hammer. Sweat and blood matted his ruddy mane. "Every time we face each other in these little fights, you get the worst of them. You're going to make me believe the Cherazii aren't so unbeatable after all."

With a snarl, Dougal surged past Orias and leapt. Rotoss struck out wildly, and, with a yelp, the lion crumpled into the bloody snow.

Rotoss spun back. "Why not send the Rievers in too? Get all the distractions out of the way, so we can get to business." His blade descended.

Orias's sword gave way beneath the blow.

Rotoss held its tip trapped in the snow. He leaned over until his face was inches from Orias's. "Well, well. Here we are again, aren't we, with your life at my mercy? What'll our bargain be this time? How about groveling on your knees and begging?"

Orias's blood pulsed from his side. Sweat beaded his lip. "Our covenant is over."

"No, it ain't. I know how you people work. Cherazii covenants end only in death."

"Then let it end."

His sword surged up into Rotoss's and ripped it from the man's hands. Rotoss staggered back. With a bellow, Orias lunged. The point of his sword plunged into Rotoss's side, and the man screamed in terror. Orias dragged the blade loose, then levered it up and back in to find the heart. Rotoss's mouth gaped, his eyes bulging. He toppled to his knees, and his body slid from the sword.

Once again, Orias's lungs caved in. His body threatened to collapse, and he stumbled a step. Then, thrusting his hand against the hole in his side, he turned to find Chris.

Sweat drenched Chris's clothes and burned in his wounds. The injury in his side had ripped completely open, and blood trickled down his flank. He tripped over a wounded Koraudian, and his fingers slipped against his hilt. His limbs felt as though they were dragging buckets of cement. He could barely keep up with Mactalde's attack, much less plot the next move.

He reeled backwards, always backwards, on the defensive, fighting for nothing more worthy than his life. This was a battle he could not win. It was a battle he was not meant to win. He had come to this world, ravaged it with his folly, then had the arrogance to believe he had the power to put it to rights. But he did not have the power. He was only a man, after all. And, in a moment, he would die, and Lael would die with him.

Their blades skidded against each other, and Mactalde shoved in closer, almost hilt to hilt, his sword on top of Chris's. He rammed his chest against Chris's shoulder, one foot planted behind Chris, trapping him from retreat. "You fought well after all, Mr. Redston." His mace chopped into the underside of Chris's blade, and the sword ripped from Chris's hands. "But not well enough." His elbow smashed against Chris's solar plexus, and his leg smacked into the back of Chris's legs.

Chris toppled and caught himself on his hands and knees. Tiny suns burst inside his head, and the blood trickling down his side turned his innards spongy.

"Get up." Mactalde's boot thudded into his ribs. "You fought like a man. Now let us see you die like one."

Chris raised himself to his knees, every breath a marathon. Mactalde cast the mace aside and stood over him with the sword clenched in both hands. Falling stars, much closer than before, streaked through the sky. The end was coming.

"Too bad, really," Mactalde said. "I do hate to see a man die disappointed."

Chris searched for his sword. It lay half-buried in the snow, three or four yards behind him.

"If only we knew the end from the beginning, eh? Life would be much different." Mactalde's sword swung over his shoulder, the blade behind his head. He raised one foot, stepped into the swing, and opened his mouth.

But the sound that blasted through Chris's ears was the battle cry of a Cherazim.

Orias smashed into Mactalde, and Mactalde's blade hatcheted the air in front of Chris's face. Blood—red and blue—clotted the snow as Orias and Mactalde rolled to their feet.

"You," Mactalde said. "You fool! What do you think you accomplish by saving him?"

Orias snatched his dirk and axe from his belt. "Redemption."

Chris lunged for his sword and turned back.

For the first time, Mactalde was on the defensive. Orias rained blows upon Mactalde's blade. An ocean of blue blood flooded the left side of his sleeveless tunic, but he fought with juggernaut strength. Roaring, he caught Mactalde's blade between his own. His arms bulged, veins worming the skin, ligaments trembling.

But Mactalde didn't give way. Orias's cry pitched higher, and he spun away, leaving only the dirk against Mactalde's blade. He showed Mactalde his back for one long dangerous second, then etched his axe toward Mactalde's leg.

Mactalde twisted, and the axe bit into little more than skin. His sword came free of Orias's dirk. It pierced Orias's back, above the hipbone, and plunged to its forte.

Chris hurled himself forward. "No!"

Orias's arms sprang wide of his body. His back arched and his head snapped back. He plummeted to his knees.

Mactalde braced both hands on the hilt to pull it free. "Now watch the Gifted die beside you!"

Orias turned, and Mactalde's blade turned with him. Howling, he twisted his body around the steel in his back, turning until he could reach behind and grab the blade. New blood welled in his palms. Mactalde fought to pull the sword free from his grip, and Orias flung his head back and screamed to the sky.

Chris launched himself. Orias had bought him the time he needed. It would be enough. It *had* to be.

At the last instant, Mactalde released the sword and dove for his abandoned mace. Chris's cry joined Orias's, and he pounded his sword at Mactalde's head. The mace haft rose barely in time to catch the blow. Chris swung again, and the blade sliced through Mactalde's biceps and cracked into bone. Mactalde stared at his half-severed arm. His face went rigid.

Chris drew back, gathering momentum. The tip of his blade slammed into the center of Mactalde's chest, just beneath the sternum.

Neither of them breathed. They stood across from each other, three feet of steel between them, and watched as a dark flower bloomed against Mactalde's blouse.

The mace fell from Mactalde's hand. He looked up from the sword in his chest and stared at Chris. Chris pulled the blade free, and Mactalde moaned. He laid one hand to his chest and thudded to his knees. "You've killed me."

Chris cast aside his sword and caught hold of Mactalde's shirt to keep him from toppling. "This is what I was meant to do. Lael is saved."

"No . . ." Mactalde sucked at the air. His eyes rolled up to stare at the palace walls. A film spread across his pupils. "I wanted only to come home."

"Was coming home worth destroying the worlds? What did it buy you?" Chris tightened his fingers. "Was it worth the destruction? Was it worth the lives you devastated? Was it?"

"*Yes.* Every exquisite moment. Yes!"

Chris wanted to shake him. Mactalde needed to see, if only for the last moment of his life, what he had done to this world he claimed to love so much. "There would never have been an imbalance if you hadn't come! The worlds wouldn't have broken!"

"I didn't do this . . . I didn't cause this. You caused this. You—brought—me—back." Blood pooled in his cheek and spilled from the corner of his mouth. "*You* broke the worlds."

His eyes turned to glass. His body fell limp in Chris's hands.

Muted sounds of battle rained in upon Chris from far away. The Koraudians screamed that Mactalde had fallen. *Mactalde the Invincible.*

Hoofbeats pounded the earth. The wind wailed down from the walls. It swirled snow devils across the courtyard and slaughtered them against the flesh-and-blood forms of men and horses.

Mactalde's body slipped from Chris's fingers. Chris gasped for air. What had he done?

Had he really dared to think he understood this place? He had opened his eyes on this world that was a part of his every fiber, just as surely as the one he had always known, and he had rejected it. He had taken one breath of its air, tinged with the sweetness of the gloamwheat, and he had spat it back out. He had been given a second chance at life, an opportunity to make more of a difference than he could ever have imagined, and he had cast it aside.

Mactalde hadn't scorned it. *He* had.

The battle raged on as the Laelers and the Cherazii pushed back the panicked Koraudians step by excruciating step. Dark clouds edged the horizons. Lightning gouged a switchback between heaven and earth, and the wind that blew ice crystals against his face carried with it the faint, faraway detonation of thunder.

His lungs burned. Mactalde might lay dead in the snow. But the worlds were still breaking.

Allara's heart forgot how to pump. Her horse had leapt the rubble of the palace walls, and she had seen the final, furious blows exchanged between Chris and Mactalde. She had seen Chris's sword disappear in Mactalde's body. She had seen it emerge, red with his blood.

Side by side, she and Quinnon galloped across the courtyard to where Chris crouched over another body in the snow. The battle was moving away from the palace. The Laelers and the Cherazii were pushing the Koraudians into retreat. Their shouts and screams sailed back to her on the wind.

"Chris!" She dismounted. A sob and a wild burst of laughter tangled in her throat.

Mactalde lay lifeless, arms spread, his eyes fogging. She stood over him, and her body shook. She pressed her hand over her mouth. They had won. She had won. She had hung onto the cliff long enough after all. It was over.

She forced down the tears that swelled in her throat and pounded in her head. The tears of twenty years could wait. They could wait forever. From this moment forth, she would have no reason to shed them.

She turned. "Chris—"

He glanced at her. His relief that she was alive and well blasted through her mind. But that was all he could spare her.

Before him on the ground, Orias Tarn lay crumpled and bleeding. The Cherazim's mutilated hand clutched a bloodied blade. Together, Chris and Quinnon worked feverishly with bandages from Quinnon's saddlebags. Orias's chest barely fluttered, and with every breath, his hand spasmed.

"We're not going to save him," Quinnon said.

Chris emptied a vial of oronborne into Orias's side. "He saved *me*."

"Cherazii blood doesn't clot like ours. Oronborne won't stop the bleeding. Even if it could, we can't make right what's ripped apart inside."

"Just keep him alive until I get back." He left Quinnon to secure the bandages and stood up. His eyes, haggard and hollow, found Allara's face. "Get him out of here."

That was all. After his burst of relief at the sight of her, he radiated only pain and a desperate kind of fear.

She grasped his sleeve. "Chris, Lael is saved. It's over, it's all over now."

He looked at the darkness on the faraway horizon. "Is it?"

57

CHRIS REJOINED HIS men in pursuit of the Koraudians. He lofted his sword at their front and threw himself into the blind fury of the final moments of his war. Mactalde was dead, the Koraudians were dying, and the war was nearer its end than any of them had dared hope.

And yet storms gathered on every horizon. Only this morning, the first stars had fallen as far away as Lake Thyra. Now they lit up the Northern Mistgloam River, just outside the city. Beneath the feet of his rearing charger, the earth shivered.

As his men chased the Koraudians into the hills above Ori Réon, he glimpsed a flicker of fire in the water. He reached into his coat to touch the Orimere, and from the other side of the worlds, images of destruction mirrored those in Lael.

Above, a winged shadow cut across the light, and the men cheered. The Garowai, full-sized, circled overhead. Chris reined to a stop and waited at the top of the hill. His body ached, but deep inside, he felt numb. Empty.

With a great back-flapping of wings, the Garowai settled beside Chris. "Well, then." He cocked his head. His eyes were rheumy and streaks of wetness lined the bridge of his muzzle. He hobbled a few arthritic steps, then sat on his haunches and wheezed. "Won a war, have you?"

Chris's horse reared, and he dragged it back to its feet. "Have I?"

The Garowai's massive shoulders rippled. "Mactalde's dead. The Koraudians are retreating en masse. Everything looks rather victorious." One brow ridge lifted. "Don't you think?"

"What about that?" He pointed to the lightshow of falling stars. "Looks like a storm."

He made himself speak the words he hadn't even been allowing himself to think. "It looks like the worlds are still breaking."

The brow rose higher.

"I thought you said if Mactalde died, the balance would be restored?"

"I believe what was said was the imbalance was created when you brought Mactalde across. And that is true."

His hand clenched his saddlebow. "Mactalde's dead. The balance *has* been restored. Why are the worlds still breaking?"

The Garowai shuddered, as if chilled. He drew a labored breath that ended in a cough, then offered a smile. "Perhaps it's too late." The brilliant green of his watering eyes held steady. "Or perhaps Mactalde's death wasn't enough."

"Something's wrong. Just tell me what it is." He had to hear someone else say it.

The Garowai spoke patiently. "You were brought to Lael for one purpose only."

"To kill Mactalde."

"To do whatever needs to be done. Isn't that what you said you were willing to do?"

Fire crept through his innards and chased away the numbness. "It's me, isn't it? *I'm* the one causing the imbalance." The words tore from him at last and left him breathless. Something Pitch had said the first day slithered through his memory. "The Gifted are forbidden to use the Orimere to bring any living thing across the worlds." He looked at the Garowai. "I'm the one who did this. I'm the one causing the imbalance."

The Garowai smiled. "Goodbye, Master Gifted. I am pleased the God of all chose me to know you."

"Wait. I don't understand." He kneed the horse forward. "If I caused all this, if it was me from the beginning, why was I brought here at all?"

"Perhaps because you will leave Lael a better place than you found her." The smile whispered again.

His every breath wrenched his chest. "How am I supposed to go?"

"The same way any of us do. Indeed, the same way I will." The smile took on a sad twist. "My time here comes to an end as well. Soon I will pass and a new Garowai will rise from my body to serve a world that will still be here because *you* will save it."

His throat clamped. "How can you be sure? How do you know I can do what you're asking?"

"I'm sure because this is your gift. This is what you will give Lael. You are their leader now. Sometimes leading means going where others cannot follow and shouldering commitments too large to bear." The Garowai reared back on his hind legs. "Farewell, my friend." With one mighty pump of his wings, he lifted himself from the ground and surged away from the hill.

A Guardsman galloped over. Smile lines gleamed through the grime on his face. "My lord Gifted, we've captured their ranking officer! He wants to talk terms."

The Garowai flew across the lake, then wheeled to soar up past the waterfall. He topped the palace and didn't look back.

"Congratulations, sir." The Guardsman beamed. "For the victory."

Chris laid his rein to his horse's neck. "Yes. The victory."

By the time Chris galloped through the palace gates, the storm had blown darkness into the sky. Women and children and old men swarmed the courtyard to greet their victorious soldiers. Their shouts and their laughter rose above even the gale. They mobbed Chris's horse and would have carried him upon their shoulders had he not waved them aside. He left them to their celebrating and entered the explosion-shattered castle.

Allara, clad in a soft almond-colored gown, met him at the top of the stairs. Her left arm was already bound and cradled against her stomach. Her hair hung loose over her shoulders, and the shadows pitting her cheeks only amplified the brilliance of her eyes.

She smiled at him and held out her hand. "Chris."

He pressed her fingers, then let go. He wanted no part of these victory celebrations. He stepped up to join her at the top of the stairs. "Orias?"

Her head tilted to the nearby door, but her eyes held fast to his. "What's wrong?"

He shouldered past. "Nothing."

"Chris." Her hand brushed his sleeve. "You've won."

He pushed through the heavy door into Orias's room. He *had* won. He'd done what they wanted him to. He'd given everything he had to win their war. And against all the odds, Mactalde was dead. By Chris's sword, he was dead. That should have been enough. The worlds should be saved. To ask him to give more—to ask him to leave this place and everyone in it—was a price too great.

"Chris." Pitch scrambled off his chair at the foot of the bed and ran over to take his hand. In the fluttering candlelight, his face gleamed with tears. "Orias is hurt. There was blood all over—"

"I know." He held Pitch's hot little palm, and they crept across the room to the bed.

Quinnon stood behind the doctor with his arms crossed and his chin tucked against his chest. He watched Chris approach.

The doctor stepped back from the bed. "My lord Gifted. I've done all I can."

Orias lay stretched beneath the bed's canopy, his body almost too long for the bed. The green silk coverlet covered his chest, unstirred by any visible breath. On the pillow next to him, Raz sat cross-legged and shook his head gravely. Pitch clenched Chris's fingers. He peered up with tear-slick eyes, as if he believed Chris could somehow make this right.

And why not? Chris's throat tightened. He was the Gifted, wasn't he? The only reason he had been allowed to cross over at all was to make things right. Thunder cracked outside, and Pitch flinched.

The Garowai wanted Chris to leave Lael. If he left, the worlds would theoretically be safe. But what if they weren't? Maybe the breaking had already stopped. How did he know this storm wouldn't pass and the sun wouldn't return in the end? How could he leave this place forever, while there was the slightest hope of an alternative?

Pitch leaned across the bed to touch Orias's forearm. "Orias, he's come. Chris has come."

Slowly, as though his neck had rusted, Orias turned his head until his cheek lay flat on the pillow. His eyes opened, and his pupils drifted up.

Chris sank to his knees. "You saved my life."

"My—honor." Orias labored for breath enough to carry his words. "Thank the God of all." His eyelids slid shut. "I am set free. I have lived to see the evil gone from Lael."

Chris's stomach churned. "Orias—" The impossible, agonizing truth clogged his throat. "Orias, I'm sorry."

"It is as it should be."

"Everything that's happened was my fault. You're not accountable."

"It doesn't matter. We've both made it right. It is over now, and I die in peace." Orias's chest sagged.

Pitch threw a wild look at Chris.

The doctor moved forward to check Orias's pulse. He shook his head. "Not yet. But soon."

Chris reached across the bed to touch Orias's bandaged palm. Through the windows on the far side of the room, the lake thrashed all the way to the edge of sight.

It made sense now why Mactalde had spent his life plotting to return to this place. It made sense he would have preferred to die again rather than surrender to the emptiness of leaving it behind forever. This morning, Chris had asked Mactalde if coming home had been worth the deaths and the destruction. Maybe he had known the answer before he had asked the question.

He looked back at Orias's head lolling against the pillow, and he filled his nostrils with the metallic stench of blood and the sour bite of oronborne. Orias had died to keep him alive. Orias had bought him the time he needed to see this to the end. And the end was coming.

"Soon," Chris said. The word was a promise. He rose and turned to where Allara waited in the doorway. Quinnon stood several steps in front of her. "Get together Denegar, Eroll, and Cabahr Laith. And my father."

Quinnon's eye narrowed. "What for?"

He started toward the door. "You'll see."

Mactalde was dead, but the storm raged on. Why? Why did it not stop?

Allara stood before the chapel's door as Chris faced what few of his captains remained. Rain rattled the stained-glass windows, and she shivered. The day had been won. Chris had corrected the imbalance. The storm should be slackening, not worsening.

"Our battle isn't over." Chris stood on the dais at the end of the room. He propped one arm against the altar, probably to keep from swaying with exhaustion. "The worlds are still breaking."

Arrayed across the room were his men. Quinnon. Denegar. Laith. His father sat in the back where Eroll lay on a pew. They had come because their victorious leader had summoned them. But the heaviness in Chris's face and the words falling from his tongue like so much lead did not speak of victory.

The men stared at him, uncomprehending.

Allara pushed away from the door. "The storm *will* stop. Now that Mactalde's dead, it has to stop."

"The war's won." Denegar's nose shone red with the cold that filtered through dusty rents in the walls. "We should all be celebrating."

"The war may be won," Chris said. "But the imbalance hasn't healed."

Like frozen water in a flask, the cold in her bones ruptured. She could almost hear them crack. She started up the aisle. "No. Mactalde's dead. You killed him. I saw you kill him."

His features were perfectly still. He was bracing himself, preparing himself for her reaction to the truth.

She began to shake—because she knew the truth without being told. She reached the chancel.

"I did kill Mactalde," he said. "But that isn't all I have to do."

A murmur chased through the room behind her.

"If Mactalde was not to blame, then who?" asked Laith.

The patter of rain against the windows became the click of ice pebbles. Her blood thundered in her head.

Chris exhaled. "Me. I'm responsible. I caused the imbalance when I brought Mactalde across. And I'm the only one who can fix it."

"Fix it how?" Worick asked.

"I have to leave this world." He spoke as if it were the most natural thing in the world.

She breathed out. "No . . ."

"Leave?" Worick's voice turned strident. "How do you think you're going to do that? How can anyone *leave* a world?"

"No—" She crossed the few spans to the dais and clutched Chris's coat lapel. "No! This isn't right. It can't be you!"

He stepped down from the dais to face her, and his voice dropped, low and intent and determined. "This has to be."

He had already made up his mind.

"*No.*" She tightened her grip in his coat. "No, it doesn't!"

"*What* has to be?" Worick demanded. "What are you talking about?"

Tears sheeted her vision. She clung to him, every muscle screaming. She would hold him here whatever it took. Hold him by sheer force of will if she could not hold him by logic. "I will not let this happen!"

From behind, a hand warmed her shoulder, and when Chris held the man's gaze for a long moment, she knew it was Quinnon. She looked back at him, pleading, even though he had never believed in the Gifted.

Like all the rest of them, he waited for Chris to speak again. But the way his good eye opened so much wider than the bad one said he waited for something different. Or perhaps, for the first time, he was *seeing* something different.

"Quinnon," she begged.

"Life gives every man only one opportunity." He watched Chris, and a glimmer of respect eased the hard lines of his face. "To do his duty and to do it well."

She spun to the men. "You can't believe what he's saying? You can't be willing to let him throw his life away like this?"

Chris's hand against her back pushed her forward, and he limped down the aisle beside her. "The worlds are coming apart at the seams. And I caused it. I used the Orimere to bring a living thing across the worlds."

"This is madness!" Denegar said. "Why were we told nothing of this imbalance? We should have been told. This should have been addressed long ago."

Eroll dragged himself up on one elbow. He looked from Allara to Chris. "What do we do?"

"*Nothing,*" Allara said. "We have no reason to believe any of this! It's a whim. A suspicion because the storm hasn't stopped!"

"We have to send me home," Chris said.

"The Orimere will take you back?" Worick asked. Like her, he sounded unwilling to let himself believe what he knew was the truth.

"No . . ." Chris slowly shook his head. "Not the Orimere."

Her throat caved in.

Eroll stared at her. "There must be another way. There has to be."

"There isn't." Chris straightened his shoulders. "I've already talked to the Garowai."

Denegar pushed past Laith to grip Chris's arm. "Lael will never stand by and see you executed after such a victory."

"This isn't anyone's choice to make but mine." His hand pressed against Allara's back, but he looked at his father. "You understand that?"

Worick's face was gaunt. "No."

Streaks of falling gold lit the stained glass. Stars landed somewhere in the nearby hills, and their hollow thud, like an underground detonation, joined with the thunder.

"It must be done." Laith inclined his head to Chris, almost respectfully. "The Cherazii will bear your blood, if such be the Gifted's will."

"Nay," Quinnon said. "I will do it. It would be my honor to so serve him."

Chris looked at Quinnon for a long moment. "If you want to call it an honor, then the honor's yours."

Allara stared at Quinnon. He might as well have shot her. "How can you do this?"

"Because it has to be done." He spoke as if he didn't know he were breaking her heart, but she caught a glimmer of anguish that was as much his own as a reflection of hers.

She whirled back to Chris and dragged him toward the door and away from these men and their words of honor and duty.

His weight yielded in her hands. "Let the people know," he told Quinnon. "This time when a Gifted dies, they need to know why. No one is to blame but me." He nodded at Laith and the other Cherazii, then turned back to his father. "Get the family together—" finally, his voice did waver, "—so I can say goodbye."

She flung the door open and spun around to wait for him in the deep shadows of the corridor. He followed her and pulled the door shut behind him.

"Chris—"

"Not yet." He took her elbow and walked her down the passage.

"No, now." She yanked free. "We have no time for *not yet*. You're not giving me time!"

His own pain and frustration twisted his face. "Allara, I don't have any time to give you! Look outside. Everything's going to fall down on our heads any minute. We've got maybe an hour before the heart of that storm reaches us."

"It's a storm. It's just a storm. It's not a part of the breaking. The breaking is over. It ended with Mactalde!" A sob caught in her throat. He blurred in front of her, like a painting left in the rain.

"Alla." He pulled her against him. "I've done this to you. I've betrayed you in more ways than one. To leave Lael, to leave you—it's unthinkable." His arms tightened around her, as if he could pull her into himself and take her with him. "But you know I'm right. There's no other answer."

"There has to be." Her fingers cramped in the back of his coat.

"I caused the breaking. It was my fault, and I'm the only one who can fix it." Resolution steadied his voice.

"No—" She wouldn't listen to this, and she wouldn't believe it. She pushed away. "It wasn't you. You didn't cause this. You didn't know! How could you? It was Orias!"

He shook his head.

"Orias lied to you. He baited you, he gave you no other choice than to bring Mactalde across!" If someone had to be the sacrifice here, then let it be Orias. He was dying already. He maybe even wanted to die. Death would bring him peace. But if Chris left her—if he disappeared back into the world of her dreams—how would she ever find peace for herself?

His face was still. "Maybe I didn't know exactly what would happen if I brought him across, but in my gut I knew it was wrong. I knew Mactalde was dangerous. This is my fault, there's no way around that. You and I both accepted that from the beginning. We can't hide from it now."

She pulled in breath after breath. She had to be calm, she had to think. "You *want* to die? You want to leave Lael?" The tears came anyway. "Do you want to leave me?"

"*No.*" A look, like fractured glass, filled his face. "But I don't have a choice."

"There's always a choice!"

He turned to the window and braced his arms against the sill. "All right, yes. And what I have to choose is to take responsibility for what's happened. What I choose is to save this place. What we talked about the other day is true. We *are* part of a bigger plan. And, even if I didn't believe that, I still have to do this if for no other reason than because all of this means too much to me now to let it die."

Her body shook. "Nobody ever said anything about slaughtering a Gifted!"

He shoved away from the windowsill. "I am going to die anyway! When that storm gets here, we're all going to die. *You* are going to die. You think I'm going to stand by and do nothing when there's a chance I can do everything?"

Tears burnt her face. "Please. Please don't leave me all alone."

He approached her; he took her shoulders in his hands. "Maybe I'm wrong. Maybe the Garowai lied to me. Maybe my death won't make a cent of difference. But I have to try. *We* have to try. You've worked and prayed for this all your life. You can't give up now just because the final step isn't the way you want it to be."

She leaned into his chest, and her injured arm throbbed between them. At last, the sobs tore free. "I cannot bear it."

"You can." His breath warmed the air above her ear. "You can because you're strong. Because you gave your life to fulfill a destiny you didn't even want. You've worked for twenty years for this victory. Don't surrender now." He pulled her closer and whispered almost too low for her to hear, "Don't make this harder than it is."

"Please, wait." She pressed her forehead against his chest. "Wait until Orias dies."

"I can't."

"He can't live much longer. He may even be dead now. Just in case, just in case it isn't you . . . please wait."

His chest rose and fell against her.

"Please."

"All right." The stubble on his cheek scratched her temple. "But we both know it won't matter."

58

FOR THE NEXT thirty minutes, Chris waited for a friend to die, because maybe, just maybe, that death would give him life. He sat in front of the fire in Orias's room, the Rievers seated to either side of him. He leaned his chin into his hands, his elbows propped against his knees, and tried to shut out the whistle of Orias's last breaths and the howl of the storm. Behind the closed door, people crowded the hallway, rustling and whispering.

He shouldn't have listened to Allara's panic. But life was a precious thing, and second chances even more so. He could not throw them away while hope remained. Was it only a few months ago he had fought tooth and nail to escape this place? He had wanted the dreams to just *stop*. That's what he had said over and over. He buried his face in his hands.

Somebody should have clocked him every time he'd opened his mouth that first day. He had been such a fool. He had tried to blow this world away like dust off his hands. Of course it *would* turn out to be gold dust.

And now he would give his right arm, his right eye for Quinnon to use as a spare, even ten years off his lifespan, just to make this world his reality. Let him live the other one in dreams as he had this one most of his life. Let him stay here forever. Oh God, just let him stay.

Beside him, Pitch flinched and stood up on the bench. Chris looked up.

The doctor laid Orias's arm at his side and turned to nod, his mouth a compressed line. He knew by now what hinged on Orias's death. Everyone knew.

Allara, standing at the window, cast the curtains aside, and the pewter light of the storm flooded the room. In silence, they waited. They held their breaths, listening, straining to see a streak of sunlight.

He counted the time in his head. He had agreed to wait five minutes after Orias's death. That was as much time as they could afford.

"Is it stopping?" Pitch whispered.

Stone and ice rattled against the parapet. Falling stars burned across the sky. The wind crashed against the glass.

Allara looked back at Chris. Her skin clung to her face in a death's mask.

He held himself very still. Nod. That's all he had to do. Nod at her and agree to stay and forget the consequences. And if the worlds broke apart, at least they could die together—and he would die only once. Walk away from his mistakes. Walk away from his responsibilities. Just walk away. But that was the one thing he couldn't do.

He swallowed, and he turned from her. He forced the stiff muscles in his neck to nod at Quinnon, where he stood guard at the door. "It's time. Tell them."

Allara choked on a breath and hurried past Quinnon. The door opened upon the noisy hush of a hundred waiting people and clicked shut once more to mute Quinnon's voice.

As the doctor and his aide closed the curtains on either side of the bed, Chris walked to the end of the bedstead. Shadows covered Orias's face. The hard angle of his mouth remained unsoftened.

"It wasn't you," Chris whispered, and he laid his fist to his heart.

The Rievers padded over to stand on either side of him. Raz clutched a fistful of Chris's trouser leg. "What happens now?"

He steeled his voice. "Now we have to say goodbye."

"Had enough goodbyes." Raz stared straight ahead.

Pitch gripped Chris's hand in both of his. "You can't go away unless I give you permission."

Chris lifted Pitch's skinny body. "Today I've got to answer a higher call than Riever law."

"I know." Pitch wrapped his arms around Chris's neck. "And that is why I am setting you free."

Only Parry remained in the hallway when Chris emerged from Orias's room. The boy stared at the floor. "I'm supposed to tell you they're ready." He tilted his head toward the stairs.

At the bottom, Chris's family waited, their faces tight and afraid.

Chris gave Parry's shoulder a shake, just enough to make him look up, then offered him his hand. "You were the finest manservant I ever had."

Parry shrugged and looked down once more.

Chris scanned the landing below. "Where's Allara?"

"She ran off as soon as the Cherazim died."

"I need you to find out where she went." He waited until Parry nodded, then he turned and walked down the long, long stairs to where his family waited.

"My son." Lauria took his face in her hands. "My only son. I won't even be able to dream of you." Her voice crumpled.

He kissed her fingers. "I got to see you once more, and that's more than I ever thought I'd get."

Tielle's cheek churned. "What about me? Will I dream about you?"

"I promise." He looked to where Worick stood, strong and stead-fast. "And so will you. Especially you." For a long moment, they stood facing each other, until finally Chris leaned forward to wrap his father in his arms. "Goodbye, Dad."

"What can a man say?" Worick crushed him with his strength, then backed away. The tears ran down his face. "I'm proud you were my son, Talan Malchor Bowen."

Sirra locked her arms around his body and refused to let go. She hiccupped. "How will I live without you?"

"You have to," he murmured.

"I knew." She pushed away, her face damp. "From the moment I saw you that day when the Searcher brought you home, I knew you would do something great, but not this. Not this."

Parry reappeared in a doorway at the far end of the chamber, and Chris backed away from his family. He tore himself, one step at a time, from the second chance he was never going to have.

"I love you," he said. "All of you."

In the doorway, he met Parry, and the youngster pointed at the floor. "I found her. Down there in the armory. Want me to show you the way?"

"I remember."

He followed the passageways, one after the other, down into the heart of the fortress. The wind against his face led him to the open-ended gymnasium, where he and Allara had sparred so many times. She stood at the far end, where only the columns separated her from the waterfall. Hailstones smashed to the marble at her feet, but her face remained tilted to the wild water.

He crossed the gymnasium, his footsteps silenced by the howl of the wind and the thunder. He stopped behind her, so close he could smell her hair. And suddenly, he found himself empty of words. He'd said them already, a dozen times in the last ten minutes.

"I've always loved storms," she said. "Ever since I was a child. Why, I wonder? Why should I, of all people, love the storms?"

He touched her shoulder. "I have to go now."

She bowed her head, and her hair curtained her face.

"Are you going to let me go?" he whispered.

She turned. Tears glittered against her face. "In my heart, I always knew it couldn't end well."

"It *is* ending well." He touched her cheek. "Just not the way we wanted."

"I wanted . . . I wanted so much. I thought everything would be made right. I thought I wouldn't be alone any longer. But I'm still hanging onto the cliff, fighting for even a shred of peace." Her tears welled over. "You told me it would end. You said, when it did, you wanted me to be there. It's at an end, and I need *you* to be here."

"I can't. I want to, but I can't." He bowed his head and tilted her forward until their foreheads touched. "That cliff you're trying to hang onto is crumbling, Allara. It's time to let go."

She shook her head. "There's no one left at the bottom to catch me."

"Maybe it's time to let go and find out." He took the Orimere from his coat's inner pocket. It shone its golden light against their faces. "I know I wasn't the Gifted you wanted. If I could have stayed away somehow, like you asked me to, I would have."

"No." Tears clotted her lashes. "You did save Lael. Mactalde is gone, Nateros is gone, the Koraudians have been forced back." Her tears spilled over. "You've made it possible for peace to come again." She turned his hand so the Orimere lay against his chest. It pulsed in time with his heart and surged impossible energy through his veins.

"But what if you die too late to make a difference? What if it's all in vain?"

"I was meant to do this. And so were you."

Her mouth trembled. "I shall never see you again."

"Maybe you'll see me in the lake. Maybe you'll dream about me."

A laugh choked her. "How can I? I will never find you in your world. My other self will not even know to look for you."

He closed her in his arms and pulled her to him. "Somewhere far away, in my world, you're asleep. You think all of this is a dream. But it's a dream you're going to remember." He rested the side of his head against hers. "You're going to remember when I tell you a phone number."

"I don't even know what that is."

"Part of you does, and you're going to remember this number, and you're going to call it as soon as you wake up, understand?"

"Chris—" Her head started to shake. "I can't. It won't work."

"Ssh." As the storm crashed down all around them, he whispered Mike's phone number in her ear, over and over again.

Outside, fire and ice rained from the sky.

"It's time," he said.

"Yes," she whispered. Her hand behind his neck pulled him down to her. She lifted herself onto her toes, and her face hesitated in front of his, her eyes closed, her breath warm against his skin. She kissed him: a kiss for everything that would never be.

Then she backed away, the Orimere clamped against her chest.

He looked at her one last time: the whirlwind of her hair and her gown, the shocking blue of her eyes, the impossible straightness of her body even after all she had endured these months.

And then he looked beyond her at the storm-torn world, and he filled his lungs with the cold, wet air. "Goodbye."

He left, and his strides lengthened into a run as he crossed the cracked tile of the armory floor. He ran up the stairs two at a time, and pain throbbed through a dozen wounds he would never feel after this day. Life ticked away, every second standing in for the years he would never live and the dreams he would never again see. He ran because he had no more time to waste, and he ran because if he could not stay, he had to leave before he lost the courage to go.

His people waited for him in the chapel. They parted before him, and women and men alike reached to brush a hand against his clothing. The Cherazii, ranged along the walls, laid their fists to their chests.

Eroll lay on a bench in the front.

Chris stopped beside him and gripped his hand. "You'll take care of her."

His face twisted into disbelief and grief. "You know I will."

At the front of the church, Quinnon waited with a two-handed sword. "You'll have to kneel. It will be over in a minute."

Chris shook his head. "Not here. Let me see Lael before I die."

Quinnon glanced at the Guardsmen standing beside the double doors in the northeast corner. "Let him out."

The doors swung open upon the second-story parapet, and Chris walked into the storm. He shucked his coat and his jerkin and tugged loose the drawstrings at his throat so he could pull the collar away and leave the back of his neck unobstructed.

Quinnon stood beside him, just outside the door. "Let's get this over with, laddie." He gripped Chris's arm. "And may the God of all be with you."

"I thought you said you didn't believe in the God of all."

Quinnon hefted the sword in both hands. "So I did."

Chris dropped to his knees. The stone jarred against his kneecaps and shot cold up his skin. The muscles in his back clenched. His blood pounded, aching in his shoulder and his side.

Behind him, the grit on the parapet scraped beneath Quinnon's boots. The sword multiplied into a dozen shadows and rose overhead.

One long breath whispered past Chris's mouth. The blurred glitter of Ori Réon's wind-torn waters swept out before him. This was his lake, his city. This was his home. It would always be his home.

The sword's shadows descended, coalesced, and vanished. He filled his lungs. The blade bit into the back of his neck, and for one blinding second, the sun's warmth burst against his face.

59

CHRIS OPENED HIS eyes to darkness. His head throbbed. He tried to roll over, but the confines of a nylon sleeping bag trapped him. Cold air slapped him in the face. His mouth tasted hot and stale, and the room's smell of dog hair and corn chips wasn't much of an improvement.

Wherever he was, it wasn't Lael. His stomach cramped. It was over. Lael was gone. Allara was gone. He closed his eyes again and eased his breath through his lips.

"Finally. Thank heavens." The voice was Brooke's.

"Sheez, bro." Mike's big hand groped for his arm. "You had me about ready to call the morgue. You've been out almost twenty-four hours."

Chris worked a hand free and scraped it over his face. "Where are we?"

"Our basement. Just be glad you're not back at the nuthouse. And be even gladder those cops never figured out I lied about you tripping and knocking yourself out. If I'd had to spend the night in jail, waiting until you woke up to come bail me out, this boy would not have been happy."

"The power's still out?"

"Not a bad observation for a man with a concussion. Of course it's still out. You think I always huddle in the basement with the lights out and the heat off just for fun?"

"Oh, stop." Brooke sat next to Chris and laid the back of her hand against his forehead. "He's probably still woozy." She, at least, seemed back to normal.

He clawed at the sleeping bag's zipper. Pain swirled through his head, and he caught himself on his elbow. "What happened to the storm?"

"Just rest." Brooke took hold of his shoulder. "Everything's going to be all right." Only the faintest note of fear touched the end of her sentence.

He struggled upright. Somewhere in the darkness, Pluto growled.

"You should be in the hospital," Brooke scolded.

"I drove you by there as soon as the cops got off my back," Mike said. "But you wanna talk about a madhouse."

"I have to know what happened to the storm." If the storm was still raging, then everything he'd done had been in vain.

"It's even worse than yesterday," Mike said. "I don't want to think about how much of my house got spun off to Kansas during the night."

Chris pulled free of Brooke's hand and braced himself on his hands and knees on the concrete floor. Silence, not wind, blared in his ears.

"Just lie back down." She tugged at his arm. "We're not going anywhere."

"Yeah," Mike said. "The whole stinking world's coming to an end, for all I can tell. We just need to keep warm, conserve our bodily energy, that kind of stuff." An aluminum bag crackled. "I emptied the fridge and all the cupboards, so at least we don't have to go up in the cold to get food. Want some chips?"

"The storm has to have stopped." Chris fumbled in the dark, caught hold of the corner of a desk, and toppled a stack of CDs as he heaved himself to his feet. "It's over."

"I don't think so. I had to climb up the stairs just ten minutes ago to stuff a towel under the door 'cause the cold was pouring in."

He tripped across the basement and slammed into a wall. The blue glare of a flashlight cut across the room in time to show him the stairwell.

"Where are you going?" Brooke asked.

"Will you sit down already?" Mike stood, and the chip bag crinkled to the floor. "Every time you make a move these days, you start a national emergency."

Chris grabbed the handrails on either side of the narrow stairwell and dragged himself up.

"C'mon. Why is it I listen to you, but you don't even hear me?" Mike's voice swung away from Chris. "Sic him, why don't you?"

Pluto only growled.

"Now, now." Brooke and the flashlight worked their way toward him. "Maybe it's best to let him see for himself."

He found the towel beneath the door and wrenched it free.

Behind him, the stairs creaked and the flashlight's beam swung up to glint off the brass doorknob.

"You're going to let all kinds of freezing air down here," Mike groused.

He opened the door, and a wall of cold smacked against his face. Slits of gray highlighted the window in the kitchen. Snow had drifted in the sink, and an icy trickle of air rattled the blinds. He lifted his foot over the final step, and broken glass cracked against the linoleum. Glass and hail, table and chairs, dishes and trash littered the floor.

"Satisfied?" Mike called.

"It's over. It has to be."

"Since when are you a meteorologist?" Mike tromped up the stairs after Brooke.

Chris pushed a chair out of the way and stumbled into the living room.

"What a mess." The beam of Brooke's flashlight glanced across the front door. "I hope your new storm windows came with a warranty." The blue light filled the detritus-strewn living room. "Chris, now what are you doing?"

He snapped the deadbolt clear on the front door, then stopped. If the storm hadn't ended . . . if he'd been too late . . . He dropped his forehead against the wood for a second, then opened the door.

Framed in the ripped screen door, the street lay in silence.

He rattled the screen. It refused to budge against the snow piled on the step. He slammed his shoulder into the frame and snapped it off its hinges.

"Hey!" Mike said. "We don't have a warranty on *that*!"

He climbed over the fallen door and sank up to his knees in the snow. Shingles and shutters and tree limbs cluttered the street and the yards. The green of the remaining leaves dazzled against the snow. A single snowflake twirled in front of him, and he reached out to catch it in his palm. A breeze, soft like the caress of silk, brushed his cheek. The storm was over.

"I don't believe it." Mike scrambled over the fallen screen door.

Brooke's suddenly superfluous flashlight swung around and hit Chris in the face. Her mouth hung open. "How'd you know?"

The snowflake glinted against his hand, then melted into nothing. He looked back up. Faraway, a rim of sunlight gleamed against the clouds' edge. A tiny warm spot touched the core of his body. It didn't grow or spread, but it flickered, strong and bright.

If Chicago was safe, so was Lael. So was his family. So was Allara. He *hadn't* been too late.

"I didn't know," he said. "I just hoped."

"No, you *knew*." Brooke floundered through the snow until she could grab his shoulder and pull herself the rest of the way.

Mike followed, scowling. "When I knocked you out yesterday, and you fell into that hole, all that stuff down there disappeared."

Chris looked at him. "What stuff?" Now that it was over, there was no reason to explain it all. What was done was done, and no one had to believe him if they didn't want to.

Mike flung up his arms. "What do you mean *what stuff?* I mean whatever that old man had under that tarp. It all disappeared."

Chris slogged through the snow. "We should check if people are okay."

"That dream thing." Brooke struggled to keep up. "It wasn't true, was it?"

"No way," Mike said. "All this crazy stuff going on, it's just coincidence. It has to be."

"That's it," Chris said.

Brooke huffed. "That's the best job of convincing you can come up with? Because I can't tell you how much I'd love to be convinced. Even coincidences that end with me buying a new car are better than what you've been trying to tell us."

He leaned against the mailbox and squinted through the pain in his head. "No, it isn't better."

On the horizon, the rim of light spread. The breeze swirled through what was left of the trees, and all along the street, people began easing their heads outside their front doors.

It really was over. The battle was won. And Lael was lost to him forever.

60

CHRIS DREAMED ONE more dream.

From the mist and the rush of a waterfall, the Garowai spoke to him, disembodied, floating. He was perfect and whole, and yet he wasn't. He was complete, but the glimpses Chris caught were only out of the corner of his eye. It was a dream like the dreams he remembered from before the crossing.

"It worked." That seemed to be the most important thing to say.

"Aye, it worked." The Garowai's smile filled the dream. He seemed younger. The whorls on his muzzle were now a smooth steel blue, sleek and vibrant. His eyes shone, and his movements betrayed none of the flinches of arthritis. His voice was calm and clear. He didn't sneeze.

"I can't go back, can I?" Chris asked. If he could see the Garowai, even after dying in one world, perhaps he might somehow be able to return after all.

The Garowai shook his great head. His mane moved gently in the breeze. "No, my friend, that's not the way of it. That I speak to you now is a gift, to both of us. I told you I would be following you in leaving Lael, and now I am."

"You're dying?"

"Not dying. Just moving on."

"And what about Allara? She's losing you too?"

"Allara will live. Allara will dream. And she will not be without a Garowai." The black expanse of his wings spread. "You brought a new era to Lael. It is only right that the world have a new Garowai with which to enter it."

"Is that what you came to tell me?"

"Partly. Partly also to tell you that what has happened to you may now feel like anything but a gift. Or worse: a gift that was snatched away after the giving. But that isn't so, is it? Once given, a gift will always be. So take your gift, and live your life, Chris Redston."

The mists rolled over him, the water rushed in his ears, and the Garowai gave one flap of his wings and swirled into the clouds. In his place sat a wet blue-black cub with nubbly wings behind his shoulder blades. The cub looked at him through green eyes, and when his mouth gapped, the smile was almost familiar.

That was the last dream.

———

Two weeks after the storm, Chris left the office building of Mike's publisher friend and entered the sunlight. Mike had written him a letter of recommendation, and, against even Chris's own expectations, he had gotten the opportunity to pitch the idea of a book about the survivors of fatal car accidents.

His dad had agreed to check into a rehab center, and somebody had to make sure he stuck it out. Chris was that somebody, which meant he had to stay in Chicago. It was time, after all. If he couldn't live life in both worlds, he could live it here the way he should always have had the courage to live it.

He walked down the sidewalk, hands in his pockets. The world was finally beginning to put itself back together. The snow had melted. New grass glinted beneath the brown of the frozen blades. The streets had been cleared, the smashed windows boarded up, and the broken streetlights covered in duct tape. Traffic buzzed along, same as ever, horns blaring at the intersections. The power had finally come back on last week, and, one by one, businesses were reopening their doors.

He lifted his face to the sun. The temperatures hadn't returned to the expected norms of early fall, but the cold had fled. It felt like spring, the warmth against his face fresh and tentative. Even this deep in the city, the air smelled clean.

After that last dream of the Garowai's farewell, he went to bed every night and slept the sleep of the dead. He woke, rested and refreshed, his mind a blank. He still closed his eyes and dared to hope that somehow, impossibly, he would open them again to find himself back in Réon Couteau.

He wanted to see Lael repair itself. He wanted to see the beads of silver and green pearling the hills as the new grass responded to the warmth. He wanted to watch the people trickling back to their homes and to their lives, free from war and politics and tragedy. He wanted to see his mother and his sisters. And the Rievers—and Crea Quinnon—and Parry—and Eroll Leighton. And Allara.

At the intersection, the bumblebee yellow of a taxi swung around the corner, and he flagged it down. He gave the driver directions to Mercy General, where his dad was still recovering from his gunshot wound, then leaned back and watched the traffic blur.

Allara hadn't called him. He had known giving her Mike's number was an impossible gamble. Even if the dream had made any sense to her in this world, she would have to take a huge leap of faith to pick up the phone and call a man she had never even heard of.

He fingered what was left of the bruise Mike had inflicted behind his ear. Half of him had died in Lael, perhaps the better half. He felt continually at a loss, like a man who looked over his shoulder and couldn't find his own shadow. And yet he would have traded the shadow all over again, would have sold himself twice over, for those months. He'd been given a chance to know the truth, a chance to see the glorious possibilities behind his dreams. Most people never saw beyond the veil of their own lives. He was one of the few. A Gifted.

Life was suddenly more than just what he could see stretched in front of him. There was a purpose, there was a plan. He no longer had to drift in the mire of apathy, absorbed in his own futility. He could open his eyes to the warmth of each new morning and embrace it as a gift of ineffable potential.

He had succeeded and he had failed. He had lost much, gained more, then somehow, impossibly, after all these years of clinging to his shriveled sense of the scope of life, he had learned to give it all away . . . because letting go was sometimes the only way of holding on.

What he had found in Lael had been worth the price. He would pay it again if he had no other choice. But acknowledging that didn't kill the emptiness. For the rest of his life, he would be looking for his shadow, and he would never find it.

The cab stopped in front of the hospital's main entry, and he paid the driver and climbed out.

His dad was sitting up in bed, his arm in a sling, reading the newspaper. His hands shook a little, but he smiled a welcome. "Mike's looking for you. He went down the hall to get me some ice."

Chris dropped his jacket on the foot of the bed. "You should get out of here. Enjoy the sun."

"Sounds good to me." His dad tossed the paper on top of Chris's jacket and inched himself off the bed. "This room ain't got much up on a jail cell." His lower lip caught between his teeth, and he darted a glance at Chris, his cheeks hollowing a little bit more.

Chris ignored the comment and steadied his dad's good elbow. He waited until Paul could stand without wobbling, then walked back across the room to hold the door open. "C'mon. Jail's no place to spend a morning like this."

The corner of Paul's mouth pulled up, and he hobbled across the room.

In the hall, Chris flagged a nurse and asked her to send Mike out to them. He and his dad wandered outside to where wooden tables had been interspersed along the sidewalk.

"So . . ." Paul eased himself onto a bench. "You're going to stop globetrotting and stay here to write a book?"

"Yeah." Chris sat next to him, his back to the table, and propped his elbows against the edge. "About Mom and Jenifer. And us—you and me and Lisa."

Paul interlocked his fingers, pulled them apart, then locked them again. "That's not something you're going to regret, is it? I mean, that's not going to hurt you all over again? Like . . . I've hurt you all these years."

"We hurt each other." He looked at his dad. "As soon as you're settled at the center, I'm going to make a quick run out to Los Angeles to see Lisa and the girls. Then I'm coming back to be with you while you're in rehab."

The silence stretched. Paul cleared his throat and turned his head away. Without looking, his hand reached out to pat Chris's. For just a second, Chris laid his hand on top of it. It was a touch of both repentance and forgiveness.

Through the sun glare on the exit's glass doors, he could see Mike's approach.

"You know," his dad finally said, "the nightmares . . . they did go away."

"I know."

"You do?" His dad looked back, surprised.

Chris shrugged. "You agreed to go to the center, didn't you?"

A can of diet soda in one hand and a plastic cup of ice water in the other, Mike lumbered down the sidewalk. "There you are. If I didn't know better I'd think you were trying to avoid me." He set the water on the table next to Paul and looked at Chris. "Some woman called my cell a little while ago, asking for you."

The back of Chris's neck went cold.

"Not that I mind being your personal answering service or anything, but don't you think it's time you got around to finding wherever it is you lost your phone?" Mike pushed his sunglasses up his nose.

"Did she leave a message?" He had to concentrate to hear himself speak over the sudden rush of blood in his ears.

"No, didn't even give her name. Just wanted to know if you were there. I said no, but I'd pass the message along. She hemmed around a minute, then hung up."

"Give me your phone." He stood.

"Why?" Mike's eyebrow appeared over the rim of his sunglasses. "She didn't leave a message." He dug the phone out of his shirt pocket anyway.

Chris took the phone. His hands shook as he thumbed back through the call log. "Who else called you this morning?"

"Nobody. Just her and the radio station. What's going on?"

He found the first out-of-state call and hit send.

The phone rang once, then twice. He stood up from the bench and walked down the sidewalk, his hand pressed against his free ear to block out the rattle of traffic in the parking lot. The phone rang twice more, then picked up.

"Hello?"

His lungs stopped working, and he lurched to a stop.

"Hello?" From the other end of the line, Allara spoke to him. Allara Katadin, Searcher, princess of Lael, spoke to him, her voice bouncing off satellites and skipping through transmission towers to whisper in his ear.

He cleared his throat. "You called this number a minute ago. I wasn't here. My friend picked it up."

"Oh." Her voice quieted, the way it did whenever she was keeping something back. "Yes, um, sorry, I didn't mean for you to have to call me."

"No, no, I don't mind." Everything was in her ball court right now. In this world, he didn't know her name or where she lived. If she wasn't willing to take a chance and admit she'd called this number on nothing more than a gut feeling, he'd lose her all over again. He pulled in a breath. "What did you need?"

"Um—" She laughed. "Look, this is going to sound really crazy, because I don't know you, and you've never heard of me, but . . . I had this dream I was supposed to call you." She laughed again. "Crazy, I know. I'm sorry."

"Not so crazy." His grip on the phone relaxed. He turned his back to the sun and looked at the shadow stretched in front of him. A smile warmed his face. "I'm a firm believer in dreams."

Silence touched the phone, and when she spoke again, her voice was soft, and he could almost see the intensity of her blue eyes.

"So am I," she said.

Note From the Author: Reviews are gold to authors! If you've enjoyed this book, would you consider rating it and reviewing it on Amazon.com?

Join the discussion: #dreamlander

ABOUT THE AUTHOR

K. M. WEILAND LIVES in make-believe worlds, talks to imaginary friends, and survives primarily on chocolate truffles and espresso. She is the author of the historical/dieselpunk mashup *Storming* and the medieval epic *Behold the Dawn*, as well as the Amazon bestseller *Outlining Your Novel: Map Your Way to Success* and *Structuring Your Novel: Essential Keys for Writing an Outstanding Story*. When she's not making things up, she's busy mentoring other authors through her blog *Helping Writers Become Authors* (helpingwritersbecomeauthors.com). She makes her home in western Nebraska. Visit her website: kmweiland.com.

Also by K.M. Weiland

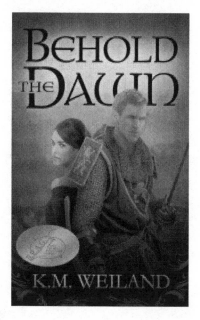

The sins of a bishop.
The vengeance of a monk.
The secrets of a knight.

Sometimes even pilots
have to wing it.

www.kmweiland.com

WANT MORE?

Use the following link to visit a hidden webpage, designed especially for fans of *Dreamlander*.

kmweiland.com/dreamlander-extras

ACCESS EXCLUSIVES SUCH AS:

Desktop Wallpaper

Story Soundtrack

Deleted Scenes

Character Interviews

World-Building Notes

Extra Maps

And more!

Made in the USA
San Bernardino, CA
14 September 2018